High Praise for *The Eyes of God*:

"A cracking good read." —*SFX*

"Marco offers a sprawling tale of military battles, personal and political intrigue, magic, and star-crossed love set against a richly detailed land of warring kingdoms and hidden magic." —*Library Journal*

"Mr. Marco has delivered an epic fantasy with heart and pathos. His characters are flawed and believable, wholly sympathetic to the reader. He paints a landscape of palace grandeur and desert desolation where magic is a reality and winning a battle is not winning the war." —*Romantic Times*

"The greatest strength of this novel remains in the way in which the author manipulates and alters his original Arthurian-based landscape to serve very different ends, as well as his refusal at times to take his story where expected. The reader *will* be in for some surprises." —*SF Site*

"Marco paints characters with a deft hand . . . all the plotlines are clearly thought out and interesting. Marco's fans should look forward to his next installment." —*The Davis (CA) Enterprise*

"It's a classic tale of triumph and tragedy, well written with great depth of emotion. As I was reading this novel, I had the feeling I was reading something important. In 20 years, I wouldn't be surprised to hear Marco, and this book, mentioned alongside the icons of the fantasy genre." —*The News Star* (LA)

"This epic fantasy novel, first in a brand new series, is a well-crafted addition to a much-beloved genre. The book's characters are well-drawn, and although the plot is fairly dense, the story moves along at a smart pace . . . the author creates a compelling and entertaining read." —*Voya*

"This is no lightweight book. Marco's characters are complex and multidimensional, and his seemingly simple story is a rich, complex exposition of high fantasy with an underlying brutal reality. This brutality is punctuated with Marco's skill as a military writer—the battle scenes in *The Eyes of God* are massive in scale while remaining rich in exquisite, personal detail." —*Editors of Amazon.com*

THE
EYES
OF
GOD

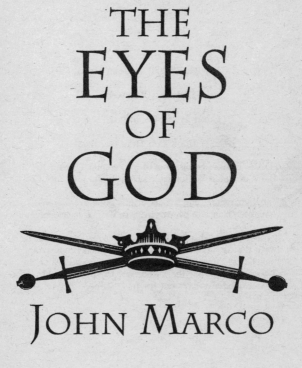

JOHN MARCO

DAW BOOKS, INC.
DONALD A. WOLLHEIM, FOUNDER
375 Hudson Street, New York, NY 10014

ELIZABETH R. WOLLHEIM
SHEILA E. GILBERT
PUBLISHERS
www.dawbooks.com

First Paperback Printing, January 2003
12 13 14 15 16 17 18 19 20

DAW TRADEMARK REGISTERED
U.S. PAT. OFF. AND FOREIGN COUNTRIES
—MARCA REGISTRADA
HECHO EN U.S.A.

PRINTED IN THE U.S.A.

ACKNOWLEDGMENTS

Writing is a solitary business, but no book is truly born of a single person. This book had many midwives, some new to my life and some old, and I want to thank them all for their support and dedication.

Thanks—and love—go once again to my wife Deborah, and to my entire family. They are my staunchest defenders and most loyal fans.

As always, thanks goes to my agent, Russell Galen, who saw this book for what it could be and found a good home for it.

Thanks to fellow fantasist Kristen Britain, for exchanging ideas and an impressive number of emails, and for being there through frustrating times.

Thanks to Jack Bilello, a fine writer and a good friend, who constantly reminds me that the true value of books lies in their power to move the human heart.

Thanks to Debra Euler, Sean Fodera, and everyone else at DAW books. Though there are bigger publishers in the world, there are none with more dedicated, dependable people. It's been a pleasure working with them.

Special thanks to my wonderful editor, Betsy Wollheim, for welcoming me into the DAW family and for always being gracious. No writer could have a better patron.

And finally, thanks to all of my readers, all around the world, for continuing to invite me into their lives and letting me tell my stories. Their support has been amazing, humbling, and greatly appreciated.

PART ONE

THE
BRONZE KNIGHT

1

He was a giant.

His horse was a giant too, and layered in hammered bronze like its rider, so that the two formed a centaur in the ebbing light. On his head he wore no helmet, just a short-cropped blond mane, but every other inch was armored, reflecting the sinking sun. He rode at the front of his legion, abreast of his king and a full pace ahead of the standard bearer whose blue flag stood flaccid in the breeze-less air. Two lines of cavalry stretched out behind him, proud in the face of the dreaded city. They had traveled for days across good roads and bad, had drunk from the prized river Kryss, all to endure the company of enemies.

Lukien, the Bronze Knight of Liiria, looked across the valley toward the waiting city of Hes, capital of Reec. Hes the Serene, it was called, and its walls and domed towers bespoke an easy quietude. He had seen the city before, had battled on this very plain, but he had never heard the wind whisper through the valley as it did today, and the sound startled him. Today there were no screams, no thunder of swords. Lukien lifted his face toward Hes, satisfied. Today was a good day after all.

"They see us by now, surely," said Lukien. "Yet they do not come to greet us?"

Akeela shrugged off the implication. "We are far off yet," he said. "When we're closer, they will meet us." The young king smiled as if nothing could sour his mood. "Put your suspicions away, Lukien. Nothing will go wrong."

Lukien nodded, because everything Akeela said was true. He was seldom wrong, this new king of Liiria, and that's why his people adored him. It was why they called him "Akeela the Good." And it was why men like Lukien and the other Royal Chargers followed him, even into the heart of Reec. Lukien settled into his saddle, trying for some of Akeela's abundant confidence. Behind them, the cavalry rode at attention, unnerved by the sight of Hes. The Bronze Knight stole a backward glance at his men. Behind the standard bearer he saw Lieutenant Trager. Unlike his underlings, Trager showed no trace of fear, but his silence belied his anxiety. Lukien leaned toward Akeela.

"Trager seems . . . uneasy."

Akeela put up a hand. "Not today, please."

"You should have left him at home. He'll disrupt things."

"He won't," said Akeela. "You're just trying to irritate him. Stop it now."

Like many of the Chargers, Trager hadn't wanted to come to Reec. Behind Akeela's back he had secretly sneered at the notion of peace, sure that King Karis would snub the offer. Yet here they were, on the road to the Reecian capital, invited guests of the king. For Lukien, who had battled the Reecians since graduating war college, it seemed a miracle. Akeela was right to be proud. He had done something his dead father had never dared dream. If the meeting went well—if they weren't riding stupidly into a trap—then years of bloodshed might end and Lukien's Royal Chargers could at last sheath their swords. The decades of war had made them hard and suspicious, but the light in Akeela's eyes had convinced them that peace was in fact possible. Like Lukien, they quested for Akeela's dream.

Lukien knew his world was about to change irrevocably. Under Akeela, they all faced an uncertain future. Even if it was one of peace, it would still not be perfect for the Bronze Knight. Lukien was still a young man, and peerless with a sword. He had earned his reputation the hard way. War was his life, his best and truest calling. Without war he would change, and the idea chafed him. To sit at home with a dog at his feet simply didn't interest him. Barely twenty-seven, he still had a soldier's lust for life. Were it up to him, he would never make peace with Reec. That way, Liiria would always need him.

But it wasn't up to him. Akeela ruled Liiria now, and this was a matter he had decided alone. If war was Lukien's calling, then peace was Akeela's. Lukien glanced at his king and was pleased to be with him. If a trap did lay ahead of him, he would welcome death at the side of such a good man.

High in a tower of Castle Hes, Princess Cassandra of Reec cocked an eyebrow toward the window, marveling at the soldiers approaching her home. It was nearly dusk but she could see them faintly in the dimming light; their silver armor, their well-bred horses, their blue flag stirring listlessly on a pole. They were very many, much more than she had expected. She wiped the mist from the glass, spying the front of the column. Akeela would be there, leading his men, as brave as the stories said.

"Come away from the window, Cassandra," the girl implored. Jancis was nervous, and her voice quavered a little. The handmaiden had laid out Cassandra's dress and continued fussing with it, smoothing out wrinkles that weren't there.

"They're coming," said Cassandra.

"You'll see them soon enough. Come on, Cass, we must dress you."

"Come here, Jancis, look at them."

With a sigh Jancis did as her lady asked, going to the window to stand beside Cassandra. The princess, still in her undergarments, stepped aside so Jancis could see.

"Look, at the front. The two riding alone."

Jancis nodded. "Uh-huh," she said dully.

"Do you see them?"

"Barely."

"Do you think Akeela's at the front?"

"Probably," said Jancis. The handmaiden frowned. "I suppose that brute Lukien is with him."

"I suppose," agreed Cassandra sourly. No one had wanted her father to allow the Bronze Knight into Reec, but Karis had insisted, for King Akeela would not come without him. "I bet he's an arrogant-looking bastard, too."

"Too far away to tell." Jancis bit her lip. "Hmm, I wonder what Akeela looks like. I can't wait to see him."

Cassandra's curiousity spiked. She went back to the window, nudging Jancis aside. Akeela was much too far away to see, and that frustrated her. It frustrated her, too, that she'd been obsessing over his appearance. He was a great man coming to Reec, with a great offer, and that should have been enough for her. But Cassandra knew she was special, and had long dreamed of a special husband. It was a childish thing, she supposed, but the dream was still with her. Cassandra thought it very strange that no one knew what Akeela looked like, or had faced him in battle. Most princes were warriors, but not this one. He let his infamous knight make war for him, while he himself stayed safe behind castle walls. Was he a coward then? Cassandra didn't think so. It took courage for a Liirian to ride into Reec.

"He's a mystery," Cassandra purred. The idea intrigued her. She moved away from the window and drifted toward her bed, an oak four-poster with ruffled sheets and perfumed pillows. The dress Jancis had made for her lay across the mattress, looking pristine and beautiful, the perfect garment for seduction. The princess looked down at her smock-clad body. She was seventeen and had filled out nicely. She knew this from the way the men at court looked at her, and she loved to play games with them. But Akeela was a king. Surely he had been with many women, and would judge her critically. A touch of inadequacy—something Cassandra rarely felt—began to tug at her. She had accepted her father's request to marry the Liirian gladly, because she was tired of Hes and loved the idea of being a queen. But she had made sure that she supported her father's plan with just enough restraint to keep her modesty. However, that had been a month ago, and now Akeela was at her doorstep. Worse, the Liirian king didn't even know what her father had planned.

More than anything, Cassandra wanted this peace to work. She had seen the disbelief in her father's eyes when Akeela's message had arrived, imploring a summit. Her father had never seemed so happy, or so grave. To make this peace he would do anything, even give her away. Cassandra pretended to care for her father's sake, but to be away from Hes—away from the shadows of so many sisters—was her fondest dream. And to be a queen! Which of her sisters could say that yet?

"We should dress you now," said Jancis, "before they get here. Your father may want you to greet them."

Cassandra nodded but said nothing. Jancis picked up on her silence and shot her a questioning look.

"How are you feeling?" Jancis whispered.

Cassandra groaned. She didn't want anyone finding out about her pains, not today when she was so close to leaving. "You promised you wouldn't speak of that today."

"You're all right then?"

"Yes, and keep your voice down." Instinctively Cassandra looked toward the closed door, hoping no one was outside. "I'm fine. I haven't felt the pain for days."

"I don't believe you," replied Jancis. "I heard you this morning. If you're feeling fine, why were you vomiting?"

"Oh, you're such a witch sometimes!" snapped Cassandra. "Stop ear-wigging on me." She sat down on the edge of the bed, knowing she couldn't escape her friend. The sickness had come upon her a week ago, and had gotten worse before it had gotten better. Now it came in fits, a burning pain in her stomach that made her retch and sometimes turned her water red. She didn't know what it was, and truly didn't care to find out. She only knew that if her father discovered it, her marriage—her chance at greatness—would vanish. "It hurts sometimes when I eat, and that's all," she admitted. "I was nervous at breakfast. It's made me a little sick." She looked up. "Don't worry, Jancis. And don't you dare say a word to anyone."

The girl remained troubled. "I'm afraid for you, Cass. You should let Danette look at you, at least. She won't tell anyone, and maybe she can give you something for the cramps."

"Danette has a mouth as wide as the Kryss. I can't tell her anything, and neither can you. And besides, you make it sound like my moon blood, which it's not. What's that old midwife going to do for me?"

"I don't know," Jancis confessed. "That's why I'm worried. Maybe you'll need a real physician. Maybe—"

"Jancis, stop," bade Cassandra. She help up one finger, the way she always did when Jancis rambled. "That's enough. You promised to keep quiet about it, and I expect you to do so. Now . . ." She stood up and tucked her long hair behind her ears. "Let's dress me."

Jancis was about to take the garment from the bed when a knock came at the door. Dressed only in her undertunic, Cassandra jumped at the intrusion, wrapping her arms about herself. "Who is it?" she asked.

"Your father, girl. Open up."

As expected, the king had come to fetch her. Cassandra replied, "I'm not dressed yet, Father."

A laugh came from behind the door. "I bathed you myself and know every inch of you. You're going to show modesty now? Fetch a robe and open the door."

Jancis hurried a dressing robe out of the wardrobe and hustled Cassandra into it. As the princess tied the garment's belt around her waist, Jancis opened the door. King Karis stood alone in the threshold. His pepper-black beard was split with a wide grin, and his body was swathed in crimson velvet, kingly attire for the meeting to come. He wore all his rings today, great gemstones that twinkled in the torch-light, and when he saw his youngest daughter across the room he beamed. Jancis had brushed Cassandra's hair till it shone and had carefully painted her face and nails. Even in her plain dressing robe, Cassandra was beautiful.

"Daughter, you look lovely," said the king. He stepped into the room. Jancis curtsied and kept her eyes averted. Karis hardly noticed her. He was taken by the vision of his daughter, which always filled Cassandra with pride.

"Father?" she asked innocently. "What is it?"

Karis turned to Jancis. "Would you leave us, please? I need to talk with my daughter."

"Talk? But Father, we're dressing."

"Jancis, go," said the king. The handmaiden didn't wait to be asked again. Quickly she left the room and closed the door behind her, leaving Cassandra to stare blankly at her father. The ruler of Reec took a step forward, his eyes revealing an inner sadness. Cassandra had expected the visit, and had dreaded it.

"You've seen them from your window?" asked her father. His voice was soft. With her, it was always soft.

"Yes. That's why I must dress."

Karis shook his head. "No, not yet. I'll be meeting with them when they arrive, but briefly. Akeela will be tired, too tired for even you to seduce him." His eyes traced over his daughter. "I want him to be as impressed as I am when he sees you."

"Then I won't be meeting him now?" asked Cassandra.

"Tonight," said the king, "after they've rested. When we dine, you'll meet him."

The princess drooped. She had waited so long to meet her new husband, and couldn't bear more delays. But she didn't argue with her father. Instead she let out a dramatic sigh, going back to the bedside and sitting down.

"I wanted to talk to you before tonight," said Karis. He sat down next to her on the bed, then picked up her hand and placed it in his own. His skin was rough against her petal-soft fingers. But his eyes were soft and affectionate.

"A father shouldn't have favorites, I know," he said. "But I'll tell you something now, Cassandra. I've loved you best of all."

"I know," said Cassandra. "You don't have to say so, Father."

"I want you to understand why I'm doing this," he said. "You do understand, yes?"

"For peace," Cassandra replied. It was what her father wanted to hear. "For the good of Reec."

"And everyone in it, including all your sisters and their children. And even for my own good." Karis squeezed her hand. "This is a great favor, daughter. Perhaps I'm selfish to ask it. So let me give you one last chance to refuse me. If you don't wish to marry this Liirian, say so now, before I make the offer."

Cassandra squirmed. Her father didn't know how she really felt, because she hid it so well. "You would think less of me if I refused now, Father."

"Never. I could never think less of you." He looked deep into her eyes. "The truth, Cassandra. There'll be no going back for you, not once the offer is made. And life in Liiria will be hard for you."

"Not so hard, probably."

Karis chuckled. "Ah, you don't know yet, daughter. You think only of being a queen. But we don't know this man, not nearly as well as we should. He may breed you like a bitch, one pup after another. Liirian men can be brutal."

"He is kind," said Cassandra. "You said so yourself. Only a kind man would offer peace, you said."

"True," admitted Karis, reminded of his words. "But it won't be a fairy tale. You know that, don't you?"

"Father, what is this?" Cassandra asked, laughing. "Now you don't want me to marry him?"

Karis' face was firm. "I want you to be sure of your decision, because it is your decision, not mine. I have no greater gift to give this king than you, Cassandra, but you are no slave. Say no to me now, and there will be no harm to it. I'll find another way to seal the peace."

For a moment, Cassandra almost told her father the truth. She almost confessed her great desire to leave her city and country behind, to finally be her own woman and not just one of Karis' daughters. But she didn't tell her father that, because it would have broken his heart.

"You said that Akeela is special," Cassandra reminded him, "and that any woman would be lucky to be his queen. I believe that it is so, Father."

Karis studied her with a grin. "You parse words like a barrister, Cassandra. Don't do this thing just to spare my feelings."

"Father, I am Reecian," said Cassandra. "If Akeela will have me, then I will marry him, because I love you and I love our land."

It wasn't really a lie, and it made her father's face shine. Karis patted his daughter's hand and said, "You're special to me. You always will be. And you will always be my daughter, even when you are a queen." The king rose from the bed, straightening his stunning tunic. "Rest for now. Tonight, when the banquet begins, I will send for you. You will dance for King Akeela, and he will fall in love with you."

Cassandra smiled. Since she had blossomed into womanhood, every man seemed to love her. It gave her power, the taste of which was sweet.

When her father left the chamber, Cassandra rose from the bed and went back to the window. Outside, she could see Akeela's little army, now just outside the city gates.

The Reecian capital rose in a splendid arc before them. Lukien had never been so close to the city before, and as he rode beside Akeela, nearing the tall iron gates, he marveled at the simple, natural architecture and the grace of

his enemies. Hes wasn't like Koth, Liiria's capital. It was smaller and had fewer tall towers, so that light fell easily on its white and brown cement, giving it a shimmering appearance. As the sun dipped down, the city came alive with candles, blinking in the round windows and lending the place an orange sheen. Lukien slowed his column as they neared the city gates. The dentate portals were opened wide in welcome. Beyond them, mounted soldiers sat at attention, their swords sheathed and their shoulders rigid. A procession of Reecian citizens stretched out behind them, disappearing down the avenues and watching the newcomers in silent awe. Lukien heard music, the brassy parade tunes the Reecians favored. An uneasiness grew in his stomach. Despite the obvious welcome Hes was giving Akeela, the Bronze Knight cringed inwardly. In the five years since becoming a full-ranked Royal Charger, he had clashed with these people dozens of times.

"You see?" said Akeela. "They welcome us. As I told you they would."

The king rode a bit faster toward the waiting city. Lukien spurred his horse to keep up.

"Slowly, Akeela," he warned. He brought his chestnut charger to a trot beside his king, steering the beast toward its brother to block its stride. "Let me go first."

Akeela relented, checking his eagerness. He brought his horse to a halt. The winding column behind him stopped. Lukien waved his lieutenants forward, and Trager and Breck trotted out of the mass.

"We'll go first," he told the pair. "The king will follow."

Breck nodded his red head. Trager's face didn't change. The two rode beside each other but behind Lukien, ready to lead their king and his procession into the city. As he turned back toward Hes, Lukien noticed a group of well-dressed nobles at the gate's threshold. Karis' counselors wore red and gold tunics and uneasy smiles on their bearded faces. One of them, taller and more regal than the others, stood a pace ahead of his companions, a black cape around his shoulders and sword at his side. The smile on his face twisted when he noticed Lukien coming toward him, and soon the contagion spread through the others. The soldiers along the avenue cocked their helmeted heads; a murmur rippled through the crowds.

The Bronze Knight had come.

Lukien squared his shoulders. He was Akeela's herald, and that meant he needed to be fearless. His armored horse snorted its disdain, and Lukien rode across the threshold of Hes, into the midst of his enemies. The music grew as the musicians lining the avenues strummed their guitars and blew into their horns, and the red flags of Reec were every-where, hanging down from apartment windows and held aloft by proud teenagers. Yet to Lukien's surprise the Liir-ian flag was displayed too, held by a Reecian honor guard resplendent in crimson tunics and white gloves. As Lukien approached the nobles just inside the city, the foursome bowed deeply, putting their hands over their hearts and lowering their eyes to the cobblestones. They did not lift themselves until Lukien's shadow fell upon them.

"I am Lukien of Liiria," he declared. "Herald of King Akeela and Captain of his Royal Chargers."

The four noblemen raised their eyes to Lukien. The tall one's smile was inscrutable.

"Welcome," he said. He spread his arms wide, looking past Lukien to where Akeela waited behind Trager and Breck. "I am Earl Linuk of Glain. On behalf of King Karis and all of Reec, I welcome you."

"Thank you," said Lukien. He remembered the name Linuk, sure that he had faced the Reecian in combat be-fore. As Earl of Glain, Linuk ruled one of Reec's largest territories and was one of Karis' closest advisors. Akeela had expected him at the meeting, but his presence dis-tracted Lukien nonetheless. Hurriedly he spun his horse around to reveal his king. Trager and Breck parted, and Akeela rode forward. Again the four noblemen bowed, honoring the young ruler.

"My lord Akeela," said Linuk. His voice rang with awe. "This is a great honor for us. We welcome you to Hes, and grant you all our city has to offer."

Akeela looked regal atop his horse, and his expression warmed with good humor. "Earl Linuk, the honor is mine. Rise, please."

The earl did as Akeela commanded, and Akeela sur-veyed the soldiers and citizenry that had gathered to meet him. Except for the music the huge crowd was remarkably quiet. Even the children hanging out of the nearby windows

were silent. Akeela cleared his throat, then raised a hand
to them all, just as he had practiced. He declared, "Thank
you all for this warm welcome. I am truly glad to be here,
and to be honored by you. This will be a great day, a great
moment in history for both our nations."

And with that, the crowd erupted. The people clapped
and the children shouted, and the musicians played louder
to compete with the clamor. Earl Linuk and his fellow nobles beamed at Akeela, looking relieved. Lukien felt a sudden calm. If this was a trap, it was ridiculously elaborate.
He glanced back at his friend Breck, who gave him a wink,
then at Trager, who simply looked disbelieving. The
second-in-command of the Royal Chargers spun around
toward his men, signaling them to enter the city, and slowly
the column of horses came forward, led by a wooden wagon
covered with a white tarpaulin and flanked by four armored
chargers. As the wagon rolled forward, Akeela pointed at
it.

"We bring gifts for your king, Earl Linuk," he said. "May
we present ourselves to him?"

The earl nodded. "King Karis awaits you at his castle,
my lord," he said, then gestured toward the center of the
city. There, on a hill of green lawns and fruit trees, stood
Castle Hes, a twin-towered citadel of gray stone slicing
across the sky. The castle dominated the capital, throwing
its two shadows down upon the baroque city. The main
road from the gate seemed to lead directly to the castle,
and the entire way was lined with onlookers and more of
the ubiquitous musicians.

"It's been a long ride," said Akeela, "and I would like
to meet your king as soon as possible. I think our gifts will
please him, as will our news."

"The king wants nothing more than to speak with you,
my lord, I assure you," said Linuk. "If you'll follow us, you
will see him presently."

"Then lead on, Earl," chirped Akeela.

Linuk and his courtiers turned and went to their horses,
a group of brawny beasts with crimson blankets waiting at
the side of the avenue. At the earl's command the Reecian
soldiers prepared to fall in line behind the Liirians. Akeela
brought his horse forward, waving to the eager crowds. Lukien hurried alongside his king, followed directly by Trager,

Breck, the wagonload of gifts, and the forty Royal Chargers accompanying them. The gates closed silently behind them, and Castle Hes beckoned them forward. Lukien looked about, spying the Reecians lining the street. All met his eyes with a distinct scorn. Though they loved Akeela, apparently, they hated his herald. The knight leaned toward Akeela.

"You were right," he confessed. "Look at them. They adore you."

"They adore the thought of peace," said Akeela, his lips barely moving as he continued to smile and wave. "They are as weary of war as we are."

"We?" chuckled Lukien. "You, perhaps."

"All right then, me," said Akeela. "You're not king, Lukien. If you were, you'd feel differently."

Lukien decided not to ruin the moment. Of all the Chargers, only he himself craved war, because it defined him and because he knew nothing else. He said, "I'm happy for you, Akeela. I'm happy you're right."

"Be happy for Liiria," said Akeela. They were passing a crowd of young children, all boys, all excited and pointing at them. "Look there, you see those boys? They would have all grown up to be Reecian soldiers, with nothing more to look forward to than war. But they can have a future now. They won't have to face you on the battlefield."

Akeela's logic was flawless and cruel, and it made Lukien stiffen.

"As I said, I'm glad you were right."

The two rode in silence for minutes afterward, Akeela enjoying the crowds, Lukien enduring their stares. Earl Linuk and his party had brought them to the very edge of the castle hill, to another open gate leading to the outer ward of the citadel. Here, the crowds of citizens thinned, replaced by more soldiers and servants of the king. Stableboys and milkmaids had gathered in the yard, and the wide portcullis of Castle Hes had been raised, bidding them enter. The long columns of horsemen snaked into the ward, where Linuk and his men dismounted, handing their steeds off to waiting grooms. Akeela glanced up at the two towers, impressed by them. They were suitably grand, and the lichens climbing up their walls made them look ancient. Now that the sun was nearly down, the palace was lit with braziers. Grim-faced guards with feathers in their helms flanked the portcullis. Lukien waited for Linuk to fetch them. He dismounted, along with Trager and Breck.

Earl Linuk stepped forward and carefully took Akeela's reins. "My lord, if you'll come with me, I'll take you to King Karis. He's in his throne room, waiting for you."

Akeela dismounted, eager to follow the earl. "Will, see to the wagon, will you?"

Lieutenant Trager said, "Yes, my lord," and went to work. Like Lukien, he had known Akeela for years, and hated being ordered about. But he always did as ordered, and with Breck's help pulled back the tarpaulin from the wagon. Atop the wagon's bed was an iron chest with stout rivets and a padlock. Akeela gestured to it, asking Linuk if he could bring it with him to the throne room. The earl agreed without hesitation, but when Linuk called some of his men forward to carry it, Akeela said, "Don't bother, Earl. My lieutenants will see to it," then followed the earl through the portcullis. Lukien hurried after him.

"Breck, Trager," he ordered, "bring it along. The rest of you, stay behind."

Quickly he caught up with Akeela, falling in step behind him. The earl's men surrounded them, talking idly about how pleased they were to have Akeela in Reec. The young king nodded and smiled, well suited to his first diplomatic mission. Lukien was proud of him, the way an older brother would be proud of a younger sibling. They had talked about this moment for months, and all the while Akeela had fretted about the task. Yet the new king seemed every bit as polished as his late father.

The halls of Castle Hes were marvelous. High ceilings swallowed them, decorated with mosaics of colored marble and gilded glass. Huge windows revealed the night outside as it came alive with stars, and glowing torches stood like sentries along the walls. The stableboys and milkmaids had gone, and now only well-dressed nobles greeted them, bowing to Akeela as he passed. Lukien caught the eye of a comely noblewoman just in time to see her snicker. He sighed and looked away. Just ahead a pair of carved oak doors hung open on iron hinges.

"The throne room," said Linuk. He paused outside the chamber, stepping aside and gesturing for Akeela to enter.

Akeela took a breath, then turned toward Lukien, giving
his champion a nervous smile. Lukien encouraged him with
a wink. Then, with Akeela leading the way, the two Liirians
stepped inside.

The throne room spread out before them, high and
barrel-vaulted, with stout iron chandeliers and grand tapestries and a formidable dais at its far end. On the dais was
a throne of ebony, with carved runes through its form and
feet like the paws of a lion. Perched on the throne, his eyes
as hard as diamonds, was King Karis of Reec. Akeela and
Lukien took careful steps toward him, not averting their gaze.
Karis' face was emotionless. He studied the pair dispassionately, barely twitching his ringed fingers. Two more Reecians,
dressed similarly to Linuk, stood on the dais beside him. Lukien guessed they were Raxor, the king's war minister, and
Arnod, the Reecian treasurer. Raxor was the king's brother,
and the family resemblance was striking. To Lukien's eye,
they could have been twins. Not so with Arnod, who was
much shorter than Raxor and fair-haired. Both advisors
were quiet as Akeela approached, waiting for their king to
speak first. An anxious silence filled the chamber.

Then, unexpectedly, Akeela dropped to one knee before
the Reecian king. He bowed his head, put an arm across
his knee as if being knighted, and said, "Great King of
Reec, I am Akeela of Liiria. By accepting me into your
home, you honor me."

Lukien couldn't believe the sight, nor could Karis. From
the way the Reecian's eyebrows lifted, he seemed stunned
by the greeting. Noticing that Lukien was still standing,
Akeela casually reached out for his hand and gently
dragged him downward. Reluctantly, Lukien joined in the
bow, keeping his eyes on Karis. The King of Reec looked
first at his advisors, then back at Akeela.

"King Akeela," he said finally, "Thank you."

Akeela and Lukien rose. The young king offered his host
one of his warm smiles, which the Reecian did not return.
Karis merely studied them. Thinking the stillness of the
chamber would suffocate him, Lukien nudged Akeela to
say something. But the king remained silent.

"You're very young," said Karis. "My advisors tell me
you are twenty-four years old. Is that so?"

"Your advisors are accurate, King Karis," said Akeela. "I am twenty-four."

"How many years have Reec and Liiria been at war?" pressed Karis. His tone was featureless, neither threatening nor mild. "Do you know?"

"Since before I was born, my lord," replied Akeela. "For twenty-eight years, since the battle of Awalak."

"That's right," sighed Karis. "A very long time, your whole lifetime and more. So tell me then why a scholar like yourself is so anxious to end a war his father loved, so soon after taking his place."

Insulted, Lukien stepped forward. "You presume a great deal, King Karis," he said. "King Balak never loved war. To say so is to slander him."

"Lukien," said Akeela, taking his shoulder. "Be easy."

King Karis rose from his throne. For the first time, anger flashed in his eyes. "You are the Bronze Knight," he declared. "*Butcher.* I should warn you to be silent, Lukien of Liiria. You are not so welcome here as your king."

Lukien wanted to speak but Akeela's insistent grip on his shoulder stopped him. Akeela stepped forward, saying, "Lukien is my champion, my lord. I go nowhere without him, and you've already agreed to let him accompany me."

"Yes," said Karis. "I did agree, because I wanted to speak with you, King Akeela, and to hear your offer." His eyes went to Lukien. "But I warn you, Bronze Knight—I tolerate you only for the comfort of your king."

Akeela said calmly, "And I should warn you, King Karis, that Lukien was as close to King Balak as a son. Speaking against my father will invite his ire. And mine."

Karis grunted suspiciously. "You are brothers, then?"

"Of a kind," replied Akeela.

"All right, then," agreed Karis. "We are here to talk peace, after all."

Before Akeela could respond, a clamor sounded in the doorway. Lukien turned to see Trager, Breck, and four others of their brigade toting the iron box. Earl Linuk was before them, smiling at his king.

"My lord, forgive me, but King Akeela has brought this for you."

Karis looked perplexed, and also strangely pleased. He

stepped down from his dais just as the sweating men dropped the chest to the floor with a thud.

"What is it?" Karis asked.

"Gifts," said Akeela brightly. "From Liiria to you, King Karis. I think you'll like what we've brought you. In fact, I have something very special to give you."

Lukien bristled, realizing what Akeela meant. But Karis seemed intrigued. Instantly he had lost his dispassion toward Akeela, and now seemed to share the young man's exuberance. Raxor and Arnod gathered near him as he peered at the box. To Lukien, they looked like a bunch of children waiting for Akeela to open a toy chest. Then, as if he'd suddenly come to his senses, Raxor put out a hand.

"Wait, my lord," he told Karis. His eyelids narrowed on Akeela. "Tell us first what is in there."

"Raxor . . ."

"Brother, it could be dangerous," advised the war minister. "I'm sorry to say this in front of our guests, but they are Liirians, after all."

The king flushed. "Forgive my brother, King Akeela. He means no offense, I assure you."

Akeela produced a shiny silver key from beneath his cape. "I promise you, my lord, there is no danger in the box. Only good things. May I proceed?"

"Of course," said Karis, ignoring his brother's concern. He stepped closer to the box in a show of goodwill. Raxor stood beside him, but Arnod kept back a pace. Curiosity got the better of Earl Linuk, who came to stand next to his king, and as Akeela clicked open the padlock and tilted open the iron lid, the faces of the Reecians took on an amber glow, bathed in the reflected glow of the contents. Nearly everything in the box was gold; coins and candelabras and carving knives, rings and plates and picture frames, all shimmering in the chest. It was more than a fortune, more than a king's ransom, and it made Karis' jaw drop. The Reecian king hovered over the box, dumbfounded. Akeela swelled proudly.

"For the people of Reec," he said. "From the people of Liiria. There's something in here from nearly every citizen of Koth, my lord. These are not only valuables from my own coffers, but from farmers and blacksmiths, even from my own soldiers, here." He gestured to Lukien, who himself had tossed a gold-hilted dagger into the chest.

Karis could barely speak. "They did this for you?" he asked.

"They did this for peace," said Akeela. "Not for me."

"My king is modest," said Lukien. "They would not have done this for any other ruler, not even his father."

King Karis shook his head in disbelief. "In Liiria they call you Akeela the Good," he said. "I know this. And now I know why."

"It is the people of Liiria that are good, my lord. I asked them to contribute and they did so willingly." Akeela brightened. "But that's not all. Look closer at the chest, my lord."

Puzzled, Karis did as asked, staring into the box and its lustrous contents. "Yes?"

"That bunch of cloth. Pick it up."

Laying atop the golden heap was a piece of blue linen, wrapped securely around a hidden item. Karis reached out and plucked it from the pile, holding it carefully.

"What is it?" he asked.

"Go ahead, unwrap it," urged Akeela. Lukien cringed. Like Trager, he had dreaded this moment. It was the one thing he and his lieutenant agreed upon. He watched Karis peel the blue linen back until its contents was revealed—a little crystal bottle filled with clear liquid. Karis held it up to the light. His advisors gathered around to see it.

"Forgive me, King Akeela," said Karis, "but your gift is . . . baffling."

"That's water from the river Kryss," said Akeela. His voice quavered, and Lukien knew he was nervous. After this, there could be no going back. "It's yours, my lord."

Karis looked at him, not quite understanding, or not daring to believe.

"My lord, you said it yourself," said Akeela. "Since before I was born, Reec and Liiria have battled, and all because of a river. We've always thought the Kryss was ours, and you've always thought it belonged to you. I don't know how many people have died for that bloody stream; I don't think anyone could count. But I'm king now, and I won't let it go on." He shrugged, and for a moment he looked more like a boy than a monarch. "The river Kryss is yours. If you'll allow Liiria free trade on the western side, we will quarrel with you over it no more."

King Karis of Reec blinked, mute with surprise. He didn't move, but merely stared at Akeela with his mouth open.

"Fate above," said Linuk. "Do you mean this?"

"Everything my king says is the truth," said Lukien. "Akeela the Good does not lie."

"You would give us the Kryss?" asked Raxor. The war minister seemed dazed. "Just like that?"

"No," said Akeela sharply. "Not just like that. For peace, and peace only. That's the price for these gifts. You may keep all this gold, but if you break this pact there will be bloodshed again. And I'm gambling that none of us wants that. Do you want war, King Karis?"

Still Karis didn't reply. Clutching the bottle of river water, he climbed back to his throne, seating himself. Lukien knew Akeela's gift had astonished him. After nearly thirty years of war, the Kryss was suddenly his, and now he didn't know what to do with it.

"Do you know the cards of Noor, King Akeela?" he asked.

Akeela nodded. In Liiria, fortune cards were common, just like all other arcane trappings. "I know of them, but that is all," he replied.

"When your father died, I read the cards," said Karis. "I wanted to know what kind of man was succeeding him. The cards told me that you were a man of peace. It was the first time I thought they were lying to me. Now it seems the cards have shamed me. I should have listened."

Akeela stepped toward the throne. "We have an agreement, then?"

Karis gave a huge grin. "Oh, young king, we have so much more than that. We have peace, for the first time in my memory. You have made an old man very happy."

The Reecians in the room cheered, and Akeela and Breck joined them. Even Lukien grinned. Akeela clapped the shoulder of Earl Linuk, then embraced Raxor and Arnod in turn. Finally, he climbed onto the dais to take Karis' hand, but Karis rose instead, took Akeela's hand in his own, and placed a gentle kiss on it.

"Tonight we will celebrate," he declared. "There will be music and we will feast. All your men must attend, and we will show you how Reecians celebrate!"

"Thank you, my lord," said Akeela. To Lukien, he looked gigantically relieved. "Then we will see you tonight. And if you have rooms for us, we would be grateful. 'Twas a long road from Liiria."

"Rooms are already prepared for you," said Karis. "Earl Linuk will escort you, and my servants will see to your needs. Rest well for tonight, King Akeela. You are not the only one with gifts."

Akeela squinted at him. "My lord?"

Karis laughed and released his hand. "You'll see what I mean. For now, just rest and enjoy my home."

2

Akeela had been given chambers in the south tower of Castle Hes, overlooking the city and its vast marketplace. They were well appointed rooms, fit for a royal visitor, furnished lavishly with silk and tapestries. A cavernous collection of hallways connected the rooms, so that Akeela not only had a bed chamber, but also a dressing room and a separate room for bathing. A huge bed of iron and brass decorated with plush pillows had been prepared for him, along with a platter of fresh breads and cheeses. Earl Linuk, who had escorted Akeela to the rooms, had told him to rest and make ready for the banquet being prepared for him. Linuk had seen to Akeela personally, while Karis' servants tended to the other Liirians, finding them rooms on lower floors. Linuk had not expected Lukien to insist on sharing the rooms with Akeela. Cordially, Linuk explained that he had prepared a nearby room for the king's "bodyguard," but Lukien had ignored him, choosing instead to remain with Akeela.

Lukien was always with Akeela.

Sometimes, it seemed to Lukien that he had been with Akeela his whole life. They were nothing alike, really, but over the years they had become like brothers, and had even been raised as such by Akeela's father, Balak, who adored Lukien. Abandoned by his father and orphaned by the death of his mother, Lukien had lived in the streets of

Koth, with only his ten-year old wits to protect him from the big-city predators. He had been a thief, stealing what he needed to survive or working for pennies in the slave-like conditions of smithies. By eleven he was emaciated from this grueling life, but by thirteen he was becoming a man, and life in the smithies had strengthened his body and hardened his heart. Then, at fourteen, he had met Akeela.

Akeela, who was three years younger than Lukien, had been touring the Liirian capital with some of his father's advisors. A contingent of guards had accompanied them, but Akeela, curious about things even then, had wandered off to explore on his own, blundering into the alleys Lukien called home. It hadn't taken long for the roughs in the area to find the well dressed stranger. Even for his age Akeela was short, but he had defended himself against the youths that had robbed him, swearing when Lukien found him that he'd bloodied the noses of two of them. Of course it was Akeela who was truly bloody. Thoroughly drubbed by the boys, Akeela needed help finding his way back to his royal guardians. And when they had located the guards and gotten Akeela safely into his carriage, the boy-prince had told his protectors not to go looking for the youths that had robbed him, because they were poor and knew no better.

In all the years since then, Lukien had never forgotten that moment. Had he been the victim, he would have tracked the rabble down and killed them, but not so this forgiving youngster. Instead, Akeela had insisted that Lukien return to the castle with them, to get some clean clothing and a good meal, and to meet his father, the king. There, the young Lukien was greeted as a hero for helping the prince, and King Balak had practically adopted him. He hadn't left the castle since; as he had never left Akeela's side, because the young prince needed him.

But Lukien always remembered the hard-won lessons of the street, and he had never forgiven his drunken father for leaving him, nor his mother for dying. Those were burdens he carried with him everywhere, even onto the battlefield, and it was an unfortunate enemy indeed who came upon the Bronze Knight and his unwieldy emotions. In Koth's castle he had grown to manhood, had studied in the Liirian war college, and graduated at the top of his class.

He had become the paragon of a horse soldier, rising to command the Royal Chargers. Still Lukien brooded as he recalled his miserable life on the streets of Koth.

All these things Lukien considered as he sat by the window overlooking Hes' marketplace, absently chewing an apple. From high in the tower, Hes looked much the same as Koth, and the similarity triggered unpleasant memories. Lukien stretched out, holding back a sigh. Inside the dressing chamber, Akeela was preparing for the celebration. Lukien himself had already dressed, choosing a tunic of plain brown and some stiff black boots that Karis' servants had provided. Already Lukien felt himself growing anxious. He didn't like the idea of eating with Reecians, or of spending the evening being stared at. But Akeela was in a fine mood, for he had brokered his peace with Karis and was ready to celebrate. As the young king readied himself in the nearby chamber, Lukien could hear him whistling.

Whistling. Lukien couldn't help but laugh. At twenty-four, Akeela still resembled the boy he had rescued in the alley.

"Akeela the Good," he whispered, shaking his head. An apt name for such a blameless man. Suddenly, Lukien was pleased with his life as Akeela's champion. Sometimes brothers are less than friends, he knew, but that didn't mean there was love lost. Putting aside his half-eaten apple, he got out of the chair and strode toward the dressing chamber. "Almost ready?" he called. "They'll be expecting us."

Akeela stepped out of the small room, his hair shining with oil, his blue tunic stunning. Across his waist rested a silver belt with a small, ceremonial dagger, while on his feet were a pair of thigh-high boots, polished to a gemstone-like luster.

"I'm ready," he declared. "And I'm starving."

"Let's hope these Reecians can cook," said Lukien. He glanced down at Akeela's dagger. "You're taking that?"

Akeela caught his meaning. The Reecians had requested that Lukien himself bear no arms to the banquet. "It's just for ceremony," he explained. "Besides, you'll be sitting next to me. If anyone tries to harm me, you can grab my dagger and save me, all right?"

Lukien didn't laugh. Without his weapons he felt naked.

"I think they'd try to poison you first. Not much good I could do you then."

Akeela found a mirror in the hall and adjusted his collar. "You don't trust them, I know. But you'll see. The time for peace has come. The time for a new Liiria, maybe a whole new world."

"A grand dream."

"Nay, not a dream, Lukien. A plan." The young king smoothed down his hair. "Shall we go?"

With Akeela leading, Lukien followed him out of the chambers and into the hallway where two Reecian guards were waiting, ready to escort them downstairs. They explained that King Karis was already in the banquet chamber, and that many of Akeela's men had gathered there, too. Akeela walked with eager strides as the guards led them down a flight of stairs, then into another hall, wide and tall. The hall was decorated with flowers, and as they neared the banquet room the strains of music reached their ears. Lukien could see Trager and Breck waiting for them just outside the banquet room. Breck wore a grin while Trager was unreadable, but both had dressed for the evening, sporting long capes trimmed with wolf fur. They looked fit, fine examples of Liirian excellence, and Lukien was proud of them. They bowed to Akeela as he approached.

"How's it look in there?" Lukien asked Breck, peering over his lieutenant's shoulder. The chamber was crowded with people and pipe smoke.

"You should see the feast they've laid out for us," Breck replied. He was a big man who loved food, and his appetite shone in his eyes.

"King Karis is already inside, waiting for you, my lord," Trager told Akeela.

Akeela nodded. "Go on, all of you, go first."

With a shooing gesture he ushered Trager and Breck into the banquet chamber, then asked the Reecians to proceed. Akeela steadied himself with a breath. Then, with Lukien at his side, he stepped into the tumult of the banquet. Instantly, every head in the chamber turned toward him, and the music grew. A crescendo of applause erupted and the Reecians banged the long banquet tables with their metal tankards and cheered for the foreign king. Servants with platters in their hands stopped in mid-service to gape, and the children of the castle nobles, who had been carefully outfitted in royal finery, pointed and giggled. At the end of the vast chamber, at a raised table against the far wall, King Karis stood and joined the applause. There was a huge goblet in his meaty fist and his beard parted in laughter. Around him were Earl Linuk and a dozen other nobles, while at a table to his left sat a group of lovely women all sharing a striking resemblance. These, Lukien guessed, were Karis' daughters. He had heard that they were very beautiful, and now he saw the rumors were true. Each wore a long velvet dress and twinkling jewelry, and each had a husband or suitor seated beside her. As Akeela moved into the center of the room, his Royal Chargers, who had already gathered for the feast, gave a large round of cheers, drowning out even the whistling children. The hero's welcome made Akeela flush. The young king gave a humble smile as he approached the table where Karis waited, two empty chairs directly on his right. Akeela thanked the crowds, trying to speak over the clamor, gesturing for quiet. But there was too much exuberance in the room for that, so he simply made his way to the head table with Lukien. There, with everyone watching, he and King Karis embraced. It was a light embrace, more like a handshake, but the peck the Reecian gave Akeela's cheek told Lukien it was sincere.

"A great day!" said Karis over the din. "And now, a great night to celebrate!" ·

Akeela swept an arm over the room, moved by the celebration. "This is wonderful, my lord," he said. "I'm grateful."

"It's well deserved," replied Karis. "All Reec should celebrate tonight. Now sit, my new friend, and enjoy yourself. Tonight is for getting drunk."

Akeela sat down next to the king, then Lukien took his own seat beside Akeela. Trager and Breck, who had been waiting for them beside the table, sat down next to Lukien. A pretty serving girl offered him some ale. Lukien held out his goblet, giving her a wink. Trager noticed the flirting and shook his head with disgust.

"What?" asked Lukien.

Trager scowled. "Why would you pretend to want one of these Reecian she-wolves, Captain?" he asked, careful that Akeela did not hear him. "Once she got you in bed she'd emasculate you with her teeth."

"Sure," Lukien scoffed. "And how would you know that? Has a Reecian wench gotten to your stones, Trager?"

"They're our enemies," said Trager simply. "Piss-filled bags of misery, the lot of them. You of all people should know that, Captain."

"Times are changing, Trager," said Lukien simply. "Have some ale."

The lieutenant folded his arms over his chest. "I won't drink with these swine."

"Suit yourself."

Turning his attention toward the floor, Lukien noticed a clearing between tables. The space just in front of their own table had been left bare, but an instant later an acrobat tumbled into it. As the crowd laughed and clapped, the man somersaulted backwards, landing on his feet again and again. A juggler joined him, then a violinist, and soon the floor was full of entertainers. Lukien settled back to enjoy the show.

From a tiny alcove just beyond the banquet room, Cassandra peered out from behind a velvet curtain, breathless with anticipation. In a moment the soft music would start and her father would call her forth. Cassandra smiled inwardly. She was a fine dancer, and the dress Jancis had made her was tight in all the right places. Even if Akeela was accustomed to beautiful women, she knew she could seduce him. Men were like that when she danced, so pliable, even the hardest of them. Next to her, Jancis was smiling mischievously, enjoying the excitement. From their place in the alcove they could barely see Akeela past the crowds, catching only glimpses of him and his bodyguard, the Bronze Knight. The Liirian king was drinking and laughing. He had dark hair, not unlike Cassandra's own, and his smile was blinding. Cassandra thought him handsome. Not stunningly handsome, but serviceably so, and that heartened her. She had heard too many stories of duchesses married to beastly brutes, who did nothing but breed them for sons.

From the little she knew of the Liirian, he didn't seem that type at all. And, to Cassandra's great surprise, neither did his knight.

Lukien of Liiria was easily the more handsome of the pair. He was tall and lean, with the look of a wolf about his sharp face, and his hair was honey-colored, making him seem less threatening than Cassandra had imagined. Like everyone in Reec, she knew the stories of the legendary knight. On this side of the river Kryss, they were evil tales. Yet as she spied him from behind her curtain, Lukien didn't look evil. He looked remarkably tame.

"Look," Jancis whispered, pointing toward the head table. "The tumblers are leaving."

As the entertainers left the floor, Cassandra finally got an unobstructed look at her husband . . .

No, she corrected herself. Not her husband. Not yet. He would have to accept her first, and for that she needed to be perfect. How many women had Akeela been with, she wondered? And she, still a virgin, had to seduce him. The challenge made her pulse race.

"God's death, what's taking Father so long?" she muttered.

"Easy," bade Jancis. "The musicians are coming, see?"

Cassandra craned around the curtain and saw the violinists moving toward the floor. When they made their soft music, her father would call her out. She closed her eyes, summoning her skill, and waited for his call.

Lukien watched with interest as the acrobats cleared the floor. He had been enjoying their antics, and they gave the Reecians in the room something other than him to stare at. A group of musicians were taking the floor, a lute player and a pair of violinists. The lute player tested his instrument, plucking off a string of gentle notes. The sight of them made the knight groan.

"Oh, no," he muttered softly, prepared to be bored.

Next to him, Akeela still had a smile plastered on his face. He was talking to King Karis, but when the musicians came forward their conversation abruptly stopped. Karis seemed distracted.

"More music, my lord?" Akeela asked him. Strangely,

the room had quieted. The violinists drew their bows across their strings, readying themselves.

"King Akeela, I have a special treat for you now," said Karis. "The sweetest date in my orchard—my daughter, Cassandra."

"Daughter?" said Akeela. With his chin he gestured to the nearby table. "Aren't those your daughters?"

"They are. But there is one you haven't met yet." The monarch's face glowed with pride. "She is the most special thing I have, King Akeela. Now she will dance for you."

Before Akeela could reply, Karis clapped his hands loudly. The violinists began to play, drawing out a soft melody. The lute player joined them, plucking slowly on his strings, and the music they made was beautiful. Lukien felt suddenly calmed. Like candlelight, the music bathed him. Even Trager was pacified. The glower on the lieutenant's face melted away, replaced by a blankness. Akeela looked around the chamber, wondering where this prize daughter was hiding. Then, from behind a velvet curtain, she emerged.

Gliding into the center of the chamber came a lithe and delicate figure with raven-black hair and a twirling dress of green and crimson. She floated, barely grazing the floor in her passage, her face lightly flushed, her dark eyes lustrous. Lukien slowly lowered his goblet, his eyes narrowing. She was a vision. Perfect in every way. The folds of her dress wrapped around her flawless figure, showcasing her hips and perfect breasts, and as she spun slowly toward them her hair twirled in seductive ribbons about her face. The music drew her nearer, filling the room, and every eye watched her, admiring her grace. Lukien glanced over at Akeela and saw his king mesmerized. He too had lowered his goblet, and now was clutching the arms of his chair, entranced by the lovely girl.

"Cassandra," Karis whispered. "My youngest daughter." Akeela nodded dumbly. "Cassandra."

The music grew. The dancer drifted closer. As the rhythm quickened so did she, her movements bewitching. Soon other instruments joined the song, another lute and a flute player. Cassandra tossed her body into the music, twirling and falling and throwing back her head as though an unseen lover caressed her. Lukien swallowed hard, unable to take his eyes from the girl. She radiated beauty, and her seductive turns made his blood race. She was very near their table now. Lifting her face toward them, she gave Akeela the slightest smile. The gesture made the young king swoon. He tilted toward Lukien slightly, whispering in a starstruck voice, "Look at her. She's beautiful."

Lukien nodded. In that moment, Cassandra of Reec was the fairest thing he had ever seen. Her seductive movements touched something primal in him, something dark and carnal. And, to his surprise, something gentle stirred within him too, longing for the love of a woman. He sank back in his chair, and suddenly he was on the streets of Koth again. Alone and afraid, he could never hope for a woman like this. Princesses were the purvey of princes. Lukien picked up his drink and sipped at it distractedly. He had bedded beautiful women before, but never a royal one. Close as he was to Akeela, he was still kept from such finery.

"Oh, she's lovely," said Akeela. This time, he was speaking to Karis. "Such a fine dancer, my lord."

"My daughter dances constantly," said Karis. "It is a gift she has." He gave his guest a curious look. "You like her?"

"Like her? She's a treasure. Your daughter—all your daughters, really—are lovely."

Karis moved in closer. "Ah, but Cassandra is the fairest of them all, don't you think?"

"She's splendid," agreed Akeela, then said no more, concentrating instead on the dancer and letting the world fall away around him.

Cassandra danced until sweat fell from her brow and her long hair straggled across her face. She twirled and twirled without end, and when the music finally climaxed she collapsed to the floor in a dramatic finish, tossing back her head and panting, a giant smile on her face. Her eyes locked with Akeela's as the room came alive with applause. Akeela's gaze lingered on her. Lukien sighed breathlessly.

"Beautiful," he whispered.

Akeela rose to his feet. "Beautiful!" he echoed, clapping for the girl. His approval made Cassandra glow. Still on her knees, she tilted her head to the Liirian king.

"Thank you, my lord," she said. Out of breath, her voice was soft as a breeze.

"Rise, daughter," said Karis.

Cassandra did as her father commanded, getting to her feet. She did not look away from them as Lukien expected, but rather faced them head on, still looking at Akeela. Then, oddly, her eyes flicked toward Lukien for a moment. The gesture startled Lukien and it was he that looked away, but by the time he looked back her gaze had returned to Akeela.

"You are a very fine dancer, Princess," said Akeela. "The finest I've ever seen, I'd say. Wouldn't you agree, Lukien?"

Lukien said, "I would, my lord."

"Good!" said Karis. "Then you will be pleased with what I have to tell you. Sit, my lord, please."

They all returned to their chairs, and while Cassandra stood before them, Karis picked up a pitcher of ale and began refilling Akeela's goblet. Akeela put up a hand to stop the king.

"No, no more for me yet, my lord."

"Oh, but we may have something to toast, I think, King Akeela," said Karis. He filled the goblet to the brim, then sat back. A pensive expression crossed his face.

"My lord?" Akeela probed. "What is it?"

"King Akeela," began Karis, "you have given all of us a great gift. You have brought gold to us and the goodwill of your people, and have given us the river Kryss to use as our own. Most of all you have brought us peace, a thing I had never expected to see in my lifetime."

Akeela shifted, embarrassed by the praise. "Thank you, my lord."

"You are remarkable, King Akeela. For such a young man, you are very wise. So different from your father."

"Please, my lord . . ."

"No, let me say this," Karis interrupted. His face was grave. "I never met your father, not even on the battlefield. But I know from my advisors that he was a brutal warrior and a hater of Reec, and I think it's extraordinary that a man like that could sire such a wise-hearted son. You are remarkable, King Akeela, and I have almost nothing of equal value to match the gifts you have given me."

"I ask for nothing in return, my lord Karis," said Akeela. "Just the chance to rule Liiria in peace."

Karis nodded. "I believe that. I know you want nothing

from us but peace. And to seal that peace, I offer you the greatest thing I possess, something that means more to me than anything." He pointed at the waiting Cassandra. "I give you a queen. My daughter, Cassandra."

Akeela's ubiquitous smile faded. "How's that?"

"A wife, King Akeela. To seal the peace between us."

Lukien was stunned. Akeela looked at him for an explanation, but the knight merely shrugged. Before them, Cassandra wore a confident smile.

"A wife?" blurted Akeela. "For me?"

"You are surprised, I know," Karis admitted. "But you are young, and unaware of how we do things in Reec. Peace is made in such ways, my lord."

"Yes, but . . ."

"She is the greatest gift I can give you," said Karis. "And if you accept her, she will please you. She will give you children as beautiful as herself, and a link to Reec, so that we will never war again. Isn't that what you want, my lord? Peace?"

Unable to speak, Akeela looked at Cassandra. She was still breathing hard from her dance but met his gaze head-on. Akeela chewed his lower lip, overwhelmed by the offer. Lukien put a hand on his shoulder.

"It is a great gift, my king," he said diplomatically. "But a surprising one. And surely you will need time to think on it."

"Yes," agreed Akeela quickly. "Time to think on it, consider things."

"Of course," said Karis. There was a trace of disappointment in his voice. "Such a union shouldn't be entered lightly, and while you're my guest you can think on it."

"It really is a great gift, King Karis," said Akeela. "Truly, I am humbled. But what does your daughter think of this, I wonder?" He turned toward Cassandra. "Princess Cassandra? Do you agree to your father's proposal?"

The questions shocked Lukien. Was Akeela actually considering the offer? He kept his hand on Akeela's shoulder, giving it a cautionary squeeze. Surprisingly, Akeela shook it off.

"My father is very wise," said Cassandra. "And I don't object to his offer. If you will have me, King Akeela, I'll be your queen."

Akeela grinned. "Very well, then. I will think on it. Thank you, Princess. And thank you for your beautiful dance."

Cassandra curtsied and dismissed herself, disappearing back behind the curtain. Akeela watched her go, admiring her all the way. Once again Lukien put his lips to the young man's ear.

"Steady," he whispered. "She's just a girl."

Akeela shook his head. "Not just a girl, Lukien. Perhaps *the girl.*"

"You've had too much ale," said Lukien. The music had started again, and the servants went back to work, delivering steaming platters of bread and meat. Akeela's eyes lingered on the velvet curtain. Lukien sighed. "Fate above," he muttered. "What have we gotten into?"

If Akeela heard him, he didn't show it.

3

Night fell on Koth with a hammer-blow of rain. Wind from a summer squall shook the panes of glass in the single window of a tiny bedroom. And Beith Toms, in her thirteenth hour of labor, turned her eyes toward the storm outside and began to sob.

"Easy, now," said the midwife, Gwena. The old woman's hands touched Beith's thighs, massaging the aching muscles. Next to her, Beith's friend Meri squeezed her hand, so hard that Beith thought her fingers would crack. But that pain was nothing compared to the agony inside her. Beith choked back her tears and concentrated on Meri's earnest face and the rain pelting her window.

"Oh, yes," said Gwena. The old woman was peering between Beith's legs as if looking at something fascinating. "Not much longer, girl. Push now!"

"I can't!" groaned Beith.

"Yes, you can. Do it now. Not much more."

Beith shut her eyes and tried to expel her infant, wailing with the effort. For thirteen hours she had been like this, first losing her water, then crying for Meri and Gwena while the contractions overtook her body. Eventually, they had come like the storm, quickly and with unexpected fury. Beith bit down hard as she gave the infant another push. Sweat fell from her face. Meri put a cool cloth to her forehead, wiping away the perspiration. Her friend was smiling, but Beith could tell she was afraid. These days, Beith recognized fear easily. It always stared back at her from mirrors.

"All right, breathe now," directed Gwena. She nodded, satisfied with Beith's effort. "Not much longer."

"You keep saying that," gasped Beith. "For god's sake, how much more?"

"Not much more."

"Argh!"

"Be easy, girl," said Gwena. She had a towel in her hand that had once been white but was now stained with blood. The sight of it made Beith queasy and she looked away, back toward the window. The hard rain frightened her— she wished it would stop. She wished the baby would come out and stop torturing her, and she wished that her husband were with her, but he was dead. Meri kept squeezing her hand, but Beith felt profoundly alone. She had no one else now that Gilwyn was gone, and she wondered if King Akeela would let her remain in the castle. Her child was being born fatherless, and that was the greatest pain of all.

"Damn it!" she cried.

Old Gwena ignored the outburst. She had been the castle's midwife for years and had heard far worse from her charges, even from the royal ladies she tended. Beith wasn't royal but she could swear like a devil, and as a contraction seized her she let out a string of curses. Her emotions were galloping in all directions. Gilwyn's face came to her every time she closed her eyes. He had been a good man and had died too young, and some were saying his death had sparked Akeela into talking peace with the Reecians. He had been one of Lukien's best. Lukien himself had brought her the terrible news, which had shattered the pregnant Beith and drove her to depression. But Akeela had promised her she could remain in the castle, and Akeela was a good man, wasn't he?

"I don't know," moaned Beith, tossing her head back. She felt delirious, and didn't care what she said or who heard her.

"Beith, stop now," said Meri. Her friend wiped her face, blotting up the perspiration. "You'll be all right. It's all going well, right Gwena?"

"It's going perfectly," said the old woman. "This child's

sliding out smoother than the devil in velvet trousers. It
hurts, I know, but this is nothing. I brought King Akeela
into the world, you know, and if there was ever a child
that didn't want to come out, it was him. Twenty hours of
sheer agony . . ."

"Gwena!" snapped Meri. "Watch what you're saying!"

For the first time in hours, Beith laughed.

"Don't laugh, breathe!" the midwife commanded. Once
again she tucked down to inspect the birth. Beith could see
the top of her head bobbing. "Yes, it's good. You're doing
well, child. That's it, now. Keep helping it along."

Beith strained to breathe the way Gwena had taught her.
She saw a flash of lightning outside the window, then felt
the room shake with thunder. Outside, the rain had smothered the moon and stars, so that only torchlight lit the
chamber. She could smell her own foulness, the stench of
blood and sweat and effort. Every breath was laborious.

"I want a boy," she gasped. "You hear, Gwena?"

The midwife scoffed. "That's not what I do."

"A boy," Beith insisted. "So I can name him after his
father."

"And if it's a girl?" asked Meri.

"It won't be a girl," snapped Beith. "God owes me. He's
taken everything else from me. The least He can do me is
this favor!"

Another contraction came. Beith gasped, feeling her
birth canal move within her and the awful pain of the insistent child. She clutched at the stained sheets, gritting her
teeth.

"All right now, this is it," said Gwena. She put her hands
between Beith's legs. "Give me another push, girl. One
more big one."

Beith clamped down on her pain, banishing it from her
mind. As thunder crashed outside the tower she let out a
determined cry, focusing on expelling the child from her
womb. The pain was enormous, and the simples Gwena
had given her had done little to ease her suffering. Now it
had all come down to this final, monumental effort. But
she was nearly done now and she knew it, and that gave
Beith strength. With all her waning energy, she pushed.

"Yes!" urged Gwena. "Yes, yes!"

It will be a boy, Beith told herself. *And he'll be handsome*

*and strong like his father, and he'll be a great knight for
Akeela. He will be!*

Even through the pain, a little smile curled the girl's lips.
There would be some reward for her loss, after all. When
this was done, she would have a wonderful little child.
Beith kept her eyes closed and summoned the image of her
husband. She had loved Gilwyn Toms with all her heart,
and now she would pass that love to their offspring.

"There's its head," said Gwena. "You're doing perfectly,
girl. Keep it up now."

"It's coming, Beith," said Meri. She peered over Beith's
belly and let out a delighted yelp. "I can see it!"

The last moments were hellish. Beith held her breath, using
all the air in her lungs to expel the baby, and as it slipped
out of her, inch by torturous inch, the final contraction came.

"Oh, lord," Beith wheezed. "Come on, please!"

Heaven heard her prayer. The baby that had racked her
body dropped out in a sudden burst, right into the waiting
hands of Gwena. The pain slackened, and Beith's body
seemed to shrink, sore but wonderfully lighter.

"Beith, you did it!" cried Meri. The girl was staring at
the infant, her eyes wide with wonder.

"I did it," Beith sighed. Suddenly she laughed. "I have
a baby!"

Gwena's next words were like a miracle. "It's a boy,
Beith. A beautiful boy."

"A boy?" Beith struggled to sit up. "A boy!"

Gwena lifted the baby toward Meri. "Take the child,"
she ordered. Meri stepped to the foot of the bed, then
Gwena set to work tying off the umbilical cord. The exhausted Beith caught her first glimpse of her infant. Smothered with afterbirth, he was nonetheless astonishing. As
Gwena clamped and severed the cord, Meri held the child
carefully, wiping away its slick coat and cooing to it gently.
When the cord was cut, Gwena took the baby and quickly
tapped its bottom until the smallest noise issued from it—
its first astounding cries.

Beith brushed the sweat-soaked strands of hair from her
face. The crying infant mesmerized her, cradled in old
Gwena's capable arms. The midwife's proud smile lit the
room. "Ah, look at you, little soldier," she sighed. "How
many is this for me now? You are my hundreth, at least!"

"Let me hold him," Beith implored. "Please."

Gwena was about to bring the child around to Beith when suddenly her expression dimmed. Her eyes narrowed on the infant, studying him. Beith's heart tripped.

"What?" she asked. "What's wrong?"

Gwena didn't answer. She picked up the baby's tiny hand, cocking her head as she inspected it.

"Gwena, what is it?" Beith demanded. "What's the matter?"

"I don't know," replied the midwife. She brought the baby closer to its mother. "Look at his hand."

Beith leaned forward, focusing on the boy's little appendage. At first she could see nothing wrong, it was so tiny. But looking closer revealed an oddity in its fingers. The thumb was strangely close to the index finger, and both seemed shorter than normal. Beith reached out for the little hand. Studying it, she discovered that the thumb and finger were fused together.

"Oh . . ."

Baby Gilwyn, as he had already been named, began to cry again.

"His foot, too," said Gwena. She looked worried, even pale. "It's the same."

Beith looked and found that his left foot was indeed the same, slightly clubbed and curled into a ball. The two smallest toes were together, merged by shared flesh. Beith felt her world collapse, and suddenly a dire future flashed before her eyes for the child she had birthed. In Liiria, as everywhere on the continent, cripples were usually beggars.

"Oh no," said Beith. "Please . . ."

"Beith, don't worry," said Meri quickly. "He's newly born. I'm sure it's nothing." She looked at Gwena for support. "Right?"

The midwife grimaced. "I don't know," she said softly. "I don't know what it means. Maybe—" Abruptly she stopped herself. Beith looked up instantly.

"What?"

Gwena glanced down at the child and sighed. "It may not just be his foot and hand. It could be worse than that."

"What? What could be worse?"

"Beith," said Gwena gently. "It could be his brain. He may not be . . . normal."

"Don't say that!" railed Beith. "Don't you dare say that!"

"I've seen it before, girl. Sometimes a deformed child has other problems, problems with his mind. Your little one here could be like that."

"He isn't!" snapped Beith. She sat bolt up, ignoring her nakedness and the filth of the bed. "Gilwyn's fine," she insisted. "He's going to be a Royal Charger, like his father. He's . . ."

Her voice constricted and she couldn't speak. Withered and drained, she reached out for her child. Gwena handed him over carefully. Beith took him in her arms, holding him close to her breast. She smiled at the child. He was so beautiful, even with his clubbed hand and foot. But she worried, too. What life could there be for a crippled boy? She had seen them in the streets, how they begged for food because they couldn't work or support themselves. Her little boy—her new Gilwyn—might become a wastrel.

"No," she said, shaking her head. "No, I won't let that happen to you."

"Beith, give me the child," said Gwena. She reached out for the infant but Beith pulled him away.

"I want to hold him," said Beith.

"He needs to be cleaned," said Gwena. "He's filthy, and so are you. Give him here. Let me wash him. I'll bring him right back. Meri, clean up Beith, will you?"

Beith agreed, reluctantly, and handed her newborn over to Gwena. She was exhausted and her body ached; even talking was a chore. Gwena took the child in a clean wrap and left the room. Beith leaned back, not caring how soiled the sheets were. Meri began dipping towels into a basin of water and dabbing the fabric between her thighs, cleaning off the worst of the afterbirth. It might have been embarrassing, but Beith was a thousand miles away, fretting over her infant's fate.

"Don't worry, Beith," said Meri as she worked. "You need to rest. Gwena will see to the baby. You should try to sleep."

Sleep. It sounded wonderful to Beith, but she was sure her slumber would be filled with nightmares.

"Meri?"

"Yes?"

"What if Gwena's right? What if the baby isn't normal?"

Meri smiled, trying to cover up what she really felt. "We don't know that."

"But his hand, and his foot. They're . . ." Beith could hardly bring herself to say the word deformed. "What if his brain is like that too?"

"Beith, he's too young. No one can tell by looking at him, not even Gwena."

"But if he is? What then?"

"Then you will raise him, and you will love him as if nothing is amiss. He's your son, Beith."

Beith nodded. Already she loved little Gilwyn, and he wasn't yet an hour old. But love couldn't move mountains as the poets said, and she couldn't save him from the cruelty of the world. If her child was simple, only the king's grace could help him.

"Akeela is a good man," she told herself. "He will have a place for Gilwyn in the castle. I know he will." She glanced at Meri. "Right?"

Meri wrung a dirtied towel into the basin. Her face was serious. "Akeela *is* a good man, that's what everyone says. He was a good prince, and he'll be a good king."

"Yes," agreed Beith. "Even if Gilwyn can't be a soldier, Akeela will find a place for him, don't you think?"

"Beith, close your eyes now. Rest."

Beith knew she'd get no answer from her friend. Succumbing to her exhaustion, she closed her eyes and let Meri freshen and comfort her, wondering what would become of her son in the world the new king of Liiria was making.

4

Three days after coming to Hes, Akeela had made his decision.

It was a warm day in the Reecian capital, perfect for proposing marriage. The marketplace on the south side of the castle was teeming with people and livestock, and the streets were filled with children and cats, which to Lukien's surprise were everywhere in Hes. The sky was perfect, blue and cloudless, and the rains that had soaked the city the day before had utterly vanished. Over the balcony, Lukien could see Hes stretching out for miles. He could see the city gates and the long, winding road that would eventually lead him home to Liiria. Lukien gazed at the eastern horizon, longing for home. For Akeela, their trip to Hes had been a complete success, but for Lukien it had been surreal. Things had moved too quickly, and too many decisions had been made. Decisions, Lukien believed, that Akeela had made hastily.

Together they waited on the balcony for Princess Cassandra. It was a meeting King Karis himself had arranged, and they were very early. Even if she were on time, Cassandra wouldn't arrive for another half hour. But Akeela had wanted Lukien to come to the balcony with him, because the young king was nervous. He had also claimed the need to explain his bold decision. Yet now that they were together, Akeela wasn't talking. Like Lukien, he stared out over the city, lost in thought.

Lukien didn't blame Akeela for wanting to marry Cassandra. She was beautiful, after all, and Akeela himself was less than beautiful. What Lukien hated—what he had protested for days—was the suddenness of it all. Cassandra had merely danced, and her movements had bewitched Akeela so that he had forgotten all propriety. He didn't know that there were many women in the world, and that as king he could have his pick of them. Or, if he knew this, he simply didn't care. Lukien stole a glance at his king, watching him furtively. Akeela was young, and woefully inexperienced. He had spent too much time with his nose in books and not enough chasing kitchen maids, and Lukien regretted that. He was angry that old King Balak hadn't insisted his son become a soldier after graduating war college. If he had joined in at least some campaigns, then perhaps he would have known what it was like to be with a woman, and he wouldn't be so enamored of the first one to flutter her eyelashes at him.

But no, that wasn't right, either. Lukien knew he couldn't blame Balak for Akeela's lovesickness. Balak had been a good father, wise enough not to push his bookish son into a military life. And that wisdom had paid off handsomely for Liiria, because her new king was cultured and committed to peace. That he was starry-eyed was simply an offshoot of his goodness, the very thing that made him special. Lukien sighed, shaking his head. Akeela heard the lament and glanced over at him.

"What's wrong?" he asked.

"Nothing is wrong," lied Lukien. "I was merely thinking."

"Thinking about me?"

Lukien nodded. "That's right. You've given me little else to think about these past three days."

The young king crossed the balcony to stand beside his champion. It was a huge balcony, just off a conservatory decorated with tall plants and cracked plaster statues. Several bird cages hung nearby, their occupants serenading the two men. The balcony afforded them a flawless view of the city, but Akeela had lost interest in the view.

"I know you don't approve," he said. "But at least try to understand."

"I have tried. And I still can't understand."

· "Then you haven't tried hard enough," said Akeela. He was agitated; his left eyelid twitched slightly. "Look at me, Lukien. I'm not like you. I'm not tall or handsome, and I'm certainly no hero. You've always had your pick of women, while I'm still a . . ."

Akeela hesitated, and Lukien was glad that he didn't say the word.

"It takes more than a strong jaw to win the love of a woman, Akeela," said Lukien. "You think I'm some great lover because I tell tales about the harlots I've been with, but I'm just a braggart. And I leave out the sordid bits, like all the lice-ridden beds I've slept in."

"So?"

"So you can have any woman you want. Not some whore, either, but a good woman, one with breeding."

Akeela laughed. "One like Cassandra, you mean?"

"No, not like Cassandra. Someone you love. And someone who loves you. Haven't you wondered why the princess wants to marry you?"

"I know why," argued Akeela. "For peace."

"No," said Lukien ruthlessly. "Because she is a woman and her father wills it, that's why. And because she has the chance to be a queen. She doesn't love you, Akeela."

"Lukien, this is how royal marriages are arranged," said Akeela. "If my father were alive, he would have made a marriage for me by now anyway, and probably to someone far less beautiful than Cassandra. He would have given me Dralla of Marn or some other girl that looks like a warthog, because he was too stubborn to consider peace with Reec. But why should I be saddled with a girl like Dralla? Why shouldn't I have Cassandra?"

Lukien groped for a good reason. Cassandra's beauty wasn't something to be argued over—it was a fact, like the beauty of a sunrise. And it had captivated Lukien just as it had Akeela. Maybe that was why he was opposed to the marriage. It wouldn't be the first time he'd been jealous of his royal "brother," a brother in small talk only.

"Can't you at least wait?" said Lukien. "Just a little longer? Let's go back to Liiria. Maybe the familiar air will clear your head."

"There's no reason to wait. I'm not going to find a prettier girl, or a better reason to marry. And it would be an insult to King Karis to refuse her. I won't jeopardize the peace like that."

"That's rubbish, Akeela. Karis wants peace as much as you do. More, even. That's not why you want to marry Cassandra."

Akeela looked at him, surprised at the outburst. "I thought you would be happy for me," he said. "You of all people know how lonely I've been. Why would you keep this from me, my one chance at a beautiful wife?"

"I . . ." Lukien stumbled over his answer. "I am happy for you, Akeela. I'm just worried."

"Well, don't be. I'm a grown man, Lukien, and I don't need you to protect me anymore." Akeela turned and looked out over the city. His hands gripped the stone railing of the balcony hard, turning his knuckles white. "I think I'd like to be alone now," he said.

"I can stay with you," said Lukien. "She won't be here for a while yet."

"Yes, but I need time to think, to consider what I'm going to say."

"What's to consider?" said Lukien. "She's been offered to you, and all you have to do is take her."

"Oh, yes, that's very romantic," replied Akeela dryly. "Look, don't try to help me with this, all right? Just let me think."

Lukien turned to go, angry at being dismissed. But before he took three paces, Akeela called after him.

"Wait, I forgot something." He wore a sheepish grin. "A favor, actually."

Lukien scowled. "What?"

"If Cassandra accepts my proposal, I'm going to be leaving for home at once. I want to prepare the castle for the wedding, and I won't be taking her with me."

"So?"

"I'll need someone to look after her, someone to escort her back to Koth for me." Akeela's eyes twinkled as if nothing had just happened. "Would you do that for me?"

The question astonished Lukien. A little voice warned him to refuse, but instead he said, "If that's what you want . . ."

"Yes," said Akeela. "You're the only person I trust. Who better to look after her than you?"

Lukien hedged, saying, "She may not like my company. To her I'm still the Bronze Knight."

"Don't worry about that; I'll explain it to her. I want her to have the best, and you're the best soldier I have. You'll protect her, I know." Akeela's smile was all-forgiving—and terribly naive. "Thank you, Lukien. You're a good friend."

Friend. Were they friends, Lukien wondered? At times like this, when Akeela was his most petulant, it was hard to believe they truly loved each other. Giving his king a half-hearted nod, Lukien turned and left the balcony, hoping Princess Cassandra refused her royal escort.

Cassandra moved through the hallways of Castle Hes, floating with anticipation. It was nearly time for her meeting with Akeela, and Jancis had told her that the Liirian was already on the eastern balcony, waiting for her. Because the balcony was very large and studded with statues, Jancis had been able to spy on Akeela quite effectively. Apparently, he had been waiting for her for some time now, first talking with his bodyguard Lukien, then pacing nervously among the statues. According to Jancis, he had even been talking to himself. Cassandra slowed her pace as she neared the balcony, taking the time to smooth down her dress and adjust the braids in her hair. She wore a velvet gown of midnight blue and just the right amount of make-up to highlight her eyes, and she already knew from the way the young king had stared at her that he was attracted to her. He had done a very poor job of hiding his attraction, in fact, but Cassandra was flattered. Soon she might be leaving Hes behind. She would be the first of her sisters to become a queen.

Queen Cassandra. Cassandra tried the title on and liked the way it fit. And she had a thousand questions for the Liirian king. She wanted to know everything about Liiria, about its people and customs, and she wanted to know what her new home, Akeela's castle, was like. Was it tall, she wondered? She had heard everything in Liiria was tall, so much the opposite of squat and stubby Hes. Supposedly, Liirians were great architects. Their culture had influenced much of the eastern continent. Once, Cassandra had considered that a terrible thing. But now she was about to marry

a Liirian, and she hoped they were the most powerful, most
renowned nation in the world.

Cassandra paused in the middle of the hallway and
looked around. Castle Hes wasn't spectacular, but it was
home and she would miss it, and the realization startled
her. She had been too busy planning her escape to appreciate her home, because for too long the castle had simply
been a prison. Under her sisters' shadow and father's
watchful eyes, there had been little freedom here. Now, she
would be totally independent, or at least subservient only
to Akeela.

"What will that be like, I wonder?" she whispered. She
ran her hand along the rough stone of the wall, sliding a
finger into the joints between bricks. Karla, the maid who
looked after the upstairs rooms, rounded the corner and
spotted her.

"My lady?" the maid asked, her round face concerned.
"Are you all right?"

Cassandra nodded. "I'm fine, Karla. I'm just . . .
thinking."

"Well, there's a lot of that about, my lady." She looked
over her shoulder, then whispered, "Your young man's
been very pensive, too."

"You mean Akeela?"

"Aye, King Akeela. I spotted him near the conservatory." The maid smiled as if she had a great secret. "He
seems lost in thought."

The princess laughed. Was everyone spying on poor
Akeela?

"Thank you, Karla," said Cassandra, then hurried past
her toward the balcony. The balcony where Akeela waited
was at the front of the castle, in the southern tower. In less
then a minute Cassandra was there, arriving in the vast,
rounded conservatory boasting plants and birds from across
the continent. One huge birdcage rose up out of the center
of the room, reaching the ceiling. Cassandra stalked toward
the birdcage, then peered around it to see out to the balcony. The balcony shutters were all open wide, and she
noticed Akeela standing outside, sunlight striking his dark
hair. He had dressed for their meeting, which pleased Cassandra, and his spotless tunic shimmered with golden trim.

For the first time, she got an uninterrupted view of him. She lingered near the birdcage, watching him. A curious canary inside the cage hopped onto a branch beside her face and studied her, then let out a surprisingly loud song. Cassandra stepped back from the cage, startled, just as Akeela heard the commotion and turned around. Their eyes met. Cassandra smiled sheepishly.

"Umm, hello," she said.

Akeela stood motionless. For a moment he seemed not to recognize her, but then he righted himself by stepping forward, and said, "Princess Cassandra, hello. I . . . uh, you startled me."

His voice was very light, nervous but melodious. With his sweating forehead and shaking voice, Cassandra thought him sweet-looking.

"Forgive me, my lord," she offered. "I didn't mean to frighten you."

"Frightened? Oh, no, I wasn't frightened—not at all. The bird surprised me, that's all."

The bird continued to sing. Cassandra moved away from the cage, going to the balcony to stand before Akeela. She noticed with satisfaction the way his eyes moved along her body. She took the opportunity to study him as well. He was shorter than he'd seemed at the banquet table, about her height, and despite his fine clothes he didn't look like a king at all. In fact, he could have easily passed for a squire. His unimposing appearance made her comfortable at once.

"My father said you wanted to speak to me," said Cassandra. She gave him an encouraging smile. "I was happy to come."

"Yes, thank you for that," said Akeela. "I thought it would be best if we could talk alone, without others eavesdropping."

Instantly Cassandra thought of Jancis, wondering if her friend was somewhere in the conservatory, listening. "No one can hear us out here, my lord."

Akeela turned toward the city. "Yes, we are rather high up." He looked over the stone railing, down at the people milling below. "Your father's castle is beautiful, my lady. As is your city."

"I'm pleased you think so, my lord."

The young man heard the uncertainty in her voice. "Don't you think it's beautiful?"

"Yes," replied Cassandra. "Yes, I do."

"Hmm. I wonder then what you would think of leaving it." Akeela looked at her hopefully. "Am I making myself plain, my lady?"

Cassandra understood perfectly. "Is this a proposal, my lord?"

"Would you accept if it were?"

"I would. But I don't understand why you would ask, when I have already been given to you. It is your choice to accept or decline, not mine."

Akeela said, "I want a wife, not a slave. I want you to enter this marriage willingly, or not at all. I want to hear the words from you."

"Do women decide such things for themselves in Liiria?" asked Cassandra. Because she was a princess, and her father's favorite, he had given her a choice. But that wasn't always the case in Reec. Her country had a long tradition of bartering women away.

"In Liiria people don't always have choices," said Akeela. "There are barons and dukes who make decisions for them, who decide where they will work and how much wheat they'll produce. It's been that way forever, I think." He came closer to her. "But I'm going to change that, Cassandra."

"Are you? How can you?"

"I'm serious," said Akeela. A strange light came on in his eyes. "I'm going to reform Liiria. I'm going to make it the greatest country on the continent."

Cassandra grinned. "Ah, you want to be a great king."

The Liirian shook his head. "No, that's not it at all. I don't care about myself or what history will think of me. I care about changing things, the entire social order. Why should a woman marry a man she doesn't love? And why should a man work a field his whole life, just because a baron says he should? I'm talking about freedom, Cassandra. The ability to do whatever you want. Do you see?"

It was a difficult concept for Cassandra. What good was freedom without food? Someone had to work the fields. But she was intrigued by the man and his bold ideas, and wanted to hear more.

"How will you do this?" she asked. "How will you make these changes, my lord?"

"It won't be easy. There will be people who oppose me, strong landowners mostly, and old aides of my father who think things should stay the same. There were many who didn't even want me to make this peace with Reec. They said it couldn't be done, but I've proven them wrong. And I will prove them wrong about all my ideas." He rubbed his hands together, satisfied with himself. "I have dreams for Liiria, Cassandra. Great dreams."

She closed the gap, the last few inches separating them. "We all have dreams, Akeela," she said softly. "Tell me yours. What will you do in Liiria?"

Akeela loved being close to her. She could sense it in him. "There is one thing," he said. "My biggest dream of all. My Cathedral of Knowledge."

"Cathedral? You mean a temple?"

"No," laughed Akeela. "That's just what I call it, my Cathedral of Knowledge. I'm talking about a library. The biggest, most extensive library in the world!"

Cassandra frowned, confused. "How will that help Liiria, my lord?"

"Don't you see? It's knowledge that changes things, Cassandra. How many people in Hes can read and write? Not many, I'd bet. Probably half the servants in this castle have never even held a book. That's just plain wrong; it's keeping them ignorant. They need to be educated. Knowledge gives people power."

The idea was scandalous. "My lord, knowledge is a dangerous thing. If all the commoners had knowledge, what would they need with kings and queens? Such ideas are for the royal, surely."

"Why? Why should you and I and our privileged families be the only ones to read and write? Why can't a farmer become a teacher if he wishes to?"

"Because . . ." Cassandra fumbled for a reply. "Because it's the way of things, that's why."

Akeela's smile grew sly. "Ah, that's the very thinking I'll have to battle, Princess. The thought that just because things have always been one way, that they won't be better another. But my library can change that. When it's done, it will be filled with books and scrolls from all over the world. Then people will come to Liiria, making pilgrimages to study there. They'll bring more new ideas with them, too, and then there will be knowledge for everyone. And when that happens, all Liirians will have opportunities they can barely imagine!"

Cassandra chuckled, struck by his fantasy. Even if he built his library, there was no way it could have its intended impact. He was just a man, more like a boy really, and his youth had clouded his judgement. For a moment, Cassandra wondered if she really did want to be queen to Akeela's king. Instead of setting Liiria on a brave new path, he might be herding it toward chaos.

"I think your dream is very grand," said Cassandra. She smiled, not wanting to hurt his feelings but not wanting to encourage him too much, either. He sensed her elusiveness at once.

"I'm not naive, Cassandra," he said. "I know that changing things won't be easy. I'll have a great deal of opposition. But I'd like a queen that can share my dream, at least a little." He stayed close to her, looking into her eyes. "Tell me what you dream," he asked.

The question was too probing for Cassandra. How could she confess her dreams? Compared to Akeela's, her own seemed so greedy. She replied, "I want peace for my people and a good life for myself. That would satisfy me."

"That's it?" pressed Akeela. "Nothing more?"

Cassandra thought for a moment. She decided to confide in him, just a little. "What would you say if I told you I wanted to be free of this place, my lord? How would you feel if you knew I was anxious to see new places?"

"And new people?"

Cassandra gazed out over the city. "Yes," she sighed, brooding over a world that had become too familiar.

"I would say that you and I are not so different," said Akeela. "You see? You were right—everyone has dreams, Cassandra. The people of Liiria have dreams, all of them. I will help them meet those dreams. And as queen you will help me."

"You are going to be a very odd king, my lord," said Cassandra. "I wonder what kind of queen I will make in a land of scholars and wise men."

"A fine one, I'm sure," said Akeela. "Having you for

my queen is part of my dream now, Princess. You'll love Liiria, and my people will adore you. And you'll see—this isn't some delusion. I'm going to build my library, and I'm going to change Liiria forever."

It was a frightening thought, but it was also compelling. Compared to her stagnant life in Castle Hes, with its suffocating walls and tiresome chatter, Cassandra's new life in Liiria might be magical. She would be wife to this good man, and she would be happy.

She hoped.

"I want to be your wife," she said without thinking. "I want to marry you and go to Liiria and be away from Reec forever. And I want to go now, my lord."

Akeela was stunned by her forwardness. "Are you sure? I mean, have you really thought about it?"

"I have thought about little else since your messenger came with your peace offer. I have made my decision, and I know I won't regret it. If you'll have me, I will be your queen."

"Oh, my lady," sighed Akeela. "You've made me very happy. I promise you, you will adore Liiria."

It sounded dreamy, almost too perfect. "Yes," Cassandra agreed. "We can marry as soon as you wish. I'm anxious to see your country."

"Good," said Akeela. "Then I will leave at once and prepare a place for you."

"*You'll* leave?" asked Cassandra. "But won't I be going with you, my lord?"

"Eventually, of course. But not right away. I have a wedding to plan. I have to ready the castle, send invitations—the list is endless, really. Oh, but don't worry, Princess. It won't take more than a month, I shouldn't think."

Cassandra was crestfallen. "A month? That long?"

"Well, three weeks at least. Then you can come to Liiria, and all the capital will be ready for you. And you'll have a contingent of Royal Chargers with you, my lady." Akeela smiled proudly. "Lukien will be your escort."

The princess' eyebrows went up. "That one? Oh, no, my lord. I don't think that's a good idea."

"Lukien is my best knight, my lady," said Akeela. "He's the only one I trust to protect you."

"We have plenty of soldiers in Hes that can escort me,"

Cassandra argued. "I don't need your infamous knight to keep me safe."

"I'm sorry, my lady, but it's already arranged," said Akeela firmly. "I'll feel better knowing that Lukien is here, looking after you. And the road can be treacherous for a woman. If there are highwaymen about, Lukien will deal with them. Or worse, there may be garmys on the road. They come out in the wet weather."

Cassandra shook her head. "You're not understanding me," she said. "The Bronze Knight is an outlaw here, worse than any highwayman. Worse even than a garmy. He may be a hero in Liiria, but in Reec he is a butcher."

The young king looked wounded. "Princess, Lukien is like a brother to me. He *is* my brother, really. My father took him off the streets and raised him as his own. We went to war college together, and we're rarely apart. Forgive me, but if you're going to be my wife, you're going to have to accept him. And I can think of no better way to start then by letting him escort you to Koth."

Her argument lost, Cassandra sank back. Riding with Lukien was inconceivable, but losing Akeela's approbation—that was unthinkable.

"Very well," she conceded. "I'll let your knight take me to Koth, because it's your wish and because I trust your virtue, King Akeela, not his. But I don't want him speaking to me. He may escort me, and that's all."

"My lady . . ."

"Those are *my* wishes, my lord," said Cassandra. "Please."

Akeela relented without arguing. "Then that is how it will be," he said. "I'll leave for Koth the day after tomorrow, and will send word when I'm ready to receive you. Until then, Lukien and some others will stay behind in Hes."

Cassandra nodded, hating the idea. "Will I see you again before you go?"

The young king came closer, his eyes jumping. "I'd like that very much," he said. Then, without waiting for an invitation, he kissed her. Cassandra was startled by the gesture but didn't resist. His soft lips brushed her own, and the sensation was sweet, almost too gentle for the kiss of a man. When he was done, he leaned back and smiled at her.

"Your father will want us all to get together before I leave," he said. "I will see you then."

"Yes," agreed Cassandra. "All right."

He left without another word, departing the balcony and disappearing through the conservatory. Cassandra's eyes lingered on him for a long moment, then she turned toward the city and the eastern horizon. Somewhere out there, beyond the city walls of her gilded cage, Liiria beckoned. The old enemy of her people, with all its myth and fantasy. In a month she would finally be there. She would emerge from under her sisters' shadows, the queen of a fabled land. Suddenly she felt like dancing, and turned in a pirouette on the balcony, laughing. When she did the smallest movement caught her eye, something unseen in the conservatory. Cassandra stopped twirling.

"Jancis?" she called. "Is that you?"

There was no answer. Cassandra squinted, sure that someone was watching. She took a step forward, enough to startle the intruder, and for a moment caught a glimpse of Lukien peering at her through the foliage. The Bronze Knight's face was blank, unreadable. When he realized the princess had seen him, he backed away quietly, then turned and left the conservatory.

A chill passed through Cassandra. She thought of pursuing him, but didn't. She thought of telling Akeela about the intrusion, but knew she wouldn't. She simply stared at the place that Lukien had been, enchanted by his strangeness.

5

Aral Vale sat alone in the corner of the Red Lion, staring at his reflection in a tankard of ale. It was his third drink, at least, and the liquor embraced him warmly, like a lover. Outside, night had seized the city, suffocating all sound. It was well past midnight, and the inn had lost most of its patrons to sleep. Now it was very quiet, the way Aral needed it. He supposed his wife would be worried about him, but he didn't really care. Presently, Aral Vale cared about very little. He had his ale to keep him company and a gallery of ugly images in his mind, and all he could do was focus on the dreadful reflection in his ale and remember the grievous thing he had done.

Being a farmer wasn't easy. That's what Aral's father had told him. It had been intended as a warning not to leave the family coopery in Marn, but Aral hadn't listened. His father was a drunk and Aral had been anxious to be rid of him, and when he had learned that a parcel of inexpensive land had opened up near Koth, he had snatched the opportunity eagerly. Aral smiled forlornly. It all seemed like a very long time ago. In the intervening years he had married and poured his heart into his little farm, only to have weather and pests eat his profits. He had dreamed of being a landowner, like the Duke of Marn, but his land had given him precious little, mostly calluses. Worse, his wife had been as barren as his farm, giving him one still-born child after another. She was only twenty-four now, still young enough to bear children, but she was cursed, and that was the truth of it.

"Cursed," Aral whispered. "Like me." He picked up his tankard and drank a deep mouthful, enjoying its soothing burn. In a minute the beer was gone. Aral fished into his threadbare trousers and pulled out another coin. Slapping it down loudly on the table, he called for the barman to bring him another. The fat proprietor obliged, eager to keep his only customer drinking, and set a fresh tankard with a foaming head down in front of Aral. He took the coins and, at no extra charge, gave the young man a sympathetic look. Aral scowled at him.

"Something you want to say to me?"

The barman replied, "I'm sorry about what happened to your newborn."

Aral looked down, ashamed to face the man. "It's the way of the Fate."

The barman sighed. "It's a shame, though. She finally carried this one the whole way. To have it die so suddenly . . ."

"It's over," snapped Aral. He felt his face redden suddenly, not with rage but with guilt. "There's nothing to be done about it now."

The barman went back to work, leaving Aral sulking at the corner table. Aral watched him suspiciously. He didn't suspect anything, did he? The idea made his heart race. And anyway it was hardly murder. More like a mercy killing, really. For farmers like Aral, having a girl child was disappointment enough, but having a blind one was unthinkable. Just another mouth to feed, and no help tending the crops. Vara, Aral's wife, had insisted that she could be taught to clean house when she got older, but what kind of daughter was that, banging around blindly with a broom? He needed sons. Or at least daughters with open eyes.

Aral picked up his mug and found that his hand was shaking. With his other hand he tried to still it.

"Damn it," he hissed. "Damn everything."

He went back to drinking.

A minute later, the door of the Red Lion opened, letting in an unwelcome gust of wind. On the threshold stood two figures, one a giant, tall and wide, the other a woman, short as a child. Aral blinked at the sight of them. The woman wore a long coat of patchwork leather, colorful and dramatic. She stood barely four feet tall in her tiny shoes, and her eyes lit the room with cold radiance. The man towered over her, a great brute with a bald head and broken teeth that hung over his slack jaw in an overbite. Aral had never seen anything like him, or his miniature friend. Neither, apparently, had the barman. The sight of them made the proprietor drop a glass, sending broken shards skimming across the bar. The little woman took notice of his shock and smiled.

"Oops! Careful now," she chirped.

She had a dazzling smile, unnaturally bright. The many colors of her coat seemed to move around her. Aral shook his head, sure that the drink had gotten to him. He suddenly felt nauseous. He pushed aside his drink, watching as the tiny woman and her beastly companion entered the inn. The giant stayed a pace behind the woman, his wide shoulders hunched, his broad back slightly curved. The little woman walked lightly toward the back of the inn, near the fire. Of all the empty tables, she chose the one next to Aral. She and her companion each pulled out chairs and sat down. The barman stared at them.

"I . . . uh. . . . Can I get you something?"

The woman looked over at Aral's table and gave him the most disquieting grin. "We'll have what he's having."

Aral's head continued to swim, yet he could not bring himself to look away from the strangers. The woman was remarkably small, with long white hair and a peculiar face set with elfin features. Two bewitching eyes looked back at him, deep and uncannily black. As the barkeep brought them their drinks, Aral finally managed to pull his gaze free of the pair. He stared down at his drink, hoping the woman wasn't watching, but when he lifted his head again he discovered those mocking eyes, studying him.

"What?" he asked defensively.

The woman didn't answer. Her monstrous companion hardly stirred.

"Please," Aral said. "Stop staring."

But the woman didn't stop. Instead she casually opened her patchwork coat, revealing a curious amulet around her neck. Hanging from a chain of braided gold, the amulet blinked like an monstrous eye, its ruby gemstone twinkling in the firelight. Aral stared at it, mesmerized. His nausea left him immediately, replaced by a sudden warmth. It was the drink, he told himself. Good, soothing ale.

"Yes," said the woman. "It's the drink."

Aral puzzled over her statement. Had he spoken? He hadn't thought so.

"Aral Vale," the woman whispered. "That's your name?"

Aral nodded. Somehow, she knew him.

"Oh, I know a great deal about you, Aral Vale," said the little woman. Aral could barely hear her. Her words were soft, like a breeze, sounding only in his head. He wondered if the barkeep was listening. Remarkably, the woman answered his query.

"He can't hear us," she said. "I'm talking only to you."

She was talking, yet she wasn't talking. Her lips moved as if by illusion. Aral watched the amulet around her neck. It was pricelessly beautiful. It seemed to pulsate as she spoke, echoing her words. He suddenly felt giddy, completely unafraid. They were an odd looking pair, but he didn't feel threatened by them— not the way he had when he'd first seen them. The woman had a gentle look about her and the man, if that's what he could be called, never said a word.

"Trog doesn't speak," the woman explained. She continued to scrutinize him, her eyes narrowing. "You have been here a long time, Aral Vale. You were difficult to find. But then, men who are hiding are often difficult to find."

Aral stiffened. "I'm not hiding."

"You have a wife at home who worries over you."

"That's none of your business. I just want to be alone. To think."

The little woman's black eyes flared. "Yes. You have much to think about, don't you?"

Aral's puzzlement grew. He lifted his gaze from the amulet, back toward the stranger's face. Her mute companion brooded over him, his jaw slack, his breathing raspy. Aral noticed the barkeep across the room absently cleaning glasses with a rag, pretending not to be listening.

"Who are you?" Aral whispered. "How do you know me?"

"It's not important," replied the woman. She sat back and closed her coat, shutting away the amulet and its radiance. Instantly, Aral grew alarmed as reality snapped back into focus. He coughed, shaking his head, sure that the ale had sickened him. The woman was no longer staring. Instead she and her companion sipped their drinks, ignoring him. The woman made small talk, chuckling convivially. Aral loosened his collar. The room was very warm and he felt flushed. He tried to relax and catch his breath.

"Barkeep," called the woman. She banged her tankard on the table. "Another, please."

The proprietor drew another ale and brought it to their table. As he set it down, the woman said to him, "You have a nice place here."

"Thank you," replied the man suspiciously.

"Koth is very nice."

"Yes." He shrugged. "It is nice here."

Aral couldn't help but overhear their strange conversation. He toyed with his drink, pretending not to care.

"Such a tragedy at the castle, though," the woman continued. She spoke too loudly, deliberately raising her voice. The barkeep frowned. "Tragedy? What would that be?"

"Hadn't you heard? The castle has a new baby. One of the king's servants gave birth just the other evening." The woman shook her head as if it were the saddest thing in the world. "Deformed."

"Is that right? I wouldn't know much about the castle folk." The barkeep laughed. "They don't come in here much! How do you know about it?"

The woman slowly turned toward Aral. "Oh, I make it my business to know such things," she said softly.

The barman shrugged and strode away. Aral swallowed hard under the woman's accusing gaze.

"What are you staring at?" he demanded. His tone finally got the big man to stir. The woman held up a hand to keep her companion down.

"No, Trog, it's all right," she said. Her expression lost all its prior grace, and her little mouth curled back in a snarl. "Like I said, I make it my business to know things about the children born around here. And I know what you did, Aral Vale."

Aral could bear no more. He rose from the table, shoving back his chair so hard that it tumbled over, and headed for the door. He was eager to be away from the bizarre woman, eager to escape her incriminating gaze. Pushing open the door, the night and its cold air swallowed him instantly. He took a deep, cleansing breath, then ran down the abandoned street, fleeing the Red Lion and its freakish patrons.

Aral walked for an hour more, ignoring the chill and the lateness of the hour. A breeze blew down the avenue, sending bits of rubbish tumbling toward him, and the candles in the windows above had all been snuffed out long ago, lending the street an eerie stillness. In the distance, Akeela's castle rose above the common housing, sending a moonlit shadow over the city. Aral considered the castle. He was sick with himself, sick with what he had done, and he thought about the words of the odd woman in the inn, and how a deformed baby had been born within the castle's walls. An epidemic of bad luck had hit the city, apparently, and he wondered what the parents of the newborn felt. Rage? Enough to drive them to . . .

"Forget it," he growled. It was done, and he wouldn't torture himself about it. It was time to go home.

He rounded a corner and headed to the south side of the city, where he hoped to catch a carriage home to his farm. He was far too tired to walk the whole way again, and he had just enough money left to pay the fare. Moving quickly, he went the way most familiar to him, heading for the alley that would shorten his time. He was in a bleak part of Koth, where the buildings were close together and smelled of decay. As he reached the alley, the slime-covered walls of the structures rose up around him. He closed his collar around his throat and decided to hurry. The alley was long and narrow and spattered with garbage. The rain barrels along the gutters gurgled with filthy water from the rooftops after last night's downpour. Aral quickened his pace, but before he took another step he saw something up ahead, a shimmering along the left-hand wall. His heart began to pound. Out of the wall, or emerging from its shadow, stepped the woman from the Red Lion. Her patchwork coat writhed around her, changing colors, mimicking the alley. She stepped out into the center of the street, facing Aral, and once again the fractured smile appeared.

"You left before we finished our conversation."

Aral panicked. He whirled to dash away, but discovered the monstrous bald man behind him, blocking his path. The behemoth stalked toward him, his arms outstretched. Aral stumbled backward. The woman remained in front of him. Determined to push her aside, he turned and started toward her—until she opened her coat.

The amulet around her neck glowed furiously. Aral's feet stuck to the floor, glued in place by its compelling aura. A strangling terror seized him. He tried to scream but couldn't, and soon the big man was upon him, wrapping his massive arms around his chest and pulling him from the ground. Aral struggled but his attacker was impossibly strong, and his iron grip squeezed the air from Aral's lungs. He lifted Aral effortlessly, hauling him toward one of the rain barrels. The little woman scurried alongside them, looking up at Aral as he squirmed.

"You shouldn't have done it," she said. Her face was set with sad anger. "There was no reason to kill her."

Aral finally found his voice. "I had to!" he screamed. "Please!"

"Had to? An infant?"

"Yes! She was blind! She would have been nothing!"

"She would have been your daughter," snapped the woman.

They had stopped near one of the rain barrels. Aral lay pinned over the giant's shoulder, unable to break free. His terror peaked.

"Don't do it!" he pleaded. "Don't!"

The tiny woman sighed dolefully. "People like you make my work so much harder," she said. "Now you will learn a lesson, Aral Vale. We are all beautiful in the eyes of God."

With a small nod from his mistress, the giant took hold of Aral, inverting him and plunging him headfirst into the barrel. Cold water rushed down his throat; blackness enveloped him. He screamed, releasing a stream of bubbles. The giant's viselike grip held his legs, driving him again and again against the bottom of the barrel. Aral felt his lungs exploding, then watched an image of his wife flash before him, cradling their newborn daughter.

It was the last thought he had before dying.

6

After a week of easy travel, Akeela arrived home to Koth.

The capital city of Liiria gleamed like a white diamond at his homecoming, the spring sun setting it alight with the pure glow of morning. It had been an uneventful journey for the young king and his party of Chargers, except for a minor detour forced by the swelling river Kryss. The solitude had given Akeela time to consider things, too, like his peace with Reec and his perfect new wife. For the first time Akeela could remember, his life was flawless. He missed his father, but that emptiness was ebbing fast, filled by the day-to-day burdens of kingship. Now he reveled in his title and in the sweeping changes he intended to make. He had daydreamed throughout his entire journey home, whistling while he rode with his comrade and soldier, Breck, and staring up at the stars at night, looking for Cassandra's face. But he had never really found her in the heavens, because she was more beautiful than that, and no constellation could rival her. He was already lovestruck and he knew it, and despite Lukien's warnings, he planned to give his love to Cassandra completely.

As Akeela approached Koth, his heralds rode forward to the castle, informing them of his arrival. He had a huge staff in Lionkeep, just as his father had before him, because Liiria had interests varied and wide, and there were always civil servants needed to attend the minutiae of government.

Akeela sat up in his saddle—as tall as he could—as he entered the city. Beside him, Breck's face shone with pride, an emotion reflected by all in their company.

"You're a hero, my lord," said Breck. "It took your father years before anyone called him that, and you've done it in mere months." The cavalryman raised his face to the sun, now almost hidden behind the alabaster structures of Koth. "It's good to be home."

"Home is always the best place," agreed Akeela.

Koth had not yet fully awakened. An hour past dawn, the city was only now rubbing sleep from its eyes. Shopkeepers began opening their doors, dragging tables of linens and other wares into the avenue, and a spring breeze sent the signs of the inns and taverns along Capital Street swinging. Early rising bankers rode in carriages from their posh homes on the west side for the money-lending south district, where the bulk of crucial commerce took place. It was the bankers who had donated the lion's share of gold to Akeela's gift chest. Eager to open new avenues of trade, they were among the new king's most ardent supporters. As Akeela and his men rode into the city, he watched as the carriages and their well heeled occupants stopped to wave at him. Like all of Liiria, they had heard the news of his success in Hes and were overjoyed. Akeela smiled and nodded at them, careful not to seem too boyish. The bankers, his father had always said, couldn't be trusted when the money dried up.

Aside from the carriages and shopkeepers, Capital Street was mostly deserted, affording Akeela's company ample room to maneuver their armored horses and wagons. The street fingered off in all directions, leading to the affluent west side and the squalid northern districts, and, most importantly, to Chancellery Square. There, in the center of the city stood Lionkeep, Akeela's residence. And around the royal castle, circling it like vultures, were the Chancelleries. Here the countless ministers and bureaucrats bickered and bartered and supposedly made Liirian life easier with their logjams. It was where the War Chancellery stood in a stout building of brick and black iron, and where the Chancellery of Treasure towered nearly as tall as Lionkeep itself, an edifice of gold leaf and marble gargoyles. Next to the Treasury stood the House of Dukes, a five-storied fortress of quarried rock and the home of Baron Thorin Glass, the House's minister. There, huddled around tables of oiled oak, the landowners of Liiria drank expensive wine and occasionally made important decisions. The sight of the House of Dukes soured Akeela's good mood. Baron Glass had been his major critic since he'd ascended the throne, always opposed to the changes Akeela wanted to make.

But today, Akeela wasn't interested in the bold baron. He kept his eyes locked on Lionkeep. The royal residence had housed his family for more than a century, and had been built when Liiria was young, carved from the continent by wars and treaties. Koth, having been the only town of real consequence, had been named capital of the new nation, and Lionkeep had been constructed shortly thereafter. For the people of Liiria, who worshipped many gods and so had no national temples, Lionkeep was something of a church, a holy relic to be revered. Unlike Reec or Marn or Liiria's other neighbors, the Liirians were a mixed bag of peoples. When the nation was new it had attracted tradesmen and pilgrims from across the continent, promising a good life away from the wars plaguing the world. In the dreams of its founders, Liiria was to be a place of peace and opportunity.

Akeela's mood continued to slip as he rode toward Lionkeep. His forefather kings hadn't fulfilled the vision of the founders. For them, it wasn't long before the good days of peace were replaced by war. Constant border skirmishes and broken treaties had turned Liiria into little more than its neighbors, one more country struggling toward the future. The thought made Akeela grit his teeth.

"Breck," he said. "I'm going to change this land."

Breck smiled. "Yes, my lord, you've told me."

"A dozen times at least," Akeela admitted. "But I mean it. Things are going to be different."

"Things *are* different," Breck said. He was soft-spoken for a career soldier; had been since their war college days. And he always had a reassuring word for anyone who needed it. "You've made peace with Reec, my lord. I'd say that's a good start, wouldn't you?"

"A good start," agreed Akeela. "But not enough."

Breck looked forward, considering the mass of government buildings in the distance. "It won't be easy," he sighed. "Even your father had trouble dealing with the chancellors, and they feared him."

"And they don't fear me," said Akeela. "I know that. But I don't want to rule out of fear, Breck. I want the ministers to follow me willingly, because they believe in where I'll take them." He gave his horse a commanding spur, urging him forward. "Come. I'm eager to get to the castle."

The column rode for long minutes more, filling the echoing streets with the noise of their homecoming. Windows opened at the sound of the horsemen and the people of Liiria leaned out of their homes, eager for a glimpse of their king. An occasional woman blew Akeela a kiss, which made him blush. Finally, they passed the open-air market and entered Chancellery Square, where the Chancelleries loomed and Lionkeep's shadow darkened the avenues. The streets were narrow and cramped, jammed full of carriages and civil servants rushing to their jobs. At the Chancellery of Treasure a pair of long-robed ministers stopped in mid-argument to notice the king. They bowed with big, inscrutable smiles. Akeela nodded politely but hurried along, urging his horse toward Lionkeep and the hill holding it aloft. The gray wall of the fortress rose up around him, comforting him. He heard the familiar sounds of castle life from the battlements above. The main gate had been raised for his arrival, its spiked portcullis hanging open like the jaws of a shark. Hanging lanterns lined the way, still glowing orange in the growing light of day.

Akeela looked past the gate to the courtyard. It was practically empty save for a few young pages walking and brushing horses. The castle doves, which were everywhere in Lionkeep and were treated like royalty, hobbled along the yard in search of food, clawing at the green grass. At the top of the hill a contingent of Lionkeep's Wardens waited, rigid in their uniforms of gold and crimson. Unlike the Royal Chargers, who were under the command of Lukien and who fought Liiria's wars, the Lionkeep Wardens were autonomous troops from the Chancellery of War. Their sole responsibility was the protection of the castle and its royal inhabitants. As usual, the halberdiers were stiff at attention as Akeela approached. At the front of the guardians stood Graig, a welcoming smile stretched across his face. The Head Warden had obviously received Akeela's heralds and had arranged the guard to greet him. Graig was an old man but his eyes still twinkled, and he still looked daunting in his crimson uniform.

"Ho, Graig!" Akeela called. The king trotted forward and dismounted. A page appeared instantly to take care of his horse. Akeela ignored Graig's ceremonial bow, taking his hand instead. It was the usual ritual since Akeela had become king, and it was over in an instant. They shook, then embraced. "Good to see you," said Akeela.

"Ah, good to have you back," laughed Graig. He slapped Akeela's shoulder, then kissed his cheek. "You've done well! I'm proud of you!"

"We're all proud of the king," said Breck, bringing up his horse. "You should have seen him, Warden. He dealt with Karis like an old hand."

"I always told your father you'd be a diplomat." The warden spied the line of Chargers curiously. "Where's Lukien?"

"I had him stay behind with Trager and some others," said Akeela. He smiled slyly. "They're looking after something for me. You've heard about my other good news, I suppose?"

The old man guffawed. "Yes, you're a rascal now I hear. You've fallen into the wrong crowd with these Chargers!"

"You'll love her, Graig. Cassandra's a real beauty. Isn't she, Breck?"

"My lord could have done worse," Breck replied with a smile.

"Well, when do I get to see her?" asked Graig. "Why the wait?"

"Because I have a wedding to plan, you romantic old fool," said Akeela. "There's a lot to do, and I want to get this place ready for her." He rubbed his hands together. "But first, I'm starving. Did you consider my need for breakfast, by any chance?"

"I've got the kitchens on it already," smiled Graig. Then he shrugged, adding, "I'm still your houseboy, as usual. Come . . ." He turned and headed toward the gate, then shouted at the pages to attend the soldiers and their horses. Akeela followed him, but Breck remained behind, seeing to his men and mounts. The courtyard was quickly coming

to life at the king's arrival, and the warming sun felt good
upon Akeela's face.

"So?" he asked as they moved through the courtyard.
"What news since I left? Nothing too bad, I hope."

"Bad?" scoffed Graig. "I've had this place running like
a timepiece. Not even a leaky roof to worry about."

"And the chancellors? What of them?"

"Behaving themselves. Baron Glass has been making
some noise, but nothing unusual."

"That's good news," said Akeela. They passed under an
archway and into a hall heading toward the kitchens. The
smell of frying bacon made Akeela's stomach rumble. "You
did a fine job looking after things, Graig. Thank you."

"I wish it could all be good news," said Graig.

"Isn't it?"

"No, I'm afraid. Beith had her baby."

Akeela stopped walking. "Stillborn?"

"Gods no, nothing like that," said Graig. "Just, well, deformed. Bad hand and foot, like this . . ." The warden
made a crumpled ball of his fist. "Clubbed, I guess you'd
call it. And Beith's all upset that it might be more."

"More?"

"You know," said Graig. He tapped his skull. "Its mind.
The child might be simple."

All the levity went out of Akeela's face. Beith had already lost her husband, and Akeela knew how much she
was looking forward to her baby. Like the midwife Gwena
had said, it was going to fill her "empty spaces." "I should
go to her," said Akeela. He glanced around, unsure what
to do. "Is she up yet?"

Graig grinned. "I don't make a habit of calling on her,
my lord."

"We'll talk later, Graig," said Akeela, then dashed off
in the direction opposite to the kitchens. Breakfast could
wait; he needed to see Beith.

He hurried through the halls then up a staircase, dodging
servants and taking the steps two at a time. Beith had a
chamber on the third floor of the main keep. She had
shared it with her husband, Gilwyn, and together they had
planned for their infant's arrival, gathering blankets and
baby clothes from the women in Lionkeep and decorating

a corner of their tiny apartment with toys. Gilwyn had been
Lukien's friend, mostly, but on the few occasions that
Akeela visited the apartment he had always found it
cheery. He supposed it would be appallingly cold now.
Reaching the third floor, he braced himself as he entered
the hall. Most of the doors were closed. Beith's room was
at the far end. Akeela went to it and listened, but didn't
hear anything. Unsure if he should interrupt, he went ahead
and knocked.

"Beith?" he called softly. "Are you awake?"

There was a stirring behind the door. Akeela fixed a
smile on his face.

"Who is it?" called a voice. It was hoarse from lack of
sleep, but Akeela recognized it.

"Beith, it's Akeela."

After a hesitation, the startled voice returned. "The
king?" There was more fumbling behind the door. Akeela
imagined Beith smoothing out her night clothes. "My lord
Akeela, a moment, please . . ."

Akeela waited patiently until finally the door opened,
revealing Beith in a disheveled robe and unkempt hair, her
red eyes rimmed with sunken bags. She forced a sunny
smile, stepping away from the door so he could enter.
Quickly she dipped into a curtsey.

"My lord, this is a surprise. Forgive me, I wasn't expecting you. My appearance—"

"Is perfectly fine, Beith, don't worry." Akeela stepped
into the room. As expected, the apartment's cheerfulness
had fled. "I apologize for bothering you, but I've only just
arrived home. I'd heard . . . well, that you've had your
child."

"Yes, my lord," said the woman. She wrapped her robe
about herself, obviously embarrassed. Since he'd become
king, Akeela had noticed the way ordinary people squirmed
around him.

"Please," he implored. "Be at ease. I just wanted to see
you, and your little one."

Beith brightened. "You've come to see Gilwyn?"

"Gilwyn?" laughed Akeela. "Is that his name? I didn't
even know you'd had a boy! I know you wanted one." He
looked around the room and spotted the crib beneath the

room's only window. Sunlight poured onto its whitewashed wood; a cottony blanket fell over its rim. "Ah, that must be him."

"Yes, my lord," said Beith. Pride crept into her tone. "He's sleeping, I think."

Akeela tiptoed toward the crib. "May I see him?"

"Certainly," answered Beith. "But he's . . ." Her voice trailed off.

"I know about his problems, Beith. Warden Graig told me. I'm sorry."

Beith said quickly, "Oh, but he's a beautiful baby, my lord. He's got his father's eyes. And he's smart! He can already tell when I say his name." Beith moved toward the crib. "Here, let me show him to you."

"If he's sleeping . . ."

"No," said Beith anxiously. "I want you to see him."

Akeela followed her to the crib, watching in fascination as she lifted the little bundle out of the blankets. Baby Gilwyn squirmed in protest at being awakened. Beith's expression lightened as she held out the baby for Akeela to inspect.

"Ah," said Akeela, enchanted. He stuck his face closer to the child, amazed by his smallness. Little Gilwyn fixed his bleary eyes on the king and gave a tiny cry.

"No, don't cry," said Beith, bouncing the baby in her arms. "That's the king!"

Akeela put out a finger, touching the baby's stomach. Gilwyn reacted by wrinkling his nose, which made the king laugh.

"He's beautiful," said Akeela. He noticed the clubbed hand but pretended to ignore it. "Congratulations, Beith. If your husband were here, he'd be very proud."

"Yes," said Beith sadly. "I wish he could see him. But Meri says he's here in spirit, watching."

"And perhaps he is," said Akeela, not believing a word of it. Like some in the castle, Meri believed that the dead lived on as spirits, walking among the living. It was just one of the varied religions represented by Lionkeep's staff. "Like I said, Gilwyn would have been proud of this little soldier."

Beith blanched. She hugged the baby a little tighter.

"Oh, blast," said Akeela. "I'm sorry, Beith. That was stupid of me to say."

"No, it's all right," said Beith. "But I don't think he's going to be the little soldier. He won't ever be a Charger like his father."

"No," Akeela agreed. With the baby's infirmities, being a soldier was impossible.

"But he's smart, my lord," Beith insisted. "He's not slow or simple. Gwena says he might be, but I just know he's not."

Akeela nodded. "I'm sure you're right."

"He'll be able to do things, my lord. He won't be a burden to anyone." Beith was looking at Akeela fretfully. "I swear, I'll teach him to take care of himself. He'll be a good member of this castle. I mean, if you'll allow it."

Suddenly Akeela understood her fears. Her eyes reflected her dashed dreams, and her motherly concern for a son that might grow up a beggar.

"Let me hold the baby," said Akeela. Carefully Beith handed the infant over. Akeela, who had seldom held children before, cradled the child in the crook of his arm. Little Gilwyn squirmed but was silent, looking up at him. For Akeela, it was like holding a miracle, just like Gwena had always described. The warm little body curled in his embrace, enjoying the safety of the king's protection.

"He likes you," said Beith. She glanced up at Akeela hopefully. "See? He already knows what a good king you are."

"Beith, stop. There's no need." Akeela kept his gaze on Gilwyn. "I would never abandon this child to the streets. I don't care if he's simple or a genius. Lionkeep is his home. As long as I am king, it always will be."

"Really?" asked Beith. "Will you promise me that, my lord?"

"I promise," said Akeela. He leaned down and laid a gentle kiss on the infant's forehead. "And not just to you, but to this little fellow here. He will always have a place in Lionkeep."

Beith could barely find her voice. "Thank you, my lord. Thank you."

Akeela took the baby over to a nearby chair. He sat

down and rocked the child, loving the paternal feeling. Gilwyn's little mouth turned upward. Akeela took the gesture for a smile. He cooed to the baby, speaking softly.

"Little Gilwyn, Liiria is going to be a great nation. I'm going to make it special, the way the founders intended. There will always be a place for you here, and for all the other children, too. And you're going to grow up strong and smart, and whatever you can dream, you can be."

Beith spent the rest of the day feeling lighter than air. The good news Akeela had given her put a smile back on her face, and she bragged to Meri and her other friends about the king's promise, and how her son would grow up in Lionkeep just as she and her dead husband had always planned. For Beith, who hadn't known real joy since her husband's death, the lightness in her heart felt wonderful. Now, with her baby safe, she could begin mourning her beloved properly, without fretting over the fate of her newborn.

That night, Beith slept sound and deeply. She had retired early, putting Gilwyn to bed in his crib and taking a cup of tea before drifting off to sleep. For the first time in weeks, her dreams were unpolluted.

Then she awoke for no apparent reason. Her eyes fluttered open to catch moonbeams slanting through her window. The mist of sleep was on her, and for a moment she couldn't place the time. It was very late; dawn was still many hours away. Realizing this, she listened for Gilwyn. He was a good baby and surprisingly cooperative about sleeping, but she knew it was time to check on him. Desperate for the pillow, she nevertheless rose from the bed and started toward the door, shambling through the darkness in a groggy haze. Then she saw the figure in the threshold.

Beith stumbled backward, about to scream, before an amazing calm overtook her. Unable to move, she merely stared at the figure, enchanted by a strange light emanating from its chest.

"Don't be afraid." The figure took a tiny step forward. Everything about it was tiny, in fact. Beith had never seen anyone like her, not outside a carnival. She realized that the stranger was a woman, and that the woman was a midget.

"Who are you?" Beith asked. "What are you doing here?"

The woman smiled. Beith could see her impish face in the red glow of her necklace. "Fair questions, Beith," she said. "But first, your child is safe. Do not be afraid for him."

To her surprise, Beith wasn't afraid. She knew—somehow—that no harm had come to Gilwyn. She squinted at the little woman and saw her multicolored coat swirling as if it were alive.

"Are you magical?" she asked.

The question delighted the intruder. "Why, yes I am."

"I'm not afraid. But I should be. Am I under a bewitchment?"

The woman floated closer, until she and Beith were standing face to face. Only they weren't really, because Beith towered over the stranger. The woman looked up at Beith. She seemed to be studying her.

"Let us talk." She gestured toward the bed. "Sit."

Beith heard the warnings in her mind, telling her to run and to rescue Gilwyn, yet the voices were very faint, pushed way back in her brain. So instead of running, Beith obeyed the stranger, sitting down at the edge of the bed. She noticed the amulet around the woman's neck, glowing ruby red. The remarkable coat she wore no longer swam with life, yet Beith knew she was in the power of a magician.

"Why are you here?" she asked again.

The woman replied, "For the sake of your child, Beith. I can help him."

"Gilwyn? Gilwyn needs no help."

"Does he not?" asked the woman. "I have heard about him. He is deformed, quite probably crippled. He is not well, dear Beith. But I have a safe place for him."

"No," said Beith. "Lionkeep is a safe place for him."

A sympathetic expression lingered on the stranger's face. "If only that were so," she sighed. "Your child is not like others. He may not be safe here in the castle, or anywhere in Liiria. But I know a place where all like him are safe. I can take him there."

"What is this place?" Beith asked. Vaguely her memory returned, recalling a story she had heard as a little girl.

"It is a secret place, far from here, far across a desert. There are people like me there, and people like your child."

"Magical people?"

The woman's smile dimmed. "Yes, all right. Magical people."

Suddenly a memory bloomed in Beith's mind. She gasped, "You're the Witch of Grimhold."

"No," said the woman. "I am no witch."

"You are," Beith insisted. "My mother told me the story, when I was very young."

"Your mother was mistaken," said the woman. She closed her eyes for a moment and seemed to be concentrating. The awesome calm within Beith increased. As quickly as she had recalled the old legend, she forgot it.

"Now, tell me," the woman continued. "Will you let me take your child? I will look after him for you. I will take him to a place where no one will harm or ridicule him."

Beith struggled to stay awake. "There's no need. Gilwyn is safe here. The king has promised it."

"The new king?"

"Yes, Akeela. He's told me this very day that Gilwyn is safe here. He will always have a place here in Lionkeep. It is the king's promise."

For a moment the woman said nothing. She turned away, considering the moon outside the window. "I have heard about your new king," she said at last. "I have heard that he is very good; very wise."

"He is good. And he has been kind to me and my baby."

"And he will look after your child, even when he is grown?"

"He will."

"Even if he is crippled?"

"Yes."

"And simple?"

Beith hesitated, but only for a second. "Yes, even then."

There was no sound from the stranger. The light from her amulet lit her face, revealing concern. Beith, still in the hold of the bewitchment, couldn't help but smile at the tiny figure who for some reason was concerned about her little boy. She reached out for the amulet around her neck, but the little woman pulled gently away.

"What is that you wear?" asked Beith.

The woman smiled down at her amulet. "This is Inai ka Vala," she replied. "You would call it the Eye of God."

"God? What god?"

"You are full of questions, Beith." The tiny woman studied her. "I think your son will be like you—inquisitive."

Talking to the woman was like floating in a dream or on a gentle lake of calm water. All the fear had left Beith now, so that there were only questions.

"Will you tell me your name?" she asked.

"Minikin," replied the woman.

"Minikin?" Beith chuckled. "Your name is Minikin? That's funny."

"Yes," said the woman. "The people who named me that thought so, too." She turned from the window, heading for the door. "Follow me."

Once again Beith obeyed, following the woman out of her bed chamber and into the main room where Gilwyn's white crib rested in the moonlight. The woman hovered over Gilwyn, her thoughts unfathomable.

"Very well," she said. "I will trust your new king to help this child." Then she bent over the crib, giving Gilwyn a kiss and speaking a single remarkable word.

"Grimhold."

When Beith awoke the next morning, she remembered nothing of the strange intrusion or of her remarkable conversation with the midget woman. She felt refreshed and hungry, and that was all. She rose from bed at her usual hour and saw at once to Gilwyn's feeding, sitting down at her chair near the window and putting the baby to her breast. Still feeling wonderful over Akeela's acceptance of her child, she laughed as her son fed, loving the communion of nursing. Gilwyn fed hungrily but gently, latching on without discomfort to his mother. The morning sun was bright and warmed the room. Beith considered what a fine day it would be.

"Oooh, you're a hungry little scholar this morning, aren't you?" she asked.

Gilwyn kept feeding. For some reason, seeing his earnest face reminded Beith of a story she had heard when she was younger. She puzzled over the memory, trying to recall it clearly, deciding to entertain herself with the tale.

"There's a story my mother told me once," she began. She then proceeded to tell Gilwyn about Grimhold, a place where monsters live, led by a witch who steals children.

7

Lukien sat at the end of a pond, absently tossing stones into the water. The sky was bright but his mood was heavy, and as the ripples disappeared he watched them pensively, his mind a hundred miles from his halcyon surroundings. Not far away, Trager sat on a blanket on the green grass, sipping a drink and picnicking on the pheasant Earl Linuk had provided. With him were Durwin and Benn, two Royal Chargers who, like Lukien and Trager, had been left behind in Reec to look after Princess Cassandra. Both men wore broad smiles and greasy smudges on their shirts. Trager was talking and laughing too loudly. The lieutenant had been over-enjoying his wine; Lukien had seen him empty more than one bottle over the course of the afternoon. The Bronze Knight suppressed a sigh and flicked another stone into the lake.

For two weeks now he had been in Reec, missing home and enduring Trager's company. He had been treated well by his Reecian hosts, but he longed to return to Koth, and every day he waited impatiently for word from Akeela, summoning him back. So far, word had yet to come. Akeela had warned him that it could be at least a month before he would return, and the wait was interminable. Castle Hes had been a prison for Lukien, a very pleasant place to die slowly. With only Trager and a handful of Chargers for company, Lukien had been forced to bear the stares of Reecian soldiers and stableboys and the whispers of the castle gossips. Worse, he had been too close to Cassandra. Since Akeela's departure, the princess had occupied his every thought, and his proximity to her was irksome. Because he was her bodyguard, he was never very far from her, accompanying her to knitting sessions and tea with her sisters and other mind- deadening activities, all the while trying to avert his eyes from her flawless face and figure. Cassandra had remained aloof, mostly, yet she had insisted that he perform his duties as her protector, making sure he was always nearby. From the moment Akeela had gone, they had shared Castle Hes like two uneasy house guests.

But now they were no longer in Castle Hes. They were in Glain, the seaside estate of Earl Linuk. Princess Cassandra, evidently a spoiled brat, had wanted a last holiday. She had left behind her overprotective father for the watchful eyes of Linuk, whom Lukien quickly discovered was something of an adopted uncle to the girl. Linuk doted on Cassandra, opening his house to her and her handmaidens and providing them with all the splendor of Glain in springtime. Of course, Lukien had been given no choice in accompanying Cassandra to Glain. Earl Linuk had made it clear they were all going to spend a week at his estate, and Lukien's protests had fallen on the earl's deaf ears. So he had relented, and now sat in warm sunshine as Cassandra indulged herself with a picnic and Linuk's musicians entertained them. It would have been a good day for Lukien if they were in Koth, if Trager was somewhere else, and the music was Liirian. If Cassandra wasn't so near.

Lukien lifted his gaze from the pond. On the other side of the water, past the narrow bridge that spanned it, Cassandra was with her friend Jancis. The princess had set up an easel and was painting, enjoying the light of the sun. She seemed to be hard at work, occasionally stepping back from her masterpiece and cocking her head, then lifting her brush again to make corrections. She wore a white dress that caught the sun and contrasted with her raven hair. She had dressed well for their picnic and that surprised Lukien, and occasionally she stole glances across the pond. He watched her for a long moment, and when she discovered him staring at her, the princess frowned. Quickly she returned to her painting.

To Lukien, Cassandra was an enigma. She was barely

more than a child, but she had the body of a woman and a keen look in her eyes that belied her innocence. In his many campaigns, he had met women like Cassandra before, those with iron under their soft skin, who longed for a wider role in life. Cassandra was like that, Lukien guessed. After only two weeks with her he knew why she had accepted Akeela's proposal. She was bored with life in Castle Hes. She was tired of being King Karis' daughter. The princess wanted to be a queen.

"And of course she will be," muttered Lukien. That was how it was for royalty—they always got what they wanted. Akeela had blundered into a beautiful wife, and Cassandra, not satisfied with one castle, would soon have two to call home. Lukien leaned back on his palms, a scowl forming on his face. Why was it then that men like him desired things they couldn't have? Being called a "brother" by Akeela simply wasn't enough. Women of refinement—women like Cassandra—were kept from him.

"Captain?"

Lukien heard the word as soon as the shadow crossed his face. Over him stood Trager, looking down with a queer smile. The lieutenant had a plate of food in one hand and a bottle of wine in the other. It was plain from the dullness in his eyes that he was drunk.

"You haven't eaten anything," said Trager. He handed the plate down to Lukien. "I thought you might be hungry."

Lukien hesitated. Taking the plate might invite Trager to sit down. Since he was indeed hungry, he took his chances by accepting the food—and lost the gamble. Trager sat down immediately, letting out a giant sigh as his rump hit the grass.

"Two glasses," he called to one of Earl Linuk's servants.

"Just one will do," said Lukien.

The servant hesitated. Trager smiled wickedly, then held up two fingers.

"You heard me," he said.

The servant scurried off. In a moment he returned with a pair of crystal goblets, which he handed to Trager before quickly disappearing. Trager didn't thank the man but commenced pouring. Lukien glanced down at his food, his appetite gone.

"You've been very quiet today, Captain." Trager handed him a glass of wine. "Are you unwell?"

The question irritated Lukien. "I'm fine," he replied.

"Then why not enjoy the day?" Trager gestured to their beautiful surroundings. "I know you don't like this duty, but there's nothing we can do about it, so why be bothered? There's wine, music . . ." He glanced across the pond. "And pretty ladies to enjoy."

Lukien looked up. "What does that mean?"

"It's just a pretty day, that's all." Trager sipped at his wine. He let out a grotesque belch and leaned back on his elbow. "Eat, Captain," he urged. "It's very good. Earl Linuk certainly knows how to care for his guests."

"I thought you said you wouldn't drink with Reecians," Lukien reminded him. "Or have you changed your mind?"

Trager shrugged. "Change of heart, I suppose. Free food and drink. Only a fool would pass that up."

The answer reminded Lukien why he disliked his lieutenant so much. Inwardly he cursed Akeela for leaving Trager behind with him. He was a jealous, petty man, and had been since their war college days. He held grudges longer than anyone Lukien had ever known, too, and had never really forgiven Lukien the good fortune of being King Balak's favorite. Though they had graduated together, posting almost identical grades, Lukien had become Captain of the Chargers. Some, like Trager, thought it was because of his closeness to the king. To be honest, Lukien suspected there was some truth in that theory. But it was also because he was the best soldier the college had ever produced, and because he had proven himself in battle many times. But Trager never considered that.

"It's very nice here, don't you think, Captain?" Trager continued to sip his wine as he studied the area, swaying to the strains of the music.

"Yes, it is," Lukien conceded. He began picking at the food on his plate, nibbling at the meat of a pheasant joint.

"I'm grateful to be out of Hes," said Trager. "The castle air was getting stale." He took a deep breath. "This is how a man should live. You can smell the sea here."

"Very nice."

"It will be good to get back home to Liiria, though. I miss it."

Lukien nodded. Trager's voice was tiresome.

"I suppose King Akeela's wedding will be quite an occasion," the lieutenant went on. "He seemed excited about it. You'll be there, of course, his steadfast man."

"I suppose."

"And it will be tournament season. He'll have it at the same time, I suppose, to celebrate the occasion." Trager looked at him. "Some jousting perhaps?"

"Oh, I'm sure," said Lukien. He returned his lieutenant's sharp smile.

"I've been practicing, Captain."

"Really? Good for you."

"In the apple orchard near Lionkeep. Before we left for Hes, I was practicing most every morning. The spring tournament should be enjoyable this year."

Lukien laughed. "I will beat you, just as I do every year. And this time everyone at Akeela's wedding will be on hand to watch you kiss the mud. You're right—that will be fun."

"Big words," said Trager. "I have the feeling that all this bodyguard duty will make you soft." He tapped the rim of his goblet, making it ring. "This just might be the year the Bronze Knight shows his glass jaw."

"We shall see," said Lukien. "Just keep practicing, and maybe you'll have a chance against the squires."

Trager's eyes began to smolder. "I came here in friendship, Captain."

Lukien yawned. Friendship was a subject Trager knew nothing about. "Yes. Well then, thanks for the food."

But Trager didn't leave. He merely leaned back again, staring at Cassandra across the pond. A low whistle crossed his bearded lips.

"She's a beauty, isn't she?" he asked. "Akeela's going to be a lucky dog when we get back home."

Lukien said nothing.

Trager leaned in closer. "I wouldn't mind taking her to my bed, I'll tell you that."

"Lieutenant," began Lukien coldly, "you've had too much to drink. She's to be the king's wife, remember."

Trager grinned. "Don't tell me you haven't noticed her, Captain. I've seen you looking at her. You're like a bitch in heat when she passes by."

"That's enough," Lukien snapped. He snatched the wine bottle from Trager's hand. "Go dry out, Lieutenant, and I'll try to forget that insult."

For a moment, Trager didn't move. His eyes kept a challenging watch on Lukien. Then he smiled again and rose from the grass, letting the goblet drop from his hand. It shattered when it hit the ground.

"You know, Captain, you're a very arrogant man," said Trager, then turned and walked off.

Lukien watched him go, his heart racing. He suddenly felt sick. Had his attraction to Cassandra been so obvious? He hadn't thought so, but now he wasn't sure. He gazed across the pond again to where the princess was painting. The music of the lutes surrounded him. She was very beautiful, and he simply couldn't look away.

On the other side of the pond, Cassandra played with her paint pots, pretending to ignore the strange knight across the water. It was a perfect day and her holiday from Castle Hes had been delightful, yet still she was restless, unable to get Lukien out of her mind. She glanced past her easel, moving only her eyes. He was alone again. The sharp-tongued one, Trager, had left him. Now he was sipping a glass of wine. He looked pensive, as if he was staring at nothing in particular. But Cassandra knew better. The Bronze Knight had been watching her since they'd met, rarely taking his eyes off her. In every sense of the word he had become her bodyguard, and to her dismay she liked the way he coveted her. Her stomach fluttering, she returned to her painting, using a dull yellow to complete his uniform. He wasn't in his armor today but she liked him best that way, and since no one but Jancis had come across the bridge to disturb her, she had painted what she desired, without fear of being discovered. With a thin brush, just a few horse hairs thick, she detailed his brilliant, bronze armor. The sun shone on his golden hair. To Cassandra, he was strikingly handsome.

"He's looking at me again," she whispered. A few yards away, Jancis sat on a blanket, knitting absently. Her friend's observation made her raise her head. "No, don't stare," snapped Cassandra. She kept her eyes on her painting.

"Trust me, that's all. He's been looking at me all afternoon."

Jancis, who was appalled by Cassandra's painting of the knight, made a disgusted sound.

"If anyone sees what you're doing . . ."

"No one will see," Cassandra chuckled. "It's private here. That's why I wanted to come. At least I don't have my sisters looking under my bed."

"But the earl, Cassandra. This is his home."

"So? He doesn't care what I get up to just as long as I'm happy, the old dear." The princess smiled at her painting. It was very good considering her amateurish skill, and she was proud of the way she had captured his expression. Earnest, with just a touch of danger.

"You should be painting your new husband," Jancis chastised. She lowered her knitting angrily. "And just what will you do with it when it's done? Give it to Lukien?"

"Don't be silly."

"Me?"

"Yes, you. Stop fretting now, I'm trying to work."

Cassandra stole another glance across the water. Lukien had looked away again, which deflated her. She frowned. Another of his men came to join him, not Trager this time but the one called Benn. He sat down next to Lukien and the two began talking.

"He's not at all what I expected," said Cassandra finally.

Jancis rolled her eyes. "I can see you won't let me get any of my knitting done today."

"He is though, isn't he, Jan? Handsome, I mean?"

"Stop being wicked," said Jancis. She looked around for unwelcome ears. "You're engaged, Cass. Have you forgotten?"

Cassandra hadn't forgotten. In fact, she kept drawing comparisons between Lukien and her husband-to-be. Akeela was sweet and charming in his own nervous way. And he was a great man, at least that's what everyone was saying. She knew she was lucky to have him. But he was also bookish and overly polite, with none of Lukien's roughness. All her life Cassandra had been surrounded by people like Akeela. She realized suddenly how tired she was of men with breeding.

"It's nice to daydream," she said softly. She put down her brush, plainly staring now across the water. Benn and Lukien were laughing and sharing some cheese. A lute player was nearby, as were several of Linuk's friends. Everyone seemed to be enjoying the picnic—except Cassandra. It wasn't the pain in her stomach that bothered her anymore. Since coming to Glain that had mostly subsided. Now it was a different ache that seized her, much less physical than the one that had kept her on the chamber pot.

"I want to go riding," she decided suddenly. "With Lukien."

"What?" Jancis put down her knitting and stood. "Cass, don't."

"Why not? It's my only opportunity. No one here will care."

"What about your father?"

"My father's twenty miles from here." Cassandra pulled the canvas over her painting, hiding it from prying eyes. "I want to talk to him."

Jancis huffed forward. "That's why you wanted to come here, isn't it?" she asked. "You just wanted a chance to be alone with him."

When Cassandra didn't answer, Jancis sighed.

"Please, Cassandra, don't be stupid. Just forget it, all right?"

"I don't want to forget it," said Cassandra. "I want to find out why he's been staring at me." She looked at her friend imploringly. "I want to find out about *him.*"

Jancis shook her head in resignation. Cassandra gave her a smile.

"You're a dear. Look after the painting for me, will you?" she said, then started back across the bridge. Lukien noticed her at once. He stood up, as did the others, bowing his head in greeting.

"I want to go riding," Cassandra declared. She looked at Linuk's servants. "Fetch me two horses, please." Then she looked at Lukien. "You'll come with me."

The knight's face drained of color. "What?"

"You'll ride with me, keep me safe. You're my protector, aren't you?"

"Yes, but—"

"Then protect me. My father wouldn't want me riding off without you."

Lukien swallowed hard. "All right, my lady," he managed. "I'll ask some others to come with us as well."

"No," said Cassandra, brushing past him. "I came to Glain to get away from the noise of the city, not to drag it along by the tail. You alone will be quite enough, Lukien."

As she passed, heading toward the house to change into her riding gear, she heard Lukien's astonished gasp. A small, satisfied smile crept onto her face.

To Lukien's surprise, Cassandra was an excellent rider. She hadn't needed his assistance to mount or guide her horse, and in fact she led the way through the rolling hills of Glain, hardly speaking or even turning to regard him. Her silence was a pretense, Lukien knew, and it bothered him. She had surprised him with her request to go riding, then had once again turned into her stony, familiar self. As she rode a few paces ahead, taking full notice of the meadow and none of him at all, Lukien watched her in fascination. He even felt a little nervous. Or was it guilt?

They were far from Linuk's house now, far from the other picnickers and servants, in a meadow of swaying grass surrounded by gentle slopes. Lukien could see no one for miles, just the birds and creatures that called the meadow home. They rode at an easy pace, Cassandra occasionally pausing to gaze at the open sky or steal a leaf from a tree. It had been nearly an hour since they'd left the others and her mood had quieted. She wasn't quite the insistent princess she had been earlier, but she wasn't a companion, either. It was as if she were riding alone, and Lukien kept a respectful distance, silently spying on her. A warm breeze blew across the meadow, stirring her hair. Cassandra tucked the ebony strands behind her ear, then looked around with a satisfied nod.

"We'll stop here," she said.

Lukien shifted in his saddle. "Stop? I thought you wanted to go riding."

"I want to rest now," she said as she slid from her horse. She smiled as she surveyed the meadow, enchanted by the sunlight on the grass. There was a patch of buttercups nearby. Cassandra sat down next to it and folded her legs beneath her. She stuck her nose into the flowers, became frightened by a bee, then plucked one of the blooms. Seeing Lukien still mounted, she sighed, "Please come down. I won't hurt you."

Embarrassed, Lukien dropped from his horse and towered over her. "Earl Linuk will be worried about you. We should head back."

"We haven't been gone that long," said Cassandra. "And I have that old dear Linuk wrapped so tightly around my finger he can barely breathe. I could be gone for a week and weasel my way back into his graces in a minute. Now relax. You're making me nervous."

Lukien remained standing over her, unsure what to do. He felt awkward. He looked around for something—anything—to occupy him. Cassandra noted his nervousness and chuckled.

"Sit, Lukien," she said. For the first time she gave him a genuine smile as she gestured to the grass beside her. "Here."

Lukien at last sat down. His eyes darted around the meadow, praying that no one could see him. Cassandra gazed across the plain, sighing happily. Her face glowed with sunlight and a look of deep satisfaction. It was easy to tell how much she enjoyed being away from Hes. Without her father or sisters shadowing her, she didn't seem like a child anymore. Lukien let his eyes linger on her a bit too long.

"You're staring at me," she said.

Lukien turned his head. "I'm sorry."

"You've been looking at me a lot, I've noticed," said the princess.

"Forgive me, my lady. I meant no offense." Lukien groped for an explanation. "I'm supposed to protect you, after all. It's hard to do that unless I look at you."

Cassandra's smile grew sly. "Oh."

Lukien picked a blade of grass andtwirled it between his fingers. "It's my job, you see."

"Yes, I see. Thank you for explaining it to me. I was curious."

"Well, that's all right, then."

Cassandra didn't stop smiling. "Yes."

Lukien cleared his throat. For some reason, he couldn't keep himself from asking, "But you were curious?"

"Oh, yes," said Cassandra. She played with the flower in her hand. "I mean, you were staring at me so intently across the pond, I was wondering why. I thought perhaps you found me . . . interesting."

A tiny terror seized Lukien. He knew he'd crossed a line suddenly, and didn't know how to respond. Cassandra was baiting him. Bolstered by the privacy and ignoring his guilt, he said, "You are interesting, my lady. You're different from most women I've known."

"Am I? Tell me."

Lukien tried a smile. "You are very beautiful and talented, and no man can resist that. But you are also refined."

Cassandra laughed. "Oh, but you live in the king's castle. You are surrounded by refined women, sir."

Yes, thought Lukien blackly. *Surrounded and doomed to never touch them.*

He didn't tell Cassandra how he longed to be with a princess instead of a harlot, or how Liirian women of breeding were reserved for dukes and barons. He said instead, "Still, you are different. You can paint and you can dance. You can even ride a horse. I think you are a mystery, my lady. And that interests me."

Cassandra brightened, not showing the slightest hint of offense. "And you interest me, sir. Here in Reec you are the Bronze Knight."

"I'm called that in Liiria as well, my lady."

"Ah, but in Liiria you are a hero, while here in Reec you are a villain."

Lukien bristled. "I am no villain."

"But you kill people. I have heard the stories. They say you are a berserker in battle. My Uncle Raxor once told me that you killed twelve men in the battle of Redthorn, even after he had called retreat." Cassandra looked at him squarely. "Is that so?"

"I'm a soldier, my lady. I do the bidding of my king. When there's war, I fight."

The girl's eyes narrowed on him. "But you love it, don't you? I can see it in you. You love to fight."

"It is what I am best at," Lukien replied. He studied

the blade of grass in his hand, then noticed the flower in Cassandra's. The comparison made him laugh. He was like the grass—utterly common. And Cassandra was certainly a flower. But he had tried to be more than just a blade of grass. He had tried to distinguish himself through battle. "I won't apologize for what I am, my lady," he said. "You are royal. You don't know what it means to be a commoner."

Cassandra seemed perplexed. "But you're not a commoner. You're a knight."

"I am a knight now, true. People call me 'sir,' but it wasn't always so."

The princess leaned closer. "Tell me. I want to know about you."

"I was an orphan, living on the streets of Koth. My father abandoned us and my mother died shortly thereafter. I was alone and had to fend for myself. And Koth is a big city, my lady. Bigger than Hes. It's not a place for a boy to grow up alone."

"How did you survive?" asked Cassandra.

"How does anyone survive on the streets? I stole. And I worked, when I could. The smithies were always looking for boys to exploit. They drove us like slaves. I lived like that for almost four years, all alone." A smile cracked Lukien's face. "Until I met Akeela."

Cassandra noticed his grin. "You're very fond of each other, aren't you?"

Lukien nodded. Despite all the arguments he'd had with Akeela, he truly loved him.

"And you are Akeela's champion? You protect him?"

"I protect him because I love him, because he is the closest thing I have ever had to a brother," said Lukien. "And I protect him because he is the son of King Balak, whom I adored."

"But he is a mystery to me," said Cassandra. "I know so little about him, and who better to tell me about him than you? Do they really call him 'Akeela the Good' in Liiria?"

"They do," said Lukien, laughing. "And it's a name he deserves, believe me."

"So he is a good man?"

"Oh, yes."

"And will he make me a good husband?"

Lukien looked at her again. Her face had changed, set with worry. He told her, "My lady, Akeela is the dearest man I've even known. It's why I pledged myself to him, and why I followed him here to Reec. There is no evil within him. He's not capable of harming anyone, least of all you. Are you looking for a gentle husband? A man who will honor and worship you, and ask himself every day how best to make you happy? If you are, then you have found him, my lady."

Their eyes remained locked, and for a moment they shared a thought, wondering exactly who Lukien had just described. Lukien felt his face grow warm with embarrassment. He looked away.

"Akeela will be a good husband, and a good king," he said. "You will be happy with him, my lady."

Cassandra was quiet. The flower in her hand had dropped to her lap. Now she was the one who was staring.

"You are not what I expected," she said softly. "You aren't a villain. I think you are . . ." She stopped herself, changing direction. "I'm sorry for the way I've treated you, Sir Lukien. You must think me a shrew."

"Don't apologize, my lady. If your Uncle Raxor came to Koth, I'd probably treat him the same way."

"No," said Cassandra. "I must apologize." She reached out and touched Lukien's hand. "Since Akeela is so fond of you, then you and I should be friends, too."

The touch of her hand was magical. Slowly Lukien let his eyes drift back to her, and saw in her expression something far worse than friendship.

"Yes, my lady," he said. "Friends."

Cassandra's lovely face shone, but then went horribly twisted. She jerked back her hand with a cry, putting her hands to her stomach and doubling forward. Startled, Lukien rose and knelt beside her.

"My lady?" he asked. "What's wrong?"

The girl let out a horrible gasp. Her eyes were clamped with pain.

"Princess? What is it?"

Barely able to put up a hand, Cassandra moaned, "Nothing . . . I'm all right."

"No you're not." Lukien took hold of her arm. "Tell me what's wrong."

"It's nothing," Cassandra insisted through gritted teeth. She was on the verge of tears.

"It's . . . my moon blood, that's all. That must be it."

"Your moon blood? No, that can't be it."

"And how would you know about my blood?" she snapped. She rose to her feet unsteadily, pushing him away, stumbling toward her horse. Her face was colorless. Before she could reach her mount she collapsed to her knees.

"Cassandra!" Lukien rushed forward, putting his arm around her. "God, let me help you."

The princess shook her head. "It will pass. It always does." She took deep, painful breathes, steadying herself. "Please, just let me rest a moment."

"What's wrong with you?" Lukien insisted. "Tell me, please."

Cassandra's expression was poisonous. "There is nothing wrong with me. Just my monthly cycles, that's all. And don't you dare tell anyone about this, do you understand? Don't utter a word of it."

"My lady . . ."

"Not a word," sputtered Cassandra. She closed her eyes to compose herself. The worst of it seemed to pass as quickly as it had come. Lukien released her, watching her fretfully. Carefully she got to her feet, her head drooping, one hand still pressed against her abdomen. "I must get back to the house," she said. "Help me to my horse."

Unsure what to do, Lukien obeyed, getting the weakened Cassandra into the saddle. He checked her for steadiness, then mounted his own horse. Cassandra found the strength to ride and urged her mount forward, returning the way they'd come. Lukien followed closely, watching her. She was already much better, but her color hadn't returned and her shoulders remained slumped. He had never seen a moon cycle do *that* to a woman, and he was sure the princess was lying. But he said nothing as they rode, and eventually they arrived back at the lake where the picnic was still going on. They were on the far side of the water, where Cassandra had been painting. As they neared the gathering, Cassandra straightened in her saddle, putting on a counterfeit smile. Jancis saw them at once and came to greet them.

"Did you have a nice ride?" the maid asked, taking the reins of Cassandra's horse.

"Yes, nice," said Cassandra. She frowned at her companion. "But I want to go inside now. I'm tired."

The worry on Jancis' face was plain. "Get down," she ordered, helping Cassandra off the horse. Lukien dropped down after her, shadowing her as Jancis led her away. It was then he noticed the painting, still sitting undisturbed on its easel.

"Let me get your painting for you," he said, going towards it.

"No!" shrieked Cassandra. She wrenched free of Jancis and dashed forward. Lukien had picked up the painting, its canvas cover still draped over it. He looked at Cassandra in shock.

"What's wrong with you? Just get inside. I'll look after this for you."

With a lunge Cassandra snatched the painting out of his hands, but it slipped from her grip and fell to the ground— just in time for a breeze to blow off its canvas covering. Cassandra went as still as stone. She glanced down at the exposed painting, then up at Lukien. Lukien's eyes studied the painting, and for a moment he didn't recognize himself in the work. But when he did, he gasped. Slowly he knelt down and picked it up. It was him, sitting by the water in his golden armor.

"Oh, my God," Cassandra gasped. She put her hand to her mouth, mortified. "Jancis . . ."

Jancis hurried forward and took the painting from Lukien. The knight and the princess stared at each other. Cassandra's face collapsed with grief.

"I'm sorry," she whispered. "I'm . . ." When she couldn't find her voice, she turned and dashed away. Jancis lingered a moment longer, offering Lukien an apologetic smile.

"Don't tell anyone, all right?" the girl asked. "Please, she's embarrassed enough."

"I . . . I won't," Lukien said.

He watched Jancis go after the princess. Across the pond, Trager was looking at him. But Lukien didn't care. Something told him his life had just become a lot more complicated.

8

As the morning sun rose over Koth, Akeela walked alone through a field of bricks and limestone, enchanted by his strange surroundings. A mountain of quarried stone lay to one side of him; to the other, a span of earth cleared of trees and grass. The foundation of a tower had been laid, and the outline of a main building could be seen cut into the dirt, a huge, rectangular footprint that could easily swallow most of the chancelleries. Akeela arranged his cape around his shoulders to stave off the morning chill, his chin held high with satisfaction. Not far away, the constructs of Koth threw shadows onto the work site. He could see Lion-keep on its hill, surrounded by the government halls of Chancellery Square, and knew that he had picked the perfect place for his Cathedral of Knowledge.

"Perfect," he whispered over the breeze. No one heard him. He had come alone, except for Breck, who was on the other side of the site marveling at the mountain of limestone. It was an ambitious project and Breck had voiced his doubts, but upon seeing the work that had been accomplished in the past few weeks, the soldier was becoming a convert. They all were, even the stodgy lords of the House of Dukes, and that pleased Akeela. His enthusiasm for his library was contagious.

He strode through the site toward the foundation of the tower. The first inklings of its construction revealed a round base that would one day rise high above the main building, looking down upon the rest of Koth. It would be a symbol to all Liirians, calling them to knowledge and its bond-breaking power. A thrill went through Akeela as he studied the tower's base. For a moment he wondered if his father would have been proud of him, then decided not. His father had been a strong king, but not a visionary. The same blindness that had made peace with Reec impossible had also robbed him of dreams. Akeela's good mood flattened.

"He would have said this was folly."

But it wasn't. Now Akeela would have to prove it, not only to his father's ghost but to the entire world. Even to Cassandra. She had laughed at his plans for his library. It had been an innocent chuckle, but it had hurt Akeela. He worried that his new wife would be like his dead father—pragmatic and short-sighted.

When Cassandra arrived from Hes he would take her here, he reasoned. He would show her the tower being built and the enormous main library, and she would marvel at the number of books it would hold, and realize then that he was building something grand. After years of awkwardness, he was finally becoming an impressive young man. He was sure it was the reason Cassandra had agreed to their marriage so quickly. She had seen the emerging greatness in him.

"You're right, my lord," called a voice from across the plain.

Startled, Akeela turned to see Breck trudging toward him. "Eh? Right about what?"

"It's impressive," said the soldier. "It will be splendid when it's done."

Akeela sighed, letting his eyes drift over the site. So far it really wasn't much, just a gaping wound in the earth with some rocks strewn around, but it was huge and had a good view of the city, and that made it impressive. Already it could stir the heart.

"I wish Lukien were here to see it," said Akeela. "And Cassandra."

Breck looked at him curiously. "When will you be sending for them, my lord? Soon?"

"In a day or so."

"Ah, so you've made ready for your wedding then," said Breck. He gave his king a small smile.

Akeela laughed, understanding the man's meaning. "I have to admit I'm a little nervous. But Graig and the others have been making most of the arrangements, so I haven't been thinking about it. Not about the wedding, anyway. But I have been thinking about Cassandra. I'm going to bring her here as soon as she arrives. I told her about the library when I was in Hes, but I don't think she grasped it. She needs to see it to understand."

"I'm sure she'll be impressed, my lord."

A flash of movement caught Akeela's eye. He turned toward the city and saw two horsemen riding forward, approaching the library site. The lead man was instantly recognizable. Graig, the Head Warden, wore his typical gold and crimson uniform. He waved to Akeela across the distance. An excited smile bloomed on Akeela's face.

"Who's that with Graig?" Breck asked.

"That," said Akeela hopefully, "just might be my new librarian."

Riding a pace behind Graig was a man not much his junior, a fiftyish fellow with dark hair and a brightly-colored cape caked with the dust of the road. He had a thin face with darting, eager eyes. The clothes he wore were foreign to Akeela, full of crimson and silk, bespeaking someplace far away. Akeela had expected him to be dressed as a Marnan, but the man was different than he'd imagined, like a mismatched collection of colorful rags. Atop his head was a threadbare hat, wide-brimmed with a golden band, and his cape was fastened around his neck with a bejeweled clasp that seemed extravagant against his shabby shirt. But most curious of all was the thing on his shoulder. Perched on his right side, its eyes wide with mischief, was a small, sable-haired monkey. The creature's head bobbed excitedly, taking in the strange surroundings as it chattered in its master's ear. The man took a nutmeat from his pocket to quiet the monkey, which the creature happily devoured.

"That's your librarian?" asked Breck. "My lord is joking, surely."

Akeela cringed. This man was nothing like he'd expected. He had come highly recommended by the Prince of Marn. Supposedly, he was a scholar of great renown. But seeing him made that hard to believe. His trampish clothes and silly grin disappointed Akeela. He raised his

hand to Graig, beckoning him closer. At least they weren't
late. Graig had promised to bring their guest to the site the
moment he'd awoken. When at last the duo reached the
waiting king, Graig slid down from his horse and gestured
to the stranger.

"My lord," he said simply, "this is Figgis."

"And friend, apparently," said Akeela. "Good day, sir.
Thank you for coming so far to see me."

The odd man surveyed the area as he said, "You're welcome, my lord. A pleasure, really. Looks like you've got
something big going on here."

Graig cleared his throat. "Fellow, you're addressing the
King of Liiria."

Figgis got down from his horse, then offered the king a
small bow. "I'm sorry, King Akeela. I'm not accustomed
to meeting royalty."

"Indeed?" asked Akeela. "Yet you worked for Prince
Jarek?"

"Worked for, yes. Spoke to, almost never. I was his clerk,
my lord. That means I spent my days surrounded by books
and ledgers. I had very little company. I'm afraid it's made
me a bit unpolished."

Breck gave Akeela a sideways glance. Akeela ignored it,
trying to smile.

"Well, you're here now," said the king. He looked him
up and down. "Your clothes look travel-worn. Didn't you
arrive last night?"

"I did, my lord, and slept like a baby in your home.
Thank you."

Akeela's smile waned. Obviously, Figgis didn't think
much of bathing or washing his clothes. He decided to look
at the monkey instead.

"And your little friend?" he asked. "What's his name?"

"This is Peko," replied Figgis. He put out his hand and
let the tiny creature climb on, then watched as it wrapped
its long tail around his wrist and fell backwards, dangling
like an ornament.

"He's charming," said Akeela, laughing. He came closer,
enchanted by the animal. Figgis noticed his interest and
held the monkey out for him.

"Here, give me your hand," Figgis offered. "He'll climb
right on."

Akeela drew back. "I don't know. His teeth look pretty sharp."

"Ah, he won't bite you, King Akeela. Go on."

Akeela did as instructed, putting out his hand for the monkey. Without hesitation Peko leapt forward, grabbing hold of Akeela's hand and wrapping his quick tail about his wrist. The sensation of warm fur made Akeela chuckle. Carefully he stroked the monkey's head.

"He's so soft. And look at those eyes."

The little monkey cocked its head, directing Akeela to scratch its ear.

"He's wonderful," said Akeela. Already he was growing to like the strangers. "Now tell me, Figgis. What do you know of my project here?"

The man snapped up the brim of his hat and glanced around. "Well, it's big. But where's the library going to be?"

"You're standing in it."

"What, all of this?" Figgis looked aghast. "You mean this whole area?"

"That's right," said Akeela. "What do you think?"

"Gods above, it's enormous." Figgis twirled around to study the site. "This'll be the biggest library in the world."

"Many times the biggest, I should think," said Akeela. "It will be filled with books from across the continent, a place where scholars can meet and discuss great ideas. And I need someone to run it, someone with brains and vision." The young king grimaced. "To be honest, I'm not sure you're up to the job."

The man straightened indignantly. "My lord, in Marn I am a renowned scholar and mathematician. I may not look like much . . ."

"No, forgive me," said Akeela quickly. "That was rude of me. It's just that you're not what I expected. When Prince Jarek wrote to me about you, he left me with a different impression. I was expecting someone . . ." He shrugged. "Well, different."

"If you mean my appearance, my lord, I am not offended. I'm often thought of as odd."

"Odd? Oh, no," said Akeela. Then he thought again. "Well, yes." He looked down at the creature in his hands. "I mean, after all, a monkey?"

"A friend," Figgis corrected. "Everyone needs a friend, my lord." Figgis put out his hand and whistled, summoning Peko to him. The monkey obeyed at once, leaping between Akeela and its master and scurrying up the librarian's arm. "Go ahead, my lords," said Figgis, addressing them all. "You must have questions. Ask me anything. As I said, I'm very good with numbers."

"Eighteen times twenty-seven," said Breck quickly.

"Ridiculous. A hard one, I mean." Figgis turned to Akeela. "My lord?"

Akeela thought for a moment, then challenged, "Six hundred eighty-four times nine hundred twenty-seven."

"Six hundred thousand sixty-eight," replied Figgis.

The others went blank. Akeela asked Breck, "Is that right?"

"Oh, it's right," answered Figgis. "I assure you, my figures are always accurate."

Akeela laughed and said, "So you're good with numbers. But I need a man of ideas, Figgis. Someone who can fill my library with books. Do you know much about books?"

"Books?" blurted Graig. "You should see the crates of them he arrived with, my lord. Not a stitch of clean clothes, just stacks and stacks of parchments and scrolls."

"My collection," Figgis explained. "I don't go anywhere without my books."

"You seem quite certain that I'll hire you, fellow," Akeela observed. "You came all this way with your things. What makes you think I won't turn you away?"

Figgis gestured to their surroundings. "Look at this place. You're obviously pouring treasure into it. You want the best person you can find to run your library, King Akeela. That's me."

Graig snickered. "That's a bit cocky."

"Not at all," said Figgis. "I'm accomplished, that's all."

"Tell me," said Akeela.

"My lord, before working for Prince Jarek I was head scholar at the College of Science in Norvor. That's when I began collecting books, and I venture to say I have a bigger collection than you yourself. I have a nose for finding special papers, and I invented my own cataloging system."

"So you're an inventor, too," said Graig dryly.

"Yes. I am also an astronomer and can predict the movements of the heavens." Figgis looked at Akeela. "Science, my lord. Not theology."

"I understand," said Akeela. "Go on."

"Well, he's an expert on monkeys," said Graig.

Breck laughed. Figgis scowled.

"I'm an expert on many things," said the librarian. "I know cultures and I speak four languages, and I'm an authority on Jador, my lord."

"Jador?" Akeela's brow creased. Jador was a mystery to the rest of the continent, a little known territory across the Desert of Tears. In all Akeela's life, he had never met a Jadori, nor anyone who had. He was immediately intrigued by Figgis' claim. "What do you know about Jador? Have you been there?"

"No, but I have studied it all my life. It's a passion of mine. I have some Jadori texts, the prize of my collection. And I've got some tools from there as well. I even have a Jadori scimitar." Figgis put up a finger for Peko to grab. "Even my little companion here came from Jador. A breeder I knew in Ganjor gave him to me."

"Really?" Akeela was instantly fascinated. As a lover of books himself, he had read many fanciful tales of the Jadori. "Is it true they ride lizards?"

"They're called kreel," said Figgis. "And yes, it's true. Look at this . . ." He dug under his shirt and fished out a necklace. On it was a serrated tooth, as long as a shark's. "This is a kreel's tooth. I got it from a Jadori trader when I was in my twenties."

Akeela was wide-eyed. He reached out and ran a finger over the tooth's edge, feeling its sharpness. Pride flickered in Figgis' eyes.

"If I take this position I'd like to continue my study of Jador," he said.

Akeela looked up. "You mean if I give you the position."

Figgis nodded. "As you say."

He was an arrogant man, certainly, and his eccentricities were obvious, yet Akeela was intrigued.

"Walk with me, Figgis," he said, then strode away from the others. After a moment he heard Figgis' footsteps on the gravel, following. Akeela didn't turn around to summon Graig or Breck; he wanted to talk to the stranger alone.

"My lord?" asked Figgis. "Where are we going?"

Akeela didn't answer. Instead he led Figgis toward the giant heap of quarried stone, which his workmen had been bringing to the site in cartloads. The pile was now well over the height of a house, and would only grow larger as the project continued. Akeela paused before it, considering its enormity.

"Look at that," he said. "Figgis, I need someone who can help me turn this pile of rocks into a great library."

"I'm not an architect, my lord."

"Don't be obtuse. You know what I mean." Akeela smiled at him. "You seem like a very learned man. There's a lot of knowledge locked in that head of yours, and I'm sure it would be useful. But this project will require more than just brains."

"What do you mean?"

Akeela thought for a moment. How could he explain a dream?

"This isn't going to be just a library," he said finally. "I call this my Cathedral of Knowledge. It's going to be a beacon, a place that isn't reserved just for scholars and royalty. It's for the people, Figgis. All the people. I want this library to help me change things. For that I need a man of vision."

Figgis gave a wicked grin. "Vision is a dangerous thing, my lord."

"So then I need a brave man, as well. Someone who can take the rough weather of politics and not be scared away. I won't lie to you; there are men in the House of Dukes that will oppose me. But so far they've given me the funding I need, because I've made peace with Reec and they admire me for that. I don't know how long their goodwill will last, though. When it fades, I may have to fight them to keep this project alive. And I'll need someone to stand with me."

The librarian removed his hat and ran his fingertips over the brim, considering Akeela's words. His big bald spot shone in the sunlight. His eyes shifted to his simian companion. Peko seemed to sense his master's dilemma and began to squawk. Figgis nodded at the monkey.

"Don't tell me he's talking to you," said Akeela.

"Let's just say Peko and I understand each other."

"Really? All right, then. What does he tell you to do?"

Before Figgis could answer, Graig appeared over his shoulder. The Head Warden waved to get Akeela's attention.

"Pardon me, my lord, but I think you should be heading back now. It's almost time for Mercy Court."

"I'll be with you presently, Graig," said Akeela. He continued to stare at Figgis. "Well, old fellow? What's your answer? Are you up to the challenge of my library?"

Figgis put his hat back on and glanced around. "I've been a lot of places, my lord. I've seen a lot of things and had a lot of jobs. I'm old and I'm tired, and I could be dead by the time this project of yours is completed."

Akeela's expression fell.

"Still," Figgis went on, "Sooner or later a man has to settle down and call a place home. Let's build your cathedral, my lord."

Akeela arrived at the Chancellery of Justice five minutes late for Mercy Court. His small tardiness was punished by a logjam of petitioners.

Mercy Court was one of Akeela's first and best accomplishments, a chance for the people to see and speak to their young king and to seek pardons for crimes both petty and large. Since taking the throne a few months ago, Mercy Court had been a weekly ritual for Akeela. He would arrive at the Chancellery of Justice, take his place in the red leather chair usually reserved for Chancellor Nils, and wait for the petitioners to fill the courtroom. It had been a fairly simple thing when it began, never taking more than a few hours. But word had spread quickly of the new king's benevolence, and now his weekly ritual was an all-day duty. Today, with a huge congregation already gathered outside the chancellery, Akeela knew he wouldn't return to Lionkeep until sundown. And that was the rule of Mercy Court; that the king would listen to petitions until the sun fell. Those unlucky enough to miss his judgement could return the following week or take their chances with Chancellor Nils and his judges.

This day, as Akeela made his way through the chancellery, a crowd of Liirians pushed toward him with gifts and offerings and petitions written on parchment, begging him to listen to their pleas. As always, Akeela told the crowd that they would each be seen in turn, and would receive his fairest judgment. Not wanting to be corrupted, he politely declined the gifts shoved under his nose, even refusing an apple tart an old woman had baked. At the other end of the hall, Chancellor Nils waited, his old, grim face tight with anxiety. Nils was a good man and a fair judge, and he had served Akeela's father wisely. But like many of Liiria's chancellors, he had trouble with the new king's idealism, and he did not like Mercy Court at all. Nils bowed cordially as Akeela approached, then had his gray-robed assistants open the courtroom doors. Akeela pushed his way through the throngs and greeted Nils with a smile. The old chancellor returned the grin crookedly.

"Another crowd this morning, my lord," said Nils. He stepped aside for Akeela to pass.

"Yes. It's good to see the people coming out, don't you think, Chancellor?"

"It's like bedlam in a broom closet, my lord."

Akeela walked into the courtroom. The chancellor's assistants closed the wooden doors behind him, and suddenly the world went silent. The trial chamber of the Justice Chancellery was a grand, even frightful place. A majestic judge's bench stood at the far end, looming darkly over the petition box, a small, barred area with a single wooden chair. There were rows of benches for the petitioners to use while they waited, and busts of past chancellors lined the rosewood walls, staring down at Akeela with cold detachment. Akeela made his way to the bench and sat down in the leather chair. He suddenly felt imperious, then remembered why he had begun Mercy Court. In Liiria, men like Nils held all the power.

"All right, bring them in," he told the assistants. The men in their charcoal robes opened the courtroom doors again. The petitioners surged forward. They had each been given a wooden tag with a number painted on it, but that didn't stop them from fighting for the front seats. Akeela settled in for a long day.

The first hour was unremarkable. Akeela heard the cases of farmers and housewives, coopers and landowners and merchants, all with similar gripes. They were mostly petty squabbles, but Akeela gave them all his full attention, never letting the dullness of their stories make him irritable. He loved the work of Mercy Court and gave out judgements liberally, making sure that no one guilty ever suffered cruelly, or that an innocent should bear an unfair burden.

But Mercy Court wasn't all about petty squabbles. There were real crimes to be dealt with, particularly thievery. Just before noon, Akeela heard the case of a man named Regial, who had been convicted of stealing sheep two years ago and had since served in Borior, Koth's infamous prison. Regial had gone into prison at the age of twenty-three. Now, only two years later, he easily looked Akeela's senior, with gaunt skin bleached white by prison walls and speckled eyes that searched the courtroom suspiciously. He licked dry lips as he stood before Akeela in the petition box, unable or unwilling to sit down. He had no barrister to defend him, just Assistant Chancellor D'marak, who read all the charges against prisoners and who, presumably from his tone, thought Regial deserving of his steep sentence. Akeela looked at Regial curiously, wondering how such a young man could waste away in prison. His father's justice had been harsh. He offered him a glass of water.

"Here," said Akeela, holding out his own glass. "Drink."

But Regial was manacled and couldn't come forward, so Akeela gestured to D'marak. "Give this to him," he directed.

The Assistant Chancellor raised his eyebrows for a moment, then reached up to the bench to take the glass from Akeela. He handed it to Regial, who was barely able to bring the glass to his lips for the cuffs around his wrists. Sloppily, he drank the entire contents, then let D'marak take the glass away. The Assistant Chancellor put the glass down with some annoyance before continuing to read the charges in his book.

"As I said, my king, he has served two years of his eight year sentence. He's here because he heard about Mercy Court and wouldn't give his jailors any peace until he spoke to you." D'marak scowled at Regial. "Well, you're here now, thief. Speak your plea."

Regial shuffled forward awkwardly. His jaundiced eyes looked up at the bench. "My king, I don't know what to say. How do I plead for myself?"

Akeela replied, "This is Mercy Court. Tell me why you deserve mercy."

"Because I've served two years in Borior," said Regial. "That should be reason enough to free any man."

"Your sentence is eight years," D'marak reminded him. "Now stop wasting the king's time."

Regial became flustered. He held up his manacled hands. "My king, I am twenty-five years old. I stole some sheep and have regretted it every moment since. But I'm fit and I can work, and I shouldn't be shut away like some leper."

"You stole nineteen sheep, to be precise," said D'marak. "From the Baron Glass' own herd."

"Ah well," said Regial with a grin. "Not the smartest move, no."

The courtroom laughed. So did Akeela.

"If Baron Glass found out you'd been freed, he'd demand payment for his stolen sheep," he said.

"He got his bloody sheep back," said Regial. "When I was caught."

"Still, you've a debt to pay," said Akeela. "You say you're able-bodied, and you look fit enough to me. A little thin maybe, but nothing some food and sunlight couldn't cure."

Regial's face brightened. "I'm free, then?"

"I see no reason for you to waste away in Borior," said Akeela.

Assistant Chancellor D'marak cleared his throat loudly, shooting Akeela a cautioning glance. Akeela looked at him askance.

"Is something wrong, D'marak?"

"My king," said D'marak, "this man is a felon, beyond redemption. He got eight years because he deserves it." He tapped his book. "It's all in the records. He made his livelihood as a thief. If you let him go he'll just steal again."

Akeela thought for a moment, leaning back in the big chair. Mercy Court wasn't supposed to be a mockery, and releasing dangerous men was the last thing he wanted to do. But Regial didn't look dangerous to Akeela. He looked dirty and that was all, the way Lukien had looked as a boy.

"Regial," he said, "Mercy Court means a great deal to me, but it's also important to all these others. If I release someone who then goes out and repeats the same crimes, it would ruin this court. I'd have to stop granting leniency and hearing petitions, and then everyone would lose. Do you take my meaning?"

The young man nodded quickly. "I do, my king."

"So you won't return to thieving?"

Regial crossed his heart. "I promise."

"Promise," sneered D'marak. "King Akeela, please . . ."

Akeela held up his hand. "It's done. Release him and take him to Lionkeep." He glowered at Regial. "We're going to put you to work in the castle, fellow. I'm going to keep an eye on you. And I warn you—I know every stick of silverware in my home. If so much as a spoon goes missing, it's back to Borior with you."

Regial smiled, D'marak sighed, and the crowd of petitioners broke into murmurs, surprised by Akeela's trust.

"Thank you, my king," said Regial, bowing. "I won't disappoint you, you'll see."

"See that you don't," said Akeela. He was pleased with himself, pleased with the respect he saw reflected at him from the crowd.

For the rest of the afternoon, the petitioners were ordinary. Two more prisoners were brought in from Borior, but neither of them had stolen from a baron and that made them less appealing to the crowd. D'marak, still stung by Akeela's refusal of his advice, remained quiet throughout the proceedings, simply reading charges and answering Akeela's inquiries. Akeela could sense D'marak's disquietude.

Finally, near sundown, D'marak called the last number for the day.

"Forty-three."

A man stood up from the crowd, his wooden number tag in hand. He was well dressed and groomed, with shining jet black hair combed carefully to one side and a well tailored jacket around his slim frame. He stepped forward, bowing first to D'marak then to Akeela. He presented himself with an earnest smile and a whiff of nervousness.

"Thank you for hearing my petition, my king," he said. "My name is Gorlon, from Koth."

"Welcome, Gorlon," said Akeela. It was late in the day now and he was weary, but he was determined to give this last case his full attention. "You look afraid. Don't be. This is Mercy Court, after all." He glanced at D'marak. "Assistant Chancellor, what are the particulars?"

D'marak paged through his book until he came to number forty-three. Half-laughing, he said, "Adultery, my lord."

Akeela's smile waned. "Adultery? Is that true, Gorlon?"

Gorlon swallowed. "I'm sorry to say so, my lord."

In Liiria, adultery wasn't a crime like rape or thievery, but it was a transgression for which a man could expect restitution. He could put his wife away for it, or demand that damages be paid as compensation for his broken home, if not his broken heart. So far in Mercy Court Akeela had dealt with thieves and whores and even a rapist, but this was his first adulterer. For some reason he couldn't explain, he disliked the man.

"I don't think we should waste your time with this, my king," said D'marak. "I'm sure Gorlon here is sorry." He turned to the young man. "My ledger says the offended wants twenty sovereigns for damages. You can pay half that, yes?"

Gorlon nodded. "Yes, gladly."

D'marak made a mark in his book. "Fine. Then we're done here, I think. My king, if you'd—"

"Stop," said Akeela. He looked at D'marak acidly. "We're not done here, *Assistant Chancellor*."

D'marak blanched, and Gorlon, who hadn't expected the king's tone, stepped back a pace.

"Explain yourself, Gorlon," Akeela ordered. He leaned forward, gazing down at the man. "I want to hear about your crime."

"My king, there's really nothing to explain," stammered Gorlon. "I loved a woman who was married. That's all. It was my foolishness that brought me to this place."

"And your lust," added Akeela.

"Aye, and that," agreed Gorlon. "But I did the lady no harm. She was with me willingly, and has even told her husband so."

"No harm?" said Akeela. "You believe that?"

Gorlon nodded. "Yes, my lord. But I don't have the twenty sovereigns to pay the man I've wronged. If ten is agreed . . ."

"It is not agreed, sir," said Akeela. He closed his eyes

and rubbed his temples against a rising headache. The way this arrogant Gorlon pranced into court . . .

"My king," said D'marak. "Why not let him pay the ten sovereigns and be done with it? It's late, after all. And it's only adultery."

"Only adultery?" Akeela erupted. He stood up suddenly, forcing a gasp from the courtroom. "Adultery is a crime in Liiria."

D'marak chuckled. "It's hardly the same as murder, King Akeela."

Akeela turned to Gorlon. "What is marriage?"

"My lord?"

"Come on, man, tell me. What is marriage?"

"It's . . ." Gorlon searched for an answer. "It's a union, my lord."

"What kind of union?" snapped Akeela.

Gorlon was lost. "My lord?"

"It's a legal union! It's two people committing themselves to each other before the Court of Liiria. Before *me*. And it isn't something that can be broken just because a man feels an urge or a woman agrees to spread her legs."

"My lord, I never . . ."

"Quiet." Akeela turned to D'marak. "What is the husband asking for? Twenty sovereigns?"

"Yes," said D'marak. "Quite a bit, actually."

Was it a lot, Akeela wondered? How much was a marriage worth? And how much should this scraper pay to repair one? Suddenly Akeela didn't know himself. All the mercy blew out of him like a wind. He saw Gorlon standing before him, prideful and handsome, cocksure that he could come to Mercy Court and bargain a better deal, and Akeela remembered how awkward he had been as a youth. In his mind's eye, it was all he could see.

"Right," he said, nodding. "Gorlon, you will pay the husband you wronged forty sovereigns."

"Forty?" Gorlon shrieked. "But my lord, he's only asking for twenty!"

"Forty," Akeela repeated. "And don't raise your voice to me."

Gorlon looked at D'marak for support, but the assistant only stared at the king, his mouth agape.

"You think I'm being cruel, don't you?" Akeela asked the petitioner. "You're lucky I don't toss you into Borior."

"King Akeela, please . . ."

"Look at you, standing there in your fine clothes with your perfect face. I've seen fellows like you all my life. You think that smile of yours lets you get away with anything."

Stunned, Gorlon said nothing.

"Well, not this time." Akeela rose from the bench. "D'marak, forty sovereigns. Not a penny less."

He left the courtroom, suffering the shocked expressions of the crowd.

9

Lieutenant Will Trager shook cold rain from his face, cursing his bad luck. The storms that had surged through the valley the past few days had turned the road to muck and swallowed the sun with clouds, and though he suspected it was very near noon, he could barely see the path past the blinding rain. He drew back the reins of his horse, bringing the beast to a stop. A canopy of sable hung overhead, windswept and miserable. Trager's uniform clung limply to his body, soaked through with rain. Behind him, the muddy road snaked through the forest, back toward his company and the warm fires of camp. Ahead of him lay a fork in the road, both branches leading to darkness. The thick forest weaved a mesh of tangled limbs, warning him away.

Trager shook his head, muttering to himself and hating Lukien for sending him scouting. The captain and the others were back at camp, enjoying food and the cover of pavilions, while he was out in the storm, enduring the cold and filth. For three days they had traveled, heading west toward Koth, and for three days it had rained, slowing them to a crawl. Worse, the swelling river Kryss had flooded the Novo Valley, forcing them to detour down unfamiliar roads. It had taken a lot of scouting to get this far, and Trager was sick of the duty. He was tired of the rain and the endless mud, but mostly he was tired of Lukien and his orders. Beads of rain fell into his eyes as he considered the forking road.

"Bloody hell, this figures. Which way now?"

Only the wind replied, lashing his face. He suddenly felt alone, and the murkiness unnerved him. Again he thought of his arrogant captain, and his patience snapped.

"God damn it, I'm a lieutenant! Why send me out in this swill?" Then he laughed bitterly, adding, "Because the captain is a bloody bastard, that's why."

He could turn back, he supposed, but then he would have failed in this simple task, and that would give Lukien pleasure. So he squinted through the rain, surveying the routes carefully. Both directions looked equally eerie; not at all hospitable, especially since they had the princess with them. And Lukien had told him to find the safest route. But Trager wasn't even sure where they were. Somewhere lost in Reec, south of the Novo Valley.

"Left then," he decided. It was more southerly and would probably lead them closer to Koth. He urged his mount forward again, his mind polluted with thoughts of Lukien.

The captain had been very quiet lately. Since leaving Hes, he had hardly spoken at all. He simply rode at the point of the company, occasionally giving orders to the men and checking on Princess Cassandra's carriage, which rolled along in the middle of the company, comfortably housing the young woman and the maid Jancis. Despite the wind and rain, Trager smiled as he thought about Cassandra. She was comely, more than Akeela deserved, and the image in his mind made him hunger. He didn't wonder why Lukien was always looking at her—the answer was obvious. The lust in Lukien's eyes was plain enough for anyone who cared to see it. And Trager didn't blame his captain for coveting Cassandra, either. He was a man, with a man's urges. To Trager, that was forgivable. What wasn't forgivable—what haunted Trager day and night and had for years—was the arrogance with which the captain carried himself. Apparently he thought nothing of craving the king's property, because he was like a brother to the stupid Akeela and the king was blind to everything. When it came to Lukien, Akeela was like a little boy, hero-worshipping an undeserving bag of pus.

"It's time to puncture that bag, I say," muttered Trager.

He would do it with a lance. When the spring tourney came, he would be ready for it. Finally, he would tarnish the vaunted knight of bronze.

Trager rode on, heartened by the image of Lukien dangling from the tip of his lance. Overhead the tangle of branches thickened, blocking out the worst of the rain. He would ride another mile before turning back, he decided. Ahead of him, the forest road widened slightly. Trager congratulated himself for choosing the right direction. Reecian roads were good, at least as good as those in Liiria, but the rainy season turned them all into slop. This year, the rains had come earlier than expected. A slick of mud blanketed the road, making travel hard for his horse. The stallion's hooves disappeared into the earth with a sucking sound. Trager listened to the noise, wondering if he should stop. Then he heard something else. A hissing sound, very faint. His eyes seized on something dead ahead. Abruptly he jerked back the reins.

For a moment he saw nothing, then caught a glimpse of something green slipping through the mud. The darkness of the storm and trees shaded the road. He held his breath, afraid to make the smallest sound, realizing that a garmy was ahead, one of the rarest and most deadly creatures that called the forest home.

The creature lay very still. Trager mimicked its silence, not daring to move. Thankfully, his horse had yet to see the beast. Carefully he scanned the surrounding trees, looking for others, then saw two more pairs of yellow eyes glowing in the thickets. His heart thundering, Trager considered his options. He had to flee, that was plain enough, but garmys could be quick, and might strike if he tried to run. He pretended to ignore the creatures, knowing they would come as close as possible before striking. Predictably, the one in the road began to slither forward.

It moved like a cat through the mud, its reptilian body barely visible, its spiked tail rising like a dorsal fin above the water. Beneath the filth, two webbed hands pulled it forward. Its head was smooth, covered with scales, and its lidless eyes shone a sickly gold. Each swish of its tail brought its wide mouth closer, while its brothers in the trees watched in silence, ready to spring.

"Mother of Fate," Trager whispered. He knew the tales of the garmys, how they looked like people and preyed on human flesh, and how they could hypnotize a man with their preternatural eyes. Now, caught in their watery nest, he believed every word. His horse finally caught the scent of the monsters and began to snort wildly. Trager squeezed his thighs against its flanks to quiet it. Only one thought occurred to him—escape.

"Now!"

Drawing his sword in one hand, he wrenched his mount around with the other, bringing the stallion snorting to its hinds. The garmy in the road sprang forward; its hideous face filling Trager's vision. He swung his sword wide, catching the creature's neck and slicing the head from its sinewy body. A shriek filled the air, then silence. Trager spun his horse around. The garmys in the trees dropped from the branches. Trager heard them sprinting through the mud. But his horse was already bolting away. He turned to see the creatures scurrying over their fallen brother, slowly dropping back. They were monstrously ugly—like monkeys in the skin of snakes.

"Hurry!" Trager urged his mount, praying his horse wouldn't stumble and break a leg.

Two hours later, Trager approached the camp. His ride back had been uneventful, and he had neither seen nor heard anything more of the garmys. He was proud of himself for having slain one of the beasts, and was looking forward to boasting about it when he returned. The fear that had seized him earlier was gone now, and all he could think about was Lukien, and how the captain would look when he told him about the garmys.

But not far from the camp, Trager remembered how much he hated Lukien, and how unendurable his life had become in the Bronze Knight's shadow. He remembered also how much Akeela loved Lukien, and how Lukien was a hero in Liiria, something that Trager would never be. And then he remembered how Lukien always took the point when they traveled, careful to protect the king's new bride.

When at last he entered the camp, he reported directly to Lukien. He told the captain how he'd scouted the forward area, and that there was no trouble on the roads save for the muck that had plagued them for days.

He mentioned nothing of the garmys.

The next morning, Lukien gave the order to break camp and led the company once again toward Koth. It was a clear morning, the first any of them had seen in days, and Lukien took the sunlight as a good omen. Now they might finally start making some real progress. As was his custom, he rode at the head of the company, with Trager and the other Royal Chargers behind him. Cassandra's royal carriage rumbled along in the center. So far, it had been an uncomfortable ride for all of them, and Cassandra's once lovely carriage was now spattered with mud and windblown leaves. The roads were still soaked with rain, which made traveling slow, but as the sun rose higher the day began to warm and the puddles slowly dried, revealing the road beneath. Lukien kept a relaxed pace, careful not to tax their horses. If they were lucky, they would reach the Liirian border in a day or so. From there it was at least another full day's ride to Koth.

To Lukien, it seemed like a lifetime ago that he had been with Cassandra at the picnic. Since then, he had seen precious little of her. She had been shunning him, and he supposed it was embarrassment that kept her silent. He had tried several times to speak to her while in Hes, but always she had feigned tiredness or some pressing business, and she never seemed to require his bodyguard services anymore, the way she had during their first weeks together. Now she was lost to him, and the loss disturbed Lukien. Soon enough, he would turn her over to Akeela. They would marry, and he would be forever cursed to see her with another man. Irritated, Lukien gave an angry sigh. The sound of it summoned an unwanted visitor.

"Captain?" asked Trager. The lieutenant rode up alongside him. "Is something wrong?"

"Nothing's wrong," answered Lukien, struggling to be civil. The last month with Trager had been unbearable. "I was just thinking."

"You should be pleased," said Trager. "We're making good progress. And look at that sky. Not a cloud."

Lukien nodded. "Yes. Finally." He looked over at his

lieutenant. Trager wore a peculiar grin. He asked, "What are you smiling at?"

"The day, Captain," replied Trager. "That's all. And I'm glad to be getting closer to home."

"Mmm, yes," agreed Lukien. "But the roads are still bad. We won't cross the border till tomorrow at the earliest. There's a fork up ahead, you say?"

Trager looked around, seemingly puzzled. "It was dark in the rain," he mused. "I can't quite recall. But it's around here somewhere."

A few minutes later, they found it. Lukien considered the fork, not liking the looks of either route. Both were canopied with trees and laden with mud. He brought up a hand, calling the company to a halt. Trager relayed the order and watched as the horsemen and carriage came to a stop.

"All right, we'll rest here for a spell," said Lukien. He spied the two lanes, unsettled by them both. "Trager, which way did you take yesterday?"

The lieutenant didn't reply. Lukien turned and saw that he had already dismounted and was leading his horse away.

"Trager," he called. "Which way?"

"Captain?" the lieutenant asked.

"Which way did you go yesterday?"

Trager thought for a moment, then said "Left."

Still atop his horse, Lukien studied the leftward route. It was dim and foreboding, like its twin, and something told him to be cautious. He said, "I'm going to ride ahead and scout it out. Tend to the men and see that they water their horses. Then look after the princess, make sure she's all right."

"Good idea, Captain," said Trager, then quickly turned and walked away.

Cassandra sat inside her carriage, absently watching the world through her dingy window. Though Jancis was with her she felt completely alone, just as she had for weeks. The carriage rocked from side to side as it rolled along the muddy roads, slowly pulled forward by a team of horses. The horses had been white when they'd left Hes, splendid looking beasts to herald her arrival in Liiria. Now they were mud covered, like everything else, and they matched

Cassandra's mood perfectly. For days now she had been stuck inside the carriage, only taking breaks when her escorts did, or when she needed to relieve herself. The vehicle's claustrophobic walls were driving her mad. Jancis, who constantly occupied herself with knitting, made small talk as they traveled, daydreaming about Koth and King Akeela, and what it would be like for Cassandra to be queen. But Cassandra hardly thought about those things anymore. As it had for weeks now, her mind turned to Lukien.

She had embarrassed herself with the knight, and now could barely face him. She remembered with horrible clarity his expression when he'd seen the painting, and though Jancis had asked him not to tell anyone about it, Cassandra didn't trust him. She fretted that he had bragged to his comrades about the incident. Worse, she wondered what he might tell Akeela. And though she had desperately wanted to talk to Lukien, to apologize and beg his silence, she could not, for being around him stole her voice. She feared him. Worse, she feared she loved him. She kept reminding herself that Akeela was a good man, and how fortunate she was to have been chosen by him. Any of her sisters would have willingly traded places with her. But the love she had hoped to feel for Akeela had yet to take root, constantly stunted by her infatuation with Lukien.

Have I ever loved? she wondered as she watched the trees pass by her window. *Do I even know what love is?*

She loved her father, but this was different. When she looked at Lukien—or when he looked at her—she felt peculiar, and the feeling was wonderful. None of the boys in Castle Hes had ever stirred such emotion in her, and she knew that was because they were simply boys, while Lukien was a man. He was accomplished and strong, and his skin bore the scars of a life hard-lived. In a matter of weeks he had taken over her mind. That was love, surely.

"I don't know," she whispered.

Jancis looked up from her knitting, eyeing her friend suspiciously. "What's that?"

Cassandra didn't reply. She merely stared out the window. Jancis laid her knitting aside and leaned forward.

"You've been very pensive lately," she remarked. "Are you feeling all right?"

It was the same tired old question. Jancis watched her like a midwife these days.

"Yes," Cassandra lied. "I'm fine."

"No pains?"

"No," said Cassandra. Another lie. "I was just thinking."

"Oh, I'm sure. About what? Should I guess?"

"Don't be a pest, Jancis," said Cassandra. But she sighed theatrically, inviting her friend's attention. "Oh, Jan. I don't know what to do . . ."

"There's nothing to be done, so don't fret over it. I told you—he's probably forgotten all about it. And even if he hasn't, I don't think he's going to tell anyone. He's as guilty as you, Cass. Don't forget that."

"He's not," said Cassandra.

"He is. He was the one looking at you, remember. He couldn't take his eyes off you!" Jancis frowned. "Bloody wretch, that's what he is. Going over his king's wife like that. Maybe Akeela should find out about it, teach him some manners."

"I have to talk to him," Cassandra resolved. She thought for a moment, her eyes narrowing. "Yes. If I could speak to him I could explain things, before he says anything to Akeela."

Jancis' face hardened. "Don't talk to him. That's how you got in this mess in the first place."

"I have to," said Cassandra. She gave her maid a sad smile. "I want to, Jan."

Just then the carriage came to a stop. Jancis massaged her neck in relief.

"Thank God," she said, stretching. "I could use a walk."

"We're stopping," said Cassandra absently. The seed of an idea began to bloom. She cranked up her courage. "Yes, all right."

"What?"

Cassandra stood up, stooping, and opened the carriage door.

"Cass, where are you going?"

"To talk to Lukien," said Cassandra quickly. "I have to speak to him before we reach Koth."

"No!"

Cassandra hardly heard Jancis' plea. She was out of the carriage in a second, her boots splashing into the boggy earth. The entire company had come to a halt, and the men were already dismounting. She strained to see toward the head of the column, searching for Lukien, but he was nowhere to be found. Puzzled, she glanced around. The men were all stretching and seeing to their horses. Jancis jumped out of the carriage beside Cassandra.

"I don't see him," said Cassandra. "Where'd he go?"

Jancis was relieved. "I don't know and I don't care. Now forget about him, will you please?"

Cassandra had no intention of forgoing her plan. She intended to speak to Lukien now, while she still had the courage.

"Stay here," she ordered, then made her way to the front of the company where a number of Liirian soldiers were caring for their mounts. Noticing her at once, the soldiers stopped working.

"My lady?" asked one of them, a young man named Tomas. "Can I help you?"

Cassandra hesitated. "I'm looking for Lukien," she said. "Do you know where he is?"

The soldiers glanced at each other. Cassandra tried to look confident.

"He's just gone off, my lady," said Tomas, pointing down the road. "He's gone to scout the way ahead."

"Well, I must speak to him," said Cassandra. "It's important."

Tomas smiled. "He'll be back soon, my lady."

"No, that won't do. I have to speak to him now." Cassandra returned Tomas' smile, heaping on the charm. "Could you take me to him, Tomas?"

"Me? Oh, no, my lady. I don't think I should. He'll be back presently."

"But it's urgent, Tomas," said Cassandra. She took a step closer, fluttering her long lashes. *"Please?"*

Tomas almost blushed. "I suppose we could ride ahead. He's only just gone. It shouldn't be a problem catching up to him." He gestured to one of the horses. "You can ride, my lady, can't you?"

Cassandra wasted no time in mounting the horse.

Trager waited until he had watered and fed his horse before checking on the princess. She was a spoiled brat anyway, so he took his time sauntering to her carriage. When he arrived, he found the princess' handmaid leaning against the vehicle, her face drawn. He took the time to leer at her before she noticed him.

"Handmaid Jancis?" he asked.

The girl jumped at the intrusion.

"Yes?"

"Is your mistress about?" Trager asked. "I'm here to see if she needs anything."

The maiden blanched. "No."

"No, she doesn't need anything, or no, she isn't around?"

Jancis hesitated. "She's . . . away."

"Away? What exactly does that mean, girl?"

"I'm sorry, Lieutenant," said Jancis, "but she's gone off after Captain Lukien."

"What?" blurted Trager. "Why'd she do that?"

The girl shrugged. "To speak to him. She—"

"Fate above, I don't believe this!"

Trager didn't spare a moment. He dashed back to his horse, tossed himself onto its back, then raced like the wind after Lukien and the princess. As he galloped past his bewildered men, he sneered, "You stupid brat. I'm supposed to help protect you!"

Ten minutes after riding off, Lukien was satisfied the route was safe. He glanced around at the trees, unnerved by their thickness but convinced that they held no dangers. He drew back the reins, bringing his horse to a stop. Ten yards away, the road disappeared under a pool of murky water. Lukien studied it, gauging its depth, and was sure it was passable. Suddenly nothing could spoil his good mood. Liiria was close now, far closer than it had been for weeks, and he was anxious to make up lost time. He spun his mount around to return to the company—and saw Tomas riding toward him. To Lukien's shock, the soldier wasn't alone. Riding a pace behind him was Cassandra, her faced fixed with a peculiar grimace.

"What the . . . ?" Lukien trotted toward them. "Tomas, what's going on?"

Tomas held up his hands. "Don't be angry, Lukien," he said. "I'm only following orders."

"Orders? Whose orders?"

"Mine," said Cassandra. She brought her horse up before Tomas'. "It's not his fault, Captain. I made him take me to you. I have to talk to you."

The princess was resolute. Her forwardness annoyed Lukien.

"My lady, you're very foolish," he said sharply. "Coming out alone like this is dangerous." Then he turned to Tomas, saying, "And what business have you taking her here, away from the others? What's wrong with you?"

"I'm sorry, Captain," stammered Tomas. "But she insisted . . ."

"She doesn't give you orders, soldier. I do!"

The man lowered his eyes in disgrace. He was one of the youngest in the troop, about Cassandra's age, and he had obviously been influenced by the princess. Though Cassandra's pretty face was no excuse for stupidity, Lukien understood its power, and so tried to soften his tone.

"All right, no harm done," he said. "Now turn around, both of you. We're heading back."

"What? No . . ." Cassandra protested. "Lukien, I must speak to you privately."

"We'll talk back at camp."

The princess' expression became earnest. "Now," she urged. "Please."

Just as he knew it had beguiled Tomas, Cassandra's soft voice made Lukien relent. Regrettably, he found her plea irresistible. "All right," he nodded. "Tomas, give us some privacy, will you?"

The young man said, "Should I ride back to the others?"

"No. Just out of earshot."

Tomas did as Lukien asked, trotting past him and coming to a stop several yards away, near the flood in the road. Lukien looked at Cassandra and spoke in a whisper.

"My lady, why have you come out here? It's unseemly for you to come calling after me."

"I'm sorry," Cassandra offered. "It didn't occur to me what others would think."

"Obviously not," said Lukien. He shook his head and sighed. "You're very young, Princess. But not so young as to be so silly. You mustn't ever come after me like this again, do you understand?"

Cassandra stiffened. "I'm not a child, Captain," she retorted. "I'm a princess, and soon to be your queen. I will go where I wish, when I wish. And I won't be ordered about by you. Do *you* understand?"

Lukien tried to stay calm. "My lady, why are you here?"

"To speak with you alone," replied Cassandra icily.

"Then speak and let's be done with it." Lukien leaned forward and lowered his voice again."And please, go back to being that lady you were during our ride. I much prefer her to the harpy you're being now."

The sharpness vanished from Cassandra's face. "All right," she said. "I wanted to come to apologize. I've been dreadful to you the past few weeks, ever since you saw my painting. . . ."

"Shhh," Lukien cautioned. He looked over his shoulder at Tomas. Satisfied the man couldn't hear them, he said, "Keep your voice down, my lady. I haven't told anyone about your painting, and I don't want the world finding out now."

Cassandra smiled in relief. "I was worried you might have told your men," she confessed. "Thank you for honoring my privacy."

To Lukien's great annoyance he felt himself smiling. "To be honest, I was flattered. Surprised, but flattered."

"It was wrong of me," said Cassandra. "I shouldn't have painted you, with or without your permission. But I don't want King Akeela finding out about it, you see. You won't tell him, will you?"

She was dancing around the subject. They both were. Lukien desperately wanted to speak the truth.

"Tell him what, my lady?" he asked. "That I've been staring at you across lakes and meadows? That you've painted secret portraits of me?" He let his horse take one step closer to her. "Is that what we should keep from him, Princess?"

Cassandra nodded. Her eyes were wide with understanding. "Yes," she whispered. "And more."

"What more?" asked Lukien. "What else is there to admit?"

She watched him, unwilling or unable to speak. Yet Lukien could sense the unspoken words. There was affection in her eyes, plain and true. He wanted to hear its confession. Cassandra opened her mouth to speak . . .

"Aiiiieeee!"

The sound was Tomas, screaming. Lukien saw Cassandra's eyes widen in terror, then turned as a slimy body rose from the flooded road. Already the creature had one arm twisted around Tomas' leg, dragging him from his horse. The stallion whinnied, bucking and tossing Tomas from its back, sending him crashing into the water.

"God!" cried Lukien. He drew his sword and bolted forward. "Cassandra, stay back!"

The garmy wrapped its arms around its prey. Tomas writhed in its grasp, struggling to lift his mouth from the filthy water. A gurgling scream tore from his throat.

"Lukien . . . . !"

Lukien rushed toward him, bolting past his frightened horse, desperate to find the garmy in the water. All he could see was parts of Tomas wrapped in reptilian flesh, tossing and splashing as he fought to get free. Beneath him, Lukien's horse shuddered, refusing to go into the water. Lukien leapt from its back and waded in—then saw the other garmy fall from the trees.

It was on him too quickly, knocking the breath from his lungs and the sword from his hand. For a moment he saw its inhuman face, hissing, then tumbled backward into the muck, the creature's arms flailing after him. He felt the powerful limbs seize him, heard the gnashing of teeth again his armor, but he was suddenly blind and realized he was underwater, his face buried in the mud. A cold appendage snaked around his neck; the garmy's tail. Lukien panicked, found a strength born of terror, and exploded upward with a shout.

"No!"

The garmy fell backward, its tail still coiled around Lukien's throat. The appendage pulled, dragging Lukien after it. He dug desperately into his belt, finding his dagger. As he fell forward he plunged the weapon down. The blow stunned the monster. Lukien drove the blade with all his weight, puncturing the scaly hide and releasing a spray of stinking blood. He was suddenly a savage, a berserker, and the beast bellowed as he thrust the dagger again and again, stabbing it repeatedly. In the distance he heard Cassandra's voice, calling to him. He heard Tomas gurgling nearby, screaming for help. And then he heard another voice, familiar yet surprising.

"Tomas! Hold on!"

A black stallion splashed into the flooded road, madly flailing its hooves. Atop the steed was Trager. The lieutenant's face was furious. His blade sprang from its scabbard as he searched the foaming water. Lukien saw it as if in a dream. His own fight was almost over. The garmy's tail slipped slowly from his neck. Now it was the garmy that was desperate to flee. It twisted its wounded body and began crawling away, slashing its spiked tail at Lukien's face. Lukien grabbed hold of the tail and jerked the creature backward.

"Come here, you bitch!" he spat.

The monster's face turned and snapped at him. He punched his dagger forward, sending it through the garmy's open mouth. The creature cried in agony, tumbled backward into the mud, then lay there twitching and dying. As Lukien turned to help Tomas, he watched Trager dive from his horse, falling against the last garmy. The creature had risen against its new adversary, bringing up its head and arms even as Tomas dangled from its tail. The young man's face was purple. He wasn't moving. Trager's sword slashed, slicing the garmy's shoulder. The creature's arms flew at him, raking his armor with its powerful nails. Exhausted, Lukien stumbled forward, his dagger still in hand. The garmy noticed him and let down its guard—a fatal mistake against the skilled Trager. The lieutenant saw the opening and lunged, burying his sword in the monster's chest. The garmy's shrill scream tore through the forest. Its arms flailed, its tail slackened, and its yellow eyes dimmed as it collapsed. As he fell from the creature's grasp, Tomas collapsed beside it.

"Tomas!" Lukien cried.

Trager was already over the man, lifting him from the mud. It was plain that Tomas was dead. His head lolled back in Trager's arms, lifeless. Lukien stopped mid-step, dropped his dagger, and let out an anguished moan.

"Oh, no," he sighed. "Don't tell me he's gone."

Cassandra brought her horse to the edge of the water. She looked at the corpse in Trager's arms. Her face contorted with sorrow.

"It's my fault," she whispered. "Fate forgive me."

"No." Lukien looked squarely at Trager. "It's not your fault, my lady. It's the fault of this incompetent fool!"

"What?" Trager blurted. "Captain, I tried to save you!"

"Fool!" Lukien said again. "You said this road was safe!"

"It was safe!" Trager roared. He still had Tomas in his arms. "I didn't see the garmys yesterday. It was raining. It was dark!"

"Dark?" Lukien laughed horribly. "You were on scout duty, you ass. What does it matter that it was dark?" He pointed at Tomas. "*You* killed him, Trager. Not those garmys."

"You arrogant bastard," Trager sneered. He turned and walked off, holding Tomas in a dismal embrace. He passed Cassandra without regard, put Tomas onto the back of the dead man's horse, then took the stallion's reins. When he had gathered up his own horse, he led them both away. Lukien watched him go.

"Lukien?" asked Cassandra. "Are you all right?"

Lukien stood in the mud amidst the dead garmys. He closed his eyes, fearing he might weep. "Let's get back to camp."

10

To Cassandra, who had never seen a city larger than her home of Hes, the Liirian capital was a marvel. It was everything Akeela had promised, everything Lukien had bragged about, and it humbled the princess with its beauty. Koth was a hub of activity, a meeting place of businessmen and scholars, its streets filled with carts and carriages, its buildings tall and gilded. Cassandra fell in love with it immediately. After her dreary ride from Hes she was ready for the luxuries of a city again, and so spent her days in the castle with Akeela, preparing for their wedding. Even after a week had passed, there was still more of Lionkeep to explore, still dozens of servants whose names she hadn't learned. And there were ministers, too, scores of them. They constantly came to the castle to vie for Akeela's attention, most of them old, somberfaced men with trains of civil servants, their hands nervously scribbling in ledgers. In those first days of her arrival, it seemed to Cassandra that the chancellors of Koth could do nothing without Akeela, for they monopolized him day and night, and even when he was away from them, he was exhausted.

But Cassandra took it all in stride. She adored the freedom of her new home, and Akeela's busy schedule gave her time to investigate Lionkeep and to think about what had happened on the road to Koth. She had not seen much of Lukien since their arrival, yet she still thought of him often. True to his word, the Bronze Knight had mentioned nothing of their encounters to Akeela, and for that Cassandra was grateful. Despite the tragedy of Tomas' death, Akeela had greeted her with a smothering smile, and she knew that he suspected no infidelity of her, not even of the daydreaming kind she had committed. Before her arrival, Akeela had ordered the city gates trimmed with ribbons and flowers and the streets lined with white horses. The chancellors had come out to greet her, filling Chancellery Square and showering her with praise. There had been music, too, with honey-voiced minstrels and a choir of children arranged for her by the one-armed Baron Glass, head of the House of Dukes. Koth had turned out in force to welcome its new queen, and Cassandra had melted at the outpouring of emotion. At that moment, she knew she had made the right choice in accepting Akeela's proposal.

Mostly.

For though she seldom saw Lukien, he was never far away. Akeela had named Lukien her champion. Sweetly, her soon-to-be husband seemed not to notice the way Lukien's eyes flashed when he was near her. The young king was too preoccupied in exhibiting the sights of Koth. When they had arrived at Lionkeep, he had shown her their apartments, a vast collection of chambers occupying an entire wing of the castle. It was more than anyone should have, even a queen, but Cassandra loved the excess. Afterwards, he had taken her to a ledge of the castle, very high up on the north side, Koth spread out like a blanket beneath their private perch.

"On the tenth day of spring we will be married," he had told her. His voice had been as soft as down. "It will be a special day, the kind of wedding you deserve."

She had looked at him and smiled, and in the moonlight he seemed a little boy, starstruck. He was lovesick for her, in a way that Cassandra feared she could never return.

With the tenth day of spring only a week away, Cassandra finally settled into a routine. Because she was not yet married, she had a room of her own in Lionkeep, away from the cavernous wing she would soon share with Akeela; Jancis had a room nearby. The sickness that had plagued her for months continued to trouble her, but she ignored it, confessing nothing of it to Jancis. The handmaid was giddy with the attention the Liirians showed her. She accompanied Cassandra everywhere, relishing the newness of her surroundings even more than her princess.

On a perfect morning bright with spring sunshine, Cassandra and Jancis toured the avenues of Koth, conveyed by an opulent carriage and guarded by a host of Royal Chargers. Lukien chaperoned them, pointing out attractions along the boulevards and directing them to the best shops. Because he was away from the castle his mood had improved. He no longer avoided Cassandra's eyes. Cassandra and Jancis relaxed in the coach, whispering like two conspirators.

"He loves you, I think," said Jancis.

Cassandra nodded. The carriage moved through a crowded street. She could see Lukien atop his horse, proudly ferrying them through the traffic.

"It doesn't matter," she said sadly. "In a week I will have a husband, and it will not be Lukien."

"Then forget him, Cassandra," said Jancis. "Think of Akeela."

"I will," said Cassandra.

But she knew it was a lie. She would never be able to forget Lukien. He was too close, and he had done something to her. Now when she thought of her impending marriage, she did so joylessly.

As promised, the wedding took place on the tenth day of spring.

Neither Cassandra nor Akeela could have asked for a more splendid day. The sun was warm but not oppressive, the sky bright without being glaring. A gentle breeze moved through the city and the lilacs around Lionkeep bloomed. Cassandra wore a dress of white and emerald, was veiled with silk and followed by a long, elaborate train. The dress had been made for her by Akeela's royal tailor, who had promised the young bride she would look stunning in his creation. As she walked down the aisle of Lionkeep's throne room, she knew the tailor hadn't lied. The faces of those gathered reflected her loveliness. At the throne stood Akeela, resplendent in an outfit of black and crimson. Atop his head was his golden crown, still looking out of place upon his young brow. He wore a ceremonial sidearm and a nervous smile. Even from across the chamber, Cassandra had seen him perspiring. Next to him was Lukien. The knight wore his bronze armor, outshining all of them, even Cassandra. She had let her eyes linger on him for a moment.

After the ceremony, the new bride and groom had gone off to the yard for the tourney. The courtyard of Lionkeep was decorated with flags and colorful pavilions. Hundreds of people, mostly Liirian nobles, milled through the yard with goblets in their hands, nosing around the tables laden with food and wine. Musicians and jesters entertained the guests while the knights readied themselves for the tournament. Akeela had explained to Cassandra that Liiria had such a tournament each spring, and that it was one of the best times in the city, a sort of holiday for the countless civil servants and their noble masters. All the chancellors had come, bringing their wives and children with them, and had taken seats either near or within the royal gallery, where Akeela and Cassandra sat in the first row, flanked by Lukien and Warden Graig. Cassandra had removed her train and veil and took a seat next to her new husband, eyeing the crowds as they nodded and smiled at her. Before the gallery was the tournament ground, busy with the activity of knights and squires as they prepared their weapons and horses for the show. It was a test of skill, Akeela had told her. The lances and swords were blunted. He had also told her that Lukien was the champion of the tourney, and had been for the past three years. He would be defending the title later in the day, partaking in the jousts against his rival, Trager. Cassandra stole a glance at Lukien. He sat beside Akeela with a goblet in his hand, laughing as a jester told jokes. To Cassandra, he looked remarkably calm. She leaned back and let a servant fill her glass. Next to her, Jancis gave her a nudge.

"Well?" her friend whispered. "How do you feel, my queen?"

Cassandra frowned. "Queen." The word felt strange to her. "It's all too much, isn't it?"

"I don't think so," chirped Jancis. She took a sip of wine, happily studying the platters of food. "I think it's wonderful. Look how many people there are!"

But the new queen was unable to brighten, because they were all strangers. None of her own family had come, for

King Karis was a private man, and despite the new peace between Reec and Liiria he still felt unwelcome in the land of his old adversary. Surprisingly, Cassandra missed him. As eager as she'd been to be gone from him, she wished he had seen her married.

"Look how fat they all are," she whispered. "These ministers; they are all the same everywhere."

"Shhh," cautioned Jancis. "What's wrong with you, Cass? You should be happy. This is what you wanted." Her brow furrowed. "Are you feeling all right?"

"Fine," said Cassandra. She didn't tell her friend about the fire in her bowels. It was making her feel out of sorts. Before she could change the subject, Akeela took her hand.

"Cassandra?" He gave her a great smile. "What are you two chatting about?"

The others in the front of the gallery turned to hear her answer. Even the old man named Figgis seemed intrigued, dropping his mutton joint to listen. Cassandra mustered up a beautiful smile.

"Forgive me, my lord," she said. "We were merely talking about all the people that have come. It's quite a crowd of ministers you have. My father didn't have nearly so many advisors."

"No," agreed Akeela sourly. "Nor all the problems they bring, I'd wager."

Cassandra tried to lighten the conversation. "Forget your troubles with the chancellors, my lord. Remember the spirit of the day."

"Of course," said Akeela. Yet his eyes lingered on the second row, where Baron Thorin Glass was seated. The Chancellor of the House of Dukes sat nearby, as his station demanded. With him was his wife, a woman much younger than he, and a gaggle of unruly children. The Baron was a big man, barrel-chested and ruddy, with unkempt red hair and an oiled goatee combed to a sharp point. Cassandra guessed his age to be in the mid-forties. Like all the nobles, he had dressed for the occasion in expensive clothes and jewelry that twinkled in the sunlight. But most remarkable of all was his left arm, which wasn't there at all. In its place hung an empty sleeve, pinned up at the shoulder. Glass poured himself more wine, and when he noticed Akeela looking at him he smiled and raised his goblet in tribute.

Akeela returned the gesture, drinking with the Baron, but Cassandra caught the glare of contempt in his eyes. The emotion looked misplaced in Akeela.

"My lord," she said softly, "you could do a better job of hiding your feelings for the baron."

Sure that Glass couldn't hear him, Akeela replied, "The baron knows my feelings, my lady. There's no reason to hide them."

"For the sake of your kingship, then," Cassandra suggested. "You will need the baron's goodwill for your many projects."

"He opposes me, Cassandra. He makes it plain in the House of Dukes." Akeela lowered his goblet, his eyes shifting angrily. "Mark me. Before this day is over, he will spoil it with politics and bad news."

Cassandra had never seen Akeela so agitated. His mood surprised her. "Akeela," she said mildly, "this is our wedding day. It's time to celebrate, not brood." She passed him a bowl of grapes. "Forget your duties for one day. Enjoy yourself."

He chose a grape and popped it into his mouth. Before them, a group of knights and young pages were readying for the first bout. Akeela seemed not to notice them.

"He is a bitter old fool," he whispered. "He's jealous of me because I'm young. Tell her, Lukien."

Lukien looked up. "My lord, please don't make me speak against Glass. You know how I feel about him."

"How, Lukien?" asked Cassandra. "Do you know him well?"

"Yes, my lady," said Lukien, keeping his voice low. Next to him, Figgis strained to hear. "He is a hero in Liiria. Once he was a great soldier."

"A long time ago," Akeela reminded him.

"Still, I honor him. As do most of the Chargers. He fought in the war against Norvor, and against Marn. That's where he was wounded."

Cassandra snuck a peek at Glass again, and at the peculiar way his empty sleeve dangled at his shoulder. "Remarkable."

"He is remarkable," said Lukien. "As I said, he is a hero."

"Hero," scoffed Akeela. "You are twice the hero Glass ever was, Lukien."

Lukien shook his head. "No."

"Yes," Akeela insisted. "Twice and more."

"The king is kind."

"I know something of Baron Glass," said Figgis suddenly. The old man shifted eagerly forward. "I learned about him when I was in Marn, during the war. Sir Lukien is right, my lord; he was a great soldier. And if I'm not mistaken, he served your father well."

Akeela rolled his eyes. "You are an expert on too many things, friend Figgis."

"Good," said Cassandra brightly. "Then let us change the subject. Figgis, my husband tells me you are a learned man, a great scholar."

The old librarian puffed up at the compliment. "The king does me proud to say so, my queen. But yes, I would agree with his description. I have studied many subjects all my life. Languages, the patterns of the stars, poetry." He thought for a moment. "To be true, it is hard to think of a subject that bores me."

Cassandra laughed. He was a peculiar man, but she liked the twinkle in his eyes. "And Jador," she added. "The king says you are an expert on that land."

"Ah, now you have touched on my greatest passion, my queen." Figgis' face lit up. "If anyone can be called an expert on Jador, than I suppose it is I. Since I was a boy the Jadori have fascinated me. When I—"

"Figgis, stop," said Akeela, smiling. "Really, the queen was just being polite."

The old man looked hurt, but soon found solace again in the food and entertainment. The knights who had taken the field were ready for the first bout. Lukien shoved his plate of pheasant away, sitting up to watch the joust. Behind him, Baron Glass told his children to take their seats as he, too, relished the coming combat.

The tournament stretched into the afternoon, as knight after knight took to the field for the honor of the king and queen and the ladies in the audience. There were jousts and archery exhibitions, feats of swordplay and horsemanship, and Cassandra watched it all with disinterest, feeling queasy and exhausted. Then, finally, it was time for Lukien to fight.

The Bronze Knight had left the gallery an hour earlier, to prepare for his bout. Now he was at one end of the parade ground, sitting atop his charger with his helmet in the crook of his arm. He was splendid in his bronze armor. The horse he rode shared the same bronze outfitting, protected with layers of metal along its breast and flanks and bearing an ominously forged headpiece. A page stood beside him, lance in hand. Akeela had explained that the lance was dulled and tipped with a protective head—a coronal, he'd called it. Lukien reached for the lance and inspected it, then looked over the other weapons arrayed nearby. A mace awaited its use, as did a broadsword. Another page held Lukien's shield, emblazoned with the crest of Liiria. Lukien nodded to the boys, then looked across the field at his opponent. There sat Trager, his head hidden beneath his dark helmet, the reins of his stallion held tightly in gray gauntlets. Unlike Lukien, Trager wore the traditional silver armor of the Royal Chargers. His helmet bore the likeness of a ram's head, replete with curling horns.

"I think neither of them cares for the other," said Cassandra absently. She remembered Lukien's rage when Tomas had died, and how he had called Trager a fool. The lieutenant's face had twisted horribly at the insult. Cassandra was sure he wore the same expression now under his dark mask. Her heart raced with worry. Akeela took her hand, surprised to find it trembling.

"My lady, you're shivering," he said.

Cassandra frowned. "It is a barbaric sport, and I hate it," she said. "Look at them, one just as eager to kill the other. I can't watch this."

Akeela laughed. "Ah, but it is sport, as you say. And it's what these people have come to see—a spectacle. Look, see how they watch?"

The hush over the crowd was remarkable. Everyone waited for the outcome of the duel, which Trager had boasted he would win.

"Lukien tells me Trager's been practicing," Akeela remarked. "We shall see."

"Lukien will win, won't he?" asked Cassandra. "I mean, he won't be hurt, will he?"

Akeela looked at her askance, and for a moment she regretted her question.

"No," said Akeela. His eyes narrowed. "But your concern is refreshing."

Out on the field, Lukien put on his helmet. The officer of the tournament, a plump, middle-aged man, came to stand in front of the gallery and summoned the jousters. Both Lukien and Trager trotted forward, bringing their mounts to stand beside the officer, then removing their helmets as they faced the king and queen. For a moment, Lukien's eyes met Cassandra's. He seemed to wink at her reassuringly. Trager's face was furious, his jaw clamped tight.

The officer proclaimed, "My King and Queen, these two gentlemen have come into your presence, recommended by your good grace humbly, beseeching you to find the best jouster. To him, a diamond will be the prize. To the second, a ruby."

Akeela held out both hands. In the right was a brilliant diamond. In the left, a blood red ruby. He said, "To the best shall go the diamond, and to the second the ruby. And when the tournament is done, we shall retire to the banquet rooms of Lionkeep, and dance and drink." He handed both gems over to Cassandra. "Who will win the diamond from the fair hand of the queen?"

Lukien said, "I think we know the answer to that, my lord."

The gallery laughed, as did the rest of the crowd. Cassandra saw Trager's face twitch, and for a moment she pitied him.

"Sir Trager, good fortune to you," she said. Then she looked at Lukien. "And to you, my champion."

"I will make you proud, my queen," said Lukien.

"Then to your stations," ordered the officer. He watched as both men bowed to the gallery, replaced their helms, and rode back to their positions on the opposite ends of the field. Lukien's page offered him a lance, which the Bronze Knight tested for balance before tucking beneath his arm. Across the field, Trager did the same. The pages

fell away. The combatant's horses snorted. The officer of
the joust stepped off the field, heading to the side of the
gallery to stand with Breck and some other Royal Chargers.
And Cassandra, sick with anxiety, clutched the gemstones
in her fists until her knuckles turned white.

Lukien and Trager lowered themselves into riding
stances. Akeela raised his hand, held it aloft for a moment,
then let it fall. Lukien's charger bolted forward. Trager
raced toward him, his lance aimed. The air filled with clods
of dirt and the noise of hammering hooves. The two jousters devoured the distance between them, each pointing a
lance at the shielded heart of his opponent. The air
sounded with the report of cracking wood. Lukien's lance
drove into Trager's shield and Trager's into his, and Cassandra saw her champion's weapon buckle, sending up
shards of wood. The jousters roared past each other, neither unhorsed. The crowd cheered wildly.

"Another lance!" Lukien cried. He whirled his horse
around, anxiously waiting for his pages to bring him a fresh
weapon and clear the debris from the ground. From the
opposite end of the field, Trager waved at him

"Ha!" the lieutenant crowed. "You are clumsy this
year, Captain!"

The folk in the gallery loved the banter. They shouted
at the jousters, urging the combat to continue. Lukien fixed
his new lance beneath his arm and spurred his horse forward with a cry. Trager matched his moves, bolting forward. This time the clash sent Trager's lance skidding off
Lukien's shield. Again, neither man went down. Their
horses came to skidding stops.

"Well done, Trager," called Akeela. He favored the soldier with a smile. "This year you are truly worthy. Will the
diamond be yours at last?"

"It is as good as won, my lord," replied the knight. He
turned to his bronze opponent. "What say you, Captain?
Again?"

"Again," replied Lukien. He raised a guantleted hand,
waving Trager forward. "Now, come and get your lesson."

Incensed, Trager crouched and drove his boots into the
flanks of his mount, spurring the charger onward. Lukien
joined him, racing forward. Again their lances closed, again
the crowd was wide-eyed. And this time the Bronze Knight

found his mark, burying his lance in Trager's shield. Trager rose off his horse and tumbled backward, crashing into the ground. The crowd cheered. Without thinking, Cassandra jumped from her seat and joined them.

Lukien quickly brought his horse around and hovered over Trager. The lieutenant rose unsteadily to his feet.

"Well?" Lukien asked. "Are you injured?"

"Sword!" Trager cried, answering the knight's question. A page hurried onto the field and tossed Trager his broadsword. Lukien laughed.

"Yield, Trager," he said. He raised his lance toward Trager's chest. "You've already lost."

"No!" Trager swiped at the lance with his sword. "Come down and fight me!"

Lukien brought his horse forward, pushing the lance into Trager and knocking him over. Again the crowd crowed. Trager scurried backward in the dirt, trying get up, but each time he did Lukien's horse took another step forward, pushing him back down.

"It is done!" cried the officer of arms. "Lukien has won."

Still on her feet, Cassandra applauded loudly. Akeela joined her, as did the others in the gallery. Lukien dropped down from his horse and stood over Trager, then offered out his hand.

"Are you all right?"

"Get away from me!" spat Trager. His pages rushed out, helping him to his feet. When he finally righted himself, he snapped up the visor of his helm and glared at Lukien. All around them the crowds were clapping, but not for Trager.

"Both of you, come here," called Akeela. He turned to Cassandra. "My lady, I think you have something for our knights."

The officer came forward, escorting Lukien and the disgraced Trager to the gallery, both of whom bowed before the king and queen. Cassandra noticed how Trager kept his helmet on, a breach of etiquette, surely. He couldn't even look at her, so strong was his shame, so she let the lapse pass.

Said the officer, "Sir Trager has jousted well, but Sir Lukien has jousted better. So to him goes the diamond."

"Sirs," said Akeela, "These gentle folk thank you for your great labor. Trager, since you are second best, you get this ruby." He glanced at Cassandra, nudging her to bring out the gem. Cassandra complied, holding out the ruby for Trager, who took it reluctantly.

"Thank you, my lord and lady," he said.

Akeela continued, "And Lukien, once again you have jousted best of all. Once again, the diamond is yours, my friend."

Cassandra needed no encouragement this time. She held out the diamond for Lukien, placing it in his outstretched hand. But before he released her, he bent and gave her hand a kiss.

"For the honor of my queen," he said.

That evening, the celebration continued inside the halls of Lionkeep. The ladies danced and the minstrels strummed their instruments, and children played beneath the tables with the dogs, enjoying the atmosphere fostered by the king. Festoons of flowers hung from the walls, scenting the air with lilac. Akeela sat with his new wife at a gigantic ebony table covered with platters of game birds and flagons of wine and beer. Out on the floor, Lukien was dancing with the daughter of Chancellor Nils. Cassandra watched them, frowning slightly. Akeela noticed the expression and wondered.

"You do not eat, my lady," he said, offering her some food from his own plate. Cassandra turned her nose away.

"I've already eaten enough for a week."

"Is the music too loud for you? You look uncomfortable."

"I'm fine," replied Cassandra. Then she smiled apologetically, adding, "It has been an exciting day, that's all. I'm just tired."

"Yes, exciting," Akeela agreed. "But you don't look well, Cassandra; your color." He studied her, wondering why she was so white. "Perhaps you should excuse yourself, get some rest."

She shook her head. "It's our wedding night."

"Cassandra," he whispered, "I'm not going to force myself on a sick woman. If you're not feeling well . . ."

"I'm fine." She smiled weakly. "Really."

Before Akeela could reply, Lukien hurried over from the dance floor. Perspiration covered his face. He took up

Akeela's goblet and drank down its contents furiously, then wiped his hand across his brow.

"Whew! That girl can dance!"

Of course, thought Akeela blackly. *All the girls want to dance with Lukien.*

"Sit, Lukien," he offered. "You look about to collapse."

"Indeed I am," said the captain. He came around the table and fell into a chair beside Akeela. He had doffed his armor once again and now wore a crimson tunic. When a servant brought over a full pitcher of beer, Lukien took it and drank without a glass. He was in fine spirits after his victory in the joust, and wore the diamond around his neck to prove it. Trager, on the other hand, was conspicuously missing from the banquet. His lieutenant's absence only buoyed Lukien's mood.

"So?" asked the knight. "Why aren't the happy couple dancing, eh?"

"The queen is tired," Akeela explained. "The excitement of the day."

"Tired?" Lukien looked at Cassandra. "Is that all, my lady?"

Cassandra grimaced. "Yes," she said. Yet her eyes seemed to say more.

"Well, then," said Lukien awkwardly. "You should rest."

"She is resting, Lukien."

Akeela and Lukien looked at each other. Lukien's smile sagged. He nodded and returned his attention to the pitcher of beer, filling Akeela's goblet again.

"Good beer," he said. "Let's drink a toast to the two of you."

"Yes," agreed a new voice. "Let's drink to the young lovers!"

Akeela looked up and saw Baron Glass approaching the table. He had a goblet in his only hand and a smarmy smile on his bearded face. He had left behind his pretty young wife and undisciplined children, and he bowed slightly to Cassandra as he came forward. Cassandra forced a pleasant countenance.

"Baron Glass," she said, "you are welcome to drink with us. Come, sit yourself down."

"The queen is gracious," said the baron. He looked around for a chair, then found the one that Figgis had vacated. Coming around the table, he pulled the chair close to Akeela, but before he sat he lifted his glass. "To you both," he said. "May Fate grant you a long and happy marriage."

"Here, here," toasted Lukien, still drinking from the pitcher.

"Thank you, Baron," said Akeela. He took a sip of beer, watching Glass as he did so. If the baron hadn't been so near, he would have reminded Cassandra of what he'd said earlier—before the day was over, Glass would ruin it with politics.

"So," said Akeela cordially, "how did you like the tournament this year, Baron?"

"Well played, as always," replied Glass. This time he raised his goblet to Lukien. "Good jousting, Sir Lukien. You are as skilled as I ever was, maybe more so."

"Thank you, my lord," said Lukien. "You honor me."

"And the banquet . . . so lavish!" Glass looked around the chamber. "To be honest, I had expected a smaller affair."

"Oh?" asked Cassandra. "Why is that?"

Akeela braced himself. *Here it comes* . . .

"The expense, my lady," replied Glass. "With all the projects your husband has been championing, I didn't think the treasury had enough in its coffers for such luxury."

Akeela stiffened. "Baron Glass . . ."

"It's a special day," interrupted Lukien. "And I think it's worth the expense, don't you, Baron?"

"Of course." Glass grinned. "Tell me, Queen Cassandra, have you seen your husband's library yet? It's quite impressive."

Cassandra began to answer, but Akeela said quickly, "I've taken her there, yes."

"Did you think it was very grand?" asked Glass.

"I think it will be marvelous when it's done," said Cassandra. To Akeela's surprise, she took his hand. "And I think it's worth any expense to bring light to the world, Baron."

"Hmm, Chancellor Sark may not agree with you, my lady. He doesn't like watching the coffers of his treasury bled dry."

"It's not his treasury," snapped Akeela. "And it's not

yours or mine, either, Baron. It belongs to the people of Liiria. They want the library. They know it will bring them knowledge."

Baron Glass looked down into his goblet, considering his words carefully. "Knowledge," he sighed. "Knowledge is for men like you and I, King Akeela. Knowledge is for people who can handle it." He gestured around the chamber. "Look about this room. What do you see here but nobles? These are the elite of Liiria, my lord. They already know how to read and write. They don't need your library."

"Precisely," argued Akeela. "The library is for all those people who aren't here; the people left out to celebrate my wedding in the streets." He smiled slyly at the Baron. "I'm building the library for your servants, Baron Glass, so that maybe they can do something better than swill your pigs and shear your sheep."

Glass' face reddened. "King Akeela, not everyone can be noble. Fate chose my birthright."

"Nonsense," said Akeela.

"It's not nonsense," said Glass. "And the same power that made me noble put you on the throne. Do you think my servants tend my herds because I keep them from something better? No. They tend my herds because they can do no better. It is Fate's will."

The notion incensed Akeela. Like many in Liiria, Glass was Fateist, part of a cult that believed the world controlled by an unseen force, neither god nor devil. It was just one of many faiths accommodated by Liiria, but it was influential in the country, and Glass believed its myths devoutly.

"Baron," said Akeela carefully, "this is my wedding day. I don't want it spoiled by politics and religion, and I don't want to argue with you."

"You should listen to me," Glass warned. "I am not alone in these thoughts. There are others who are concerned with your ideas, my lord. They think they are dangerous, and so do I."

"The people support me," said Akeela.

"The people do not run the chancelleries," Glass countered. "You and I are of noble birth; we know how to govern. At least that's what your father believed."

"I am not my father!"

The music suddenly stopped. Akeela shrank back in his chair as the eyes of the celebrants fell upon him. Baron Glass smiled, amused, and rose from his seat.

"No," he said, "you're not."

Before he could go, Akeela got to his feet. "Wait."

Glass stopped and turned around, looking at him questioningly. Angry, Akeela decided the time had come to make his statement.

"Everybody, please listen to me." He already had the crowd's attention. "I want to make an announcement."

"Announcement?" asked Lukien.

"Akeela?" probed Cassandra.

"I'm going away for a while," Akeela told them. "I'm going on a journey, a goodwill tour, you might say. I want to introduce myself to our neighboring nations. I want them to see me, and know that they have an ally in Liiria."

"What?" erupted Glass. "My lord, you've only just returned. The ink on the Reecian treaty hasn't dried yet!"

"Even so," Akeela continued, "I'm going. Countries like Marn and Norvor need to know they still have an ally in Liiria. This is going to be the start of a new relationship between our nation and the rest of the continent."

The crowd began to murmur. As Akeela expected, the chancellors in the audience shook their heads.

"My lord," said Glass, "don't you think you're going too quickly? Don't be reckless. Let us send emissaries first."

"Reckless?" asked Akeela. "Like I was in Reec, you mean? Or do you think I was merely lucky on that mission, Baron? More of your Fate nonsense?"

Glass sighed miserably. "I'm only thinking of your safety, my lord. And the good of Liiria."

"Fine. Then we're agreed that the good of Liiria matters. Therefore, I am going on this tour. It's important."

"King Akeela—"

"It's important," Akeela repeated. He glared at Glass. "Now, make your fellow lords understand that, Baron."

Baron Glass was flabbergasted by Akeela's tone. They stared at one another in challenge, Akeela determined not to blink. Then, the baron smiled.

"Well," he said, "perhaps there is more of your father in you than I thought, King Akeela. Excuse me, please."

Akeela watched him turn and go, then sat back down.

He realized suddenly he was shaking. Lukien hurried a goblet into his hands.

"How'd I do?" he asked.

"Drink," advised Lukien.

"Akeela?" Cassandra asked. "Are you really going away on this . . . tour?"

"I'm sorry, Cassandra, I should have told you," said Akeela. He took a few gulps of beer, steadying himself. Blessedly, the minstrels had started playing again. "But Glass got me so angry I forgot myself. I had to say something to change the subject."

"Well, that certainly did it!" joked Lukien.

"So you're going?" asked Cassandra crossly. "Just like that?"

"I must. I'm king." Akeela took her hand. "Please try to understand. It's as I told you in Hes—I'm trying to accomplish something. And it won't be so bad; I won't be gone that long. You can get things ready for us here in Lionkeep. And Lukien will look after you."

Cassandra's face clenched. Lukien put down his beer.

"Me?" he blurted. "But . . . shouldn't I go with you, Akeela? I mean, who'll protect *you?*"

"Come now, Lukien, you're not the only Royal Charger in Liiria. And you're Cassandra's champion now. Your first duty is to the queen."

Cassandra pulled back her hand. The expression on her face was dreadful. "I'm not feeling well, Akeela," she said. Yet as she spoke, she looked at Lukien. "I think I need to be alone."

The celebration went on for hours more, though Cassandra had retired early to her private chamber, feigning a headache that had become remarkably real. Her private chamber was a very grand room, with silk window dressings and velvet chairs and her own bed for those nights when Akeela didn't require her. She stared at the bed from one of the plush chairs, listening to the ebbing revelry in the banquet room far below and wondering what it would be like to share her sheets with Akeela. Despite her illnesses—real and imagined—she had promised him his wedding night, and as king he had a right to expect her compliance. She hadn't thought she would dread the experience, but as the night wore on and the celebration ended, she began to fear the inevitable knock at her door. If she had gone to her window, she would have seen the exhausted nobles streaming out of Lionkeep, their enormous appetites slaked by Akeela's kitchens and wine cellars. She could hear them faintly though the glass, bidding farewell to friends and enemies they wouldn't see again for ages, and she knew that her virginity would soon be at an end.

He's a good man, she reminded herself. *I should be proud to give myself to him.*

But she wasn't proud at all. Cassandra's feelings bounced between dread and guilt, because she feared Akeela's clumsy touch and longed for Lukien's experienced hands instead. She had hardly been able to look away from the Bronze Knight all day. He was compelling, like the sun, and watching him warmed her soul.

And she was cross with Akeela, because she thought his plans were stupid and she resented him for leaving so soon. He was a man but he acted like a boy sometimes, and despite the hours she had spent brooding alone in her chamber, she could not understand his desire to tour the nearby nations.

Or did she simply fear being alone with Lukien?

Yes.

The answer cut through her mind, crystal clear. Without her husband close, Cassandra knew Lukien would tempt her. Akeela wasn't the only child in Lionkeep. She too was like a youngster, accustomed to getting what she desired.

On the table beside her chair stood a flagon of blood red wine. Cassandra picked it up and poured herself another glass. She had been careful with the wine throughout the night, sipping just enough to ease the pain in her stomach while still keeping her senses clear. There was a point of drunkenness she hoped to reach, though, a point where it would be easy to go naked into Akeela's arms and feel his hard body atop her. She knew what it would be like; her maids in Hes had warned her all about it.

Then, at last, the knock came. With it came the voice of one of Akeela's many stewards.

"My lady? Are you awake?"

Cassandra put down her wine glass slowly. "I am."

"How does my lady tonight?" came the question through the door.

Well enough to bed the king. That was the answer the steward sought.

"I am well," replied Cassandra dully. "Where is the king?"

"King Akeela requests your presence, my lady. I am to bring you to him if you are well and willing."

Cassandra couldn't help but smile. Too many men wouldn't have given her the choice. "Come in, then," she said and stood up to greet the steward. He was a little man with perfect clothes and a gentle twinkle in his eyes. He smiled at Cassandra, as if to soothe her fears. Cassandra felt at ease with him and returned the smile. She looked down at her dress, which she hadn't changed, and suddenly hoped she looked all right. But she could tell by the steward's approving nod that she still was beautiful. Without a word the steward stepped aside, revealing the torchlit hallway beyond her chamber. There was no one in the hall at all, just the soft glow of light bidding her forward.

There was nothing to be done, Cassandra told herself. And she had so wanted this marriage, and to be away from Hes. It would be well to be Akeela's lover. He would not hurt her, at least. So she let the steward guide her from the chamber, and not a single word passed between them as they walked the glowing hall. At the opposite end was another chamber, also very grand, with two ornate, rounded-top doors and a pair of brass braziers standing beside them like sentries. Cassandra felt herself flush from the heat of their fires and her growing apprehension. The wine worked on her brain, making it swim. Akeela was beyond those fabulous doors, waiting for her. And she knew that she would not emerge intact, and that a piece of her would be left behind, never to be reclaimed. When the steward paused outside the doors, he noticed Cassandra's troubled expression and offered her a little nod, the way her father might have done.

Then he opened the doors. With two hands he pulled both doors open slowly, revealing a chamber awash with candlelight. Much larger than Cassandra's own private chamber, this one disappeared deep into the keep, with hallways and doors of its own spoking out from the central hub. A gigantic window let starlight into the room, revealing the dark silhouette of a man gazing out over the city, his hands clasped behind his back, the fingers twitching nervously.

"My lord," said the steward softly, "the queen."

Akeela nodded but did not turn around. Instead he waited for the steward to leave the room, closing the doors again behind him. It seemed to Cassandra that Akeela was preparing himself. She watched his shoulders rise with a deep breath. When at least he turned he had a smile on his face, and she could tell he was afraid. For some reason she couldn't fathom, she resented his fear.

"I'm glad you've come," he said. He drifted across the carpeted floor, going to her carefully. "How are you feeling now?"

"Better now," Cassandra lied. She glanced around the chamber but saw no bed, then supposed it was in another of the rooms. She had already learned that Koth was a place of excess, and Akeela's chambers were no exception. But he looked splendid in his royal garb, and it was hard to be angry against his earnest expression. He came and stood before her, and looked into her eyes for a long moment. The longing in his face was frightening. The deepest, angst-filled love burned in him. His eager lips came down to kiss her.

Cassandra closed her eyes. Like a brave soldier she stood her ground as his mouth glided down her cheeks to taste her neck and his hands came around to encircle her waist and pull her greedily forward. She felt herself stiffen at his clumsiness, begging herself to relax and not offend him, yet he seemed unaware of her dread, so lost was he in his own needs. He took her hand and squeezed it tight, his embrace cool and trembling. Breaking off his kisses, he led her toward one of the archways into another chamber of orange candlelight where a huge bed awaited them, already turned down, piled with colorful pillows and immaculate sheets. One by one Akeela blew out the candles as he forged toward the bed, until only a single light burned by the bedside. Then he sat himself down at the edge of the bed, looking up at Cassandra expectantly.

For a moment Cassandra hovered there, watching him

watching her, adoring and loathing him at the same time. It was supposed to have been so different. She had always dreamed of a lover with skills. All of Akeela's talents were in his head, though, and she knew his hands couldn't bring her joy.

But there was nothing to be done for it. She was his now.

She smiled, struggling to love him, and reached back to undo her dress. When she was done and it fell in a pile at her feet, Akeela's hands reached out again and pulled her onto the bed.

11

With the absence of King Akeela, Liiria moved quietly into late spring. The king had gone on his goodwill tour weeks earlier, leaving the work of government to his chancellors and the task of protecting his queen to Lukien. To most men, chaperoning Cassandra seemed an enviable task. But for Lukien, whose passion for the young queen had grown insatiable, the duty was hellish. In the days, then weeks, of Akeela's absence, he spent increasing amounts of time with Cassandra, seeing to her needs and escorting her to courtly functions, all under the guise of the impeccable champion. They were seldom alone, but that didn't keep the tension from rising between them. Lukien loved Cassandra and now he knew it. She kept him awake at night, intoxicated by the faint smell of her perfume on his clothes, and she was his first thought in the morning. An awful guilt accompanied him everywhere. His love was a betrayal, a corruption of his loyalty to Akeela, yet he could not control it. It wasn't lust that drove him on—he knew that because he had tried to satisfy it with Kothan prostitutes. There was more than just a manly yearning goading him toward Cassandra. To him, she was perfect. And the fact that she was unattainable only drove him harder.

Cassandra, too, was burdened by their love. Lukien knew it when he looked at her. Despite a room full of people, she always had a glint in her eyes that belonged only to him. She walked with deliberate slowness when they were alone, never anxious for their solitude to end, and she seldom spoke of Akeela, himself far away and unable to watch her. There were dozens of hints that betrayed Cassandra's love for Lukien, and the Bronze Knight cataloged them all each night, lying awake in his bed.

But their love for each other remained unspoken.

And it maddened Lukien.

Five weeks after Akeela's departure, Lukien had made a decision. He was desperate to be with Cassandra, to spend at least one hour alone with her. That afternoon he was absent from the training grounds, feigning illness. He remained in his chamber in Lionkeep the entire day, hunched over a tiny table with a quill in his hand. Balls of crumpled paper littered the floor, the half-written remains of a dozen terrible love poems. Somehow, he had to reach Cassandra. He had to convince her to see him, and that his love for her was real. But he could find no words, and his stunted poetry frustrated him. He sighed and leaned back, staring out the window. The days were longer now, growing warm. Eventually Akeela would return. Lukien closed his eyes, summoning words that would not come. He was an artist with a sword, but with a pen he was a buffoon, and he feared that any poem, no matter its sincerity, would make a fool of him.

"How do I say it?" he whispered. "How . . . ?"

Unlike Akeela, he had never been a man of letters. He realized suddenly that if he were ever to express his love for Cassandra, it would need to be face to face. So he took up one last sheet of paper and wrote a note instead. And when he was done he folded it carefully, sealing it with wax and placing it in the pocket of his shirt. Then, determined not to waver, he left his rooms in search of Jancis.

Cassandra was in her bathtub when she got Lukien's note.

It had been a long day for the queen, spent listening to the prattle of civil servants and the complaints of kitchen staff. With Akeela gone, she was surprised at how many of his responsibilities had fallen on her shoulders. There were always countless questions to answer and decisions to make, and endless invitations to tea at the chancelleries, where the ministers interrogated her for insight into her husband. Nervous about his costly library and his revisionist views, they were always eager to speak to Cassandra, hoping for some gaffe or juicy bit of gossip to pass her lips. They were always disappointed. Despite her youth and inexperience, Cassandra knew she was loyal to Akeela. At least politically.

She sunk down into the iron tub, burying her chin beneath the warm water, soap bubbles clinging to her breasts and hair. The room was blessedly quiet, for the wing Akeela had prepared for them in Lionkeep was gigantic, and only certain servants were allowed in its halls. If she listened very closely, Cassandra could hear their footfalls in the distance, tapping on the marble floors. It was a very grand home she had now, and she adored it. But mostly, on days like today, she enjoyed the silence. Too tired to dance the way she had in Hes, she spent a good deal of time in her prized bathtub, letting the perfumed oils draw the knots from her muscles. So when she heard Jancis' insistent call, she groaned.

"Cass? Where are you?"

Cassandra considered not answering, but it was too late. Jancis rounded the corner, peeking her head inside the chamber. A peculiar excitement lit her face.

"I'm tired, Jancis," said Cassandra listlessly.

"Oh, you won't be after this," said the girl. She held up a piece of folded paper.

"What's that?"

"A note," said Jancis. "From Lukien."

Cassandra jerked upright, splashing water over the edge. "What?"

"He just gave it to me." Jancis hurried over and knelt down next to the tub. "While I was in the kitchen, helping Beith. He called me aside and handed it to me."

"Just like that? Did anyone see?"

"No," Jancis assured her.

She gave the note to Cassandra, who took it warily. Cassandra's wet hands saturated the paper. She looked at it blankly.

"Open it," pressed Jancis.

"I'm afraid," said Cassandra. "What do you think it says?"

"How should I know? Find out for yourself!"

Jancis hovered over her friend eagerly, waiting for her

to read the note. Cassandra slid her nail under the wax seal, breaking it, then unfolded the paper. On it was Lukien's penmanship, broad and rambling.

"What's it say?" Jancis asked.

Cassandra read in silence.

My Queen,
When the dawn is new, look for me at the southern gate.

It was signed simply, *Your Adoring Servant.*

Confused, Cassandra stared at the paper, biting her lip. "He wants to see me," she said. "In the morning. He wants me to meet him at the southern gate at dawn." Cassandra let the note drop from her hand and fall to the floor. "Jancis, what am I to do?"

"I don't know," said Jancis blankly. "Cassandra, you're ..."

"Married. I know."

It was a miserable prospect, and it made Cassandra sag until her chin was once again in the water. She stared at her knees poking above the bubbles. What was she to do? Lukien had made his move. In a hundred daydreams she had hoped for this moment, and now that it was here she was speechless.

Dawn, she thought blackly. *When no one can see us.*

"What a grand conspiracy I make," she whispered. "What a terrible queen I am."

Lionkeep slept. A gentle fog hung about the keep, shrouding the bricks and grassy fields. Up in the sky, starlight struggled through the haze. Sounds of wildlife heralded the coming morning, the buzz of insects and the songs of birds. Off in the distance, a sentry called all clear.

Lukien rounded the corner of the granary house, quietly approaching the gate. The hooves of his horse, Ghost, clopped on the cobblestones. He wore no armor, just a gray doublet and trousers, and he carried no sword at his belt, for he did not wish to look suspicious or arouse a sentry to alarm. As always, the southern gate was unmanned. A winding avenue led to the main houses, up a hill and out of sight in the fog. Past the gate, the avenue fanned out into a green and rolling field, which also disappeared in the mist. Lukien paused just past the granary, staying to the shadows. It was very near dawn, yet he could hear no one else, just his own nervous breathing. He peered toward the gate and the avenue, waiting for Cassandra to appear. Surely she had received his note. But that didn't mean she would answer his odd request, and her absence worried Lukien. He had taken a dangerous chance in sending his note. The die was cast.

"Come on," he whispered. "Please . . ."

The first rays of sunlight crawled over the keep. Lukien was grateful for the fog. The morning was warm, perfect for spiriting away. But he didn't intend to ride alone. If Cassandra didn't show . . .

He heard footfalls up the avenue, very faint. He cocked his head to listen. Someone was approaching. Carefully he backed Ghost against the wall, enough to still glimpse the gate. Down the hill a figure approached. Small and slight, it moved with grace through the fog, head hidden beneath a shawl. Lukien's heart leapt. It was Cassandra. She looked around furtively, clasping the shawl around her face, her body dressed in a colorless frock. When she reached the open gate, she paused. Her eyes darted nervously about the avenue. Lukien urged his horse out of the shadows. Cassandra noticed him immediately.

"Shhh," he cautioned, putting a finger to his lips. He did not speak again until he was just before her. "My lady, you've come." Unable to control his smile, he beamed. "Thank you."

"Lukien," she sighed. "This is . . ." She shrugged. "Wrong."

"I know, but I had to speak to you. I swear, my lady, I couldn't bear another moment of silence." He glanced around. "This is no place to talk. Here, take my hand."

"No," Cassandra refused. "I can't go with you. Say what you must, but say it here."

"Cassandra . . ."

"I am the queen, Lukien. I am Akeela's wife." Cassandra's eyes betrayed her misery. "Will you make a whore of me?"

The words cut Lukien. He sat up straight, summoning his remaining dignity. "I love you," he declared. "I loved you when I saw you in Hes, and I love you now more than ever. And you love me. I can see it in you."

Cassandra shook her head. "No . . ."

"Yes. It is too plain to hide, my lady. For both of us. Well, I will not hide it from you any longer. I confess it gladly." Lukien looked at her, waiting for a reaction. All he got was an anguished groan.

"Don't make me do this . . ."

Lukien thrust out his hand. "Take it."

"I cannot!"

"I know you've tried to love Akeela."

"I do love him," said Cassandra bitterly.

"Like a brother," said Lukien. "Yes, I know what that's like. That's not what I mean."

She looked up at him, her expression shattered. "If we do this it will kill him. It will, and we will be to blame."

Lukien kept his hand outstretched. He had already considered the pain it would cause his king. "He'll never know," he said softly. "I would die before letting him find out. Come now, before the light comes."

Still Cassandra wouldn't take his hand.

"If you don't come with me, then you'll be saying you don't care about me," said Lukien. "I will tell myself that what I saw in your eyes was an illusion, and I will not come to you again."

A terrible expression overcame Cassandra. She took another look around the grounds, studying the fog for unwanted faces. When she was convinced that no one was about—that not a soul could witness her adulterous act— she took Lukien's hand and let him sweep her onto the back of his stallion.

They rode. Heedless of the mist, they fled the keep and plunged into the gardens of Akeela's estate, leaving the avenue for the rolling hills. Cassandra kept her arms wrapped around Lukien, and she did not speak or utter the smallest sound. She could feel the heat coming off his body, the strength of his shoulders as he pushed his steed further into the green fields. Morning was coming, slowly breaking the haze. Cassandra listened to the sound of horse hooves, bearing her away. Lionkeep and Chancellery Square fell off in the distance, replaced by wildflowers and fruit trees. She felt weightless, bodiless, and as Lukien rode she laid her head against his back, smiling. Ahead of them lay an apple orchard, inviting them into its private folds. Lukien hurried toward it. For Cassandra, the rest of the world dissolved away.

What she was doing was a crime. She knew it and hated herself for it. Now she thought of Akeela, sweetly ignorant and blindly trusting her with Lukien. But he appeared to her as a distant memory, something easily forgotten in Lukien's embrace. More, she *wanted* to forget him. Just today; just for this morning. A giddiness overtook her, and she laughed with delight. The breeze struck her face and suddenly the sun appeared, warm and yellow. In the embrace of the apple trees they were alone. For a moment at least, she could be with Lukien.

"It's so beautiful here," she said in his ear. "Let's stop."

Lukien did as his queen requested, bringing his horse to a halt within the orchard. The cessation of riding heightened the silence of the place. Cassandra heard birds in the trees. She took a breath of the sweet air. It smelled of springtime.

"It's lovely," she said. She slid down from the horse, looking around, and all she could see were green fields lined with apple trees, like soldiers stretching out into the morning. Not another soul stirred amid the orchard.

"No one will see us here," said Lukien as he got down from the horse. He stood before Cassandra. "Don't be afraid, my lady."

"I'm not," said Cassandra. She had never been less afraid in her life. She reached out and took Lukien's hand. "Come," she told him. "We will . . . talk."

Without a word she led him beneath a great apple tree bursting with pink flowers. There she sat herself down on the dewy earth, dragging him down beside her. He yielded to her easily. She saw pain in his eyes.

"Cassandra . . ." His voice was a whisper. "I don't know what to say."

He didn't have to speak a word. Cassandra could read it all in his expression.

"You love me," she said.

He nodded.

"And I you, I fear."

Lukien stroked her face. His touch was warm, like `the coming sun. Cassandra felt the stirrings in her body, dreading them yet following their lead. She lowered her head in offering.

"What are we doing?" she asked. "We will be damned for this."

"No." Lukien leaned in closer. "No one will ever know. Not ever."

"Just this once, then."

He didn't answer. She was glad he didn't. Once, she knew, could never be enough.

Will Trager rode through the field, plagued as always by a black mood. The sweetness of the apple orchard did nothing to soften his expression, for he was possessed this morning of a familiar hatred, one that had dogged him relentlessly since the tournament. He was tired of coming to the orchard in the morning, waking at the crack of dawn to practice in secret. And he was tired of not getting any better, and of losing every joust to his captain. But mostly he was tired of the laughter, still ringing in his ears these many weeks later. The endless chorus of catcalls drove him deeper into the orchard.

He was alone, as he always was when practicing, but had two horses with him: one, the black charger he always rode, the other a smaller beast of burden, laden with the equipment he would need for practicing. The smaller beast held his lance and jousting armor, and the quintain he would ride against. The quintain had a red target painted on a swing arm; when the target was struck, the arm would whip around, catching him in the back if he weren't swift enough. Trager was very swift now, and was almost never tagged by the arm. But he wasn't swift enough. Before the summer ended there would be more tourneys, more chances to best the Bronze Knight. He was determined to be ready.

The sun was barely above the horizon when he came to his usual practice place, a long strip of flat ground between the sentrylike apple trees. He stopped his little caravan, dismounted, then took a look around, confident that no one could see him. He was about to unload his equipment when he heard something echoing through the orchard. Trager froze, sure that he'd been discovered. His first suspicion was Lukien.

"Son of a bitch," he spat. The captain would just love to see him practicing. The jokes would go on forever.

Trager tried to locate the sound. For a moment it disappeared, but then it returned, stronger, more urgent. It didn't sound like a human precisely, more like an animal. A low groan. Trager decided on its direction and took a wary step forward. Sound carried far in the orchard, and the silent morning played tricks on it, making it louder. He stalked through the trees, examining each one, but saw nothing. The sound was louder now, definitely human. Trager recognized the noises of lovemaking. A mischievous grin swam on his face. Very quietly he picked his way toward the unknown lovers, careful to be quiet. He rounded a stand of trees, hid himself behind a stout trunk, and peered with one eye into the distance.

There he saw them, beneath a tree. Two lovers, more naked than clothed, their arms tangled around each other. The man was on top, his face hidden. Beneath him the woman squirmed, letting out the calls that had summoned their unwanted visitor. Trager snickered, putting a hand over his mouth. He didn't recognize the man, but he was sure he was from Lionkeep. A Royal Charger, most likely. He thought about interrupting the couple and disciplining the man right there, but then he reconsidered. What harm was there in getting a leg over a kitchen girl?

He was about to leave when the man tossed his head back. A handsome head, unmistakably blond. A voice pealed from his throat, crying in lust, as recognizable as his pretty face.

"Fate above . . ."

Trager staggered back. It was Lukien, and it was no kitchen girl beneath him. His eyes bulged at the sight of Queen Cassandra, chest thrust out, mouth open in passion. The vision burned itself into Trager's brain. He shook his head in disbelief, but when he looked again the couple was the same.

As fast as he could Trager turned and went to his horse, mounting the beast and dragging its little sibling after them. He rode quickly but quietly, not wanting to be seen or heard. He had a great prize now and didn't want it discovered, not until the perfect moment.

"Oh, Captain," he chirped gleefully. "You've really gotten your hands dirty this time!"

12

When Akeela arrived home, it wasn't in triumph. There were no musicians to greet him, no fanfare of any kind. As always, the streets of Koth were busy with commerce, but were almost oblivious to the return of the king. His royal carriage, flanked by honor guards, rolled into the capital without announcement, having sent only one herald ahead to Lionkeep. Akeela himself reclined in his carriage, alone. It had been an exhausting trip and he was glad to be home. To his great surprise, his goodwill tour had been disastrous. He'd been greeted warmly in Marn and Ganjor, but in Norvor he had been shunned, a reaction that had shocked him. Because he hadn't sent emissaries to Norvor before his arrival, he hadn't known of King Mor's anger over the Reecian treaty, and had borne the brunt of the old ruler's ire. Now, instead of returning to Liiria in celebration, Akeela stole into Koth like a criminal, ashamed to show his face. Tonight he would have to deal with the consequences of his trip. He would have to summon a meeting of his chancellors and explain what King Mor had told him—that there might be war between their countries.

"Stupid," he chided himself, closing his eyes against a burgeoning headache. "Too fast . . ."

He had done everything too fast, and his eagerness had made an unwanted enemy. Norvor had always sided with Liiria in the arguments with Reec, sure that their own claim to the river Kryss would be honored in any eventual deal.

But Akeela had been too anxious for peace with Reec, and had barely considered Norvor in his plans.

And now they threaten war, he thought miserably. *What a fool I am.*

He opened his eyes to look at the city. In the distance he saw the foundation of his library, slowly rising from its hillside. Akeela sighed, wondering if his cathedral would ever be built. Seeing its foundation reminded him of himself— incomplete, even rash. It was a trait he was only now starting to recognize, but he was sure Baron Glass would remind him of it. He dreaded seeing Glass, almost as much as he savored seeing Cassandra. Weeks of traveling had withered Akeela's good mood, making him hungry for companionship. He imagined the smell of Cassandra's dark hair. Tonight, after his council, he would take her to bed.

She makes a man of me, he thought.

That evening, Akeela supped with Cassandra alone, telling her what had happened during his tour. She listened distractedly, hardly touching her food. Akeela commented on her lack of appetite, but the queen laughed off his concern. Still, she seemed preoccupied, and was unconvincing when she simply told Akeela she was glad to see him. Akeela didn't mind her awkwardness. He was with her again and he was glad, and he used the quiet supper to prepare himself for his meeting with the chancellors, who were presently gathering in the council chamber. According to Warden Graig, Baron Glass had already arrived, and was anxiously awaiting Akeela's presence. But Akeela didn't rush his meal. He explained almost everything to Cassandra, including the dangers of a war with Norvor. His new queen merely nodded.

"You will deal with it," she assured him. Her face was hidden behind her wine glass. The room was very quiet.

"You are my good luck charm, Cassandra," Akeela told her, reaching across the chamber to take her hand.

"No," said Cassandra. "You don't need me."

"If you were with me in Norvor you would have charmed that arrogant ass, Mor. No man can resist you, Cassandra."

Cassandra's eyes widened. "What?"

"You're a jewel, that's all," said Akeela. He got up from the table. "But now I must go. I can't keep Glass and the others waiting too long. I'm sure they're anxious to crucify me." He bent down and kissed his wife's forehead. There was a chill on her skin. "Good night, my love. Don't wait up for me. This meeting will take some time."

He made to leave, but Cassandra stopped him.

"Akeela . . ."

"Yes?"

She hesitated, then said, "I'm glad you're home."

To Akeela, the words were like music. "We've been apart too long, I know," he replied. "But now I'm back, and I won't be going away again."

A peculiar expression flashed in Cassandra's eyes. "No," she whispered. "Well, off with you. And don't be afraid of Glass."

"Afraid?" said Akeela. "Cassandra, I'm not afraid of him."

"All right," said Cassandra. "Good luck, then."

When Akeela had gone Cassandra waited in their chambers for a very long time. The servants cleared away the remnants of their meal as she watched them, politely questioning her about her uneaten food, a very fine pheasant one of the keep's huntsmen had snared. Cassandra did not answer the question, instead smiling and asking the woman to find Jancis.

"Have her come to my reading room," said Cassandra, then drifted out of the chamber.

In the reading room was a large window cut into the turret, ornately fabricated with panes of stained glass that painted patterns on the opposite wall when the sun was strong. Tonight, however, moonlight put on the show. Cassandra sank down into a plush velvet chair and watched the pale beams as she waited for Jancis. Seeing Akeela again had increased her guilt a thousandfold, and she could barely lift her head or even think of herself without the deepest self-loathing. Such a good man, with so much on his shoulders. Yet she had betrayed him easily, and continued to do so almost every night, stealing ecstatic moments with Lukien without the slightest regard for her husband. What kind of monster had Akeela married? She had no answer to that question, and she cursed herself. She had always thought of herself as clever.

But it's dreadful to be clever, she thought. It was like a revelation suddenly, as clear as any of the moonbeams. To be clever was to be a bitch, or a betrayer like Lukien. Akeela wasn't clever. He was moral, and moral men were never clever. It was why they were better than everyone else, and why Akeela was a better man then Lukien. Even Lukien knew it, and the truth of it tormented him.

Yet despite the torment they hadn't stopped. Now Cassandra feared nothing could ever stop them, or save her soul from her own crimes.

It took long minutes for Jancis to arrive. When she did she found Cassandra staring pensively into the stained glass, out toward the muted city beyond. A tear was rolling down Cassandra's face, but she didn't bother wiping it away. She wanted Jancis to see how truly bad she felt.

"I'm not a monster, Jan," she whispered without turning around. "I'm just . . . trapped."

Jancis came closer and placed a hand on Cassandra's shoulder. To Cassandra's great relief there were no chiding words this time, only mildness. Cassandra thought she would sob.

"You should have seen him," she went on. "He has so much to deal with, maybe even war, yet he brightens like a firefly when he sees me."

"He's a good man," said Jancis.

"Better than I deserve."

Unable to face her friend, Cassandra waited for the counsel she knew would come. Jancis kept her hand on the young queen's shoulder, until the gentleness of the touch grew firm.

"You have to stop, you and Lukien both," she said. "Akeela's home now. It's time to give yourself to him, and no one else."

Cassandra shook her head. "I can't."

"Cassandra, you must." Jancis went around the chair to face her. "Enough, now. The two of you have enjoyed yourself, but it has to end, right now. Tonight."

There was no way for Cassandra to explain it, so she didn't try. How could one explain love? Everything Jancis said was true, but love like this didn't yield to logic. It was beyond the sensible. It was like lunacy.

"I don't want to end it, Jancis," said Cassandra. "I'm not strong enough."

And as she spoke, the tear trailing down her face fell at last into her lap.

There was a strange quiet to the castle as Akeela made his way through the halls. His council chamber was on the other end of the keep, near the main gate and easily accessible to travelers. Unlike his father, who always held council in his throne room, Akeela shunned the throne as just another trapping of authority. He preferred to deal with his chancellors as equals, even if they really weren't. He was king by blood-right, had authority over all the ministers in Chancellery Square, but that didn't mean he would abuse his station—not even against men like Glass.

Akeela was halfway to the council chamber when he saw Trager. The lieutenant was leaning against a wall, alone, his arms folded over his chest. The torchlight revealed an odd expression on his sharp face. Akeela slowed but Trager noticed him, coming quickly to attention.

"My lord," he said with a slight bow. "Welcome home."

"Thank you. Shouldn't you be in the council chamber with the others?"

"Yes, my lord, but actually I wanted to speak to you first." Trager looked around, his voice dipping to a whisper. "It's important."

"I have business with the chancellors, Will. I really can't dally."

"I know, my lord, but this will interest you," Trager insisted. He continued blocking Akeela's path. "I have news for you."

"Can't it wait? Really, you should be going through Lukien with news. This is improper."

Trager's eyes seemed to laugh. "Improper, hmm . . ." He thought for a moment. "No, I think I'd better tell you this directly, my lord."

"Very well," Akeela relented. "After the meeting, then. Now, do you mind?" He shooed Trager out of his way. "Is Lukien already there?"

"Yes," replied Trager, following after him. "So is Baron Glass and Chancellor Hogon."

"And Nils? I sent for him as well."

"He's there with D'marak," said Trager.

Akeela nodded, bracing himself. Nils was a reasonable

man, and he would need his goodwill against Glass and Hogon. Hogon was also a reasonable man, but he had a temper and was an old ally of Baron Glass. The two had soldiered together, and almost always took the same side in arguments. As Chancellor of War, it was Hogon's responsibility to oversee the Liirian military, including the Royal Chargers. Akeela was suddenly glad he'd invited Lukien to the meeting. They would listen to Lukien, he knew. It was valuable just having the Bronze Knight by his side.

Trager followed Akeela like a dutiful dog, pulling ahead of him only when the reached the council chamber. The door to the chamber was already open. Akeela could smell Glass' pipe. Muted voices issued over the threshold. Trager entered first, announcing the king.

"King Akeela," he said simply.

The men all rose from around the oval table, all except for Baron Glass, who was already standing, pacing around the room. The baron stopped and turned to Akeela, neither a smile nor a scowl on his face. Determined not to be intimidated, Akeela hardened his expression. The chancellors and their underlings all bowed in greeting, welcoming him home. Akeela shook outstretched hands as he made his way to the opposite end of the chamber, where a chair awaited him, slightly larger than the rest. The air was already stale from overcrowding and the obnoxious smoke from Baron Glass' pipe filling the room. Glass was the last to greet Akeela. He did not put out his hand as the others had, but merely nodded deferentially. Lukien, however, greeted his king with a warm embrace.

"Akeela," he said, kissing both his cheeks. "It's good to see you. Welcome home."

Akeela smiled, loving the attention. "Lukien, I missed you." He patted the man's back then whispered, "Thank you for coming."

As always, the Bronze Knight had a chair at Akeela's right side. He dropped into it just as Akeela sat down. The chancellors and ministers did the same. And just as he was first to stand, Baron Glass was last to take his seat, doing so noisily only when all the others were seated. As expected, Glass sat next to Hogon. The War Chancellor's expression was anxious, as if he'd already heard Akeela's news. Nils and D'Marak sat at the far end of the table, both dressed in their usual drab robes, while Chancellor Sark sat apart from the others, surrounded by three silent ministers of the Treasury. Trager, along with Breck and Lukien, sat near Akeela. The closeness of the chamber made the young king queasy. Servants had set the table with pitchers and goblets. Akeela took a long drink before beginning.

"Thank you for the welcome," he said finally. "I know it was short notice, and I appreciate you coming to see me. I have news of my trip, you see, and I thought you should all hear it at once."

"Bad news, no doubt," said Baron Glass. "Or you would have waited until tomorrow."

Akeela stiffened. "I'm afraid you're right. My news is dire. My goodwill tour wasn't all that I'd hoped it would be. It caused some . . . trouble."

Chancellor Hogon leaned forward. "What kind of trouble, my lord?" His watery eyes filled with concern.

"Norvor," said Akeela. "King Mor took some offense at my peace initiative with Reec. He thinks the Kryss belongs to Norvor as well as Reec, and he wasn't happy about us giving control of our side to the Reecians."

"Wasn't happy?" said Glass. "You mean he was angry, don't you?"

Akeela nodded. "That's right."

"How angry?" asked Hogon.

"Angry enough to threaten war," replied Akeela.

"I knew it!" erupted Glass. He slammed a fist down on the table. "King Akeela, didn't I tell you? Didn't I warn you not to go so quickly?"

"I'm not a little boy," hissed Akeela. "Yes, you did warn me. And I'm not a damn bit sorry about the Reecian peace. Are you?"

Smouldering, Glass looked down at his wine goblet, refusing to answer.

"Now listen," said Akeela, "I don't want to argue. I called this meeting because you have to know of Mor's threat. He told me that he won't let our peace bargain with Reec stand, that he plans on taking the Kryss back from Reec, with or without our help."

"Did he threaten Liiria?" Hogon asked.

Akeela hesitated. So far, he hadn't told this part to anyone, not even Cassandra. "Yes," he admitted. "He said that he'd be stationing troops on the Norvor side of the river, and that if we tried to cross or help the Reecians maintain the river, he would attack us."

"That snake," sneered Hogon. "How dare he speak to you like that. You're the King of Liiria!"

"And he's the King of Norvor," Akeela countered. "To be honest, I don't think my title impressed him. I expected to be greeted like a friend, not like a ruler. Instead I got a cold, stiff breeze." The memory hardened Akeela. "Well, it won't stand. We can't let Norvor move against Reec, and we can't have our treaty threatened, or our rights to use the Kryss."

Baron Glass shook his head, muttering, "I told you."

"We have to plan, Baron Glass," Akeela insisted.

Glass looked up at him. "You are willful, King Akeela."

The insult stunned Akeela. Lukien rose to Akeela's defense.

"Baron Glass, forgive me, but you're out of order," he said. "Remember—you're talking to your king."

"No, Lukien," said Akeela. "Let him speak his mind. Go on, Baron. Get the poison out of your blood."

"Very well." Glass sat up straight. "I warned you against the Reecian peace, King Akeela. I told you that you were going too quickly, and that you should at least tell King Mor of your plans. But you didn't listen to me. Then I warned you against going on this goodwill tour, and again you refused my counsel." He tried to smile, but it came out crooked. "You think of me as a bitter old man. You think I resent you for having the throne at so young an age . . ."

"I don't," Akeela protested.

"You do. But I don't resent you, my lord. You're my king, and I serve you the best I can. But you won't listen to any of us. You always do what you want, and I think that serves you poorly." Baron Glass looked around at the other councilors. "We are not bitter old men, my lord. We are experienced, and we should be heeded. Your father listened to us."

Akeela sat back in his chair, feeling insufferably small. The invocation of his father shattered the defensive wall he'd erected, and he suddenly felt naked, exposed and

weakened by these men who pledged to serve him. He did
not appreciate the baron's honesty.

"All right," sighed Akeela. "You've had your say, Baron.
Now, give me your counsel. We have to deal with King
Mor. What do you suggest?"

"It's obvious," said Glass. "He's planning to mass troops
across the Kryss? Then we must do the same. We must
match his force, show him we cannot be intimidated."

Akeela's expression soured. He glanced at Lukien, but
the knight's face was unreadable.

"Chancellor Hogon?" he asked. "Do you agree with
Baron Glass?"

The old man frowned. "If what you say is true, my lord,
then Mor is not to be trusted. Given cause, he will move
against the river. Will you give him cause?"

"He wants the treaty with Reec rescinded," said Akeela
bleakly. "And that's something I will never do."

"Then he will have his cause," said Hogon. "I agree with
Baron Glass. We must act."

"But I don't want to provoke a war," said Akeela.

"You already have," said Glass sharply. "Face it, King
Akeela. And if I may say so, I think it's time to halt construction of your library. It's too expensive. We can't afford
to bleed our treasury with war on the cusp."

"The library?" Akeela was aghast. "Oh, no. That's out
of the question."

"Please, King Akeela," Glass implored. "War may be
coming. Don't continue with this folly—"

"It isn't folly!" sneered Akeela. He felt Lukien's hidden
hand on his leg, coaxing him down, but he stood up anyway. "I won't let you use this trouble with Norvor as an
excuse to stop the library. The monies have already been
allocated. Isn't that right, Sark?"

Chancellor Sark, who had been listening with varied interest, now froze under the king's glare. "My lord?"

"The money for the library, man," said Akeela. "It's all
been allocated, right?"

Sark grimaced. "Well, yes and no."

"What does that mean?"

"Akeela, be easy," whispered Lukien. Akeela ignored
him.

"Chancellor, does the Treasury have the money or not?"

"Not if war comes, my lord, no," said Sark. "I'm sorry, but your library is very expensive."

Glass smiled. "And so is paying for a war. King Akeela, I beg you to listen to reason."

But Akeela couldn't listen. All around him were enemies.

"We will build the library," he declared. "And we will not provoke a war with Mor. I didn't make peace with Reec just so we can battle Norvor."

"So?" pressed Glass. "What's your plan, then?"

"We wait," said Akeela. "Mor may be bluffing, and I don't want bloodshed if it can be avoided."

Baron Glass sighed with disgust. "You're just protecting your library."

"No," Akeela shot back. "I'm trying to protect lives. Apparently that means nothing to war-mongers like you, Baron."

Rising from his seat, Glass said, "That is a terrible thing to say to me, King Akeela."

"If you're standing for an apology you'll have a long wait," said Akeela. "Sit down, Baron. You're making a fool of yourself."

Glass' eyes shifted around the room, now engulfed in charged silence. Chancellor Hogon reached out and grabbed Glass' sleeve, gently drawing him back into his chair. It was not going at all as Akeela had hoped, but suddenly he didn't care any more. He was king, and he demanded respect.

"Now listen to me, all of you," he said. "We're not going to match Mor's troop movements, and we're not going to break the treaty with Reec." His eyes widened dramatically. "And we're absolutely not going to stop building my library. Do you understand?"

The chancellors and their underlings gave non-committal nods—all except for Glass.

"And what of Norvor?" asked the baron. "Will you just ignore them?"

"I will deal with Norvor if and when the time comes." Akeela pushed back his chair and started out of the council chamber. "That is all."

Out in the fresh air of the hall, Akeela caught his breath. His hands were shaking and his mouth was dry and he could hear the disparate voices of the chancellors still in the chamber. Akeela licked his lips, suffocated with panic. He stalked off without thinking, not waiting for Lukien or the others. Lukien caught up to him within a few strides.

"Akeela," he called. "Are you all right?"

Akeela paused, his head swimming. "They oppose me, Lukien. Everything I do, they question!"

"They're just concerned," Lukien said. He smiled warmly. "We all are."

Akeela returned his comrade's grin. Good Lukien, the only one Akeela knew he could trust. He put a hand on the knight's shoulder. "It's wonderful to see you," he said. "The only friendly face in this whole damn city."

By the next morning, Akeela's temper had quieted. He had spent the night with Cassandra and had breakfasted with Graig, going over small matters that required his attention. Since they were easily dealt with, Akeela felt accomplished after the meal. He was refreshed from a good night's sleep and his anger at Baron Glass had subsided, at least temporarily. Because he had been gone from Lionkeep so long, he decided to visit with Beith and see how her new baby was faring. Little Gilwyn was now almost three months old, and Akeela had heard from Gwena that he was growing well, showing no signs of the mind damage they all had feared. His hand and foot were still clubbed, but according to Gwena he was a happy child, and that pleased Akeela.

Beith's room was in the servants' area, so Akeela left Graig after breakfast and headed for her chambers. But he hadn't gone far before he saw Trager, patiently waiting for him at the end of the hall. Suddenly he remembered his promise to the lieutenant, one that he'd forgotten in yesterday's rage. Trager smiled at him from across the hall. Like yesterday, the hall was empty. Akeela realized with discomfort that Trager had planned it that way.

"Will, I'm sorry," he offered. "I forgot you wanted to speak to me."

"No matter, my lord, it could keep until today." Trager glanced around. "Is there somewhere we can talk in private?"

"Private?" asked Akeela. "Is it so important?"

"Oh, it is," Trager assured him. "I'm sorry to say so, but I think it will trouble you."

"Why am I not surprised? Very well; we can talk in my study."

Akeela led Trager in the opposite direction of Beith's rooms, promising himself he'd check on her and the baby later. Trager's expression was earnest enough to worry Akeela. The lieutenant said nothing as they walked through the halls, but he scanned every face they passed, apparently worried about being seen. Finally, when they reached Akeela's small study, Trager spoke.

"Thank you for seeing me, Akeela," he said as he entered the room.

Akeela bristled the way he always did when Trager addressed him in the familiar. They went back a long way, but they had never really been friends. Akeela wondered if Trager considered him one now. Or was he trying to become a friend?

"It's all right," he said. He directed Trager to a well-worn leather chair. "Sit down."

"Thank you." Trager took the chair and sighed. He shook his head as if not knowing where to begin. Akeela sat down on the edge of his desk, facing Trager. There was something insincere about the man's expression.

"You're troubled?" Akeela asked.

Trager nodded. "My news is heavy."

"Tell me," Akeela insisted.

"It's about . . . the queen."

"Cassandra?" Akeela stood up. "What about her?"

"My lord, it pains me to tell you this . . ."

"Tell me!"

"She has been . . ." Trager grimaced. ". . . unfaithful to you."

It was as if Akeela hadn't heard the word. It hung in the air, out of reach and understanding.

"What?"

Trager looked heartbroken. "I'm sorry, Akeela, but it's true. While you were gone she was with another man. I saw them."

"That's impossible!" Akeela cried. "She wouldn't dare betray me like that. Tell me what you saw!"

"It was in the apple orchard, not even a week ago," said Trager. "It was very early and I was in the orchard, practicing my jousting. That's when I saw her." He looked away. "With her paramour."

"What paramour?" asked Akeela. "Did you see him?"

"Yes," said Trager. "Akeela, it was Lukien."

The name fell on Akeela like a hammer. He staggered back against his desk, strangled with disbelief.

"No," he said desperately. "No, I don't believe it. You lie!"

"I saw them, Akeela. They were making love right before my eyes."

Akeela shot forward and grabbed Trager's lapels, pulling him from the chair. "How dare you speak of Lukien like that. And the queen!"

"It's the truth!" Trager spat. "Akeela, I swear it . . ."

"Do not address me in the familiar, you rat! I am your king!"

"Forgive me," cried Trager. He took Akeela's hands, prying them from his clothes. "But you had to know the truth."

Akeela shook his head wildly. "It's not the truth. You've always hated Lukien. You'd do anything to ruin him!" He released Trager, shoving him backward. Trager fell over his chair and sprawled onto the floor. Akeela stalked after him. "I won't believe your lies. And don't you ever speak them again. If you do, I'll kill you."

Trager's eyes were wide. "It's the truth," he insisted. "I swear, I saw them!"

Enraged, Akeela kicked the writhing man. "Quiet!"

"Stop!" Trager pleaded. He crawled away, clutching at the chair for support as he struggled to get upright. "King Akeela—my lord—listen to me!"

"Your lies sicken me," said Akeela. "Now get out of here. And don't you ever speak such filth again. If I hear the smallest rumor about Cassandra, you'll hang for it, I promise."

Trager paused halfway to the door, his eyes fixed on Akeela. "You're mad," he hissed. "Truly mad."

Akeela grabbed a book from his desk and flung it at Trager. *"Out!"*

Trager left, slamming the door after him. Akeela fell

against his desk, nearly collapsing. He felt sick suddenly, about to retch, but he swallowed it down and caught his breath. His heartbeat exploded in his temples, and all around him the room seemed to swim with color, until he could no longer stand. Clumsily he reached for the chair Trager had toppled and sat down. Everything was happening too fast—the battles with Glass, the coming war with Norvor, everything. And now this horrible accusation. Akeela closed his eyes, fearing he might weep. Trager's charges were . . .

What? Unbelievable? Akeela had acted as if it were impossible, but inside something needled him. His little voice was speaking again. Cassandra and Lukien had been remarkably civil to each other since coming to Koth. More than civil, really. Akeela hated to admit it, but part of him believed Trager's tale.

"Cassandra . . . why?"

If there was an answer, Akeela didn't know it. He felt remarkably alone.

"I'll not hide from the truth," he whispered. "Cassandra, I'll find out if you've been unfaithful. And Lukien, if you've betrayed me . . ."

A rage like he'd never felt before rose up within him, making his heart pound and his temples quiver. He would not be made a fool of by Lukien or Cassandra or anyone, no matter how much he loved them. Akeela knew he had to discover the truth.

Somehow.

13

Just as Cassandra had predicted, she did not stop seeing
Lukien. He was everywhere in Lionkeep, and on everybody's lips, and because he was her champion he was impossible to ignore, accompanying her to every royal
function, constantly by her side.

It was much the same with Akeela too, for Lukien had
sway with the nobles of Koth and was useful to Akeela,
who had need for influence in the House of Dukes now
that Norvor was threatening. Cassandra attributed Akeela's
recent mood changes to the trouble with King Mor, because
her husband had been distant and quiet since his return,
and had never once asked her back to his bed. Truly, that
was a relief for Cassandra, who now thought constantly of
Lukien and his fiery touch, and who hated to compare
Akeela's sober lovemaking to that of her bronze champion.
She stole every moment possible that she could with Lukien, though they were seldom alone, and when no one
was looking she let him kiss her or whisper poetry in her
ear, rhymes so bad that she had to fight against giggles.
Since her first time with the Bronze Knight, Cassandra had
discovered the remarkable lover within him, generous and
patient, and skilled in bringing the woman out of her
young, inexperienced body. What had started as a curious
infatuation was now an inferno of love, and though she
knew she risked everything by being with him, Cassandra

could not stop herself. Or would not stop herself. She still didn't know which was the truth.

But there was always the guilt. No matter how much love or pleasure she felt, remorse was her ever-present companion, and she lived in constant fear of being discovered. She did not fear for herself, though; she knew the weight of her crimes and accepted it. And she did not fear for Lukien, either, confident he could weather any disgrace. Rather she feared for Akeela, and what the discovery of her indiscretion would do to his fragile confidence. The world saw Akeela as good and kind, but they did not see the softness that made him so generous, and Cassandra knew how easily he could be broken.

One night not long after Akeela's return, Cassandra told herself she'd had enough. She had traveled to Merloja on a goodwill tour of her own, a Liirian city not far from Koth. There was a duke there named Jaran who was very influential with some in the chancelleries. Jaran had been an old friend of Akeela's father and as such was sympathetic to the new king's predicament with Norvor. Jaran also respected Lukien. So Cassandra tried to do Akeela some good and had gone to Merloja willingly. With her went Lukien and a host of Royal Chargers, as well as the ever-present Jancis. At Jaran's castle they had gotten a warm welcome and the duke's assurances that he would side with Akeela, no matter what the young king's choice was. But Jaran had warned Cassandra that his voice had little weight with Baron Glass, and that in the end Akeela would have no choice—war with Norvor seemed imminent. It was, Jaran said, just a matter of time.

Cassandra stayed in Duke Jaran's castle for three days. She was grateful for his hospitality, and dreaded returning to Koth to tell her husband of Jaran's dire prediction. Akeela was hardly a political strong man, and she doubted his ability to prosecute a war. Worse, she felt more guilty than ever over her infidelity, for she knew the weight of things was crushing Akeela, and he needed her loyalty more than ever.

Yet on the road back she found herself alone with Lukien, in his arms once again. A hard rain had come from nowhere, forcing them off the road and into a small village.

Though the villagers were overjoyed to see their queen, they had little to offer but basic food and shelter, and put Cassandra and her entourage up where they could, splitting up the force between a dozen different households. Cassandra found herself that night in the grandest house in the village, situated on a hill overlooking farmland. The home was owned by a wealthy merchant and landowner whose children had moved out years earlier and who eagerly offered his extra chambers to the queen and her handmaid. Unable to leave Cassandra alone, Lukien had chosen to sleep on the floor outside Cassandra's room. When the night was thick and the old merchant lost to sleep, he had come to her. With only a disgruntled look from Jancis he slipped into Cassandra's chamber and found her there, waiting for him. She had been unable to keep her brief promise to herself, for the longing to be with him overwhelmed her. As lightning flashed outside their window, they came together, clasps of thunder drowning the sounds of their lovemaking.

And when it was over and they both lay in the other's arms, exhausted, Cassandra asked Lukien about war with Norvor. The question startled the knight, who laughed.

"Cassandra, am I such a poor lover that you think of politics when we're together?"

"No," she said with a smile. The thunder over the village made the shutters rattle, but she felt remarkably safe in Lukien's arms. "I can't help thinking about what Duke Jaran said, though. And I don't know what Akeela's planning, either. He won't talk to me about it."

Hearing the king's name made Lukien shift. "He's got a great deal to consider, Cassandra. There are a lot of people watching him, waiting for him to make a mistake."

"But if war comes you will be there for him, won't you?" asked Cassandra. "If he can't avoid it, will you protect him?"

"I should be offended by that question but I'm not," said Lukien with a yawn. "You know I'd never let anything happen to him."

For a moment Cassandra didn't answer. Lukien stopped yawning and stared.

"Cassandra? You do know that, don't you?"

It was hard for Cassandra to nod. "Yes. I know that you'll protect him."

"I've always protected him," Lukien reminded her. "That's been my duty from the time King Balak took me in. I won't abandon that duty, not even now. And for you to think so hurts me."

"No," said Cassandra, rushing out a hand to stroke his face. "I know you love him. I know you'll make sure nothing happens to him."

It was a horrible thing to say as they lay together naked. They had already harmed Akeela more than any Norvan sword could. Lukien was quiet for a long moment, turning away from Cassandra to stare out the dark window. When at last he spoke his voice was shallow and hard to hear over the thunder.

"I have spent my life looking after Akeela," he said. "And he adores me for it. I know how he admires me, I can see it in him. Sometimes it's hard to bear. Sometimes . . ."

His words trailed off. Then he put his head back on the pillow and closed his eyes. "Let me sleep now, just for a little while."

Cassandra stared at Lukien as he drifted off to sleep. She would have to wake him soon, she knew, but she loved looking at him in the darkness, the way the lightning flashed off his blond hair. In that moment she knew there would never be peace for her. She could make a hundred pledges to herself, promise never to be with him again, but her will would always buckle in the end. Such was the terrible power of this love.

Less than a week after Cassandra had returned home, word reached Akeela of Norvor's troop movements. At first there were merely rumors—fearful, insubstantial whisperings from the border. Traders from southern caravans told of unusual activity along the River Kryss and near Hanging Man, the formidable tower of rock Norvor had long ago turned into a fortress. It was said that King Mor had stationed an unusual number of soldiers on the borders with Liiria and Reec, and that earthworks were being built which could be seen on the Liirian side of the river. Like all rumors, the first ones started slowly, but within a week all of Liiria was buzzing with the news. By the end of another week, Akeela's own scouts confirmed the worst of them. Along with the earthworks, barracks and other structures for the support of many troops were being erected. King Mor's own banner, an ugly flag featuring a two-headed hawk, was flying nearer the borders of Liiria and Reec than ever before. But worst by far was the cessation of shipping. Liirian and Reecian trading ships were being refused passage down the river, which was now blockaded by Norvan barges. Two ships, both Reecian, had already been boarded. Their cargo seized and their ships scuttled, the crews of the vessels had been sent back to Reec with one dismal message—the Kryss belonged to Norvor.

With the threat of war hanging over Liiria, the city of Koth was transformed. The good mood that had endured since the treaty with Reec evaporated, leaving the capital under a pall. Chancellery Square became the center of debates, and the House of Dukes rang with calls for action. Led by Baron Thorin Glass, the chancellors were nearly unanimous in their desire for war, and each day saw new declarations sent to Lionkeep for Akeela to sign, directing the Chancellery of War to make battle plans. Even King Karis, Cassandra's father, had hurried emissaries to Koth, begging Akeela for action. Karis wanted reassurances. He wanted to know what the young King of Liiria would do if Norvor crossed into Reec. But Akeela could not answer him. He simply didn't have answers.

The last two weeks had passed in a haze for Akeela. Still reeling from Trager's stunning accusations, he had shut himself away in his study, depressed and drinking more than he should, rarely eating or seeing anyone. Unable to face his wife, he had feigned business as the reason for avoiding their bed. And Cassandra had not seemed to mind, because she herself was ill these days, losing weight and color to some ailment of the stomach she refused to discuss. Akeela still loved Cassandra and he added her ill-health to the pile of worries crushing him. He had no proof of her infidelity, but he suspected Trager had told the truth. Cassandra adored Lukien. If he hadn't been so blind with love for both of them, he would have seen it sooner. Surprisingly, he held Cassandra little umbrage. Lukien was as beautiful as she was herself. No woman could resist him—

or ever had—and the power of his allure had simply overwhelmed her, the way it had countless girls in Lionkeep over the years.

And Lukien? Akeela still didn't know how he felt about his old companion. Brothers always fought, and they were no exception. It had been a hard relationship sometimes, but Akeela had always felt Lukien's love. It assured him. When he was around Lukien he felt taller than his normal stature. He needed Lukien, and he always had. And because Lukien fed that need willingly, Akeela had always loved the Bronze Knight, no matter how differently they viewed the world.

Yet now there was something like hatred blooming inside Akeela, something ugly. He felt betrayed, as though an unforgivable wrong had been done him. The only thing saving his feelings for Lukien was a lack of surety. Despite the feelings in his gut, Akeela had only Trager's word as proof.

"Not enough," Akeela muttered. He was alone, as he always was these days, finally leaving the confines of Lionkeep for the open spaces of his unbuilt library. It was a gray day, matching his mood. Raindrops fell periodically from the sky, dampening his hair and face. Since news had come of Norvor's actions, work on his Cathedral of Knowledge had slowed to a crawl, and the rain had conspired to stop the rest. There were no workers on site today, not even Figgis, who was overseeing much of the library's construction. In the distance, Koth looked like a hobbled giant. She needed a king, Akeela knew, someone to lead her boldly into the future, someone who could take on Mor and his arrogance and silence the protests from the chancellor. She needed a decision maker, the king that Akeela had been once, however briefly. Where was that young man now, he wondered?

"Gone?" Akeela asked himself. Beneath his feet stone dust crackled as he walked aimlessly through the foundations of his dream.

No, not gone, he decided. Just confused and betrayed. But he would be back. And when he returned he would show the world he was not to be trifled with, that he could be as much a hero as Lukien or Baron Glass had ever been.

"Akeela the Good," said Akeela. The sobriquet made

him smile. He was still good. The people still loved him.
Everything he did was for them and they knew it, and that's
why they weren't joining in Glass' violent chorus. They
were waiting for their king to speak.

Akeela went to the center of the foundation, where a
particularly large rock stood out from the rest. Akeela had
seen Figgis sitting on the rock countless times as he con-
sulted his plans and directed the workmen. Akeela ran his
hand over the smooth stone, pushing off little puddles of
water before sitting down. He looked around, studying
Koth, wondering what to do. He didn't want war. More
than anything, his was to be a reign of peace. But he
seethed at King Mor's actions, and hated the old ruler for
ruining his peace. Mor was a very arrogant man. Akeela's
own father had complained about him more than once.
Now he was testing the son.

"Yes," said Akeela, agreeing with his own theory. "He's
testing me." He scowled. "They all are."

King Mor, Baron Glass, Chancellor Hogon; they were all
part of the same conspiracy, eager to tear down what little
he had built. They wanted power for themselves and nothing more, but Akeela would not let them succeed. He
glanced around the construction site, knowing in his heart
that his library would be built.

Somehow.

He heard a sound at his back. Turning, he noticed a lone
horseman riding through the drizzle. The Bronze Knight
wore a golden cape and a concerned expression. His eyes
narrowed, focusing on Akeela as he brought his horse to a
stop just outside the foundation's stone border.

"May I come ahead?" he asked.

Akeela thought for a moment. He wanted to be alone.

"Yes, if you must."

Lukien dropped down from his horse. He drew his cape
about his shoulders. Looking into the sky, he said, "It's a
bad day for daydreaming out here, Akeela. Why don't you
come back to Lionkeep with me? We'll have something hot
to drink."

"Not yet."

From the corner of his eye Akeela saw Lukien frown.
"You're brooding," said the knight. "What's preoccupying
you so?"

"I have things on my mind," said Akeela. Finally he looked at Lukien. "Why did you come? To check up on me?"

"Yes, and to give you some news. The House of Dukes has sent another declaration to Lionkeep, Akeela. Baron Glass has brought it himself. He's waiting for you back at the castle."

Akeela's already sour mood curdled. It was the fourth declaration of war the House of Dukes had authored, and each one had the signatures of more Liirian lords than the one before. Eventually, Akeela knew, he would not be able to ignore them.

"Baron Glass is insisting on an answer," Lukien went on. "I think you should at least see him."

"I have nothing to say to him yet. That's why I'm here, thinking."

Lukien came closer, sitting down on the rock next to Akeela. He had a gentle smile on his face. "What will you do? Sit here in the rain all day?"

"If it will help, yes."

"You're being very cross. Please don't take your anger with Glass out on me. I have nothing to do with it."

Akeela bit his lip. The innocence on Lukien's face told him Trager might actually have lied.

"I have a lot to deal with right now, that's all," he offered. "This business with Norvor is plaguing me. I think we have no choice but to mobilize troops."

Lukien nodded. "Agreed. Then you can talk to Mor about it, maybe get things settled. Once he sees that you're serious, he'll be in the mood to bargain."

"Bargain? Oh, no. That's not what I have in mind at all."

The knight blinked. "No?"

"Mor has insulted me, Lukien. He's threatening my peace with Reec. I won't let him ruin all my work, or make a fool of me."

"So what will you do?" asked Lukien.

Akeela looked away. For the first time in his life, he didn't want to tell Lukien his plans. He let his eyes linger on the library site, and a thin smile came to his face.

"It will be very grand when it's done," he said. "You'll see, Lukien. So will Cassandra and Baron Glass and everyone else. This library will be something special."

Lukien studied their bleak surroundings. "It doesn't look like much now, though, does it?"

"Not yet, maybe. But soon."

"Akeela, I've been thinking . . ." Lukien leaned back on the rock. "Maybe Glass is right about the library. Maybe you should stop pouring money into it."

Akeela raised his eyebrows. "What?"

"Until this business with Norvor is over, I mean."

"No, Lukien," snapped Akeela, getting to his feet. "Glass is not right. Not about the library, not about anything."

Lukien put up his hands. "I'm just making a suggestion, that's all."

"This library is going to be built. Damn Norvor, and damn Baron Glass." Akeela pointed a finger in Lukien's face. "And damn you, too."

"What?" Lukien leapt to his feet, swatting Akeela's finger away. "I'm not one of your little serving wenches, Akeela. Don't you ever say that to me again. I'm on your side, remember."

Akeela scoffed. "Are you?"

The knight's expression tightened. "Yes. Why don't you know that any more? Why don't you trust me?"

Seeing himself in a losing argument, Akeela shook his head and sighed. "All right. I shouldn't have said that to you." He sat back down on the rock. "I have too much to deal with, I guess. It's maddening me."

The explanation appeased Lukien, who nodded. "I know you're worried about Cassandra, too. How is she?"

Akeela couldn't help himself. He asked, "Why do you ask that?"

"Because I haven't seen her for days," said Lukien.

"She isn't well," said Akeela. "Something with her stomach; I don't know."

"Then she should see a physician." Lukien's tone was brittle. "Quickly, don't you think?"

"She doesn't want to see a physician, Lukien. She doesn't do everything I tell her, you know."

"You're her husband. You can insist on it."

Akeela laughed bitterly. "I'm her husband! I don't think that makes much difference to Cassandra."

"Akeela, what are you talking about?" asked Lukien in exasperation. "You're not making sense."

Akeela waved him away. "Go back to Lionkeep, Lukien. Tell Baron Glass to leave his declaration with all the others. When I'm ready to talk, *I* will send for *him*."

"Won't you come back with me?"

"No. I'm not done here yet."

Lukien stared at him for a moment, but Akeela would not meet his gaze. Finally the knight turned away. Dejected, he returned to his horse and rode off. Akeela watched him go. He didn't like shunning Lukien, but he didn't know if he could still trust the knight.

"Damn it all," he muttered. "I have to know!"

His brief time with Cassandra had taught him something about her. She loved trinkets, and never got rid of anything. If there was any evidence linking her to Lukien, she would still have it, squirreled away somewhere.

Sure that he would go mad without the truth, Akeela resolved to find it.

An hour later, Akeela was once again inside Lionkeep. Still in his damp clothes, he went straight to the private wing he shared with Cassandra, skirting his underlings along the way and refusing to speak to anyone but Warden Graig, who told him that Baron Glass had gone. When Akeela asked the Head Warden about Cassandra, Graig reported that the queen was gone, too. Apparently her handmaid Jancis had convinced her to leave her sickbed behind and get some air. Relieved, Akeela headed toward his lavish rooms, telling Graig not to disturb him. He was nervous suddenly, and wondered if his furtiveness showed. But Cassandra was out of their chambers very rarely lately, and Akeela knew he had to move fast.

The hallway leading to their wing was empty. His boots fell hard on the floor, echoing through the hall. The servants had gone, for without Cassandra to look after they had a much needed break, letting Akeela make his way undisturbed to their bedchamber. It was an elaborate, many-chambered room featuring a high ceiling and wide hearth. A canopied bed draped with linens stood against the western wall. Akeela didn't bother to strip off his wet things.

He could smell sickness in the air, the staleness of Cassandra's lingering breath, and for a moment he felt ashamed. She was ill, and he still loved her, no matter what she might have done. But illnesses passed. Adultery was forever.

He looked around the room, studying the shelves and mantle. Both were lined with trinkets Cassandra had collected from her years in Reec. There were urns and pretty plates, etched glassware and statuettes, all in feminine patterns and colors. But none of these things were unusual or new, and Akeela knew any evidence against his wife wouldn't be on public display. Studying the room, he took stock of the furniture. She would keep her private things very close to her, he decided. Discounting the bed, his eyes came to rest on Cassandra's wardrobe in the dressing room. He had never been into her wardrobe because there had never been a need to, and that made it the perfect hiding place.

Akeela listened for a moment then, sure that no one would disturb him, went into the dressing room and opened the wardrobe. The tiny chamber smelled of perfume. Unsure of what he was looking for, he began rifling through Cassandra's garments. She had brought a lot of clothing with her from Hes, and many more items had been given to her by the noblewomen of Koth. The wardrobe bulged with garments, making the search difficult. There were tiny drawers filled with jewelry and shelves with hairpins and brooches. Akeela searched these, too, finding nothing extraordinary. He even found the bracelet Baron Glass had given Cassandra when he'd met her. It was a pretty thing, but Cassandra hadn't thought so, relegating it to her wardrobe with her less cherished items. Akeela felt suddenly foolish. There was nothing in the wardrobe linking Cassandra and Lukien.

"Who's betraying whom?" he wondered. He shook his head, laughing. "What a fool I am."

He was about to close the wardrobe when a slim, white item at his feet caught his eye. There, barely visible beneath the wardrobe, was a piece of paper. Akeela's heart stopped. His eyes lingered on the sliver.

Not in the wardrobe, he told himself. *Under it.*

He went to his knees and reached beneath the hulking furniture, barely able to squeeze his hand into the space. With his fingers he tried prying out the paper, but found

that it wouldn't yield. Lowering his head to the floor, he
peered beneath the wardrobe with one eye and discovered
why. There were dozens of similar papers, all stacked upon
each other and corded together with yellow ribbon. Each
had been carefully folded in the same exact fashion. Akeela
struggled to get his hand into the space. Finally he seized
the bundle and pulled it forth. Sitting up with the papers
on this lap, he undid the yarn and unfolded the first one.
What he read made his heart sink.

It was a love note. It described a brief and beautiful
interlude in an apple orchard, using words like "honey"
and "rapture." Akeela's hand trembled as he read. Cassandra's name was all over the page, but Lukien's was nowhere. Even the signature was furtive. Lukien had simply
called himself "your adoring servant." But it was unmistakably the knight's script, and it proved Trager's every detail
correct. Unable to stop himself, Akeela read another letter,
then another, all written by the same treacherous hand.

He felt sick. He had believed the worst, but only partially. There had always been hope, and that had kept him
alive. Now he was truly alone, and he was enraged. There
were no tears this time, only an endless ocean of madness.
He slammed the letters down into his lap and clumsily
began tying them together again. When he was done he
shoved the packet roughly under the wardrobe. Let Cassandra wonder if she'd been discovered—he didn't care.

"Bitch!" he spat. "After all I've done for you."

And then there was Lukien; sweet, deceptive Lukien.
What could be done with a man like that? Akeela closed
his eyes, imagining punishments. He could execute Lukien
for what he'd done, but he knew he could never order such
a thing. Like Cassandra, he still loved Lukien.

"Betrayal," he whispered. "It is everywhere."

Very slowly he got to his feet. He heard voices in the
distance, footsteps coming closer. He straightened. It would
be Cassandra, returning from her walk. His anger cresting, he
stepped out of the dressing room and into the bedchamber,
resolving to confront her. Jancis' voice rang down the hall,
coming closer. Akeela went to the door and flung it open . . .

. . . and saw Cassandra's death-white face.

"Cassandra!"

Cassandra's body hung limply at Jancis' side, propped up

by the maid's arms. She was stooped and groaning, holding her midsection and straggling toward the bedroom.

"What's wrong?" Akeela demanded. "Cassandra?"

Cassandra shook her head, able to speak only in moans.

"She's very ill," said Jancis. "Help me get her to bed."

Akeela took over, carefully lifting Cassandra into his arms. She let out a wail, closing her eyes. Tears squeezed past her eyelids. Akeela rushed her into the bedroom.

"Jancis, what happened? What's wrong with her?"

As Akeela placed Cassandra into the bed, Jancis explained, "We were in the garden, talking. I thought she should get out for a while, get some air. Then she started moaning." The girl looked at her mistress, her eyes full of worry. "I'm sorry, my lord. It's . . ." She stopped herself.

Akeela whirled on her. "What?"

"It's an old sickness, my lord. She's been this way for months." Jancis bit her lip. "I think it's getting worse."

"Months?" Akeela erupted. He turned to Cassandra, who was breathing hard. "Cassandra, is that so?"

His wife nodded weakly. "I'm sorry, Akeela." She began to sob. "Please help me. It hurts . . ."

Akeela hurried a hand onto her face. "All right," he soothed. "I'm here, love. Don't worry." He turned to Jancis. "Get Gwena in here. And send for my physician!"

The maid raced out of the room. Akeela took Cassandra's fragile hand in his own. It was bony from lack of food. Her eyes were sallow.

"Cassandra, why didn't you tell me you were so sick?" he begged. He was angry again, this time at the thought of losing her. "Tell me why."

"I . . ." Cassandra swallowed. Her voice was thin. "I wanted to come to Koth. If I was sick, my father wouldn't have let me."

The confession rattled Akeela. So did her sunken cheeks. She began crying in earnest.

"Akeela, I'm frightened." She put her hands to her stomach. "My insides . . ."

"Don't worry," said Akeela. He stroked her hair. "The physician is coming soon. It's going to be all right."

She opened her eyes. "Will it, Akeela? Do you promise?"

Akeela's smile was inscrutable. "I promise. I'm never going to let you go, Cassandra."

14

A cancer.

Physician Oric had been with Cassandra less than an hour before making his diagnosis. The dreadful conclusion turned Akeela white. He knew what tumors were, of course, but up until that moment he had only heard it used in regard to strangers. No one meaningful to him had ever perished from such growths, and it seemed impossible that it should strike so young a woman. Physician Oric had come out of Cassandra's bedchamber looking gray and harried. Akeela had been waiting in the hallway. Gwena and Jancis and some of the other castle women were with him, and when he'd heard it was a tumor the young king had fallen against the wall, nearly collapsing. In that moment, he could have forgiven Cassandra anything, and the adultery she had done was as nothing compared to the love he felt for her. Barely able to speak, he had made old Oric repeat the word again to be sure he'd heard it.

"It's a cancer," said the physician. "And it will spread."

Oric was a learned man and had been the family's healer since Akeela could remember. Like most Liirian physicians, he had been educated in Koth's renowned colleges. But when it came to Cassandra, Akeela trusted no one, and so called on every physician in the city to examine his wife. Over the following days they came to Lionkeep at the king's request, poking and prodding the queen, their faces long with concern. And all of them confirmed Oric's opinion—Cassandra was dying. She had a growth that had advanced beyond any surgery. It had begun somewhere in her gut and was reaching into her bowels, slowly clawing out a fatal foothold. Despite their combined knowledge, none of the physicians could offer any hope. All they could do was make her comfortable, they said, and wait out the weeks before she died. Most believed she would be dead within two months, but Oric was generous enough to say three, maybe slightly more. "The queen is young and otherwise strong," he told Akeela. "She will live longer than most."

But three months was hardly time at all.

"She will have good days and she will have bad days," Oric went on to say. "And her bad days will be very bad indeed."

Akeela didn't have the strength to listen to any more. For days he kept the worst of the news from Cassandra, but he knew that she had guessed it, and when he returned to their bed chamber to tell her, she said the words for him.

"I'm dying," she whispered.

Akeela tried to smile. "That's what Oric says, but I don't believe him."

"Then you're a sweet fool, Akeela."

Her voice was a rasp; her eyelids drooped with drowsiness. Oric had prescribed a regimen of strong herbs and medicines, and now Cassandra seemed to be in no pain at all. She looked pale, and that was all.

"How long?" she asked.

"I won't answer that," said Akeela.

Cassandra opened her eyes. "Akeela, how much time do I have?"

"As long as I say so. I am your king and husband. You can't die without my permission."

Cassandra laughed. "Even a king can't save me now."

"I won't let you die, Cassandra. Remember my promise?"

"Your promise is forgiven, Akeela. What kind of wife would I be to hold you to something so impossible?" She turned her head and buried her face in the pillow. Then she began to sob. "What kind of wife. . ?"

"Rest," said Akeela. "I'll be back later. There are visitors waiting to see you, but I'll send them away."

Suddenly Cassandra faced him. "Visitors? Who?"

"Jancis wants to see you." Akeela hesitated. "And Lukien."

"Lukien?" Cassandra's eyes darted away. "He knows, then?"

"The whole city knows, Cassandra, and would be at this door to see you if not for me." Akeela turned to leave. "But you need rest. I'll tell them to go."

True to his word, Akeela dismissed all of Cassandra's visitors. Even Lukien. He guarded Cassandra like a mother, keeping everyone but Oric away from her, relenting only when his wife cried for Jancis. The handmaid became the queen's lone visitor, for all others were barred from the royal couple's wing.

Days passed, and Akeela grew more despondent. The isolation that had plagued him since returning from abroad had reached a dangerous peak, and he shunned all overtures of friendship and support. Baron Glass stopped sending war declarations from the House of Dukes, but there was still talk of battle with Norvor, and whispers that Akeela had become impotent and unable to act. It was said that his courage was withering along with his wife. Work stopped on the great library. Akeela attended Cassandra day and night. And he brooded. He had made an impossible promise. Akeela knew he would need a miracle to save Cassandra.

Then, one afternoon, Figgis came to see him.

It was eight days after Cassandra's illness had been discovered. Akeela, weary beyond words, had sought shelter from the world in his study, the only part of Lionkeep that was truly his alone. He sat at his desk listening to the breeze outside his window, threatening a storm. In one hand he held a book, in the other a brandy. Akeela swirled the brandy absently as he read, losing himself in the rhymes of some Liirian poet. For the moment, he had put aside Cassandra and his thousand troubles, and the brandy deadened his pain. The sound of the wind gave him something like contentment.

But an unwelcome knock at the door shattered his solitude.

"My lord? Are you in there?"

Akeela recognized Figgis' voice. He put his down his book with a sigh. "I'm here," he called. "Come in."

Figgis the librarian pushed open the door and licked his lips nervously. He, too, had a book in his hand, very old from the looks of it and covered in dust. His hair was matted and his clothes were customarily wrinkled, and his eyes had the same tired droop as Akeela's own. He gave his king an apologetic smile as he peered into the study.

"Sorry to interrupt, my lord, but I found something I thought would interest you."

Akeela looked at the item Figgis had brought. "A book? Figgis, I have my mind on bigger things these days than books." He waved it off. "Add it to the collection."

"Uh, no, my lord misunderstands. This isn't just a book. May I come in?"

"I'm very tired, Figgis . . ."

"Really, this is important, my lord," said the old man.

He waited on the threshold. Akeela hesitated. The last time someone had come to his study with "important" news he had learned of Cassandra's infidelity. More news like that and Akeela knew he'd collapse.

"All right, but close the door, will you? I don't want a parade marching in here. Brandy?"

Figgis shook his head. "Uh, no, my lord, thanks."

"Pity. I find it the only thing that helps my headaches these days." Akeela drained his snifter then poured himself another. He could already hear his slurred speech, but didn't care. "Be seated, Figgis, and tell me what's so urgent you simply had to disturb me."

"Yes, thank you, my lord," said Figgis. He slid out a chair and sat down, laying his book on the desk. "Now, about this book—"

"Where's your monkey?" Akeela interrupted. "I like that little fellow."

Figgis smiled gently. "My lord is drunk."

"So I am."

"Peko is resting in his cage." Figgis reached out and nudged the book beneath Akeela's nose. "I have something special here, my lord."

Through bleary eyes Akeela studied the book. It had a cover of worn brown leather, frayed at the corners, with numerous dog-eared pages. There were strange markings in the leather, like Reecian runes, but foreign. Akeela reached out and ran his fingers over the embossed lettering, trying to decipher it.

"It's from Jador," Figgis explained. "It's very old and rare. It's written in Jadori, my lord. You won't be able to read it."

"No?" Akeela slid the book back toward Figgis. "Then it's not much good to me, is it? I really wish you wouldn't bother me with this, Figgis. I told you, I have things on my mind."

"But that's just it, my lord," said Figgis. "I'm here to help you. And help Queen Cassandra."

"What do you mean?"

"This is a text of Jadori history and folklore, my lord. Like I said, it's very unusual, maybe the rarest book I own. I've been reading it for years now, trying to make sense of it. The Jadori language is very different from our own. It's difficult, and I've only been able to translate some of the text."

"So? What's this to do with Cassandra?"

"My lord, when I heard of the queen's illness, I started going through my books, trying to find out what I could about her tumor, anything that might help her. I wanted to ease her suffering you see, maybe even cure her."

Akeela smiled at the librarian. "No one can cure what Cassandra has, my friend. Not even you with all your books can do that."

"No, you don't understand," said Figgis. "While I was looking through my books, I remembered something I'd read a long time ago. Sort of a legend, you might say." He tapped the Jadori manuscript. "Something in here, my lord."

"Something about her cancer?" asked Akeela.

"Better." Figgis opened the book to one of its yellowed pages. He read for a moment, mouthing the words with effort, trying to find the right passage. Then he smiled and looked up at Akeela. "My lord may think me mad for this."

"I already think you're mad, Figgis. Go on."

Figgis continued, "I've been able to translate most of this passage pretty well. It speaks of the Kahan and Kahana of Jador, and two amulets that they wear."

"Kahan and Kahana? Who are they?"

"Like a king and queen, my lord. That's what the Jadori call their rulers. These amulets they wear are called Inai ka Vala—the Eyes of God."

"God? What god?"

"That's the Jadori word for it, my lord. The Jadori have one main deity they call Vala; he's like the great spirit worshipped by the Reecians, or the Fate here in Liiria."

"And what of these amulets? What are they?"

"Let me read it to you, my lord." Clearing his throat, Figgis read, "The master of the hidden place across the desert wears an amulet of red and gold." The hidden place, Figgis explained, was Jador. He continued, "His wife wears the amulet's twin. The Eyes of God protect them, saving them from all disease." Figgis looked at Akeela excitedly. "See, my lord?"

"See? See what?"

"The Eyes of God, my lord. They're magic amulets. They can save Queen Cassandra!"

Akeela rolled his eyes. "Are you mad? I thought you were coming here with real hope, that you had found something that might help my wife. But this . . ." He gestured to the book in disgust. "This is ridiculous."

"My lord, I'm telling you the truth. The book speaks of these amulets as having real power!"

"My wife is dying, Figgis! I don't have time for fairy tales."

Figgis seemed surprised by Akeela's reaction. Scowling, he said, "My lord is foolish to deny the existence of sorcery."

"I don't deny it, Figgis. I just don't approve of it."

"Ah, but it exists, my lord. You've seen it yourself. Hiding from it won't make it go away. The fortune cards of Noor are magical. And what about the holy relic of Marn? Can you explain why it weeps?"

"I cannot. But if it is sorcery, then I do not wish to understand it."

Figgis got to his feet, clutching the book. "My lord, I've studied Jador all my life. The Jadori are very different from us. They have skills we know nothing about."

"Bah, the world is plagued by sorcery these days," Akeela scoffed. "The poor and ignorant use it as a crutch. But not me. I'm a man of science and knowledge, Figgis. That's what you're supposed to be."

"I *am* a man of science, my lord. That's how I know about Jador, and how I know these amulets just might be real. Isn't it worth a chance if it will save the queen's life?"

"What chance? Jador is hundreds of miles from here. Even if these amulets are real, how would we find them? How would we cross the Desert of Tears?"

"You forget, my lord, I know something of that part of the world. I lived in Ganjor, remember. The Jadori trade with the Ganjeese. Sometimes the Jadori travel to Ganjor, and sometimes the Ganjeese send caravans across the desert to Jador. They both cross the sands without incident."

"The Jadori have their lizards for crossing the desert," said Akeela. "We do not."

"Not all of them ride kreels, my lord. Most of the caravans are from Ganjor, where they use drowas. If they can do it, surely we can find a way."

Akeela thought for a moment, studying the librarian's earnest face. He certainly seemed to believe his wild tale. And there was sorcery enough in the world, that was certainly true. The stew of Liirian culture had shown Akeela that already. But he had never heard of any sorcery like these amulets, these so-called "Eyes of God." To Akeela, it smacked of folly. He closed his eyes and sighed.

"Figgis, I wish I could believe you," he said. "But how can I? This story is incredible. It's like something from a bedtime story. Soon you'll be telling me Grimhold is real!"

"Why not?"

Akeela opened his eyes. Before him, Figgis stood as sure and straight as an arrow. There was not the smallest trace of jest in him.

"Figgis," said Akeela, "what kind of man believes in fairy tales?"

"It's hope, my lord, that's all," said Figgis. "It's not insanity or folly. I believe in these amulets."

"Do you? Or do you simply *want* to believe? You're very keen on Jador, Figgis. Might this not be some delusion of yours, a false hope?"

Figgis shrugged. "Even if it is, what else can we do? Cassandra will die in months, and nothing on this side of the desert can save her."

For Akeela, any hope, however insane it sounded, was welcome. For days now he had been in a dark tunnel, groping through the blackness with no way out. Now came Figgis bearing a candle.

"Figgis, if I agree to this they will call me mad. The chancellors already think me a lunatic. How can I tell them about magic amulets? It sounds like nonsense."

Once more the librarian tapped his book. "It's in the text, my lord. That's all I need to know."

"That's not good enough. You said yourself you haven't read the whole thing. Why can't that book of yours be nothing more than a collection of lies? Why must it be the truth?"

"Because I've studied Jador, my lord," argued Figgis. "And everything else I've read out of this book is true. It speaks of the kreel, and we already know they exist, and it talks about the city across the desert. That's Jador, my lord. And Jador is no myth. Why should the amulets be the only thing the book lies about?"

Akeela couldn't answer. Perhaps it was the drink, but he was starting to believe the old man's fantasy. Like most Liirians, he knew almost nothing about Jador, just that it was far away and mysterious. And he had seen sorcery before, or at least a semblance of it. Koth's streets were littered with fortune-tellers and rune-carvers. If they could do magic, why not the Jadori?

"If only it were so," he whispered. "I would do anything to save Cassandra."

Figgis seized the opportunity. "The amulets can save her, my lord. If they exist, she can live forever without disease, as young and beautiful as she is now. And you with her!"

"I have no wish to live forever, Figgis."

The librarian shifted, looking down at his feet. Akeela raised a suspicious eyebrow.

"You're not telling me something," he said. "What are you hiding?"

Grinning, Figgis said, "My lord is perceptive."

"Tell me," Akeela demanded.

"Well, there is something else." The librarian grimaced. "Something about a curse, my lord."

For a moment Akeela thought he'd heard wrong, then he burst into bitter laughter. "A curse? You mean those bloody amulets are damned?"

"My lord, let me explain . . ."

"No, Figgis, don't you see? A curse is just perfect, for I myself am cursed. Giant lizards, magic amulets, and now a curse! How fitting."

"King Akeela, please," said Figgis. "It's not what you think." He began running a finger along the page of the book, scanning it quickly. "Here it is," he said, then began to translate the text. "The wearer of Inai ka Vala—the Eyes of God—shall not be looked at by human eyes. To do so breaks their power, inviting death." Figgis looked up from the book. "That's all it says."

"And you don't think that's bad? Are you mad? Are we to be shut-ins, Cassandra and I? Never looked at with human eyes! How are we supposed to live like that?"

"But my lord, think for a moment. It can't be that simple. Does the Kahan of Jador live alone, without his subjects laying eyes on him? Does his wife?" A sly smile crept over Figgis' face. "Don't you see? There's got to be more to this story than what's written in this book. If we go to Jador, we can find out the truth of the amulets, discover how they're truly used."

"Oh, yes," drawled Akeela. "I'm beginning to see perfectly. You're just dying to get to Jador, aren't you? You said it yourself; you've known about these amulets for years. Now you have the perfect opportunity to seek them out, with me to fund your little excursion."

Figgis' smile melted away. "My lord is unjust if he thinks me so selfish. What I'm suggesting is for the good of the queen."

"But you will accompany a party to Jador, won't you?"

"Well, of course," said Figgis stiffly. "I'm the only one that speaks even a smattering of the language. To not send me would be foolish."

"How convenient," smirked Akeela. He poured himself another glass of brandy, angry with himself for being duped. He hadn't thought the librarian so ambitious. But he was also sincere; Akeela had learned that much about him. As he sipped his drink, he wondered about the amulets, their stupid curse, and how he could take them from Jador. Figgis watched him curiously, not interrupting his dark thoughts. After a long minute Akeela lowered his glass to the table.

"I love Cassandra very much," he said. "I know we

haven't been married long, but she's already the moon and stars to me. I can't lose her, Figgis. If this tale of yours is some lie just to get yourself to Jador, I will hang your pelt from a wall."

"It isn't, my lord, I swear," said Figgis. "This book says the Eyes of God exist, and I believe it. I'll bring them back for you, if you'll let me." He looked pleadingly at Akeela. "Will you let me, my lord?"

For a moment Akeela couldn't speak. All he could think of was Cassandra.

"I must be drunker than I thought," he said. "Go. I give you leave for this mad mission, Figgis."

The librarian's face lit the room. "Well done, my lord. Thank you! But I'll need men, and money and supplies. And I'll have to leave as soon as possible. By week's end, I'd say."

"Get your things together quickly, and come to me for your finances. I'll pay whatever you need." Akeela leaned back in his chair, a wicked smile cracking his face. "And as for men, I know just who to send with you."

15

At the crack of dawn, Lukien arrived at the stable and found Trager and Figgis waiting for him. His traveling companions had already packed and dressed for their long trek south, and the grooms had readied their mounts, three brawny stallions that would take them as far as Ganjor. Lionkeep was barely awake, and a mist rolled over the castle. The air was wet with must and hay. Still exhausted from a night of worry, Lukien entered the stable without a trace of a smile. Figgis, the old scholar, was rummaging through his saddlebags and mumbling to himself. He wore an unusual ensemble of mismatched riding garb and his customary wide-brimmed hat. Trager stood imperiously at the stable's far end, looming over a stableboy and shouting.

". . . and what did I tell you about packing my horse? Not too heavy, isn't that what I said?"

The boy nodded. "You did, sir."

"And didn't I tell you we needed to be swift?"

"Yes, sir, you did."

"So then what's the use of all that garbage, eh?" Trager pointed accusingly at his horse. "He'll be lame before we get out of Koth! Now unpack him and do it over. And leave off that cooking gear. I'm not going on a bloody picnic!"

Lukien tried to ignore Trager, but caught the lieutenant's eye. There was an immediate iciness between them. Lukien strode toward his own horse. The stallion had been outfitted just as he'd ordered, with all the things Figgis had said they would need. A groom near the horse noted Lukien's satisfaction and smiled.

"Good work, Gill," said Lukien, rubbing the horse's neck.

"He's all ready," said Gill. He shot a glance at his fellow groom, being berated by Trager. "But I guess you'll have to wait before leaving."

"Yes, about that . . ." Lukien turned to Trager. "What's wrong with you, Lieutenant? I told you I wanted to get going at dawn. Stop wasting our time."

"Me?" flared Trager. He pointed at the young groom, who was unpacking his horse. "It's this waterhead! He packed my horse so heavy we'll never make it to Jador."

"He packed the damn horse just like I asked," said Lukien miserably. He turned back to his own mount, cursing. Akeela still hadn't told him why Trager was going with them. It seemed the worst choice for their impossible mission. Figgis was obvious, of course, but Trager would be an endless nuisance. Lukien began looking over his saddlebags. It had been days since Akeela had come to him with the fantastic story of the amulets, begging him to go on this quest for Cassandra. And Lukien had agreed willingly, because he would do anything for Cassandra and her illness had shattered him. But he still didn't believe in their ridiculous mission. Over to one side, Figgis wore an excited smile as he surveyed his horse, checking off items on a square of paper. The librarian had worked day and night putting together their itinerary, but he didn't look tired at all. His face glowed with a child's exuberance.

"We're ready, I think," said Figgis. "We have everything—maps, food, gold for the trade caravans . . ." He nodded, satisfied with himself. "We've done a very good job. We're well prepared."

"I'm glad you think so," said Lukien dryly. He returned to fussing with his horse, hoping Figgis would leave him alone. They had a long trip ahead of them, and if the old man was going to be talking through the whole thing . . .

Closing his eyes, he took a deep breath. Cassandra was counting on him. He was her only hope now, and this mad mission might just save her. He couldn't—wouldn't—let his feelings interfere.

Yet still he brooded, for the whole thing smacked of folly. He wasn't a thief, but that's what Akeela was asking him to become. Somehow, they were supposed to steal these magic amulets from the Kahan and Kahana of Jador. Under the guise of friendship they would pose as emissaries, working their way into the kahan's good graces. Then, if they could, they would steal the amulets and race back to Liiria. And all in time to save Cassandra.

Tired of waiting, Lukien went outside for some air. The dawn was creeping fast over the horizon. They were losing time, and Lukien was losing patience. He was about to slip back into the stable to hurry Trager when he saw Akeela approaching out of the mist. The young king's expression was grave, the way it had been for weeks now. He wore a cape of crimson around his slight shoulders. Lukien's black mood lifted slightly. He had hoped Akeela would come to see them off.

"Ho, Lukien," called Akeela.

Lukien waved back. "So you decided to say good-bye, eh?"

Akeela stopped before him. He looked weary beyond words. His eyes betrayed a wildness that hadn't always been there. "I've come to wish you luck," he said. He peered into the stable and saw Trager and Figgis. "Looks like everything's ready."

"Everything but Trager. Why do you have that buffoon going with me, Akeela? He'll only slow me down."

"Because he's a good soldier, believe it or not," said Akeela. "And I need good men for this mission."

Lukien said, "You need good men against Norvor. If there's going to be battle, that's where I should be, not traipsing around solving riddles."

"Lukien, we've already settled this," said Akeela. "If this quest is going to succeed, I need my best men on it. That's you, like it or not."

"But what about Norvor? If a fight comes, what will you do without me?"

Akeela laughed. "You're not the only knight in the world, you know."

"Akeela, I'm serious . . ."

"I can handle them."

Lukien wasn't satisfied, but he knew Akeela would brook no arguing. They had already agreed on this mission. A sadness overcame Lukien suddenly. Akeela was changing, rapidly and day by day.

"I'll do my best, you know," said Lukien, "but I can't promise anything. Even if we find these amulets, it's a long way back from Jador. We may not be quick enough."

"Cassandra hasn't much time, Lukien."

Lukien nodded. "I know." He couldn't say any more. Akeela's eyes bore down on him, as if they could see the shame eating his soul. Thankfully, Trager and Figgis emerged from the stable to end the awkward moment.

"We're ready," Trager pronounced. He looked at Akeela with a curious trace of scorn. "My lord."

Akeela ignored him. "Do you have everything you need, Figgis? Can you think of anything more?"

Figgis shrugged. "No, my lord, I think we're ready. We've mapped out our route and shouldn't have too much trouble. First Farduke and Dreel, then on to Ganjor."

"It would be fastest if you went through Nith," Akeela observed.

"Maybe faster," said Figgis with a grimace, "but more dangerous. They don't care for strangers in Nith, my lord."

"Going around Nith will waste time."

"A bit of time, yes," Figgis agreed, "but it's better this way. We don't want to bring too much attention to ourselves. And going around Nith will only lose us a day or so. Then we'll go to Ganjor for drowas and a desert guide. That should get us to Jador in a month or so."

"Just so you hurry," said Akeela. "Remember the queen, all of you. She's depending on you."

"We will, my lord," said Figgis, climbing onto his horse.

Gill led Lukien's horse out of the stable and into the misty morning. He handed the beast over to the knight. Lukien took a last look at Akeela. Trying to reach across the chasm that now separated them, he said, "Take care of yourself. Don't let King Mor take advantage of you, and don't let Baron Glass push you into anything you don't want to do, all right?"

Akeela's smile twisted. "Always with the advice."

The answer stung Lukien. "Yes, well, take care of yourself." He climbed onto his horse's back then led Trager and Figgis away from the stable, not looking back.

*   *   *

Akeela remained behind at the stable, watching as the mist swallowed Lukien and his party. He was glad to be rid of both his troubles, and the sight of their departing backs eased his mind. Now, with Trager gone, he wouldn't have to worry about him spewing his poison all around Lionkeep, true though it might be. And Lukien? Akeela would miss him, but it was necessary. He was the Bronze Knight, a hero. He was the perfect man to quest for the amulets.

Akeela glanced around, struck by the quiet. Once, he had loved coming to the stables with Lukien. They would ride together for hours, laughing and exchanging stories, but they hadn't done that in a very long time, and probably never would again. Even if Lukien returned from Jador, there was still the matter of adultery. Akeela knew he couldn't forgive it. When Lukien returned—if he returned—he would deal with it.

Just as he would deal with Norvor.

He hadn't lied when he'd told Lukien he would handle Norvor himself. In fact, he meant every word precisely.

"You're not the only one that can be a hero, my friend," he whispered. He would show Cassandra that he could be a hero, too.

"Gill!" he called.

The young man hurried out of the stable, a grooming brush still in hand.

"Yes, my lord?"

"Go find Warden Graig for me. Tell him I want a meeting with Baron Glass and Chancellor Hogon. Tell him it's very important."

Two hours later, Glass and Hogon arrived at Lionkeep. The sky had lightened considerably since the early morning and the windows of the council chamber were open wide, letting in a needed breeze. Glass sat in his usual seat, next to Chancellor Hogon. Both men wore scowls. Akeela had kept them waiting many days for an answer to their war declarations, and they did nothing to hide their ire. Glass fidgeted with his wine glass but did not drink, occasionally rubbing at the stump of his arm in irritation. Hogon sat back in his chair, watching Warden Graig, who had called them to this important meeting but didn't know why. Other than those three, the room was empty.

But the door was open and Akeela could see them all as he strode toward the chamber. Surprisingly, he wasn't nervous at all. He felt exhilarated. Having made his decision had lifted a weight from his shoulders. It didn't matter now what they thought of him or his bold plan—he was king, and he would command them to follow orders. In his fist he held the latest declaration from the House of Dukes. He held it out before him, making sure it was the first thing the chancellors saw when he entered the council chamber. The three men—Glass, Hogon, and Graig, all stood as the king entered the room. Glass' gaze fell on the rolled up paper in Akeela's hand.

"Be seated," Akeela commanded. He took his place at the end of the table but did not sit. When the men had finally taken their seats, Akeela tossed the roll of paper onto the table.

Baron Glass reached for it hesitantly, looking at Akeela.

"Go on, read it," Akeela directed.

One-handed, the Baron struggled to unroll the parchment. His eyes immediately darted to the end of the page where Akeela's signature rambled along the bottom. Hogon leaned over and spied the signature. Together the two lords looked up at Akeela. So did Warden Graig, whose mouth hung open.

"Say something, gentlemen."

"My lord, I don't know what to say," stammered Graig. "This is war!"

"You did the right thing, King Akeela," pronounced Glass. He held up the paper and shook it in the air. "Now we can move against those Norvan snakes."

Graig got out of his chair. "My lord," he sputtered, groping for words. He tried to smile. "Akeela . . ."

Akeela kept his expression cool. "You have something to say, Warden Graig?"

Graig looked at him in disbelief. "Are you sure you want to do this?"

"As sure as I've been about anything," said Akeela. "King Mor has left me little choice."

Chancellor Hogon nodded soberly. "Very well, my lord. Then I will make ready at once."

"Yes, at once," agreed Akeela. "I have a plan to deal with

the Norvans, and I want to begin quickly. The sooner we make arrangements, the sooner we can leave for the Kryss."

Hogon blinked, confused. "*We*, my lord?"

"I'm going with you, Hogon. I'm going to lead the attack on Norvor."

"What?" Baron Glass rose from his seat. "King Akeela, you cannot."

"I've made up my mind," said Akeela, "and no amount of arguing can change it."

"Great Fate, no!" snapped Glass. "You're not a military man. You're the king! What put this idea into your head?"

Akeela started to respond, but was quickly interrupted by Hogon.

"King Akeela, Baron Glass is right. I'm sorry, but I can't agree to this folly." The old man looked genuinely concerned. "This is war, my lord, serious business. You realize that, don't you?"

"I'm not a child, Chancellor," said Akeela. "I know exactly what I'm doing."

"Then explain it, King Akeela, please!" said Glass.

So Akeela explained. First he insisted that Glass and Graig take their seats, and when they did he walked around the table for a moment, composing his thoughts. He told them that he was the King of Liiria, and that his word was law, no matter how much any of them cackled. He told them too that he was not a weakling; that despite the popular opinion that his dreams of peace had made him impotent, he was his father's son and not afraid of battle.

"And King Mor is like the rest of you," he said. "He also thinks me a weakling. He thinks I'll do anything for peace, even bend to his ridiculous demands."

"My lord," said Glass, "none of us think you're a weakling."

"Please, Baron," said Akeela. "Don't lie. You're too easily discovered. I know what you and the other nobles think of me. And I plan to use that misconception against Mor. He thinks I want peace at any cost. He thinks moving troops against our border will force me to his table. So let him go on believing it. Let's talk peace with King Mor." A crafty smile stretched across Akeela's face. "And when he's most trusting, we'll strike."

Baron Glass contemplated the scheme. "Yes," he said. "It's not a bad plan at all . . ."

"It's treachery, that's what it is," protested Graig. "Akeela, how could you consider such a thing? You disappoint me."

"How do we proceed?" asked Glass, ignoring Graig.

"We send a messenger to Norvor," said Akeela, "asking for a meeting between Mor and myself. We tell him I want to meet near our border, so I'll feel safe. Somewhere just outside of Norvor, perhaps near their fortress at Hanging Man. Chancellor Hogon, start mustering your men. Some will accompany me to the meeting. Just a handful of them, so not to worry Mor. The rest will march with you to Reec."

"Reec?" asked Hogon. "Why Reec?"

"Because that's where you'll be attacking from," said Akeela. "King Karis has been asking what I have planned. He says he wants to help. Well, Reec's border should hide our troops nicely, don't you think?"

Baron Glass nodded in understanding. "And then when you're clear, they attack."

"Yes," said Akeela, "and Reecian soldiers with them, if Karis agrees. The rest of the soldiers, the ones with me, will join them, cutting off any escape from Hanging Man. The Norvans won't have a chance."

"They'll be slaughtered," agreed Hogon. "Quite a plan you have, my lord."

"Treachery," said Graig. "My lord, I can't believe you'd do this. You said yourself you're known as a man of peace. Is that what it means to be 'Akeela the Good?' You've hardly been king for a fortnight and already you've turned backstabber."

"Don't be an idiot, Warden," sneered Glass. "The king's showing real mettle! Personally, I'm proud of him."

The baron smiled, and the smile sickened Akeela. He'd known his plan would disappoint Graig, but he hadn't counted on Glass' praise. It sounded horrible to him.

"I want to get moving on this quickly," he said. "Let's arrange that meeting with Mor. And send messengers to Reec with all speed. Chancellor Hogon, you've got a lot of work to do. Make sure the treasury releases the funds you need. If they argue, tell them to speak to me. And Baron Glass, I have something special for you to do as well."

"Anything, my lord," said Glass. "I'm yours to command."

Akeela wanted to laugh, but instead said, "Liiria will need a ruler while I'm gone. I'm leaving that to you."

"Me?" Glass flushed. "Forgive me for asking this, King Akeela, but why?"

"I have no regent and no heirs," said Akeela, "and obviously the queen is in no condition to rule. You, Baron, are my only choice."

The reasoning deflated Glass, yet still he said, "I'm honored, my lord. And I won't disappoint you. While you're gone I'll rule Liiria as wisely as I can."

"I should warn you, Baron, there's a price for this favor," said Akeela. He walked toward Glass' seat. "There's something you must do for me while I'm gone."

Glass grimaced. "I'm afraid to ask."

"The library, Baron. I want its construction to continue. You're to see to it."

"The library? But . . ."

"No, no arguing," said Akeela. "That's my order. Rule Liiria while I'm gone, but see to it that work continues on my library. I want your commitment to this project, Baron."

"Obviously," said Glass. "And if I don't give it to you?"

"Then you'll have no place in my plans. You won't rule in my stead, and you won't accompany us to Norvor, either. Commit to my library or be insignificant—those are your choices, Baron."

Trapped, Baron Glass nodded. "You have me, King Akeela. Well played."

"And I have your word? You'll see to the library in my absence?"

"I will," said Glass. He smiled sourly. "I was wrong when I said you were nothing like your father, King Akeela. You can be a serpent sometimes, just like him."

Warden Graig stood up. "You're all very happy with yourselves, but aren't you forgetting something? What about the queen, my lord?"

"That's your duty, Graig," said Akeela. He turned to his

old friend. "I'm trusting her to you. Look after her while I'm gone. Make sure nothing happens to her. She mustn't die until Lukien returns, do you understand?"

Graig barely hid his anger. "My lord, you're her husband. You should be looking after her, not me."

"I would if I could," said Akeela, "but I have to go. It's the only way to defeat Norvor."

"Yes," said Graig disgustedly. "Trickery."

"It's necessary!" Akeela shouted. "Why can't you see that?"

"All I see is the change in you," replied Graig. His old face wrinkled crossly. "What happened to that young man of peace? Is he completely dead already?"

Embarrassment colored Akeela's cheeks. He said to Glass and Hogon, "Would you excuse us, please?"

Without a word the two noblemen left the council chamber, closing the door behind them. Graig remained seated, refusing to look at Akeela, who felt ashamed and hurt by his old mentor's disappointment.

"Graig, you have to understand," he implored. "They think me weak. They all think me weak."

"Who, Akeela?" asked Graig. "Who are you trying to impress with this dangerous game? It's not just Glass, is it? It's not even King Mor. It's someone else."

Akeela stiffened. In all their years together, Graig could always see the truth in things.

"You're a very clever old man," said Akeela with a forlorn smile. "Is it so obvious?"

"Just to me, Akeela. I've known you a long time. I know when something's bothering you."

"I won't lose her, Graig," said Akeela. "Not to sickness, and not to some notion of cowardice. I can't let Mor get away with this, because that's all she'll ever see in me if I do."

Graig shook his head miserably. "You're talking foolishness. Cassandra's your queen."

"Oh, yes," said Akeela bitterly. "And if that were the answer to everything I'd have no troubles at all." He picked up Baron Glass' untouched wine and took a deep drink, drowning his need to confess. He couldn't tell anyone of Cassandra's infidelity, not even Graig. Finally he lowered the glass and said, "Look after her for me, Graig. See that nothing happens to her while I'm gone. That's the most important task I'm giving anyone, and I'm trusting you with it."

"You don't have to do this, Akeela," said Graig. "You don't have to go."

"Yes I do." Akeela moved toward the door. "I only wish I could explain it to you."

Graig shouted after him, "But you're no soldier!"

Akeela didn't reply. *No soldier,* he thought blackly. *No Lukien . . .*

16

Ganjor glistened like gold in the sun. The long trek south had finally paid off for the weary trio, and now they were rewarded with the sight of the city, perched on a sea of sand that stretched out endlessly beyond it. Sunlight made the dry earth seem to shimmer, and the breeze carried the smells of Ganjor, the first human habitat the travelers had seen in days. They had passed through Farduke and Dreel, avoided the principality of Nith, had slept in the forests of Dalyma and followed the Agora River, all to be led to this ancient crossroads.

To Lukien, who had never before ventured further than Marn, Ganjor seemed a remarkable ruin. The city reeked of age, even from a mile away. He could see the tall walls of Ganjor's fortress, now abandoned. The funerary temple rose above the streets in a golden dome, just as Figgis had described. On the south side of the city grew olive groves, making do with the little rain that fed the harsh soil, and from the east came the trading caravans, well-stocked with goods and laden with dark-skinned children. A second, less-traveled road came from the north, bringing visitors from Dreel and Marn and, on rare occasions, Liiria.

Lukien reined in his horse, pausing in the shadow of the city. He removed his neckerchief and dabbed the sweat from his forehead. The southern sun had toasted his fair skin. The tips of his ears were burned red. He looked past

Ganjor to the Desert of Tears, a vast expanse of blistering sand. The awesome sight crushed his already waning spirits.

"Great Fate, look at that," he said. "It's like an ocean."

Figgis wore an exuberant smile. "Beautiful, isn't it?"

"Beautiful?" said Trager. "Are you mad? How are we supposed to cross *that?*"

The old man's smile didn't wane. He gazed at Ganjor in a kind of happy homecoming. He had done a good job of guiding them this far, and Lukien was pleased. But he didn't understand the librarian's fascination with these southern cultures. During the days and nights of their long trek south, Figgis had taught them what he could of the Ganjeese, never tiring of his own tales. He had told them that the Ganjeese were a desert culture, like the Jadori, and how they were different from northerners. The hot climate made them quiet, easy-going people, never prone to wasting effort. Even their speech was simple, Figgis had explained, another means of conserving strength. No one of Ganjor ever used two words where one would suffice, nor spoke when a lack of words would do. They were a proud and ancient people, and thought themselves the center of the world. Liirians, Figgis had warned, would not impress them.

But Lukien didn't care about impressing the Ganjeese, and didn't plan on staying in their city more than a day. He needed to get to Jador, and that meant crossing the formidable desert. To do so they would need to trade their horses for drowa. Figgis had promised it would be an easy bargain to make, for drowa were everywhere this near the desert. If Lukien sniffed hard enough, he could smell their peculiar musk in the air. He had already seen some of the humped beasts on his way south. They were atrociously ugly and, according to Figgis, ill-tempered. Lukien didn't relish riding one across the desert.

"I'm exhausted," he said with a sigh. He took notice of the sun high overhead. "Come on. Let's get into the city before we roast. I could do with a bed for the night."

"That would be a nice change," said Trager sourly. The lieutenant drew a hand across the sweat on his brow. He was a fit man, but the journey had wearied him. He turned to Figgis, saying, "Lead the way, old man."

Figgis started off in a trot toward Ganjor. Lukien and Trager followed close behind. The city beckoned them, and Lukien felt his mood lighten. His ears quickly filled with the sounds of the bustling crossroads, and as they approached he could clearly see the white towers dotting the city, poking up from the thousands of squat, closely-spaced buildings of brown brick. Golden domes and silver spires with keyhole windows graced the ancient skyline, throwing sweeping shadows into the streets. The road widened as they reached the city outskirts, opening like a mouth to swallow them. Lukien swiveled in his saddle, suddenly enraptured by his surroundings. He had been many places in his many battles, but he had never seen anything like Ganjor. He slowed, eager to see it all. Even Trager seemed enamored by the city. The clay walls of ancient structures rose up around them, and the wide street quickly choked with travelers and the stalls of pottery and silk merchants. Barefoot men sat in clusters around small tables, sipping drinks and tossing dice, while others worked diligently with looms and hawked passersby to buy their weavings. White-faced monkeys like the one Figgis had left behind in Koth were everywhere, perched happily on the shoulders of children and shoppers, and exotic smells from cooking stalls suffused the air. Lukien's stomach rumbled at the aromas. He saw a boy eating chunks of meat on a stick and wondered where he could get one of his own. Trager pointed at the boy.

"Food, Figgis," he said. "Get us some."

The librarian scowled. "Manners, Lieutenant. You're not in Koth anymore, remember."

"I'm hungry!"

"Yes, we all are. Just calm down and don't make a spectacle of yourself. First we have to find a place to stay for the night. And we'll have to get clothing."

"Clothing?" asked Lukien. "What do you mean?"

"For the desert," said Figgis. "We can't go across like this. We'll have to dress like everyone else, in gaka." He pointed to a group of men, all similarly garbed in long white robes and headdress. "See? Those robes are called gaka. They keep out the sand and reflect the sunlight. They'll keep us cool."

"Cool?" Trager laughed. "Wrapped from head to toe like that? You're joking."

"Do you think they'd wear it if it didn't work?" asked Figgis. "Believe me, they've lived here long enough to know what they're doing. We'll have to wear gaka or we'll never make it."

"And a guide," Lukien reminded him. "What about that? We'll need someone to guide us to Jador."

"All the shrana houses have guides, Lukien, don't worry. We'll find someone to take us."

"All right, what's a shrana house?"

"Like a tavern, you might say. Shrana is a popular drink here. It's a hot liquor made from roasted beans. You'll see people drinking it all day long."

"Hot drinks, hot clothes; what's wrong with these people?" snapped Trager. "Don't they feel the bloody sun? What are they made of, leather?"

"You'll learn, Lieutenant," said Figgis. "Come. Let's find a place to rest."

Figgis led them through the crowded streets, gingerly maneuvering his horse past throngs of carts and people. Most of the folk were Ganjeese, olive-skinned and dark-haired, but there were northerners in the mix as well, and the knight recognized the crests of Norvor and Dreel in the crowd, carved into the sides of battered wagons that had chosen to trade this far south. They were a welcome sight to Lukien, who was quickly feeling foreign among the southerners. But he didn't feel unwelcome, for there was a curious easiness about the Ganjeese, as though they had seen it all and outsiders held little interest for them. Curiously, most of the people crowding the streets were men, but there were also women sprinkled through the crowd. All wore robes similar to their male counterparts, and all had a veil of black cloth covering their faces, so that only their eyes could be seen.

"The woman all cover themselves," Lukien remarked. "Why, Figgis?"

The librarian smiled. "Because Vala has told them to."

It was another of the scholar's riddles. "Vala? Is that their king?"

"No, not a king. Remember the Eyes of God? They are called Inai ka *Vala*."

"Ah, so Vala is one of their gods?"

"Not *a* god, Lukien. *The* god. The Ganjeese and the Jadori worship only one deity, whom they call Vala. It is the will of Vala that women cover themselves."

"But why?" Lukien spied the women in the street. Young and old alike were hidden behind dark veils.

"The Ganjeese believe that men and women should be modest, and should not show their bodies. This way, they can be judged on their skills and intelligence, and not by the way they look. Women in particular must be modest, and not be flirtatious or corrupt a man. The holy book of Vala instructs women to guard their modesty, and not display their beauty to any but their husbands."

Trager laughed. "You hear that, Lukien? That's what the veil is for—to keep sniffing dogs like you away!"

"Still," said Lukien. "It seems unfair. This would never happen in Liiria."

"No," agreed Figgis. "But then what's in Liiria to believe in?" The librarian regarded Lukien. "Do you have a god, Lukien?"

Lukien thought for a moment. He had never really considered the question. Growing up in the streets hadn't given him much time to ponder such things. As a Liirian he had his pick of religions. He could believe in the Fate as Baron Glass did, or the Great Spirit of Reec or the serpent god of Marn. But to him they all seemed empty, without truth.

"I believe in this," he said, patting his sword. "And I believe in myself. Other than that, who knows?"

"That is the answer of a Liirian," said Figgis. "And it won't win you any friends here, I assure you. These people are devout. Say whatever you wish, but do not criticize their beliefs. If you do, they will kill you."

"Figgis, I intend to say as little as possible to these people," replied Lukien. "I just want to get back home as soon as possible."

They rode in silence until the road widened into a village square, now converted into an open market. Lukien was stunned by the market. He had never seen such an exotic array of goods, not even in Koth. A young boy with a colorful bird perched on his shoulder caught his attention, as did a shapely young lady walking unhurriedly through the square. His eyes followed her. Like the other women, she was dressed in long white wraps that trailed behind her, but he could make out the curve of her body beneath the robes, and a trace of dark hair falling beneath her veil. She held a basket in her hands, full of bread. Two small boys scurried after her, but to Lukien she didn't seem old enough to be their mother. In a moment she disappeared through a beaded curtain, entering one of the buildings.

"There," said Figgis, pointing in her direction. "That looks like a shrana house. I'll go in and ask around, see if I can find us shelter for the night."

"And food," added Trager. "Before we all collapse."

"And a guide," said Lukien. He looked at the entrance to the shrana house. "Shouldn't we go in with you, Figgis?"

"No," said Figgis. "Stay outside and watch the horses. There's a lot of thievery in this city. If we lose the horses we'll have nothing to trade for drowa, and it's a long walk across the desert."

Lukien was about to agree when he saw the most amazing creature emerge from the crowd. He stopped his horse just outside the shrana house, staring as the beast rounded the corner. A huge, reptilian head wrapped in leather tack stared back at him, its two black eyes blinking beneath membranous lids. It had four legs and a long, slender tail, and was as tall as a horse but much broader across, its muscles bunching beneath its scaly skin. There was a rider on its back, robed in crimson and black, his face hidden behind a cloth wrap. Dust and sand clung to every inch of him. Lukien's horse noticed the creature and snorted in alarm.

"Great Fate," Lukien gasped. "What is *that?*"

"That," said Figgis, "is a kreel." The librarian got off his horse as the beast and rider approached, moving with a graceful gait toward them. Too stunned to move, Lukien and Trager simply watched the kreel in disbelief. They had talked about the great lizards during their ride south. Figgis had said they were not to be feared, but seeing one close up made being afraid easy. Lukien's hand fell instinctively to his sword. The crowd outside the shrana house parted as the lizard sauntered near, but they did not seem surprised or frightened by the creature. Figgis smiled as if a stray dog was approaching.

"Beautiful, isn't it?" he said. "It's been years since I've seen one."

The kreel and its rider noticed Figgis and stopped before him. The rider's dark eyes studied the old man.

"Uh, Figgis, I think you should get out of its way," Lukien suggested.

But the librarian held up his hands towards the man and beast in a gesture of peace, then began to say words Lukien didn't understand, speaking with effort as he pronounced the words.

"Jadori?" Trager guessed.

Lukien shrugged. He didn't know Jadori from Ganjeese, nor any other of the strange tongues he heard around him. But remarkably the rider seemed to understand Figgis. There was no malice in his eyes, only a sort of surprised humor. Figgis struggled with the language, pausing in long stretches between each sentence as he groped for the right words. The rider waited patiently, amused by the old foreigner.

"Figgis?" probed Lukien. "What are you doing?"

"He is from Jador," said Figgis. Childlike exuberance shone on his face. "And he understands me!"

"Yes, all right," said Lukien. "Just be careful what you say to him." Lukien slid slowly off his horse and went to stand beside Figgis. He whispered, "Remember why we're here."

"Of course I remember." Figgis smiled at the Jadori, then began to speak again. The man nodded. "He says he has come for trade," said Figgis. "He's only just arrived from Jador."

"Will he be staying long in the city?" asked Trager. "Maybe he could take us back with him."

"I'm afraid not. He says he will be going east from here. We don't have the time to wait for him."

"Agreed," said Lukien. "Then we'll find a guide in the shrana house."

Figgis kept talking to the Jadori, asking questions. The man answered each one, patiently waiting for Figgis to form his sentences, and when he spoke he did so slowly, making sure the old man understood. Figgis had told them during the journey that the Jadori were peaceful people, gracious in every way, and now that seemed true. The rider didn't even have a sword, and his great reptile seemed as docile

as a pony. It lowered its head onto the sandy ground as its
rider spoke, oblivious to the conversation.

"Come on, Figgis," growled Trager. "What are you going
on about? Hurry up."

Figgis ignored the lieutenant. He exchanged smiles with
the rider, who then got down off his kreel and looked at
Lukien and Trager. Amazingly, he bowed to them. Not
knowing how to reply, Lukien bowed, too.

"Lukien, he is thanking you for looking after his kreel,"
Figgis explained.

"What?"

"We are going into the shrana house. I'll buy him a drink
and find out what I can about Jador. I told him you'll be
outside looking after our horses, so—"

"So you thought I'd look after this big lizard? Are you
mad?"

Figgis tried to cover Lukien's anger with a smile. "Easy,"
he said. "I won't be long, and the kreel won't be any trouble. I told you—they're peaceful creatures. Just stay out
here and look after it, all right? Make sure the children
keep away." Figgis turned toward the beaded curtain, parting it for his new friend. "I'll bring you back something
to eat."

"Figgis!"

The librarian disappeared into the tavern with the Jadori,
leaving Lukien and Trager with the kreel. The two soldiers
looked at each other, aghast. The kreel had closed its eyes
and laid its giant head in the sand. Its broad back rose and
fell with easy breathing.

"Well?" asked Trager sharply. "What do we do now?"

Lukien looked at the resting kreel. "Hope it doesn't
get hungry."

An hour later, Figgis finally emerged from the tavern. The
Jadori man was with him, smiling and laughing as the two
spoke among themselves. Figgis held two packages of food
in his hand. As he approached Lukien and Trager, he held
them out.

"For you," he said, then went back to talking to the
Jadori. Lukien looked at his food—a large, flat circle of
bread stuffed with meat and spices. He gave it a wary sniff,

decided it smelled good, then bit down hungrily. Trager did the same, glaring angrily at Figgis.

"What took you so long?" he asked through a mouthful of food.

"I had things to discuss with Tamaz. I learned a great deal."

"Tamaz?" asked Lukien. "Is that his name?"

The Jadori looked at him, then pointed at himself. "Tamaz."

Trager wasn't satisfied. "You leave us out here starving, looking after that monster?" He gestured to the kreel. "What were you thinking?"

"Easy," scolded Lukien. The kreel hadn't been a problem. Only now did it rise, seeing its master return. "No harm done. What did you learn, Figgis?"

"First, I got us passage to Jadori," said Figgis happily.

"Really?" Lukien looked at Tamaz. "Is he taking us there?"

"No." Figgis looked back toward the shrana house. "He is."

Coming through the beaded curtain was another man, big and dark-skinned with a weathered face and beard. He was older than the Jadori man, almost as old as Figgis himself, and carried himself with an air of authority that made Lukien stop eating. As the Jadori man mounted his kreel and said his good-byes to Figgis, the new stranger stepped up and gave the trio a slight bow. His drab robes rustled as he moved, but he never took his eyes off the foreigners. Then another figure emerged out of the tavern, directly on the heels of the first. To Lukien's surprise, it was the young woman he'd seen earlier.

"Who's this?" asked Trager.

Figgis stepped between them and introduced the man. "This is Jebel. He is the leader of a caravan that will take us to Jador. The girl with him is his daughter, Cahra."

"Caravan?" asked Lukien. "You mean they're traders?"

"They are like nomads, Lukien. They travel from place to place, living off the land and bartering for what they need. They live in the desert mostly, but come into Ganjor when they need things. Now they are going to Jador. Tamaz introduced them to me."

Trager's face lit with alarm. "What? You mean you told Tamaz we're going to Jador?"

"It seemed like the thing to do."

"Figgis, that was very stupid," said Lukien. "He could have warned them—"

"Stop," said Figgis, putting up his hands. He took Lukien by the arm and turned him away from Jebel and his daughter. "Watch what you say. Jebel speaks our language."

Lukien looked at the man, who stared back with a hard expression. "Jebel. Forgive me," he offered. "I am Lukien. This is Trager."

Jebel nodded at them. His daughter Cahra did not.

Lukien smiled awkwardly. "You will take us to Jador, Jebel?"

The dark man said, "My family rides in the morning. You may come with us, and we will guide you. But you will need your own drowa."

"I've already explained that to them, Jebel," said Figgis. "We will trade our horses for drowa. Then we'll meet you back here and go to your caravan. Agreed?"

"It is agreed." Jebel looked at Trager, who was still eating with both hands, and cringed in disgust. He said to Figgis, "Teach them something of manners before you return." Then he turned and went back into the shrana house, calling his daughter after him. Cahra hesitated a moment, studying the three strangers before hurrying after her father.

"What was that all about?" asked Trager. Meat drippings dribbled down his chin.

"It's my fault," said Figgis. "I should have explained this to you before I brought the food. We're in Ganjor now; we can't eat like we usually do."

"Bah," scoffed Trager. "If I'm too messy for them, screw 'em."

"That's not it," said Figgis. "You don't eat with both hands here, Trager. You eat with the right hand only."

Puzzled, Lukien frowned. "The right hand? Why?"

"Because that's your clean hand. Your left hand is for . . . well, you know."

"No, I don't know. What do you mean?"

Figgis smiled. "In this culture, the left hand is used for bodily things, Lukien. You know, cleaning yourself?"

Suddenly Lukien understood. He looked down at his hands, then at all the Ganjeese people around them.

"I don't get it," said Trager. He continued eating with both hands. "What do you mean, clean yourself?"

Figgis sighed hopelessly. "Forget it. Let's just get those drowa."

That night, Lukien and the others rested with Jebel's caravan on the outskirts of the city. They had traded their horses for three drowa, then had met again with Jebel in the tavern, who took them out to his caravan near sundown. There they had met with the rest of the desert leader's huge family, a similarly-featured band of some hundred people spanning multiple generations. Jebel introduced them perfunctorily to his wife and his brother, then had his youngest children line up for inspection. He explained to them that they had visitors from far away, and that they were to teach them what they could of their culture and their god, Vala. Because they were foreigners, Jebel explained, they could not be expected to know how to eat and clean themselves. Lukien listened to Jebel's speech in embarrassment, and more than once saw Cahra giggle. Now that she was with her family again she had doffed her veil, revealing her pretty face. She was not glamorous, but she had dark, deep eyes that reminded Lukien of Cassandra.

Jebel's caravan was an impressive sight, easily seen from the city. There were at least two dozen wagons, strangely designed vehicles with large, wide wheels and a high clearance beneath them. There were also numerous, humpbacked drowa laying lazily around the camp. Torches and candles had been set in the sand, and the moonlight shone on the dunes. Lukien, Trager, and Figgis had all taken their ease at the camp, supping with Jebel and his wife and sharing his water-pipe, a strange but pleasant device that Lukien had never seen before. Now they were full and content as they sat around a fire, listening to the odd music of the desert and gazing at Ganjor in the distance. To the west lay the Desert of Tears, an endless stretch of forbidding sand. The setting of the sun had cooled the world considerably, and all of them wore the gakas that Figgis had purchased. Lukien found the garb remarkably comfortable. He stretched with a yawn, yearning for sleep. Tomorrow they would begin their trek to Jador, making their way along the caravan routes, the well-traveled lanes that Figgis had promised could accomodate the wagons as long as they weren't swallowed by sandstorms. Lukien wasn't sure he was up to it. Of the three, only Figgis was eager to break camp. He sat slightly apart from Lukien, talking with Jebel on the far side of the fire. Trager had his eyes closed, half asleep. Around the wagons, children giggled in hushed voices and played with mangy dogs. Lukien watched Figgis converse with Jebel, amazed by his stamina. He knew that without the strange librarian, their mission would have been hopeless.

While they had shopped for their drowas, Figgis had explained his conversation with Tamaz, the Jadori. He had learned from the lizard rider that Jador was still at peace, just as Figgis had suspected, and that they still had a kahan and a kahana, just as they did decades ago when Figgis was a young man in Ganjor. Back then, Figgis had recalled, the kahan had been a man named Kadar. So it had surprised and elated Figgis when Tamaz told him that the Kahan of Jador was still Kadar, apparantly the very man who had ruled Jador all that time ago. It might have been his son, Figgis supposed, but he prefered to think it was still the same man, and that a magical amulet was keeping him alive. Kadar's wife, the kahana, was called Jitendra. This news draped a pall over Figgis' theory, because he remembered Kadar's wife as having a different name. Still, it was enticing.

Deciding there was no harm in explaining their pretense to Tamaz, Figgis had told him that they were emissaries from King Akeela of Liiria, and that they had brought gifts for the Jadori kahan in hopes of opening up diplomatic relations. The news had pleased Tamaz, who told Figgis that Kahan Kadar would welcome the Liirian visitors. But he had refused to speak more about Kadar, and that puzzled Figgis. The librarian had decided not to push the man further, but had taken his evasiveness as a good sign.

"Perhaps they are not allowed to speak of the kahan's magic," Figgis had theorized.

Lukien didn't really care. He was just glad they were on their way to Jador, and that soon he might confront this Kahan Kadar. If he and his wife did indeed have the magic amulets, he would steal them. In the quiet of the desert, it seemed a remarkably simple plan.

For Cassandra, Lukien reminded himself.

He wasn't a thief, but for Cassandra he would become one. For Cassandra, he would do anything, and that troubled him. He was far from home now, maybe about to die. He had risked his brotherhood with Akeela and imperiled his soul, if indeed he even had a soul, and as the wind played across the sand Lukien wondered what life would be like without her. In the little time they had spent together, he had fallen deeply in love with her. He imagined he could accept her as Akeela's wife, as long as she was close and he could look at her. But if she died. . . .

She will not die, Lukien told himself. *I won't allow it.*

With Cassandra's face filling his thoughts, Lukien closed his eyes and went to sleep.

17

At the bridge of Roan-si, Chancellor Hogon and his army of Liirians paused to look across the glistening River Kryss. They had traveled many days to make the rendezvous, and the infantry and horses were exhausted from the march. But the sight of the river heartened them, and the opposing army that had come to meet them put a smile on Hogon's face. He narrowed his eyes against the strong sun, recognizing Raxor's flag. The Reecian war minister's standard was a green flag embroided with a snarling lion, in the same colors as his brother. From the looks of Raxor's camp, the Reecians had arrived at least a day earlier. Tents and pavilions had already been erected, and a few small cooking fires burned among the huddled troops. The scouts that Hogon had sent ahead had reported that Raxor was anxious for his meeting at the bridge. Already Reecian soldiers were riding out of camp to greet them. Hogon put up his hand and bid his company to remain calm. He had five hundred infantry with him and almost a hundred heavy horsemen, all of whom still distrusted their new allies. But Raxor had come just as his brother had promised, and Hogon had his orders. So far, at least, Akeela's plan was working.

"Dusan, you will accompany me," said Hogon. "Kass, stay back with the others."

The chancellor's aides frowned at each other.

"Sir, is that wise?" asked Dusan, the younger of the two.

He had been with Hogon for five years, yet still saw fit to question him. "You should have at least two men with you, for protection."

The Chancellor of War chuckled. "Protection from what? They're our allies now."

Lieutenant Kass snorted, "Allies. Who believes that, truly?"

"Your king believes that," said Hogon sharply. "And look, they have come."

"So you trust them?" asked Kass.

Hogon didn't answer. He didn't have to trust the Reecians. Like Liiria, they had a stake in defeating Norvor, and that would keep them honest, at least for now. And despite his violent history, Raxor was known as a man of his word, not only in Reec but throughout the continent. Hogon had battled Raxor many times, but he had never hated the man. He respected him.

"See that the men rest, Kass," said Hogon, "and that the horses take water. Dusan, come along."

With Dusan following close behind, Hogon trotted toward the bridge. Roan-si Bridge was wide and sturdy, and would easily accommodate bringing the army across. It had been built by the Reecians long before Akeela had come to power, but had been abandoned during the bitter stalemate, used mostly by traders and merchants. Roan-si, Hogon knew, was an old Reecian phrase meaning "meeting place." The irony of the name wasn't lost on the old man. Those who had built the bridge had supposed it would bring the two nations together, but only Akeela had been able to do that.

As he neared the stone bridge, Hogon recognized Raxor among the approaching soldiers. When the Reecian noticed Hogon's single companion, he paused for a moment, ordering all but one of his soldiers to stop and wait as he himself rode on. He wore a surcoat over his black armor and metal studded greaves, and his ebony warhorse matched his own dark hair, combed back and slick with oil. He was a big man, like his brother, and as he trotted onto the bridge his eyes met Hogon's with an air of mistrust. Hogon remained arrow-straight in his saddle, not even blinking as he rode to face his longtime enemy. Never before had he been this close to Raxor. The urge to draw his sword was almost irresistible. There was no sound on the bridge, only the clopping of horse hooves on stone. Behind Hogon, Dusan was silent.

The two men rode toward the crest of the bridge, their aides keeping back a pace. Hogon stopped his horse and raised his hand in greeting.

"Raxor."

The War Minister of Reec nodded. "Hogon."

They looked at each other without the smallest hint of friendship. Raxor was unreadable. Hogon felt the breeze strike his face and decided he should say something.

"You've come," he said. "To be honest, I didn't know if you would. Thank you."

"My king commanded it," said Raxor. "Is that not why you are here, Hogon?"

Hogon nodded. "It is."

"You look tired," the Reecian remarked.

"It is a long march from Koth."

"And from Hes," agreed Raxor. "But we have rested. We arrived yesterday."

"Good. Then you are ready to march on Hanging Man?"

"We are." Raxor hesitated, sizing up Hogon. "Chancellor, I have a question from my brother. He wants to know how his daughter fares."

Hogon grimaced. In the tension of the moment, he had forgotten that Karis had been told of Cassandra's illness. The messenger that had asked for his help against Norvor had delivered that bad news as well.

"I'm sorry," said Hogon, "but the queen does poorly. She has some good days, but she is very ill. Her physician says she may be dead in a month or two."

"And the quest your messenger spoke of? How does that go?"

"No word yet. But we have sent out our best knights in search of the amulets. If they exist, our men will find them."

Raxor's face betrayed his sadness. "It is a fool's errand," he said. "If Cassandra has so little time, how can your knights save her?"

"They will do their best," said Hogon. He did not believe in Lukien's quest either, but thought it best not to say so. "As I said, if the amulets exist, our men will find them."

"Then I will dispatch that news to my brother, and tell him to begin mourning his daughter," said Raxor bitterly. "Now, what news of your king?"

"King Akeela still rides for Hanging Man. He will arrive there on the morrow. We will attack the day after, just past dawn."

"Will there will be a signal?"

Hogon shook his head. "No. My orders are to attack an hour past dawn. Akeela assured me he would be ready."

Raxor grimaced. "With respect, I have met your king, Chancellor. He doesn't seem capable of this mission."

"Maybe. But he's not alone. He has fifty men with him, including one of his best Chargers. When we attack, they will be ready."

Raxor looked over Hogon's shoulder, toward his Liirian army. "You have brought a goodly force with you."

"Five hundred infantry and a hundred cavalry." Hogon surveyed Raxor's troops in the distance. "Almost as many as you, it seems."

"Indeed. We will be formidable . . ." Raxor almost smiled. "Together."

Hogon returned the crooked grin. "Together," he echoed. The word felt odd to him. "We live in strange times, Minister," he said, then proceeded across the bridge with Raxor.

18

The Norvan fortress of Hanging Man clung to the edge of a cliff, one sheer face turned toward the churning river below. Defiant flags overhung its battlements, snapping in the wind, while countless scores of armored men milled about its courtyard, barely visible through the surrounding iron gate. A single turret rose from the fortress, its gray stone weather-pitted, its arrow slits perpetually watching the River Kryss. Beyond the fortress lay Norvor, a land of formidable mountains and hot southern summers. Hanging Man's shadow fell across the River Kryss like a drawbridge. The fortress had stood for six decades, guarding Norvor and its diamond mines from its Reecian neighbors. It had earned its name during the first Reecian'Norvan war, when Norvan soldiers hung their Reecian captives on the wall facing the river, so that any who approached would see their grisly trophies and be warned. The name had stuck, but not the practice, for there had been no war between the uneasy neighbors for many years, and Norvor had quieted as its brutal leader aged. Akeela knew very little about King Mor, but he knew that he was very old, and that now he was very angry. Angry enough, it seemed, to return to his warlike ways.

It was just past noon when Akeela and his contingent of Chargers arrived at Hanging Man. The sun beat down on his cape-clad shoulders. His horse moved sluggishly, eager for a rest, and the warmth had wilted Akeela's spirits, which withered further at the sight of Hanging Man. For eight days they had ridden, finding what shelter they could in Liirian villages, until they had crossed the Kryss and entered Reec. After that they had been on their own, and the lack of sleep and decent food had plagued Akeela. He wasn't as hearty as Breck or the others, and he knew that it showed. Breck rode very close to him, watching him like a concerned brother.

"They see us, my lord," said Breck. He ambled his horse alongside Akeela's, pointing at the great turret.

"No doubt," said Akeela. His insides clenched. From the looks of the fortress, King Mor had been busy. There were catapults and heavy wagons and stables housing war horses, all plainly visible and meant to send a message. Akeela no longer doubted Mor's intentions. It was expensive to move so many men and so much equipment; Mor wasn't bluffing. He intended to attack Reec if his demands were not met, even if it meant war with Liiria.

"Keep riding," Akeela told Breck. The lieutenant called the order down the line, and the fifty horsemen kept moving. The men in Hanging Man's courtyard began opening the great gate.

"My lord?" Breck whispered.

"Yes?"

"Are you all right?"

Akeela nodded. "Yes."

Breck leaned in closer. "You don't have to do this. We can still turn around. Just say the word."

But Akeela couldn't say the word. Frightened as he was, he knew there was no turning back. Hogon was already prepared, and Raxor with him.

"I can't explain this to you, Breck. It's just something I have to do."

"But you've never done anything like this before." Breck kept his voice low, but his tone was earnest. "Forgive me for saying this, but you're not a soldier, my lord."

"Shhh," Akeela urged. "No more talk, all right? It's done, and I'm not backing down."

Akeela took a breath to still his doubts. Mor's arrogance had brought them to this, and if Mor died in the battle, then Akeela wouldn't shed a tear for him. There was more at stake than one man's life—there was Liiria, and Akeela's rule over it. He couldn't let Mor or Baron Glass or anyone else think him a weakling.

Cassandra doesn't want a weakling for a husband, thought Akeela. *She wants a hero, like Lukien.*

He rode ahead of Breck, checking himself as he approached the fortress. He felt the slender length of his dagger against his breast, his only protection. Up ahead, the great gate of Hanging Man beckoned. A contingent of soldiers waited there, dressed in the peculiar armor of Norvor, their heads hidden beneath winged helmets. Akeela searched the crowd for Mor, but did not see the old man.

"Ho," he called to the men. "I am King Akeela of Liiria. May we come ahead?"

"You may come," answered a sentry, "and ten men with you. No more."

Akeela shook his head. "I won't walk into a lion's mouth without protection. I have fifty tired men with me, and they all need rest and food."

"And I have my orders, King Akeela," said the sentry. "King Mor has said ten men only may enter."

Breck leaned over, whispering, "Refuse."

Akeela hesitated. If his plan was to work, Mor needed to think him a coward. He called to the sentry, "Twenty men. Otherwise I will not enter."

The Norvans mumbled amongst themselves. Finally their leader relented. "Twenty men is agreed. Come ahead."

"And you will see that the rest are fed?"

The sentry agreed, and Akeela had Breck count out twenty of the Royal Chargers. Together they rode forward. Akeela took careful notice of the gate as he passed through it. If their plan was to succeed, they would have to keep the gate open as long as possible. The sentries in the courtyard bowed slightly to Akeela as he entered the courtyard, taking his horse. Akeela dismounted, surveying his surroundings.

"This is Lieutenant Breck," he told the wing-helmed sentry. "He will accompany me everywhere, is that understood?"

"King Mor expected you to have a bodyguard," replied the leader. There was a trace of humor in his tone. "He's waiting for you inside." He began to order the fortress gates closed. Akeela quickly interrupted him.

"Don't you dare close those gates until my men are taken care of," he said sharply. "I want them fed, and I want feed for their horses as well."

The sentry reluctantly agreed, telling his companions to see to their "guests." "The rest of your men can take their ease here in the yard," he said. "We'll see to their horses as well, but they're not to accompany you to the meeting. And they're not to draw their weapons for any reason."

"Then don't give them reason to do so," said Akeela.

The guard seemed to smile beneath his helmet. "Your bodyguard may accompany you to the meeting. And as I said, King Mor is expecting you."

With Breck beside him, Akeela followed the sentry out of the yard, through a portcullis and into the main keep. A wide hall full of torchlight greeted them. Soldiers and servant boys walked the stone floor. Akeela felt his pulse quicken. Up ahead was a large pair of wooden doors guarded by two more soldiers. Both wore the ornate armor of Norvor, polished to a luster, and sported winged helmets. As Akeela approached, they uncrossed their halberds and bowed, then turned to open the creaking portals, revealing a large, dark chamber. Akeela stepped across the threshold. In the room was an oval-shaped table, laden with bread and cheese and flasks of wine. Three men were seated at the far end. Two of them rose when Akeela entered. Mor, seated in the center, did not. His watery eyes watched Akeela; his thin lips parted in an amused smile. A spotless white cat lay in his lap, purring as Mor stroked its long hair. Mor had dressed for the meeting, wearing a resplendent emerald cape and an elaborate collection of gem-encrusted rings. His pate was speckled with age spots, making him look even older than the last time Akeela had seen him. His dark gaze drifted over his guests.

Akeela bowed. "King Mor. It's good to see you again. Thank you for agreeing to meet with me."

Mor inclined his head. "You've come quicker than I'd suspected, young Akeela. Anxious for peace, are you?"

"I am, my lord," said Akeela. "I'm hopeful we can come to some sort of arrangement."

The Norvan king continued stroking his pet. "You know Nace and Fianor."

The two men remained standing, bowing slightly to

Akeela. General Nace was Mor's top military man, now in command of Hanging Man fortress. The younger man, Fianor, was Mor's son. As next in line for the Norvan throne, he accompanied his father everywhere. The prince had strange, mismatched eyes and platinum hair that harkened back to what his father might have looked like in youth.

"This is Breck," said Akeela, "a lieutenant of my Royal Chargers and one of my closest aides. He'll be staying with me inside Hanging Man."

The sentry that had brought them to the chamber said, "My lord, King Akeela has brought about fifty men with him. Twenty of them have been allowed inside the courtyard."

King Mor smiled. "Twenty? Bargaining already, King Akeela?"

"They make me feel safe, my lord," replied Akeela. He remembered how he needed to play the weakling. "I'm sure you understand."

"Yes," drawled Mor. He stroked his cat and studied Akeela. "Sit, my friend."

Akeela took a chair across from Mor. Breck remained standing. The significant distance between the two kings added to the air of mistrust. Akeela took notice of the room and the placement of the chairs. Tomorrow, he would have to be much closer to Mor. A servant came from the corner of the room, filling Akeela's goblet with wine. King Mor raised his glass toward his guest.

"To you, King Akeela," he said. "And to our meeting. May it be fruitful."

"That is my fondest hope," said Akeela. When he had drank, he put down the glass and looked at Mor earnestly. "King Mor, you know why I'm here. You threaten war with Reec, and even with Liiria. I've seen the buildup of your forces here at Hanging Man. But I can tell you honestly, there is no need for this."

"No need? King Akeela, you surprise me. You make a treaty with my enemy, and yet you say there is no need for me to worry?"

"I made a peace treaty with Reec, my lord, that is all."

"Words, King Akeela." Mor waved off his remarks. "You gave them rights to the Kryss. You didn't even think about us here in Norvor. We are like nothing to you. Well,

as you can see, we will not ignore such shabby treatment.
And we will not let Reec have the Kryss. If we must, we
will take it." King Mor leaned forward threateningly. "And
not even Liiria will stop us."

Incensed, Akeela wanted to spit across the table. Mor's
arrogance was boundless. But Akeela held his tongue, summoning the coward Mor expected him to be.

"No, my lord, please. We must avoid such a thing. Liiria
doesn't want war with Norvor any more than we wanted it
with Reec. We must do what we can to stop it."

Mor sighed, considering the cat in his lap. "Frankly, I
am out of ideas. I made my anger plain to you in our last
meeting, yet you have chosen to offer us nothing.
Unless . . ." He looked up with a smile. "Have you come
to offer something?"

"Since I cannot have war with you, I'm prepared to
bargain."

"I am listening, King Akeela."

"First, the Kryss is no longer mine to give. You know
that. We traded it for peace with Reec, and to take it back
would invite war with them. But we still have rights to it,
rights assured us by King Karis. If you are willing, Liiria
will pay you tribute for use of the river. If you allow our
ships to sail south past Hanging Man, each one will pay a
toll of gold."

Mor looked intrigued. "And Reec? What of their ships?"

"We will pay their tribute as well," said Akeela. "It will
come from our own coffers, provided you make no aggres-
sion against them. And provided you move your army back
from the border."

"Your own coffers? You would pay for Reecian ships
just to avoid war?"

"My lord, you have given me little choice," said Akeela.
"If you attack Reec, Liiria will be forced to intercede. And
we have no wish to fight you. I'm not happy about it, but
I see no other options."

Prince Fianor snickered. "You could act like a man."

His father glared at him, warning him to be silent. But
when he looked back at Akeela, he said, "My son talks out
of turn, King Akeela, yet I fear he's correct. Your father
wouldn't have come here with such an offer. He would
have fought. But you're not your father, are you?"

"My father sent thousands of men to die in useless wars, my lord. I am trying to avoid such waste of life."

"By bleeding your treasury?" Mor laughed. "Well, if you are willing to offer such a deal, I am willing to accept it. Will you sign a treaty saying so?"

"Of course. Have your people draft a paper of intent. Have it ready in the morning, and we will both sign it before I leave. We can work out the particulars of the payments later."

Mor's grin lit the room. "Then we are concluded, my friend. But you must stay the night in Hanging Man, of course. And your man here with you."

"Fine. But I must leave on the morrow," said Akeela. "I'm eager to return home."

"Yes, I'm sure you are." Mor hid his disdain very poorly. "The papers will be drawn tonight. We'll wake early and sign them, and you can be on your way. But I should warn you, King Akeela, I will hold you to your word. If payment is not made on every ship that passes south, my army will return. And I will not be so willing to bargain."

Akeela frowned. "I am a man of my word, King Mor. You should know that by now."

"Indeed." Mor lifted the cat from his lap and held it to his breast, then rose from his chair. "You should rest now, King Akeela. You look exhausted."

Akeela got to his feet. "Yes, I am. But so are my men. We've ridden for many days, my lord. I'm wondering—may they come inside as well? They need rest, a proper roof from the sun and wind. If you could see fit to letting them stay within the courtyard at least, I would be most grateful."

Mor chuckled. "You try to be so strong, King Akeela. Yet here you are, in my council chamber with just one man to protect you. What will you do if I refuse your request?"

"To refuse would be unjust, my lord, for as you've chosen to point out, I'm no threat to you. I'm only concerned about my people."

Mor thought for a moment, turning again toward the sentry. "Fifty men, you say?"

"Yes, my lord. And twenty are already inside the courtyard."

"I would say that twenty Liirians are quite enough," Mor

concluded. "But they may shift if they like. When the first twenty are rested, twenty others may take their ease in the yard."

"My lord, that's not very helpful," said Akeela.

"But it's all I am willing to grant." Mor gestured to the door. "Take your rest tonight, King Akeela, and be glad I've allowed even that many of your cowards into my fortress."

At dawn the next morning, Akeela and Breck waited for Mor's men to come for them. Akeela had hardly slept at all. He had dressed and he had planned, and he had checked and rechecked the dagger beneath his cape. The room Mor had given them was on the north side of the fortress, and Akeela had spent much of the night staring off at the dark horizon, hoping that Hogon and Raxor were prepared. They were to use the cover of night to advance on the fortress, ducking behind the hills and mountains to hide their advance. An hour past dawn, they would attack. Now that it was dawn, Akeela supposed they were very near. But he couldn't see them from his window, and he wondered if they were there at all.

"It's almost time," he noted. The sun was rising, exposing the terrain. The dark mountains took shape and the river began to glow, but there was no sign of Hogon. Akeela turned from the window. "Maybe they haven't come. Maybe Raxor wouldn't join them."

"No, they're out there somewhere, my lord," said Breck. Throughout the night he had been the voice of reason. Now he sat in one of the chamber's spartan chairs, waiting. He watched Akeela with the cool gaze of a seasoned soldier. "Don't worry about Hogon. Just keep your mind on the task at hand. And remember, you have to get close to Mor."

"I know," said Akeela impatiently. "I'm just worried about the timing."

"Don't be. Mor loves to talk, so keep him talking. Start him bragging about his army or something. We just need enough time for them to get a glimpse of Hogon."

"And Raxor," added Akeela. It felt odd for him to be taking orders from Breck, but the reversal of roles was necessary. As he was too often reminded, he wasn't a soldier. He said, "I just hope he's come as well. Do you think—"

A knock at the door interrupted Akeela. He jumped, staring at the portal. "Yes? Who is it?"

The door opened and Fianor appeared. The prince was alone. He smiled wryly at Akeela. "Good morning, my lord. I see you are ready for your meeting with my father."

"I'm ready," Akeela replied. "Have the papers been drawn?"

"Drawn and awaiting your signature, my lord. May I escort you downstairs?"

"Is your father already there?"

The prince seemed to laugh. "My father is anxious to see the treaty signed, my lord, and hardly slept at all last night. You said you wanted to leave early, so he made himself ready for you."

"And my men? What of them?"

"Your men are still in the yard," said Fianor. "They've been fed and sheltered." The prince snickered. "They seem eager to be on their way."

Akeela took the insult without flinching. "Yes, well, they're a long way from home." He clapped his hands together and rubbed. "Now, let's go sign that treaty."

Chancellor Hogon was exhausted. He and his army had marched hard through the night, following the river and ignoring the dangers of darkness. With Raxor's army beside them, they had kept close to the hills bordering the Kryss, periodically sending forth scouts to make sure their advance went unnoticed. Their horses were tired and in desperate need of rest, and the feet of the infantry bloomed with blisters. Hogon himself had hardly been able to keep himself erect in the saddle. Desperate for sleep, he had nevertheless pushed his old body to its edges, for time was his enemy and Akeela needed him.

Dawn was coming, and that meant battle was near. In the growing light, Hogon could see the first hint of Hanging Man on the horizon, its ugly turret poking out of the rocky earth like a cobra. He ordered his company to come to a halt. His six hundred men silently obeyed. Raxor, who rode beside Hogon, repeated the order to his own men, and down the line the order went. Together they surveyed the terrain.

"So?" asked Raxor. "Do we wait or do we ride?"

Hogon wasn't sure how to answer. He wanted to give Akeela enough time to meet with Mor. At just past dawn, it seemed unlikely they would already be meeting. But Akeela had given him clear orders. He looked at the sun rising in the east, echoing his king's words.

"Just past dawn."

Raxor nodded. "We're already close enough to be seen. If we don't ride, we'll be discovered too early."

Still Hogon hesitated. Even from such a distance, Hanging Man looked formidable. Between himself and Raxor, they had over a thousand men. Akeela's company added fifty to their ranks, but still. . . .

"I hope Akeela knows what he's doing," muttered Hogon.

"Don't fret for your king," said Raxor. "All he has to do is get the gate open. If he succeeds, we will triumph." He looked at Hogon for an answer. "Chancellor, there isn't much time."

Hogon didn't argue. He gripped the reins of his horse tightly, raised one hand above his head, and gave the order to advance.

King Mor and his ubiquitous cat were already seated when Akeela arrived in the council chamber. As before, there was food on the table and wine to toast the treaty. General Nace was present with several other soldiers, all bearing the same smug expression. The general and his underlings rose when Akeela entered. Breck kept close to Akeela. Akeela looked about the room, disappointed that none of his other men had been invited. On the table sat the treaty Mor had ordered written, a single piece of parchment rolled out flat. Next to it was a quill pen in an inkwell. Mor's face hovered over the treaty, smiling triumphantly.

"Welcome, King Akeela," said the old ruler. "I trust you slept well?"

The incongruous question vexed Akeela. "Well enough. Is that the treaty?"

"Indeed." Mor pushed it across the table toward Akeela.

"It reads just as you said it should. You will pay us a tribute of gold for every Liirian and Reecian ship that passes south of Hanging Man. It says that the price of the tribute will be determined at a later date by our factions, likely based on tonnage, and that you, King Akeela, take full responsibility for seeing this agreement implemented." Mor picked up the pen. "Ready to sign?"

"No," said Akeela. "You have these soldiers here to witness for you. All I have is Breck. I think I should at least have more of my men present, don't you?"

Mor made a sour face. "Yes, I suppose," he sighed. He looked past Akeela toward his son, Fianor. "Go and bring three of King Akeela's men. Tell them to leave their swords. Be quick."

Prince Fianor did as he was asked, disappearing down the hall. Akeela tried to relax, sure that he had bought himself some time.

"General Nace," he said cordially, "would you mind giving up your seat for the signing? I should be next to King Mor, I think."

The general was about to sit down but stopped himself. He gave Akeela a peculiar look, then glanced at his king.

"It's tradition, Nace," said Mor. "Sit at the other end, will you? Let King Akeela have your chair."

Akeela thanked the general and took the seat to Mor's right. This close to Mor, he could smell the old man's breath and the odor of his cat, still perched lazily in his lap. Breck remained standing. Knowing that he needed to stall for time, Akeela leapt on the first idea that came to mind.

"Great Fate, I'm starving," he said. "And look at all this food! Shall we break our fast together, my lord?"

"Certainly, my friend," said Mor. Then he took the pen from the inkwell. "But let's eat after we take care of business, hmm?"

Akeela reached across the table for a loaf of bread. "Well, my witnesses aren't here yet, so we have some time." He held the loaf out for Mor. "Bread, my lord?"

Mor shook his head. "No."

"Well, I hope you don't mind if I help myself." Akeela tore off a great hunk of bread and stuffed it into his mouth. Seeing a servant in the corner, he said, "You there. Pour

some wine for me, will you? I'm as dry as the Desert of
Tears! Breck, sit down and eat. We've a long ride ahead
of us."

"King Akeela," said Mor, "don't you even want to read
the treaty?"

"Ah, yes, of course," said Akeela. As the servant filled
his glass, he pulled the paper closer to him. "Yes, have to
read this carefully indeed."

"As I said, it's not complicated."

"No, no, you're right, my lord. Let me read this carefully.
Don't want to sell my country into slavery, now do I?"

Mor sat back impatiently. "No, of course not."

With both eyes on the treaty, Akeela pretended to read.
As he did he snuck a peripheral glance at the chamber's
only window. The stained glass began to lighten, warning
him. Soon he would get his signal. He quelled his growing
nervousness by draining his glass.

"Yes, well, this looks fine, mostly," he said. "But we'll
have to work out a payment schedule, to make sure Liiria
isn't cheated. The treaty should address that, I think. Perhaps I could leave a man or two behind to account for the
ships that pass?"

"Cheated?" The word made Mor bristle. "Why would
you say such a thing? Norvor only wants what it deserves."

"Oh, I'm sure you're correct, my lord," said Akeela.
"Still, a strict accounting is necessary. Do you think you
could have some changes made before I sign it?"

"Changes? No, King Akeela, I don't think so. I—"

Before Mor could finish, Fianor returned with three of
Akeela's men. The Royal Chargers greeted their king, then
bowed to King Mor. They were, as Mor had insisted, without swords. Breck quickly explained to them about the
treaty, and how they were to witness its signing.

"Yes, the signing," Mor insisted. Again he held out the
pen for Akeela. "Or are you changing your mind, my
lord?"

"No," said Akeela. He wanted to stall further, but
couldn't think of another ruse. Just as he reached for the
pen, his salvation came.

"My lords!" cried a voice. "Soldiers!"

Akeela moved like lightning. While Mor sat up, confused
by the call, he dashed his hand beneath his cape and freed

his waiting dagger. Breck and the three Chargers did the same. Akeela exploded out of his chair, took a handful of Mor's shirt, and put the dagger to his throat.

"Don't you bloody move!" he ordered. "Or I swear I'll cut your throat."

Breck had his own blade at Fianor's throat. A panicked page boy stumbled into the chamber, crying that soldiers were approaching. Outside the chamber, men were shouting amid sounds of struggle. General Nace and his men stood still as stone, unsure of what was happening.

"Get out of the chair!" Akeela roared, pulling Mor from his seat.

"What is this?" Mor sputtered.

"Shut up and listen," said Akeela. Quickly he maneuvered himself behind the gasping man, wrapping an arm about his throat and keeping the dagger to his cheek. "Do as I say, you stinking toad, or you're a dead man."

"Let him go!" barked Nace, even as the Chargers held him, too. All three of Mor's men were subdued, as was Fianor. The prince fought violently against Breck.

"You cowardly scum!" gurgled Fianor. "What are thinking? You can't get out of here!"

"Quiet!" snapped Breck, pressing hard against Fianor's throat.

"Release us!" the prince wailed

Breck dragged him roughly around, faced him against the wall, and drove his head into the hard stone. Akeela heard the crack of his skull, then watched him slump slowly to the floor, leaving a smudgy trail of blood down the bricks. Mor writhed in Akeela's grasp, crying out for his son. Breck turned like a wildcat on Nace and his men.

"Still don't believe us?" he hissed, brandishing his dagger.

Mor's fingernails tore at Akeela's arm. "You won't get out of here! You won't escape!"

Akeela pushed the blade against Mor's cheek so that the old man wailed. "We will, and you're coming with us." He barked at the page, "Get in here!"

The boy stepped into the room. He looked at his king helplessly, then back into the hall where the commotion was rising.

"How many men are approaching?" Akeela asked.

The page barely stammered a response. "I . . . don't know. Maybe a thousand . . ."

Satisfied, Akeela dragged Mor toward the door. "Now listen to me, General Nace. We're going to leave here, slowly and in order. I promise you, nothing is going to happen to Mor unless you disobey me."

"I don't take orders from you!" Nace spat. With the blade of a Charger still at his throat, he laughed defiantly. "Go ahead and kill us. You'll never get out of here."

"No?" Akeela tightened his arm about Mor's thin neck. The tension in the chamber had overcome him, drowning him in a flash of madness. "Is that what you want, you greedy old reptile? You want to die?" Again he pricked Mor's cheek with the dagger.

"Stop!" wailed Mor.

"Who's the coward now, eh?" Akeela asked, jerking him backward. "You dirty bastard. I should kill you for what you did to me!"

"My lord, stop!" ordered Breck. "We have to get the gate open!"

Still breathing hard, barely able to think, Akeela glanced at General Nace. "You heard him, General. You're going to order the gate open, understand?"

"Never!"

Breck cursed, took hold of Nace's hairy head, and put his dagger to his throat. "Mor, do you think we're bluffing you? Do you think we actually won't hurt you?"

Mor was panting in fright, unable to answer.

"Well, watch then," said Breck, and quickly ran his blade over Nace's throat, slicing it open. The general's eyes widened as blood poured down his chest. The Charger holding him let go, and Nace hovered in shock for a moment before falling in a gurgling pile to his knees. Stunned by the murder, Akeela almost dropped his dagger. Before Nace was dead, Breck rushed to Mor and put his own blade to the king's throat.

"Believe me now?" he asked.

Mor erupted into cries. "Great Fate, don't kill me!"

"Are you going to open the gate?"

"Yes!"

Breck looked at Akeela, instantly in charge. "Get him

out of here." He whirled on the rest of his men. "Get their weapons and come with us."

The Chargers took the swords from their captives, then lowered their daggers and hurried toward Breck. The terrified page went to the Norvans, who all stood in shocked disbelief.

"Follow us and the old man dies," Breck promised them. His men were armed now, and having Mor as a hostage buoyed his confidence. With only his dagger in hand, he said to Akeela, "All right, let's move. Slow and easy, my lord. They'll let you pass once they see you have Mor."

Akeela barely heard Breck's orders. Still riveted by Nace's corpse, he stood like a cold statue near the door.

"My lord, what's wrong with you?" shouted Breck. "Get going!"

Collecting himself, Akeela fixed his dagger beneath Mor's chin and inched to the door. He began to perspire and shake, but he kept his blade against his frightened captive and stepped out into the hall. The fortress rang with sounds of battle, the screams of men and clashing steel. Breck and the others formed a ring around Akeela as they slowly crept out of the room. Breck took the lead, waving frantically when he saw his men up ahead, battling their way into the fortress.

"Randa!" he called. "Randa, Hanas, here!"

When the two soldiers saw Breck and Akeela, they shouted at their Norvan opponents. "Look there! Your king is captured!"

The Norvans continued pouring against the Chargers. Akeela knew he had to act fast.

"Lower your weapons!" he cried. "Or your king dies!"

One by one the Norvans noticed their captured king. Slowly the combat ebbed. Randa, Hanas, and the other Chargers fell back, joining Akeela. Mor continued sputtering, blood trickling down his slashed cheek.

"Stop!" he gurgled. "They'll kill me!"

"Open the gate," Akeela ordered them. "Now!"

The Norvans simply stared. More of them entered the hall, ready to fight, but their brothers held them back, gesturing to the king.

"My lord," called one of them. "Are you all right?"

"Do I look all right, you idiot?" spat Mor. "Open the gate!"

"But my lord, there are soldiers coming!"

"Open the gate and surrender," Breck ordered, "Or Mor dies."

"Surrender?" gasped the Norvan. "My lord?"

"Seven hells, Virez, they've already killed Nace. Just do as they say!"

The soldier stood in mute shock, then reluctantly ordered his men to open the gate. Relieved, Akeela started forward again, protected now by a wall of Chargers. Virez and his men slowly parted as they approached, careful not to imperil their king.

"The gate's being opened," Virez said. "Now let him go."

"When we reach the gate he'll be released," countered Breck. "Not before."

King Mor let Akeela guide him through the hall, clumsily keeping step with him. His breath came in nervous rasps. "Akeela, you won't get away with this, you vile little snake. You'll pay for what you did to Nace. And my son!"

"Quiet," said Akeela, "or I'll kill you."

Remarkably, Mor began laughing. "You won't kill me. You're a coward! You'll have your dog soldiers do it for you!"

Akeela tried not to listen, concentrating instead on reaching the courtyard. At last they came to the double doors of the fortress, both open wide and letting in the morning sunlight. Akeela could hear the calls of his men outside the fortress gates, and the thought that Hogon was near eased his fear. The yard itself was full of Norvan soldiers, but none moved against Akeela and his band. Akeela spied the gate in the distance and saw that Mor's orders were indeed being heeded. A handful of men were opening the great gates. And beyond the gates, sitting triumphantly upon his horse with a broadsword in hand, was Hogon. The chancellor looked harried and proud, and when he saw Akeela emerge from the keep a disbelieving smile lit his face. Beside him was Raxor, stunning in his black armor, an army of his fellow Reecians at his back. Breck, who had taken a sword from one of the Norvans, waved the weapon at Hogon. A rush of exhilaration passed through Akeela.

Like Hogon, he couldn't believe he'd actually succeeded. His thoughts were suddenly of Lukien, and how impressed he'd be when he learned of this day.

As Akeela moved toward the gate, Hogon and his men began entering the huge courtyard. The feeling of victory overswept Akeela. But only for a moment. Mor began squirming angrily in his grasp, staring at the gate and rasping hatefully.

"Reecians?" he growled. "Reecians!" He exploded, thrashing wildly to escape Akeela. "No Reecians will ever take my fortress! Never!"

Akeela struggled to control the old man, but Mor's sudden anger gave the old man strength. He kicked at Akeela and elbowed him, fighting to get free. As Akeela hurried him toward the gate, Mor began screaming at his men, "Virez, it's Reecian scum! Stop them!"

Breck shouted, "King Akeela, shut him up!"

"I'm trying!"

"Virez! Attack!"

"Akeela!"

Panicked, Akeela looked toward Virez and knew that he could hear his king. The soldier lifted his gaze toward the gate and realized that Reecians rode with the Liirians.

"Virez!" Mor cried. "Fight them!"

"Quiet!" Akeela pleaded. "We're almost free!"

But Mor would not be silent. With Akeela's dagger still at his chin, he continued to call for attack, screaming against his strangled throat for his men to fight. Breck was screaming too, shouting for Akeela to silence their captive. Akeela looked around impotently, wondering what to do. To one side was Hogon and his army, struggling through the gate. To the other side was Virez, finally comprehending his king's cries. There was no time to waste. Akeela panicked. Mor was bellowing, ordering their deaths. Akeela's tenuous control snapped.

"Quiet!" he cried, and drove his dagger through Mor's windpipe. The flesh exploded with blood. Mor fell backward into Akeela, who stood in horror at what he had done, watching as Mor clutched at his throat. Blood sluiced from the wound, drenching both of them. Akeela dropped his dagger and began to scream.

"Breck!"

When Breck saw Akeela, his jaw fell open and his face went white. Akeela was out in the open, unarmed and wailing, Mor crumpled at his feet. The world around Akeela slipped into darkness. He heard voices, saw men charging at him from both directions, and all he could do was stand there. Terror seized him; Mor's blood drenched him. And Virez and his men were streaming forward, clashing against his own shocked troops. Breck threw himself into the melee, joining his outnumbered men as Hogon and the others struggled forward. The air filled with screams. Akeela realized suddenly that he was screaming, too. A man was charging toward him, sword drawn, legs pumping as he fought to reach his quarry. Akeela raised his hands uselessly against his attacker, sure that he would die.

"King Akeela, run!" screamed a voice. Chancellor Hogon thundered forward on his horse. With one smooth move he arced his broadsword through the air, slicing off the offender's arm. The man screamed and fell backward. Hogon spun his horse toward Akeela.

"Run, my lord, run!" he commanded. "Get to safety!"

So Akeela ran. Finding just enough courage to flee, he headed for the gate just as Raxor came through. The War Minister of Reec gave him a disgruntled look, then moved his horse aside to let the young king pass.

The armies of Hogon and Raxor easily outnumbered the Norvans. Without a king or general to lead them, the defenders of Hanging Man could muster only a clumsy defense. They had been caught unaware by Akeela's deception, and with the gate of their fortress open like a wound, it didn't take long for their enemies to overwhelm them. What might have been a long, bloody siege lasted only hours, as the determined Norvans barricaded themselves in the many structures of the fortress, refusing to surrender to their long-time foes. Raxor, eager to avenge the many wrongs Mor had done his people, saw no reason to give quarter. He was as merciless as he'd been in his battles against Liiria, and he relished the fight Akeela had brought him, cherishing it like a long-anticipated gift. Prince Fianor awoke just in time to join the battle, but didn't survive long. The blow to his skull made him sluggish with his sword, and he died shortly after he awoke, run through by a Reecian spear. Hogon and Breck and the other Liirians joined the bloodletting without reluctance, for they were soldiers and believed in the righteousness of war.

Akeela had run far from the fortress, but not far enough to drown out the screams of the dying men. He had run until his lungs burned and his legs turned to water, and when he could run no longer he collapsed on a hillside overlooking Hanging Man. For hours he lay there, still covered in Mor's blood, which would not come off no matter how hard he rubbed. He wept at the ruins of his plan and watched the men battle for the fortress with the detachment of a dream, his eyes blurry with tears. Finally, when the battle was over and the afternoon sun was high overhead, he saw Hogon and Raxor emerge from the iron gates. A train of defeated Norvans streamed out of the courtyard. Without food or horses or weapons, they began the dismal trek into the interior of Norvor. Akeela knew the wounded among them would die on the way, because Hanging Man was remote and Norvor was rugged. Yet he didn't seem to care that more men would die, and he puzzled over his lack of sympathy. Not long after, he heard Breck calling his name. He did not answer, but Breck discovered him anyway, sitting alone among the rocks of the hillside. Akeela had his arms wrapped about his knees.

"My lord?" Breck asked warily.

Akeela said nothing. His eyes blinked lifelessly.

Breck's voice softened, gently prodding, "Akeela? Are you all right?"

"You won," replied Akeela. His tear-stained face smiled awkwardly. "I saw it all from here."

"Yes." Breck chanced a step closer. His sword was sheathed and his hair was matted with filth, but he was uninjured. "My lord, why didn't you answer me when I called?"

Akeela shrugged. "I don't know." He held out a bloodstained hand. "It won't come off. I've tried all day, but I can't get it off me."

Breck came and knelt before him. "Oh, Akeela," he sighed. "Don't worry. You'll be all right."

"Me?" Akeela laughed. "Why shouldn't I be all right?"

"I warned you," said Breck. "I told you not to do this. You're not a bloody soldier!"

"Why are you looking at me like that? I told you, I'm fine."

But even Akeela knew he wasn't fine. Something inside had snapped the moment he'd killed Mor, the moment the old man's blood spurted against his face. "We have to get back to Liiria," he said. "I have to see Cassandra." His smile was fractured. "I'm going to tell her how we conquered the fortress."

Breck took Akeela's hand and gently pulled him to his feet. "All right, my lord. Let's just get you home."

19

The desert, Lukien quickly learned, was a place of mirages.

Each day when the sun rose, the sands shifted with the wind, forming pools of watery sunlight on the earth. The dunes seemed to move as if alive, and the dust storms sang in the distance, warning of their approach. There were no trees or rain clouds, only occasional, life-giving cacti; the sun was a constant companion, blithely watching the caravan invading its burning realm. Scorpions and lizards skittered along the rocks, and the bleached bones of unlucky drowa stuck out like guideposts among the shifting sands. Time moved unhurriedly, like syrup, and the vast expanse of nothingness drowned every thought. For five days the travelers had endured the rigors of the desert. Now, unbelievably, their journey was nearing its end. The caravan leader Jebel had told them that Jador was very near, maybe another half-day's ride, maybe less. But the news did little to buoy the mood of Lukien and his companions. Despite the gaka and headdress he wore, the exposed flesh of his hands and around his eyes had been burned red. Old Figgis had fared no better, and Trager never spoke at all, except to curse the heat. Lukien knew they needed to reach Jador quickly, or else be sick from heatstroke. They didn't want water or the temporary shelter of wagons any more; they wanted an end to the taunting sands.

Lukien kept his drowa near the strange wagons as he

rode, letting Jebel and Figgis lead the way. Trager kept to
the rear of the caravan. After five days of riding, he still
hadn't mastered the ill-tempered drowa, and occasionally
grumbled at the beast to behave. Lukien himself had grown
accustomed to the humped monster, though his back ached
from its loping gait. He had named his drowa Mirage in
honor of the shimmerings on the horizon. The beast already
seemed to know its name and didn't question Lukien's
commands. Surprisingly, Lukien liked his silent companion.
Drowas were remarkable, and far better suited to the desert than horses. They were powerful and swift when they
had to be, and, according to Jebel, the females gave milk
to feed their masters. Lukien had already tried drowa milk
and thought it disgusting, but it didn't keep him from admiring the beasts. In the deathlike Desert of Tears, he was
grateful for them.

At mid-afternoon the sun was hottest, and Lukien drew
his headdress around his face so that only his eyes peered
through. Beneath his gaka, sweat poured from his body. In
the wagon next to him, Cahra and two of her younger sisters were watching him, swaying lazily to the rhythm of the
caravan. Cahra wasn't like her siblings. She was the oldest
of Jebel's children and so enjoyed a measure of freedom
that made her talkative. She had already exhausted Figgis
with questions of Liiria and the lands to the north, surprising them all by speaking their language. Jebel explained
that all his children spoke the tongue of the northern lands,
because they were traders and needed to be fluent. Cahra
had a surprising command of the language. The idea that
desert people were quiet simply didn't apply to her.

"Lukien is thirsty," she said. She had a peculiar way of
addressing him, but he had gotten used to it. "Water?"

"Yes," said Lukien. He sidled up to the wagon, careful
to avoid its wide, sand-churning wheels. Cahra told her sister Miva to fetch a waterskin. The youngster did so and
held it out for Lukien with a smile. "Thank you," said
Lukien, then lowered his face wrap and took a conservative
drink. The water was remarkably cool, and Lukien didn't
want to stop. But he capped the skin and handed it back to
Miva. Neither Miva nor her sisters took a drink themselves.

"Your father says that we'll reach Jador by tomorrow,"
said Lukien as he fixed the cloth about his face.

"Or sooner," said Cahra. She continued to watch him.

"By nightfall?"

"Maybe."

Lukien looked ahead. All he could see was more and more rolling sand. "Tomorrow, I'd say."

Cahra chuckled. "The desert fools you. Do not expect things. Jador could be right in front of us, and the desert would hide it."

"It's perfectly clear today. If Jador were ahead of us, I'd know."

The girl continued to study him, her dark eyes full of curiosity. Because the wagon provided cover, she no longer wore her headdress. Instead she let her hair fall around her shoulders. More and more, she reminded Lukien of Cassandra. "You are strange," she said. "You do not talk like the old one."

"You mean Figgis? No, no one talks like Figgis. He's impossible to shut up."

"You are quiet, like the other one." Cahra spied Trager. "That one is sour like a grape."

Lukien nodded. "That's our Trager."

"You do not like each other." Cahra leaned forward. "Why?"

"It's a long story, girl, and not very interesting."

"He calls you captain. He is your servant?"

"Something like that," said Lukien. "He serves under me, in the Royal Chargers."

"In Liiria," said Cahra brightly. "Figgis told me about Liiria. He says that your king is a great man, and that he wants to make peace with the world. That is why you are going to Jador, yes?"

Lukien hated to lie to the girl, but he said, "Yes, that's right. We're emissaries from our king."

Cahra struggled with the word. "Em-a-sair-ee?"

"Emissaries. Like friends. We're going to make friends with Jador." He gestured to the packs hanging from his drowa's haunches. "We've brought gifts for the kahan and kahana, to show them we want peace and friendship."

"Your king is generous," said Cahra. "Tell us about him. We are all interested."

Miva and the other girl, Yilena, had gathered closer to listen. "What do you want to know?" asked Lukien.

"A story."

"What?"

Cahra smiled. "Ganjeese are story people. We tell our history in stories. So now you tell us about your king and his story. If he is a great king, he will have a great story."

Lukien thought for a moment. Was Akeela a great king? A great humanitarian perhaps, but he had ruled Liiria too short a time to be called a great king.

"There are no stories about Akeela," said Lukien. "I've known him all my life, and can't think of a single one."

"But *that* is a story," argued Cahra. "You and him, together. If you have known him all your life, then that is his story, and yours. Tell us. It will pass the time."

Knowing that he had nothing but time on his hands, Lukien agreed. He told them of Akeela, and how he was a good man with big visions for Liiria, a man of peace and justice, and he told them how he had met Akeela in the streets of Koth. Cahra and her sisters listened, enthralled, as Lukien told of growing up in Lionkeep as ward to King Balak, like a brother to Akeela, and how they had attended war college together. Lukien bragged about his own exploits as a soldier. He had posted almost identical grades as Trager, he said, but he was the better soldier by far, and that was why he was Captain of the Royal Chargers. Cahra smiled at the boast but let Lukien continue, and for almost an hour he regaled them with tales of wars and soldiering and his comradeship with Akeela, which he explained was stormy at times but was quick to point out how much they truly, *truly*, loved each other.

"Brothers are like that, you know," Lukien stressed, knowing it was for his own sake that he took such pains to explain things. Cahra listened and seemed intrigued by this, even suspicious, yet still she said nothing. Finally Lukien came to the part in his story where King Balak died, leaving his throne to Akeela. He told them about Reec, and how Akeela was determined to make peace with them, and how King Karis had greeted Akeela warmly, even after years of war. Finally, he told them about Cassandra.

"Ah, so your king has a woman," said Cahra. "Tell us about her. Is she very beautiful?"

"Oh yes," said Lukien softly.

Cahra's eyes narrowed on him. "The queen is special to you."

"Why do you say that?"

"Your voice. It changes when you speak of her." Cahra looked at her bare feet dangling off the side of the wagon. "Forgive me. If you do not wish to speak of her . . ."

"No," said Lukien. "I don't mind. It's just that Queen Cassandra is very ill. She may not survive. I'm worried about her, that's all. And I'm worried about Akeela."

"Yes, I can tell. You think of them often. They are both special to you."

Lukien grinned. "You should be a fortune-teller, Cahra." Then he sighed. "I don't want to talk about Liiria any more. It's your turn to talk. Tell me about Jador."

"You will see Jador soon enough."

"Prepare me, then. What's it like?"

The girl thought for a moment. "It is pretty."

"Like Ganjor?"

"No. Ganjor is dirty. Jador is clean and beautiful. All white."

"But how do they live in the desert?" asked Lukien. "Ganjor is near the Agora River. What do the Jadori do for water?"

"Jador has a river. It comes from the mountains. And Jador is not in the desert. It is like the start of a new world."

"New world? You mean there's more beyond the desert than Jador?"

Cahra looked away as if being caught in a lie. "There is always more," she said evasively.

"What's beyond Jador?"

"I told you—the mountains."

"And after the mountains? What's beyond them?"

Cahra shrugged. "I do now know. I have never been."

Lukien could tell the girl was hiding something. "But you must have some idea. Are there other countries past Jador? More people like them, perhaps?"

"There must be people beyond the mountains," said Cahra simply. "The world is large."

"Yes," said Lukien. "I suppose." He wasn't satisfied with the answer, but decided not to push. He was about to change the subject when he heard a shout.

"Lukien, Trager, look!" cried Figgis gleefully.

Lukien looked at the librarian. He was pointing to something ahead, something vast and long on the horizon. After days of endless sand, Lukien had to think for a moment before recognizing the things for what they were—mountains.

"I'll be damned . . ."

Cahra laughed. "You see? The desert is a trickster."

Lukien shielded his eyes with a hand. "Jador?"

"Almost," said Cahra. She spied the mountains coming into view. "You will see it soon."

Kahan Kadar's city of white and gold sprawled at the base of a brooding mountain range, shining like a beacon across the burning sands. It was tall with towers and domes and lined with limestone streets, and it rivaled Koth in size and beauty. There was no city gate to guard it, only a welcoming avenue down its center. Green trees served as sentries to the city, bursting with fruit and swaying lazily in the desert breeze, while a winding aqueduct roamed above the roads, bringing water down from the distant mountains. The streets of Jador bustled with caravans from around the desert, swarming in and out of the city's many streets. There were drowa everywhere and dark-skinned people much like Jebel's clan. And there were kreels. From his place on the outskirts of the city, Lukien could see the fleet-footed lizards scrambling through avenues, some being ridden, others pulling trading carts. After five days in the desert, it was like a dream to Lukien, and he watched it wide-eyed from the confines of his cowl, eager to reach the gleaming city.

"Great Fate, it's amazing," said Figgis breathlessly. As he rode at the head of the caravan with Jebel, he kept his gaze fixed on Jador. Lukien and Trager rode beside him. Both were equally struck by the amazing city, but only Figgis seemed unable to look away. "I've waited all my life for this," said the old man. "All my life . . ."

Lukien smiled at him. "I'm glad for you, Figgis. Enjoy this moment."

Jebel overheard the conversation and looked at Figgis oddly. "All your life? To make this simple trip?"

"Simple for you, maybe," said Figgis. "But not for me,

or anyone else from the north." He smiled at Jebel. "You have done me a great service, my friend, and I'm grateful. Seeing Jador was always my greatest dream. And now . . ." He sighed, taking in all of the desert city's glory. "Now I feel like I could cry."

"Please, don't," said Trager. "Spare us that at least, will you? We have a mission, old man. Remember that."

Lukien shot Trager a warning glance. "Easy."

"Yes, your mission," said Jebel, nodding. "You will want to see Kahan Kadar quickly."

"If possible," said Lukien. "But will that be difficult? He's the kahan, after all. Where do we start?"

Jebel pointed toward the city. "The green tower," he said simply.

Lukien squinted and saw a cylinder of lime-colored stone rising from the city streets. "What is it?"

"Kadar's palace. You will go there, speak to the kahan."

"And he will see us?" asked Trager. "Just like that?"

Jebel laughed. "You do not know Kahan Kadar."

"No, I don't," said Trager. "Tell me."

Jebel looked at Trager. He replied, "Even you will be welcomed by Kadar."

Lukien didn't laugh. "I just hope you're right, Jebel. We've come so far; I don't want to be turned away now."

"When Kadar learns you are emissaries, he will welcome you," said Jebel.

"Emissaries," said Lukien sourly. "Right."

None of them had told Jebel the truth of their mission, and now that they had reached Jador Lukien felt a familiar pang of guilt. As they rode toward the city's main avenue, he noticed that none of the men were armed. Just as there were no soldiers or gates barring the way, there were no swords or daggers, and none of the drowa or kreel were armored, the way horses often were in the north. Lukien recalled what Figgis had told him—that the Jadori were peaceful. Now, seeing their serene, unarmed city, he believed it completely. He realized suddenly that his plan to steal Kadar's amulets would be easier than he'd thought. For some reason, the realization saddened him.

Dressed as they were in the Ganjeese gakas, no one took particular notice of Lukien and his companions as they neared the city, but by the time the caravan entered Jador the people in the streets began to surround the wagons, shouting at Jebel and his family and holding out silver coins.

"Figgis," whispered Lukien, "can you understand what they're saying?"

"Only a bit," the librarian replied. "I think they're asking what the caravan has to sell."

"Look at them," spat Trager. He glanced down at the people milling about his drowa, plainly disgusted. "Like animals."

But Lukien didn't think they were animals. He thought they were beautiful. Like their Ganjeese cousins across the desert, the Jadori had dark skin and shiny, dancing eyes. The women wore multicolored robes and silk veils over their faces, and the children laughed as they played. Lukien looked around at the structures of white and gold, awed by their sunlit beauty. Overhead the aqueduct gurgled, bringing its life-giving water. He saw a fountain at the end of the street, marveling at the way the water cascaded over its limestone tiers. Exotic looking trees stood around the fountain, almost completely bare of limbs except for sprouts of fanlike leaves at their tops. A warm breeze tumbled down the avenue, bearing the scent of strange perfumes. For Lukien, the noise of Jebel's bartering fell away; he felt remarkably happy.

"You're right, Figgis," he said. "It's beautiful."

Figgis sighed. "It's paradise. Just like I knew it would be." He turned to Lukien and Trager. "You see? I was right. It's just like I told King Akeela."

"Fine," said Trager. "Now let's find those amulets and go home."

Lukien nodded. "Sorry, Figgis, but Trager's right. We can't dally. Let's get on to the palace and find Kadar."

Figgis didn't argue. He went to Jebel, asking him to take them to the kahan's palace. Jebel agreed, telling Cahra and the others to see to their business. The wagons came to a stop in the street and were soon surrounded by eager Jadori. Jebel said good-bye to his daughters and brother, then rode out ahead of his charges, leading them out of the bustling street and down a quieter corridor shadowed by tall buildings. The Jadori that passed them did not stop to stare this time, and Lukien made sure to keep his face covered. As they rode through the avenues, changing course with the flow of the streets, the palace of Kahan Kadar came into view before them. Sunlight played on its copper dome, aged through countless years to a green pa-tina. The main tower rose high above the city, a twisting spire of emerald and gold. People and drowa and kreels choked the square outside the palace. But once again there were no soldiers baring the way, only men in dark gakas milling around the open archway. Lukien took careful mea-sure of the palace. The main archway led to the huge square, and the square led to the crowded streets. Fleeing the palace would be difficult, even if stealing the amulets wouldn't be. He realized at once they would have to flee at night, when the streets would be less crowded.

Once Jebel had led them into the square, he dismounted, telling them all to do the same. He pointed at the archway to the palace. "Kadar."

"Yes," said Lukien, understanding. "But how will we see him?" He got down from his drowa. "We can't just walk in and ask for him."

"Come," said Jebel. "Let me show you."

Jebel led his horse through the archway onto a carpet of cool grass just outside the palace. Lukien and the others followed him warily. There were children on the grass, playing with a leather ball, and men and women sitting around in little circles, happily ignorant of the nearby for-eigners. The shadow of the green tower fell gently on the field. Jebel cleared his throat to get some attention, then began to speak. All around the yard people turned to look at him, then at the strangers with him.

"Figgis?" Lukien asked. "What's he saying?"

The old man shrugged. "I don't know."

Jebel turned to them. "Uncover your faces," he said.

"What?"

"Your face wraps," said Jebel. "Take them off."

Lukien hesitated. The people in the yard were staring at him. Some began to inch closer. Very slowly he reached up to his face cloth and pulled it down.

One by one the Jadori stood and gaped. Figgis and Trager both uncovered their faces, and soon the children in the yard began to point in astonishment. But they weren't horrified the way Lukien had feared. Instead, their smiles lit the yard.

"I told them you are visitors from far away north," said Jebel.

"By the Fate," hissed Trager. "Why'd you do that?"

Jebel laughed. "To show you how stupid you are to be afraid. Look! I told you they would welcome you."

Ignoring Lukien's orders to keep back, Figgis raised his hands in friendship to the crowd, then began to speak in his broken version of Jadori. The men and women listened carefully, trying to understand. But enough of the meaning was clear to them. They returned Figgis' greeting, putting their hands together and bowing to him. Figgis laughed in delight.

"You see, Lukien?" he cried. "I told you they were peaceful. Jebel was right—they're welcoming us!"

His suspicions ebbing, Lukien followed Figgis forward. A crowd of children gathered at his legs, looking up into his striking, pale face. They pulled at his garments, urging him down. Lukien knelt and let them touch his face. A little boy stared into his blue eyes and gasped.

"Liiria," said Lukien to the children. "That's where I'm from. Liiria."

The boy frowned. He tried to say the word, but could not. Lukien laughed.

"It's all right, I'll teach you later," he said. He rose and looked back at Jebel. "So?" he asked. "What now?"

"Now we wait for Kadar," replied Jebel. He didn't move from his spot on the grass, but nodded toward the palace. Lukien listen carefully and heard people shouting Kadar's name. Excitement rippled through the yard and into the open halls of the tower.

"Shouldn't we at least go in?" Lukien asked. "Surely the kahan won't come to us."

Jebel simply shook his head. Lukien watched the opening in the tower, swelling now with curious people. A few moments later, a man came skidding into the yard, stopping short when he saw the visitors. Instantly his face went from astonishment to glee. The people in the yard parted to let him pass, but he merely stood there, staring, his youthful face fixed with a joyous smile. He wore regal robes of gold and crimson, the sleeves hanging in loose loops from his arms. His hair was jet black without the slightest hint of gray and slicked back against his head. He was neither tall nor short, but he was striking nonetheless. And most striking of all was the item hanging from a chain around his neck. Lukien's jaw fell open when he saw it—a beautiful, jewel-encrusted amulet.

"Figgis . . ."

"I see it," whispered Figgis.

Lukien could only stare back at Kahan Kadar. He was just as Figgis had expected—amazingly youthful, as if disease had never touched him. Merely yards away, he regarded the strangers with silent awe. His dark eyes darted toward Jebel, who bowed and spoke to the kahan.

"Bow, bow," urged Figgis, who followed Jebel's lead. Lukien and Trager did the same. To their astonishment, Kahan Kadar put his hands together and returned the gesture. Then he clapped like a school boy, laughing in delight.

"Tell him who we are, Jebel," said Figgis. "Tell him we mean no harm, and that we're on a peace mission."

As Jebel explained, Kadar nodded. The kahan had an almost comic exuberance about him, like a younger version of Figgis. Not surprisingly, Figgis was the first of the group to step forward. With all of Kadar's people watching him, he again tried out his poor Jadori. Kadar listened, sometimes nodding, sometimes frowning. Jebel hurried to his aid, explaining that Figgis was from Liiria, and that he and the others had come bearing peace offerings from their own king, Akeela. Kadar beamed at the news. He began speaking quickly to each of them, his voice as melodious as it was confusing.

"I'm sorry," Lukien offered, "but I don't understand you. I—" He snapped his fingers. "Wait," he said, then went to his drowa. The children surged around him as he unpacked the gifts they had brought, gold coins and flasks of perfume and ruby rings, all donated by Akeela to appease Kadar. Eager little hands reached for the items, but Lukien held them out of reach as he gave them to Kadar, who nodded before handing them out to his people. Surprised, Lukien looked at Jebel.

"Kadar thanks you for the gifts," said Jebel, "but he does not need them. Do not be offended. The kahan is very generous."

"Apparently," said Lukien. The children squealed happily as Kadar doled out the gifts. The Jadori men and women smiled. Kadar continued talking, letting Jebel translate for him.

"The kahan says he is honored that you would come so far to see him, and that you would cross the Desert of Tears for peace."

"Tell him it's our pleasure," said Figgis. He was plainly enchanted with Kadar.

"Yes," added Lukien. "Tell him the honor is ours, and that we're pleased that he and his people have welcomed us."

Jebel told Kadar what Figgis and Lukien had said. He did not bother looking at Trager, who was customarily quiet as the children milled around him. Kadar replied by saying they were all welcome in his palace, and that he was eager to hear about Liiria and its great, generous king. But before Jebel could finish translating another figure emerged from the palace, a striking young woman with straight black hair down to her backside and her stomach swollen with pregnancy. She had Kadar's warm smile and a dark, regal look, and when the people saw her they greeted her with bows.

"Jitendra," whispered Jebel. "The kahana."

Kahan Kadar stretched out a hand for his wife, gesturing to the strangers. Jitendra looked at them each in turn, smiling graciously but obviously uncomfortable. She looked tired, and very far along in her pregnancy. Lukien studied her belly, then realized something was horribly amiss. Unlike her husband, she wore no amulet.

"Figgis, is that really his wife?" he whispered.

Figgis grimaced. "It can't be. She's supposed to have the other—"

"Shhh, not now." Lukien stepped forward and bowed to Jitendra, then asked Jebel to tell the lady how honored he was to meet her. Jitendra smiled lightly at the compliment, keeping her hands on her belly. Kadar leaned over and gave her an affectionate kiss. Then he turned to his guests and spoke.

"Kahan Kadar asks you to come inside," said Jebel. "He wants you to rest and to take food."

"Gladly," said Figgis. He tried to thank Kadar in Jadori. Kadar merely smiled, then led the way back into his palace, still holding his wife's hand. As Figgis and Trager followed him, Lukien grabbed hold of Figgis' sleeve, leaning close to him.

"Where's the other bloody amulet?"

Figgis shrugged. "I'm sorry, Lukien, I don't know."

Lukien looked over his shoulder, making sure Jebel was out of ear shot. "We don't have time to waste. If we can't locate it in a day or so, we'll just have to take the one Kadar's wearing."

Figgis nodded somberly. "All right. But we'll need a plan. It won't be easy."

"Are you kidding?" Lukien chuckled. "Look at these people. No guards, no weapons. We're like wolves in the fold here, Figgis."

20

When the first tower of Koth appeared on the horizon, Akeela knew he was finally home. The long trek back from Norvor had wearied his body and spirit, and he yearned for home and the clean sheets of his bed. For too long he had endured the wind and hot sun. His skin cracked with blisters; his backside ached with saddle sores. Beside him, Chancellor Hogon rode at the head of their army. The chancellor looked fit despite the long ride, and when he saw Koth his old face split with a smile. Breck, who always rode alongside Akeela, let out a joyous whoop that was picked up by the rest of the company. But Akeela himself said nothing. He was simply glad to be home.

Since leaving Hanging Man, he had been haunted by the ghost of King Mor. He saw Mor when it was dark, peeking out from behind trees or waiting for him at the side of the road, staring. No one else ever saw the murdered king, but Akeela knew he was there, taunting him. Worse, Mor's blood would not leave Akeela's hands. He had spent an hour at the banks of the Kryss rubbing his hands raw, but all he had gotten for his troubles was Mor's reflection gazing back at him from the water. As he looked toward Koth, he hoped it would be a haven from the dead king. Cassandra would be there, sick in bed, but she would be a friendly face. He had not forgotten nor forgiven her adultery, but he longed for her comfort. He was tired of Hogon and the others, tired of the way Breck had been watching him.

"We're home, my lord," said Breck. "You can rest now."

"Rest." Akeela sighed. "Yes."

"Don't worry—you'll be all right. You can take it easy now, get your mind off things."

Akeela shifted. Breck was always saying things like that now, and Akeela wasn't sure why. He glanced down at his hands. He couldn't see the blood stains anymore, but he could feel them.

"I'm not a child, Breck," he said. "I don't need to nap like a baby."

"Yes, well . . ." Breck shrugged. "We all need rest after what we've been through, my lord."

Akeela continued toward Koth. Admittedly, rest sounded wonderful, but there was business to attend to first. Overlooking the city was the hill where his library was being built. Akeela could see it in the distance. The clear afternoon sky displayed the outlines of the library's foundation.

"You go on," Akeela told Breck. "All of you. I'll meet you back at Lionkeep soon."

Hogon started. "My lord?"

"Take the men into the city, Chancellor," said Akeela. "Give them my thanks again and let them rest and eat good food. I want to go and check on my library."

Breck and Hogon exchanged troubled glances. Breck said, "My lord, think for a moment, please. You need to get home. Cassandra, remember?"

"I'm not addlebrained, Breck. Of course I remember her. That's why I want to check on the library now, while I have the chance. Once I get back to Lionkeep I'll be attending her. I won't have time to ride out to the site."

"Do it later, then," said Hogon. "Really, my lord, you need to get back to Lionkeep."

"I've been gone for weeks, Chancellor. Why the hurry?"

"Because you're not . . ." Hogon stopped himself. He tried to smile. "You need rest, my lord, that's all."

"I'll rest when I'm done," said Akeela. "Now, do as I say and return to Lionkeep. Tell Warden Graig that I've returned and that I'll be home presently." He started to turn his mount toward the library hill, but Breck hurried alongside him, blocking his way. Akeela glared at him. "What are you doing?"

"My lord, listen to me. The queen needs you. Let's go back to Lionkeep. We can check on the library later."

"I'm the king, damn it!" Akeela yanked his horse away from Breck. "Stop treating me like an infant. I gave you an order, Breck. Follow it!"

"All right," said Breck easily. "I'll go with you, then. We'll check on the library together." He turned to Hogon. "The rest of you go on. We won't be long." He looked back at Akeela, smiling. "All right?"

Akeela studied Breck, not quite trusting him. He was a good man, but lately he'd been too close.

"If you must," said Akeela, then rode off toward the hill. Behind him, Breck and Hogon exchanged some words that he couldn't make out, and soon Breck was galloping up behind him. They rode in silence, avoiding the main road into the city and keeping instead to a less traveled path that led into the heart of the hillside. Akeela avoided looking at Breck, sure that he would see the familiar, concerned expression.

Before long they reached the library's hill, riding up a sloping road. Akeela listened but could hear nothing, not even the voice of a single workman. As the trees thinned and the site came into view, he saw that it was empty. His eyes narrowed, sure that he was missing something. But there was nothing to see. He had a picture perfect memory of the place, and he knew that nothing had changed from the last time he'd seen it. His jaw began to tighten and his head throbbed. Not a single additional tree had been cleared; not one brick had been laid. Beyond the hill, Koth still loomed in the distance, its skyline unobstructed. Akeela gripped the reins of his horse with shaking fists.

"He's done nothing," whispered Akeela.

"My lord—"

"Nothing!" Akeela's voice tore through the hillside. "That motherless liar! He's betrayed me!"

"Akeela, stop," said Breck sharply. The order, overly familiar, shocked Akeela. "Just take it easy. I'm sure there's an explanation."

"Oh, I'm sure you're right," seethed Akeela. "I'm sure Baron Glass has his reasons. That bloated toad never wanted my library built. And now he's defied me! Well, he won't get away with this . . ." Angrily he spun his horse around, heading back toward the road. "That lying whoreson will pay for disobeying me!"

Blind with rage, he spurred his mount forward, sending up clods of earth. Behind him, Breck shouted for him to stop. But Akeela's mind was wrapped like a bear trap around a single goal—destroying Baron Glass.

When Akeela reached Lionkeep, he found Graig in the courtyard, waiting for him. The warden's grin disappeared when he saw Akeela's twisted face. Akeela galloped into the courtyard. He tossed himself from the back of his lathered horse and thundered toward Graig.

"Where's Glass?" he demanded.

"My lord?" Warden Graig studied Akeela with alarm. "Are you all right?"

"Damn it, can't anyone give me a straight answer any more? Where is he, Graig?"

"My lord, stop," ordered Breck. He rode into the courtyard after his king. "Just wait, damn it, please!"

Graig was stupefied. "What's this all about? Akeela, what's wrong?"

Akeela could barely find his breath. He managed, "I want to know where that pustule Glass is hiding."

Breck dropped down from his horse. "My lord . . ."

"Shut up!" roared Akeela. "Graig, answer me. Where is Glass?"

"In your council chamber, my lord, meeting with Chancellor Hogon. The chancellor just arrived a short while ago."

"Then come with me," snapped Akeela, pushing past the warden. He didn't ask Breck to come, but the lieutenant did so anyway, following him through the doors of Lionkeep. Soldiers and servants greeted Akeela, smiling and welcoming him home. Akeela gave them each perfunctory waves. Graig and Breck walked briskly behind him, trying to keep up. Breck urged him to calm down. Akeela ignored him completely.

At the end of the hall lay the council chamber. The doors were closed. Akeela didn't bother to knock. He quickly grabbed the handle and swung open the door. It crashed against the wall, bringing Glass sputtering to his feet. The baron leapt from his chair, spilling the wine in his one good hand. Hogon turned toward the threshold, aghast.

"King Akeela," said Glass. He put down his goblet and brushed at his stained tunic. "By the Fate, you startled me!"

"How dare you?" hissed Akeela. He stalked into the chamber, staring at Glass. "How dare you!"

Glass stepped back. "My lord?"

Akeela's hand shot out and slapped the baron across the face. The blow stunned Glass, sending him backward. He looked at Akeela in shock, then his face contorted in rage.

"You little . . . !"

Hogon grabbed his arm to keep him back.

"You lied to me," spat Akeela.

"What are you talking about?"

"I've just been to the library, Baron. There's been no work done since I left. You've done nothing!"

Glass gasped in astonishment. "Is that all? You struck me over *that*?"

"You promised that you'd help construct the library. You betrayed me!"

"I did nothing of the kind," said Glass, shaking off Hogon's grasp. "I halted construction of your library for a reason!"

"Lies!" cried Akeela.

"My lord, please," said Breck. "Let him talk."

Akeela whirled on him. "You would listen to this snake charmer? Of course. Why doesn't that surprise me?"

"Just listen," pleaded Breck. "Let Glass explain."

"All right," said Akeela. "Fine." He folded his arms. "Go on, Baron. Explain. This should be good."

"King Akeela, I didn't betray you," said Glass. He put his hand to his chin and massaged the reddened flesh. "It's true—I ordered work on the library stopped. But I had to. It's like I was trying to tell you before you left for Norvor—there are no funds for it."

Akeela scoffed. "A lie."

"It isn't a lie! I've spoken with Chancellor Sark. The treasury doesn't have the money. All of it's gone to pay for the battle with Norvor."

Akeela sneered, "Don't cloud the issue, Baron. You know how much that library means to me, yet you chose to disobey me."

"Yes," admitted Glass, "or risk seeing Liiria ruined by debt. That's the choice you left me with, Akeela! I did what I had to do." ·

"Indeed. You've made your choice, Baron. Now you'll have to pay for it." Akeela turned to Warden Graig. "Arrest him."

Graig's mouth dropped open. "My lord?"

"You heard me, Graig. Baron Glass is a traitor. Let's see how long he lasts in Borior prison."

"My lord, no!" cried Breck.

"King Akeela, this is madness!" said Hogon. He stepped between Glass and his king. "I won't allow it!"

Akeela glared at him. "You won't . . . ? Listen to me, old man—you serve *me*. You follow my orders." He looked at all of them, at all their shocked faces. "Do you hear me? I'm the king!"

Breck hurried out a hand. "My lord, enough, now . . ."

Akeela swatted him away. "No! I'm done listening. That's all I've been doing for months, listening to all of you tell me what to do, thinking you can run Liiria better than me and talking behind my back. Norvor threatens and I do nothing. Glass plots against me, and I do nothing. Well not this time." He put a threatening finger in Glass' face. "This time you're going to pay, Baron. You won't stand against me any more."

"My God, he's mad," whispered Hogon. He stared at Akeela in disbelief. Akeela realized they were all staring.

"Graig, get that ridiculous expression off your face. Arrest Baron Glass. That's an order."

"Akeela, don't make me do this. . . ."

"Don't disobey me," warned Akeela. "I'm warning you, I won't tolerate this lawlessness any more."

"Great Fate, King Akeela, think for a moment," said Glass. "I'm not your enemy!"

Akeela ignored him. He kept a steely gaze on Graig. "Do it, Graig."

"Akeela . . ."

"Do it!"

Graig looked around blankly. Chancellor Hogon grimaced uselessly. Breck had turned the color of milk. Finally, the Head Warden relented.

"I'm sorry, Baron," said Graig. "I have no choice."

Baron Glass nodded. "Very well." He looked at Akeela. "Akeela the Good? Is that what they call you?"

"The people call me that," said Akeela proudly. "Not fat noblemen like you."

"You're going to ruin us," said Glass. Graig took his arm and began leading him to the door, but Glass wouldn't leave until he had his say. "There's no money for your library, you fool."

"Oh, but there is, Baron," said Akeela. "You're going to pay for it. You and the rest of your cohorts in the House of Dukes."

"What?"

"Enjoy your stay in Borior, Baron."

"Don't you dare touch my property!"

Graig hurried Glass out of the chamber. The Baron's threats rung down the hall. When he was gone, Akeela closed his eyes and took a steadying breath. His head was pounding. If he didn't rest soon, he knew he would collapse. When he opened his eyes again he saw Breck and Hogon staring at him.

"I had to do it," he said. "He was a traitor. He betrayed his word to me."

"He's a good man," said Hogon. "And you. . . ." The chancellor shook his head. "You're not well, my lord."

"Chancellor, I am as fit today as the day I was born. It is the queen who isn't well." Akeela went to the door. "So if you'll excuse me, I must see my wife now."

Alone in her enormous bed, Cassandra listened to the voices outside her chamber. It was like awakening from a dream. The narcotics Physician Oric had prescribed had done a remarkable job of curbing her pain, but they had the terrible effect of leaving her like a drunken fool. For more than a week now she had been unable to leave her bed or take solid food. Her cancerous growth had progressed rapidly in Akeela's absence. She had dropped weight and was now featherlight, and her hair had lost its sheen, falling around her shoulders in lusterless strands.

She expected to be dead soon and didn't really mind. Without her beauty, she was only half the queen she had been. And now that she was losing her mind, she wasn't even that. She opened her eyes at the sound of the voices, trying to focus. Oric's simples were very strong, and often made seeing difficult. Her groggy head tilted upward to listen. The offensive smell of her own body assailed her nose. How long had she been asleep? She couldn't remember, but she had dreamed of Lukien.

"Cassandra?"

Cassandra turned toward the voice and saw Jancis in the doorway. Her friend's pretty face glowed.

"Good, you're awake." Jancis floated toward the bed and sat down on the mattress. She put a hand to Cassandra's face and brushed the hair out of her eyes. "How are you feeling?"

"I . . ." Cassandra swallowed, finding it hard to speak. "I was sleeping. I heard voices."

Jancis reached for a glass of water on the bedside table. She put it to Cassandra's lips, carefully cradling her head as she sipped.

"I've got good news, Cass. Akeela is back."

Cassandra pushed the glass away. "He's home?"

"He's just arrived. He's coming up to see you."

Cassandra shook the fog from her mind. She struggled to sit up. "Is he all right? Did he say what happened?" She had a hundred questions suddenly, and it surprised her how worried she'd been about her husband. Then she remembered her horrible condition. "Look at me," she groaned. "I'm a crone. I don't want him to see me like this."

"You look fine," said Jancis, "and I don't think it will matter to him anyway. He just wants to see you."

"I look like a dead cat on the side of the road. Fetch a hairbrush."

"Shhh," urged Jancis. "Don't tax yourself. Remember what Oric said—you have to rest."

Jancis went to the side table and pulled a hairbrush from the drawer, then helped Cassandra sit up. Even that small effort exhausted Cassandra. Her eyes blurred and the pain in her stomach flared anew. Jancis began gently brushing her hair.

"The whole castle is talking about him," said Jancis, smiling. "They knew you'd be happy to see him back."

"Yes," said Cassandra sadly. "Happy . . ."

"Oric is outside waiting for him. I'm sure he'll tell him how you've been doing."

Cassandra laughed mirthlessly. "He'll tell him I'm dying."

"Cass, stop now."

Cassandra could barely keep from crying. She sat up in bed, too weak to brush her own hair, too blind to see clearly. Then she heard his voice. As the king stepped into the chamber, Jancis stopped brushing and gasped.

"My lady?"

Cassandra strained to see him, blinking to focus her eyes. "Akeela. You're all right?"

"Yes," he replied.

As he came to hover over the bed, she finally saw him clearly. Even through her blurred vision she could see the poison in his features. His eyes were sunken and his cheeks were hollow. A twisted smile curled his lips. Cassandra's eyes widened, hardly believing she was seeing Akeela.

"Jancis, leave us," Akeela ordered. When she hesitated, he snapped, "Stop staring and go."

Jancis hurried from the chamber. Akeela took her place on the bedside. He gazed at Cassandra, taking her hand.

"My love . . ." His voice was edgy. "I was so worried about you."

"Akeela," gasped Cassandra, "what has happened to you?"

"Happened?" Akeela frowned. "Oh, you mean in Norvor. We won, Cassandra. Haven't you heard?"

"No." Cassandra shook her head, which was swimming with confusion and pain. "I mean, what happened? You look different."

"Oric told me you're not seeing well. Don't worry, Cassandra. I look the same as when I left."

Cassandra didn't believe him. Her eyes were blurry, but she wasn't blind. He looked older, and vastly tired. Something in his expression warned her he had changed.

"It was glorious, Cassandra." Akeela tried to smile, but his voice betrayed the truth. It shook as he spoke, and Cassandra knew he was near tears. "We won. I beat them, Cassandra. I led the army and beat them. What do you think of that?"

"Yes," said Cassandra, not knowing what to say. "You won."

"And Mor isn't a threat to us any more. I killed him, Cassandra." He held out his hands. "I killed him with these, all by myself."

"No . . ."

"Yes I did." Akeela's breathing was shallow. "I killed him, just like a real solider. Just like Lukien."

Then he began to sob. And in that instant, Cassandra knew she'd been discovered. There was nothing left to confess—her adultery was known. She was sure of it. She reached out for Akeela, putting his head against her chest.

"I'm sorry," she said. "I didn't mean to do this to you."

Akeela didn't answer. Cassandra knew he wouldn't, for there was nothing now to say. Suddenly she remembered her warning to Lukien, how she had begged him not to come to her, sure that their tryst would ruin Akeela.

She had been horribly prophetic that day.

21

Lukien sat beneath a tree in Kadar's garden, slowly eating a handful of dates. He had discovered the place during his first day in Jador, when Kahan Kadar had showed off his royal residence, telling his Liirian guests that the garden, like all of the palace, was theirs to enjoy. Birds with exotic plumage chirped in the trees. Jadori children wrestled on the manicured grass. A blue sky swept above him, perfectly cloudless. Lukien heard a fountain gurgling in the distance and the noise of the city beyond the palace walls, but here in the garden he could not see the pressing streets of Jador. All he could see were green trees and flowers, the vista broken only by the range of brooding mountains in the east.

Kahan Kadar's palace was a remarkable haven from the bustle of Jador. It had the peace of the desert and the coolness of shade, and it didn't surprise Lukien at all that Kadar never seemed to leave it. He and the others had been the kahan's guests for three days now, enjoying his hospitality and the graciousness of his people, and while the palace seemed to be open to everyone, neither Kadar nor any of his underlings ever ventured from its confines. Lukien supposed it was because his wife was pregnant, and that Kadar wanted to be near to tend her. Kahana Jitendra was, in fact, *very* pregnant. To Lukien's eye, she looked ready to drop at any moment.

He took another date from his palm and bit into it, studying the children in the yard. Since coming to Jador, he had seen a number of Kadar's children. Many of them were young, like the wrestlers in the garden. But others were much older, easily in their teens and twenties. It was just one more puzzle about the kahan, one more tantalizing hint. Kadar himself looked too young to have fathered them, and there was no way Jitendra could have birthed them. As he ate his date, Lukien pondered Kadar's true age. Fifty? Sixty, maybe? He didn't look a day over thirty. Perplexed, Lukien took a sighing breath. The air was sweet with flowers.

Magic, he told himself. *It's got to be.*

The notion heartened him. Now he could save Cassandra. If she was still alive. And only if he could get the amulet away from the kahan. Worse, they had not been able to locate the second amulet. They had seen Kahana Jitendra twice more since coming to the palace, and never once did she wear any jewelry like Kadar's. Though Figgis clung to his belief in the second amulet, he could not explain why his precious texts had lied about it being in the kahana's possession. But time was running out, and they could wait no longer. They had found one of the Eyes of God, and that would be enough to save Cassandra.

To the east, the great, unbroken mountain range ruled the horizon. Lukien studied it as he swallowed his one date and popped another into his mouth. The mountains were just one more of Jador's riddles. Cahra hadn't wanted to talk about them, and it seemed that no one in the palace wanted to, either. He had tried to ask Kadar about them, but the kahan had merely smiled and changed the subject, pretending not to understand. Now Cahra's caravan was gone, probably back to the sands of the desert, and Lukien still had no answers. Lukien smiled, knowing he'd never have the chance to unravel the mountains' secret. Tonight, if all went well, he would be on his way back to Koth.

He sat alone for a few minutes more, finishing his dates. When he had swallowed the last one, he noticed Trager making his way through the garden. Lukien wiped his hands and leaned back against the tree. The people in the garden smiled at Trager, but the lieutenant ignored them. His dark eyes darted about suspiciously as he stopped to hover over Lukien.

"Where's Figgis?" he asked.

"He'll be here. Sit down."

Trager clucked at the lack of chairs, than sat down on the ground before his captain.

"Well?" Lukien asked, keeping his voice down.

"Nothing. I tried to keep close to the kahana, but she's been in her chambers a lot, and none of her maidens seem to have the amulet, either."

"All right," said Lukien. The bad news wasn't a surprise. "We tried."

"We've wasted enough time. That waterhead Figgis probably read his texts wrong."

"That *waterhead* just might have saved the queen," said Lukien sharply.

"Yes," drawled Trager. "It's all about the queen, after all."

Lukien glanced at him."What's that supposed to mean?"

"Mean? Nothing, Captain. We're all just worried about the queen, that's all. I know you're worried, aren't you?"

"Of course," said Lukien. He struggled not to look away. "I'm the queen's protector, after all."

"And you do a fine job of looking after her. Really admirable."

"Trager, if you've got something to say. . . ."

Trager's smile grew. "I think I've said it all, Captain."

Their eyes locked. Lukien could feel Trager's burning gaze. For a moment he couldn't speak, terrified that Trager had discovered his affair. But that was impossible.

Wasn't it?

Suddenly, Trager leaned back against his palms and sighed. "It's a beautiful day, isn't it? So much nicer here than in Koth. Do you think it ever rains here? It must, I suppose; all these flowers."

"Trager . . ."

"Don't worry, Captain." Trager grinned. "We'll be leaving soon. You'll see Cassandra soon enough."

Lukien groped for a response, but before he could Figgis appeared. The old man approached with a dejected expression.

"Ah, here's our court jester now," said Trager. "Come, old man. Sit down before you fall down."

In the way he had of always ignoring Trager, Figgis said

to Lukien, "I'm sorry, Captain. I looked all over." He lowered himself to the grass, shaking his head. "I just don't know where it could be."

"In your imagination, maybe?" Trager suggested.

"I'm not wrong about the other Eye," Figgis snapped. "The text was very clear. It says that one amulet is worn by the kahan, and the other is worn by his zirhah."

"His what?" asked Lukien.

"Zirhah. It means wife."

"Well, Jitendra doesn't have the other amulet, and we don't have time to keep looking." Lukien glanced around, making sure no one could overhear. He whispered, "We have to take Kadar's amulet tonight."

Trager nodded. "Yes. Let's stop wasting time and get home. What's your plan, Captain?"

"Surprise. I think we've already earned Kadar's trust. I'm sure he doesn't expect any trouble from us."

"I'm sure," said Figgis sourly.

"That means we'll be able break into Kadar's chambers without much trouble."

"Shouldn't be a problem," Trager agreed. "The fool doesn't even guard himself."

"Because he doesn't have to," flared Figgis. "Because this is a peaceful place."

Trager grinned. "It won't be so peaceful tonight."

"No," said Lukien. "I don't want anyone hurt. We'll just slip into Kadar's chamber, take the amulet from him, and be on our way as fast as we can. Figgis, you'll need to get the drowa ready for us. Stay with them and wait. As soon as we reach you, be ready to ride."

Figgis nodded glumly, but said nothing.

"And what if Kadar doesn't want to give us his precious amulet?" Trager asked. "What do we do with him then, Captain? Ask him nicely?"

"We won't hurt him," Lukien insisted. "We'll force the amulet from him if we have to, but I want no violence. Kadar's been too good to us for that. Once he sees our weapons and knows our intent, he'll give it to us."

"Right. Then as soon as we're gone he'll scream like a maniac. Face it, Captain—we have to kill him."

"No!" Lukien leaned forward angrily. "Now you listen to me, you idiot. Kadar is not to be harmed, not if we can help it. We'll tie him up and gag him, but we're not going to hurt him. And we're certainly not going to kill him, understand?"

Trager looked away. Lukien kicked him.

"Lieutenant, I said do you understand me?"

"I understand," said Trager through gritted teeth.

"Good. Now be ready tonight. Get the rope from our supplies and bring a dagger and a sword."

Trager rose and glared down at Lukien. "Am I dismissed now . . . *Sir?*"

"Yes," said Lukien, then watched as Trager stormed off. He watched until Trager left the garden and disappeared into the palace, and when he was gone he cursed and leaned back against the tree. "That son of a bitch," he muttered. "I wish Akeela had kept him home."

Figgis didn't answer. He simply stared off into the distance, completely lost in thought.

"Hey," said Lukien, snapping his fingers in his face. "What's wrong with you?"

"I was just thinking," replied Figgis. "I wish there was some other way to get the amulet."

"I know, but there isn't. So stop thinking about it."

"It's just that these people are so peaceful. They've never harmed anyone, and here we are, ready to steal from them—"

"Shhh, keep your voice down," Lukien scolded. Then he softened, adding, "I don't like it any more than you do. I'm not a thief, Figgis. But this was your idea, after all. And we can't back out now."

"I don't want to back out," said Figgis. "I just wish we didn't have to hurt these people."

"We're not here to hurt these people. We're here to save Cassandra."

Figgis smirked. "Oh, yes. Does that make you feel better, Captain?"

"Figgis?"

"Yes?"

"Stop talking, please."

Sometime past midnight, Lukien awoke. Trager was standing over his bed. Lukien's eyes opened to the soft glow of candlelight on Trager's face. The lieutenant wore his gaka, with his head dress pulled down around his chin. When he noticed Lukien awaken he said two simple words.

"It's time."

Lukien sat up and took a breath, letting his booted feet dangle off the silky bed. He too was already dressed. His sword belt waited nearby. He looked toward the keyhole-shaped window and saw the pale moon outside, lighting the distant mountains, and for a moment he wondered how long he had slept. Trager put the candle down on a nearby table and picked up Lukien's sword belt.

"Here."

"What time is it?" Lukien asked. He stood and took his weapon from Trager, lifting his gaka to belt it around his waist.

"It will be dawn in three hours," whispered Trager. "I've scouted out the halls around Kadar's quarters. They're empty."

Lukien noticed a bag dangling off Trager's sash. "That the rope?"

"Yes. And a cloth to gag him."

"Good. What about Figgis?"

"He's already down with the drowa, waiting for us near the gate. I told him to keep to the shadows. Far as I could tell, there wasn't anyone else around. The whole palace is asleep, Captain."

It took a moment for the words to come clear in Lukien's mind, but when they did he smiled grimly. Trager had done a surprisingly good job of arranging things. For the first time since leaving Koth, Lukien was glad he'd come. He went to the basin by his bed, splashed his face with rosewater, then ran his fingers through his hair. There wasn't much time, but he was nervous and unsure. After days of planning, it had come down to a simple act of pilferage, and he was irritated that Akeela had reduced him to a thief. Behind him, he felt Trager's impatient eyes.

"Captain?"

"I'm ready," said Lukien. He took one final look around the chamber to make sure he hadn't left anything behind, but he and Figgis had already packed everything they would need. This was water, mostly, for the long trip through the desert. Almost everything else had been disposed of, in hopes of making their drowa lighter and faster.

Still, Lukien surveyed his chamber sadly. Kadar's palace was comfortable, and the kahan had been very gracious. The silk sheets, the perfumed water, the fresh flowers brought in daily; it was all so different from his spartan quarters back home. When he returned to Koth, he wouldn't be a welcomed diplomat anymore. He'd just be a soldier again.

"All right," he sighed. "Let's go."

He went to the door and slowly pulled it open, peering out into the hall. Listening, he heard nothing, only Trager's eager breathing in his ear. Moonlight came in through the hall's many windows, lighting a pale path through the palace. The golden walls shimmered. Lukien stepped out cautiously, waiting for Trager to follow. The lieutenant lightly closed the door behind him, then pointed leftward.

Lukien knew the way. Soundlessly, he tiptoed through the marvelous hall, taking care as he passed each closed door. The quiet of the desert infused the palace—not a single servant stirred in its halls. Lukien made his way past the chambers Figgis had vacated, heading toward a rounded staircase spiraling up into the main tower. Kadar's personal chambers were higher than the rest, but it wouldn't take long to reach the kahan's perch. Trager snickered when he saw the unguarded staircase.

"The fool," he whispered. "He flaunts his amulet, and doesn't even bother guarding himself. He deserves to lose it, I say."

"Yeah, well it isn't yours," Lukien hissed. "It's Cassandra's, and don't go forgetting that."

He peered up the twisting stairway. Glowing sconces of scented oil lit the way. The silence encouraged him upward. Deciding not to draw his weapon yet, he kept his hands out before him as he climbed, his boots scuffing softly on the stone. Trager followed close behind, one hand on the dagger beneath his gaka. The bag of rope bounced against his knee. Together they made their way up the spiral, eyes wide, ears alert to any tiny sound. The burning sconces stretched their shadows against the wall. Lukien steadied his breathing as he climbed. His heart thundered in his temples. Slowly and with effort, he made his way toward the top of the staircase, emerging into another wide hall.

Jadori artwork and vases lined the walls. At the end of the hall were a trio of archways, each one black with emptiness. As Trager reached the last stair, Lukien shrugged at him.

"Which one?" he whispered.

Trager's eyes narrowed. "The center one."

The choice seemed logical. The center arch was the biggest and partially curtained with beads. Lukien slunk toward it, keeping close to the walls and deftly avoiding the tall vases. Now that he was close, he let his hand slip down and retrieve his dagger. Its blade jumped in the moonlight. Prowling toward the curtained arch, Lukien held his breath. He fixed his eyes on the chamber past the beads and caught a glimpse of light streaming through a window. The room ahead was large, and probably connected to other rooms. He would have to find their bed quickly, and hope that Kadar and his wife were asleep.

"Go on," Trager urged, his voice barely audible.

Lukien spread the beads with his dagger and poked his head into the room. His eyes scanned the darkness, picking up the outlines of soft pillows and ornate furniture, the kinds of things that adorned all the rooms. But there was no bed, and the chamber was empty. Lukien spied another beaded doorway at the far side of the room. Without a sound, he moved through the beads and bid Trager to follow, then stalked toward the next door. Dagger in hand, he repeated his actions, parting the new curtain with the blade. This time, he was rewarded.

In the center of the room, lit by moonlight from a nearby window, stood a bed with saffron sheets. And in the bed was an unmoving mound, all but hidden among the fat pillows. Lukien moved aside for Trager to see. The lieutenant nodded. Lukien's eyes darted about, but he could see no one else, only another doorway leading to yet another hidden room. From the looks of it, Kadar and his wife were asleep. Lukien and Trager shared a soundless glance. Both men held their daggers out before them, then floated toward opposite sides of the bed. The sheets didn't stir. Lukien reached out, his hand hovering over the pillows, hoping he was on Kadar's side. Blinded by blackness, he carefully took the sheets and pulled them down . . .

. . . and heard a shout behind him.

Lukien jumped back and whirled toward the doorway.

Kadar was standing there, dumbstruck. The figure in the bed rose suddenly. Kahana Jitendra's eyes shot around the room in a panic. She scrambled upright, clutching the sheets.

"Damn it!" Lukien growled. Barely thinking, he turned on the kahana and dragged her out of the bed. Kadar rushed forward, but stopped abruptly when he saw Trager vault the bed toward him. Trager's dagger warned him off, and Kadar backpedaled.

"Quiet!" hissed Trager. "Don't say another bloody word!"

Lukien struggled to bring Jitendra to her feet. He wrapped his arm around her throat as gently as he could, careful to keep the dagger from the throat, yet close enough to give the kahana the message. Jitendra gasped.

"All right, nobody move," Lukien said. He was panicked, unsure what to do. Kadar's shouts might have awoken the palace, but so far no one was coming to his aid. Kadar seemed to understand Lukien's demands and fell silent. He held up his hands, wordlessly pleading for Jitendra's release.

"Yes, that's it," Lukien encouraged. "Keep quiet and no one gets hurt." He twirled his dagger, making sure Kadar saw it. "I don't want to hurt her, Kadar. Just give us the amulet and we'll be on our way."

Kadar looked at his pregnant wife, confused. He said a soft plea that Lukien didn't understand.

"The amulet, you idiot," whispered Trager. He slid toward Kadar. "Give it to us."

Kadar looked bewildered. Lukien bit his lip. His plans were unraveling, and he didn't know the Jadori word for amulet. Then, like a miracle, it struck him.

"Inai!" he cried, remember the word Figgis had taught him. He pointed at Kadar's chest. The amulet dangled there, glowing furiously. He repeated the phrase, unsure if it was right. "Inai ka *Vala!*"

Kadar looked at him, then nodded, still holding out his hands. But Jitendra understood, too. As her husband began removing the amulet, she shrieked.

"Inai ka Vala! Kadar!"

"No!" Lukien struggled to hold her back.

Jitendra went on screaming.

"Stop!" Lukien snapped. "Please!"

Not wanting to hurt her, he lowered his dagger. Jitendra fought off his grip. Lukien lunged toward her, reaching for her arm. Jitendra slipped away, hurrying toward Kadar. Seeing her escape, Trager whirled, slashing his dagger. The threat surprised Jitendra. She screamed, stumbling backward, falling into Lukien—and his brandished blade.

"No!" cried Lukien. He fell back, too late to pull the dagger from the woman's back. Jitendra hung there as if suspended, her eyes wide with shock, the back of her night garb blooming crimson. A second later her knees buckled, and she collapsed to the floor.

"Jitendra!" cried Kadar. He dropped the amulet and ran to his wife, falling beside her. Lukien watched, horror-stricken. His dagger erupted from Jitendra's back.

"Captain, let's go!" said Trager. He raced toward the abandoned amulet and scooped it up. "We got it!"

"Oh, no," Lukien groaned. "Oh, Fate, help me. I didn't mean it. . . ."

Kadar was sobbing, lifting Jitendra. Jitendra writhed in his arms, still alive but losing blood in waves. Neither looked at Lukien, or even seemed to hear him.

"Captain, come on!" urged Trager. He hovered in the doorway, ready to bolt. "Let's move before we're discovered!"

But Lukien couldn't move. He could only stare. Jitendra let out an agonized wail. Kadar was covered in her blood. Jitendra's pregnant belly swelled with gasps.

"Damn it," swore Trager, then raced into the room to grab Lukien. He dragged his captain toward the door. "Figgis is waiting for us, you fool. Now come on!"

"I didn't mean it," whispered Lukien desperately. He continued watching Jitendra. "You saw. I didn't mean it. . . ."

"God almighty, will you shut up and hurry? We have to go!"

Something in Trager's voice snatched Lukien from his stupor. Jitendra was as good as dead, and there was nothing to be done now but flee. With one last look at the kahan and kahana of Jador, Lukien turned and hurried from the chamber.

* * *

By the gates, Figgis kept to the shadows. A remarkable hush had fallen over Jador, and the grassy courtyard was abandoned, occupied only by statues and buzzing insects. Past the open gates, Figgis could see the empty streets of the city, so calm and beautiful. A handful of straggling figures moved along the avenues, shopkeepers getting ready for the morning. They would pose little trouble to the trio when they fled the city, but Figgis knew the real trouble would come in the desert. They would be out in the open there, an easy target for Kadar's men. Their only hope was to make good time, as much time as possible before the inevitable hunters came after them.

The three drowas stood ready in the moonlight, peacefully chewing their cuds. They were far more at ease than Figgis, who shifted uneasily from foot to foot, anxious for Lukien and Trager to arrive. Lukien's plan had been a good one, he supposed, because Kadar and his people were far too trusting, and they had learned to like their visitors from Liiria. Figgis felt ashamed. All his life he had wanted to reach this place, and it had not disappointed him. It had been the paradise he'd imagined. Now he had poisoned it.

"Figgis!"

The cry startled Figgis from his daydream. Out of the darkness came two figures, racing desperately toward the gate. Figgis waved, then hurried to bring the drowas out of the shadows. Trager's face was a mask of mania, dripping sweat and smiling wildly. He skidded toward Figgis, holding up the amulet like the severed head of an enemy.

"You got it!"

"Indeed I did! Now get on your ugly beast and ride, old man!"

"Lukien?" asked Figgis, studying the Captain. "What's wrong?"

Lukien's expression was vacant. He was breathing hard and his eyes were glazed, and his skin was the color of curdled milk.

"No time. Got to move . . ."

"What? What happened?"

"Shut up and ride!" bellowed Trager. The lieutenant threw himself onto his drowa, then watched as Lukien and

Figgis did the same. "Follow me," he ordered. A snap of the reins sent his mount galloping out of the yard. Figgis followed, with Lukien close behind. Figgis glanced back at the knight, who had tucked himself behind the drowa's neck.

"Lukien?" he pressed. "What happened?"

Lukien could barely speak. "I killed her, Figgis," he managed. "Jitendra." His eyes closed in pain. "I'm not a thief. I'm a god-cursed murderer. . . ."

Kahan Kadar stood over his wife, fretting as her maidens dabbed her forehead with cool clothes and Argadil, the healer, packed her wound. They had managed to remove the dagger and lift her into the bed, and now the sheets were soaked with blood. Jitendra barely clung to life, but the infant inside her belly fought to escape. The shock of her stabbing had induced labor. The kahana's midwife was at the foot of the bed, white-faced as she stared into the womb, wondering if the child could be coaxed out before Jitendra expired. Kadar held his wife's hand. It was soft and cold and trembled; its familiar strength was gone. Jitendra's breath came in wailing pants. Each groan bloodied her bandage anew, yet she was determined to fight on for her unborn baby— her first with Kadar.

"You will live," Kadar told his wife. She was decades his junior, but he loved her more than any of his previous mates, and the thought of losing her was crushing. "Hold on for me, Jitendra. Hold on for our young one."

Jitendra squeezed his hands. "They have taken the Eye," she moaned. It was the same thing she'd been repeating since the northern thieves had fled. "You must stop them, Kadar."

Kadar tried to smile. "It doesn't matter."

Jitendra winced as Argadil worked, feverishly trying to stem the bleeding. The midwife studied her womb, her face twisted with concern. Yet Jitendra seemed to ignore these things. Remarkably, her concern was for Kadar.

"Why, Kadar?" she gasped. "Why don't you stop them?"

"It is no matter," said Kadar.

"It does matter." Jitendra began to sob. "Without the Eye you will die."

"I will not die," said Kadar. "I will grow old."

"Thieves," cried Jitendra. "They must pay. Send men after them. . . ."

Kadar shook his head. His wife was dying, and that was all that mattered. "They will pay, beloved. I do not need to hunt them for that."

22

Lukien and his party fled through Jador, expecting Kadar's men to follow. But they did not. And when Lukien reached the edge of the desert, he paused to look back at the golden city; all was silent. So they plunged into the desert and were soon swallowed by its blackness. They rode as quickly as they could, always waiting for Jadori men and kreels to hunt them.

But they did not.

After hours of endless riding, Lukien, Trager, and Figgis finally paused to rest. Even their hearty drowas were exhausted. When the beasts came to a stop, the silence of the desert enveloped them. It seemed to Lukien that he could hear for miles, but all that reached him was the soft whisper of the sand crawling over the dunes. Dawn was edging nearer. Jador had disappeared in the distance; even the mountains were gone. They were alone in the world. As Trager and Figgis slaked their thirst with water, Lukien scanned the horizon.

"Why don't they come?" he whispered. He took a step toward Jador. The desert sand pulled at his boots. "I don't understand."

"Don't argue with it, just be glad," said Trager. He had emptied the rope from the sack at his belt, replacing it with the stolen amulet. Now he patted the sack happily. "We got what we came for, and got to keep our skins in the bargain. A good night, I'd say."

"Yes," said Lukien gloomily. "You would say that."

In the east the sun was rising, beginning to paint the sky with light. But toward Jador the world remained dark. Lukien could feel the blackness, the misery. Kadar's cries still rang in his head. His gaka was stained with Jitendra's blood.

"She was pregnant and I killed her," he said. "Almighty Fate, what have I become?"

Figgis put a hand on his shoulder. "There's no sense in this, Captain. It's done, and we have a long ride home. We're not safe yet."

Lukien stared into the distance. "Why don't they come, Figgis? What are they waiting for?"

The librarian shrugged. "I don't know."

"I do," said Lukien. "You weren't there, you didn't see Kadar. I think I killed him too, in a way. I don't think he can follow us. I think I crippled him."

"That's a good enough reason for me," said Trager. He climbed back onto his drowa. "Either way, I don't want to stay in the desert any longer than I have to. You two lovers can die out here if you wish, but I'm going home."

Trager began riding off. His pace was light, like his mood. Lukien watched him, knowing that he was right. Koth was a world away, and Cassandra needed the amulet. Though he had killed Jitendra, there was still a chance to save Cassandra. That, at least, he could do.

The trio made good progress the first day. Without Jebel's caravan to slow them, they crossed the miles easily, following a crude map Figgis had drawn on their first trek through the desert and heading east toward the waiting oasis of Ganjor. The second day was much the same as the first, and by the third day even Lukien was convinced they would make it. None of Kadar's men had entered the desert after them, and all was peaceful among the dunes. Loneliness and heat plagued them, but nothing more. The Desert of Tears seemed to forgive their crimes and did not conspire to keep them in its grasp. There were no sandstorms and few mirages, and though the sun was hot, they had almost grown accustomed to its brutal company. Finally, by the seventh day out of Jador, they reached the end of the desert.

In Ganjor they rested, desperately needing sleep and proper food. They spent a day in the city, mostly asleep, and traded their drowa for horses. Jebel and his family were not in the city, and Lukien found himself missing their company. But the soft, clean bed of an inn eased his melancholy nicely, and he awoke the next morning refreshed and eager to head north.

From Ganjor they followed the Agora River until they reached Dreel, and from Dreel they skirted Nith and continued on to Farduke. They were far from the dark-skinned southerners, and the language was once again familiar. The city of Farduke provided another badly needed respite. They were nearly out of funds now, but were able to trade their exhausted horses for fresh ones. It had taken nearly two weeks to reach Farduke from Ganjor, and the horses they had purchased there were almost beyond use now. Their last few coins went into three fine stallions, well-bred beasts that could swiftly take them to Liiria and Koth. In Farduke, they spent some time in a local pub, listening to the gossip and hoping to hear a hint of Cassandra's health. But instead the talk was of Norvor and King Mor, and how Akeela of Liiria had slain the Norvan king. Lukien stiffened when he heard the news, barely believing it. Figgis' old eyes widened, and Trager frowned in disbelief.

"Did you hear that?" Trager asked. He cocked his head to listen to the conversation. The men around the nearby table laughed and shook their heads, all agreeing that the new king of Liiria was not what they expected.

"Akeela killed Mor?" said Lukien. "That's impossible."

But it was true, or at least that was the consensus of the pub's customers. Mistaking Lukien and his companions for merchants returning from the south, they explained how Akeela had arranged for Mor's destruction at Hanging Man, ambushing the Norvan army with help from the Reecians. Akeela, they said, had killed King Mor himself. The news shattered Lukien, who sank back in his chair and refused to talk about it any more.

They were only days from the Liirian border, and so set off the next morning for Koth. The simple thought of returning home quickened their pace. Two days after leaving Farduke, they entered Liiria. They stopped infrequently, barely sleeping or eating, taking meals from their packs as they rode, and quickly crossed the southern grain fields and fruit orchards. Finding a main road, they joined the many travelers heading to Koth, making inquiries into the health of the queen and being met with odd stares. Because they had doffed their uniforms for simple riding clothes, no one recognized them, nor did anyone seem to know of the queen's illness. Lukien supposed that was good news. If Cassandra was dead, it would have been common knowledge by now. If she was merely ill, then Akeela had done a good job of concealing her fading health.

The road to Koth was wide and quick, and within a day the companions saw the capital. Seeing Koth, Figgis let out an enormous sigh. He was hearty for his age, but the difficult trip had exhausted him. The outlines of the chancellery buildings rose above the city, and Library Hill glimmered in the distance, easily recognizable by the construction rising from its surface. It seemed to Lukien that much had been done on the library since they'd left. Figgis, too, took notice of the progress, grinning happily.

"Ah, look at it," he said proudly. "My library. It's going up!"

"Your library, Figgis?" asked Lukien playfully. "I thought it was for the people."

"Yes, well, it is," Figgis corrected himself. "But I designed it. And I can't wait to see what's been done. Come on."

Now Figgis led the way into the city. Lukien let him go, knowing that he himself could afford no detours. He had the amulet safely at his belt, having taken it from Trager, and he wanted to reach Lionkeep as soon as possible. Trager rode at his side, eager to take some credit for their prize. The lieutenant kept pace with Lukien as he hurried forward. The gates of Koth were open for commerce and the streets were typically choked with traffic. As he entered Lukien heard the cries of friends, waving and welcoming him home. He smiled, despite his aches and sunburn. Near the center of the city he met up with two more of his Royal Chargers, Jiri and Neel. The men embraced, leaving Trager conspicuously out of their huddle. Jiri and Neel told Lukien that Cassandra was still alive, though only barely. Lukien almost chuckled at the good news. He told Jiri and Neel to accompany them to Lionkeep, and the four horsemen rode triumphantly through the city, Lukien carefully guarding his secret prize. Soon they reached Chancellery Square, which was remarkably quiet for the hour. Seeing the great buildings, Jiri turned to Lukien.

"Captain, there's something you should know."

"I've already heard," said Lukien. He shook his head sadly. "I told Akeela not to make war on Norvor without me. But he's like a child sometimes; he never listens."

Jiri and Neel looked at each other, confused.

"No, Captain, that's not it," said Neel. "It's about Baron Glass. He's been arrested."

"Arrested?" said Lukien. "Why? What happened?"

"Akeela's orders, Captain. He says the Baron betrayed him, went against his demands while he was in Norvor."

"*Akeela* ordered Glass arrested?" said Trager. "Come now—I don't believe that."

"It's true, sir," said Jiri. Because they were nearing Lionkeep, the soldier kept his voice low. "The king's changed since you've been gone. Something's wrong with him. He doesn't leave the keep anymore, and he barely speaks to anyone."

"And he's confiscated Baron Glass' property," added Neel. "That's how he's funding his library."

Lukien couldn't believe it. He rode on, a bit slower now, wondering what had happened to his king. Cassandra's illness was a burden, surely, but how could it have affected Akeela so badly? It didn't make sense.

"I have to see him," he said. "I have to talk to him, make sure he's all right."

"He isn't all right, Captain," warned Jiri. "Even Warden Graig thinks he's lost his mind."

"Don't say that," snapped Lukien. "He's your king."

Driven on by the shocking news, Lukien hurried his mount toward Lionkeep. He entered the courtyard, throwing himself off his horse and not talking to anyone. Jiri and Neel rode into the yard after him, but only Trager followed Lukien into the keep, where they immediately found Warden Graig.

"Lukien!" Graig cried. "I wasn't told you were back. When did you get home?"

"Just now. Where's Akeela, Graig?"

"Akeela's in the throne room, Lukien. But listen—".

"The throne room?" said Lukien incredulously. "What's he doing in there?"

Graig's eyes darted between Lukien and Trager. Then he took Lukien around the shoulder and led him a little way down the hall.

"Lukien, listen to me," he whispered. "Akeela's not well. Something happened to him in Norvor."

"I know. He killed Mor."

"That's right, and he hasn't been the same since. He's demented, Lukien. He doesn't trust anyone, not even me. I just want you to be prepared when you see him."

Lukien was crestfallen. "Great Fate," he sighed. "It's that bad?"

"It is. I'll go and tell him you've returned and that you have the amulet. I'm sure he'll want to see you, but . . ." Graig shrugged. "Just don't expect the old Akeela, all right?"

Lukien couldn't answer. He and Trager followed Graig toward the throne room, which had always been vacant since Akeela's kingmaking. The hall outside the throne room was filled with civil servants. They avoided Lukien as he milled among them. Graig went to the huge doors of the chamber, opening them and slipping inside. The great portals closed behind him.

"What's going on here?" Lukien asked, looking around at the drawn faces of the crowd. He recognized a number of the men, remembering them from meetings they had with Akeela. They were all servants of the chancelleries. "This looks like Mercy Court."

"Mercy? We'll get no mercy here!"

Lukien turned to see who had spoken. A small, bald man in the purple vest of the treasury looked up at him, but didn't seem to know who he was.

"Why do you say that?" Lukien asked. "What's happening?"

"Thievery and tyranny, that's what's happening," said the man. "Where have you been hiding for the last month? In a cave?"

"What are you talking about?"

Before the stranger could reply, the doors of the throne room opened again and a man stepped out. It was Chancellor Sark of the treasury. Sark's expression was grim. Warden Graig followed after him.

"Lukien? Come in," said Graig. "Akeela wants to see you."

Lukien found it hard to move. He stared at Sark, wondering what bad news had befallen him, then fixed his confused gaze on Graig.

"Graig, what's happening? Why are all these people here?"

"I'll explain it later," said Graig. "Hurry, now."

Lukien pushed through the crowd toward the door. Trager made to follow, but Lukien told him to stay behind. Trager agreed reluctantly, and as Lukien crossed the threshold he heard Graig close the doors behind him. The garish throne room spread out before him, all painted murals and iron candelabras. A red carpet ran toward the dais, where the carved throne sat imperiously between two burning braziers.

"Welcome home," said the man on the throne.

It was Akeela, yet it was not. He sat with his hands on the armrests, smiling insanely as his dark gaze bore down on Lukien. The skin of his face was pale and taut, an emaciation imitated by his bony fingers. His eyes were bloodshot, his hair a tangle, and his wrinkled shirt hung limply around his slight shoulders. He was alone in the chamber, and the sounds of the men outside echoed off the gilded walls. His smile grew as Lukien approached, but there was no warmth in the expression.

"Akeela," Lukien gasped. "What . . . what happened to you?"

"You are the thousandth person to ask me that question. Frankly, it's tiresome." Noticing the bag dangling from Lukien's belt, Akeela waved him closer. "You found the amulets?"

"I did."

"Let me see them."

Lukien hesitated. The man on the throne was hardly Akeela at all. He seemed vastly older, with a face ruined by troubles.

"Akeela, you look so different," said Lukien. He took a step toward the dais. "I heard about what happened in Norvor. Are you all right?"

"The amulets, Lukien. Give them to me."

"What's going on outside? Why are all those chancellery people here?"

"Paying their debts," said Akeela.

"Their debts? You mean paying for your library, don't you? Jiri and Neel told me about Baron Glass, Akeela. How could you arrest him?"

A flash of anger crossed Akeela's glassy eyes. "Barely home a minute and already you're telling me how to do things. Thank you, Lukien. I don't know what I'd do without you. Now please—give me the amulets."

"How is she?" Lukien asked. "Is she worse?"

"My wife is fine," said Akeela. "Or at least she will be once you've given me the bloody amulets."

"There's only one, Akeela," declared Lukien. He took the bag from his belt and dumped the contents into his hand. Then he lifted the amulet by its chain and held it up for Akeela to see. "I'm sorry, but this one was all we could find."

Akeela's expression fractured. "One? That's all?"

"Yes. We looked for the other one as long as we could, but we had to get back in time to save Cassandra." Lukien took yet another step toward the throne. He saw despair in Akeela's eyes, the depth of which he had never seen before. "But this one will work, Akeela. Figgis was right. I saw Kahan Kadar, and I saw his children. He's young. Unbelievably young, really."

"It will save Cassandra . . ."

"Yes," said Lukien. He went to the dais to be with Akeela. "It's only one, but it will save her. At least until Figgis can find the other amulet."

Akeela's thin hand reached out and took the Eye from Lukien. He let it dangle from its golden chain, watching it pulsate. For a moment, Lukien thought Akeela would weep. The pain on his face was enormous. But it fled as quickly as it had come, replaced by a brooding anger.

"Thank you, Lukien," he said. "You've probably saved Cassandra's life. But there's something you just don't seem to understand. Cassandra is *my* wife. She's not yours. She never will be."

"What . . . ?"

"I know, Lukien. I know what you did."

Lukien's heart froze. He took a step back from the throne. "Akeela . . ."

"You just couldn't be satisfied, could you? It's not enough that every maid in Lionkeep wants to bed you. You had to take the only woman I ever loved."

"Akeela, it's not like that. Cassandra loves you. I know she does!"

"And you?" thundered Akeela. "What do you think of me, Lukien? Do you love me so much you would rut with my wife behind my back? Is that your love, *brother?*"

"No! I would never do anything to hurt you."

"Brother," Akeela sneered. He stalked after Lukien, his eyes wild. "And so you steal from your brother, and break his heart, and ruin the only thing he loves in the world. That's how street scum treat their brothers, is it?"

"Akeela, just listen. . . ."

"Street scum. That's what you are, Lukien. My father should have left you there to rot."

"I'm not!" Lukien flared. For the first time in his life, he wanted to strike Akeela. "I'm just as good as you, Akeela. I'm better than you ever were! And I didn't take Cassandra to hurt you. I did it because I love her. And she loves me too."

"Of course she does," spat Akeela. "Everyone loves Lukien. Well, no more." He whirled and sat back down on his throne. Glaring down at Lukien, he said. "I'm the King of Liiria, and I'm making a decree. You're banished, Lukien. You're never to set foot in Liiria again. If you do—"

"Akeela, stop! This is madness!"

"If you do," Akeela continued, "you will be killed."

"You wouldn't do that," said Lukien. "Not to me."

"Be assured, Lukien—if you can defile my wife, I can banish you from Liiria."

The statement struck Lukien like a hammer. "I'm sorry, Akeela. You're right—I did this to you. But I never wanted to hurt you."

"I don't want your apology, Lukien," said Akeela. "All I want is for you to be gone. And I can do that. You see? I'm stronger than you are. I can make you disappear."

Lukien nodded. "If that's what you want, then I will go. But promise me you'll take care of Cassandra."

"Of course I'll take care of her. She's my wife. I'll never let her go."

Somehow, Lukien knew it was true. Akeela's obsession with Cassandra was boundless. Slowly, regretfully, he started toward the doors. As he walked away he heard Akeela's haunting voice behind him.

"Good-bye, Bronze Knight."

23

Akeela waited until dark before going to see Cassandra.
It was almost midnight, and except for the occasional footfalls of sentries, Lionkeep slept. The private wing he shared
with his wife was all but abandoned, and Akeela had left
strict instructions with Jancis and the other maids not to
enter the area or interrupt him in any way. He was told
that Cassandra was sound asleep, and that was perfect. He
wanted to awaken her with the amulet. But the amulet's
curse dictated certain priorities, and Akeela wanted to ob-
serve them flawlessly. It might be years until he found the
second Eye of God, years before he could ever look at his
beloved again. Tonight, he would savor her.

He walked alone through the empty hall, lighting his way
with a taper in a candleholder. The shades of all the windows had been drawn, by his orders, and the torches along
the walls had been extinguished. Only the flicker from the
candle guided him. Beneath his cape he held the amulet.
He could feel its power glowing warm against his side, but
he was not tempted to wear it. If it indeed had magic, he
would not waste it on himself. At the end of the hall he
saw the bedchamber, now Cassandra's private sick ward.
The door was closed but unlocked, and he turned the handle slowly, careful not to make a sound. As the door slid
open he caught a glimpse of the room. Cassandra lay in
the bed. Moonlight from the open curtains played on her
gaunt face. Akeela stepped inside and closed the door be-

hind him. It clicked softly, but did not awaken her. Careful
not to blow out the flame, Akeela floated toward the windows and closed the curtains one by one, shutting out every
small moonbeam. The candle flickered in its dish, throwing
his shadow against the wall. He went to the bed and looked
down at Cassandra. She did not stir. Her chest rose softly
with her breathing. She had lost considerable weight and
now looked skeletal. But to Akeela, she remained beautiful. He studied her, adoring her dank dark hair and her
cracked, sickly lips. Soon she would be whole again. Akeela
smiled. He reached out and brushed her cheek.

"My love," he whispered, "wake up."

Cassandra stirred, but did not awaken.

"Cassandra, it's me, Akeela." He gave her shoulder a
gentle nudge. "Wake up."

This time Cassandra's eyes fluttered open, focusing on
him slowly. "Akeela?" She squinted against the piercing
candlelight. "What . . . ?"

"Don't be afraid, Cassandra. You'll be all right now."

Cassandra struggled to rise. "Is something wrong?"

"No, don't sit up," said Akeela. "Just listen. You're
going to be all right now. They found the amulet, Cassandra."

Cassandra gasped. Not surprisingly, her first word was,
"Lukien?"

"Yes," said Akeela sourly. "Lukien found it." With his
free hand he reached beneath his cape and drew the amulet
out by its golden chain. Cassandra's eyes widened in awe.
The amulet's jeweled center pulsated, throwing a crimson
glow around the room. "It works, Cassandra. Lukien said
so. It will save you."

"Oh, thank the Fate," moaned Cassandra. She reached
out for it, but Akeela pulled it away.

"No. Not yet."

"Why not?" Cassandra asked.

Akeela did not answer her. He had never told her about
the curse.

"There is only one amulet, Cassandra," he said. "They
were not able to find the other."

"But it works, yes? It will save me?"

"It will. But you will be alone with its magic. I won't be

able to join you until I find the other Eye of God. And I will find it, if it takes me forever."

"Akeela," pleaded Cassandra, "let me have it, I beg you."

Akeela smiled. "Now you will never die. You will be strong again, young and beautiful forever."

Again she reached for the amulet. "Please. . . ."

"Yes," said Akeela. "All right. I'll put it on you. But first. . . ."

He blew out the candle. The room went dark; he could no longer see her. Cassandra jumped at the blackness.

"Why'd you do that? I can't see."

"Nor can I, my love. Now keep still."

"But the light . . ."

"Shhh . . ."

Akeela widened the loop of chain, groping for Cassandra's head. When he felt the softness of her hair, he closed his eyes and dropped the amulet around her neck. Then he quickly turned away, facing the door. Cassandra said nothing. Akeela shook with excitement.

"Well?" he asked. "What do you feel?"

There was an awful silence, then a sudden, sharp breath. Akeela didn't dare turn around.

"Cassandra, are you all right?"

"I . . . I feel heat," she gasped.

"What's happening?"

Cassandra cried out, but the sound was full of joy. "It's working! I can feel it, Akeela."

Akeela wanted to see her, to throw open all the curtains and let the moonlight flood inside, but he didn't dare invoke the amulet's curse. It was working!

"What else?" he asked. "Tell me, please."

"Akeela, I am free." Cassandra's voice was a beautiful whisper. "I feel nothing. No pain."

"No pain," Akeela sighed. He could hardly believe the words. "It's a miracle. . . ."

Cassandra laughed. "Look at me, Akeela!"

"A miracle," said Akeela. He did not turn around.

"Akeela, bring back the light. Look at me!"

"No. Stay in bed, Cassandra. Don't move."

"What? Why not?"

"Just don't," ordered Akeela. "I have something to tell you."

A gigantic feeling of loneliness engulfed him. But Cassandra was his now, completely. There was solace in that. He stared at the wall, avoiding the temptation to look at her.

"The amulet has saved you, Cassandra, but there's a price you don't know yet."

"Tell me," Cassandra demanded.

"There is a curse. I don't know how it works or why, but if you're ever looked on with human eyes, the spell that's keeping you alive will be broken." Akeela sighed miserably. "No one must ever see you, Cassandra. Not even me."

"What? You mean I'm a prisoner?"

"Until I find the other amulet, I can't look at you. No one can."

Cassandra bolted up in the bed. "No!" she cried. "This can't be!"

"Don't worry, my love. I've already thought about it. We'll take out all the windows in this wing and brick them up. And I'll hire blind servants for you, so you won't be alone. . . ."

"Are you mad?" Cassandra shrieked. "I can't live like that!"

"Oh, but you will. You're well now, and I won't risk losing you again."

"No! I won't live like this. If that's how it will be, I won't wear this damned amulet!"

Akeela had to stop himself from turning around. "Don't you dare take it off. Don't you dare."

"You *are* mad," said Cassandra. "Oh, Akeela, please listen to me. . . ."

"No, Cassandra, I will not listen. I have decided." Akeela closed his eyes and turned back toward the bed. "You will wear the amulet and wait for me to find its twin. Then we can be together forever."

"I don't want to be with you forever," said Cassandra. "You're insane, and I don't love you."

"Yes," hissed Akeela, "I know. You love Lukien. But you'll have all eternity to forget about him, Cassandra."

Cassandra was silent at the accusation.

"Nothing to say, my wife? You must think me a great fool. But I know what's happened between you and him. And I've dealt with it. Lukien is gone now. You shan't be seeing him again."

"You killed him?" gasped Cassandra.

"No, but I will kill him if I must. If you take off that amulet, or if you let yourself be seen, or if anything should happen to break the spell that keeps you, then I will hunt Lukien down and I will kill him."

"*No* . . ."

"And if he ever returns to Liiria for you, he will be executed."

Cassandra began to sob. "Akeela, please . . . listen to yourself!"

Akeela had listened, and he'd liked what he'd heard. He was powerful now, something he had never been before. Men feared him. Men like Baron Glass. Men like Lukien. With his eyes still closed, he reached out and touched Cassandra's cheek. He felt her tears and liked them, too.

"I told you I would never let you go, Cassandra."

Then he turned and went to the door. Fishing a key out of his pocket, he opened the door and closed it fast behind him. He had to struggle in the darkness to find the keyhole, but when he did he quickly turned the tumbler, locking away his shrieking wife.

PART TWO

THE

Librarian's Apprentice

24

Gilwyn Toms sat in a chair with his leg outstretched, staring at the contraption in Figgis' hands. It was a shoe, essentially, but with a spring mechanism on its heel and a long series of straps up its neck. Its leather had been worked into unnatural curves. To Gilwyn, it looked more like a torture device than a shoe, but since it was a birthday gift he tried to smile. He was sixteen today, and if his mother was still alive she would have been here kissing him. But his mother had been dead two years now, and could give him nothing. Figgis beamed as he presented his gift, his rheumy eyes twinkling. He had worked long and hard on the thing and was proud of it, Gilwyn could tell. The boy kept his clubbed foot outstretched, hardly moving his fused toes. The appendage had been that way since his birth and its appearance no longer bothered him, nor did the look of his similarly useless hand. He sat back as Figgis eased the shoe onto his foot. There was no pain, just awkwardness. Teku, Gilwyn's monkey, bobbed excitedly from her perch on a shelf, her golden tail swaying like a snake.

"Just relax," said Figgis. With one hand he held Gilwyn's ankle; the other shifted the shoe back and forth. "I know it looks strange, but you'll thank me if it works."

Gilwyn was already thankful. Figgis had been like a father to him for years. Or a grandfather, really. And now the promise of walking without a cane. . . .

"If it works will I be able to run?" he asked.

"Let's start with walking, hmm?"

Teku squealed excitedly. She wrapped her tail around a spindle and swung down for a closer look.

"If this works as well as I hope," said Figgis, "you won't need your little friend so much. You'll be able to reach the highest scrolls yourself."

Gilwyn smiled. "Hear that, Teku? You might be out of a job soon."

"No, no," said Figgis. "There'll always be a place for her here, just like the rest of us." He gently eased Gilwyn's foot further into the shoe. Gilwyn felt his bent toes reach the leather sole, then noticed it was curved to match his deformity. Unlike a regular, flat sole, this one was humped. Surprisingly, it seemed to match the contour of his foot perfectly.

"All right so far?" asked Figgis.

Gilwyn nodded. "I think so."

"Good. Now don't fight it—just let your foot slip into place."

Gilwyn relaxed his clubbed foot the best he could and let the shoe fall in place around it. It was a snug fit, but Figgis had explained that was necessary for support. Figgis tested the fit by wiggling the shoe. Finding no play in it, he smiled.

"Perfect," said the old man. "This just might work."

He began tightening the straps around the neck of the shoe, which ran up Gilwyn's calf almost to the knee. Gilwyn spied the door to Figgis' study. He could hear voices down the corridor, and hoped no one would come in and see them. As usual, the library was crowded. It was noon, a peak time for visitors, and a contingent of scholars had come from Marn. They had been polite to Gilwyn when he'd met them, but had pitied him when they saw his limp.

"That's too tight," Gilwyn complained. "It's pinching my skin."

"It has to be tight," said Figgis. "I told you; otherwise it won't support you." His old fingers worked the leather straps carefully, not wanting to hurt the boy. When he was finished, he leaned back to study his work. "There," he pronounced. "What do you think?"

Gilwyn stared at the shoe. It looked odd, with its hinged heel and springs and tangle of buckles, but it felt fine. A bit tight, but otherwise a good fit. Even Teku seemed to approve of it. The little monkey jumped from the bookshelf to Gilwyn's chair and climbed up on his shoulder, focusing her yellow eyes on the shoe as Gilwyn wiggled his foot.

"I like it," Gilwyn decided. It was strong looking, like the boots the Royal Chargers wore. "Thank you, Figgis."

"Don't thank me yet," said the old man. "Now comes the real test." He rose and went to Gilwyn's chair, then took him by the arm and pulled him gently to his feet. "Steady now . . ."

Gilwyn kept his weight on his right foot first, his good foot, then slowly tested the shoe. The hinged heel squeaked as he pressed down on it. Figgis shrugged.

"A little oil."

Gilwyn tried a bit more weight. To his surprise the shoe held firm, keeping his ankle straight. He felt the leather bulge around his calf, straining against the strong straps. Buoyed, he brought down his full weight.

"Easy," urged Figgis, still holding his arm. "I've got you."

For Gilwyn, who had never really stood on two feet before, it was a triumph. He couldn't keep the smile from overcoming his face. With Figgis' help, he chanced a step forward and found to his delight that the shoe continued to hold. When he lifted it from the ground, the springed heel pushed him gently forward, providing power to muscles that had atrophied years ago.

"It's working," said Gilwyn excitedly.

But as soon as Figgis removed his grip, Gilwyn began to wobble.

"Careful," said Figgis. "You'll have to get used to it."

Gilwyn struggled to balance himself, favoring his good foot. When he stopped wobbling he laughed with delight. Again he tried a step, and again the remarkable shoe urged him onward. Holding his arms out for balance, Gilwyn took the first real steps of his life.

"You did it, Figgis. I can walk!"

Figgis glowed. "Happy birthday, my boy."

Gilwyn turned a bright smile on his mentor. "It's a wonderful gift, Figgis. Thank you."

Figgis sat himself down in Gilwyn's vacated chair, admiring his handiwork. He smiled, not hiding his missing teeth.

"Look at you, standing there straight as an arrow. Your mother would be proud."

Gilwyn nodded, wishing his mother could see him. Beith Toms had never had a lot of money, but she had one thing she'd always been proud of—her son. He hadn't seen his mother as often as he would have liked in the last years before her death; he had always been busy with Figgis, learning the librarian's trade. But his mother hadn't minded. She had served in Lionkeep nearly all her life, one of countless servants who kept the castle running, and she had always known that her boy was barely a mile away, safe under Figgis' tutelage. It had been that way since Gilwyn was old enough to read; Figgis had become a surrogate father. But Beith was always there, not far, proud of her son, the scholar.

"You'll need to practice," Figgis cautioned. "Take it easy at first, don't push yourself. Your leg might be sore until the muscles get used to it, but soon it will grow strong."

"Yes, all right," said Gilwyn. He was still shaky but immensely pleased. He took a small step toward the door, hoping the Marnans would see him now, without his cane. But there was no one in the hall. A few figures straggled through the bookshelves, not noticing him.

"Now you can come and watch the moon shadow with me," said Figgis, "let everyone see you walking."

Gilwyn grimaced. With the excitement of his birthday, he had forgotten about the eclipse. "Uhm, about that, Figgis, I'd meant to tell you. I'd really rather not go with you, if that's all right."

"What?" The old man's expression fell. "Why not? Everyone from the castle will be there. Even General Trager." Figgis smiled slyly. "Don't you want to meet the general?"

Gilwyn shook his head. He had given up wanting to be a soldier, and no special shoe could change things. "Really, I'd rather not."

"But this is a big night for me. You know how hard I've worked to predict the moon shadow." The old librarian's face softened. "You can't hide in the library forever, you know."

"I'm not hiding," said Gilwyn. Again he turned toward the door. Holding himself up in the threshold, he looked out into the corridor, wishing someone would come and save him from the conversation. The fact that all of Lionkeep was turning out to see Figgis' prediction was precisely why he wanted to avoid the show. He wasn't like the boys of the keep. Even if he could walk now, they would still make fun of him. If he went with Figgis tonight, the moon shadow wasn't the only thing that would attract attention. "Go without me, Figgis," he said "You don't need me there."

"But I *want* you there. This could be important for both of us. It's a chance for us to show Koth that we're just as important as the army, that we're not just a couple of bookworms."

"I know," said Gilwyn. "But I don't like the crowds. They stare at me."

"They'll be too busy staring at the sky to give you a second look." Figgis rose from the chair with a dramatic sigh. "Still, if you want to miss the moon shadow. . . ."

"I won't miss it," said Gilwyn. "I'll be able to see it just fine."

Figgis went to his desk and started toying with the little model he'd built. It was called an orrery, and represented the movements of the heavenly bodies. Along with mathematics and books and the culture of Jador, Figgis also had a passion for astronomy. He alone had predicted tonight's moon shadow, and all of Koth was buzzing about it. Absently he pushed at the tiny planets, making them spin lazily on their rods.

"Ah, so I'll just go by myself, then," he said. "And when everyone starts applauding I'll take all the credit, too." His twinkling eyes turned to Gilwyn. "Is that what you want, apprentice?"

Gilwyn wouldn't answer. Instead he inched carefully toward the desk, studying the intricate model. Figgis had used the orrery to explain his prediction to King Akeela. And the king had been impressed. According to Figgis, he had even smiled.

"Will the king be there tonight?" Gilwyn asked. He flicked the little metal globe that represented the sun, sending it spinning. From the corner of his eye he saw Figgis' face sour.

"No," replied Figgis. "You know he doesn't go outside."

"Not even for the moon shadow? I thought you said he was excited about it."

"You're trying to change the subject. But if you must know, King Akeela told me he'll be watching the moon shadow from the castle."

"Pity," said Gilwyn. King Akeela's presence was the only thing that might have tempted him to the gathering. But then, an appearance by the king would have been a far greater event than the moon shadow. Akeela the Ghost almost never ventured out of Lionkeep. Gilwyn had never even seen him. Like his wife, the grotesque Cassandra, he shunned people, seeing none but his closest advisors. Surprisingly, old Figgis was one of those advisors; despite his madness, the king loved his library. But the subject of the king was never to be broached with Figgis. When it came to Akeela, he was as closed as a coffin.

"You know," said Figgis as he toyed with his model, "there'll be a lot of pretty girls at the gathering tonight."

"So?"

Figgis shrugged. "Nothing really. Just a thought. But Chancellery Square will be packed with them, I'd imagine."

Chancellery Square. The name made Gilwyn chuckle. It was never called that any more, not since the king had abolished the chancelleries years ago. Some of the old chancellery buildings were still there, but they had mostly been taken over by General Trager's army. Figgis seemed to forget that sometimes. Or did he just prefer the old name?

"No girl wants a fellow like me," said Gilwyn. He held up his clubbed hand. "This isn't very attractive, you know. And you said yourself—there'll be plenty of other boys there. Squires and pages. Real boys."

"You are a real boy, Gilwyn. Don't ever let me hear you say that again."

"Yes," said Gilwyn softly. "Yes, all right."

Turning his gaze to the orrery on the desk, Figgis said, "You don't have to go with me tonight. I don't want to push you." He began moving the sun globe with his finger, distracting himself.

"I won't miss it, Figgis," Gilwyn promised. "I wouldn't

miss it for anything. I know a place where I can watch the moon shadow perfectly."

Figgis didn't seem to care. "That's nice."

He was disappointed; his disappointment stabbed at Gilwyn. Gilwyn looked down at his foot, at the remarkable gift the old man had given him, and felt ashamed.

"Well, no matter," said Figgis suddenly. He rose and started toward the door. "We have a lot of work to do; the library is crowded. We'd best get to it."

Gilwyn started after him, his monkey Teku still on his shoulder.

"Take your cane," Figgis directed. "At least until you're more accustomed to the shoe."

"Yes, sir," said Gilwyn. He went to the chair where his cane was resting and retrieved it. When he turned around again, Figgis was smiling at him.

"Happy birthday, my boy," he said warmly.

On the south side of Lionkeep, the afternoon sun beat down on the bricked windows and barred balconies, just as it had done for years. It was midsummer, and the rooms in the castle's southern wing were furiously hot, making it all but unbearable for the queen and her blind attendants. Since there were no windows in the wing, or at least none that could be opened, fresh air was a rare commodity. It was just past noon, the hour when the sun did its worst, and the wing was eerily quiet. There was no sound from beyond the thick walls, no singing birds to ease the monotony, and Cassandra wondered as she sat by her mirror if she would ever hear a bird again. Sometimes, she couldn't even remember what they sounded like. She had some birds in cages, of course—Akeela never let her want for anything. But the music of her captives was stilted, not at all the same as she remembered from the meadows of Hes.

Just once, she thought dreamily. *To hear a bird. To see a tree. . . .*

Akeela never spared any expense in making her prison exquisite. He had built new rooms for her, new wardrobes, even an inside garden for her amusement. She had plenty of servants, all remarkably skilled despite their disabilities. She herself had seen dozens of human beings in her sixteen

years of captivity, but no one had ever seen her. Not one.
Not ever.

To see the sky.

Even with all his fortune, Akeela could not construct a
sky for her.

Cassandra sat back, letting Jancis brush her hair. Jancis
was nattering cheerfully about the moon shadow, and how
all of Lionkeep was turning out to witness it. Though she
couldn't see the event herself, she nevertheless seemed
happy about it, and that perplexed Cassandra. It had always
perplexed her, Jancis' happiness. Cassandra regarded their
shared reflection in the mirror. It was like a magic mirror,
showing them a fractured past. Jancis had changed in the
sixteen years. Her skin had aged. Her hair had changed,
and now bore a jagged streak of grey. But not Cassandra's.
Hers was as raven black as the moment she'd put on the
amulet. Not a single grey hair dared show itself.

Jancis continued brushing Cassandra's hair. Cassandra
felt her friend's fingers pulling through her locks, as warm
and as safe as a mother's caress. Their relationship had
almost become maternal.

". . . and Megal will be there, and Freen from the
kitchen," continued Jancis. "And General Trager too, I
heard. It will be like a celebration." Jancis gave a sad smile,
then paused in her brushing. "I wish I could see it."

Cassandra turned to look at her friend. Her eyes were
white with blindness but hadn't lost their depth. Right now,
they were deep with regret. Cassandra took the hair brush
from her friend.

"Others will tell you all about it," she said, "and then
you can tell me. That'll be nice, won't it?"

Jancis nodded. "Yes."

"And tomorrow it will all be over, and we can both stop
hearing about it!"

Jancis laughed. "And the others will have their memories, and you and I will have nothing!"

It wasn't funny, but it was the familiar black humor
Jancis always used to cope with her blindness. She had
never gotten used to it, not in sixteen years, but she no
longer cursed Akeela for his cruelty. It was a warped gift
Akeela had given Cassandra, but Cassandra was oddly
grateful for it. Sometimes she felt ashamed. Knowing that

Jancis had been blinded for her sake was a great weight to carry around. And there was simply no way to repay such a debt.

"We'll have Freen make us a special dinner tonight before he rushes off to the moon shadow," suggested Cassandra. "We'll eat early, and celebrate for ourselves."

"But I can go, can't I, Cass?"

"Of course. Go and have a good time. And tell me all about this bloody thing when you get back. I'll wait up for you."

Jancis smiled, a beautiful, untainted smile. She felt for the brush in Cassandra's hand, then started working again. Cassandra tried to relax. She was hot and irritated and wanted to be with people, people that could see. She wanted to kill the endless rumors about her and let all of Koth see their queen, to prove to them that she wasn't grotesque and shedding skin with leprosy, and that she didn't shun onlookers because of her ugliness. She was still beautiful.

And that was her curse.

I am old, thought Cassandra. She studied herself in the mirror. *But I do not look it.*

She had given up wondering if she was immortal. It was obvious. Nothing could touch her. Not old age, not a cancer, and certainly not a man. Akeela longed to be with her, but he didn't dare. He had tried it once, in a fit of lust, wearing a blindfold so not to invoke the curse. The results had been an embarrassing disaster for Akeela, who wasn't a skilled lover even when he could see. Blinded, he had been worse than a crippled old man, groping madly for her body, hurting them both. He had left in shame and rage. And he had never come back to her bed. Now he only came to her in darkness, to talk and sometimes to read to her, and she could hear the change in him, too. He had grown weary and mad, but his lust had never been sated. Cassandra saw herself in the mirror and wanted to spit. Her beauty remained her greatest malady.

A desperate hatred grew inside her. Jancis obliviously brushed her hair. Cassandra wanted to scream from the heat.

"Stop!"

Jancis jumped back. "What?"

Cassandra snatched the brush from her and threw it against the mirror, cracking it.

"I can't take it any more!" She rose from her chair and stared at Jancis, who stared back blankly. "This bloody heat, this bloody moon shadow, this whole bloody prison! I want out, Jancis."

Jancis smiled very calmly. "You broke the mirror."

"Damn the mirror!" said Cassandra. She turned and began pacing, the way she always did when anxious.

"Sit down, Cass," said Jancis. "Be at ease."

But Cassandra couldn't relax. This wasn't one of her typical tantrums. She felt different, near a breaking point. The incessant talk of the moon shadow had driven her mad.

"I'm sick of this place," she said. "I don't want to stay here."

"I know," said Jancis.

"You don't know! None of you know what it's like for me. You can all come and go as you please, but I'm stuck in this place. *I* want to see the moon shadow, Jancis. Everyone is going to see it. Even you're going to see it!"

Jancis lowered her head, and Cassandra felt an immediate stab of guilt.

"Oh, Jancis, I'm so sorry. That was stupid of me. . . ."

"It's all right. . . ."

"It isn't." Cassandra went to her friend. "Forgive me. But I'm going insane in this place. I want to get out so bad. I want to see the moon shadow, like everyone else."

"Me too," joked Jancis.

Cassandra's bitterness rose up like a wave. "Then let's."

Jancis laughed. "Cass, stop being silly."

"I mean it, Jancis. Let's go see this thing for ourselves."

"Cassandra, it's impossible."

"But it isn't, don't you see? You said yourself everyone's going to the parade ground to watch the moon shadow. The castle will be empty. We can watch it from the old garden."

"Cassandra, the heat is getting to you. You can't risk being seen. And I'm not going to help you get killed."

Cassandra took her friend by the shoulders. "No one will see us; it'll be dark and the castle will be empty. And no one goes to the garden any more, especially at night."

"You don't know that."

"Yes, I do. I remember how it was. And I bet it's still the same, right?"

Jancis turned her face away. "You're upset because of the heat. . . ."

"No, I'm mad with boredom! I have to see the outside, Jancis, just once."

"It's too dangerous, Cass. . . ."

"I don't care. I'll risk it."

Jancis frowned. "Oh really? And will you risk *him,* as well?"

Cassandra lowered her arms. She didn't have to ask who Jancis meant. Turning toward the broken mirror, she said, "No one knows where he is, Jancis. He might even be dead."

"Would you risk that? Have you forgotten Akeela's promise?"

"I haven't forgotten," said Cassandra dreadfully. The image in the mirror showed her pretty face, cracked in two by the fracture she'd dealt the glass. She still thought of Lukien sometimes, but he was just a memory to her now, no more tangible than air. If she were seen tonight, she would die. And if she died Akeela would try and kill Lukien—he had repeated that promise many times over the years. But he would have to find Lukien first, and that seemed very unlikely.

"I can't go on like this," Cassandra whispered. "I have to see the sky. Just once. Just for a moment."

Jancis floated up behind her, putting a soothing hand on her shoulder. "Don't, Cass, please."

"I have to," said Cassandra. "It's worth the risk. I don't care if it kills me." She turned toward her friend. "No one will know, Jancis. We'll sneak out when everyone else has left for the grounds. And I can describe the whole thing for you. Wouldn't you like that?"

"Yes," said Jancis, her voice shuddering. "But—"

"No," said Cassandra. "No arguments. I'm going to do it. With or without you."

Jancis was quiet for a long moment. Then she reached out and felt for the amulet beneath Cassandra's garment. "If you break the curse, this won't keep you safe. Aren't you afraid?"

"Yes," said Cassandra. "I'm afraid that if I don't see this damn moon shadow, I'll lose what's left of my mind."

As the sun went down on Koth, the great castle of Lionkeep began to empty. The moon shadow would not begin until hours after dusk, but the king's servants were eager to celebrate and so began gathering at the parade ground early. They'd been promised music and food and acrobats to entertain them, and people throughout the city began to swarm the streets in anticipation of Figgis' prediction, bringing traffic to a standstill. It was like a holiday had come, for only the king's great librarian had been able to predict such things, and he had promised that such knowledge of the heavens would usher in a grand new age of science. Even the soldiers, who were everywhere in Koth these days, anticipated the moon shadow. Old Chancellery Square, now the almost exclusive purview of General Trager and his army, had been flattened and turned into a huge parade ground, big enough for his forces to drill on and big enough to be seen from the towers of Lionkeep.

Gilwyn himself had tried very hard not to be seen. He didn't have any books or scrolls to deliver to Lionkeep tonight, but he knew Lionkeep as well as anyone, for he had explored it copiously as a child. Except for the forbidden wing of Queen Cassandra, Gilwyn knew every inch of the place. Until he had been old enough to join Figgis in the library, exploring Lionkeep had been his only solace. He knew the place better than most of the servants, better than the king himself, he suspected. Tonight, he wanted his best, most private spot.

With Teku perched on his shoulder, Gilwyn made his way through the empty halls. He had slipped past the wardens at the southern gate, feigning a message for a minor official, and because the wardens knew his face and familiar limp they let him pass without question. He soon found himself in the quietest part of Lionkeep, near Queen Cassandra's rooms. Because most of the eccentric queen's servants were blind, he always had little problem making his way up through the tower. Hindered only by the noise from his shoe, he climbed the spiral steps with remarkable ease, no longer needing his cane. And when he came to the third level of the castle, he paused at the doorway of the turret to look around. The hall, like the rest of the tower, was empty. Gilwyn smiled at his luck. His destination was on the third level, just beyond a storage area used for tools and old, useless junk. It was usually deserted at this time of day, and tonight was no exception. He passed the narrow hall, making his way to the storage room where he found the door unlocked. The room was dark, and the shutters on all its windows had been closed. Most of the shutters had been locked with heavy, rusted padlocks. One window hadn't been, and it was just big enough for Gilwyn to squeeze through. He picked past the collections of old wares, feeling his way through the dark. Teku chattered anxiously in his ear. Gilwyn put a finger to his lips.

"Shhh."

He reached the window and undid the rusty latches, then pulled open the shutters. There was no glass, just an oval-shaped opening above a wide ledge. The window overlooked a tired old garden far below and the remnants of Chancellery Square in the distance. Gilwyn could already see the crowds gathering on the grounds in the moonlight. He leaned down and let Teku drop from his shoulder. The little monkey hopped through the window and clambered out onto the ledge. Ten feet to the left was an abandoned balcony, overgrown with lichens and penned by stone gargoyles. There was no door to the balcony. Gilwyn supposed there had been one once, but it had been bricked up years ago. So the balcony stood abandoned and neglected, and no one seemed to remember its existence, leaving it free for Gilwyn to discover. It had been his private retreat for years, with a spectacular view of the parade ground and the sprawling capital. On summer nights he would come here to read, and when his mother had died he had come here to weep. And he had never told anyone about the balcony, not even Figgis. It was the perfect hiding place, but it had one dangerous drawback—it was difficult for a lame boy to reach. But Gilwyn had risked it, many times. The ledge was strong and wide enough to support him, and the castle wall was rough with good handholds. And now that he had his new shoe and could walk with relative ease, Gilwyn wasn't frightened at all. He started to follow Teku out onto the ledge, then remembered the food in his pockets.

"Oh, wait," he said, rummaging through his pants. Any small thing might disturb his balance, so he pulled the apple out of his pocket and held it out for Teku. "Here, this is yours."

The monkey took the apple, bouncing in approval. She quickly ran with it to the balcony, set it down, then returned for a dry sausage and Gilwyn's folding knife, both of which she deposited near the apple. When she was done, she climbed onto the head of a gargoyle and urged her master forward.

"I'm coming," said Gilwyn, slipping through the window. With his good right hand he took a firm hold of the ledge. Leaning against the castle wall for support, he set his foot down gently. Slowly, carefully, he shuffled along the ledge toward the balcony, hidden like a wraith in the darkness. The ledge was slippery with moss but Gilwyn was used to it. Though he couldn't walk without limping, he proved remarkably athletic at crossing the ledge; he soon reached the balcony. He wrapped his arm around the gargoyle for support and dragged himself to safety.

It was a beautiful night. The Fate had given Figgis a beautiful venue for his moon shadow. Gilwyn looked up at the moon, which was amazingly bright on his face, and wondered at the precision of the heavens. Figgis was very smart, smarter than any of the scholars that came to his library, but Gilwyn still found it hard to believe that the world was round, as Figgis had claimed. It was like a ball, said Figgis, and the sun and the moon were like that too. Sometimes, according to Figgis, the world blocked the sunlight, casting a shadow on the moon. Moon shadows weren't magic, and they weren't the will of the gods. They were scientific, Figgis claimed, and they were predictable.

"Amazing," whispered Gilwyn. He strained to see past the trees, trying to pick Figgis out of the distant crowd but it was impossible to sight the librarian among the throngs. Gilwyn did see horses though—the brilliant, armored steeds of the Royal Chargers. Their banners were everywhere, blowing in the breeze. And their pages were everywhere, too. Gilwyn sank back from the rail and sat down on the cool stone of the balcony. Teku squatted down in front of him and held out her apple. As Gilwyn unfolded his knife and began slicing off pieces of the fruit, he began daydreaming. Once, a long time ago, he had wanted to be a Royal Charger. He had wanted to ride a horse like the great Lukien. He had even foolishly thought his foot and hand might heal. But by his tenth birthday he knew that could never be, and had given up the dream forever. To this day he had never even ridden a horse.

"Maybe someday," he said, regarding his strange new shoe. It had already done wonders for his walking. Of course, he could never join the Chargers, not with a hand like his, but maybe riding a horse wasn't completely impossible any more. "We can have our own horse," he said to Teku. The monkey grinned at him through a mouthful of apple. Gilwyn sliced off a wedge for himself, adding, "Then we can ride through the parade ground like the rest of them, just like Lukien would have."

Teku chattered, but Gilwyn knew it was only for another piece of fruit. He surrendered, handing the rest of the apple to Teku and putting aside his silly dream. Lukien was gone and had been for years. Only his legend remained.

Barely ten minutes before the hour of the moon shadow, Cassandra stalked through the darkened halls of Lionkeep, her heart pounding in her temples, her ears tuned to every tiny sound. The sound of her own anxious breathing alarmed her as she led Jancis by the hand, searching for the garden she could barely remember. It had been sixteen years since she had left her elegant prison, and her eyes were wide with wonder at seeing Lionkeep again. As she inched forward, stealthily avoiding human eyes, Cassandra felt a rush of fear and exhilaration. With Jancis' help she had slipped past her blind servants, not even breathing as Jancis explained how the queen was sleeping and didn't want to be disturbed. Megal and Ruthanna, her young chambermaids, had believed Jancis' lie entirely and had smiled at the news, saying how sad it was that Cassandra wouldn't be able to see the moon shadow, as if they had forgotten their own blindness.

Because no one with sight except for Akeela was allowed in her private wing, Cassandra was confident she wouldn't be seen. But the abandoned garden, she recalled, was just beyond her forbidden rooms, near the first floor scullery. She had gambled that the kitchen girls had left for the moon shadow, and so far her bet had paid off—she could see no one. More importantly, no one could see *her*. She was free, for the first time in memory, and it was wonderful. Akeela had shackled her but she had picked the lock, damn him, and would at last see the stars again.

"Stay with me, Jan," she whispered. "Not much further."

Because Jancis rarely strayed from their private wing, she was unfamiliar with this part of the castle and had to be led by the hand. Jancis' grip was cold with fear and her breathing came in nervous gasps.

"I want to go back," said Jancis. "Please, before we're seen."

But they were so close now, Cassandra knew they would make it. "No," she said. "Keep walking."

"Cass, please. . . ."

"Shhh!"

There was moonlight streaming through the windows and smoky torches in the hall. The scullery doors were just up ahead—the hardest hurdle they would need to leap. Before Cassandra could peek inside, a figure emerged suddenly from the scullery, startling her. Her pulse exploded with fear as the man's eyes turned to her.

"Hello?" he asked. "Is someone there?"

It was Egin, Cassandra's fuller. His dye-stained hand held a chicken wing that he'd stolen from the stores. Cassandra held her breath, forcing down her panic. Egin was blind, and his sightless eyes passed over her without recognition. Cassandra quickly pulled Jancis forward and nudged her to say something.

"Uh, yes, it's me," said Jancis awkwardly. "Is that you, Egin?"

"Jancis?" probed Egin. The fuller's face relaxed, knowing that Jancis couldn't see the food he'd stolen. "What are you doing out here, girl? Why aren't you gone to see the moon shadow with the rest of them?"

"I'm . . . on my way there now," said Jancis. Then she frowned. "And why aren't you there?"

"What good would it do me? I don't need to hear everyone ooh and ahh over something I can't see." He stuffed the chicken leg into his trouser pocket. Unlike Jancis, he had been blind since birth and didn't seem to care much about the things he couldn't see. He was well-adjusted and friendly, and his blindness never seemed to bother him at all. "But you should get going if you're gonna catch the moon shadow yourself." He stood aside, knowing instinctively that Jancis was right in front of him.

"Yes," said Jancis. "All right . . ."

Cassandra urged her gently forward.

"Good night, Egin," said Jancis.

"G'night," Egin replied, then wandered back toward the private wing. Jancis' shoulders slumped as she heard him walk away.

"You see?" she snapped. "We almost got caught!"

"Keep your voice down," said Cassandra. Quickly she grabbed Jancis hand and began dragging her away from the scullery. There was little time until the moon shadow, but they were close to the garden now and past the worst of their journey. Cassandra quickly located the door that would take them outside. It was just as she remembered it, just past the scullery and neatly hidden behind a bend in the hall. The door was rusted, like everything else in this rarely used area, but Cassandra forced it open with a tug. Flakes of rust fell from the hinges as the door screeched open, revealing a dark and overgrown patch of weeds. Startled by the state of the garden, it took Cassandra a moment to remember its layout. There had been a lawn here once, well-manicured and lined with lilies. Recalling a simple path of cobblestones, she looked down and caught a glimpse of its remains, a ribbon of neglected stones beneath the encroaching grasses, winding its way into the darkness of the garden.

"This way," said Cassandra. She led Jancis into the weed patch, then shut the door behind them. "It's a bit overgrown. . . ."

"A bit? Cassandra, I can feel the grass up my skirt!"

"It'll hide us better," said Cassandra, then plowed ahead with Jancis in tow. Her eyes adjusted to the darkness, and up above she saw the stars. They winked at her like long lost friends. The moon was stout and bright in the heavens, throwing its light on the forgotten garden. Cassandra stopped, unable to move, unable to pull her gaze from the sky. She let her hands drop to her side, and all at once forgot the curse of the amulet and the danger of being outside.

"It's beautiful. I had forgotten how amazing it is."

The stars were abundant, too numerous to imagine. They swept across the sky in a milky arc. Cassandra's legs wavered beneath her.

"Cass? Are you there?"

"Yes," whispered Cassandra. She looked at Jancis, at her confused face and unseeing eyes, and she pitied her. Smiling, she took her friend's hand again. "Come. I'm going to explain it all to you."

They walked alone through the tall weeds, brushing aside the grasses as they made their way at last to the abandoned garden. The tower rose over them, but that was abandoned too, so they were not afraid of being seen. Cassandra spied the small stone bench in the center of the garden, where once she had sat and dreamed of Lukien, and where Akeela had bored her with love poems. The bench, like the rest of the garden, was thick with moss and lichens. Rows of dandelions rose up through the brickwork, and the beds of lilies and other perennials overflowed with tall, choking weeds. A few gallant rose bushes bloomed among the tangles of unpruned fruit trees, and rotting apples littered the grounds, chewed to pieces by insects. The place stank of ferment. But Cassandra didn't care. She was mesmerized by it all, and even the decay enchanted her.

"We're here," she whispered.

Jancis' blind eyes maneuvered over the garden. "Are we alone?"

"Oh, yes."

There was not a soul to be seen or heard. Cassandra marveled at the silence. Far in the distance, she could hear the dull murmur of people on the parade ground, gathered for the coming moon shadow but Lionkeep itself was a tomb, with only the breeze creeping through its halls. Cassandra looked up at the moon, so perfect in the sky, ready to be devoured in the shadow of their world.

"Can you see the moon shadow?" Jancis asked.

"Not yet," said Cassandra. But then the smallest sliver of darkness came across the moon. "Wait . . ." Cassandra squinted, then heard a cheer go up from the parade ground. "Yes! It's starting."

Jancis smiled and squeezed Cassandra's hand. "Tell me."

Without fear, Cassandra draped an arm around Jancis and began to tell her everything she saw.

Gilwyn waited an hour for the moon shadow to begin, mindlessly cutting off slices of sausage as he sat back against the cold stone of the balcony. Teku had finished her apple and amused herself by jumping from one gargoyle to another. A pleasant breeze stirred through the balcony; all was silent but for the far-off merriment from the parade ground. Gilwyn glanced at the moon. Figgis had been very precise about the time of the shadow, but Gilwyn had no timepiece to test the old man's accuracy. Still, he suspected it would be very soon. Then he saw the first brush of shadow. He put down his knife and struggled to his feet.

"Look, Teku, it's starting."

Darkness slowly crept across the moon's surface. Gilwyn heard a cheer rise up from the parade ground and knew that somewhere in that throng, Figgis was smiling. He laughed, delighted for his mentor.

"He did it," he said. "He was right."

Excited, he went to the edge of the balcony and leaned out over the rail. Teku climbed onto his shoulder, as if to get closer to the sky. Together they watched as the moon shadow took hold, gradually inching its way across the distant orb. The world fell silent. And in the silence Gilwyn heard something remarkable.

Voices.

Startled, he looked down from his perch and saw two figures in the garden far below, cloaked by the overgrown plants. Gilwyn took a quick step back, not wanting to be seen. But the figures in the garden had not discovered him. They spoke in hushed voices, their faces turned toward the moon. Once again Gilwyn peered over the balcony to steal a better look. They were women. One was much older than Gilwyn, at least thirty, with plain brown hair streaked with gray and clad in unremarkable clothes. But the other was a vision, and stopped Gilwyn's gaze cold. She was young and remarkably beautiful. Her raven hair tumbled down her back like a waterfall. Her skin was perfect, vibrant and glowing with health, and her skirt clung to her in the breeze, revealing her alluring shape.

"Who . . . ?"

In all his visits to the castle, Gilwyn had never seen her before. He supposed she was a visitor to Lionkeep, a diplomat's daughter, perhaps. But whoever she was, she was far more interesting than the moon shadow. Gilwyn sank down behind the balcony, spying her through the space between rails. Her hand was raised toward the moon—she seemed to be describing it to her companion. Gilwyn realized suddenly that the older woman was blind, no doubt one of Queen Cassandra's servants. But the younger girl was no servant, certainly. Her clothes were far too expensive, her face and hands too regal.

"She's beautiful," whispered Gilwyn. There was a sudden pain in his heart. He wanted to call down to her, to rise from his hiding place and wave for her attention, but he knew that he was only a librarian's apprentice, and no one as beautiful as she could ever care about a clubfooted boy.

The moon shadow continued for almost an hour. The figures in the garden watched the celestial show. Gilwyn missed it entirely. Too enamored with the dark-haired girl, he hardly noticed the passing of time. And when the moon shadow was over, the two strangers fled the garden, disappearing quickly into the confines of the trees. When they were gone, when he was sure they couldn't see him, Gilwyn emerged from his hiding place and stared into the empty garden.

"Teku," he said softly, "I have to meet that girl."

25

Night after night, Gilwyn returned to his little hiding spot, hoping to catch a glimpse of the dark-haired girl. Night after night he would brush his hair, smooth down his clothes, and go with Teku to the balcony, anticipating her arrival. And night after night he was disappointed.

The girl had captivated Gilwyn. He spent his days in the library daydreaming about her, causing him to bring the wrong books to the scholars or to forget his chores entirely. And though Figgis repeatedly asked what was troubling him, Gilwyn kept the knowledge of the girl to himself, sure that Figgis would berate him for skulking around Lionkeep looking for her. So he did what he could to finagle plum assignments out of his mentor, anything that involved delivering books or messages to the castle. There were always manuscripts being requested by Akeela and his staff. Still, Gilwyn's many trips to the keep went unrewarded, and after a week of pining he knew more drastic measures were needed. Since the girl wasn't blind, she could be anywhere in the keep. Yet the hope of running into her in the castle's "open" spaces had proved fruitless. Gilwyn realized that his best chance of seeing her meant trespassing into the queen's forbidden wing. Her servants were blind anyway, he reasoned, and so would never detect him if he was careful. But he couldn't speak to anyone—he couldn't risk being recognized, not until he knew the girl would actually meet with him. It was a dilemma that seemed to have no answer.

Then Gilwyn remembered Teku.

Teku had many talents. She was a monkey, but Figgis had trained her to be much more than a pet for Gilwyn, and her time with the old librarian had made her intelligent and resourceful. And she was a Ganjeese monkey, an extra special breed. Ganjeese monkeys were expensive and sought after, because they could learn anything, and not just tricks. They could understand language and reply in rudimentary grunts and chirps, and they bonded with their masters in an unusual, almost preternatural way. Teku had been Gilwyn's right arm. More precisely, she had been his crippled left hand. When he needed a book or scroll he couldn't reach, she fetched it for him. She scaled the library's bookshelves faster than Figgis ever could with his ladder, and she had made the daunting task of navigating the place easy for the crippled apprentice. In many ways, she was Gilwyn's best friend. Now, he needed a favor from her.

It was forbidden for Gilwyn or anyone else to enter the queen's private wing. But Teku was a monkey, so she wasn't really confined by such rules.

Was she?

Gilwyn didn't know, and he was past caring. He would write a note to the strange girl, address the paper to her alone, and hope that whoever found Teku would know to bring his message to her. It was risky, because anyone might find Teku's note and read it themselves, but he wouldn't sign the letter with his own name. He would be more crafty than that, asking the unknown girl to meet him in the abandoned garden. There he would spy from his private perch, and if she came alone he would meet her. If she came with others, he would hide. And if she didn't come at all. . . .

Gilwyn quickly suppressed that idea. His one hope was to lure the girl into a secret rendezvous, a hope that rested on the little shoulders of a monkey.

Years of working with Figgis had made Gilwyn good with words, but in the end he settled on the simplest of sentiments for his note. He addressed it to the "dark-haired beauty," explained how he had seen her in the garden the night of the eclipse, and asked her to meet him tomorrow night in the same spot. And when he had finished he sat back and considered what he had written. He decided that his note needed at least some sort of signature, so at the bottom of the paper he wrote, "Your Adoring Servant."

Satisfied, he folded up the paper and stuck it in his pocket. Calling Teku to his shoulder, he emerged from the study and went in search of Figgis. He found the old man laboring with a stack of manuscripts that had just arrived from Paaral, a city north of Liiria and well-known for its poetry. Figgis' wrinkled face glowed happily as he pushed the wooden cart full of papers down the hall, searching for just the right place among the endless leaves of poetry. When he saw Gilwyn, he waved him over.

"Gilwyn, they've come," he said. "I need your help cataloging them."

"All right," said Gilwyn. "We'll do it as soon as I get back from Lionkeep. You said there were some books to deliver, right?"

"That can wait." Figgis hefted his ledger and began scanning the shelves, tabulating the book numbering system he himself had created. "It's going to take all day to get these Paaral poems in order."

"But you said King Akeela was waiting for the books."

Figgis shrugged. "No hurry."

"But I always deliver the books to Lionkeep around noon. Graig is probably expecting me."

Figgis turned to regard the boy. "You're very keen on going to Lionkeep lately." His eyes narrowed. "Why?"

"No reason. Just trying to get my work done on time." Gilwyn smiled, sure that Figgis suspected something. Mercifully, Figgis didn't pursue it.

"All right then, keep your secret." Figgis shooed Gilwyn away. "Off to the keep with you. But don't dawdle—there's work to be done."

Gilwyn tried not to grin. "Thanks, Figgis," he said, then turned and started back down the hallway.

"Don't forget the king's books!" Figgis hollered after him.

"I won't," Gilwyn called.

If not for Figgis' reminder, he would have forgotten his delivery entirely.

*　　　*　　　*

In less than an hour, Gilwyn was outside of Lionkeep with his sack of books. Because walking remained difficult for him, and because the load of books would have tired out anyone, he always rode to the keep on a wagon drawn by a single, worn-out horse named Tempest. The horse and its master had become a familiar sight at Lionkeep over the years, and were mostly ignored when they entered the parade ground and main courtyard of the keep. As usual, there were soldiers drilling on the grounds and boys and girls in the yard, grooms and servants mostly, who looked after the keep and the soldiers they worshipped. A few familiar faces smiled and waved at Gilwyn as he arrived. He made his way through the yard, carefully avoiding the groups of boys, and brought his wagon to a stop at the entrance to the keep, where a pair of guards with halberds granted him entrance. With his sack of books over one shoulder and Teku on the other, he went in search of Warden Graig. The warden had been in charge of Lionkeep since anyone could remember. He was warm and friendly, and always welcomed Gilwyn when he came to the keep. He was also Gilwyn's only conduit to King Akeela. The king saw very few people, and of course couldn't be bothered with apprentice librarians, so whenever Gilwyn delivered books to Lionkeep they went through Graig.

The Head Warden had an office on the keep's ground floor, near the main entrance. In earlier days, before age had enfeebled him, he would regularly patrol the courtyard. Since he could barely walk without a cane now, General Trager had asked for his retirement, but Graig had pleaded with King Akeela to let him stay, and Akeela had relented, relegating him to paperwork in a shabby little room. Warden Graig was in his chair when Gilwyn arrived, serenely staring out the window as he smoked his pipe. His office door was open, and when he heard Gilwyn enter he turned to smile at him.

"Ah, you're late," said the old man. "I expected you earlier."

"Sorry," Gilwyn offered. He hobbled into the room and set his bag of books down on the Warden's cluttered desk. "I was busy at the library with Figgis. He just got a delivery of poetry scrolls from Paaral."

"You look tired." Graig gestured toward a chair near his

desk. "Sit and rest a bit." He reached for the bag and started nosing through the texts Akeela had ordered. Graig pulled one of the books from the bag, a collection of love poems much like the ones that had arrived from Paaral.

"More nonsense for him to read to the queen," he said with a sigh. He leaned back, taking a long drag on his pipe. Gilwyn took the opportunity to rest, sitting down and rubbing his aching ankle. The shoe Figgis had made him was working remarkably well, but its straps had left welts on his skin.

"I can't stay long," he said. "Lots to do."

"That old maniac works you like a dog," said Graig. He began leafing through the poetry book, clucking at the sugary passages. "The queen likes this drivel," he said. "And Akeela adores reading it to her."

"The queen has very little else," said Gilwyn.

Graig nodded. "Yes, I suppose so."

"She's lucky to have a husband who reads to her." Gilwyn glanced at his crippled hand. "Not everyone knows what it's like to be ugly, Graig. I feel sorry for the queen."

There was a silence between them. The awkwardness made Gilwyn clear his throat.

"You know, I've been thinking about the queen," he said suddenly. "About her servants, I mean. They're all blind, aren't they?"

"Of course," said Graig. "You know that."

"Yes, but how do they manage? I mean, they must have some sighted people to help them."

Graig shrugged and blew a ring of smoke from his lips. "I suppose."

"You mean you've never seen them?"

"Who?"

"The people who help Queen Cassandra."

"Are you kidding? Not even I'm allowed in that part of the castle." The warden's suspicious nature rose up. "You're not thinking of snooping around there, are you?"

"Don't be silly. I'm just wondering, that's all."

"It's not good to wonder such things, boy," Graig warned. "Just do your job, deliver your books, and don't get underfoot. And don't go near the queen's wing. Her servants may be blind, but they'll sniff you out like bloodhounds."

Gilwyn rose from his chair with a smile. "All right," he said, calling Teku to his shoulder.

"I mean it, Gilwyn." Graig looked straight though the pipe smoke at the boy. "Stay away from there. If the king finds out you're poking around, he'll murder you."

"Don't worry," said Gilwyn. "I was just curious. I thought maybe the queen had some sighted servants, that's all."

"Why would you think that?"

Gilwyn didn't know how to answer. "I'm a librarian," he said. "I'm supposed to wonder about such things."

"You're an apprentice librarian and a pain in the backside. Now go on, get back to work."

Gilwyn didn't return to the library. Not long after meeting with Graig, he found himself near the southern wing of the castle—Queen Cassandra's wing. He had been this close to her quarters many times before, for it was where his secret balcony lay, and he knew that the grounds around the wing were unkempt and abandoned, just as they had been that night he'd seen the girl.

He skulked into the garden where he had first seen the girl, at once noticing the overgrown rose bushes. The thorns tore at his shirt and he brushed them aside, shielding Teku as he walked. When he parted the branches, Lionkeep rose up like a fortress before him. His mouth dropped open in surprise, for he had never seen the keep from this vantage before, and it frightened him. It looked haunted, a great ruin slowly being devoured by time. There were no windows, only bricked up spaces where glass had once been, and all the balconies had been torn down, so that only their rubbled remains lay at the base of the wall. A stony silence entombed the garden. The afternoon sunlight struggled down through the thickets, but the southern wing of Lionkeep seemed immune to its warmth.

"How do we get in?" Gilwyn whispered.

He saw doors with padlocks and knew they hadn't been opened for ages, but then he remembered that the visitors to the garden had made it outside, and knew that one of the portals must be unlocked. He stepped forward, emerging from the thickets until he spied a broken path of cobblestones winding through the weeds and bushes. After a cautionary glance around, he and Teku plunged forward, ducking to avoid the worst of the branches. Teku chattered uneasily on his shoulder. The path had obviously not been used for ages, but it seemed to lead directly toward the southern wing. Soon Gilwyn discovered the terminus of the path—an abandoned, broken door.

"Well, hello there. . . ."

Teku bobbed on his shoulder, understanding their discovery. Gilwyn didn't waste a moment. He reached for the door and pulled it open, revealing the forbidden confines of Lionkeep. A hallway greeted him, wide and lit by torches. Up ahead were voices. He froze, afraid to go further, but remembered what Graig had told him—all of the queen's servants were blind.

Time to find out. . . .

He stepped across the threshold, closed the door behind him, then turned to face the room. The torches were warm on his face and the voices in the distance coaxed him onward. He put a finger to his lips, and Teku understood the gesture perfectly. A surge of excitement coursed through him, pushing him onward. He took a few steps, rounded a bend in the hall, and blundered into a room full of people.

Fear froze him in place. One man and two young girls stood just yards away, talking to each other. The girls were laughing and holding trays of half-eaten food. The man busied himself knocking about pots and pans in a steaming wash basin and talking to the girls. Remarkably, none of them had seen Gilwyn enter their midst. Gilwyn's eyes darted about the place, taking it all in. He was in a scullery, with cooking utensils hanging from the walls and wraps of dried meats and vegetables dangling from the low ceiling. The place glowed with warmth and good humor as the blind servants went about their work, oblivious to their intruder. Gilwyn studied the girls quickly, but knew at once that neither of them was the one he'd seen in the garden. He inched forward, floating like a wraith toward them, the sounds of the man's activity covering his approach as he scrubbed his pots and pans. He was an older fellow with dark skin and oily hair, but he smiled at the girls as he spoke, as if his blind eyes could appreciate their beauty.

"Give it all here," he told them, directing them to put their dirtied dishes into his basin.

"Just a moment," said one of the girls. She walked past the man and set her tray down on a table very near Gilwyn. Gilwyn held his breath, fascinated as he watched her scrape the plate into a waste bin. She was young, probably no older than Gilwyn himself, and he could tell by her frilled uniform that she was a chambermaid, just like her companion. The girls could have been twins, they were so similar. Both had red hair and fair skin and blue, sightless eyes. When she had cleaned off the plate she turned and went back to the man, dropping all the tray's contents into the steaming water. Like her companions, she moved without hesitation, not missing a step. Then she pulled a chair out from the table and sat down.

"Come on, let's take a rest," she said.

The other girl smiled obligingly, sitting down opposite her friend. She said, "Anything to eat, Freen? I'm hungry."

The man looked up from his washing, considering the foods hanging from the walls. "I've been curing some sausages. They're probably ready, if you'd like to try a bit."

The girls eagerly agreed. One slipped off her shoes, making herself comfortable. Freen, who was obviously a cook, dried his hands on a nearby towel then pulled a stout ring of sausage off the scullery wall. Quickly he located a knife from his workbench and sat down at the table, proudly setting the sausage down before them. Gilwyn took a step closer, delighted by not being seen. Because they were blind they didn't gawk at his deformities. He was like a ghost to them, and he loved the anonymity. Perhaps he would come here again, he considered. Perhaps he belonged here with the blind.

Freen sliced the sausage, handing some to each of the girls and sampling a medallion for himself.

"Good," said one of the chambermaids.

"It's hot," said the other. "Any beer?"

Freen nodded and rose unexpectedly from the chair. Gilwyn backed away. The man went to a cupboard and pulled out a stout bottle with a cork in its neck. Then he deftly collected three short glasses, which he quickly distributed as if he were dealing cards. One of the girls took the bottle from him, finding each glass with her fingertip before pouring. Gilwyn watched, enthralled, as the three drank and ate, completely unaware of him. And just when he felt his confidence grow, when he was sure he would never be discovered, another stranger entered the room. Startled, Gilwyn sank back. The woman faced him, and for a terrifying moment Gilwyn stared at her, afraid he'd been seen. But soon he noticed the same blindness in her eyes as all the others. More importantly, he recognized her.

"Jancis?" said the cook. "Is that you?"

It's her, Gilwyn realized. *The other one. . . .*

He recognized her instantly. She wore the same plain clothes she had donned the night of the eclipse, and her hair retained the unforgettable, jagged steak of gray. The woman smiled as she approached the table. The man held out the ring of sausage toward her.

"Sausage, Jancis. Want some?"

"No, Freen, thank you. I came for Megal and Ruthanna."

The two girls rolled their blind eyes. "Oh, no," said one of them. "What's wrong?"

"Nothing is wrong, but King Akeela will be coming tonight. Let's make sure the place is clean, all right? Megal, you can start with Cassandra's rooms."

The girl Megal nodded and got to her feet. "Yes, ma'am."

"Not just now," said Jancis. She was obviously the head of the staff and commanded respect. "Sit and finish up. There's time until the king comes. Just make sure you do a good job, right?"

"We will," replied the other girl. She smiled mischievously. "The king's coming to read to the queen again, hmm?"

"Yes, and get that filth out of your mind," said Jancis sharply. "Freen, the king might want something to eat or drink while he's here. Be ready, all right?"

"I'll be here," said Freen. Then he laughed, adding, "Where else would I be?"

The woman Jancis said good-bye, then turned and walked off. Gilwyn panicked. He knew he needed to reach her, for only she could lead him to the dark-haired girl. But King Akeela was coming; there wasn't time to waste. Carefully he followed Jancis out of the scullery, trying to match her footsteps so not to make a sound. The others around the table returned to their conversation. Gilwyn caught a curious snippet of it as he left the room.

" 'course he reads to her," Freen was saying. "What else would he do with a crone like Cassandra?"

Gilwyn ignored the comment, following Jancis as closely as he could, dodging behind furniture and open doors. The deeper they went into Lionkeep, the more beautiful and elaborate the place became. There were still no windows but the hall was effusive with light, brightened by candles in ornate candelabras and iron sconces clasping smoky torches. Brocaded tapestries covered the walls, and soon the stone floor gave way to thick, crimson carpet that smothered the sounds of Gilwyn's footsteps. A wide archway beckoned up ahead, revealing a royal-sized chamber beyond. Gilwyn knew he was leaving the servants' area and entering the queen's own. Jancis continued on through the archway, into a round room with a high, domed ceiling where suits of armor and royal crests decorated the walls. But she didn't pause to regard them, continuing instead through the huge room into another, equally elaborate hallway, much narrower than the first. Gilwyn ducked behind one of the armored displays, trying to remember the way he'd come. The wing was vast indeed, and with King Akeela coming he had no time to waste. If he lost his way, he'd certainly be discovered. So he spied Jancis from behind the empty armor, and when he saw her round a corner he followed her once again, hoping she would soon lead him to the dark-haired girl.

But she did not. Instead, she passed through another arch and entered a room that took Gilwyn's breath away. It was flooded with light, and Gilwyn had to squint against the brightness. He realized suddenly that it wasn't torchlight he was seeing this time. This was sunlight, pure and white, and it streamed in from the roof of the chamber through an elaborate glass ceiling, a gigantic web of windows and panes arranged to catch the traveling sun. The chamber was alive with plants and blooming flowers, colors and varieties Gilwyn had never seen. The strong perfume of the lilac and honeysuckle wafted over the threshold. Gilwyn slowed to an entranced crawl as he followed Jancis into the chamber. He had heard that the queen had a private conservatory, but he had never imagined one so vast and lovely. The expense alone was staggering. As he crossed into the chamber, feeling the warm sun on his face, he glimpsed Jancis near a stand of rose bushes, smiling as she blindly admired their red blooms. Her hand moved over them smoothly, feeling their petals and nimbly avoiding their thorns. Nearby was a bench strewn with gloves and an old pair of shears, while beside the bench sat a bucket, filled with freshly cut flowers. Jancis located the roses she wanted to cut, then felt around for the gloves and shears and went to work, humming happily to herself in the peace of the conservatory.

Gilwyn slipped soundlessly into the chamber. Dazzled by the light, it took a moment for his eyes to adjust. He looked up and noticed great shades on all sides of the conservatory, huge sheets of white canvas that could be pulled across the glass ceiling to block out the sun—or unwanted eyes. Queen Cassandra's legendary shyness was once again evident, but because the shades were open he didn't expect to see the queen here now. He had hoped to find the dark-haired girl, but Jancis was alone in the chamber, and Gilwyn knew he was out of time. He had to act now, before the king arrived.

Moving quickly, he dropped behind a stand of fruit trees and dug the note out of his pocket. The little roll of paper was perfect for Teku's small hand. The monkey spied the paper inquisitively.

"Here," Gilwyn whispered, holding it out for his friend.

Teku obediently wrapped her hairy fingers around the note.

"Now, bring it to her," said Gilwyn. He stepped out from behind the squat trees and pointed at Jancis, still humming and pruning her roses. Teku took her master's meaning at once. Without a sound she slipped down from Gilwyn's shoulder and bounded toward the unsuspecting woman. Gilwyn braced himself. Jancis might scream when Teku touched her, or run with fear. But Teku was a very gentle creature, and when she reached Jancis she sat and stared up at her for a moment, considering the best way to get her attention. Finally, the monkey let out a small cry.

"What . . . ?" Jancis started at the sound, turning her head in confusion. Having gotten her attention, Teku reached out with her free hand and gave Jancis' skirt a tiny tug. Jancis shrieked. She dropped the shears, barely missing Teku, and pulled the work gloves off in a panic. Teku continued chattering, trying to tell Jancis of her presence.

"What is that?" Jancis cried. "Get away!"

Gilwyn was aghast. He wanted to shout at Jancis, to tell her not to be afraid.

Just take the blasted note!

Teku, seeing Jancis' panic, quickly took another tact. She put the note in her mouth, jumped onto Jancis' leg, and quickly scrambled up onto her shoulder. Now Jancis was frantic. Her arms flailed, trying vainly to dislodge the unknown creature, but Teku held tight. Like a well-trained acrobat, the monkey wrapped her tail around Jancis arm, then stretched out to force the note into Jancis' hand. When Jancis realized what was happening, she stopped fighting. Her fingers quickly felt the paper in her hands. Teku leapt quickly off her arm and darted across the conservatory back to Gilwyn.

"What's this?" said Jancis. Slowly she unrolled the note. And although she could not read it, she seemed to know what she was holding—and what had attacked her. "A monkey."

Gilwyn's jaw dropped. Fearing he'd somehow been discovered, he began backing out of the chamber.

"Is someone there?" Jancis queried. "Please come out. Don't be afraid."

But Gilwyn was afraid, so afraid that he bolted out of the conservatory without looking back. Teku clung to his shoulder as he maneuvered out of the conservatory, through the carpeted hallway, back past the ornate domed room, and finally toward the scullery where Freen and the two chambermaids were finishing up. There he stopped, panting, just out of earshot of the trio. Finally, when they all went back to work, he slid out of the scullery and through the forbidden doorway, back into the freedom of the abandoned garden.

His heart galloping, he struggled to catch his breath. Teku teetered on his shoulder, dazed from the mad dash to escape. The sunlight struck Gilwyn's face; he laughed when he felt its touch.

"I did it!" he exclaimed.

Teku tugged his ear in annoyance.

"Oh, sorry," Gilwyn corrected. "*We* did it."

He leaned against the wall of the keep, a huge smile on his face. Now that his note was delivered, the dark-haired girl would read it. She would know to meet him here tomorrow night. At last, he would see her again. An odd feeling of pride stirred in him.

"I've got things to do," he said absently. If he were to meet her, he would need a bath. And clean clothes. "And a gift," he told himself. She was a lady; he couldn't meet her empty-handed.

"Teku, we have to go into town," he told his companion. His eyes narrowed in thought. "And I have to think of something I can sell."

Cassandra had just finished her midday meal and was relaxing with a book when Jancis breezed into her chamber. The look on her friend's face startled Cassandra. She lowered her book into her lap. Jancis seemed out of breath. Her skin was pale and her movements were clumsy as she entered the room.

"Cass?" she probed. "Are you in here?"

"Jancis?" Cassandra studied her friend. "What's the matter?"

Jancis drifted closer to Cassandra's chair. "I don't know. Maybe nothing. Maybe good news." She shook her head. "Something strange just happened to me."

"What?" Cassandra asked, alarmed. She got out of her chair. "Are you all right?"

"Yes, I'm fine. I . . . I just had the oddest experience."

"Jancis, you're not making sense," said Cassandra. She went to her friend and made to guide her to the vacant chair, then noticed the roll of paper in her hand. "What's that?"

Jancis began to laugh. "That's what the monkey gave me!"

"Monkey? Jan, you'd better sit down. . . ."

"It's a note, Cass." Jancis put the paper into Cassandra's hand. "I was in the conservatory cutting flowers. There was a monkey—at least I think it was a monkey. It gave me this paper."

Cassandra was hardly listening. "What would a monkey

be doing in the conservatory?" she asked, guiding Jancis toward the chair.

Jancis wouldn't sit down. "No, Cass, listen to me. A *monkey*. Who else has a monkey but that old librarian, Figgis? And who would have Figgis send you a note?"

It sounded like babble to Cassandra. Then, horribly, she understood. She looked down at the note. Her hand began to tremble.

"No," she whispered. "That's not possible. . . ."

"Read it, Cass," Jancis urged.

"No . . ."

"Read it!"

Cassandra couldn't read it. She couldn't believe what Jancis was suggesting. But suddenly it all made sense. If Lukien was going to write to her, he would need to deliver the note secretly. And only Figgis knew Lukien well enough to risk himself. It had been years since Cassandra had seen Figgis, but she remembered the little monkey he always had with him. Could that creature still be alive?

"Why give it to you?" Cassandra wondered. "Why not just send me the note?"

"I don't know," Jancis confessed. Her smile suddenly melted with concern. "Cass, do you think . . . I mean, could it be?"

To find out, Cassandra had to read the note. She paused, staring at it, then took a deep breath and unrolled the paper. The note was very brief and she read it in moments. But it wasn't the contents of the note that caught her breath. Rather, it was the signature. Cassandra turned and collapsed into the chair.

"It's from him," she said. She hardly believed her own voice. "It's his signature."

"Is it?" asked Jancis incredulously. "What's it say?"

"Your adoring servant. . . ."

"What?"

"That's how he signed it—'Your adoring servant.' Just like last time." Cassandra's mind skipped back through the years, recalling another note she had received, way back before she was immortal. She had never forgotten that first note from Lukien, nor the way he had signed it and all the notes thereafter.

"He saw us in the garden the other night," said Cassandra. "The note says so. He wants to meet me there tomorrow night."

"The garden? How's that possible? How could he have possibly seen us?" Jancis pried the note from Cassandra's hand, frowning because she couldn't read it for herself. "It's incredible. Why would he risk coming back?"

"I don't know. Maybe that's why he didn't use my name." Cassandra smiled forlornly. "He called me his 'dark-haired beauty.'" She looked up at her friend. "He's come back for me, Jan. He wants to see me again."

"But you can't go," said Jancis.

"Tomorrow night," said Cassandra dreamily. "After all these years."

"Cass, don't even think it. You'll die if he looks at you!"

Beneath her blouse, Cassandra felt the warm glow of the amulet. Its immutable power pulsed against her skin. She put her hand to her chest, feeling the Eye of God under the fabric. It had kept her alive for sixteen years—but it had also kept her prisoner. She wanted desperately to see Lukien again.

"We don't even know there's really a curse," she reasoned. "We've never tested it."

"Of course we've never tested it! If we did you'd die."

"I don't care," snapped Cassandra. She leapt from the chair, wanting to tear the amulet from around her neck. Around her rose the walls of her splendid prison— beautiful, unyielding stone without a single window, without a single shaft of sunlight.

"Cass, don't be mad," said Jancis. "You can't risk it."

Cassandra closed her eyes, considering her choices.

To see Lukien again, or live forever as Akeela's prisoner.

She made up her mind in an instant.

26

At night, the streets of Koth were no place for a crippled boy. They were crowded and dirty and dangerous, and they had been that way since the early days of Akeela's reign, when the king had first hidden himself from his people. In the sixteen years following Akeela's madness, all manner of thieves began to stalk the streets of Koth, sure that the Ghost of Lionkeep would do nothing to stop them. Commerce continued as it always had, choking the city's avenues and spilling over its sidewalks, and travelers still came from miles around to marvel at Koth. In many ways Koth was the center of the world. She had decayed during Akeela's reign, but she had also prospered. Money poured into her, but it wasn't money from Akeela's treasury. It was the silver and gold of businessmen, opportunists who saw the diversity of Koth as a well to be drained dry. So they had come, unabated, and Akeela's great library became both a beacon and a curse. For every scholar it beckoned, it brought one more thief into Koth's streets. For every boy or girl it freed from ignorance, it lost one to the mills and pits of industry.

But not Gilwyn.

Tonight, Gilwyn was uncommonly happy. He had delivered his note to the dark-haired girl and his hopes were high—too high to notice the darkness creeping through the streets. Instead of returning to the library to help Figgis as he'd promised, he and Teku had made only a quick detour at home, stopping just long enough for Gilwyn to retrieve his cane, the only item of value he had to sell. It had been a good cane, valuable enough to earn him eight copper sovereigns from a pawnbroker on Bleak Street. Because his new shoe was working so well, the cane had been an obvious choice for sale. Despite his proximity to the riches of Lionkeep, Gilwyn owned very little, and the death of his mother had only added to his poverty. The library was rich with valuable manuscripts, of course, but Gilwyn could never consider selling one of them. In the end, only his cane could fetch him some money, and not very much at that. Eight coppers were a pittance, but to Gilwyn they were a fortune. They were enough to buy him a gift for his dark-haired mystery girl. As he walked through a grim avenue, he admired the ring he had bought her. It was bronze, very pretty, and had been very affordable. The shopkeeper had promised him that his "lady friend" would adore it.

Absorbed with the ring and his upcoming rendezvous, Gilwyn hardly noticed his surroundings. He had left his horse Tempest and his wagon on the far side of Capital Street hours ago, venturing on foot toward the west side of town in search of a pawnbroker. That had been the easy part, but finding a suitable ring for his eight sovereigns had proved far more difficult. It had taken hours, and now it was well past dusk. The moon was hidden behind glowing clouds. Shadows from the buildings grew tall in the streets, darkening every alleyway, and the commerce had slowed as the vendors cleared the sidewalks. Gilwyn could hear laughter from the distant taverns, where the businessmen retired from their long days of dealing. He paused in the street to listen. Once, Koth had been full of diplomats and civil servants. According to Figgis, they had been elegant days, but now only the bankers remained to share the streets with the criminals. The chancelleries were gone; barracks and armories had risen in their place. If Gilwyn went into the taverns, he knew he would find Liirian soldiers; they were everywhere in the city now. He frowned, glancing around at his surroundings. Koth was still beautiful, but how much more lovely had it been back then? Why, he wondered, had Akeela shunned his city?

There were no answers from the candlelit windows. And suddenly Gilwyn forgot his many questions. He realized he had been walking without thinking, so enamored with his present for the girl that he had lost his way. The brick buildings and tangled avenues became alike in the gloom. A chill passed through him. Glancing toward the sky, he noticed the clouds begin to thicken.

"Oh, great," he sighed. He hadn't expected rain. Teku shared his bleak assessment, staring at the gloomy sky. The monkey wrapped her tail protectively around his neck. "Don't worry," he told her. "I know where we are."

But after two more blocks, Gilwyn admitted he was lost. The darkness and buildings conspired to confuse him. He was in a narrow avenue of cobblestones, bordered on both sides by rows of empty shops that had closed for the night. Gilwyn heard the far-off laughter from the taverns and the occasional clip-clop of a horse, but he could see no one in the street, and he suddenly cursed himself for blundering so far afield. It was getting late. He hadn't even told Figgis where he was going. The old man would be very cross when he got home. But where was home, exactly? Engulfed as he was by Koth's tall buildings, he couldn't even see Library Hill.

A cool drizzle began to fall. Gilwyn slid the ring he'd purchased into his pocket. His foot ached in its special shoe, crying for rest. He was limping again, because he had taxed himself and not built up the muscles the way Figgis had ordered. Teku chattered nervously in his ear, sensing his fear. Gilwyn stroked her head to calm her.

"It's all right," he said. "We'll find someone and ask for directions."

Behind him he heard the noise of the taverns, deciding quickly not to ask there for help. They would take one look at his strange shoe and twisted hand, and they would laugh, he was certain. He had endured the laughter of drunks many times.

"Better to be lost," he muttered, and continued down the avenue. The avenue quickly narrowed, turning into a filthy alley, and Gilwyn was soon sorry he hadn't taken his chances in a tavern. Apprehension rose in his stomach as he spied the abandoned buildings. He was thoroughly lost and decided to turn back. Yet as he turned he heard footfalls behind him. Very faint, they bounced off the alley's grimy walls, defying direction. Gilwyn peered behind him through the darkness and fog. Suddenly he wished he had his cane with him, or any other weapon. Teku's tail coiled harder around his neck.

"Don't be afraid," said Gilwyn, as much to himself as the monkey. The footfalls grew louder, then suddenly stopped. Gilwyn struggled to see through the mist. Two figures stood motionless in the fog. Very carefully Gilwyn turned and continued down the ever-darkening street. To his great dismay, the footfalls followed him.

"Teku," he whispered, "we're in trouble."

Up ahead the alley terminated in a brick wall. Gilwyn searched the wall for a way out, any little crevice he could slip through for escape. He limped through the mist toward the terminus, his bad foot throbbing with effort. Behind him the footfalls quickened. His mind groped for a plan. He scanned the end of the alley, but only the smallest sliver of space existed between the broken buildings, barely enough for Teku to get through. There was no chance for Gilwyn to squeeze past, so he took a deep breath and turned to face the approaching footsteps.

There was no laughter from the taverns, no sound of horse hooves on the pavement. There was only the dreadful sound of boots. Gilwyn fixed his gaze on the alleyway, straining to see through the mist. The rain made him shiver. Teku shook with anticipation. Together they watched as the two figures emerged, the moonlight slowly defining them. Both were raggedly dressed, with long coats that hung in tatters around their bent frames. Their shoddy boots scraped the paving stones as they shuffled forward, their faces all but hidden in shadows. Gilwyn backed against the wall. The men continued forward, then paused when they realized he was trapped. The smaller of the two, a man with filthy blond hair, smiled through broken teeth.

"You lost, boy?"

Gilwyn shook his head. "No. I'm . . . on my way home."

"Oh yes, you should get home," said the other man. He was dark-haired and lanky, most of his face obscured by a scraggly beard. "It's dangerous this time of night."

They both stalked closer. A shaft of moonlight lit their features, revealing a sickening pall. But despite their gaunt appearance Gilwyn knew running was out of the question. He was cornered.

"What do you want?" he asked. "I don't have any money."

"No money?" said the blond man. "Ah, now that's a lie. We saw you dealing with that jeweler. What'd you get yourself?"

"None of your blasted business." Gilwyn squared his shoulders, trying to look bigger. "And if you so much as touch me I'll let out the loudest scream you've ever heard."

The man looked at his companion. "Uh-oh, Jorry, we'd better do as he says. No one ever screams here in the alleys."

Dark-haired Jorry, the larger of the two, leveled his eyes toward Gilwyn's pockets. "Give it here," he said in a voice thick with consumption.

"I don't have anything." Gilwyn held up his empty hands. The two took notice of his clubbed appendage and smirked.

"Whatever it is you're hiding, I don't think you want to fight us for it," laughed Jorry. "So be a good boy and don't make us hurt you."

Teku squealed with anger, baring her sharp fangs. Jorry stopped mid-step. "Shut that beast up or I'll skin it alive," he hissed. Gilwyn made a fist with his good hand.

"You touch her and. . . ."

Jorry drew a dagger from beneath his filthy cloak. Moonlight and rain glinted on its blade. Gilwyn felt his knees begin to buckle.

"Leave me alone," he said. "Or you'll face the wrath of the king!"

"The king?" The little blond man feigned surprise. "Oh, so you're the king's man, eh? That's good. Then you should spill a lot of gold when we shake you upside-down."

They both edged closer, Jorry's pitted dagger glinting dangerously. Gilwyn fell against the grimy wall, felt its wet surface seep though his shirt. Desperate to appease the thieves, he reached into his pocket.

"Wait!" he cried, fumbling for the ring. "I'll give it to you."

But before he could find the bauble a hand shot out and seized his wrist. Gilwyn jumped, thinking another thug was behind him, but when he looked down all he saw was the hand emerging from the wall. He sputtered, horror-stricken, as the hand held him firm. It was a small hand, hardly bigger than a child's. Jorry and his companion gaped at it, thunderstruck. The dagger in Jorry's hand went limp.

"What is *that?*" croaked the smaller thief. Like Jorry, he stared at the appendage coming from the wall. The hand became an arm, and soon a whole shoulder emerged from the shifting bricks. Gilwyn pulled free just as a face appeared in the masonry. A woman's face, with a devilish smile and a cascade of white hair around her elfin ears. He stumbled back, sure that a ghost was coming from the wall, but the wall was hardly there anymore, replaced by a dazzling frenzy of color. Out of the rainbow stepped the woman. She wore a patchwork coat that swirled around her as if alive, shifting with the colors of the brick and misty rain. As the wall grew solid again, she looked up at Gilwyn with burning, coal-black eyes.

"Hello," she said smiling. She was remarkably tiny. An amulet hung from a chain around her neck, barely peeking through her amazing coat. When she turned toward the thieves, her smile vanished in an instant. "What is this?" she asked, staring at Jorry's dagger. "Violence?"

Jorry tightened his grip on the knife. He sputtered, "What are you?"

The little woman sidled up to Gilwyn and put her arm around him. "I'm a friend of the boy. That's all you need to know."

The blond man's face twisted with rage. "That's just fine, midget. Then you can bleed together."

"Ah ah, not so fast," giggled the woman. Her strange amulet glowed furiously. "Look behind you."

Both Gilwyn and the thieves gazed down the alley. Suddenly there was no way out. Another wall had appeared, as solid as the three that had always been there. And blocking the alley, as wide and tall as the newly formed wall, stood an immense man with stooped shoulders and a shining bald head. Expressionless eyes hung atop his overbite, and the hair on his bulging, naked forearms was as coarse as a wire brush. He didn't move and he didn't speak. He merely watched the thieves, waiting like a sentry in the dark alley.

"See my friend?" asked the woman. She had taken her arm from around Gilwyn's waist and now leaned back casually against the wall. "It's one thing to pick on a crippled boy. Why not try your blade on Trog, Jorry?"

"How do you know my name?" Jorry insisted.

The tiny woman shrugged. "Reading the mind of a simpleton is easy." Then she looked at the blond man. "You are Harl," she said. "And right now you're wondering how you're going to escape. You don't even mind leaving Jorry behind to deal with us, just so long as you get away."

"Sorcery," spat the man called Harl. "Get out of my head, you little bitch!"

"Plenty of room up there for everyone," said the woman. "You too, Jorry. Your skull is as empty as Harl's." Again she shrugged. "Or as full as a chamber pot. Whichever."

The answer enraged Jorry, who whirled to face the giant at the end of the alley. He tossed his knife from hand to hand, squaring off with the silent monster. "All right, you ugly bastard, come on!"

Gilwyn inched back. The little woman held her ground, her inscrutable smile growing.

"Trog doesn't talk, Jorry," she said. "And he's already heard every insult in the world. If you want to hurt him, do it with your knife."

Jorry stalked forward, swishing his blade and moving like a sidewinder toward his adversary. Breath rasped from the giant's slack jaw. His two eyes watched Jorry with dull regard, and for a moment Gilwyn thought the quick thief would best the giant. But as Jorry swiped with the blade, the giant's hand came up in a blur, effortlessly catching Jorry's. There was a bone-crushing pop as the massive forearm flexed, forcing Jorry's hand open and shattering his wrist. The mute monster lifted his quarry off the ground, barely acknowledging him as Jorry kicked and screamed in pain. The giant held him at arm's length, looking toward the tiny woman for guidance.

"Very good, Trog," said his mistress. "Let him go now."

The order given, Trog discarded Jorry by flinging him aside. Jorry tumbled, collided with the wall, then sat up whimpering and cradling his broken arm. Trog lumbered forward, now eyeing Harl.

"Don't you touch me!" cried the thief. "I swear, I'll kill you!"

If Trog heard the threat, he ignored it. His hand shot out

and seized Harl's throat, his fingers circling like ropes around his windpipe. The thief jerked as Trog lifted him to his toes. Harl's hands working uselessly to pry off the iron grip. As he choked for air, the little woman studied him pitifully.

"You see where violence gets you?" she sighed.

Harl's eyes bulged. "Please. . . ."

"Please what? Please let you go? Please release you so you can rob some other poor soul? Is that what you want me to do?" She looked over at Jorry, still crumpled in pain. "Is that what I should do, Jorry?"

Jorry said nothing, grimacing against the agony of his broken arm. Gilwyn could see bones breaking through the skin. His right shoulder hung at an odd angle, dislocated.

"Answer me, you frog of a man," commanded the woman. Her strange amulet glowed an angry red. "Speak for your friend here, or Trog will snap his neck."

Harl let out an anguished cry. The little woman tapped her foot impatiently. "Well?"

"Let us go," Jorry pleaded. He struggled to his feet. "We wouldn't have harmed the boy."

"Why don't I believe that?"

"Please!" gurgled Harl. Trog kept his fist around the man's throat, his face emotionless.

"Don't beg," said the woman. "Give me your word that you'll harm no one else, and you may go free."

"Yes!" gasped Harl. His face had turned apple red.

The tiny woman held up a finger. "Wait. Before you make your promise, I want to show you something." She turned to Gilwyn, waving him closer. "Gilwyn, come and stand near me."

Gilwyn hesitated.

"I won't hurt you," said the woman.

Her gentle tone encouraged Gilwyn's trust. Teku slid down from his shoulder to rest in the crux of his arm. When he was safely beside her, the woman took a deep breath, closed her eyes in concentration, and spoke in a toneless whisper. They were words Gilwyn had never heard before, incomprehensible, musical words. And when she opened her eyes the fog in the alley began to shift. The wall her magic had erected disappeared, and it its place rose up two twisting pillars of mist. Jorry staggered back as the pillars took form. Harl's already bulging eyes popped. And Gil-

wyn stood in fixated horror, watching as the mists shaped
themselves into ghostlike figures. They were human and
inhuman, beautiful and terrifying, and their faces shifting
from angelic to demonic like the swinging of a pendulum.
They had no feet; gusts of fog carried them forward. Their
arms floated beside them, ending in insubstantial fingers.
As they drifted closer they outstretched their ghostly hands,
one caressing Jorry, the other engulfing Harl. Both thieves
screamed at the ghastly touch.

"Trog, release him," said the woman.

Trog's fist opened, letting Harl crash to the ground. The
spirit-thing still clung to him. He and Jorry batted at the
creatures, their arms sailing uselessly through empty air.

"Jorry and Harl, these are your Akari," said the woman.
"I have summoned them for you. They will watch you always. You will never be rid of them."

"Get it off!"

"Jorry, are you listening to me? Because it's very important. These spirits are part of you now. They will go with
you everywhere, see everything that you do."

The little woman stepped toward them, raising her hands
to heaven. Instantly, the ghosts dissipated. Jorry and Harl
looked at her, their faces drawn with shock.

"They have not gone," she told them. "They are bound
to you. You cannot see them, but I assure you they are
here now."

"Great Fate," whimpered Jorry.

"Remember our bargain," continued the woman. "If you
ever threaten another of my children, the Akari will return.
Now. . . ." She turned and gestured toward the open alley.
"Go and trouble us no more."

The thieves looked about in terror. Trog still towered
over them, but the ghosts were nowhere to be seen.

"Go!" barked the woman. The order snapped the men
from their stupor. They staggered to their feet and hurried
out of the alley, looking back in fright until they disappeared into the rainy night.

For a long moment Gilwyn couldn't speak. Fear and fascination held him stiff. He stared down the alley, his arm
still around Teku. The woman went to her giant companion
and touched his arm. Surprisingly, she asked if he was all
right. The giant nodded but did not speak.

"How'd you do that?" Gilwyn finally asked. "What were those . . . things?"

The lady smiled. "Always full of questions."

Gilwyn inched toward her, studying her peculiar coat and impish face. The glow of her amulet dimmed to a dusky crimson; the patches of her coat stopped swirling.

"Who are you?" Gilwyn asked.

"Friends," replied the woman. "Do not fear us, Gilwyn."

"How do you know my name?"

The evasive smile reappeared. "You are Gilwyn Toms, from the library."

"But you've never been to the library," said Gilwyn. "Believe me, I'd remember you." He glanced between the midget woman and her mute companion. Raindrops dripped into the giant's eyes, but he hardly blinked.

"We travel, we hear things," said the woman. "We have heard of you, Gilwyn Toms."

"But how? Who are you?"

The woman looked up into the sky. A strong breeze blew her milky hair. "It's late. The storm is just starting. You should get home before the worst of it."

The strange prediction rattled Gilwyn. "You know how long it's going to rain?"

"Questions, questions . . ."

"Tell me who you are," said Gilwyn. He studied her, then whispered, "Are you a sorceress?"

The woman's black eyes widened, "Oooh, now there's a word you shouldn't use, not in Koth these days. Protect yourself, young Gilwyn. Don't ask so many questions. And forget what you saw here tonight. Just accept our help and be on your way."

"Forget? How can I forget any of this? I—"

"Shhh," bid the woman. "Too much talk. Go to your horse and get home."

"Oh, no. My horse!" In all the commotion, Gilwyn had forgotten he was lost. "I don't know where he is."

The woman reached up and touched Gilwyn's face. She said softly, "Your horse?"

"Yes," said Gilwyn. He blinked, feeling sleepy, but when she removed her hand the dullness passed.

"Where is your horse, Gilwyn?"

Gilwyn thought for a moment, and suddenly everything

was obvious. The terrain of Koth flashed through his mind, clear as daylight.

"Near Capital Street," he said. He pointed east. "That way."

The woman smiled. "Then you should go that way."

Gilwyn nodded. "Yes." A great relief washed over him. "Yes, I need to get home. But those creatures. . . ."

"They are Akari," the woman corrected. "Spirits from a world beyond this one. Now be on your way."

Still Gilwyn wouldn't go. "Spirits? What kind of spirits? And you said they'd stay with those men. How's that possible?"

"Gilwyn, because you are troubled I will tell you this—the spirits will not harm those men. I lied because I wanted to frighten them. But there's no reason for them to be afraid of the Akari, and neither should you be. And more than that I won't say." She took her bald companion's hand and started off down the alley, sparing Gilwyn one last grin. "Get home, young Gilwyn. Before the storm gets worse."

Then they were gone, swallowed up by the gloom. Gilwyn watched them as long as he could, staring at the alley for long minutes after they were gone. The rain had thickened. His clothes were drenched and Teku's fur had flattened against her skin, yet all he could do was stare. Something remarkable had happened tonight, and he couldn't begin to explain it. He thought of asking Figgis when he got home, but quickly remembered how the strange little woman had asked for his silence. For some reason, he intended to keep her secret. Finally, unable to endure the rain another moment, Teku tugged at his ear.

"All right," said Gilwyn. "We'll go."

As quickly as his sore foot would carry him he began his long trek toward Capital Street, toward the place where he knew, somehow, Tempest still awaited him. And as he walked a strange word kept popping into his mind, a word he knew only from fairy tales and children's songs. Despite the many distractions filling Koth's streets, the word would not leave him.

The word was Grimhold.

Near midnight, Gilwyn finally returned to the library. He discovered a very cross Figgis waiting for him. Gilwyn had tried to avoid his mentor, but reaching his bedchamber meant passing the old man's study, and that's where he discovered Figgis. The old man had heard Gilwyn enter the hall and was drumming his fingers expectantly on his desk. There were bags under his eyes from staying up well past his bedtime. As soon as Gilwyn crossed the threshold, he barked, "Where have you been?"

Gilwyn didn't know how to answer. "I'm sorry, Figgis. I didn't mean to be gone so long."

"Do you know what time it is? It's been dark outside for hours!" He jabbed a thumb toward the room's tiny window. "I was worried sick about you!"

"I'm sorry," repeated Gilwyn. "I lost track of time. I had something important to do."

"What?" Figgis demanded. "What's so important that you had to leave me here fretting over you?"

Exhausted, he could only shrug. "I can't explain it."

Figgis rose from his chair. "Look at you. You're drenched!" He stared at Gilwyn, demanding an answer. "Tell me where you were."

"I went into the city," replied Gilwyn. "I told you, there was something I had to do."

"That's not an answer."

"Figgis, I'm tired. . . ."

Before Gilwyn could try to leave, Figgis went to the doorway to block his way.

"Gilwyn, I can't have you running off without telling me where you're going. I spent the whole afternoon expecting you back here. I had to deal with all the work myself. And when you didn't return by nightfall. . . ."

"I'm sorry," said Gilwyn. The worry in Figgis' eyes shamed him. Still, he couldn't bring himself to confess the reason for his trip into Koth. As much as he wanted to tell Figgis about the dark-haired girl, he knew the old man would murder him for skulking around Lionkeep. Gilwyn sighed and fell into Figgis' chair, miserable and contrite. "I didn't mean for you to worry. I didn't think I'd be gone so long."

Figgis hovered over him. "What happened to you? Trouble?"

Gilwyn looked away. His strange experience in the alley was just another thing he couldn't confess. "I'm fine," he said. "I just got caught in the rain." Then he laughed, adding, "I lost my way."

"In Koth? I could have told you that would happen. It's not a city for a boy, Gilwyn, especially not at night." Figgis brushed some clutter from his desk and sat down, smiling gently at Gilwyn. "Now, want to tell me what really happened?"

Gilwyn merely shook his head.

"Gilwyn, you've been acting odd lately. You've been ignoring your work, forgetting things. . . ."

"I know, Figgis. I apologize."

"If I didn't know better, I'd say you were in love."

Gilwyn looked up. "What?"

"Is that it, boy? Have you gotten yourself a sweetling?"

A rush of heat filled Gilwyn's face. "No," he said quickly. "No, I'm just . . . thinking a lot lately."

"Uh-huh."

"No, really."

The old man laughed. "You're sixteen now, Gilwyn. Old enough to be sweet on someone."

"I'm not!"

"And you're old enough to have some secrets," Figgis conceded. "If you don't want to tell me, you don't have to."

For some reason, Gilwyn feared he would cry. His foot was aching and Teku was half asleep on his shoulder, and all he could think of was his ordeal in the alley. He wanted desperately to talk to Figgis, to enlist the old man's help in winning the beautiful girl from Lionkeep, but he was afraid. Figgis was a good man. Sometimes, Gilwyn felt he didn't deserve him.

"Figgis, I want to keep my secret," he said. "For a little while longer, at least. All right?"

Figgis nodded. "All right." He got up and held out his hand for Gilwyn, who took it and let Figgis pull him to his feet. "We've got a lot to do tomorrow," said Figgis. "Go to sleep now, and we'll forget about it. But I want your word that you'll tell me before going off on your own again. You may be sixteen, but I'm still master of the library."

"I will, Figgis, I promise." Gilwyn moved toward the door, relieved the conversation was over. But before he could say good night, the same strange word popped into

his mind again. He hovered in the threshold. Figgis stopped
fiddling with the papers on his desk.

"Gilwyn?" he asked. "Something wrong?"

Gilwyn shook his head. "No, I'm just thinking." He
paused for a moment, then asked, "Figgis, do you know
what Grimhold is?"

"Grimhold? Why are you asking about that?"

"I'm not sure," said Gilwyn. "I keep thinking about it
for some reason. Do you know anything about it?"

The librarian shrugged. "Nothing that isn't known by everyone else. Grimhold's a myth. They say it's a place of
monsters."

"Monsters." The word intrigued Gilwyn. "And
sorcerers?"

"I suppose. The legend goes that the monsters of Grimhold are led by a witch. She steals children."

"Steals children? What for?"

"I'm no expert, Gilwyn," said Figgis. He seemed almost
annoyed at the questions. "Grimhold is just a tale. A good
story, nothing more."

"But there must be books about Grimhold, right? Somewhere in the library maybe?"

"Probably," said Figgis. He shooed Gilwyn away. "Now
go to bed. It's late."

Gilwyn took a single step out of the room, then stopped
again. "Do you think you could find me a book about
Grimhold, Figgis?"

Figgis sighed. "Gilwyn, please. It's late and we've got
work to do in the morning. I really can't have you wasting
time daydreaming about Grimhold while I do all the heavy
lifting around here."

"You're right, Figgis, I'm sorry," said Gilwyn. Then he
smiled. "But you can find me some texts about Grimhold,
can't you?"

"Great Fate, you're a pest sometimes! All right, I'll dig
up something for you. But it might take me some time.
Until then, try and lend a hand around here, will you? For
old times' sake?"

Gilwyn bowed. "Promise. Thanks, Figgis. Good night."

"Good night!"

Satisfied, Gilwyn left the study and made his way to his

little bed chamber. He put Teku into her unlocked cage, stripped off his wet clothes, and slipped lazily into his night shirt. Outside his window he could see the fractured light of the moon as he pulled the bedcovers over himself. The memory of the strange woman in the alley played through his mind, yet he was not afraid. Too exhausted for fear, he closed his eyes and dreamed of tomorrow, when he would meet the dark-haired girl at last.

27

Cassandra sat alone in her bed, her mind full of images. The tolling of a distant clock absently spoke the midnight hour, but Cassandra was wide awake as she dreamed, consumed by better days. Darkness shrouded her bedchamber. Only the flicker of a candle behind a canvas partition invaded the gloom. On the other side of the partition sat Akeela, blinded by the heavy canvas yet still able to speak to her. His voice droned through the midnight silence as he read from a book of poetry. He had been ridiculously excited by the latest books from his library, and had been reading to her for hours now. Unable to face another of his dreadful performances on the eve of her meeting with Lukien, Cassandra had protested, feigning a headache. But Akeela had insisted. Like a child, he never gave her any peace. And he never seemed to tire, either, or to improve in his performance. He tried gamely to entertain her with poems and plays, but his skill was amateurish and his ebullience irritated Cassandra. Tonight, he was unbearable. His ceaseless voice tore through her like a nail, forcing her to daydream her way to freedom. Now, as Akeela worked his way through a particularly tedious sonnet, Cassandra was reminded of Lukien and the hours they had stolen together, long ago. Tomorrow she would see him again. And then, if the curse of her amulet truly existed, she would die.

A clap of thunder detonated above the tower, muffled by the thick walls of her chamber. Akeela had told her it was raining; the storm had come unexpectedly. The rain reminded her of that dewy morning when she had first given herself to the Bronze Knight. In her mind she could smell the apple orchard, the freshness of peat, and the moist spring mist. The thought brought a secretive smile to her lips. Until then she had supposed Lukien would be brutal as a lover, but he had been gentle with her. He'd had none of Akeela's clumsiness, either, and she adored him for it. And in their subsequent couplings he had learned to play her like a harp, so that her body made the most exquisite music.

And then Akeela had gone mad. And Lukien had been banished.

Cassandra opened her eyes in the darkness. As she listened to Akeela's voice, she heard the taint of insanity. He had aged. Unlike her, time had played its tricks on him. But he still had his childlike exuberance, and he still loved her, though his love was a sickness. She studied his voice as it climbed over the partition, listening to it rise and fall, imparting his words with melodrama. Surprisingly, she had never been able to hate Akeela. He had banished Lukien, Liiria's greatest hero, and he had blinded Jancis. He had neglected Koth to the point of ruin while squandering every drop of taxes on his elaborate library. In his paranoia he had crushed the chancelleries, and in doing so he had become a tyrant, imprisoning the long-dead Baron Glass and other good men and taking their wealth for his own. Baron Glass had languished for two years in Borior prison before being exiled to the Isle of Woe. Akeela had wanted him executed, but Cassandra's intercession had been enough to save the baron, consigning him instead to certain death among the savages of an island prison. He had died there, presumably, and Akeela had never spoken of him again, as though the memory of the baron was something to be expunged.

Yet for all his crimes, Cassandra still pitied Akeela. He was a fragile man, still a child in so many ways. As she listened she heard the love in his voice. Truly, he still thought she enjoyed his company. And he still craved to be near her. He hadn't laid eyes on her in sixteen years, nor had he dared to touch her in the darkness, not since that first time. But the inference in his tone was always clear. He hungered for her like a starving man, and would never take another woman to satisfy his lust. He had told her many times that their marriage was sacred. To Cassandra, their marriage was a farce. Still, she admired Akeela's fortitude. His madness had given him a peculiar strength.

Could she be just as strong, she wondered? So far, the prospect of dying hadn't frightened her, yet by midnight tomorrow she might well be dead. Would it take long for human eyes to kill her? Would there be enough time to tell Lukien all she wanted to say? A few moments was all she wanted. That would be enough to look at him, to touch his face, to see the man he had become, and to tell him that she loved him still. In her sixteen years of isolation, she had learned that love was timeless. She smiled, struck by her own poetry. Lukien was a warrior with a poet's soul. She had unearthed the truth in him. Tomorrow, if she died, she would stand before the Fate, that great and mysterious entity that oversaw the world. She would be commanded to list her life's accomplishments, and she knew that she would put Lukien at the top of that list. Loving him had changed her life. He had been worth all the dismal aftermath.

Akeela cleared his throat unexpectedly. There was a long silence, and Cassandra could hear him turn his face toward her through the partition.

"Cassandra?" he asked. His voice was a bell, crystal clear and cutting. "Are you awake?"

"Yes, Akeela, I'm awake."

Another pause.

"You haven't said anything in a while. I thought you had fallen asleep."

"No, Akeela."

There was a rustle as Akeela closed the book. "You are preoccupied tonight."

"No, I just didn't want to interrupt you," said Cassandra.

"You are preoccupied," Akeela repeated. Cassandra heard him lean back in his chair. His silhouette on the canvas seemed to slump. He was thinking, and that was always a bad thing. He could be very perceptive sometimes. Cassandra tried to mask her thoughts. When she did not reply, he asked her, "What are you thinking about, Cassandra?"

"I'm sorry, Akeela, my mind was wandering," she confessed. "It's late, and I'm tired."

"Yes," Akeela drawled. "And how is your headache?"

There was a peculiar accent on the word headache that made Cassandra cringe. He could always tell when she was lying, even through the darkness.

"Better now," she replied. She watched his shadow through the fabric, lit by candlelight. He didn't stir, but sat as still as stone. His silence frightened her, and she cursed herself for being so stoic with him. Now he was suspicious. "Keep reading," she urged. "You haven't finished the sonnet yet."

"Perhaps I shouldn't read you love poems. They make you pensive."

"No," laughed Cassandra. "I enjoy them."

"Why?"

The question hung in the air. Anything Cassandra said would be a lie, so she replied, "Because you read so well, and because it is good to hear your voice."

"No other reason?"

Cassandra frowned. She could tell he was baiting her. "Should there be another reason, Akeela?"

Akeela didn't answer. She watched his silhouette for movement, but he didn't flick a finger. She could tell he wanted to say something to her, to bring up the ugly accusation that was always on the tip of his tongue, waiting to fall off. Cassandra grew angry suddenly. Tonight, on the eve of her meeting with Lukien, the very night before her possible death, she decided to push him.

"Say something, Akeela."

Akeela's breathing quickened. "I know what you're thinking when you hear love poems, Cassandra."

"Do you? Tell me, then."

A great sigh came from behind the partition. "You're lonely. And that's my fault. I've failed you."

"What?"

Akeela rose from his chair and shook his head in despair. "It's true. You are alone because of me, because I've failed to find the other amulet."

Cassandra wanted to laugh. "No, Akeela. . . ."

"Don't spare my feelings. I know what you think of me. You're right—I have failed you. I've left you to rot in this room all alone, without a husband to comfort you. I've done my best to keep you company, but it's not enough. You need me, Cassandra. All of me. A voice in the darkness isn't good enough, not after so much time. What kind of husband is that?"

"Akeela, stop," said Cassandra. She sat up to give her voice emphasis. "I'm fine, really."

"You're not fine. You can't be. But you will be someday, Cassandra, I promise you." Akeela went to the partition and put his hand up to the fabric. His ghostly silhouette lingered there, unable to reach her. "I love you, Cassandra."

The words were terrible. Such beautiful words, warped by time and obsession.

"I know," said Cassandra softly. She closed her eyes, and again thought of Lukien.

"We will be together again, I swear it." Akeela's voice was brittle. "I'll find the other Eye, no matter what it takes."

"Yes, Akeela. All right."

"And then we can be together forever."

"Yes, Akeela. Forever."

Forever. It didn't matter anymore to Cassandra. She would be dead long before then.

28

Gilwyn spent the entire day at the library with Figgis, cataloging and shelving books and helping the scholars from Marn locate history texts. He worked diligently, doing his best to prove his industry to Figgis, who soon forgot the events of the previous night. The day was sunny and warm and the library was crowded with visitors. A large group of local farm children had come for Figgis' weakly reading class, as well as a contingent of educators from Reec who had arrived to study the library's elaborate cataloging system, a mathematical wonder Figgis himself had devised. Gilwyn was in good spirits as he worked, and he had mostly forgotten about his strange encounter in the alley. Too busy to give it much thought, he instead occupied himself with work and anticipating his upcoming rendezvous. Tonight, if all went well, he would finally see the dark-haired girl again.

By dusk, the flow of visitors finally ebbed, and Gilwyn and Figgis took a well-earned rest. Though the library remained open, they were no longer available to help patrons. They ate their evening meal together in the little kitchen off the library's main living quarters, feasting on a grand supper of chicken and biscuits that Mistress Della, their housekeeper, had cooked. Mistress Della was a stoic woman who had lost her husband years ago in the wars with Reec. She had come into Figgis' employ long before Gilwyn had arrived, when the library had first opened its

doors. She was sweet to Gilwyn and feisty with Figgis, and
the three shared most of the work of the vast place, though
sometimes Figgis requested help from the tradesmen of Lionkeep, as when the roof was leaking or some other repair
needed doing. Like Figgis, Mistress Della was paid by
Akeela himself; the king never let them want for anything.
She was comfortable in the library. Its solitude complemented her quiet nature.

After their supper, Figgis invited Gilwyn to play cards.
It was a pleasant night, and Figgis suggested they play on
the balcony of the main reading chamber, maybe even sip
some brandy. Gilwyn knew it was Figgis' way of mending
fences, for the old man had apologized to him more than
once for yelling at him the night before. Figgis' sincerity
made it all the more difficult for Gilwyn to decline his invitation. Since he didn't have an excuse handy, he simply
told Figgis that he would rather do it some other time,
suggesting that the day's labor had wearied him. Not surprisingly, Figgis saw through his pretense easily, but the old
man didn't press him. He merely smiled, saying that they
could play cards any time.

Once he left Figgis, Gilwyn hurried to his bed chamber
to dress for his meeting. He didn't own a lot of clothes, but
he had one nice shirt that he saved for special occasions. It
had a stiff collar and a bright crimson pattern, and had
been bought for him by Figgis so that he'd look good when
meeting dignitaries. Gilwyn hardly ever wore the shirt, but
it was perfect for his meeting with the girl. After he dressed
he ran a comb through his hair, checking himself in a tiny
rectangle of mirror, one that had belonged to his dead
mother. As he stared at his reflection, he was sure his
mother would be proud of him. She would never have ap-
proved of his skulking around Lionkeep, but she had always hoped he would find a girl for himself someday,
perhaps even marry.

"This might be the one," he told himself, smiling. Outside his window, the night was falling quickly. He smoothed
down his shirt, put the ring he had purchased into his
pocket, and took a deep breath. Tonight, he was taking a
giant step toward manhood, a step he had always thought
his crippled foot would prevent. Now, with the special shoe
he wore, he could take man-sized strides. A nervous flutter

turned in his stomach; excitement pounded in his temples. He looked out the window and knew that he needed to hurry, so he said good-bye to Teku in her cage and left his bedchamber, heading for Lionkeep and its long-abandoned garden.

With Jancis' help, Cassandra left her chambers shortly after mealtime, once Freen the cook had vacated the kitchen and Megal and Ruthanna had stopped working for the night. According to Jancis, the two young housekeepers had gone for a walk to enjoy the splendid evening. It was the kind of statement that could still surprise Cassandra, even after years of experiencing the extraordinary abilities of the blind. Within an hour, her private wing had fallen silent and Jancis came into Cassandra's bedchamber to report that everyone had gone off, leaving a clear run to the scullery and thus, the forgotten garden. Cassandra steeled herself. Now that darkness had come, Lukien was very near. With luck he was already safely in the garden, waiting for her. Cassandra let Jancis lead her as far as the scullery, then ordered her friend to turn around and forget everything she had done and heard.

"Admit nothing," she ordered Jancis. They were in a darkened corner near the scullery, close to the rusted doors that led outside. The rest of the blind servants were nowhere to be seen, but Cassandra held her voice to a whisper. There was a tightness in her chest; she couldn't tell if it was fear or desire. Jancis was gray. Her old friend let a tear fall from her eyes. Cassandra smiled and brushed it away. "It's what I want, Jan," she said gently. "You know I can't live like this anymore."

Jancis nodded, barely able to speak. "I know. But if you die. . . ."

"If I die, then it will have been worth it to see Lukien again. Remember that, Jancis. No matter what happens to me."

"I should come with you," said Jancis. "Maybe I could help you."

"No," said Cassandra. They had been through all this already.

"But if your sickness returns. . . ."

"Jancis, stop. There's nothing for you to do. Now I have

to go. And you have to get back to your rooms. If Akeela comes looking for me. . . ."

"I'll tell him you're in your room, sleeping." Jancis grimaced, then held out her arms. "Good luck, Cass."

Cassandra embraced her friend, a lump springing into her throat. "Thanks," she whispered. She kissed Jancis on the cheek. "I will see you again."

Jancis chuckled through her tears. "How do you know that?"

"I have faith," Cassandra said. "Now go."

With one last, forlorn smile, Jancis turned and walked quickly down the hall, leaving Cassandra hiding in the shadowy corner. Cassandra waited until her footfalls disappeared. The wing attained a cryptlike silence. She spied the doors, those magic portals that would take her back in time. But she could not bring herself to go to them.

Second thoughts, Cass? she asked herself. *No.*

It was like she'd told Jancis—she wanted this more than anything. Freedom lay just outside those doors, freedom that would flare like a shooting star before quickly burning out.

Quietly she made her way to the door. Confident no one could hear her, she opened the squeaking portal and peeked outside. Darkness rushed at her; the thick cover of weeds and branches reached for her. Her eyes fought the darkness, searching the garden for Lukien or anyone else. Not a soul was seen or heard. She stepped out into the long shadows, closing the door carefully behind her. Beneath her feet she felt the wetness of dew. Cassandra inched forward, not sure if she should call out for Lukien. How else would he find her? She cleared the castle wall and headed deeper into the garden. The moonlit faces of neglected statues startled her. She steadied her breath and looked around. Aside from the silent statues, the garden was empty. Cassandra's heart sank.

Lukien, she thought desperately, *where are you?*

She dared not shout his name, yet she wanted to scream. Had she gotten the time wrong? Or worse, had she been duped?

"No," she whispered. Lukien wouldn't lie to her. He would be here, because he had promised it. But Cassandra knew she had no time to waste. If anyone else saw her first. . . .

"Hello."

Cassandra jumped at the intrusion. She whirled toward the castle and saw a figure in the feeble light. When she saw it wasn't Lukien, her hoped crashed. And her fear spiked.

"Great Fate," she gasped. "You're not. . . ."

She turned her face away, wanting to bolt. But suddenly she realized there was nowhere to run. The figure was blocking her way.

"Go!" she cried. "Don't look at me!"

"What?" She heard the figure moving toward her, grass crunching beneath his feet. "No, don't be afraid. . . ."

"Go away!" Cassandra looked toward the trees, dashing quickly for their cover. She had been seen, but it was dark and maybe she would be all right. She hurried through the garden toward a tangled stand of pear trees.

"Wait," pleaded the figure. His voice was young, like a boy's.

Terrified, Cassandra ran for the trees and collided with a stout limb. Pain shot through her head. The world winked briefly out of existence, and when she opened her eyes again she was on her back. Wet ground soaked her legs and backside. Hurriedly she tried to sit up, but soon saw an unfamiliar face hovering over her.

"Are you all right?"

Cassandra heard the voice through a fog of pain. Her bleary eyes focused on the face, and saw the most sublime concern there.

"I'm dead," she moaned.

The boy didn't take her meaning. "No, you'll be all right," he said gently. He knelt down beside her, cradling his hand beneath her head and studying the bruise she knew was rising on her forehead. Cassandra thought of rolling free and running off, but she knew it was too late—she had been seen. All she could do now was wait until the cancer ate her insides again.

"Great Fate," she whispered, "I'm going to die. . . ."

She reached to her chest and clasped the amulet beneath her dress, expecting to feel its ruby cold with death. Instead the gem still pulsed with warmth. Cassandra took a slow, calming breath. Remarkably, there was no pain in her belly, just the sharp agony from the blow to her skull.

. "Can you sit up?" asked the boy. Carefully he coaxed
her up. "That's it. Easy. . . ."

Cassandra put her hand to her forehead and gingerly
touched the welt. Pain shot through her skull. Miserable,
she let out a defeated sigh. The boy was looking at her with
a giant smile. Then she saw his left hand. It was twisted into
a useless club, and when he noticed her studying it he
pulled it back, hiding it at his side.

"I'm sorry," she said. "I didn't mean to stare. I. . . ."
She shook her head. "I have to get out of here."

With the boy's help she rose unsteadily to her feet. Her
head swam and she thought she would faint. The boy saw
her distress and kept his good hand on her, propping her
up.

"Here," he said, guiding her toward the pear tree. "Sit
down."

Cassandra sat, knowing she had no choice. Once she collected herself she could go back inside. Then suddenly she
thought of Lukien again, and looked around expectantly.

"Are you alone?" she asked the boy.

He laughed. "Of course. Who else would I bring? I
thought you'd know I wanted to see you alone."

Cassandra looked at him dreadfully. "What?"

"My note." He studied her bruise as he spoke, obviously
concerned. "This doesn't look too bad. You'll be fine."

"Your note? You mean you sent it to me?"

The boy looked wounded. "Well, yes."

"But you're just a boy. I was expecting. . . ." Cassandra
caught herself, then shook her head and started laughing.
"I don't believe it. What a fool I am!"

The boy leaned back, grimacing in embarrassment. "I'm
sorry," he said. "I didn't mean anything wrong. I just
wanted to meet you."

"Meet me? How do you even know me?"

"I saw you in the garden the night of the moon shadow.
You were with an older woman. I saw you and, well. . . ."
He swallowed nervously. "You looked so beautiful, so nice.
I just thought. . . ."

His voice trailed off with a shrug, so ashamed he could
no longer look at her. He pulled his clubbed hand into his
sleeve. Cassandra watched him, suddenly understanding.

He was lovesick. And understandably, he thought them the same age. But he was horribly embarrassed now, and his pain tugged at Cassandra.

"Don't be embarrassed," she said. She tried to smile. "I'm flattered, really."

"But you thought the note came from someone else." The boy sighed mirthlessly. "I should have known. If you thought it was me, you wouldn't have come."

"No," said Cassandra quickly. Then, "Well, yes, you're probably right. But I was mistaken, you see. I thought the note came from someone I know, someone I care about."

"Oh," said the boy. "So you've already got a . . . well, someone special." He gave a sad smile. "I should have known that, too. You're so beautiful."

Cassandra flushed at the compliment. He seemed a kind boy, though shy. His awkwardness made her smile. Sixteen years ago, he could have been Akeela.

"What's your name?" she asked.

"Gilwyn Toms," he replied. "From the library."

"The library? Oh, yes, I've heard about you. My . . . uh, my friend mentioned you once."

"Really? Who's your friend?"

"Doesn't matter. But I have heard about you. You work with the old man."

"Figgis," said Gilwyn. "I'm his apprentice."

"And you saw me in the garden?"

"Yes." Gilwyn pointed toward Lionkeep. "I have a private place that I go sometimes, up there on that balcony."

Cassandra had to squint to see through the darkness. But there it was, a broken, abandoned balcony clinging to the side of the keep. Her heart sank when she saw it. How foolish she had been to risk her life that night. Yet now the risk seemed to be none at all. She patted her belly, feeling fine. The realization of good health made her laugh out loud.

"I'm all right," she chuckled. "I can't believe it."

"It's really not a bad bruise," said Gilwyn. "I told you, you'll be fine."

Cassandra reached out and took his hand. "Yes, Gilwyn Toms, I am fine. Fine as the day I was born!"

Gilwyn looked at her oddly. "Uhm, well, that's wonderful."

"It is wonderful!" Cassandra's laughter rang through the garden. "Oh, thank you, Gilwyn Toms!"

"For what? I don't understand. . . ."

"No, no you couldn't." Cassandra still had his hand and gave it an affectionate squeeze. "I'm sorry, I'm just so happy!"

"Why?" asked Gilwyn. "About seeing me?"

Cassandra thought a moment, then said, "Exactly, Gilwyn, about seeing you." She leaned over and gave him a kiss, a gesture that made his eyes as wide as platters. "But I have to go now," Cassandra told him. She got to her feet.

"Wait," Gilwyn cried. He rose and stood before her, his smile twisting as he considered his words. "I mean, do you have to go already? I don't even know your name."

"My name?" Cassandra thought for a moment. "My name is Megal."

Gilwyn glowed. "Megal. That's a pretty name. But I never saw you before the moon shadow. Do you work in the keep?"

"Uh, yes, I do. I work for the queen. I'm a chambermaid."

"Really? You've seen the queen?"

"From time to time. Now really, I must go. . . ."

"But I thought all Queen Cassandra's attendants were blind. That's what Warden Graig says."

"Warden Graig doesn't come to our part of the keep very much," said Cassandra, trying to be sweet. "And don't believe everything you hear about the queen. Good night, Gilwyn Toms." Again she turned to go, and again the boy stopped her.

"Wait, just one more thing." Gilwyn reached into his pocket and pulled out a small, gold-colored item. He smiled as he showed it to Cassandra. "This is for you."

Cassandra studied the thing and saw to her astonishment that it was a ring. Not a valuable one, and certainly not lovely, but the manner of its giving had a beauty all its own. She reached out and took it, twirling it in the feeble moonlight. It was fairly ornate for a simple piece of bronze, and reasonably well forged. Not expensive, but she knew expense was a relative thing.

"You bought this for me?" she asked.

"Do you like it?" asked Gilwyn.

Cassandra nodded. She did like it, very much. "Yes. I think it's beautiful. But why?"

"Because I didn't want to come empty-handed," Gilwyn explained. "I thought you would expect something." He shrugged. "I figured you get gifts all the time."

What a beautifully naïve boy, thought Cassandra. "No," she told him, "I don't. People are seldom as thoughtful as you. But you shouldn't have done it. It must have cost you a lot."

"Not a lot," said Gilwyn. "And it was worth it to see your face. Do you want to try it on?"

"I will, Gilwyn, I promise. But I can't stay long. I have to get back, before someone discovers I'm gone."

Disappointment shone on Gilwyn's face. "Oh. Well, yes, of course. You should go."

"Gilwyn," said Cassandra softly, "I know what you want to say. But I'm afraid I must refuse you. I can't see you again." She touched his cheek. The gesture made him melt. "You understand that, don't you?"

"Yes," said Gilwyn, nodding. "You've got someone already."

"That's right. But if I didn't, you would make a wonderful friend."

Gilwyn's smile was brighter than the moon. "Maybe we'll see each other again, Megal. I'm at the keep a lot. Maybe we can talk again sometime."

"Maybe," said Cassandra. "But don't tell anyone about us, all right? I'd be in trouble if the queen knew I was sneaking out at night!"

Naïve to the last, Gilwyn said, "Don't worry, I won't tell anyone. I'm not supposed to be out here either!"

"Then we can keep each other's secret," laughed Cassandra. Deciding Gilwyn deserved a gift of his own, she slipped his ring onto her finger. "Ah, look," she exclaimed, admiring it. "It's lovely."

"I'm glad you like it," said Gilwyn. He took a deep, melancholy breath. "Good-bye, Megal. Thank you for coming to meet with me."

He looked so vulnerable in the moonlight, Cassandra felt profoundly sad. "You're welcome, Gilwyn. And thank you for my beautiful gift, and for thinking me so worthy." She took a step away, and could see the heartbreak on his face. "Good night, Gilwyn Toms. I will remember you."

Cassandra turned and left him, sure that she had let him down as easily as possible. As she made her way back through the garden, she could feel his longing eyes on her back. But she did not turn back, for she knew doing so would only add to his misery. She was flattered and she was surprised, and she would have given anything to take away his misery, but that was impossible because love was always like that; out of reach and heartbreaking.

Cassandra's own heartache peaked as she reached the door to Lionkeep. Instead of Gilwyn's earnest face, she saw Lukien's, clouded by time and fading memories.

"A fool, that's what I am," she whispered as she tugged open the door. To think that Lukien would ever return for her seemed the highest idiocy. No longer was she elated over the falseness of her curse. She wanted Lukien, and that was all.

Then, horror-struck, Cassandra paused in the dark scullery, frozen by a bleak realization.

"I can't tell anyone," she whispered. "I still can't let anyone see me!"

If she did, Akeela would want to be with her. He would finally be able to take her to his bed again, and breed her like a horse for all the children he had wanted for so long. Cassandra pulled the amulet from beneath her garments and stared at it. The ruby in its center pulsed with reassuring warmth.

"Still alive," she groaned. "Still imprisoned."

29

Over the next several days, the library became remarkably quiet. The weather turned bad again with a string of summer storms, and the long lines of scholars diminished so that the halls of the vast library echoed with an unusual silence. Figgis enjoyed the solitude. The last few weeks had been chaotic, leaving him little time to acquire new manuscripts or indulge in reading, which still remained his favorite pastime. Too busy seeing to the needs of the library's many patrons, stacks of books had gone neglected in his study, waiting for his attention and never quite getting it. So when the poor weather had dampened the summer crowds, Figgis was grateful.

Still, the silence of one particular person disturbed him. For two days Gilwyn had hardly spoken a word to anyone. He had gone about his chores efficiently and had been polite to the patrons, but he had skipped meals and kept to himself, and he had lost his previous air of mystery. He no longer disappeared for hours in the evening or smiled secretly to himself the way he had just a week earlier. He did not join Figgis for cards, either, or show the slightest interest in the library's exotic books. Gilwyn's imagination seemed suddenly stunted, and it worried Figgis. But he didn't question the boy, for he supposed he already knew the cause of Gilwyn's melancholy. He had been young himself once, and he knew the symptoms of heartbreak. It was clear that whatever girl Gilwyn had been chasing at Lionkeep had discovered his affections and rebuffed them. Figgis pitied the boy. He had never been a father but he had come to love Gilwyn as a son, and he wished for some way to ease the boy's heartache. But he also knew that Gilwyn was shy and wouldn't want the attention. So he had given the boy a wide berth and just enough work to occupy his troubled mind, and he supposed that, in time, Gilwyn would get over the girl.

It was a particularly rainy night when Figgis suddenly remembered his promise to Gilwyn to locate some texts about Grimhold. In the commotion of the past week he had forgotten the strange request, and Gilwyn himself had not brought it up again. Figgis was in his office when he remembered it, yawning over a stack of paperwork. There were dozens of manuscripts that still needed cataloging and his eyes blurred from lack of sleep. Still, it occurred to him that a book of fanciful stories might take Gilwyn's mind off his troubles, so he set aside his paperwork and headed for the catalog room. It was very late and Gilwyn was already asleep, as was Mistress Della. Figgis had the entire library to himself. The many halls took on a ghostly pallor at night, illuminated only by the candle Figgis held in a holder and the occasional flash of lightning through the windows. Thunder rumbled through the corridor and a fierce rain pelted the roof and windows. The halls of the library rang with the storm, thrumming with the unearthly music.

The catalog room was on the north side of the library. Though it was on the ground floor, it was still a good distance from Figgis' study. It was one of the library's largest single chambers, larger by far than the structure's many reading rooms, and it was not accessible to anyone but Figgis. A key for the room dangled from a chain on Figgis' belt. As a thunderbolt shook the hallway, Figgis fished the key up from its chain. Down the hall stood a locked door, a round-topped guardian of iron bolted with a heavy padlock. It had occurred to Figgis long ago that his catalog was at least as valuable as the library's many manuscripts, for without a thorough record, the contents of the library were useless. There were far too many books, scrolls, journals, maps, and ledgers to be navigated without a guide, so Figgis had set upon another of his great achievements, his mathematical catalog.

Reaching the iron door, he slipped the key into the padlock, careful not to extinguish his candle. The lock clicked as its mechanism tumbled. Figgis unhooked the lock and pushed open the door, revealing a vast, dark interior. As he stepped into the chamber, his little candle swatted at the blackness, pushing it back just enough to reveal a metallic monster in the center of the room.

Figgis had accomplished a lot in his life and was proud of many things. He had invented a plethora of items, some useless, some helpful, and he fancied himself a master of the heavens for being able to predict the movement of the moon and stars. He still smiled when he saw Gilwyn walking without a cane, for the boy's special shoe had taken him months to fashion, first on paper, then in reality. But of all the things Figgis had invented, he was most proud of his catalog. The room didn't house just bits of paper and scribbled ledgers. Rather, this catalog was almost alive. It was why it was hidden from view, locked away from many curious eyes. Not even the scholars of Marn had been able to match what Figgis had created with his catalog—the world's only thinking machine.

The light of the candle played off his creation, an enormous series of armatures and springs operated from a heavy, wide wooden desk. On the desk was an oil lamp. Figgis lit the lamp with his candle and trimmed the wick, bringing it to life. The polished wood of the desk caught the glow, reflecting it around the room. There were no windows in the chamber, for the catalog was much too delicate to risk damage or theft. Figgis sat down at the desk, the head of the multilimbed, metal monster. Each armature of the device disappeared into the darkness, heading off in a hundred different directions, guided by springs and sprockets and masterminded by a bank of levers at the desk. Each lever was spring loaded and represented a different letter or number. The levers controlled the armatures through a series of notches along their lengths. Depending on where the armature rested, a unique string of letters or numbers could be sent to the machine. The machine would then match the letters and numbers against a giant scroll of copper ribbon punched with millions of dots and dashes, the machine's peculiar mathematical language. Once a matching string was found—a process that could take minutes or hours depending on the amount of information the machine was fed—a matching armature would punch out a reply in real letters and numbers on a square of copper just beneath the levers on the desk. If all went well and the catalog was asked a valid question, the reply was often quite astonishing. It was far more than a simple catalog of the books within the library. It was a vast and thoughtful cross-reference, one that could interact with its operator to answer the most vexing questions about the library's contents.

Its drawbacks, however, were equally grand. The catalog required hours of careful input each week, so that it could completely understand the mountains of new material constantly being brought to the library. Worse, only Figgis could operate the thing. Though he had tried to school Gilwyn in its use, the thinking machine required a deep understanding of its construction and an almost inhuman gift for numbers, neither of which Gilwyn possessed. In fact, no one in Koth seemed to have Figgis' extraordinary flair for mathematics, making him the sole proprietor of the strange machine's knowledge.

Yet for all its unique abilities, the catalog was less than perfect. It could still not think on its own, but could only regurgitate what it had been told. It had a remarkable memory, much better than any human's because it never forgot anything, and it could tell precisely how many books the library contained on any subject, where they were stored, and so on. But it could not answer questions about its own construction or hypothesize about its own world. And for that, it was a disappointment to its creator. Figgis still longed to make his thinking machine actually *think*, but it seemed an impossible goal. Still, he worked at it, sure that one day it would have its own cognition. If only he could teach Gilwyn to master its inner workings; then his mechanical progeny could live on, and perhaps one day reach its ultimate destiny.

"A grand dream," whispered Figgis with a smile. And a riddle he wouldn't unravel tonight. He settled back in the well worn chair, cracking his knuckles as he studied the

series of levers before him. To Figgis, the catalog was not
unlike a musical instrument. At times like these, when the
library was empty and the world was dark and quiet, he
could sit for hours and ply the levers of his odd machine,
never tiring of its precision. Tonight, though, he decided to
ask the catalog a very simple question. His fingers flew
across the console, deftly pulling levers. The springs
snapped to life and the armatures began moving, and soon
the dark spider was alive, whirring and purring under its
own mechanical power. Counterweights rose and fell, pul-
leys turned and cords unspooled, all to translate the simple
sentence Figgis had entered.

BOOKS ON GRIMHOLD?

Figgis sat back in the darkness, waiting for a reply. He
listened as the machine digested his question, then began
searching its gigantic copper scroll for answers. The scroll
made a peculiar music as the machine's brushlike fingers
danced over the punched-out dots and dashes, like the ringing of a thousand tiny bells. It took almost four minutes
for the catalog to find its references, but when it did it shot
back its reply with quick, staccato stabs. Figgis watched the
armatures punch the answer onto the square of copper.

YES, the machine replied, then printed the names and
locations of the books in its copper brain.

TALES OF GRIMHOLD A9938

FAMOUS CHILDHOOD LEGENDS AND MYTHS
C0088

TYRANT OF NORVOR, MOR'S GRIM HOLD ON
POWER L7215

Figgis studied the list, frowning when he came to the
last entry.

"Stupid machine."

He pulled another lever, this time dropping a sharp blade
across the square of copper and cutting it from the rest of
the ribbon. The machine's printed reply fell into Figgis'
waiting palm. He was about to leave the catalog when a
fanciful idea seized him. Again he worked the levers, asking
the machine another question.

DOES GRIMHOLD EXIST?

It wasn't really the kind of question the machine could
answer, but Figgis waited patiently for the catalog to search
its mechanical memory. He expected the search to take a

long while, but the machine stopped after only a minute, quickly returning its answer. Figgis looked down at the brief reply and laughed.

YES

"Yes? And how would you know?"

The answer was sadly obvious. The machine had simply found a manuscript with Grimhold in its title and said that yes, Grimhold did exist, at least in its own limited definition of existence. Figgis sighed, contemplating his grand catalog. Right now it had the brain of a stunted child, but someday it would be so much more.

"But not today."

Figgis pushed back his chair and stood up. He blew out the oil lamp, retrieved his candle in its holder and left his giant catalog, careful to lock the iron door behind him. Once out in the hallway he discovered that the rain had slackened. The windows were slick with raindrops, but the worst of the pelting had stopped and the library was eerily quiet. He reached into his pocket and glanced down at the books his catalog had recommended. Of the three names the first sounded the most promising, so he turned toward the western wing of the library in search of entry number A9938. It was, for obvious reasons, the fiction section of the library, part of a huge collection of storybooks amassed for the amusement of the local children. Each week Figgis chose one of the fiction books and read them to Koth's children, part of a ritual that had become very popular among the rich and poor alike. Somehow, Figgis had overlooked the book on Grimhold, but now that he knew exactly where to look he homed in on it easily. Section A99 was a generally popular area of the library with children, but adults shunned it and serious scholars—who were the bulk of the library's patrons—never ventured into the fictions. By the light of his lonely candle Figgis passed through the rows of manuscripts, coming at last to a bookcase stuffed with poorly bound books sporting fraying pages. He turned his head sideways to read the spines, and soon found the book he was looking for amid a group of similarly neglected titles. Its old pages smelled of must and decay. Figgis read the words on the cover, studying the faded handwriting. *Tales of Grimhold* had been written ages ago. Figgis' expert eye told him that the scribe had been from

Ganjor, an obvious graduate from that territory's school of penmanship. Satisfied, Figgis returned to his study. He would give the book to Gilwyn in the morning.

When he reached his study Figgis relit the lamp on his desk and set the book down, then lifted the mug of tea he had been drinking to his lips. The tea was cold but he sipped it anyway, considering the book. It was very old, and his penchant for antique books rose up uncontrollably. He opened the cover and within minutes was enthralled by the first chapter, a ridiculous conjecture about the origins of Grimhold. The author claimed that no one knew for certain when Grimhold had been founded, but that it was very ancient and had probably existed before most of the nations of the continent. Figgis snorted at the idea, thinking it a convenient excuse for vagueness. It wasn't science at all, but it was entertainment, and soon the minutes and pages were flying by. Figgis was enthralled by the fictions in the book, marveling like a child at the stories of vampires and werebeasts, and how they were summoned to Grimhold by the White Witch, the leader of the dark hordes. According to the book, the White Witch had a name that couldn't be pronounced by a human tongue, and that to look upon her meant certain death. Figgis laughed at the fanciful idea. There was magic in the world, certainly, but so much of this book was utter nonsense. He wondered for a moment if he really should give it to Gilwyn. After all, he was training his apprentice to be a man of logic, not a purveyor of myths.

Yet the book had the lure of all interesting tales, and soon Figgis had squandered an hour reading it. Exhausted, he leaned back and stretched, rubbing the sleep from his eyes. It was well past midnight, but he was right in the middle of a particularly interesting chapter discussing the location of the fabled place. The author didn't pretend to know the exact whereabouts of Grimhold, because that was as great a secret as any in history, but there were theories. Some said Grimhold existed in a realm beyond normal existence, behind a magical veil that could only be breached through magic or death. Others claimed that Grimhold was in fact part of the everyday world, and was simply well-hidden from human eyes.

Then Figgis read something remarkable. He read it once,

not giving it any notice until he was well past it, but then he paused and read the sentence again. He read it aloud, his whisper breaking the immutable silence.

"Most scholars of merit believe that Grimhold rests across the Desert of Tears, somewhere beyond Jador. That is why, in the Jadori language, Grimhold is called *The Hidden Place Beyond the Desert.*"

Figgis' tired eyes lingered on the page.

"Great Fate, it can't be. . . ."

Excitement seized him, the kind of thrill he had felt only once before. Years ago, when he'd discovered the first Eye of God, he had felt the same powerful stirrings. Once, he had read the same phrase in an obscure Jadori text.

"The hidden place beyond the desert!"

Figgis closed his eyes, contemplating the enormity of his theory. Had Jador ever been the hidden place across the desert? Had his quarry been Grimhold all along?

There were a thousand unanswered questions. Figgis' mind grappled with them instantly. There were things that fit perfectly and others that didn't match at all. Even so, a little voice in his head told him he had stumbled upon something monumental.

Wild with excitement, Figgis quickly took up the book and dashed out of his study. The lateness of the hour hardly mattered anymore—he needed to see Akeela at once.

Akeela the Ghost had been an insomniac for the past sixteen years. The multifold pressures of rulership had robbed him of the simple pleasure of a good night's sleep, and he had given up fighting this affliction long ago. In the first years of the battle he had ordered physicians to find him a remedy, and they had prescribed sleeping powders and herbs that had sickened him, but nothing they did brought Akeela rest. He had realized early on that his trouble was not of the body but was rather a symptom of his fevered mind, and no powders or simples could kill his demons.

Eventually, Akeela found solace in the night, the only time of day when Lionkeep was truly quiet. When the sun went down, so did Akeela's thousand anxieties. After midnight the keep became remarkably still, and Akeela could think clearly and without interruption. He had developed many quirks in the years of his kingship, one of them being an intolerance for noise. He knew the irrationality of his disorder yet could do nothing to stop it. Just like with his insomnia, he was powerless against it. It was why he waited all day for the night to finally come, and why he relished the darkness. Instead of sleeping he often wandered the abandoned halls of Lionkeep, occasionally chatting with the guards on duty, but more often heading for the balcony of the dining room with a bottle of brandy. He didn't like remaining in his bedchamber, and the cool night air of the balcony relaxed him. The brandy relaxed him, too. The liquor was a habit with him now. Over time he had acquired a great thirst for it. Other than the quiet of night, it was the only thing that brought him peace.

Tonight was a particularly cool night on the balcony. The rains had finally subsided and the clouds had parted to reveal a canopy of stars. The city of Koth rose up around the keep, shadowy and deathly still, and Library Hill beckoned in the distance. Akeela tilted the brandy bottle and refilled his glass, making himself comfortable on the iron chair. Puddles of rainwater glistened on the rail of the balcony but the little wooden table and his seat were dry, and his bottle was nearly full, so Akeela was happy. The brandy burned his throat as it reached his empty stomach. There had been no dinner for him tonight, for Akeela hardly ate at all these days. Food no longer interested him. He was gaunt from lack of appetite and his skin and eyes bore an unhealthy pallor. And though he was still relatively young, he had aged horribly. He considered this as he drank, knowing that the liquor had sped his aging almost as effectively as Cassandra's amulet had arrested her own. When he found the other Eye—if he found it—she would be young and beautiful and he would be a scarecrow.

But that was a trouble for another day, and tonight Akeela had enough to occupy his mind. He took another pull of brandy and sat back in his chair, oblivious to everything but the skyline of Koth until a shadow crossed his shoulder. Sluggishly he turned around, expecting to see one of his many guards at the threshold of the balcony. Instead he saw Figgis. The old man clutched a book in his hands and wore a disquieting grin. Behind him stood a pair of guards. The librarian's face was flushed, as if he'd run a great distance. He broke away from the two guards and hurried out onto the balcony. The guards were on him in an instant, dragging him backward.

"My lord," he called, "I have to speak to you!"

Akeela waved off his men and stood up. The guards relented, falling back without a word. Figgis snickered at them before turning back to Akeela.

"My lord, I'm sorry for the interruption—"

"Have you any sense of the time, Figgis?" asked Akeela crossly.

"Yes, my lord, I know, but—"

"What are you doing here?"

The old man held out his book. "This, my lord, will make my visit worth your while."

Akeela sighed. "Indeed?"

Figgis looked over his shoulders toward the waiting guards. They were still well within earshot, ready to protect the king.

"My lord, what I have to say isn't for everyone to hear," said Figgis. "If you could shoo away your guards. . . . ?"

"Go on," Akeela told the knights, laughing. "He's harmless."

The guards complied, dropping away from the balcony until they were almost out of sight down the darkened hall. Akeela returned to his seat, falling into it. He pushed the brandy bottle toward the librarian.

"Now then, Figgis, have a drink with me and tell me what's on your overactive mind."

"Akeela, I have stupendous news." Figgis approached the table but did not sit down. "Great, wonderful news!"

"Really? Well, perhaps *I* should have a drink then!"

Before he could tilt the bottle to his lips, Figgis grabbed hold of it. "My lord, stop."

Akeela grinned. "Ah ah, don't touch the king. . . ."

"You're drunk and you're not listening to me. Come now, this is important!"

Akeela relented, setting the bottle aside. Figgis was the only one he allowed to scold him, and he wasn't sure why. Perhaps it was because the old man wasn't afraid of him. He had never been, and Akeela respected that. "Will you at least take a seat?" he asked.

"Grimhold," said Figgis. He remained standing, staring down at Akeela.

"What's that?"

"Grimhold, my lord. Do you know it?"

"Uh, not personally, no."

Figgis carefully laid the ancient book onto the table. "I think I know where the other amulet is hidden."

All the sarcasm blew out of Akeela like a wind. His fingers reached across the table for the book. "What do you mean?"

"Grimhold, my lord. That's where the other amulet is."

"How do you know? Tell me."

Figgis shrank a little. "Well, I don't actually know for certain. . . ."

Akeela fixed him with a freezing glare. "Do not toy with me, Figgis. What have you learned?"

"A theory, my lord. An idea." Finally Figgis took a seat, dragging one of the iron chairs around to sit next to his king. With Akeela watching, he began flipping through the battered book. "This is a collection of stories about Grimhold," he said. "I was reading it tonight. I was about to go to sleep when I discovered something extraordinary."

"The book mentions the Eyes of God?"

"No, my lord, not precisely."

"Then precisely what, damn it?"

"Wait. I'm looking for it."

Losing patience, Akeela huddled closer to Figgis, watching him rifle through the endless pages. It seemed like any other book of stories and rhymes, and Akeela felt his hope fading fast. Finally, Figgis located the proper page. He traced a bony finger over the passage as he read.

"Here it is. 'Most scholars of merit believe that Grimhold rests across the Desert of Tears, somewhere beyond Jador. That is why, in the Jadori language, Grimhold is called *The Hidden Place Beyond the Desert.*'"

Figgis leaned back with a satisfied smile. Akeela stared at him in disbelief.

"So?" he roared. "What's that got to do with anything?"

"Don't you see?" asked Figgis. "The hidden place across the desert. Don't you remember, my lord?"

Akeela thought for a moment, going over the phrase. It was familiar, but it took his brandy-soaked mind a moment to remember.

"Yes," he said pensively. "I remember it. The hidden place beyond the desert. Jador."

"No, not Jador." Figgis tapped the book. "Grimhold!"

"No, Figgis, please don't tell me that," begged Akeela. "Please tell me you didn't get my hopes up over a myth."

"Myth, my lord? What is myth? Are the Eyes of God a myth? Is it a myth that Cassandra still lives, free from her illness after sixteen years?"

Akeela reached for his brandy. "Figgis, please. . . ."

"Stop," snapped Figgis, snatching the bottle and shoving it aside. "Don't hide in your bottle. Just listen to me, let me explain." He took up the book again and showed the passage to Akeela like he was a child. "This term, hidden place across the desert. I misread it sixteen years ago. I thought the Jadori text referred to Jador. But it doesn't, don't you see? It means Grimhold."

"There is no Grimhold, Figgis."

"How do you know? You didn't really believe in the amulets until I brought one back for you. Isn't that proof enough, my lord? If the amulets exist, then why can't Grimhold exist as well?"

"A place of monsters? You dream, my friend."

"A place of magic, my lord. Led by a witch. Look at Cassandra and tell me you don't believe in magic!"

"I can't look at Cassandra," said Akeela sourly. "Thanks to that damn curse."

Figgis smiled. "Ah, but now your exile from her might be coming to an end. Think about it, my lord. We always knew there must be another Eye of God. Now we may have found it. Can't you see that?"

Akeela nodded. It was implausible, but he saw the possibility in Figgis' theory. It made sense, or at least some of it did. There was no reason to doubt that the hidden place referred to in the Jadori manuscript had been Grimhold all along, but that still left dozens of questions unanswered.

"If you're right," said Akeela, "then who is the wife of Kadar?"

Figgis looked puzzled. "What do you mean?"

"Kadar's wife, remember? The Jadori manuscript says that the master of the hidden place wears the Eye, and that his wife wears the Eye's twin. So then who is Kadar's wife?"

"You remember things quite clearly when you want to," said Figgis with a grin. "The truth is, I don't know. Maybe I read the whole thing wrong. Maybe the master of the hidden place isn't Kadar at all." A light went on in his old eyes. "Maybe," he said softly, "the master of Grimhold wears the other amulet!"

Akeela rolled his eyes. "Don't be stupid, Figgis. Why would a witch have a wife?"

"I don't know," confessed Figgis. The question deflated him a little. "But we're close to getting answers, I know we are." He patted the book. "This has been a giant breakthrough. I feel it."

A wave of dizziness suddenly swept through Akeela, and it wasn't the drink or the lateness of the hour. Seeing Figgis so excited stoked a bad memory. He recalled with awful clarity a similar conversation sixteen years ago, one that had resulted in his separation from Cassandra. But now Figgis was offering hope once again, and it tantalized Akeela.

"Figgis, I can't live with this being a joke," he said softly. "Sixteen years I've waited, and I can't wait another day. I have to know that this is real."

"My lord, be fair. I've only just started researching it."

"I don't care," said Akeela. "Find out all you can about Grimhold and its location, but be quick about it. I want that amulet, Figgis. And I don't want to wait a moment more than I must."

Cassandra was deep in a dream when she heard the voice. It came from a great distance, first as part of her dream, then as something from the wakened world, calling to her. She struggled against the bonds of sleep, searching her consciousness for its location.

"Cassandra, wake up."

Her eyes fluttered open, only to be greeted by impenetrable darkness. Startled, she glanced around. There was no candlelight. Her windowless chamber coiled about her like a noose.

"Wake up, Cassandra. Wake up."

"I am up," she replied, realizing only then that the voice was Akeela's. It seemed to fill the darkness. She sat up, shaking her head. Her dream had been so vivid, yet now she could scarcely recall it. She turned toward the partition separating her from her husband, asking groggily, "Akeela, what is it? What time is it?"

"It's late," replied the disembodied voice, "but it doesn't matter. I've found it, Cassandra. I've found the other Eye of God!"

Cassandra gasped. Was she still dreaming? "What?"

"The amulet, Cassandra. The second Eye!"

"You've found it?" she sputtered. Panic took her breath away. "You have it?"

"Not yet. But now I know where it is. Figgis has located it."

"Are you sure?" she asked dreadfully. After all these years, the news was unbelievable. "I mean, where is it?"

Akeela's voice was like a bell. "Grimhold!" He chuckled in delight. "Grimhold, Cassandra! Can you believe it?"

"Grimhold?" Cassandra had to keep herself from laughing. "Akeela, Grimhold doesn't exist. It's a myth. Great Fate, don't you know that?"

"I'm not a child," Akeela growled. "Grimhold isn't just a myth. It exists, beyond the Desert of Tears. It's somewhere past Jador."

It was all too much for Cassandra, whose head began to swim. What little she knew of Grimhold was confined to fairy tales and bedtime stories, and she thought Akeela thoroughly mad for believing it was real. But believe it he did; she could hear the conviction in his voice.

"All right, Akeela," she said gently. "If you believe it, then fine. Figgis must know what he's doing."

There was a long silence behind the partition. At last, Akeela's disappointed voice said, "I thought you would be happier about it, Cassandra. We're talking about being together, finally after all these years."

"I am happy, Akeela," said Cassandra, brightening. "I'm just . . . surprised."

"Yes, I know it's hard to believe. But Figgis is confident. It's a lot to explain, but he believes he's been misreading his texts all this time. He thinks Grimhold really exists, and that they have the Eye." Akeela's tone grew excited again. "It's not madness, Cassandra. This time we're close. I feel it!"

Cassandra gave a silent sigh. It *was* madness. She decided to ply him with gentle lies.

"I believe you, Akeela," she said. "But what now? How will you find the amulet? How will you even find Grimhold?"

"Figgis will research it. But I won't depend on that. If Grimhold lies beyond Jador, then the Jadori will know where it is. They will tell us its location."

Cassandra sat up straight. "Will they? Why?"

"When they see our army marching toward them, they will tell us."

"Fate above, Akeela, you don't mean it!"

"I mean every word." Akeela drifted closer to the partition. "I will be with you, Cassandra. I will, and no Jadori filth or freaks from Grimhold will stop me. If they have the Eye of God, they will give it to me!"

"No!" shouted Cassandra. She swung out of bed and put her face to the partition, close enough to smell Akeela's liquored breath. "You're talking about a massacre, Akeela. I won't allow it!"

"I'm talking about us being together! Gods and angels, can't you see that?"

"I won't let you murder people, Akeela. Not for me!"

"Then for me!" Akeela hissed. Enraged, he put his fist through the partition, splitting the fabric like paper. His hand shot out and grabbed Cassandra's nightgown. For the first time in years she saw his face in the near perfect darkness. His eyes were closed but his mouth was turned in a snarl. "I've lived without you long enough, Cassandra. I won't live like this a minute more!"

Cassandra stared at him, wild-eyed. He didn't know that her curse had been a hoax, yet in his rage he had risked her life. "Akeela," she said evenly; "let go of me."

Slowly he opened his fist, letting the cloth of her gown slip away, but his fingertips lingered on her, brushing her. Cassandra didn't move. She stared at him, watching the twisted longing on his face. For a brief second his fingers drifted above her breasts. . . .

And then he pulled away.

"We will be together, Cassandra," he said. "No matter what it takes."

Letting his words linger in the darkness, he left her without a word of good-bye. Through the ruined partition Cassandra watched his shadow depart. She put a hand to her chest; he had torn her gown. She could still feel his touch on her skin.

"Murder," she whispered. She glanced around the black chamber, wondering what to do. Akeela was thoroughly mad. She had seen it on his face and could do nothing to cure him. But she couldn't let him lead a massacre. Somehow, she had to stop him.

And there was only one person who could help her.

30

The day after his meeting with Akeela, Figgis closed the library. He did not explain his reasons to Gilwyn or Mistress Della or to any of the library's many dependents. He merely closed the main door and locked it, putting up a sign obscurely stating that the library would reopen as soon as possible. There was no word of warning—it was simply done. And Figgis, who was always cheerful despite the many ailments of his age, quickly became an obsessed curmudgeon, locking himself in his study with piles of books and manuscripts. He had told Gilwyn he was on a very urgent mission for the king, and that he needed to do his research in peace. Warning the boy to stay close and not ask any questions, Figgis would bellow for Gilwyn to bring him books and to search through the endless racks of maps for strange, little-used charts. And when he wasn't in the study, which was rarely, he was in his catalog room, consulting with his thinking machine. He took all his meals alone, forgetting to eat until Mistress Della brought him food, and even after three days he did not divulge the purpose of his work. Gilwyn quickly grew suspicious of his mentor. He had never seen Figgis so driven, and it frightened him. The old librarian worked like a man possessed, and Gilwyn could barely begin to guess as to the task King Akeela had given him. He worried that something was very wrong in Koth. He worried also that Figgis would expire from the strain. But he voiced none of his concerns. Instead he was Figgis' loyal apprentice. He delivered the maps and manuscripts without complaint and was at the librarian's side instantly whenever he was called. For all Figgis had done for him, Gilwyn knew he owed the man service.

On the afternoon of the fourth day, a surprise visitor arrived. Gilwyn was loading up his cart in the main hall when he heard the insistent pounding at the door. At first he ignored it, thinking one of the scholars was begging entry. But when the knocking finally grew to a crescendo Gilwyn stopped what he was doing and stomped to the door as quickly as his bad foot would carry him. Angry, he threw the latch and reached for the pull.

"Can't you read?" he asked before the door was half open. "We're closed."

The austere faces of armored knights greeted him. Gilwyn stiffened when he saw them—three men, all similarly garbed in silver armor and crimson capes. They wore no helmets, but each man bore a scabbarded sword. They were a daunting trio, and the one at the center was the most frightening by far. Unlike the others, his cape was trimmed with silver and held with a golden clasp, and he had colored ribbons on his armor at the shoulders, denoting him as a man of rank. His jet hair was combed back slick against his head, its color mimicked by his meticulously trimmed beard. A pair of dark eyes smouldered in his stern face.

"I don't give a damn if you're closed, boy," he boomed. "Didn't you hear us knocking? Or are you deaf as well as—" His insults suddenly stopped as he spied Gilwyn's clubbed hand. Embarrassed, he cleared his throat. "I am General Trager. I want to see your master."

Gilwyn was stunned. "General Trager?" He stared at the man stupidly. "Really?"

Seeing Gilwyn's awe, the general puffed a little. "Yes, it is I. Now step aside."

"Of course," said Gilwyn. He had only seen the general once or twice before, and only then from a great distance while watching the knights drill on the grounds around Lionkeep. Now that he was in the man's presence, Gilwyn was tongue-tied. He stepped aside for the soldiers, then remembered Figgis' strict orders not to be disturbed. The general crossed the threshold and looked around, nodding.

"So, this is what King Akeela has spent a thousand fortunes on, eh? Very nice."

"You've never been here, General?" Gilwyn asked. The idea shocked him. "Never once?"

For a moment General Trager seemed perturbed by the question. But he indulged Gilwyn, saying, "Oh, a long time ago, yes, when I had time for such nonsense. But it's grown since then." His men followed him into the entry hall as he continued to study the structure. There wasn't much to see in this part of the library, just stone walls and torches, but the general seemed intrigued by it. He rapped on the wall with his knuckles, testing its soundness. "I've always though that Library Hill would make a good location for a fortress. Such a commanding position."

His underlings nodded.

"Good construction," the general added. "Now, boy, where is that waterhead Figgis?"

"Uhm, well, Master Figgis is in his study. But he asked not to be disturbed."

"He will see me. Which way is the study?"

"Right down that hall, sir. But really, I don't think he'll take to being disturbed. He's on a project for the king."

General Trager sighed dramatically. "The king and I are closer than two toes in a stocking. I'm here on the king's business. Now be a good boy and take me to your master."

"Well, all right," Gilwyn stammered, unsure what to do. Figgis might be very cross, but he knew there was no way to disobey the general. "This way, sir," he said as he walked down the hall.

General Trager and his silent entourage followed. But before they had taken ten paces, the general noticed Gilwyn's uneven gait.

"You limp, boy. What's that shoe you wear?"

"Figgis made it for me. Before I started wearing it I couldn't walk without a cane."

"Remarkable. Your foot is like your hand, then?"

"Yes, sir," replied Gilwyn. He didn't know how much he should tell the man. "Since I was born."

General Trager nodded. "So that is why you work in the library. Otherwise a boy your age should be in service."

"I like books, sir, and I like working for Figgis," Gilwyn

looked at the general hopefully. "But I've always wanted to be a horseman."

The general shook his head. "No chance. Not with a hand like that. Be grateful for your place here. You wouldn't last a day in the Royal Chargers."

Gilwyn continued down the hall, hiding his reddened face from the men as he walked. Suddenly he was acutely aware of his limp and did what he could to conceal it. Yet even with his special shoe the limp was always there, shouting out his malformation. He was grateful none of the knights were laughing, but he could almost sense their smug smiles. Finally, he rounded a bend in the hall and came to Figgis' study. The corridor was quiet and the study's door was closed. A tray of neglected tea and biscuits sat outside, cold and untouched. Inside, Gilwyn could hear Figgis paging madly through books. He knocked gently.

"Figgis?" he queried, pushing the door open slightly. "Can I come in?"

"Uh-huh," replied Figgis, hardly glancing up from his books. He was surrounded by manuscripts and papers. Maps and charts cluttered the floor, rising to his knees.

"Uh, Figgis, there are people here to see you."

"Tell them to be gone."

"Your attention, Figgis," said General Trager, shouldering past Gilwyn and entering the study. "I've already been delayed enough by the boy."

Figgis lifted his nose from his books. He looked exhausted. His red eyes widened when he recognized the general. "What are you doing here?"

The general sauntered into the room, his two men close behind. "I need to speak to you. It's urgent."

"No, general," countered Figgis. "What I'm doing right now is urgent. It's for the king, and you're interrupting me. Now if you don't mind—"

"I'm here on the king's business, old one," said General Trager. "It's about this work you're doing."

Figgis hissed in annoyance. "Tell Akeela I'm doing the best I can. Sending you down here to nag me won't hurry things."

"I'm not an errand boy," huffed the general. "I have important news to discuss." He paused, turning toward Gilwyn. "But it isn't for everyone's ears."

Gilwyn grimaced. "I'll go then, Figgis?"

The general said, "Quickly."

"Very well," Figgis relented. "Gilwyn, leave us for a few minutes. Why don't you go and find those maps I asked for?"

"All right," said Gilwyn. There was no sense arguing, so he left, careful not to close the door behind him. He took a few steps away from the study, rounded the corner again toward the main hall, then quietly doubled back and cocked his ear to listen. Muffled voices came to him, amplified by the stone corridor. General Trager was talking, his tone loud and clear off the stonework.

"There's no time, Figgis. Akeela's made his decision. I'm organizing my divisions now and will lead them myself."

"Divisions?" shrieked Figgis. "How many men are you taking?"

"Enough to overpower the Jadori, be assured. If they stand in the way of finding Grimhold, we'll destroy them."

"No! There's no reason to invade!"

"It's not your decision. Akeela wants it this way. He wants that amulet, and he'll brook no failure."

Amulet? Gilwyn seized on the word.

"Trager," Figgis continued, "the Jadori aren't a threat to anyone. You know that. You can tell that to Akeela."

"Akeela doesn't want a repeat of our last fiasco, Figgis. That's why he's sending an army. If the Jadori know where Grimhold is, we'll make sure they tell us."

There was a long pause in the conversation. Gilwyn pressed closer to the wall, straining to hear.

"I need more time," said Figgis. His voice was quieter now, almost despondent. "If I can find out more about Grimhold, maybe I can convince Akeela not to invade Jador. Maybe I can prove to him there's no need for an army."

"Don't waste your breath. If you argue for a peaceful solution, I will speak against you. Akeela is wise to send an army. I have already told him so."

"Oh, of course you have." There was a sound like a fist being slammed. "Anything to lead a massacre."

"Curb your tongue," warned the general. "And do what you're told. You will continue your research. And you will report your findings to me so that I may make arrangements for my army."

The conversation seemed to be ending, so Gilwyn began inching away. Suddenly the door to Figgis' study slammed shut. Heavy footfalls entered the hall. Thinking quickly, Gilwyn ducked into an alcove and crouched out of sight just as General Trager and his entourage thundered past. The men were only a pace past him when Figgis hurried into the hall after them. Gilwyn pressed against the wall, a hair's breadth from being seen.

"Tell Akeela to forget it," shouted Figgis. "I won't research the amulet anymore, not if he insists on this invasion!"

General Trager turned on his boots. His voice dipped to a threatening growl. "Oh, yes you will, Figgis. Because what do you think will happen to your precious Jadori if you don't?"

"You're a monster," Figgis sneered.

The general laughed. "You've always thought so, haven't you? You and that girl-pretty pretender Lukien. Well, let me tell you something if you don't cooperate, I'm going to show your precious Jadori just how monstrous I can be."

"Yes, you'd do that just to spite me," spat Figgis. "You're a jealous bastard, Trager. You always have been."

"Why are we arguing, Figgis? We all want the same thing. You want to find the other amulet as much as Akeela does."

"No," said Figgis. "I'd never want another massacre. Great Fate, last time we killed Kadar's wife! Isn't that enough?"

"Bah," scoffed the general. "We won't win this quest with sentiment." He turned once again and started off down the hall. As he walked he called over his shoulder, "Do your job, Figgis. And have a report to me within the week."

He left Figgis smouldering alone in the hall. Gilwyn watched his mentor from the shadows, holding his breath. Figgis shook his head, cursing softly. The exhaustion on his face melted into total despair. Then, remarkably, he spoke.

"Gilwyn, get out here."

Gilwyn froze.

"I know you're there. I saw you."

Without a word Gilwyn stepped out of the alcove. Figgis would not look at him.

"That was very stupid of you to eavesdrop. If Trager had found you he would have skinned you alive."

"Figgis, I'm sorry. I—"

"Don't say anything, Gilwyn. And don't ask me any questions about what you overheard. Understand?"

Gilwyn nodded. "All right. But—"

"That's it," snapped Figgis. "Not another word." He still didn't look at Gilwyn; he simply turned around and retreated toward his study.

Confused, Gilwyn stood like a statue in the corridor, his head full of troubling questions.

For three nights Cassandra waited for Gilwyn Toms to return to his secret balcony. And for three nights he did not show. Cassandra had risked everything in finding the boy, because she sensed that she could trust him and because he was the only one she knew that wasn't blind, other than Akeela. She had a mission for the young apprentice, a mission that couldn't be accomplished by any of her sightless servants. If Jancis or any of the others were to go missing, Akeela would surely notice. And Cassandra didn't want Akeela suspecting anything. He was lost in his new obsession over Grimhold, and was perfect for her scheme. Too enamored with the thought of reuniting with her, Cassandra knew Akeela would never suspect her plans. But her plans depended on Gilwyn, and Gilwyn was nowhere to be found.

It took Cassandra all of three days before Akeela told her that the library was closed. Figgis, Akeela explained, was doing research into Grimhold. Cassandra realized that the research was probably keeping Gilwyn occupied as well, and she supposed it was why he hadn't come to his lofty hideout. But she needed to deliver a message to the boy, and time was of the essence. Cassandra knew that she could not risk going to the library herself. Even if she could be seen by human eyes, she didn't want anyone knowing it. That left only Jancis in her sphere of trust, but Jancis was blind and the library was closed. There was simply no way to get a message to Gilwyn.

Cassandra brooded over her predicament, but only for a moment. Blindness, she decided, could be turned to an advantage.

Silence and suspicion hung over the library like a pall. Figgis continued his feverish research, refusing to speak to Gilwyn about his clash with General Trager. Gilwyn kept out of his mentor's way, dutifully performing his chores and keeping his thousand questions to himself. The conversation he had overheard played over and over in his mind as he worked, organizing the endless shelves of books after Figgis had gone through them like a whirlwind in his mad search for information about. . . .

What?

Gilwyn still didn't know for certain, but he wasn't stupid either. He had been able to add up the disparate clues and knew that Figgis was researching Grimhold. He just didn't know why. And he didn't know why General Trager and Akeela were interested in Grimhold, either, or why the Jadori were involved. It was a fascinating mystery, but Gilwyn couldn't unravel it without help, and Figgis wasn't talking. So far, he wasn't even coming out of his study. The old man's silence left Gilwyn with a feeling of impending doom, for he knew that Figgis was suddenly miserable in his work.

And then there was the question of the amulet. Gilwyn frowned as he absently went about shelving books from his cart. He knew Akeela was searching for an amulet, and that was the greatest mystery of all. The idea excited Gilwyn, who had spent a good portion of his young life reading stories. An amulet bespoke adventure and magic, and Gilwyn was desperate to find out more about it. But all the books that might have told him more were in Figgis' study, jealously guarded by the master librarian. Gilwyn sighed, blowing a fog of dust off the book rack, then glanced down at the pile of manuscripts on his wooden cart. It would take another hour or more to finish shelving the books. Teku looked down at him from the top shelf of the rack, her big eyes drooping with weariness.

"Let's take a break," he told her.

The monkey quickly swung down from her perch to rest on his shoulder, and together they made their way toward the front of the library. They had just passed the main entry hall on their way to visit Mistress Della for a confection when the hall rang with the sound of the door knocker.

"Oh, not again," groaned Gilwyn. He watched the arched doorway, hoping that the visitor would go away, but again the knocker sounded, even louder. It occurred to Gilwyn that it might be General Trager again, so he went to the door and pulled it open, prepared to apologize for keeping the man waiting. Instead, a lovely woman greeted him. Though her head was hidden behind a cowl, Gilwyn could make out curls of dark hair falling over her forehead, streaked with a lightning bolt of silver. Her eyes darted about when she heard the door creak open. A faint smile curled her lips.

"Hello?" she asked uncertainly.

"Good day," said Gilwyn. He spied her face in the shadows of her cowl. She looked familiar.

"We're closed," he told her, continuing to study her. From the whiteness of her eyes, she appeared to be blind. "I'm sorry. There's a sign on the door, but I guess you couldn't read it."

"No," said the woman. "I can't see." Yet her sightless eyes fixed intently on Gilwyn. "I'm blind."

"Yes," said Gilwyn awkwardly. "I'm sorry." Then suddenly he understood. "Oh!" He looked back to make sure he was alone, then said, "I know you!"

The woman put a finger to her lips. "Shhh. You are Gilwyn?"

Gilwyn nodded excitedly. "You're Megal's friend, the one from the garden."

"I am." Her voice was a whisper. "I must speak with you."

"How did you make your way here? Are you alone?"

"Yes, I came alone," said the woman. "Gilwyn, you must listen to me. I have news from Megal."

Gilwyn stepped aside immediately and opened the door wide. "Yes, please, come in."

"I can't. No one must see me. Can you meet Megal in the garden tonight?"

"What? Tonight?"

"It's very important. And no one must know about it. It's a great secret, all right?"

"But I can't just—"

"Please, Gilwyn, you must. Megal will meet you in the garden an hour past dusk. You have to be there."

"Why? What's so important? Why can't she just come to the library to talk to me?"

"I can't explain," said the woman. "You just have to trust me." Her blind eyes looked pleadingly at Gilwyn. "Will you be there?"

Gilwyn's head was swimming. He wanted desperately to see Megal again. Any meeting, even a secret one, was a dream come true.

"All right," he agreed. "I'll be there."

The woman's shadowed face brightened. "Thank you," she whispered. "I'll tell my lady to expect you."

"Your lady?" asked Gilwyn.

The woman turned and strode quickly down the walkway. Gilwyn made to call after her but stopped himself. He would have to wait until tonight for answers.

"Teku," he whispered, "things are getting strange around here."

Exactly an hour after dusk, Cassandra entered the forgotten garden. She wore the same brown cloak that Jancis had worn to the library and had snuck past Ruthanna and her other servants easily, for they were all involved in a word game that Jancis had arranged and were too loud and boisterous to notice the footfalls of their queen as she passed. The pretext had worked perfectly, and Akeela had been too busy making plans with General Trager to bother her much. As she stepped foot in the overgrown patch of weeds and wildflowers, she was confident her husband wouldn't come looking for her. The night was clear and Cassandra could see the garden's broken statues in the feeble light, watching her. Stars were beginning to blink to life, and the moon had settled over Koth in a mid-month sliver. Cassandra's slippers crushed moss and leaves beneath her as she walked, slowly stalking through the neglected flora. A voice from the right startled her.

"Megal? Is that you?"

Cassandra turned to see Gilwyn emerge from behind a statue. His eager face shone in the moonlight. He had dressed for the meeting, too, wearing the same expensive scarlet shirt he had at their first encounter.

"Yes, Gilwyn, it's me," said Cassandra. She glanced around. Sure no one could see, she pulled back her cowl to reveal her face. Gilwyn smiled when he saw her, all his lovesickness on full display. "I'm glad you came," she whispered.

"You look lovely, Megal," said Gilwyn.

"Gilwyn, it's not what you think," said Cassandra quickly. She took him by the arm and guided him out of the moonlight. When the concealing shadow of Lionkeep fell across his face, she whispered, "I have something to tell you, something very important. I'm afraid you won't believe me. But you must, do you understand?"

Gilwyn nodded, but Cassandra could tell that he didn't really understand. And how could she explain it to him? Magic, Grimhold, her immortality—it all sounded like a fairy tale. And Gilwyn was a bright boy, not at all like some of the keep's stablehands. He would doubt her, at the very least. She led him toward one of the benches, a seat of granite that had been worn by time and weather. Gilwyn sat, looking up at her intently. She sat down next to him and bit her lip.

"Don't be nervous, Megal," said Gilwyn. "You can tell me anything."

Cassandra chuckled. "You're a nice boy, Gilwyn. But what I have to tell you will make you think I'm mad."

Gilwyn shook his head. "No I won't. I promise."

"You will," Cassandra insisted. "Because I'm not Megal. Megal is one of my housekeepers, Gilwyn." She looked at him squarely and said, "My name is Cassandra. I'm the queen."

Gilwyn looked shocked, but only for a moment. Soon he started laughing.

"Shhh!" Cassandra scolded. She looked around in a panic. "Not so loud!"

"I'm sorry," Gilwyn managed, "but really, you're funny!"

"I'm not lying." Cassandra put a hand to his face and turned him toward her. "I *am* Queen Cassandra. I've been locked in this bloody castle for sixteen years, kept young by this!" She pulled the Eye of God from beneath her cloak. It flared an angry scarlet, lighting Gilwyn's shocked face.

"What . . . ?" Gilwyn reached out for the Eye, but didn't touch it. "I know this. I've seen it before. . . ."

Cassandra was stunned. "You have? Where?"

Gilwyn shook his head. "No, it can't be." His fingers lightly brushed the amulet's surface.

"You said you've seen it before? Another amulet like this?"

"No," said Gilwyn, pulling his hand back.

"Gilwyn, please, tell me the truth. If you've seen another amulet like this one. . . ."

"The truth?" Gilwyn smirked, an expression that looked out of place on his innocent face. "Why should I tell you anything? Who are you, really?"

Frustrated, Cassandra leapt to her feet. "I'm Queen Cassandra, damn it!"

"Queen Cassandra's an old woman! She's a crone, everyone knows that." Gilwyn frowned at Cassandra. "How could you be her?"

"Because of this amulet." Cassandra sat back on the bench, shoving the amulet beneath his nose. "This is the Eye of God. It keeps me young, keeps my cancer from killing me."

"What are you talking about?"

"Gilwyn, I'm thirty-two years old. Sixteen years ago, around the time you were born, I was wed to Akeela. We had only been married a few months when I became very ill. It was a growth, a cancer."

"That's impossible," said Gilwyn. "How can it be?"

The amulet dangled from its golden chain. Cassandra let it swing in Gilwyn's face. "Look at it, Gilwyn," she said. "It's magic. It saved me. I didn't think magic really existed until Akeela brought me this amulet. But it's very real. And I'm not lying to you. I *am* Queen Cassandra."

Too stunned to speak, Gilwyn's eyes darted between the amulet and her perfect, unblemished face. The incredible tale had slackened his jaw. When he finally spoke, his voice was toneless.

"That's why your blind servant was with you," he mused, seeming to understand. "That's why she called you her lady."

"Right. And that's why I had to meet you here alone. I couldn't risk Akeela or anyone else finding out about me."

"I don't understand," said Gilwyn. "If you're the queen, surely you can go wherever you like."

"I wish that were true," said Cassandra with a sigh. "But I'm not free. This amulet holds me captive." She glanced up at the tower that was her prison, deciding that Gilwyn needed to know everything. "Do you have time for a long story?"

Gilwyn nodded uncertainly.

"Good. Then listen and don't interrupt."

So Gilwyn listened like a loyal terrier, wide-eyed in the starlight as Cassandra began her impossible tale. She told him of her brief courtship with Akeela and how she had been anxious to marry him and be away from her domineering sisters. And she told him how she had been sick even before meeting Akeela, and how she had hidden her illness from him. But she had grown horribly ill in the following months, nearly dying. There had been no hope for her, not until Figgis had come to Akeela with his remarkable news.

"Figgis?" blurted Gilwyn. "What's he got to do with this?"

"He found the amulet," said Cassandra, hefting the Eye on its chain. "He learned of it from one of his books, and when he told Akeela about it my husband agreed to let him search for it." She let Gilwyn study the amulet again. "It's called the Eye of God," she explained. "It's what keeps me young and alive. There were supposed to be two of them in Jador, but Figgis only found one. Akeela has been looking for the other one ever since. And now he thinks he's found it."

Gilwyn grimaced. "So that's why Figgis has been so busy. He's trying to find the other amulet."

Cassandra nodded. "A few days ago Figgis came to Lionkeep. He told Akeela that he'd found the other Eye. He thinks that it's in Grimhold."

"Grimhold," echoed Gilwyn, nodding. "Now I get it."

"What do you mean?"

"Megal . . . I mean, Cassandra." He flushed. "My lady."

Cassandra smiled. "Go on, Gilwyn, tell me what you know."

"My lady, General Trager came to the library a few days ago. He wanted to speak to Figgis. I overheard them talking about Grimhold and some invasion. Figgis was upset, but he wouldn't tell me anything about it."

"No, I'm sure he can't," said Cassandra. "This mission is too important to Akeela. He won't risk anything going wrong. He's obsessed with finding the other Eye."

"But why?" asked Gilwyn. He gestured to the amulet. "Is it like this one? Will it keep him young?"

"Yes, but that's not all." Cassandra's voice grew melancholy. "Akeela is mad, Gilwyn. Do you know that?"

Gilwyn shrugged. "I'd heard that. But Figgis says he's a good man."

"Well, yes, I suppose he is. Deep down, Akeela has always been a good man. But he's changed over the years. His obsessions have maddened him. He wants to find the other Eye so that he can be with me forever, just the two of us."

"I still don't get it," said Gilwyn. "He is with you, isn't he? I mean, he's your husband."

Cassandra smiled. She had almost forgotten the curse. "You are half right, Gilwyn. I am Akeela's wife, true enough. But he cannot look upon me, because he thinks that the amulet is cursed."

The boy's eyes grew wide again. "Cursed?"

"Yes," laughed Cassandra, "the great and dark curse of the Eye. The biggest farce ever perpetrated on anyone!"

Gilwyn stared at her, clearly unnerved.

"Oh, don't be afraid of me. I can't hurt a fly and neither can this damn amulet. But that's not what everyone believes, you see. I'm not supposed to be looked at by human eyes. To do so breaks the power of the amulet, supposedly. That's the curse!"

"Not looked at? But I've looked at you," said Gilwyn. "That first night I saw you."

"Yes! Don't you remember how happy I was? That's when I realized the curse doesn't exist. But I can't tell anyone. If I did, Akeela would want to be with me, and that's something I simply cannot bear. You're the only one who's looked at me in sixteen years, dear Gilwyn."

"Great Fate," whispered the boy. "I had no idea. Everyone thinks you're a crone, my lady!"

Cassandra grinned proudly. "Vicious rumors, wouldn't you say?"

Gilwyn laughed. Cassandra liked the boy immensely. But he was still hiding something. And she still needed a great favor from him.

"Gilwyn, when you saw my amulet you said you had seen it before." She smiled gently, trying to nurture their fragile trust. "I've told you everything. Now you must do the same. Where did you see this other amulet?"

The boy turned away, contemplating the dark garden. "I shouldn't tell you this. I sort of promised that I wouldn't. But about a week ago I saw a woman wearing an amulet just like yours. It was in Koth, very late at night. I was walking home when some men attacked me. They wanted the ring that I'd bought for you."

Cassandra's heart melted. "Oh, Gilwyn. I'm sorry."

"Don't be. The woman with the amulet saved me. She had a big man with her, a real monster. And the amulet glowed when she did magic."

"She did magic?" Cassandra gasped. "You saw her?"

"That's how she saved me." Gilwyn thought for a moment. "It's all hard to remember now. But she helped me; I know she did." His eyes became two narrow slits. "Something about the amulet."

"Gilwyn, please," pressed Cassandra. "You have to remember."

"I can't. I've tried, but that's all I'm ever able to recall."

Cassandra leaned back. "It's all right," she said, unsure if she should believe the boy or not. He didn't seem the type to lie, but Figgis was sure the other Eye was in Grimhold. Why would a woman from Koth have it?

"I wish I knew the myth better," she mused. "Who can this woman be?"

Gilwyn smiled. "The Witch of Grimhold?"

They stared at each other, sharing the impossible notion.

"Oh, but that can't be," said Cassandra. "It's all just a legend."

"Is it?" Gilwyn reached out for Cassandra's amulet again, this time holding it up for her to see. "Someone who's been kept alive for sixteen years ought to believe in magic, don't you think?"

"Yes," said Cassandra. "Yes, I suppose so. But if this witch is here in Koth, then Akeela's invasion is truly for nothing." She looked hard at Gilwyn. "We have to stop him, Gilwyn. We have to warn the Jadori of the invasion."

"We?" Gilwyn reared back. "Is that why you asked me to come here?"

"I need you, Gilwyn," said Cassandra quickly. "I can't do this alone. I need to escape from here, and I need to tell the Jadori they're in danger. You have to help me."

"But I'm just a boy," Gilwyn protested. He held up his clubbed hand. "And not even a whole one at that. How can I help?"

Cassandra took his clubbed hand and held it, a gesture that calmed Gilwyn immediately. "You can do anything the other boys can do, Gilwyn. And you're the only one I can trust. I need you to find someone for me."

"Who?" asked Gilwyn suspiciously.

"Have you ever heard of the Bronze Knight?"

"Yes," said Gilwyn. "Captain Lukien."

Hearing the name made Cassandra smile. "That's right. Lukien. Before I was locked away, he was very close to me. If you can find him, he will help us. You can bring him back here, then he and I can ride for Jador."

"But how can I find Lukien? He hasn't been seen in years, not since his banishment. No one even knows where he is."

Cassandra grew curious. "How do you know so much about him?"

"I read, my lady. A lot. When I was younger I used to want to be a Royal Charger, just like Lukien. But, well, look at me."

Cassandra nodded. "I understand."

"I'm not sure you do, my lady. Lukien is long gone. He might even be dead."

"True," Cassandra conceded. "But I don't think so. Lukien was resourceful. I bet he's still alive, somewhere." She leaned in closer, whispering, "And I bet Figgis could find out where he is."

"Figgis? Why would he know where Lukien is?"

"Because Figgis went with Lukien to Jador to find the first amulet," said Cassandra. "They went with Trager sixteen years ago, just before Lukien's banishment."

"You're joking! Figgis went to Jador?"

"He did. Back then he was pretty spry, your mentor.

And he was an expert on the Jadori. He still is, I guess. He never told you any of this because it's a great secret. Only a handful of people know about my amulet and its so-called curse. Figgis is one of them."

"I can't believe it. He never said a word to me about it." Gilwyn looked disappointed, as if his mentor's secret had wounded him.

"Don't blame Figgis, Gilwyn. Akeela made him swear never to tell anyone about the amulets. But Akeela says Figgis is still sharp. If anyone can find Lukien, he can."

"I don't know," said Gilwyn pensively. He bit his lip like a little boy, the way Akeela used to. "If I ask Figgis, he'll know that I've been sneaking out of the library. He might even deny everything."

"Ask him," said Cassandra. "And when you do, you'll know that I'm telling you the truth."

Gilwyn didn't say anything. He didn't even meet her eyes. Cassandra knew he was afraid, and not just about confessing his antics to Figgis. She slid toward him on the bench, so close that their bodies touched. The nearness of her made Gilwyn twitch.

"Gilwyn, you're my only hope," said Cassandra softly. "I can't go to the library myself, and I can't send Jancis or any of my other servants after Lukien. It has to be you." She smiled, hoping she still had the power to make boys weak. "Please, Gilwyn. Won't you help me?"

Gilwyn stood slowly and looked up at the sky. "It's late. I have to get back."

But he didn't go. Instead he studied the stars, lost in all Cassandra had told him.

"Gilwyn? Will you help me?"

Still he wouldn't answer.

"Ask Figgis," Cassandra pressed. "He'll tell you the truth. He'll help you find Lukien. And I'll pay whatever it costs. You won't have to worry about money." Desperate, she rose and went to him. "Please, Gilwyn. If not for me, do it for the Jadori. They're innocent people. And you know Trager will butcher them. You're the only one that can help them."

Gilwyn looked down at his clubbed hand. A faint sigh crossed his lips. "I don't know what kind of champion I'll make you, my lady, but I'll help you if I can."

31

The familiar whirring of gears hummed through the hall
as Gilwyn made his way to the catalog room. As was customary now, the library was closed and the flames in the
oil sconces had been trimmed to a dull glow. Mistress Della
had already retired for the night; Gilwyn had passed her
room and caught her lounging with a cup of tea, her feet
propped up on a chair and a serene, exhausted smile on
her face. Gilwyn first looked for Figgis in the old man's
study, but the shabby office was empty. It had taken less
than a second for Gilwyn to deduce his mentor's whereabouts. Now he paused outside the catalog room, listening
to the peculiar machine do its work. The door was slightly
ajar and Figgis was hunched over the desk, furiously scribbling notes by the light of a single candle. He looked
wretchedly tired. He did not hear Gilwyn's approach over
the mechanical noise. His hand worked diligently, as fast
as the machine's many armatures as he took his copious
notes, his red eyes darting between the paper and a pair
of open books beneath the candle. Hard at work, Figgis
looked like any other scholar. It hurt Gilwyn to know what
he was really doing.

"Figgis," said Gilwyn, pushing open the door, "I need to
speak with you."

The intrusion startled the old man, who looked up with
his bloodshot eyes and rasped, "I'm busy."

"Sorry, but it can't wait."

"Not now," said Figgis crossly, turning back to his books. The catalog continued to whir. Figgis kept writing, ignoring Gilwyn as he appeared over his shoulder. "Go to your room. I don't need you anymore tonight."

Before Gilwyn had left Queen Cassandra, she had given him a note she had written for Lukien, carefully folded and impressed with a wax seal. Gilwyn took the note from the pocket of his trousers and dropped it squarely onto the desk.

"What's this?" asked Figgis.

It took a moment before he took full notice of the seal. When he saw the mark of Liiria impressed in the wax, his lips pursed. Gilwyn glared at him. He was too angry to be subtle or bullied by his mentor. Figgis' eyes drifted slowly from the note up to Gilwyn's face. Something like guilt laced his expression.

"Guess who that's from," said Gilwyn.

Figgis seemed unable to answer. There were only two people allowed to use the royal family's seal, and either one of them meant trouble. Figgis picked up the note but did not open it.

"Tell me," said Figgis softly. "Did Akeela give you this?"

"No. Guess again."

Figgis rose immediately and shut the door, leaving only the single candle to light the room. "Tell me where you got this," he insisted.

"You know where I got it, Figgis. I've been to Lionkeep."

"It wasn't Akeela?" asked Figgis.

"No," said Gilwyn. "It wasn't Akeela."

Still Figgis wouldn't admit the truth. "Who, then? One of the king's men? General Trager?"

"Figgis, it was her," said Gilwyn ruthlessly. "Queen Cassandra."

Figgis looked stricken. "Great Fate. . . ." He fell back against the door, staring at Gilwyn through the darkness. "How?"

"I met her. I saw her the night of the moon shadow and I've spoken to her since. She told me everything, Figgis."

Figgis was incredulous. "You looked at her?"

Gilwyn nodded. "There's no curse," he said simply. He

sighed, a sound that carried all his hurt and confusion. "Oh, Figgis. Why didn't you ever tell me?"

There was no answer from the old man. He glanced down at the note in his hand, his mouth agape. "I don't believe it," he whispered. "No curse."

Gilwyn felt a pang of sadness for his mentor. The striking news had drained the color from his exhausted face. Gilwyn went and took him by the arm, leading him carefully back to his chair. Together they laid Cassandra's note on the desk.

"It's not to you," Gilwyn explained. "Cassandra wrote it for someone else."

Figgis looked up in surprise. "Who?"

"I'll tell you, but not just yet. First, I want to know if what she told me is true. She said you knew everything, Figgis. She said you could explain it to me, and that you could prove her story and identity." Gilwyn sat down on the edge of the desk. "But I don't need you to prove it, do I? I can tell it's all true just by looking at you."

"It was a secret, Gilwyn. I swore to Akeela I would never tell anyone." Figgis' voice was softer than the candlelight, as though he was speaking the most profound confession. "If I had told you—if I had told anyone—Cassandra would have been at risk."

"So you just let the ruse go on?" asked Gilwyn. "You let the king shut her away like a prisoner? Let everyone in Koth think she was a crone?"

"Don't judge me," said Figgis sharply. "There was no other way. None of us thought it would go on this long. We thought—"

Figgis abruptly stopped himself. Gilwyn knew what he'd almost said.

"I know all about the amulets, Figgis. Queen Cassandra showed me the one she wears. She told me you've been looking for the other one for sixteen years."

The old man chuckled. "She's been busy with her stories, hasn't she? Well, I might as well confess. It's all true, every word of it. She's not lying to you, Gilwyn. She is the queen. And now that you know she's probably told others, as well."

"No, she hasn't. I'm the only one who's even seen her. She contacted me because she needs my help."

"I'm sure," said Figgis. He leaned back miserably. "She needs your help to escape, right? This note—I'm supposed to give it to someone to help her?"

Gilwyn smiled. "Figgis, it's not what you think."

"Oh, I'm sure it is. You see, I know everything about Cassandra, too. I've waited for this day for sixteen years. I don't even have to read this note to know what it says. It's for Lukien, isn't it?"

Gilwyn was amazed by the man's seeming clairvoyance. "How did you know?"

"Hmm, I wonder how much the queen actually entrusted to you, Gilwyn. Did she tell you about Lukien?"

"She did. She told me that he was banished, but I already knew that. And she told me that you had gone to Jador with him to find the amulet. She called it the Eye of God. Is that true, Figgis? Did you really go to Jador with Lukien?"

"Yes, believe it or not," said Figgis with a grin. "I was a lot younger then, and in far better shape. But what else did she tell you? Did she tell you that she and Lukien were lovers?"

Gilwyn's eyebrows went up. "Lovers? She said they were friends."

"That's why Lukien was banished," explained Figgis. "He had fallen in love with Cassandra, and she with him. It broke Akeela's heart when he discovered the truth. And it changed him." The old man fiddled with the inkwell on the desk, studying it with undue care. "He's never been the same, Gilwyn. Some people think it was the pressures of kingship that drove him mad, but that's not it. He could have handled anything if Lukien and Cassandra had stayed loyal to him. He loved them both, and they betrayed him. That's why he's the way he is. That's why everyone debates his sanity."

There was real sadness in Figgis tone. Gilwyn slid closer to him.

"Why didn't you ever tell me any of this?" he asked. "You could have trusted me. All those times I asked you about the king, you never once told me the truth. You lied to me."

"I had to. I had to protect you. You don't know what Akeela is like, Gilwyn. He's not Akeela the Good anymore.

If you knew the truth, you'd be in danger. I'm only safe because Akeela needs me. But you, well, who knows. I would never risk that. You don't know the lengths Akeela would go to." He shook his head regretfully, but then suddenly brightened. "You say there's no curse anymore?"

Gilwyn shrugged. "That's what the queen said. I first saw her days ago, and she's perfectly fine. The amulet is still keeping her safe. She said her illness hasn't troubled her."

"Remarkable. And she's still young?"

"Oh, yes. Young enough to fool me into thinking she was a housekeeper!" joked Gilwyn.

"She was very beautiful," Figgis remarked. "Still is, I'm sure." Suddenly his eyes narrowed on Gilwyn. "Is she the one you've been heartsick over?"

Gilwyn felt his face flush. "Yes," he said. The admission set Figgis into hysterics. "I don't think it's that funny!" snapped Gilwyn. "She looked my age! How was I suppose to know she was the queen?"

Figgis swiped tears away with his thumb. "I'm sorry," he managed between chortles. "You're right. It's not funny."

But he wouldn't stop laughing. "Ah, forgive me, boy," he said at last. "But it's the first time I've laughed in days. You're right, though, it isn't a joke. The truth is, you still don't know everything."

"Oh, but I do," said Gilwyn. "You're going back to Jador to find the other amulet. You think it's somewhere in Grimhold."

Figgis frowned. "My, you have learned a lot. Did Cassandra tell you that?"

"Yes, but she didn't have to, not really. I knew something was going on when I heard you arguing with General Trager. That's why Cassandra wants to find Lukien. She wants him to come back and rescue her from Lionkeep. She plans on leaving with him to warn the Jadori before Akeela's army leaves."

"Great Fate," groaned Figgis. "This just keeps getting worse and worse."

"Well someone has to do something," said Gilwyn. "Otherwise the Jadori will be slaughtered."

"Don't you think I know that? What do you think I've been telling Akeela?" Frustrated, Figgis pushed his books aside, sending them tumbling off the desk. "The Jadori are peaceful. Akeela knows that, he just doesn't care. He wants that other amulet, and he'll stop at nothing to find it."

"Well, maybe he's looking in the wrong place." Gilwyn shifted nervously. "I mean, are you really sure it's in Grimhold?"

Figgis fixed him in an insistent glare. "What do you mean?"

"Figgis, I have something to tell you. Promise me you won't get mad."

"I'm already mad, Gilwyn. What is it?"

Gilwyn grimaced. "I think I know where the other amulet is. I think I saw it."

The little color in Figgis' face drained away instantaneously. "What?" He rose from his chair, his gangly shadow falling on Gilwyn like a hawk's. "You saw the other Eye of God? Where?"

"Figgis, calm down," said Gilwyn, putting up his hands. "I'm not even sure it's the same amulet. . . ."

"Where?" Figgis insisted.

"In Koth, about a week ago. When I went missing, remember?"

"I remember. Go on."

"Well, it's hard to say exactly," said Gilwyn. "I'm having trouble recalling everything. But I know there was a woman. And a man, a big fellow. And a lot of light."

"Whoa, slow down. You're not making sense," said Figgis. He guided Gilwyn toward the chair he had vacated. "Now sit down and tell me everything. Don't leave anything out."

Gilwyn sat down, composing his thoughts. It was all such a jumble now. Every time he tried to recall the events in the alley, the memory became more and more clouded.

"It's difficult," he said, shaking his head. "It slips away from me. It won't let me get my hands around it."

"What won't?" asked Figgis.

"My memory. Sometimes I see it clearly, but when I try to talk about it. . . ." Gilwyn snorted in frustration. "Something's wrong with me, I don't know. . . ."

"Gilwyn, I want you to relax," said Figgis gently, "and tell me everything you can remember, all right?" He knelt down before the boy in the soft candlelight. "Where did you see the amulet?"

"In Koth," Gilwyn repeated.

"With a woman and a man?"

Gilwyn nodded.

"Who were they, do you know?"

"I don't know," said Gilwyn. He closed his eyes, trying to summon a picture of the strangers. All he could remember was that they were very odd looking. "Figgis, I think they may have enchanted me. I can't remember!"

"Easy," bade Figgis. "Try again."

"I can't. Every time I try it gets worse." Gilwyn balled his good hand into a fist, struggling to summon an image of the two in his mind, but the harder he tried the more distorted the images became. He knew he had seen the woman do magic, and he knew that she had helped him. But he felt like an old, senile man suddenly, unable to find his way home. "She's done something to my mind," he said angrily. "She's made me forget."

"You're sure it was a woman?"

"Yes," said Gilwyn. He looked at Figgis pleadingly. "I think it was the Witch, Figgis. The Witch of Grimhold. She was the one with the amulet. But that's all I can remember."

Figgis smiled ever so slightly. "The Witch of Grimhold. Not just a legend after all."

"I saw her, Figgis. I know I did. But I can't remember anything else about her." Gilwyn cursed and covered his face with his hands. "She's bewitched me."

"She doesn't want you to remember her," Figgis surmised. "She wants you to forget so that you can't tell anyone about her."

"Yes," said Gilwyn, nodding. "I think I promised her I wouldn't. I'm not sure. But when I try to speak about it. . . ."

"Gilwyn, look at me."

Gilwyn lowered his hands. Figgis was staring at him, his old eyes blazing in the darkness.

"Watch me closely. Don't look away. Don't even blink."

"What is it?" asked Gilwyn.

"Shhh, don't talk. Just look at me." Figgis' voice took

on the regularity of a clock. It was soft, firm, and as clear as a breeze. "Now, relax. Relax and don't think about anything but my voice."

"All right," said Gilwyn. "Yes. . . ."

"Yes," repeated Figgis. "Good. Now close your eyes."

Gilwyn's eyelids shut before he could even control them. He felt light suddenly, as though he were drifting off to sleep. The humming of the catalog filled his brain, but it did not disturb him. All was tranquil. Figgis' gentle voice reached him through the darkness.

"Be calm, Gilwyn. Breathe deeply. Nice and regular. Let everything else but my voice fall away. You're in another place. Nothing can touch you."

"Nothing can touch me," said Gilwyn. The sound of his own voice seemed strange to him. He was exhausted from all that had happened, and the darkness around him felt good. The soft warmth of Figgis' breath caressed his face. A great and pressing desire for sleep washed over him.

Figgis was talking, repeating his calming words. Gilwyn didn't know what was happening, and he didn't care. It felt wonderfully good to be like this, all alone and perfectly relaxed. He listened to Figgis' voice as if it was music from heaven.

When Gilwyn awoke he felt amazingly refreshed. He was still in the catalog room, but the great machine had ceased its whirring and now stood silent, stretching out into the dark recesses of the chamber. The single candle had burned to a nub. Alarmed, Gilwyn lifted his head and glanced around. Figgis was on the other side of the desk, kneeling next to it and quickly writing in a tablet.

"Figgis?" asked Gilwyn. "What happened? Did I fall asleep?"

Figgis kept writing. "In a manner of speaking. You told me the most remarkable tale. Do you remember any of it?"

Gilwyn thought for a moment, and suddenly a perfect picture of the little woman from the alley popped into his mind. "Yes! I can see her now. The woman."

"It's all right here," said Figgis. He stood up and held the tablet out for Gilwyn to see. "I wrote it all down, Gilwyn, every word of it. Remarkable!"

The alley, the midget woman with her bodyguard Trog,

the glowing amulet and the spirits she had summoned; everything was written in Figgis' tablet.

"It's incredible, Gilwyn," said Figgis. "You saw the Witch of Grimhold!"

"Did I?" Gilwyn wasn't so certain. "How can you be sure?"

"I've been reading about Grimhold, everything I could find. Your story matches much of what I've read. You said she was tiny, like a midget, and that she had striking white hair. That's what the stories say!"

"And she wore a coat," Gilwyn remembered suddenly. "With lots of colors."

"Like a rainbow," said Figgis excitedly. "The legends talk of that too, and how she controls spirits, like the ones you spoke of."

Gilwyn couldn't believe his ears. "All the stories say this?"

"No, not all of them," Figgis admitted. "That would be impossible. There's a lot of conjecture about Grimhold, a lot of nonsense and hearsay. But enough of the stories tell the same tale, enough to make me believe we've discovered something." Figgis sighed with deep satisfaction. "Amazing. I can hardly believe it's all true."

It was a night for miracles, no doubt about it. Gilwyn's head was reeling. "Figgis, she helped me. That's all I know for sure. We don't know that she's the Witch of Grimhold. We don't know anything!"

"*I* know," said Figgis. "I feel it in my bones."

"But why?" Gilwyn got up from the chair. "Even if she is from Grimhold, what's she doing in Koth?"

"I don't know, but she has the amulet," said Figgis. "You saw it, and it's exactly like Cassandra's. It's the one I've been searching for, the other Eye of God." Still shaking with excitement, Figgis took his turn in the chair again. His watery eyes narrowed on the nubby candle. "So many questions," he whispered. "I was wrong about Kadar's wife having the other Eye."

"Who's Kadar?" asked Gilwyn.

"Kahan Kadar of Jador. He's like their king. He was the one that had the first Eye of God. The legend said that his zirhah—his wife—had the other one. But I was wrong. I was wrong about a lot of things. You see, there's an old book I have from Jador. That's where I first learned about the amulets. It told me that the master of the hidden place wears one Eye, and that his wife wears the Eye's twin. But I was wrong about the hidden place, Gilwyn. It wasn't Jador at all. It was Grimhold all along."

"And the master of the hidden place?"

"The Witch," surmised Figgis. "She's the master of the hidden place, not Kadar."

"That would mean that Kadar is her wife," said Gilwyn. "That doesn't make sense."

"You're right," Figgis admitted. "It doesn't. But at least we know where the second Eye is now."

Gilwyn nodded. "Right. Now you can tell Akeela to call off his invasion."

Figgis shook his head sadly. "No, I can't."

"No? Why not?"

"Think for a moment, Gilwyn. What do you think Akeela would do if I told him the amulet was here in Koth?"

Gilwyn didn't have to think very hard. "He'd tear the city apart looking for it."

"Exactly. And worse, he would know for certain that Grimhold exists. People like Trager would never rest until they found it. They'd all be in peril. Not just the Jadori anymore, but the people of Grimhold."

"What people?" asked Gilwyn, almost laughing at the notion. "The stories say Grimhold is full of monsters!"

"Monsters? Like that giant you saw?"

"Well, yes, I guess so."

"People, Gilwyn," corrected Figgis. "They must be people. Magic, odd people, maybe, but still people. They'd all be in danger if Akeela and Trager discovered them. And that's not all." Figgis grew pensive. "What about you?"

"What about me?" asked Gilwyn.

"You'd be in danger, too. If I told Akeela your story, he'd pick you apart for information."

"No," chuckled Gilwyn. "He wouldn't hurt me."

"Wouldn't he? What makes you so sure? I told you, you don't know anything about Akeela. You don't know what he's become. You want to talk about monsters, start with Akeela."

A nervous dither began in Gilwyn's stomach. He had

never imagined that his encounter in the alley could lead him to danger, but now Figgis' logic seemed terribly sound.

"So what do we do?" he asked. "If we can't tell the king, and we can't warn the Jadori ourselves, what then?"

The note Cassandra had given Gilwyn still lay on the desk. Figgis picked it up. "You've got a message to deliver, boy."

"Figgis, are you mad? After all you told me you actually want to me to do the queen's bidding?"

"It's the only way," said Figgis. "Someone has to get Cassandra out of Lionkeep, and someone has to warn the Jadori. I can't do it. I'm too old, and if I left the library I'd be missed. Akeela would start asking questions, then everyone would be in danger. But if you leave, well . . ."

"I'd never be missed," said Gilwyn sourly.

"Sorry, but that's right. We need Lukien, Gilwyn. If anyone can get Cassandra to safety and warn the Jadori, he can."

"But how? Do you even know where he is? Cassandra thinks you might."

"The queen flatters me," said Figgis. "I haven't the slightest clue where the Bronze Knight has been for the last sixteen years. But there is someone else who might know. A man named Breck. He was a lieutenant under Lukien, a close friend. When Lukien was banished, Breck resigned his commission in protest."

"Oh? And where is this Breck now?"

"Still in Liiria, living on the outskirts of Koth. The last time I spoke to him was five years ago. He made a promise to Lukien to stay close to Cassandra, to keep an eye on her for him." Figgis smiled sadly. "There was nothing Breck could ever do for her, of course, but that's the way Lukien wanted it. Breck told me to come looking for him if I ever needed him, or if Cassandra was in danger."

"Well, looks like that day has finally come," said Gilwyn.

"Indeed." Figgis once more got out of the chair. He stood before Gilwyn and put his thin, bony hands on his shoulders. "I can't do this alone, Gilwyn. It has to be you. But I won't order it. If you agree, I'll stay behind and try to stall Akeela. Maybe I can throw him off track somehow. But it's up to you. You'll have the hard part."

There really wasn't anything for Gilwyn to say. Part of

him remained lovesick for Cassandra, and he had already given her his word to help.

"Will Breck take me to Lukien?" he asked. "I'll need his help—I won't be able to do it alone."

"If he knows where Lukien is, he'll take you to him," said Figgis. "You won't be alone."

"I'll need money. Queen Cassandra said she'd pay whatever I need."

"I can arrange it. I'll take the money out of the library's funds. Anything else?"

Gilwyn thought for a moment, but his mind was a jumble. There were a thousand questions, and not enough time to answer them. "Just one more thing."

"What's that?"

"Can I take Teku with me?"

The old man laughed and hugged Gilwyn to his breast. "Why not? Ah, you're a good boy, Gilwyn. I've always been proud of you."

To Gilwyn, Figgis' praise remained stronger than any magic.

32

For Will Trager, the most dreadful place in the world was his own memory. It was a palace of dark corridors and locked doors, rooms for which only he held the key. It was a place where the dusty portraits of heroes hung, watching him from across the years, mocking him. Will Trager was over forty years old now, and was considered without peer by the military men of the continent. They feared and loathed him and the war machine he had built out of Liiria's riches, but their hard-earned respect was not enough for Trager. His memories pursued him, chasing him down like wild dogs. And the leader of the ghostly wolf pack, still and always, remained his long dead father.

Will Trager had come from a long line of accomplished knights. His father had fought at the first battle of Redthorn when he was only sixteen, driven no doubt by the barking memory of his own father, Will Trager's legendary grandfather. It was like a disease of the blood passed down through generations, and it had infected Trager badly. He could not hold a sword without thinking of his legacy, and he could not ride into battle without his dead father at his shoulder, whispering slurs. The older Trager had died young, forty-five by the time a Reecian arrow found him. He had been thirty when his young wife had given birth to Will, and by then he was already well-known throughout King Balak's court. He was considered a very fine knight, and so had drilled his son relentlessly in the arts of warfare, forcing him to take up the family mantle. He had pushed young Will onto a horse almost before he could stand, had given him a dagger for his sixth birthday, and had taught him how to swing a sword rather than throw a ball. He had hounded Will day and night, toughening his body and his spirit, scarring his flesh with blows and his mind with insults. Will Trager had been an accomplished adolescent, and any father but his own would have been immensely proud. But Rory Trager was a man of small compassion. It was not enough that his son could ride a stallion or joust with men twice his size. There was an insatiable legacy to be honored, and only the best could carry the banner of the Trager family into the future.

Only the best.

Will Trager's memory palace was full of trophies, but it was also laced with defeats. He had won ribbons at fairs and the adoration of young ladies, but he had never known the respect of his father.

Despite the abuse, the first years of Will's adolescence had been good. He had been welcomed in Lionkeep by the friends of his father, good knights all. They had taught him the use of the lance and the bow, and they had given him the praise his father withheld, enough to sustain him. Even Akeela, bookish and lean, had been a friend to him. Before the bad times. Before Lukien.

Lukien had risen like the sun on Lionkeep. From the moment he'd been plucked from the streets of Koth, he had eclipsed Trager. He was younger, stronger, and better looking than any boy in the keep, and his martial abilities were natural, almost god-given. Where Trager struggled day and night to master weapons and techniques, all these things came to Lukien with easy grace. It was not long before comparisons were made between the two, and even Trager's father saw the truth of things. His judgmental voice still boomed through the corridors of Trager's memory.

"Too slow."

"Too weak."

And the worst of all, "Not as good as Lukien."

Lionkeep fell under Lukien's spell. The men adored him, the girls swooned for him, and even Akeela succumbed to his glamor. Though they could not be more different, Lu-

kien and Akeela became like brothers. King Balak showered Lukien with gifts and affection, and when he had
graduated war college there had been no question of the
Bronze Knight's path. Captain of the Royal Chargers. Remarkably, no one complained. Not even Trager. Instead he
had remained in Lukien's shadow, growing accustomed to
the dark.

It had taken Trager years to break the bond between
Akeela and Lukien, yet he still yearned for the sunlight.
The attention of the crowds, the adulation of his men, a
simple nod from Akeela—all these things soothed Trager's
burning memory and helped to quiet his father's voice. He
had made great strides in his life, and now that Lukien was
long gone the comparisons had all but stopped; still Will
Trager wasn't satisfied. There was always someone still willing to question his abilities, and his father's memory remained the most critical.

Trager was proud of his accomplishments, though. The
world credited him with spreading fear and propping up
Akeela's tyranny, but Trager knew the truth of what he'd
done. He alone had made Liiria the dominant power on
the continent. He had taken a good army and made it great,
swelling its ranks slowly, careful with his improvements.
Liiria didn't just have their vaunted Chargers anymore—
she had divisions of men, painstakingly trained, well fed
and well quartered. Trager's innovations had been the marvel of the military world, not unlike Liiria's great library
was to the world of scholars. Figgis brought education and
enlightenment to the country, and those were good things.
But Trager had never been a learned man. He was a soldier, and his best innovations were among fighting men. He
had revamped the training of recruits, choosing only the
best and making great knights of them, and he had built
facilities for his burgeoning army, gutting the abandoned
buildings of Chancellery Square and turning them into useful war schools and barracks. If there was a man of renowned fighting skills, Trager learned from him, and he
spared no expense in bringing trainers to Koth for his
knights. He had hired horsemen from the steppes of Marn
and archers from Ganjor, weapon makers from the smithies
of Dreel and mercenaries from Norvor, all for the sake of
turning the Liirian military into the greatest fighting force

in the world. In sixteen years he had risen from lieutenant to general, displaced Lukien as Akeela's favorite, and re-made the armies of Liiria. Now he was older and he guarded his accomplishments jealously, just as he guarded access to Akeela. And yet, despite the years and accomplishments, he still heard his father's voice mocking him.

General Will Trager heard his father's voice now as he looked out over his gathered troops. He was on a battle-ment of his headquarters, the former Chancellery of War. The battlement overlooked an expansive parade ground where his personal brigade, the Royal Chargers, were dril-ling and making ready for the long trek to Jador. Three hundred Royal Chargers had been rallied for the mission. They were Liiria's elite, and would lead the regular cavalry into battle with the Jadori savages, putting the total number near two thousand. Trager's eyes gleamed as he watched them, satisfied. It was late but his men were dedicated, and there were still many preparations to make before their departure. They worked by the light of dozens of torches, shoeing their mounts and polishing their long lances. To Trager's tired eyes, they looked brilliant. They were beauti-ful in the moonlight, and because they knew their general was watching them they worked with proud smiles on their faces. Trager could feel their adulation, even high up on the wall. He was as meticulous as ever in his silver armor and crimson cape, his head naked, his beard and moustache trimmed perfectly. His silver gauntlets curled around the stone of the battlement as he leaned forward, nodding hap-pily at the men below. The Royal Chargers were better than they'd ever been under Lukien. They were better trained and better led, and because they knew this they were prouder. Liiria's elite force was envied across the con-tinent, and this was another feather in Will Trager's hat. If only his father had lived to see it. If only the bastard hadn't died so early. He would have seen the strong man his son had become, a hair's breadth from the king. He would have seen how he'd become Akeela's closest advisor, closer even than Figgis or Graig. And he would have seen the lordly horsemen on the grounds of the square, looking up at Trager with admiration, calling him "sir."

But his father could see none of it. Will Trager cursed the Great Fate.

It had not been easy to live in the shadow of so many accomplished men, first his father, then Lukien, but Trager felt he had done an admirable job. Now he was about to spread his greatness to a foreign land. At last he would live out his great dream and lead men in an epic struggle. Jador was unarmed and peaceful, but that didn't matter to Trager. Proud people always fought, and he was sure that Kahan Kadar and his desert folk would resist. The thought made Trager wistful. Finally, he would use this famed weapon he had forged. Finally, he would test its blade.

The lateness of the hour made General Trager yawn. He had been up since before dawn, checking supplies for the journey and making inventory, and he longed for sleep. But Akeela was awaiting him. The king was impatient and wanted constant updates on his progress. Sleep would have to wait a few more hours. Trager waved down from the battlement, signaling Colonel Tark. Tark was three years his senior but hadn't let the age difference irritate him. He was a good and loyal man who followed orders implicitly. It had fallen to Tark to lead the Royal Chargers and, therefore, the Jadori mission. Though Trager still had ultimate control over the brigade, Tark oversaw its day to day operation. He was in a circle of officers when Trager shouted to him from the battlement.

"Tark, I'm off to Lionkeep," he called. "See that those wagons are loaded and the new mounts quartered in the eastern stables."

Colonel Tark nodded. "Yes, sir," he called back. "Will you be back, sir? I can wait up for you."

"I'm going to get some sleep, Tark," replied Trager. "I suggest you all do the same."

"Understood, sir."

Tark's smile was picked up by the rest of the officers. Like Trager, they had all been up since dawn, preparing for the mission. They nodded their good nights to Trager as he turned from the battlement, letting the noise of the grounds fall away behind him. He was on the second level of the tiered structure, and when he entered the hall of his offices the lack of sound was astonishing. A few of his aides scribbled in ledgers, counting up the vast numbers of supplies that were arriving. Only the scratching of their pens disturbed the silence. Trager walked past them without a word. Making his way down a stone staircase, he found the first floor of his headquarters as empty as the second. A pair of Knight-Guardians, his personal bodyguards, stood at the bottom of the stairway. Silently they awaited his orders.

"We're going to Lionkeep, then home," he said tersely.

The Knight-Guardians did not reply. They simply followed him out to the stables, then all the way to Lionkeep.

In the last few years of Akeela's reign, Lionkeep had become remarkably desolate. It was no longer the place of gaiety it had been in the early days, when Lukien had hordes of friends and "Akeela the Good" was available to every visitor. Now it was a shadow of itself, a vast prison for Akeela and Cassandra both, and few people entered its ancient courtyard. Despite Akeela's wealth, most of the place had fallen into disrepair. The stones were covered with vines and moss and the gates creaked with rust. Even on the clearest night the keep looked haunted, collecting pockets of fog and throwing crooked shadows across the grounds.

When Trager arrived at Lionkeep he saw the moonlight reflected in the windows and a few lonely candles, and that was all. He rode at the head of his tiny column, bidding his Knight-Guardians to remain in the courtyard as he went to seek Head Warden Graig. The Wardens still held sway in Lionkeep, and Graig had complained more than once about the Knight-Guardians, a group he viewed as competitive to his own venerable order. Trager had stopped arguing about the issue years ago. He was safe enough in Lionkeep, and needed no wardens or Knight-Guardians to protect him. He left his men in the yard, heading through the portcullis. Two wardens, dressed in the timeless uniform of their order, greeted him as he entered but Trager did not speak to them. They let him pass without question. It was very late and Trager was impatient. He wanted to get home and sleep, or at least spend some time with Dia, his mistress. Dia had promised to wait up for him, and Dia always kept her promises. But first Trager had to make a report to Akeela. And that meant seeing Graig.

Graig's office was on the ground floor of the keep, not far from the main entrance. Candlelight glowed over the threshold, telling Trager that Graig was still awake. Trager paused in the hallway, listening. He didn't like having to see Graig before visiting Akeela, but such were the rules of Lionkeep. Graig still had enough influence with the king to get his way on small matters. It was just one more reason to hate the old man.

Trager headed to the office and knocked on the open door. Graig was at his desk, smoking. On his desk were papers and a flagon of wine. Trager noticed immediately that there were two cups, one half full, the other empty. Graig leaned back in his chair and studied Trager over the long pipe in his lips. The air stank of tobacco, a substance the immaculate Trager had always detested.

"Good evening, General," said the Head Warden. There was a hint of slurring in his voice and just the trace of a smile.

"I'm going up to see King Akeela," said Trager. He turned quickly to go. Surprisingly, Warden Graig called after him.

"Wait, General, a moment."

Trager peered back through the doorway and looked at him. "What?"

Graig waved him into the room. "Don't rush off," he said merrily. "I've got myself some wine from Akeela's private cellar. A gift for my birthday."

"Your birthday? How old are you? A hundred?"

"So witty. Here. . . ." Graig hefted the enormous flagon and began pouring into the empty mug. "Have some."

"I have to see Akeela," said Trager.

"It's late. King Akeela is probably asleep."

"Akeela never sleeps, you know that."

"So then your news can wait all night, right?"

"What do you want, Head Warden?"

Graig shrugged. "Company."

Will Trager was by nature a suspicious man. He could read faces like playing cards, and Graig's face told him something was afoot. He had been waiting for Trager, and not just to bid him access to the king. Trager stepped into the little office warily. He detested Graig and always had, but the old man's forwardness intrigued him. And the late hour meant no one would see them together. Trager sensed an opportunity.

"All right," he relented. "It's been an arduous day, and

I'm as dry as the Desert of Tears." He took off his cape and laid it over the chair. From the corner of his eye he caught Graig smiling, obviously pleased with himself. "I suppose Akeela can wait for his report," he continued. "Not much to tell, anyway."

"You're still arranging your men and supplies?" asked Graig as he held out the goblet.

Trager nodded, taking the cup and sitting down. His greaves creaked as his knees bent. Resting felt wonderful. "Lots to do, and not much time," he said with a sigh. He knew that Graig wanted to talk about the Jadori mission. He decided to oblige. Like nearly everyone in Koth, Graig was kept in the dark about the happenings with Jador. He only knew that masses of men were gathering for a march to Jador; he did not know why.

"Drink," bade Graig, hoisting his own glass. "Toast my good health."

"If I must," sighed Trager. They clinked goblets and Trager took a long, exquisite pull of the wine. It was excellent, the best he'd had in months. As he lowered his cup he stared at its ruby contents. "This is very fine. Akeela gave you this, you say?"

"For my birthday," Graig repeated. "Drink up. There's more."

The old jealousy rose up in Trager like a cobra. In all the birthdays he had marked in Koth, he had never received a single gift from Akeela, and certainly nothing as fine as this flawless vintage. What did a man have to do to curry such favor, he wondered? He took another sip, not caring how much of Graig's gift he consumed, and in a moment had drained his goblet. He slammed it down on the desk.

"More."

Graig obliged, filling Trager's cup. Trager watched him, thinking him remarkably stupid. He could see the Head Warden's plan a mile away. First he would ply him with wine, then with questions. But the wine was good and Trager was tired, and he knew that he could endure the Head Warden's company. Dia would wait for him. Like a loyal bitch she would stay up until dawn for her master to return. If he still hungered for her he would take her, and she would allow it unquestioningly. He knew that she loved him, and that her love had made her weak. She always tried to please him, and Trager recognized that weakness from his own past. It was so easy to use it against her.

Trager emptied his goblet again before Graig could speak. And again the old man filled his cup. This time, though, Trager slowed his drinking.

"Good," remarked Graig. "Take it easy. We are in no rush, you and I."

"Just trying to catch up with you," said Trager. "How long have you been sitting here?"

"Oh, a couple of hours. It's nice this time of night. Quiet."

"You were waiting for me," said Trager.

Graig's only reply was a smile. He took a sip from his goblet and leaned back in his leather chair, propping his feet up on the desk. Trager took notice of his comfort and realized that Graig was not setting up a pretense. He wanted to talk, and made himself plainly obvious. Trager was glad the man credited him with some sense.

He realized suddenly that in all the years they'd served together, he had never really talked with Graig. They had argued, had fought for access to Akeela, but they had never actually *talked*. Trager instantly blamed Graig for the silence. He had been a willing part of the king's little clique, an inner circle from which Trager had always been excluded. Hatred bubbled up in Trager as he remembered all the old insults. Now, at last, he would take the chance to tell Graig what he really thought of him.

But not quickly. First, small talk.

Graig talked about the warden service and about his rheumatism, which had been acting up for years and kept him confined mostly to Lionkeep. He spoke endlessly about his service to Akeela, and occasionally dropped a question to Trager, to keep him in the conversation and, it seemed to Trager, to get him used to answering questions. The two continued drinking from the enormous flagon. Graig was liberal with his gift. He laughed and told jokes, and was surprisingly good company. Trager listened and occasionally smiled, and spoke a little about his father, whom Graig had known and never really cared for. The wine loosened both their tongues, and within an hour they were thoroughly relaxed, admitting things neither had spoken of in years. Trager felt his inhibitions slipping away. He gloried in the ability to speak the truth to this man he'd always hated.

"My father was a bastard," he said. "The first time I fell off a horse he beat me. He was embarrassed, because there were friends around. The most important thing in the world to my father was the opinion of others."

"And you hated him for that," said Graig, his voice slurring badly.

"Yes," admitted Trager. "I did."

The memory of his father overwhelmed Trager suddenly. He set the goblet down on the desk, his head swimming. Remarkably, he felt like weeping.

"I was never good enough, you see," he continued. "No matter how much I accomplished, no matter how many tourneys I won against the other squires, he was always telling me to do better, always pushing, pushing. . . ." Grinding his teeth, Trager shut his eyes. "And I was so glad when he died. I thought I was rid of that kind of jeering forever. But I wasn't, because there was Lukien to replace him. My new competitor."

Silence. Trager opened his eyes and saw Graig staring at him.

"What?" barked Trager. "Surprised to hear me say that?"

"A little," the old man replied. "I haven't heard anyone mention Lukien in years. Akeela forbids his name to be spoken."

"As it should be," sneered Trager. He picked up his cup and drank, stoking his anger. The temptation to slander his old nemesis was too great to ignore. "Akeela is wise not to perpetuate the Bronze Knight's legend," he continued. "I've done my best to bury it, and it hasn't been easy, let me tell you. I still hear men speak his name in the Chargers. Still, after all I've done for them."

"Lukien was a good man," said Graig. "You do wrong to injure him. If you had known him—"

"How could I have known him?" roared Trager. "How, when all of you shunned me? You had your little gang, your little circle of friends, so tight you couldn't slip a fingernail between you. And did you ever ask me to be part of it? Did any of you ever once show me some bloody courtesy?"

Graig looked away, unable to answer.

"I thought not," snorted Trager. "Beasts, every one of you. Just like my father. Will Trager was never good enough for you."

Now he was the one who looked away, his head pounding, bitterness choking his throat. Again the hateful need to weep crept over him, but he slammed it down hard. He would never let this horrible little man see him cry like a woman. He had already told him too much already.

Too much, he thought blackly. *More than he deserves to know.*

"I'm close with Akeela now," he said proudly. "Closer than you even, Graig. Closer even than that old fool Figgis. That makes me important in the world. And you know what you are? You're nothing."

Graig gave a thin smile. "If that makes you happy, General, I'm glad."

"No you're not. You've never been glad for me," countered Trager. "You opposed me when I became general, and you've opposed me every day since. But look at your history, old man. I'm the one Akeela listens to, not you. When I urged him to dissolve the chancelleries, he took my counsel. And when I told him to banish Baron Glass to the Isle of Woe, he listened. Akeela does what I say now, because he values my opinion. He knows I'm smarter than you or any of his other lackeys. You're the last of a dying breed, Graig. Your time is over."

Graig's face was hard as stone. He reached out for the almost-empty flagon, taking it from the desk and setting it on the floor next to him. "I think you've had enough," he said.

"Oh?" Trager flashed a menacing grin. "But it's so early, and you haven't even asked your questions yet."

"Questions?" asked Graig. "What do you mean?"

The evasive answer disappointed Trager. Apparently, Graig still thought him a fool. "Come now, Head Warden, I may be drunk but I'm not an imbecile. This was all a ruse. I knew it from the moment I sat down. You want to ask me about the Jadori mission. So ask."

"And you'll answer me?" asked Graig skeptically.

Trager laughed. "Why shouldn't I? We're old friends now, you and I."

"Old, perhaps," said Graig. "Not friends."

"Ask."

"All right." Graig folded his arms over his chest. "I don't like being kept in the dark, General. I don't like the access you've had to Akeela, and I don't like the idea of him riding off with you to Jador. I want to know exactly what's going on."

"Have you asked Akeela?"

"Of course I have. He keeps telling me to mind my own business, says that you're in charge of this mission and that it's a secret."

Trager grinned. *In charge.* He liked the ring of it.

"It *is* a secret," he whispered, leaning forward. "A great secret. And it's been going on for sixteen years, right under your nose."

Concern wrinkled Graig's brow. "What do you mean?"

"You're the Head Warden of Lionkeep," said Trager with contempt, "and yet you've no idea what's been happening all this time." He laughed, delighted by the man's ignorance. "Do you remember my last journey to Jador, Head Warden?"

Graig nodded. "Of course. You went with Lukien. You found the cure for Cassandra's illness."

"Cure. Hmm, what an odd of way putting it. What do you think it was? An herb perhaps? Some desert medicine?"

Shrugging, Graig said, "I don't know. Akeela would never say. All that I know is that it cured Cassandra."

"And made her a crone?"

"Well, a cancer will do that." Graig shook his head and sighed. "Poor girl. She was so beautiful."

Unable to contain his snickering, Trager said, "Remarkable." He rose and shut the door, much to the surprise of Warden Graig. The old man stared at him inquisitively.

"Why shut the door? Is this Jadori thing really that secret?"

"Oh, it's so much better than that," said Trager. He sat back against the desk, grinning through the haze of the wine. "Cassandra's not a crone at all, you fool. She's as bright as a penny, still and always. She's not a day older then when I left for Jador."

"What are you talking about?" asked Graig. "How do

you know what the queen looks like? No one but Akeela's seen her for years!"

"Not even Akeela, actually," said Trager. "No one has seen her. She wears an amulet, Graig, a magic pendent that keeps her young, keeps her tumor from claiming her. That's what we got for her from Jador."

Graig seemed stunned, disbelieving. He blinked with drunkenness as he tried to comprehend the amazing story. "Impossible."

"The amulet is called the Eye of God. It's one of two such amulets in the world. Akeela has been searching for the other one for sixteen years. Now he's found it, in Jador. That's why we're going back, Graig. And that's why the mission is such a secret."

"I don't believe it," gasped Graig. His old mind was reeling. "It's incredible."

"It's the truth. Only Akeela and three others know about this. Obviously I'm one of them. See? I've always been valuable to Akeela. More valuable than you."

"I don't believe you," spat Graig. "Even if it's true, why would you tell me such a thing?"

Trager shrugged. "Because it amuses me. Because I like knowing something you don't know. You see, I've always hated you, Graig. I've always wanted you to know that you're not so important to Akeela after all. To be honest, I thought Akeela might have let the truth slip out to you after all these years. But he didn't. He doesn't trust you, and that pleases me."

"Scum," hissed Graig, rising from his chair. "You're a lying piece of filth."

"I'm many things, Head Warden, but I'm not a liar. Everything I told you is true." Trager sighed dramatically. "But now I have a terrible problem. I thought maybe you already knew the truth about Cassandra. Obviously I was wrong. This is very dangerous knowledge." He winked at Graig. "A secret."

Graig seemed not to take his meaning. "So? I don't even believe it."

"It doesn't matter what you believe," said Trager. "The sad fact is that I told you." He shook his head in mock regret. "Very sad, indeed."

"General, I think you should leave now," said Graig.

Trager nodded. "Agreed."

He turned to go. Graig stepped forward to escort him out. Trager reached for the door handle, then spun with his outstretched arm, catching Graig in the throat. The old man stumbled back from the blow, his neck snapping as he fell backward over his chair. His shock-filled eyes watched Trager as his back slammed into the stone floor. A wheezing gasp escaped his throat. Frozen horror fixed his twitching face.

On the floor, unmoving, he gazed up wildly as Trager hovered over him. Trager smiled, then roughly kicked over the flagon, sending its contents spilling along the floor.

"You shouldn't drink so much," whispered Trager. "Now look at you. You've slipped and hurt yourself."

Graig couldn't respond. His neck broken, he could barely breathe.

"Such an unfortunate accident," said Trager with a smile.

Warden Graig gasped, a garble of sounds that sounded to Trager like curses.

"You should have been nicer to me, Graig," said Trager. "It would have been so easy. Well, let me tell you something now. I've got what I want, and I'm not sharing Akeela with anyone." He poked at Graig's cheek. "Do you hear me? You're finished, Graig. You, Lukien, and someday that old waterhead Figgis. *I'm* the one that tells Akeela what to do. And that's how it's going to be forever."

Trager didn't wait for Graig to die. The old man's face was already purpling. Confident he'd be dead in minutes, the Supreme General of Liiria retrieved his cape and left the office, closing the door behind him. But before he left he took his goblet with him.

"A man shouldn't drink alone," he sighed as he left the keep. "That's how accidents happen."

33

Gilwyn rode out from the library at dawn, when the sun was barely peeking over the horizon. He had his wagon and his horse Tempest to pull it, Teku on his shoulder, and a pocketful of silver coins. The letter Queen Cassandra had given him was tucked safely into his trousers. Aside from those things, he had nothing. He was alone and afraid, but he was determined to reach his destination by nightfall. So he said good-bye to Figgis and did not look back, focusing instead on the long trek ahead. Figgis had given him sparse directions to Breck's farm. Never having actually been there, the old man wasn't exactly sure of its location. It was north of the city, he'd told Gilwyn, near the town of Borath. Borath was a shire of wheat and potato farmers, and Figgis was sure that Breck grew one of those crops. Find Borath, Figgis had explained, and you'll find Breck. It seemed an easy enough task, but Gilwyn had never ridden out of Koth before. And Figgis had been unable to offer any guarantees. It had been five years since he'd last heard from Breck, and it was very possible that the old knight had moved on. Figgis didn't think so, but the possibility made Gilwyn anxious. And Borath was a full day's ride from the library. Even with good weather, it would take determination to reach the shire by dark.

Blessedly, the morning was fair. Gilwyn did not stop riding until he was well beyond Library Hill. He kept to the northern outskirts of the city, watching it peripherally and

marveling at its size. It was much bigger than it looked
from Library Hill, tall and vast and mysterious. The road
Gilwyn took afforded him an excellent view. It was cobble-
stone and lined with trees, and the day soon took on a
beautiful aura. To the south, Koth reflected the sunlight
like a mirror. To the north, a great expanse of golden grass
swayed in the breeze. Gilwyn quickly forgot his thousand
troubles. He felt remarkably free, untethered by his appren-
ticeship to Figgis or his mild deformities.

By late morning he located the river which would lead
him north to Borath. The river was called the Trident, because it split into three smaller tributaries just south of the
capital. The Trident was wide and crystal clear, and Gilwyn
took the time to stop for rest, letting Tempest drink from
the Trident's inviting bank. While the horse drank, Gilwyn
and Teku rummaged through the food Figgis had packed
for them, finding bread, meat, and fruit. Teku grabbed for
the fruit immediately, snatching herself a shiny red apple
harvested from the orchards of Lionkeep. She sat herself
down on the carriage's bench seat and buried her snout
noisily into the fruit. Gilwyn wedged some ham between
bread, then leaned back, studying the blue sky as he ate.
Though they had passed many others during the morning,
the little place he had staked out by the Trident was deserted. The place was lovely and reminded him of Cassandra. He laughed, shaking his head. How stupid he'd been
to think she was interested in him. But she had been kind,
just as he'd imagined, and she had not shunned him or
stared at his boot or crippled hand. Though she was a
queen, she had treated him like an equal. And that, more
than anything, was the reason he wanted to help her.

For the rest of the afternoon, Gilwyn, Teku, and Tempest
followed the Trident north. They stopped when necessary
for rest, letting old Tempest catch his breath, and came
upon a town where Gilwyn took the time to talk to the
locals. It was a farming village called Ferri, one Figgis had
told him about.

"If you're not making good time, spend the night in
Ferri," Figgis had said. "There'll be a bed for you there if
you want it, but don't pay too much. And don't tell anyone
why you're heading to Borath."

It was advice Gilwyn didn't need. He had no intention

of asking anyone in Ferri about Breck, but he did ask directions to Borath. A brawny pig farmer with kindly eyes confirmed what Figgis had said—Borath was only a few more hours north. Follow the Trident, head northeast where it forks, and keep your eyes open for the shire. Gilwyn thanked the man, let his young daughter play with Teku a few moments, then went about his way.

By late afternoon, they were all exhausted from the ride, despite their frequent breaks. Teku had long ago stopped chattering on Gilwyn's shoulder, and instead curled up in a sleeping bundle on his lap. And Tempest, who had pulled the carriage without complaint throughout the day, began to show signs of weariness. Gilwyn was beginning to regret his decision not to spend the night in Ferri when he saw the fork in the Trident.

"Look," he cried, waking Teku. "There it is!"

His little companion spied the forking river, squawking with relief.

"Not much farther, Tempest old boy," Gilwyn encouraged, and gently guided the horse northeast. They left behind the banks of the river and soon entered farm country again, a great flat plain with homesteads dotting the horizon. Gilwyn could barely make out the outlines of the little shire in the distance. The sun was beginning to sink, and the stone chimneys of Borath sent up evening smoke signals. Grass and fruit trees flanked the road. Up ahead, a field of wheat rippled in the breeze, like the tide of a golden ocean. Gilwyn spied the homesteads. They were acres apart, and he wondered which one was Breck's.

"Potatoes or wheat?" he wondered aloud. The wheat looked more inviting, so he headed toward the waving grain. The closest farm took long minutes to reach, and when he did Gilwyn waved down a boy just coming in from the field. The boy was younger than Gilwyn and wore clothes of the field, patched and stained with soil. He eyed the carriage suspiciously as it entered the property.

"Excuse me," said Gilwyn. "I'm looking for the home of a man named Breck. Might this be it?"

The boy didn't answer. He didn't move a muscle.

"Do you know of a man named Breck?" asked Gilwyn hopefully.

The boy nodded. "I do."

"Then would you mind telling me where I can find him? I've been on the road all day."

"You know Breck?" asked the boy. His eyes watched Gilwyn carefully.

"No, I don't," Gilwyn admitted. "But I've come to speak with him."

"Come from where?"

"Look fellow, it's getting late," said Gilwyn. "If you know where this man Breck is, could you tell me? I'd like to find him before it gets dark."

"Gordel?" called a voice. It came from the nearby house. Gilwyn turned toward the cobbled structure and saw a woman emerge from the rounded doorway. She wore a patchwork frock dirtied by labor and a smile that melted away when she noticed Gilwyn. "Gordel, who is this?" she asked.

The boy eased toward the woman. "He's looking for . . . Breck."

"I see," the woman replied. She looked at Gilwyn. "And what's your business with Breck, young man?"

"I've come from Koth, my lady, with a message for him. I don't know who he is; I've never met him. But it's important that I speak to him." Gilwyn smiled the best he could, trying to put her at ease. It was obvious she was protecting Breck. "I'd be grateful if you'd tell me where he is."

She studied him, clearly worried, but in a moment she shrugged. "Ah, what difference does it make—you'll find out soon enough. Breck is my husband. This is his home."

Gilwyn sighed with relief. "You have no idea how glad I am to hear that, my lady." Carefully he got down from the carriage, favoring his bad foot. Teku scrambled onto his shoulder. "I swear to you, I'm not here for trouble. But I do need to speak to your husband. And if you could spare a bed for the night? I can pay. . . ." He put his good hand into his pocket and retrieved a few coins. When he showed them to the woman she frowned.

"No need for that," she said. "If you've got bad news, you won't be staying."

Rebuffed, Gilwyn said, "Well, that's up to you. Can I see Breck now, then?"

"He's inside. We're just sitting down to eat. What's your name, boy?"

"Gilwyn, ma'am. Gilwyn Toms. I work in the library of Koth."

The woman's pretty face lit with alarm. "The library? You know Figgis, then?"

"I do. He's the one that sent me."

All the bravado left the woman. She simply wilted at the news. "Trouble then," she whispered. "Gordel, go on inside. Supper's on the table. Your father's waiting."

The boy spared a last, troubled look at Gilwyn before retreating into the house. When she was sure he couldn't hear, his mother stepped toward Gilwyn and said, "I've been waiting for you or someone like you for a long time. My husband told me you might come someday."

Gilwyn joked, "I'm probably not what you expected. My lady, I mean no harm to any of you. I just need your husband's help. And that supper you've cooked up sure smells good."

For the first time, the woman smiled. "Come ahead then, Gilwyn Toms. I'm really not the shrew I pretend to be."

She led Gilwyn past the flowerpots flanking the threshold and into her modest home. It was a typical farmer's house, with stone walls and stick furniture and windows with open shutters to let in the fresh air. Across the main room sat a table, near the cooking area, laden with food on iron plates. A man sat at the head of the table, talking to the boy, Gordel. The man had food in his mouth and was chewing slowly, listening intently to the boy. They both stopped when the woman entered with Gilwyn. Teku fell silent on Gilwyn's shoulder. The man swallowed and stared at them. He was rough looking, his skin tanned to leather by the sun, his hair bleached a faded orange. Though he was seated, Gilwyn could tell he was tall. He was wide, too, with shoulders made brawny from labor and muscles fed by a huge appetite, evidenced by the pile of food on his plate. He did not smile or frown as he watched Gilwyn. There was simply blankness in his face. The boy stood silently beside him.

"Breck, this is Gilwyn Toms," pronounced the woman. "From the library at Koth."

The man named Breck rose slowly. "From Figgis?" he asked.

Gilwyn nodded. "Yes. And from Queen Cassandra."

"Oh, my Fate. . . ." Breck looked at his wife and son. "Kalla, I think you two should leave us to talk."

"But I'm hungry!" Gordel protested.

"Take your plates with you," said Breck. "This isn't for your ears."

Gordel complained but obeyed, scooping meat and potatoes onto his plate and waiting for his mother, who stood staring at Breck with troubled eyes. There was a charged tension between them.

"I'm sorry, Kalla," said Breck. "I need to speak with him alone. Please. . . ."

"Get your plate, Mother," said the boy. "We'll eat outside where it's cool."

The woman touched her son's shoulder and guided him toward the door. "I'm not hungry," she said softly, then left with the boy. Breck watched her go with obvious regret. He collapsed back into his chair with a heavy sigh.

"Tell me something, boy. Was I difficult to find?"

"Not really," replied Gilwyn. He eased closer to the table. "Figgis said you'd probably be here near Borath."

"Ah, Figgis." Breck's deeply lined face cracked with a smile. "How is that old maniac?"

"Fine, sir."

"Do you work for him? Or do you work for Queen Cassandra?" Breck studied Gilwyn a moment, then answered his own question. "No, you're not blind. You must work for Figgis."

"I'm his apprentice," said Gilwyn. "I work for him in the library. But Queen Cassandra did send me, in a manner of speaking." He eyed the inviting table. "Sir Breck, if I could sit down while I tell you why I'm here, I'd be much obliged."

With his long leg Breck kicked out a chair. "Sit, Gilwyn Toms, and tell me your sad story. Is the queen all right?"

His directness surprised Gilwyn. He sat down, saying, "I'm not sure how to answer that, sir. The queen's in no real danger, not yet, but there's trouble. She sent me to ask for your help."

"Tell me," said Breck.

"It's a long story, and I'm not sure where to begin." Gilwyn stroked Teku's head as she climbed down into his lap. "To tell you the truth, it's all kind of unbelievable."

"It's not her illness again, is it?"

"No, sir," said Gilwyn. He studied Breck, trying to gauge how much he really knew—or how much he should divulge. "Sir Breck, the queen needs your help. She asked me to find Lukien."

Breck gave a small smile. "Just a matter of time," he said. "I always knew she'd ask for him someday. And you found me through Figgis?"

"That's right," replied Gilwyn. "Figgis thought you might know where to find Captain Lukien." He hesitated. "Do you know where Lukien is, Sir Breck?"

Breck looked toward the doorway, cocking his head a bit to listen. Satisfied that his wife and son couldn't hear, he said softly, "Maybe. But I need to know why Cassandra wants Lukien back. And I need proof you're who you claim to be."

Gilwyn reached into his pocket and took out the letter Cassandra had given him. "Here," he said as he handed it to Breck. "That's from Queen Cassandra, sealed with her royal mark. The only other person that uses that seal is King Akeela, and I assure you he didn't send me."

"No," mused Breck, studying the boy's clubbed hand. "I believe you. Akeela's clever, but even he wouldn't send a cripple after Lukien."

"I'm not a cripple," retorted Gilwyn. "I walk just fine now."

"Sorry," said Breck. "But you know what I mean. Besides, Akeela is smart enough to ferret out Lukien if he wanted to."

"Then you do know where he is?" asked Gilwyn. "Sir Breck, it's very important that I find him. There are lives depending on it, and not just Cassandra's. Figgis told me that you were a good man, and that if you knew where Lukien is you'd take me to him."

"Same question," countered Breck. "Why?"

Gilwyn didn't know how to answer, so he decided to tell the man the truth. Breck listened, rapt, as Gilwyn told him about the Eyes of God, and how Queen Cassandra was still eternally young. It did not surprise him that Breck knew nothing of the amulets or their remarkable charm; only a handful of people knew the truth, and they had all done well in keeping the secret. Breck shook his head in disbelief.

"It's true, Sir Breck, I swear it," said Gilwyn. "And now King Akeela thinks he's found the other Eye. He thinks it's in Grimhold, hidden somewhere beyond Jador."

"Grimhold?" Breck began laughing. "Grimhold's a myth."

"No, it's not," said Gilwyn seriously. "It's real. I know, because I've seen the Witch of Grimhold. She's wearing the other Eye."

Breck put up his hands. "Easy, boy; slow down. This is all getting a little bizarre. Grimhold? Witches?"

"I admit it's hard to believe," said Gilwyn. "But it's all true." He proceed to explain how he had seen the witch in Koth, how she had entranced him, and how Figgis had learned of Grimhold from his old texts, just as he'd learned of the amulets' existence sixteen years ago. As he spoke Breck listened, not touching his food, occasionally glancing toward the doorway. When Gilwyn was done he got out of his chair and slowly began to pace. It was getting dark outside but his little family still hadn't returned.

"Amazing," he whispered. "But I still don't see why Cassandra wants Lukien to come. Why doesn't Figgis just tell Akeela that the amulet is in Koth?"

"He can't. If he did, all of Koth would be at risk. Akeela would tear the city apart looking for the amulet, and Cassandra would be just as trapped. And it still probably wouldn't keep him from marching on Jador. Now that Akeela knows Grimhold exists, he's going to want to find it."

"No," spat Breck. "Akeela's not the one that would butcher the Jadori. It's Trager." He picked up a knife from the table and twirled it absently in his fingers. "That bastard; he's the one that's behind this. He's the one that wants to march on Jador, I'd bet anything."

"You might be right," said Gilwyn. "But it doesn't really change anything, does it? I still have to find Lukien. He has to get Cassandra out of Lionkeep somehow."

"And then they'll ride for Jador and warn them?"

Gilwyn nodded. "That's the plan." He shifted his chair around to face the former knight. "Sir Breck, Figgis told me about your promise to Lukien. He told me that you stay close to Koth, to keep an eye on Cassandra. Well, the queen needs you now. If you really made this promise, you have to help me."

Breck chuckled. "Boy, don't try to guilt me into this. I don't need you to remind me of my service. Lukien was my captain. He was also my friend. But so was Akeela, once. You're asking me to betray one for the other. Should I take such a decision lightly?"

"Well, no," said Gilwyn. He hadn't thought of it like that before.

"And who do you think those people waiting outside for me are? Just friends? They're my family. I never told Figgis about them because I didn't want to put them at risk."

"Your wife knows why I'm here, Sir Breck," said Gilwyn. "I could tell."

"Aye, she's not good at hiding it. She's been expecting someone like you to come around for years now, someone who'd drag me back into my old life. But I'm not a soldier anymore, boy. I'm a farmer."

Gilwyn feigned disdain. "Is that right? I didn't think soldiers gave up their loyalties so easily."

"Don't lay traps for me," snapped Breck. He twirled the knife in his hands, brooding over it. "You're not just asking me to deliver a note."

"Yes, I am," said Gilwyn, springing to his feet. "That's all I want from you. Just take me to Lukien. Or at least tell me where he is, and I'll do the rest."

Breck shook his head. "You don't understand, it's not that easy. You're right about loyalty. It isn't easy to give up. I can't just tell you where Lukien is and send you on your way. I owe my captain more than that. And you have no idea what you're getting into."

"Why?" asked Gilwyn, suddenly worried. "Where is Lukien?"

Breck didn't answer. Lost in thought, he walked to the open doorway and stood in the threshold. The sky had darkened considerably. Gilwyn and Teku went to stand beside him. Breck's wife and son sat alone in the distance, lounging on a bench and staring at the setting sun. They did not see Breck looking at them. They could not see the heartbreak on his face.

"If I go, they'll be alone," said Breck. "That's what Kalla's afraid of."

A pang of guilt surged through Gilwyn. "I'm sorry. If I'd known you had a family, maybe I wouldn't have come."

"You would have come," said Breck. "Because no one else can help you. Follow me. I want to show you something."

Breck turned and went back into the main chamber. Curious, Gilwyn followed him. But they didn't stop at the table again. Instead they walked past the main area into the only other room of the house, a small sleeping chamber. There was no door, only a rounded, narrow arch. Gilwyn hesitated in the threshold as he noticed the simple bed and realized this was where Breck slept with his wife.

"Come in," ordered Breck.

Against the wall were a collection of blankets and clothes. Breck shifted them aside, revealing a large wooden chest beneath them. Gilwyn drifted into the room, studying the chest as Breck undid the latches.

"What's in there?" asked Gilwyn.

Breck tossed open the lid. "This."

A dazzling display of golden metal met Gilwyn's gaze. Even in the dim light of the narrow window, the contents of the chest glistened. Gilwyn hovered closer to the box, stooping down next to it. At first he thought Breck had thrown open a treasure trove, but then he realized what he was seeing.

Armor.

Beautiful, unblemished armor, spiked and polished to a golden gleam.

No, not gold, he told himself. *Bronze.*

He reached out and touched the breastplate. It was cool and smooth, embossed with the image of a prancing stallion, the crest of the Royal Chargers. If there had been any question of Breck's ties to Lukien, they were instantly erased.

"Lukien gave you this?" asked Gilwyn.

"It was no good to him anymore," said Breck. "Not where he was going."

"Where?" Gilwyn pressed. "Where did he go?"

Breck smiled sadly. "He went to the only place he could go. He was a soldier, and that's all he ever could be."

"I don't get it," said Gilwyn. "Where's that?"

"Norvor."

The word struck Gilwyn. Of all the places he'd wished to hunt for Lukien, Norvor was on the bottom of the list.

Norvor, land of war. Land of death. A land where a heartless king and a queen of diamonds struggled for the single throne.

"Uh, Sir Breck," said Gilwyn unsteadily, "if Lukien's in Norvor, I'm going to need your help."

Breck nodded. "I told you so."

34

King Mor was dead, sixteen long years now. He had left no heirs, for his son Fianor had been murdered with him, leaving empty the throne at Carlion and leaving his army leaderless. There was no ironfist to replace King Mor, no easy means of succession. But Mor had been a man of many enemies, and there were vultures eager for his throne. Vying for the riches of Norvor's diamond mines and the fealty of her soldiers, they had fractured Norvor, spinning her into the maelstrom of civil war.

History had recorded Mor's murder as "the massacre at Hanging Man." Of the four hundred men stationed at the citadel, only a few dozen were spared. They had been forced to march back into the heart of their country with no food and water. Among these men was a Norvan colonel named Lorn. At Mor's castle in Carlion, Lorn told the court that their king was dead and his son with him. General Nace, Lorn said, was dead as well. And because he was the highest ranking man to survive the massacre at Hanging Man, he claimed the throne of Norvor for himself. Protestors to his ascension were quickly killed by the other surviving soldiers of Hanging Man, who were all too eager to avenge their defeat, even on innocent countrymen.

But Lorn's hold on power was tenuous, and always remained so. Though he continued to rule in the area of Carlion, calling himself king, there were others with ambition who saw opportunity in Mor's death.

Of all challengers for Norvor's broken throne, Jazana Carr had been the craftiest. Because she ruled the north of Norvor, and because she controlled the gem mines, she was called the Diamond Queen, a title she had purchased for herself with the help of a family fortune. For sixteen years Jazana Carr had fought King Lorn for control of Norvor, pressing her war from her stronghold at Hanging Man. With her own diamond-bought army, she had retaken the fortress when the Liirians and their Reecian allies had left, and from there had built her tiny empire, spreading her reign over more and more of the north's teeming gem mines. Diamonds and rubies made Jazana Carr rich. Ever determined to secure her reign, she spent her burgeoning fortune on the best mercenaries in the world, keeping them loyal with lucrative contracts. She was not a true queen but she would be someday, she was sure. Until then, she was content to fight Lorn for the throne of Norvor.

The Bronze Knight was no more.

He had left his armor and loyalty behind, fleeing into Norvor without looking back. He knew the depth of Akeela's hatred, knew that to return to Koth meant death for Cassandra and himself. He had tried, briefly, to live a quiet life like Breck, but he was unskilled as a farmer and clumsy as a carpenter, and so had returned to the only thing he had ever excelled at—once again, he became a soldier.

He had entered Norvor fully aware of its grim reputation, sure that the usurpers of the broken throne could use his skills. In Jazana Carr, he had found a willing employer. And so he had waged the Diamond Queen's battles, fighting for money along with countless others. He had changed his name to live among them, but Jazana Carr knew his secret and kept it, for the Diamond Queen had ambitions even greater than the Norvan throne. Lukien, now called Ryon, knew this and did not mind. Like Jazana Carr, he dreamed of one day returning to Liiria, even if it meant returning as a conqueror. Then, perhaps, he would be reunited with Cassandra. It was the one bargain he had struck with Jazana Carr—if ever they should attack Liiria, and if ever Koth should fall, he was to have Cassandra.

Lukien had quickly learned that Jazana Carr was a pragmatic woman, endlessly patient. It had been over sixteen years now, and Carr was showing her age. But she still battled King Lorn for Norvor, and she still spoke of the day when Liiria, the greatest diamond of them all, would be hers. Perhaps it was treachery for Lukien to listen to such talk. At first it had felt like the highest heresy. But the years had hardened Lukien, and he had never forgiven Akeela for banishing him. That one great insult had stripped him of everything. After a lifetime dedicated to Liiria and its ideals, the endless struggle to climb Koth's complicated social ladder, he was nothing but a freelance. Now, sixteen years and countless battles later, it no longer bothered Lukien to hear Jazana Carr speak of conquering Liiria.

But his love for Cassandra had never died. He knew that she continued to live in Lionkeep, was still Akeela's captive. And it was this more than anything that fostered Lukien's loyalty to Jazana Carr. If the possibility to see Cassandra again ever existed, Lukien was sure it would come through her.

Before that day could come, though, there were battles to fight. Lukien had become an important pawn in Jazana Carr's struggle for power. Because of his prowess with a sword he was valuable to Carr. There were borders to secure and skirmishes to fight, and towns under Carr's dominion that needed protection. Towns like Disa.

When Lukien fought, he forgot that he was just past forty. He forgot that his body was growing old or that he had lost an eye to a Norvan scimitar. He did not think of Cassandra or Liiria, or even remember that his true name was Lukien. When he fought, as he had at Disa for five dreadful weeks, he was simply Ryon, a mercenary fighting for Jazana Carr.

Disa had been a nightmare, and Lukien was well pleased to have it behind him. Once Disa had been a pretty little town, with quaint old houses and neatly trimmed gardens. But its southern location had made it a battleground. Suddenly the sleepy town of metalsmiths and shopkeepers had become tactically significant. For five weeks Lorn's soldiers had battled for Disa, trying to take its bridge. Under the command of a colonel named Ness, the southerners had put up a worthy fight. But in the end they had retreated south, back to King Lorn's territory. They had not taken the bridge, but they had exacted a heavy toll on Lukien—Ryon—and his men. The protracted fight had laid waste to Disa, sending streams of refugees north, further into Jazana Carr's bosom. Finally, when reinforcements arrived, Lukien joined the refugees. He was exhausted and longed for the peace of Hanging Man. He was confident that Layton and the others could hold Disa.

Lukien had been on the road for barely an hour when the messenger reached him. He and twenty of his fellow mercenaries had left Disa early in the morning, eager to return north. They wore no armor, nor did their horses. And they bore no lances, only shields and swords. Jazana Carr had long ago secured the northern territories, and Lukien and his men felt safe as soon as they'd left Disa behind. The road was blessedly quiet, with only the singing of birds and the good-natured banter of comrades. Young Marke, who had become a friend to Lukien since joining their ranks a month ago, rode beside him. Marke was barely twenty and reminded Lukien of himself at that age, when he had been handsome and still had both eyes. Now he wore an eye patch to cover his disfigurement, and countless skirmishes had scarred his pretty face. Marke told jokes and sang bawdy ballads as they rode, making them all forget the horrors they had left behind in Disa

And then, like the trump of doom, came the messenger's cry.

"Ryon!"

The twenty mercenaries turned in unison. A single rider thundered toward them, his black horse kicking up a furious dust cloud. Lukien recognized the rider at once. It was Garrin, one of the men he'd left behind at Disa. Marke also took notice of the man, his young face falling.

"Trouble," he said grimly.

Lukien spun his horse to face the coming rider. His companions formed a circle around Garrin as he reigned his steed to a skidding stop.

"Thank the Fate I found you," said Garrin. "Ryon, Ness is back!"

"What?" gasped Lukien. "When?"

"Soon as you left. They hit us at the bridge, not an hour ago. He's got fresh men with him, dozens of them."

The news shocked Lukien. He was sure Colonel Ness

had retreated. After such a bloody stalemate, even the stalwart Ness needed rest. Lukien cursed himself for underestimating the Norvan colonel. But he had been so desperate to get home, so very tired. . . .

"The bridge?" he asked dreadfully.

"Holding when I left," said Garrin. "Now, who knows. We need you, Ryon. There's no time to waste."

The image of home faded instantly in Lukien's mind. He knew the bridge wouldn't hold forever. And if the bridge fell, so too would Disa. Though there were only twenty of them, they would have to lend their swords to the cause.

"Every able man," shouted Lukien to his comrades. "Come on."

With Lukien in the lead, Marke and the others galloped back the way they had come, chewing up the road to Disa.

Colonel Ness sat atop his dapple gray, the visor of his winged helmet up, his eyes scanning the battleground and the town beyond. Here on the east side of the river, he was safely away from the raging battle for the bridge, on a swale of grass that afforded him an easy view of the melee. Exhaustion plagued his battered body. His armor hung on him in broken bits, dented and filthy from his countless clashes with the mercenaries. More than anything in the world, Colonel Ness wanted to return home to Carlion, to be with his wife and to forget about this worthless town that fate had catapulted into importance. But Colonel Ness could not return. He had already tried that, just yesterday. Instead he had been met by a fresh contingent of men from Lorn, one of them bearing a note from the so-called king himself. Ness hadn't really needed to read the note; he was clairvoyant enough to know what it said.

King Lorn would brook no failure at Disa. Colonel Ness was not to return to Carlion without having conquered the town. No retreat. If he failed, he would be executed.

After reading the dreadful note, Ness had let it fall from his hands into the mud. He had simply stared vacant-eyed at the two dozen new troops Lorn had sent him. Two dozen more corpses to litter the grounds of Disa. Carr's mercenaries were simply too good for them. Part of Ness had felt like weeping. But he was a military man charged with a mission, and so he had turned back with his own battle-weary men to once again walk into the lion's mouth.

It was mid-morning and the war for the bridge still raged, as protracted as ever. Ness commanded his men from the safety of the rear, but there was nothing much for him to do. The bridge was too important. And the only way to take the bridge was to throw wave after wave of soldiers at it. His cavalry still tried to ford the river in spots, but the current was too swift to make that practical. Men from both sides clashed in the water, spreading the bloody stale-mate like a stain. On the bridge itself, his cavalry had pushed through the barricade of caltrops but had failed to crush the wall of lancers awaiting them on the other side. Horsemen and infantry tumbled over each other like a bloody waterfall, slashing and screaming and plunging down into the rushing waters below.

Colonel Ness watched, unmoved. He had a very clear vision of himself dying today, because he doubted he could take the bridge and because he'd rather die here, in battle, than on the gallows back home.

When Lukien reached the riverbank, he called his party to a halt. The horsemen fell in line behind him, surprised. Garrin skidded up to Lukien with a troubled look.

"Why are we stopping?" he asked.

Lukien glanced around. They were not far from Disa and if he listened closely he could just make out the din of battle over the gurgle of the river. An ample cover of trees surrounded them, shielding them from sight. Lukien knew they'd come far enough.

"We're going to cross here," he said.

"Here?" Garrin was incredulous. "Why?"

"To surprise them," said Lukien, addressing all his men. "We'll come down from their northern flank, attack Ness directly."

Marke spied the river with trepidation. "Can we cross here? It looks deep."

"It is deep," Lukien admitted. "But what good would it do if we can't get across the river? There's only so many men who can die on that bridge at once. If we're going to finish them, we have to get across."

"Agreed," said Travis, one of the more seasoned men. "We'll go slow and careful. The first man across can string a rope for the others."

"But the horses," said Marke. "They'll be swept away!"

"No, they won't," said Lukien. "Once the first man gets across with the rope, the others can hook on through their cantle rings. We'll take it easy, a few at a time."

"Ryon, there isn't time," Garrin protested. "We need men at the bridge *now.*"

"Forget the bridge," growled Lukien. "If we don't take the battle to the east side of the river, we'll lose the bridge and Disa soon enough. Now hurry, Garrin. Tell Layton what I've planned. And tell him to send as many men as he can spare south, to cross the river there. They can ride up and meet us. We'll crush Ness between us."

"We can't spare anyone, Ryon! That's why I rode back for you."

"Do it," demanded Lukien. He was already riding down the river's shoal, testing its depth. "Quick as you can, Garrin. Like you said, there's not much time."

Seeing his commander's resolve, Garrin stopped arguing. "All right," he said, "good luck," then turned and continued riding south.

Marke sidled up to Lukien, smiling as they both guided their horses into the first few feet of the river. "You first?"

"We'll go together," Lukien decided. He called back to Travis for a length of rope, then tied the cantles of the two horses together. The added weight, he hoped, would keep the current from dislodging them. Either that or they'd both be swept away. Slowly, carefully, he drove his mount deeper into the water.

The bridge at Disa was a marvelous structure, thirty feet wide and built of granite, limestone and brick. It had stood for nearly forty years, effortlessly spanning the river and letting Norvans from either side cross in peace. Now it had became one more flashpoint in the bitter battle for Norvor. Layton of Andra watched men fight and die for the bridge, men who had become his comrades under the payment of Jazana Carr.

Layton was thirty years old, and he had never seen a

battle like this one or watched so many men die so quickly. He had arrived at Disa only yesterday, but he'd been appalled by the losses inflicted on Ryon's men, and he had been shocked to see Colonel Ness attacking once again. The incursion had caught Layton unaware and had caused the needless death of fifteen men in an instant, men who'd been guarding the bridge from the western bank. When the Norvans had broken through the caltrops, Layton's fifteen men had splintered like twigs. It had taken an hour for them to beat back the Norvans, and now they fought to a standstill on the bridge itself, the wide span choked with men and horses, both sides unwilling to yield. Ryon had warned Layton of Colonel Ness' tenacity, but to the young mercenary the colonel's attack seemed more than ferocious. It seemed suicidal.

"Layton! I found them!"

Layton turned on his horse in the streets of Disa. He and four other men were evacuating the town, helping the shopkeepers and their families into wagons for the trek north. Already whole trains of people had left, abandoning their homes as their fellow Norvans fought to reach them. When Layton saw Garrin galloping toward him, his heart sank. The mercenary was alone.

"Well?" he shouted over the noise. "Where are they?"

"North," cried Garrin. Out of breath and drenched in sweat, he wheeled his horse through the throngs of fleeing families and came to a stop before Layton.

"North where?" barked Layton. "Are they coming?"

"They're fording the river to attack from the opposite bank," Garrin hurriedly explained. "They're going to hit Ness at his flank. Ryon wants you to send more men across the river at the south, somewhere where Ness can't see them." He had to pause to catch his breath. "They're to meet up with Ryon's men, crush Ness between them."

"What?" screamed Layton. "I can't spare anyone! Look at this bloody place! I need men at the bridge!"

"Ryon says the bridge doesn't matter. He says we have to bring the battle to Ness on his side of the river, try to take him out." Garrin watched Layton, waiting for his reaction. "It's orders, Layton. Ryon is still in charge."

"Orders," spat Layton. "Right."

Layton didn't mind taking orders from Ryon. Like everyone else, he admired the older mercenary. But to spare
men for this fanciful idea. . . .

In the end, Layton could only acquiesce.

"All right," he said grimly. He turned to the four men
with him. "All of you, go half a mile south. Find some
cover and ford the river if you can. Take Kaj and his men
with you. They're already mounted up."

"Then what?" asked one of the four. "What do we do
after we cross the river?"

Layton was already heading for the bridge. "Then ride
like the wind. Go for Ness, and hope that Ryon is there to
meet you."

As soon as he thundered out of the thickets, Lukien saw
Colonel Ness' army. They were pressing their attack on the
bridge, and there were scores of them. Barely a quarter
mile away, they did not see Lukien or his men against the
backdrop of the forest, and Lukien quickly reined in his
mount to prevent from being spotted. Behind him, his men
fell into position, keeping to the trees and straining to
glimpse the battlefield. The roar of the melee rang through
the forest. Lukien and his men, all of them drenched and
exhausted, spied the fight with trepidation. They had forded
the river without incident, carefully guiding their mounts
across the treacherous waterway, but that seemed hardly a
parlor trick to the daunting task awaiting them. Lukien
scanned the Norvan troops. As before, there were both
cavalry and infantry. The infantrymen in their winged helmets and ornate armor battled on the bridge with swords
and pikes, while the mass of cavalry stood detached, some
trying vainly to cross the river.

"We're alone," Marke observed in a whisper. He spied
the field carefully, looking past the Norvans to the southern
plain beyond. "You think Layton did as you asked, Ryon?"

"I don't know," replied Lukien. Across the river, he
could barely see his fellow mercenaries in the streets of
Disa, organizing counterattacks. Townspeople continued to
pour from the narrow avenues, fleeing north. Somewhere
in that throng Layton was waiting, probably biting his nails
in frustration. He was a good man, though, and Lukien was
confident he'd obeyed the order.

"We'll charge for Ness," he decided. "Kill him, and the rest of them will scatter."

"That won't be easy," said Travis. "He's well protected, no doubt." He pointed toward a swale of grass and a collection of cavalrymen. "That's probably him."

"Doesn't matter," said Lukien. "He won't be expecting us."

There were no more questions from the men. They drew their weapons, awaiting Lukien's word. Taking his own sword from its battered scabbard, the mercenary called Ryon gave the order to charge.

Colonel Ness was about to order more men to the bridge when he glimpsed the mercenaries riding toward him. He had seen them only peripherally at first, thinking the vision a trick of the light. But as he turned slowly north, he realized with dread that he wasn't dreaming. A brigade of horsemen was riding toward him, swords drawn, steeds devouring the mossy ground. Not many of them, but enough to cause a very big problem. Ness hurriedly considered his options. Then a cry from his aide shattered his concentration.

"Colonel, look!"

Lieutenant Perrin was pointing south. Ness followed his finger and saw yet another brigade riding up the river bank.

"Assassins," he spat, knowing their mission in an instant. Taking out the enemy leader was a sound strategy. It's what he would have done.

"Colonel?" asked his aide. "What do we do?"

"What else is there to do, Perrin?" Ness drew his sword. "We fight."

Roughly sixty of Ness' men were free to fight. The rest of them were already engaged, battling on the bridge or in the churning river. Ness ordered half his men against the southern flank. All of them were on horseback and could outnumber the mercenaries. As for the northern assailants, Ness chose them for himself, for in the last moments he had spied something interesting in their ranks—they were led by a man with an eyepatch.

"Here I am Ryon, you son of a bitch!" Ness waved his blade in the air, rallying his men and taunting his attackers. He ordered Lieutenant Perrin and the other officers forward.

*   *   *

Lukien saw Colonel Ness lift his blade. The Colonel was shouting something, baiting him. His Norvan blade caught the sunlight, an ugly reminder of another scimitar that had long ago plucked out Lukien's eye. The gesture enraged Lukien. He tucked himself behind the neck of his charger, galloping forward. Next to him, Marke had his own sword drawn and his shield against his forearm, prepared to parry the Norvan spears. Travis and the others were close behind. Out on the bridge, Ness' men continued their battle against the mercs, while behind Ness another force was racing forward—Kaj's crusaders. The sight of the Ganjeese mercenary heartened Lukien. Now he knew they had a fighting chance.

"Marke," he shouted, "Get ready!"

Marke bent low for the coming clash. Ness let his men swarm forward, their weapons poised against the advancing mercenaries. Lukien watched as a young horseman took aim, a lieutenant by the look of his armor braids. As he charged forward, the man leveled his spear at Lukien's chest.

Suddenly Lukien was back at the tourneys. Suddenly it was Trager advancing on him, lance leveled for the killing blow. All the jousts in his experience told Lukien the right move. He pulled his charger hard left, letting the spear glance past him. His sword arm came up in a flash, cutting through the young man's gorget and shearing his head from his shoulders. The head rolled like a melon through the air. The body fell backwards from its saddle. And Lukien charged forward as if nothing had happened, a relentless killing machine.

On the east side of the river, Layton watched in fascination as Ryon's brigade made their charge. Apparently, they had accomplished their objective—Ness had already been distracted. From the south, dark-skinned Kaj and his crusaders were the anvil to Ryon's hammer. They screamed their peculiar Ganjeese war chant as they rode, twirling their curved blades above their heads. The sight of the counterattack buoyed Layton's sagging hopes. He was in awe of Ryon, and always had been. The one-eyed madman seemed to care nothing for his own life, yet made staying alive look so easy.

Around the bridge, the Norvans had seen the counterattack, too. Knowing they were suddenly surrounded, their assault lost its earlier precision. Men were screaming in confusion, wondering if they should retreat or push on. Instinctively Layton's men responded, counterattacking with renewed vigor.

Layton knew the time had come for full commitment. He had less than forty men to press their advantage.

"It's now or never, boys," he cried, pointing his broadsword at the armored mass of Norvans.

The last of his weary cavalry surged toward the bridge.

Colonel Ness hardly noticed the new horsemen riding for the bridge. Something deep within him told him the bridge was lost anyway. He was tired of fighting for Disa, tired of losing men for the glory of Lorn. Behind him, a small group of Ganjeese mercenaries were hacking through his tired troops, and it occurred to Ness as he watched the bloodshed that Jazana Carr must be paying very well, indeed. But like a butterfly that thought, too, flew from his mind. He had just seen Lieutenant Perrin's head fly from his shoulders. It had been surreal, and the sight had almost made Ness laugh. It was all so pointless. He began shouting orders. In his ears, his own voice sounded impotent.

"Edric, Birk, forward! Torr, Raswel, attack!"

His men slashed at Ryon's forces, fighting to reach the mercenary leader. Ness watched Ryon from three rows back, watched in detached horror as he hacked down men like weeds, his flashing blade splitting metal and brains, mindless and insatiable. Four of the mercenaries had already fallen, but Ness still didn't like the odds. Ryon and his ragtag army seemed unstoppable.

"Fight on! Fight on!" he cried. He only wanted one thing now, and that was to see the filthy Ryon fall. Forget the bridge, forget Lorn's pointless war. Just kill the mercenary scum.

Driven by hate, Ness broke from the ranks and homed in on the one-eyed berserker. Another young mercenary blocked his way, rearing up suddenly on a snorting stallion.

His blade slashed forward. Ness parried it easily. Enraged, he pressed his attack on the man, their horses dancing, their swords locking again and again. Ness had the advantage. He was stronger, fresher, and more skilled. Soon he had the ruffian in trouble. Ness saw Ryon glance toward them in alarm, heard the leader's frightened cry.

"Marke!"

Colonel Ness rained down blows. The young man struggled, his sword forced back again and again by the onslaught. At last his defenses expired. Ness' blade came down like lightning, tearing through his hand, sending fingers flying. The man-boy screamed. Ness finished him with a hack through his chest. His opponent tumbled from his horse and hit the ground.

Ness spun to see the stunned Ryon staring at him. As the melee exploded around them, the two leaders locked eyes.

Lukien watched Marke fall from his saddle, twisted and dying in the bloodied moss. It had happened so quickly he'd been powerless to stop it. A good man; a boy really. One more death for a worthless cause.

"You may keep your precious bridge," Ness spat, "but there's no way you leave here alive."

"Call retreat, Ness," said Lukien. The words sprang from him without thought. "Let's end it, right now."

Ness' face went momentarily blank. Then he snarled, "I can't end it! We're trapped, Ryon, both of us. Trapped between Lorn and your bitch-queen!"

"No," said Lukien. "Just say the word and end it."

"I can't," raged Ness. "But I can kill you, pay you back for ruining me!"

Lukien shook his head. "It's pointless, you know it is. Even if you kill me, you'll die here sooner or later. If not today, then tomorrow."

"If not here, then back in Carlion," cried Ness. "On the gallows, like a coward. Now fight me, you one-eyed filth!"

If there had ever been a choice, it vanished in an instant. Lukien knew Ness would never retreat. He glanced at Layton's men at the bridge, valiantly pressing back the Norvan advance. In the distance Kaj's crusaders were knee-deep in bodies, some of them their own. It would have to end here, right now.

"Prepare yourself then, Colonel," said Lukien heavily. "Because in a moment, you'll be dead."

As soon as the words were spoken, Lukien was charging. His sword was up and his head was down and his stallion snorted as it sprang forward, propelling him toward the waiting Norvan. Ness was ready for the attack. His own seasoned sword blocked the first blow, knocking it aside. Lukien swung his horse around, avoiding the colonel's counterblow like a dancer and thrusting his blade like an arrow toward Ness. Too late, Ness saw the sword puncture his breastplate. He gasped, his own blade falling from his grasp. Lukien plunged his sword deeper. Face to face with the Norvan, he held him aloft on his sword like a piece of dangling meat. Ness' desperate gaze stared disbelievingly at Lukien.

"Ryon," he hissed, barely able to speak. "Ryon. . . !"

"No," Lukien whispered in his ear. "My name is Lukien."

He ripped the sword from Ness' chest, then leaned forward and pushed him from the saddle. Ness hit the ground face-first. Lukien stared down at him, then at the nearby body of Marke. Around him the battle continued to rage. But for Lukien, it was over. Satisfied, he spun his horse away from the melee.

"Retreat!" he cried again and again, waving his sword so all could see. "Back to the forest! Retreat!"

His men broke off their attack and fled for the trees. As Lukien had guessed, Ness' men did not pursue. Shocked and ragged, they rode in confused circles on the field. One by one they realized their colonel was dead. Without Ness or his slain lieutenant, they were leaderless. To the south, Kaj and his men continued to fight, but Lukien knew they too would soon break off their assault. At the bridge, Layton's brigade had secured the eastern shore, while on the west bank, the fighting Norvans heard of Ness' death. Like their brothers in the flanks, the drive went out of their attack.

It took another hour for Lukien and his party to ride north, ford the river again, and return to Disa. When they did, the exhausted party saw that the Norvans had once again retreated. As it had been from the beginning, the bridge at Disa belonged to Jazana Carr. But the toll had been catastrophic. Of the twenty men Lukien had taken into battle, only twelve had crossed the river a second time. The bridge itself was slick with blood, the water beneath choked with bodies. Except for the mercenaries, Disa was deserted. An unearthly silence shrouded the place as Lukien and his men trotted into town. Layton greeted them on the outskirts, walking toward them alone along a desolate street. The mercenary was limping, a bloodied bandage tied across his right thigh. He raised his hand to Lukien as he approached.

"They're gone," he reported simply. "Back into the forest, I suppose."

Lukien brought his horse to a halt. "They'll be back."

"Probably," admitted Layton. "But we held the bridge."

"How wonderful."

In the distance, Lukien could see the mossy battlefield, polluted with corpses. He'd have to go across and retrieve Marke and the rest of the fallen. The sight of the carnage kept Travis and the others silent.

"Ryon, you did a fine job," said Layton. "You, Kaj, everyone."

"We lost Marke."

"I know," acknowledged Layton. "But you killed Ness. You held the bridge. You should be proud."

Lukien smirked. Pride was something he hadn't felt in years. "We did what we're paid to do."

"Will you go back now?" asked Layton. "To Hanging Man?"

"Yes," said Lukien, "once we've cleaned up this mess."

"Tell Jazana Carr what happened here, Ryon," Layton urged. "Tell her how we held the bridge. We'll all get bonuses."

"I'll tell her," said Lukien, then trotted his horse toward the bridge for the dirty work at hand.

35

Gilwyn Toms had spent his entire life in Koth, a city many considered the most advanced in the world. Yet he had never seen anything like Hanging Man fortress.

He had traveled the long way to the Norvan border, leaving his home behind and letting Breck, the former knight, guide him south. Along with Teku and his horse, Tempest, they had crossed south through Liiria, stopping each night at homesteads along the way. It had been a good journey, mostly, with fair weather and decent company, and Gilwyn had found Breck an amiable companion. After the first day, Breck had lost most of his gruffness and had adjusted to the pain of leaving his family. He had even begun to tell stories to Gilwyn, about Lukien and the "good days," and about the death of King Mor at Hanging Man. Breck explained how Akeela had murdered Mor, and how that one bloody act had damaged the young king irrevocably.

But despite Breck's tales, Gilwyn had been unprepared for the sight of Hanging Man. He had already known the story of King Mor, and how Akeela had killed him. Now, staring up at the fortress from the riverbank, Gilwyn was breathless. Hanging Man was a garish citadel of sandstone and iron. After years of weather and war, she remained the gateway to Norvor, and there was simply no good way to find the Bronze Knight without first knocking on her door. It had been years since Breck had heard from Lukien, but he was sure that his old friend was still in Jazana Carr's employ. Gilwyn spied the stout towers and grounds, dotted with figures in a peculiar mix of uniforms. Even from their safe distance, giant Hanging Man looked ominous.

Sitting beside Gilwyn in the wagon, Breck watched the fortress rise above them, sizing it up through narrowed eyes. "Lots of bad memories here," he sighed.

Gilwyn nodded, sure that he'd soon have his own bad memories of the place. But Breck had been sure this was the place to start their search for Lukien. Despite his misgivings, Gilwyn had agreed. But they hadn't really spoken of their strategy to deal with Jazana Carr. Breck had confessed that he knew almost nothing about her, and Gilwyn's knowledge of the Diamond Queen was spotty, also. The library didn't get many visitors from war-torn Norvor, and those that did come never spoke of Jazana Carr. It was said that she was cunning and ruthless. And of course, she was wealthy. Other than that, Jazana Carr was a mystery.

"We're no threat to her," mused Breck aloud. "Hopefully she'll speak to us, tell us where Lukien is, and let us be on our way."

"You think so?" asked Gilwyn hopefully.

The knight gave one of his tight smiles. "Let's find out."

He snapped the reins and sent old Tempest ambling down the road. The shadow of Hanging Man fell upon them, dropping down across the River Kryss. The fortress itself clung to a mountainside, one sheer face of it turned to the tumultuous river below. From this wall Norvan kings had once hung their dead enemies, dangling them as warnings to the world. It had been years since anyone had hung on the death gallery of the fortress, but Gilwyn could clearly imagine them there now. Tempest was slow but surefooted as he made his way up the inclined road. Gilwyn could hear the roar of the Kryss in the distance, churning violently down in Hanging Man's Gorge. Up ahead loomed the fortress, surrounded by a tall iron gate. Beyond the gate was a flat courtyard. Inside the yard milled scores of fighting men. The great turret of Hanging Man rose up from the fortress like an outstretched hand, its shaft spaced with arrow slits, its top crennelated with battlements. There was no flag at the top of the turret, just an empty pole where the proud standard of Norvor had once flown. The men in the yard watched the wagon as it approached, guarding the main gate. To Gilwyn's untrained eye, they were completely unlike the well-organized soldiers of Liiria, with their perfect and gleaming gray armor. Instead, the mercenaries of Hanging Man were a stew of colors and nationalities, hardly alike at all. They were a grimy, unappetizing lot, and the sight of them withered Gilwyn's confidence.

"Breck, are you sure this is a good idea?" he whispered. "I mean, look at them. . . ."

"Steady," said Breck. He kept his eyes on the waiting guardians. When they finally reached the gate, he brought the wagon to a halt a safe distance from their spears. A pair of mismatched sentries greeted them from behind the towering metal bars. One wore a chain mail coif and a dented bronze breast plate. The other wore Norvan armor with the winged helmet of Mor's loyalists. A traitor, Gilwyn surmised.

"Ho," Breck called to them.

The one in mail shifted his spear from one hand to the other. "What's your business?"

"We're travelers," said Breck. "We're looking for someone, and have need of an audience with Jazana Carr."

"Jazana Carr doesn't see strangers," replied the Norvan.

"It's greatly important," said Breck. "If you could please speak to her for us, ask her good will."

"Good will?" came a voice. From around the stout guard tower a new face emerged, long and ruddy and split with a wild smile. "Jazana Carr isn't famous for her goodwill, friend." The man stepped forward and grinned at the strangers. A black vest strained across his broad chest and a blue beret topped his red head. "And if you're looking for a bed for the night, she'll tell you to be on your way."

"Please let us explain," said Breck. "We've come a long way to speak to your warlady."

"They're looking for someone," the Norvan guard said.

"Oh?" asked the man in the beret. "Who would that be?"

"An old friend," said Breck. "A comrade of yours."

"Ah, you mean a merc," said the grinning man. He rested his hand on the pommel of his saber, a long curved blade in an ornate leather scabbard. "Well come on, what's his name? I know all the men in Hanging Man."

"I can't tell you his name," said Breck. He and Gilwyn had agreed to speak only to Jazana Carr. "I can only tell your mistress."

"Fellow," began the man, "My name is Rodrik Varl, and I am as close to Jazana Carr as her own silk sheets." He laughed at his own joke. "Well, not that close perhaps. I've not gotten so lucky yet, eh lads?"

The sentries laughed. Other mercenaries began gathering near the gate.

"You can tell me anything you can tell Jazana Carr," said Varl haughtily, "or you can just turn that fleabag horse of yours around and head back to Reec."

"We're not from Reec," said Gilwyn, riled by the insult. "We're from Liiria."

Rodrik Varl's eyebrows lifted. "Liiria?"

Before Gilwyn could answer, Breck hurried a hand onto his knee and said, "We came from the Reecian side because it was easier to cross the Kryss. But yes, we're from Liiria."

"Indeed," said the man, stroking his chin. "Are you a soldier? Jazana Carr has a thing for soldiers, especially those from Liiria."

Breck replied simply, "Why don't I just tell Jazana Carr who I am?"

Rodrik Varl laughed. "Well, you don't look like much of a threat. The boy, neither. The monkey perhaps. . . ."

More laughing from the mercenaries. Gilwyn bristled, feeling every guffaw like a knife. His face began to redden.

"Look, are you going to let us talk to your queen or not?" he said before he could help himself. "Otherwise we'll be on our way."

"Oooh, easy now, boy," cautioned Rodrik Varl. He waved a finger through the bars. "Talk to me like that again and I'll have your pet for lunch."

Breck squeezed Gilwyn's knee hard with his big hand, an obvious warning to be quiet. He said to the mercenary, "We'll tell Jazana Carr all she wants to know. But we can't tell it to you; it's too important. And if your lady wants to talk about Liiria, I'll be happy to oblige. Just let us through, all right?"

"Jazana Carr doesn't like turning away soldiers," said

Rodrik Varl. "You come on in, and I'll tell her you're here. Maybe she'll talk to you, maybe she won't."

"Good enough," said Breck. "My thanks to you."

The mercenary ordered the gate open, then disappeared into the throngs of the courtyard. As the great gates of Hanging Man swung wide, Gilwyn leaned over and whispered in Breck's ear.

"This could be a trap."

Breck shrugged. "So what if it is? We're not going to find Lukien without their help."

The sentries stepped aside and let the wagon enter. Breck drove into the courtyard, and the gathered mercenaries soon returned to their business. There were horses and barrels and stablehands in the yard and the familiar sounds of workmen cleaning stalls and women scrubbing laundry. Gilwyn glanced at the main keep, wondering where Rodrik Varl had gone. The turret of the fortress rose high above, piercing the blue sky. A handful of mercenaries stayed close, watching but not disturbing them. Like all the soldiers, they wore a varied scheme of tunics, mail, and vests from around the continent.

"Blazes, but there's a lot of them," said Breck as he spied the many soldiers. "Jazana Carr must be paying well to keep so many men."

"And they're all loyal to her?" asked Gilwyn.

Breck laughed. "Loyal? Hardly. Mercenaries are only loyal to one thing." He rubbed his thumb and fingers together. "Gold. As long as Jazana Carr pays them, they'll stay with her. But if a better offer comes around this lot will be gone like lightning." He looked around and, sure no one could hear, added, "Mercenaries are scum, Gilwyn. They're not like real soldiers, not like Lukien and I were. Remember that."

Gilwyn nodded, still confused. Hadn't Lukien become a mercenary? What kind of scum was he, then?

They waited long minutes in the shade of the turret, never leaving their wagon, until Rodrik Varl finally returned. As usual he was grinning when he entered the courtyard, strutting like a rooster and resting his hand nonchalantly on his saber.

"Well?" asked Breck. "Will she see us?"

"She will," said Varl, "but not right away. You're a very lucky pair—Jazana Carr wants you to sup with her tonight. I'm to find you some rooms. You can rest till then."

"Sup with her?" asked Gilwyn. "But we only want to talk to her."

"Ah, the warlady is a hostess without peer, boy. Don't beg off a meal with her," said Varl. Then he winked, adding, "It wouldn't be wise, anyhow."

"We appreciate it," said Breck, "but we really just need a few moments of her time. There's no need for her to go to any trouble."

Rodrik Varl, who was probably about Breck's age, gave a frightening smile. "Laddy, if Jazana Carr says sup with her, you sup."

Breck and Gilwyn looked at each other. Teku's tail coiled tightly around Gilwyn's wrist. They all came to the same quick conclusion.

"You know, I was just telling the boy how hungry I am," said Breck.

Rodrik Varl took Gilwyn and Breck to a room on the second level of the fortress. The room had a wide window covered with frilled curtains and two beds with wonderfully clean sheets. An unlit hearth graced the center of the chamber, complete with an ornate marble mantelpiece that had obviously been fitted into the spartan fortress after its construction. On the mantel were an assortment of feminine collectibles, little trinkets encrusted with gems and crystal and gold goblets overflowing with rubies. Breck's eyes bulged at the sight of them; Rodrik Varl laughed at his reaction. Gilwyn went to the mantel and scooped his hand down into a bowl of uncut diamonds, letting the gems fall through his fingers in amazement.

"Are these real?" he asked.

"Aye, they're real," said Varl. He threw open the curtains, letting sunlight flood the room. The chamber was exceptionally well appointed, not at all like the quarters of a border outpost. Gilwyn's eyes danced around the room, impressed with every detail. The rumors of Jazana Carr's wealth were apparently well-founded, and she'd spared no expense in transforming Hanging Man to suit her exotic tastes.

Breck picked up the goblet of rubies from the mantel, staring at them in disbelief. "Fate above, there's a fortune here."

"And another fortune like it in every room," said Varl. "But don't think about sticking any in your pockets. If you do, you'll be discovered. And if you're discovered, you'll be hanged."

Breck returned the goblet to the mantel. "I don't need Jazana Carr's charity," he said stiffly. "Still, I didn't know she was so wealthy."

"She wasn't always," said Rodrik Varl. "She started poor and worked for what she has, and she's been gaining wealth and territory ever since. Ah, but I'll let her tell you that herself! Jazana Carr likes to brag."

Breck scoffed at their gilded surroundings. "Apparently she likes to show off, too."

Varl merely smiled and headed for the door. "My lady usually eats at sundown," he said. "Rest until then. I'll come get you when it's time."

"Before you go," said Breck, "tell me something. What you said down at the gate, about being close to Jazana Carr; are you her man? I mean, is that what she pays you for?"

Varl tossed his head back and laughed. "Me? No, stranger, I'm not that lucky. I look after Hanging Man for her, and that's all. She's got another to look after her bed. Like I told you, she's got a thing for Liirians."

The mercenary left without saying more. Breck turned to Gilwyn with a wicked grin.

"Hear that?" he asked. "She likes Liirians. Sleep lightly, boy. Maybe she likes younger men."

"Please, don't," groaned Gilwyn. His foot was aching and he was in no mood for jokes, so he chose one of the beds and stretched out on the soft mattress. Teku nuzzled against his clubbed hand. "Close the curtains, will you?" he asked.

He heard Breck draw the fabric over the windows. The world darkened.

"Sleep now," said Breck. "Maybe tonight we'll get some answers."

Exhausted, they both fell quickly to sleep.

* * *

When they finally awoke it was much later. Rodrik Varl had opened the door, loudly calling out for them to get up.

"It's time, lads," he said. "Let's go."

Gilwyn opened his groggy eyes. Teku was on his chest, staring up at the red-haired mercenary. Rodrik Varl reached out to touch her, but she hissed at him and pulled away.

"Nice pet," said Varl sourly. "Come on. Jazana Carr is waiting for you."

Gilwyn sat up and saw Breck shaking sleep from his head. "All right," he told the mercenary. "Just give us a few minutes to clean up."

"There's a chamber pot under your bed," said Varl as he left the room. "I'll wait for you down the hall. Be quick."

When he was gone, Breck and Gilwyn did their business, washed in the basin of clean water on the table between their beds, and generally straightened themselves for their meeting. Outside their chamber they found Rodrik Varl waiting for them, leaning against the stone wall and whistling merrily. His tune carried easily down the empty hallway.

"This way," he said, waving them forward.

With Teku perched on Gilwyn's shoulder, the pair followed Varl through the hall. Like the corridors of Lionkeep, this one was narrow and made of stone, with a floor of polished timber. But Jazana Carr had added more of her feminine flourishes to the hall, brightening it with flowers and flamboyant tapestries. As they descended a staircase, Gilwyn noticed columns of weapons along the wall, all polished to a grand luster and encrusted with jewels. In fact, there were jewels everywhere. The corridors were filled with nude statues, each with a sparkling gem in its navel. Dusty portraits hung on the walls, their frames rimmed with rubies. Diamond pendants swung from the servants that passed them in the hall, encircling their necks like expensive slave collars. Up ahead, the oak doors of a great banquet room were open wide. Above the doors, a giant emerald lay in the stone arch, staring at them like the eye of an immense dragon. The emerald alone seemed priceless to Gilwyn, but beyond the doors glimmered the hints of still more fortunes. A grand table had been set with shining silverware and golden candelabras. Both ends of the table

disappeared into the unseen confines of the room. Gilwyn
and Breck approached the chamber carefully, then heard
music issuing over its threshold, the soft, pliant melody of
a lute. Rodrik Varl paused beside the doors, waiting for
them to catch up. When they did, he entered the room to
announce them.

"My lady," he said simply, "here they are."

Varl stepped aside for the pair to enter, revealing the
vastness of the chamber and the entire length of the table.
A trio of huge round windows flooded the room with sunlight, their wavy stained glass reflecting colors off the walls
and crystal stemware. Near the center window stood the
lutist, smiling as he softly plied his instrument. Dressed in
red velvet and lace, he had a woman's beauty, but he was
nothing compared to the figure that rose when Gilwyn and
Breck entered the room.

Like every one of her polished jewels, Jazana Carr was
exquisite. She rose to her feet with grace, smiling with teeth
as dazzling as the diamonds she wore on every finger. Long
hoops of gold dangled from her ears and fine chains of
platinum hung from her neck, and around her forehead was
a scarlet ribbon pulling back her auburn hair, pinned with
a golden brooch. She had a breathtaking face, mature but
flawless, with ruby-painted lips and eyes the color of the
deep ocean. When she saw the two strangers she stretched
out her arms in welcome, revealing silver bracelets beneath
her purple gown. Gilwyn stopped on the threshold to gape
at her. In all his life he had never seen a more striking
figure. Seeing her was like looking at a rainbow.

"Welcome, friends," she said. The music of the lute only
complemented her honey-sweet voice. It was a strong voice,
belying the grace of her features. Clearly she was a woman
of mature years, but her skin, like her voice, was glassy
smooth. Her feline eyes fell upon Gilwyn, bewitching him
at once. "Please come in."

Rodrik Varl guided them further into the room. Tearing
free of Jazana Carr's gaze, Gilwyn studied the table. His
empty stomach growled. The Diamond Queen had turned
out a feast, an incredible selection of breads and meats and
fish and fruit, all piled high on mirror-bright platters and
steaming porcelain tureens. As if by magic, a pair of servants Gilwyn hadn't noticed before came alive, emerging

from the far corner of the chamber. They flanked the table
on either side of their mistress, each pulling out a chair
with their white-gloved hands.

"Sit down, my friends," purred Jazana Carr.

Gilwyn sat down warily, opposite Breck. The old knight
picked up the linen napkin at his place setting. The servant
behind him plucked it from his fingers, settling it on his lap
as he took his chair.

"Thanks," said Breck awkwardly. He looked across the
table at Gilwyn, who was just as confused as his guide.

"There now, isn't this nice?" said Jazana Carr. She took
her seat again, an ornate wooden chair as tall as a throne.
Behind her, her own manservant stood at the ready, his
neck circled with a diamond choker. He was still as a statue
while his mistress spoke. "Rodrik, thank you," said Jazana
with a smile. "You may go now."

"As you wish, my lady." Rodrik Varl bowed with a
flourish then turned and walked out of the vast chamber,
leaving the three strangers alone at the table. Jazana Carr
wrapped her jeweled fingers around a crystal goblet, raising
it to her guests.

"It's so good to see you both," she said as if she'd known
them for years. "I don't get many visitors here. Drink, both
of you, please."

Gilwyn and Breck picked up their goblets, noticing they
were already filled. They exchanged wary glances, which
Jazana Carr picked up immediately.

"Oh, now you disappoint me," she pouted. "I assure you,
my dears, there's nothing in those glasses but the sweetest wine."

Teku chattered a low warning in Gilwyn's ear.

"Yes, your little friend. Rodrik told me about him." Jazana Carr leaned across the table for a better look. "I've
never seen a creature with such coloring before. Is he from
Liiria, too?"

"Uh, no ma'am," said Gilwyn. "*She's* from Ganjor."

"A girl!" chirped the warlady. "How wonderful! But you
are from Liiria, yes, boy?"

"That's right," said Breck. He still hadn't tasted his wine.

"Well, I am Jazana Carr," pronounced the woman, "And
now you must tell me what you're hiding."

Gilwyn lowered his goblet. "Hiding?"

"Your names. Rodrik told me you were a secretive pair, but I must say you're being awfully rude." She wrinkled her nose playfully at Teku, then glanced between her visitors. "Well?"

"Forgive us, Jazana Carr," said Breck. He stood up and bowed. "My name is Breck."

"Breck?" asked the woman. She lost interest in Teku suddenly. "Just Breck? Nothing more?"

Breck grinned disarmingly. "Just Breck, for now."

"A man of secrets," sighed the warlady. "You may sit." She turned her probing eyes on Gilwyn. "And you, young man—what's your name?"

"I'm Gilwyn Toms, my lady." Gilwyn made to stand but Jazana Carr waved him down.

"Don't get up. I see from that strange boot of yours that you're a cripple." Her gaze dropped momentarily to his clubbed hand. "Your hand, too. Pity. You're a handsome boy."

Gilwyn bristled. "I assure you, my lady, I'm quite capable of getting around."

"Yes," cooed Jazana Carr. "You must be to have come all the way from Liiria." She sipped languidly at her wine, letting her gaze rest on Breck, her eyes twinkling over the rim of the goblet. Her dainty fingers lowered the glass. "So, *Breck*," she began, "Rodrik tells me you're a soldier."

"That was his supposition, my lady," replied Breck.

"Rodrik knows a soldier when he sees one. He can be a boor, like all men, but he's never wrong about such things."

"He recruits for you, then?" Breck asked.

Jazana Carr replied, "Tell me about yourself."

"My lady, the boy and I are here on business. We only want to ask—"

"Yes, yes, you're looking for someone," interrupted Carr. "I know all that already. We'll get to it. But first Jazana Carr wants to know about *you*."

Gilwyn's jaw tightened at the inquisition. Even as the servants began dishing up the food, his appetite disappeared. Clearly Jazana Carr wanted something, maybe entertainment, maybe something more.

"I don't get many visitors from Liiria, you see," said Jazana Carr. "Most of my men come from Reec or Marn. I've only had a handful of Liirian men serve me, and they've all been most adequate indeed." Her perfect pink tongue slid across her lips. "If you are half as good as those men, I could use you, *Breck*."

"Ah, my lady, now you make yourself clear," said Breck. "You need another sword against your enemies."

"Hmm, something like that," said Carr. "I have many enemies. Some I haven't even made yet."

The enigmatic answer troubled Gilwyn. He said, "My lady, I don't think we can give you what you want. We're already occupied by our own important business."

"Hush, child," said Carr in a lullaby voice. She turned back to Breck. "You, sir, intrigue me. You're too old and weather-beaten to be one of General Trager's men, yet you carry yourself like a Royal Charger." Carefully she studied Breck's face for signs. A small twitch told her what she wanted to know. "Yes," she drawled. "I'm right, aren't I?"

Finally, Breck lifted his wine glass. "My lady sees very clearly."

"You were a Charger, then? In the old days?"

"Does it matter?"

"Very much," said Jazana Carr. She seemed immensely pleased by the revelation. "If you are who you say you are, then you're an enemy of King Akeela."

"Nay, not an enemy," said Breck, lowering his glass and scowling. "I'm loyal to Liiria. Whatever happened in the old days is over, and I bear King Akeela no grudges. I left the service of my own volition. Besides. . . ." He looked at Carr suspiciously. "Why would my past interest you?"

"Isn't it obvious?" said Jazana Carr. "I have need of strong men like yourself, men who know Liiria and have umbrage against King Akeela. Oh, you can deny your feelings all you like. You may lie to me about them, but I know the truth. You see, Sir Breck, I know you better than you think." Without looking, she reached out and scratched Teku's head, but her eyes remained locked on Breck. "You're not the only Liirian ever to pass this way."

Breck and Gilwyn froze under her stare. Teku purred at the sensation of her long nails.

"You know me?" asked Breck. "How?"

A servant began serving Jazana Carr oysters. The war-lady waved him away. "You're looking for someone, Sir

Breck. You're from Liiria. You used to be a Royal Charger." Her long fingers ticked off the facts one by one. "I'm not a stupid woman. I can add."

"Then you know we're looking for Lukien?" asked Gilwyn.

Jazana Carr chuckled. "I do now."

"Is he here? Can we speak to him?"

"Easy, Gilwyn," said Breck. "Let the lady tell her story."

"Thank you, Sir Breck," said Jazana Carr. "Yes, the Bronze Knight works for me. He has for many years. In fact, he's been invaluable. A fabulous fighter, that one. From the first time I laid eyes on him, I knew he was something special." The warlady sighed. "Great Fate, he was beautiful. So blond, like the sun. He's not so lovely now, I'm afraid."

"Is he all right?" asked Breck.

"Oh, yes. Don't be concerned. I think your friend is quite invincible."

"He told you about me?"

"He did. He only mentioned you once, a long time ago. He warned me that a man named Breck might come looking for him someday. Knowing he was a Liirian, I made him confess his identity. I've kept that secret for years. Around here he's known as Ryon."

Confused, Breck glanced at the servants who had just overheard every word.

"Oh, don't worry about them," said Carr. "I assure you, if they breathe a word of what they've heard, I'll cut off their stones and make them eat them."

Gilwyn almost dropped his fork. Jazana Carr laughed delightedly.

"Can we see Lukien?" asked Breck.

"First, a question," said Carr. "What news do you bring him?"

"I'm sorry, my lady," said Breck. "I can't tell you that."

"Do you mean to take him away from me?"

Breck was silent. The warlady's expression grew stormy.

"Lukien is very important to me," she warned. "If you have plans to lure him away, I must know."

Still Breck said nothing.

"You don't trust me," said Carr. "Very well. Then I will

tell you this—Lukien is not here, but he will return. He is on his way back from Disa and should return in a few days."

"And you'll let us speak to him then?" asked Gilwyn.

"I don't see why I should," said Jazana Carr petulantly. "Here I've offered you this sumptuous meal, told you the truth about your friend, yet you treat me like rubbish. You Liirians; always so damnably secretive."

"Forgive us, Jazana Carr, please," said Breck. "We mean no offense. You have indeed been gracious, and we're in your debt. But the news I bring Lukien is for him alone. We cannot tell you or anyone else."

"Is it about Liiria?" pressed Carr. "About your king, perhaps?"

Breck sighed. "My lady, you may question me all night and day, but I won't tell you what you want to know. And if you have designs on Liiria, then you best keep them to yourself."

Jazana Carr grinned. "Discovered."

Gilwyn sat up in alarm. "Designs on Liiria? You mean to attack, my lady?"

"Oooh, someday. . . ." Jazana Carr smacked her lips as if eating a confection. "Wouldn't that be grand? The greatest jewel on the continent!"

"But you can't," Gilwyn protested. "I mean, how can you?"

"Why else do you think she wanted to see us, Gilwyn?" said Breck. He was remarkably casual, swirling the wine he still hadn't tasted. "She doesn't just need swords against King Lorn. She needs insiders against Liiria. What did I tell you earlier, do you remember?"

Gilwyn had to think for a moment. "You said that all mercenaries are scum."

At last Breck drank from his goblet, toasting, "Exactly."

The insult riled Jazana Carr. She said, "You may think what you wish of me, Sir Breck. You may mistake my ambition for treachery. But I have made a life out of fighting. I started with nothing, one small diamond mine. From that I built an empire, one that even your King Akeela cannot match. While that addle-brained whelp's been spending his money like piss, I've been amassing my riches. And waiting."

"You're indeed impressive, Jazana Carr. And I take it you have King Lorn on the run, too."

"Do not patronize me, sir," she spat. "I have spent my life in the shadows of men like you. Because I am a woman you think me weak, not to be taken seriously. I am like a whore to you, because I crave success. Well, let me tell you something. I can buy anything I wish. See these men that serve me? Dogs, all of them. I throw them meat and they beg for more. Even your precious Lukien. They are the whores, sir, not I."

"Lukien is no whore," said Breck. His voice held a dangerous edge. "If he has become one, then surely you are to blame."

"Whores," said Carr again. "Like all the men that serve me." She gestured to the lute player. "Like that useless musician. I call a tune, he plays it. Why? For money. Men are the whores of the world, Sir Breck. Every last one of them is for sale."

Breck placed his napkin on the table and rose to his feet. "Since Lukien isn't here, I think we'd better go."

"I have not dismissed you!" thundered Carr. "You will sit until I have said my piece!"

Gilwyn didn't move. Nor did Breck, who remained standing. Jazana Carr fought to compose herself, putting her hands to her cheeks.

"You see?" she said. "You see how men madden me? Well, to business, then. Sir Breck, you wish to speak to my servant Lukien. And I wish men to serve me, men who are talented with weapons and have knowledge of Liiria. So we can barter, yes?"

"No, my lady," replied Breck. "I'm not looking for employment."

Jazana Carr took a diamond ring from her finger and tossed it into Breck's plate. "There," she spat, "a first payment. A single gem worth twice whatever rat hole you call a house. The first of many payments if you join me."

Breck didn't even glance at the diamond. "I have a family back in Liiria. I'm not for sale."

"Liar. All men are for sale. Their love is like a rainstorm, here one moment, gone the next. Do not profess love for a wife over your love of money. I have seen how much love means to men, how they buy and sell it."

"Nevertheless," said Breck, picking up the diamond and tossing it back at the woman, "it is true."

This enraged Jazana Carr. She stood up and glared at Gilwyn.

"That monkey. How much?"

"What?" stammered Gilwyn.

"How much for your wretched little pet?"

"I'm sorry, my lady, but Teku's not a pet. She's a friend."

"Friend?" shrieked Carr. "Are you mad? It's not even human!"

"Still, Teku is a friend. She helps me. She fetches things for me that I can't reach with my bad hand."

"Boy, with diamonds you could buy a house full of servants to bring you things. You don't need a stinking monkey!"

Gilwyn was about to speak when a new voice rang through the room.

"You can't buy everything, my dear."

A figure crossed the threshold, a giant of a man dressed in a black leather jerkin and tall black riding boots. He had a face like granite, with a gray-speckled beard and a pair of smoldering eyes. The left sleeve of his snow-white shirt looped up to his shoulder, pinned and armless. The mere sight of him wiped the venom from Jazana Carr's face.

"Thorin," she said excitedly. "You're back."

She went to him at once, forgetting her guests and their argument, throwing her arms around the man and peppering his bearded face with kisses. The man circled his single arm around her waist, drawing her near.

"Rodrik told me we had visitors from Liiria," he said. "I thought I should come at once."

Gilwyn stared at the man, purely fascinated. He wasn't Lukien, surely, yet he had the presence of a hero. His piercing eyes met Gilwyn's.

"You, boy," he boomed. "What's your name?"

Gilwyn could barely find his voice. "My name is Gilwyn Toms."

"Gilwyn Toms," the man repeated. "Well, Toms, I am—"

"Thorin Glass," said Breck. He was still standing, staring at the stranger. "I don't bloody believe it."

"Do you know me, sir?" asked the big man.

Gilwyn looked at Breck in amazement. "Do you, Breck?"

Breck nodded. "I think I do. You're Baron Glass."

The one-armed man grinned. "Ah, now that's a title that no longer applies." He guided Jazana Carr toward the table. She clung to him adoringly. "And you?" he asked. "What's your name?"

"I'm Breck. Baron, I thought you were dead!"

"And I very nearly was, no thanks to your king." The man studied Breck carefully. "Breck you say?"

"You know me, sir. I was a Royal Charger under Captain Lukien."

The man nodded as he recalled the name and face. "Yes," he said softly. "I remember you."

Gilwyn was stupefied. "Baron Glass? But how can that be? Baron Glass died on the Isle of Woe."

"Correction, boy," said the one-armed man. "*Nearly* died."

"But how?" asked Breck. "Sir, this is a shock!"

Jazana Carr led Glass to her giant chair, bidding him to sit. She took her own wine goblet and put it gently into his hand. "Thorin, these two are looking for Lukien."

Glass' face lost his humor. "Lukien? Why?"

"We have a message for him," said Breck. "It's urgent." Then he shook his head, still reeling with astonishment. "I can't believe it. It really is you. How's that possible?"

"You have a thousand questions, I know," said Glass. "And I'll tell you my ugly tale. But first. . . ." He put the goblet to his lips and drank its contents in a long quaff. "Fate above, I'm thirsty. More." Snapping his fingers brought a servant from the corner, who silently refilled his goblet before disappearing. Another servant brought out a chair for Jazana Carr, seating her beside Glass.

"Breck, I'm confused," said Gilwyn. He watched Glass as he spoke, studying him "I thought Baron Glass was banished to Woe."

"He was," said Breck. He, too, kept his eyes on the baron. "First Borior Prison, then the Isle."

"All true," said Glass. "I rotted in Borior for two years until my sentence was up. Then I was to swing from the gallows. Your Queen Cassandra intervened." Glass looked into his wine pensively. "A good woman. I suppose I should be grateful. She thought banishment on Woe was better than death. She couldn't possibly have known the horror on that barren rock."

"But you escaped," said Breck. "How?"

"Lukien," replied Glass. He put down his glass and took Jazana Carr's jeweled hand. The warlady smiled at him, her teeth like sunshine. "He was already in Jazana's employ by then. He heard about my banishment and saved me."

Gilwyn was astonished. "He went to Woe?"

"He did, with a handful of Jazana's men. They hired a ship and a crew that wouldn't talk, thanks to this dear woman." Glass lifted her hand to his lips and kissed it. Jazana Carr melted at the gesture. "It wasn't easy but they found me," he went on. "Half dead I was, a skeleton from my days in Borior and the hot sun of Woe. Fate above, that island's a giant hearth. It ripped the skin right off me."

"And then they brought you here," said Jazana Carr gently. "To me."

"I have Lukien to thank for my life," said Glass. "He rescued me because he's loyal, and because he thought I deserved a better death than the one Akeela had planned for me."

"He always thought highly of you," added Breck with a nod. "He's a remarkable man."

Jazana Carr chuckled. "I have found that all Liirian men are remarkable." Her tongue darted out and playfully licked Glass' ear. "You'd be amazed at what a one-armed man can do in bed."

Glass cleared his throat in embarrassment. "Jazana, stop now."

"Why, sweetling?" she asked, caressing his chest. "They've already guessed we're lovers." She smiled proudly at her guests. "Lukien brought a great prize back from the Isle of Woe."

Glass hurried to change the subject. "And now you're looking for him? Why?"

"We have news for him, Baron Glass," said Gilwyn.

"News we can't share with you," Breck hurried to add.

Jazana Carr's expression turned gloomy again. "You hear? They flaunt their secrets in my face."

"Easy, love," bade Glass. He looked at Breck carefully. "You and the boy have come a long way. Obviously your news is important. But we have trusted you with our identities. Surely you can trust us with your news."

Breck shook his head. "Sorry, Baron, no. What we have to say is for Lukien only. Jazana Carr has already told us he's on his way back here. When he arrives, we'll deliver our message and be on our way."

"And if my hospitality dries up before then?" asked Carr acidly. "What will you do? Rot in the wasteland outside?"

"Jazana, please," said Glass calmly. "No need to threaten. We'll let them stay until Lukien returns."

"Thorin. . . ."

"I owe Lukien a debt, let's not forget. If these two have news for him, then we must treat them as his friends."

Jazana Carr began to smoulder beneath her many gems. Through gritted teeth she said, "As you wish."

Gilwyn had never seen anything like it. Glass' ability to tame her was amazing. "Thank you, my lady," he said, trying to appease her. "We appreciate your hospitality."

"Jazana, why don't you leave us now?" said Glass. "I'd like to catch up with Breck alone, if you don't mind."

Again the anger flashed through Carr's eyes, but only for a moment. She rose from her chair, leaned down and kissed Glass on the forehead. "As you wish."

Gilwyn watched the elegant woman drift out of the chamber without another word, astonished by Glass' power over her. Glass saw the amazement in his face.

"She loves me," he explained. The words came out in a burdensome sigh. "That's why she listens to me."

"I bet you're the only one that can talk to her like that," said Breck.

Glass nodded. "Not even Lukien, though she loves him too, in a way."

"Really?" asked Breck in surprise. "She doesn't seem to care much for men."

"Oh, she's got an appetite for them."

"That's not what I mean," countered Breck.

Glass nodded. "I know what you mean. And you're right. But don't judge her too harshly. Jazana has spent her life in Norvor, remember, and Norvor is not a place that's kind to women. Men have beaten and betrayed her. She doesn't trust them."

"Yet you work for her?" asked Breck.

"In a manner of speaking. She has many men working for her, but none with my experience in military matters. I'm valuable to her, as is Lukien." Before he continued he ordered the servants out of the room, along with the lute player. As the musician retreated, Glass barked, "And close the doors."

Alone at last, Gilwyn relaxed a little. Breck continued shaking his head, still amazed by the baron's presence. Glass poured himself another goblet of wine.

"You're troubled," he said. "I can see it in your eyes."

"You work for her, and yet she plans to attack Liiria someday," said Breck. "Yes, I'm sorry, Baron. That does trouble me."

"But should it really surprise you? After what Akeela did to me? After what he did to Lukien?"

Breck was unmoved. "How long has she been planning this?"

"Forever," said Glass sourly. "Maybe that's why she let Lukien save me, I don't know. But it's why she values me so highly, and why she wants you to join her, Breck. Even the boy, if she can find a use for him."

"But Liiria's too powerful," said Gilwyn. "There's no way she could defeat them, not even with all her riches."

"Don't underestimate her, boy. Jazana is richer than you think, and she's been pushing King Lorn hard these last two years. One day she'll defeat him. And when she does, she'll finally fulfill her use to me."

The statement disgusted Gilwyn. "So you're just using her, then?"

"Like she's using me," sneered Glass. Then he softened, saying, "All right, she loves me. But she knows I'm valuable to her. Would she love me so much otherwise, I wonder?"

"I can't believe it," said Breck sadly. "You've wasted all these years, working with this terrible woman just so you can have your revenge on Akeela? What about your family, Baron?"

"My family is forfeit," said Glass. "They were lost to me the moment Akeela sent me to Borior. How could I ever return to them? Akeela would have them killed. He promised me that, your gracious king. Jazana Carr gives me hope. She's ambitious, but she's also patient. She knows she can't defeat Trager's army, not yet. But once she defeats Lorn—and she will—she'll have a real army to command, and all the riches of Norvor. And then we'll have a chance."

"That's treachery," said Breck.

"It is not!" Glass thundered. "After what Akeela did to me, it is justice!"

"And Lukien?" asked Breck. "He goes along with this?"

"Why shouldn't he? He has a score to settle with Akeela, just as I do."

Gilwyn gave Breck a sideways glance.

"Baron," said Breck carefully, "how much about Lukien do you really know?"

"I know as much as you do, I'm sure," said Glass. "Lukien's love for Cassandra is no secret to me, nor to Jazana Carr."

"And that's all you know?" Breck asked.

Glass looked puzzled. "What else is there?"

Breck shrugged off the question. "Not much. As I said, we've things to discuss with Lukien. Alone."

"And you'll get your chance," said Glass. "I owe that to Lukien. But be warned, both of you—Jazana Carr will not be keen to let you leave, especially now that you know her designs. I can protect you from her because she listens to me, but she can be quite tempting. She'll let you speak to Lukien, but if you try to take him away, there'll be trouble." The baron paused. "Will you take him away?"

"That will be up to him," said Breck.

The answer seemed to satisfy Glass. His one arm reached across the table and dragged a platter of sliced meat toward him. "Then let's eat," he said, "and have no more talk of this until Lukien arrives."

For the next hour Breck and Glass ate and exchanged histories, saying almost nothing about Lukien or the mission that had brought them here. Gilwyn listened to the banter, unable to eat, pensively feeding Teku bits of fruit. He admired Breck's casual calm, but couldn't share it. He was frightened of Jazana Carr and he missed Figgis terribly. More than anything, he wanted to go home.

36

Lukien had taken his time returning to Hanging Man.
Along with Travis and the others, he had ridden out of
Disa the day after the battle—once they had buried their
dead and satisfied themselves that the remains of Colonel
Ness' army had scattered. The forests around Disa were
quiet for the first time in weeks. So Lukien and his fellows
had headed north from Disa at dawn, making their way
deliberately toward Hanging Man but taking the time to
enjoy the peace of the road. Halfway to their destination,
Lukien had sent the others on ahead of him. They had
stopped for the night in a place called Calane, a small farming village with windmills and sheep and acres of rich, pun-
gent soil. The next morning when they were to depart,
Lukien simply couldn't bear another day on the road. He
wanted desperately to remain in the village just a little
while longer, to partake of its simple hospitality and be far
away from soldiers and their talk of battle. Travis and the
others had ridden off without him, assured that he would
follow in a day or so. After enjoying Calane for two more
days, Lukien kept his promise. He paid the family who had
put him up for his brief holiday, then headed north again
toward Hanging Man.

Now alone on the road, Lukien was spared the distractions of his fellow mercenaries. He had time to think.
Mostly he thought of Marke, and how quickly the young
man had died. Lukien had been unable to reach him in

time; Ness had chopped him down like a weed. The image of Marke slumping dead from his saddle haunted Lukien the whole ride home.

Home.

Home to Hanging Man, a fortress. Home to Baron Glass and Jazana Carr and all the comforts diamonds could buy, but not a true home at all. Home was Liiria; Lukien had never forgotten that. Sixteen years had not dulled his hunger for the streets of Koth or the accent of his countrymen. As he rode along a cool, green road, surrounded by summer flowers and chirping birds, Lukien thought of home.

The next day he reached the Bleak Territories, where the roads were rugged and splayed out along rocky hills and gorges. The River Kryss pointed the way north. Lukien followed the waterway, stopping periodically to rest and water his horse. In the whispering desolation of northern Norvor he felt alone in the world, and he relished the experience. Suddenly he was no longer anxious to reach Hanging Man. Suddenly all he wanted to do was to keep riding, perhaps to a place where no one knew his name.

But within a few more hours, Lukien put this daydream to rest. As he rounded a hill along the riverbank, the great turret of Hanging Man appeared on the horizon. The imposing fortress cut a jagged scar against the blue sky. Lukien was glad he'd sent Travis and the others ahead without him, glad that he wouldn't have to explain the battle at Disa to Jazana Carr. She would be happy with the outcome, Lukien was sure, but reciting the bloody details didn't interest him. He wanted a hot bath, a good meal, and his bed, and that was all.

Jazana Carr, however, had other plans. Still more than a mile from the fortress, Lukien caught a glimpse of two riders coming toward him. It did not take long to recognize the warlady or her bodyguard with the blue beret. Jazana Carr's horse was resplendent in flowing golden headgear and flanking skirts. Unlike a real queen, she did not ride sidesaddle but instead galloped out to greet him as though she were a man, her fearlessness buoyed by the skilled swordsman at her side. Rodrik Varl stayed a respectful distance behind Jazana Carr. The sight of the odd pair made Lukien rein back his horse. Over the roar of the river he heard Jazana Carr's call.

"Ryon! Welcome home!"

She could be such a little girl sometimes, Lukien couldn't help but grin. At times like this, when Jazana Carr forget her station and did the most absurd things, it was easy to forget she was a dictator. She waved at him across the brown earth, her long hair streaking out behind her, catching the sunlight in its gray highlights. Behind her, the gates of Hanging Man were open. Men moved casually through its courtyard. These were friends of Lukien's, mostly, and he was glad for the sight of them.

"Ho, Jazana!" Lukien called, raising a hand. He could see Jazana smile at him through the dusty haze, her smile perfect. It was easy to see why Thorin bedded her. The warlady galloped quickly forward, then brought her horse to a stop a few paces away. Rodrik Varl parroted her motion but did not pull alongside her.

"Ryon!" she cried. "We saw you from the keep. We thought we'd come and greet you."

Lukien's smile widened. "Oh? Did you miss me that much, Jazana?"

Jazana Carr trotted her horse closer. "Indeed I did," she said, then leaned over and gave his cheek a hard kiss. "It is never the same in the keep without you, Ryon. You know that."

Lukien took her multijeweled hand, bending low to kiss it. From the corner of his one eye he saw Rodrik glance away. "Is that all, my lady?" he asked coyly. "You've come all this way to greet me, nothing more?"

"Come now, Ryon, you're a fox," said Jazana. "Why shouldn't I miss you so much?"

"Because you always have a gaggle of men around you, and they keep you company well enough," joked Lukien. "Now tell me why you've ridden out, before I start worrying."

"It's a fine day for riding," said Jazana Carr evasively. She spun her horse back toward Hanging Man. "Isn't it, Rodrik?"

"Oh, that it is, my lady," replied Rodrik. He tilted his head toward Lukien. "Ryon."

Lukien returned the small gesture. "Rodrik."

The two rarely exchanged more words than these. There

was a jealousy between Lukien and Rodrik that was good-natured but very real, one that Jazana Carr herself seemed to encourage and enjoy. In his younger days, before he'd lost his eye, Lukien would have been Rodrik's better. But time had changed his opinion of himself. He had seen Rodrik in action and knew that Jazana had chosen a capable bodyguard.

"Jazana, if you have bad news for me I'd prefer to hear it quickly," said Lukien. "Is Thorin all right?"

"Thorin is always all right," said Jazana. "He's waiting for you back at the keep."

"Hmm, but he's not as anxious to see me as you seem to be. Why?"

Jazana turned to Rodrik. "Rodrik, be a dear and ride back without us, will you? I'd like to speak to Ryon alone."

Rodrik Varl lost his customary humor. "Your pardon, my lady, but I'm supposed to protect you, remember? I'll stay with you, if you don't mind."

"But I do mind," said Jazana icily. "Besides. . . ." She gave Lukien an adoring wink. "Who better to guard my person than Ryon? My safety is quite assured."

"As you wish," said Varl, turning and heading back toward Hanging Man. "I'll tell Thorin you'll be home straightaway, then?"

"Thorin is not my keeper!" shouted Jazana Carr after him.

Rodrik Varl chuckled as he rode away. "If you say so, my lady."

Jazana stared at him a moment, her eyes blazing. She had terrible tempers, but somehow Lukien had grown accustomed to them. When Rodrik Varl was safely out of range, he reached over and took the warlady's hand again. It was a good hand for a woman, soft yet strong as iron.

"He baits you, Jazana," he counseled. "Don't let him bother you."

"He doesn't bother me," said Jazana Carr. She turned her face toward him, once again full of sunshine. "Rodrik likes to play. I indulge him, that's all. And he's good enough with his saber to merit his wandering tongue."

"Ah, now you bait *me,* my lady, but I'm in no mood for your games. You've heard the news from Disa?"

"I have. Travis and the others were back two days ago. I shouldn't tell you how cross I was not to see you with them, Ryon."

"But you're pleased, I can tell," said Lukien. He began trotting toward Hanging Man. "It was not an easy victory, Jazana. Did Travis tell you everything?"

"He told me enough. Ride slowly, Ryon, I want to talk to you."

Lukien slowed his gelding. Alongside him, Jazana Carr's golden horse fell into an easy gait. "We're alone, Jazana," he said. "Rodrik can't hear us. Tell me what's troubling you."

The warlady shrugged. "It may be nothing, I don't know yet. Tell me, Ryon, are you glad to be back?"

"Of course," said Lukien. "I'm always glad to come home."

"Are you? When the others returned without you I was worried. Travis said you wanted to be alone."

"Ah, well. . . ." Lukien let his gaze wander toward the hills. "Disa was bloody. I was bothered about Marke. I needed some time to think about things."

"But you are happy here, aren't you?"

"Yes. I would say that I am content."

"And a man could do worse than be content," said Jazana. She smiled up at the blue sky. "What a day, eh? A man could slay a dragon!"

"Yes, lovely," said Lukien.

"It's a fine home, Hanging Man. I've been happy here myself. Thorin, too." The warlady regarded Lukien carefully. "I've tried to make things good for you here, Ryon. You've served me well and I've paid you handsomely for it. You know that don't you?"

"Enough, now, Jazana," said Lukien. "Tell me why you're here."

It took a moment for Jazana to reply. Her lips twisted sourly as she confessed, "There are people waiting for you in the keep. A man and a boy. From Koth."

Lukien stopped his horse midstride. "What?"

"It's true," said Jazana sullenly. "Lukien."

It was the first time in years she'd said his rightful name. Lukien felt a chill.

"Who?" he asked weakly. "Who's come for me?"

"That friend you told me about, Breck. He's got a boy with him. You couldn't know him, though; he's too young."

"Great Fate," whispered Lukien. "Cassandra. . . ."

"Easy," cautioned Jazana Carr. "They wouldn't tell me why they've come. They've already met with Thorin and know who he is. They wouldn't tell him anything, either."

"They're waiting for me at the keep?" asked Lukien anxiously.

Jazana nodded. "We saw you coming. We've all been expecting you."

Lukien didn't waste a moment. He punched his boots into the flanks of his stallion, sending the beast sprinting forward.

"Ryon, wait!" called Jazana.

Driven by panic, Lukien hardly heard her.

Gilwyn sat in a room of open windows, nervously awaiting Lukien's arrival. Sentries had seen the knight approaching from the watchtower, and Baron Glass had told him and Breck the news. Now the three of them waited in an echoing council chamber, idly milling around a giant circular table. Teku sat quietly in Gilwyn's lap, munching on a handful of grapes. Breck's face was tight with anticipation. He sat beside Gilwyn, drumming his fingers on the oak table. Baron Glass stood at one of the many windows, his one hand tightened into a fist behind his back.

As he waited, Gilwyn went over his story in his mind. He was nervous and that irked him, and he knew that the Bronze Knight would want quick answers to his many questions. Gilwyn only hoped that Lukien would believe him. He still had Cassandra's letter, which he supposed was proof enough. Carefully, he laid the letter on the table in front of him.

A few moments later footfalls rang through the hall, approaching the chamber. Breck stood at once. Baron Glass turned from the window and spied the open doors. His head full of worries, Gilwyn sprung to his feet and sent Teku sprawling to the floor, spilling grapes.

"Oh, great," he groaned. Teku shot him a nasty look then began climbing up his leg. Just as she reached his shoulder, a figure appeared on the threshold.

Lukien, the Bronze Knight of Liiria, was a shocking sight.

With his eyepatch and rough skin and thin frame, he looked nothing like the hero Gilwyn had imagined. There were scars on his face and streaks in his hair and gray speckles in his eyebrows.

"I can't believe it," he said. "Breck, it's really you."

"Aye, it's me, Lukien," said Breck. He went to his comrade and put his hands on his shoulders. "Thank the Fate we've found you."

They embraced. Lukien collapsed into Breck's arms, all the strength going out of him. Breck held him, slapping his back and laughing.

"Good to see you, my friend," he said. "You've been missed!"

"Yes," sighed Lukien. "You too." Then suddenly he collected himself. "Cassandra?"

"She's all right," said Breck quickly. "But we have news of her, Lukien."

"We?" Lukien glanced back at Gilwyn. "Who are you?"

Breck waved Gilwyn closer. "This is your messenger, Lukien. His name is Gilwyn Toms."

Gilwyn smiled awkwardly, unsure what to say. "Uhm, hello, Sir Lukien."

Lukien was plainly confused. He looked at Baron Glass for an explanation, but the one-armed man merely shrugged.

"I don't know what their business is with you," said Glass. "They wouldn't tell me and I stopped asking." He moved toward the doors. "I'll leave you to it."

Glass closed the doors behind him. With him gone, Lukien looked even less comfortable. He stood in the middle of the room, bewildered and exhausted.

"Lukien, you should sit," suggested Breck.

He pulled out a chair and guided Lukien toward it. The Bronze Knight sat down, took an unsteady breath, then asked pointedly, "Why are you here?"

"Cassandra sent us," Breck replied. He pulled out two more chairs for himself and Gilwyn. Before going to sit, Gilwyn retrieved the letter from the tabletop. He handed it to Lukien.

"Sir, this is for you," he said. "It's from Queen Cassandra."

Surprised, Lukien took the letter. "She wrote this?"

"She gave it to me to bring to you," Gilwyn explained, "the second time I saw her."

"What?" Lukien sprang from his chair. "You looked at her?"

"Easy, Lukien," said Breck. "Let him explain."

"Did you see her?" Lukien demanded. "Did you look at her?"

"Yes, I did," answered Gilwyn. "But sir, I know about the curse. It's all a hoax."

"Hoax?" Lukien hovered, staring at Gilwyn, then dropped back into the chair. "Hoax?" He studied the letter in his hand. "How . . . ?"

"It's true," said Breck. "Gilwyn Toms lives in the library. Remember Figgis? He's the boy's mentor."

"I remember Figgis all too well," said Lukien. "You work with him, boy?"

"Yes, sir," said Gilwyn.

Lukien pointed with his chin toward Teku. "The monkey, too?"

"In a way." Gilwyn showed Lukien his clubbed hand. "Teku helps me get things. We've both been with Figgis for years now."

"Well, Gilwyn Toms, you've managed to surprise me almost to death. This letter bears the royal seal of Liiria, so it could have only come from Cassandra or Akeela, and I doubt it's from Akeela. But your story makes no sense. It's impossible for you to have seen Cassandra; her curse is no hoax, I assure you."

"But it is, Sir Lukien, I swear," said Gilwyn. "Figgis had it all wrong. I've seen Queen Cassandra with my own eyes!"

Lukien frowned in frustration. "That just can't be. The amulet she wears. . . ."

"The Eye of God; yes, I know about it," said Gilwyn. "She still wears it. She was wearing it when I met her. But there's no curse on it."

"Lukien, you should believe the boy," urged Breck. "He's telling you the truth. He happened upon Cassandra one night by accident. He looked right at her, talked to her."

"More than once," Gilwyn added. "And she's as young and beautiful as when she first put on the amulet. It's amazing, Sir Lukien."

Lukien grimaced at Breck. "You know the whole story, then?"

"At first I didn't believe it," admitted Breck. "But Gilwyn convinced me otherwise."

"And we both know about your trip to Jador with Figgis, too," said Gilwyn. At last he sat down, watching Lukien carefully. "The amulet you brought back for the queen—the Eye of God—it's done its job. It's kept her young and healthy."

"I'm glad for that," said Lukien. The relief on his face was obvious. "But no curse? I can't believe it."

Breck reached out and tapped the letter in Lukien's hand. "Read her note, Lukien. I'm sure it's all in there."

Lukien looked at Gilwyn. "You came all this way because Cassandra needs me," he surmised. "Tell me why."

"Lukien, read the note," Breck repeated.

"I'll read the damn note once you've told me why you're here!" flared Lukien. "Now one of you, please, tell me what Cassandra wants!"

His outburst startled Gilwyn, but Lukien's countenance didn't soften.

"All right," said Breck easily. "I'll let the boy tell you. It's his mission, anyway. Gilwyn?"

Gilwyn didn't know where to begin. "Well, it's like Breck told you," he said. "I met Cassandra one night by accident. That was back when she still thought she was cursed."

"When was this exactly?" asked Lukien.

"About a month ago, I guess."

"Go on."

"Well, it was night when I saw her. She didn't see me that first time, but I arranged to see her again."

"Really? Why'd you do that?"

Gilwyn shifted, embarrassed. "Because I liked her, my lord. I thought she was pretty."

Finally, Lukien smiled. "She still has that effect on men, eh?"

"Yes," Gilwyn replied. "But I didn't know she was the queen, you see. She looked so young, I thought she was my age."

"Gilwyn, get to the important part," said Breck gently.

Lukien put up a hand. "No, let him tell his story." He grinned. "I'm enjoying this."

So Gilwyn continued, carefully recounting all that had happened. To his surprise, Lukien listened quietly as he spoke of his meeting in the garden with Cassandra, and how she had hit her head against the tree limb trying to escape. And when the tale turned to Akeela's madness, Lukien grew pensive. He did not interrupt Gilwyn, though. He didn't utter the smallest sound, not even when Gilwyn told him about the second Eye of God.

"Now Akeela's after the other amulet," said Gilwyn. "Figgis told him it's in Grimhold. He's raising an army with General Trager to find it. He wants to live with Cassandra forever, Sir Lukien, and he thinks the amulet will let him."

"And Cassandra hasn't told him about the curse?" asked Lukien. "Akeela still thinks it's real?"

"Yes," said Gilwyn. "She's afraid to tell him. If she does, then he'll. . . ." Gilwyn stopped himself. "Well, you know."

"Come to her bedroom," said Lukien. "But the other Eye isn't in Grimhold? You said you saw it in Koth?"

"That's right," said Gilwyn. "At least I think I saw it. I told Figgis what I'd seen, and he's convinced the Witch of Grimhold has it. He believes she really exists."

"So why is she in Koth, then?" asked Lukien.

Gilwyn shrugged. "We don't know. But Figgis didn't tell Akeela about her. He was afraid of what the king would do if he found out the Witch was in Koth."

"He'd tear the city apart looking for her, Lukien," said Breck. "I'm sorry to say, he's not the same man he used to be. Ever since you left—"

"I was banished, Breck," spat Lukien. "I didn't *leave.*"

Breck merely nodded. A sudden silence overspread the chamber. Gilwyn stroked Teku's neck, wondering what he could say to put the miserable knight at ease. He had hoped that Lukien would be pleased at the news of Cassandra's well-being, but bringing up her name had only stirred a cauldron of bad memories.

"My poor friend," whispered Lukien. "I'm sorry that Akeela's gone so mad. I still blame myself for that sometimes. I betrayed him. I've had a lot of time to think about it, and I know what I did was wrong. I knew it even back then, but it didn't stop me." He looked at Breck for reassurance. "I loved Cassandra. I still do."

"Is that why you're partnered with Jazana Carr?" asked Breck.

Lukien frowned. "What do you know about that?"

"We know enough," said Breck. "You're in league with her, you and Glass both. She's planning to invade Liiria someday, and you intend to be right there by her side."

"A dream," scoffed Lukien. "Jazana Carr's been talking about it for years, and she's never done a thing about it."

"Baron Glass says otherwise," said Breck. "He says that Carr is close to defeating King Lorn, and that when she does she'll turn her appetites toward Liiria." He was ruthless in his accusations, barely giving Lukien room to escape. "I'd rather you didn't deny it, Lukien. I'd rather you just admit your treachery."

"Treachery?" Lukien laughed. "You can call it that if you like, old friend, but you weren't the one sent away from his homeland. Akeela let you retire, remember? He gave you a farm and promised to forget your association with me. He let you *live.*" With a grunt of disdain he rose and went to one of the many windows. "Was I granted any of his famous mercy? No. Instead he banished me, practically a death sentence. If it wasn't for Jazana Carr, he'd have gotten his wish."

"You betrayed him, Lukien," Breck reminded. "You said so yourself."

"Both of you, stop, please," said Gilwyn. He lifted himself awkwardly from his chair and stood between them like an official at a tourney. "You can argue all day, but none of this matters anymore. Forget the past. We have to figure out what we're going to do."

"You still haven't told me what Cassandra wants from me, boy," said Lukien. Then he added sourly, "Though I suppose I can guess."

"Cassandra wants you to come back for her," said Gilwyn. "She wants you to take her away from Lionkeep and keep her safe from King Akeela. Then you can ride to Jador and warn them about the invasion." Gilwyn grinned. "Simple."

"Oh, yes," said Lukien bitterly. "All in a day's work for the great Bronze Knight."

Breck got out of his chair. "Lukien, we need you. Cassandra needs you. Great Fate, you said you love her! Won't you help us?"

Outside, the sun was hot on the rocks of Norvor. It dappled the rugged landscape, holding Lukien's attention. When at last he answered, his voice was soft.

"This is the only home I've known for sixteen years now. Jazana Carr may not be perfect, but she always accepted me. Now you're asking me to betray her. Believe it or not, it's not that easy."

Gilwyn stepped closer. "If you don't help us, Cassandra may die. I can't take her out of Lionkeep by myself, and neither can Breck. She needs you to protect her, Sir Lukien. And the Jadori need you, too."

"The Jadori! Now there's a people I'd like to forget."

"I know what happened with them," said Gilwyn. "I know how you killed their queen to get the amulet."

Lukien seemed shocked by this. "Figgis told you about that, too?"

"Yes," said Gilwyn. "To be honest, he wanted me to remind you about it. He hoped it might convince you to help them. Something about owing them a debt."

"That old man is a devious bastard," said Lukien with a grin. "But he's right. I do owe the Jadori a debt. And it's plagued me for years."

"Well, then maybe you'll help us," said Gilwyn. "Or maybe the letter will convince you."

"Yes, Lukien, read the blasted letter," said Breck. "Stop dallying over it, for Fate's sake. We haven't the time for—"

"No," said Gilwyn, gently interrupting. "Please, Breck. I think we've given Lukien enough to think about. Sir Lukien, Cassandra told me that you're a man of principles. And me—I'm just a kid. I can't force you to help us. I've delivered my message. I've done my part. The rest is up to you."

Satisfied, Gilwyn turned and limped from the room. He did not look back, not even to see Breck's stunned expression. As he left, a little smile crept over his face. He was proud of the way he'd handled Lukien, sure he'd laid on the guilt in just the right amount.

Working with Figgis had taught him a lot.

* * *

Lukien remained in the council chamber for another hour. Breck had not stayed with him; the old friends had nothing more to say to each other. When he was sure that he was alone and would not be interrupted, Lukien sat down in one of the dozen chairs and opened Cassandra's note. Seeing the gentle penmanship erased all his doubts. Cassandra's lilting style was as memorable to him as her voice or flawless face. And when he read her words, Lukien wept.

He had not wept for years, not when he lost his eye or saw comrades die in battle. Even when he'd been banished he had not wept, for to weep like a woman was a sure weakness and the toothy jackals of Norvor would have devoured him. But he wept now because he could not help himself. His past deluged him.

Cassandra had been succinct in her note. She had quickly confirmed everything Gilwyn Toms had told him, how she was still young and how the amulet's curse had been a horrible jest and how Akeela still longed to be with her. He was mad, Cassandra said, and his madness might mean the doom of the Jadori. Unless, of course, he helped her.

Strong as always, Cassandra had not stooped to begging in her letter. She had *asked* Lukien to come to her. But only if his love for her was still alive. If not, she claimed, she would be unable to face him.

Come and I will know you love me, read the note.

Lukien read those same words over and over, amazed that she had harbored love for him these many years. He hadn't thought himself worthy of such loyalty.

By the end of an hour he had stopped weeping. Thankfully, he had composed himself by the time Thorin Glass opened the door. The old Liirian poked his head inside the room. Spotting Lukien seated by a window, he announced himself very softly.

"Ryon, it's me. May I come in?"

Lukien nodded. "Close the door behind you."

Thorin did as he asked, shutting the big door quietly before drifting over to the window. He saw the note in Lukien's hand and immediately guessed at its contents.

"From Cassandra?"

Again a nod. "She wants me to come back for her, Thorin. All this time, the curse has been a hoax."

"So they did know about it, then," said Thorin. "I

thought they might, but they wouldn't tell me. Nor did I tell them what I know."

Lukien handed the note to his old ally. A long time ago, he had told Thorin Glass everything about Cassandra, including the remarkable tale of the Eyes of God. It took a while for the baron to read the note, so surprised was he by its contents. When he was done he simply lowered the note and gazed at Lukien.

"What will you do?"

"Go to her," said Lukien. The answer came without hesitation. "She needs me and so do the Jadori."

"You're certain? The letter speaks of Grimhold, Ryon. This may all be some wildness of Akeela's mind, some symptom of his madness."

"No, I don't think so. Akeela may be mad but Figgis surely isn't. You don't know him, Thorin. He was a brilliant man and I trusted him. I trust Breck, as well. If they believe this tale, then there's truth to it." Lukien folded the letter and put it into his shirt. "I'm going."

"Then I'm going with you," said Thorin.

Surprised, Lukien looked up at the older man. "You can't."

Thorin sneered, "I don't take orders from you, remember?"

"Thorin, there's no reason for you to take this risk. You don't owe the Jadori anything."

"No," agreed Thorin Glass, "but I owe you my life. That's a debt I've never been able to repay until now. So don't argue with me, Ryon. You need my help and I'm going. And if you say I'm too old I will poke out your other eye!"

Lukien laughed. "A one-armed baron and a half-blind knight, led by a crippled boy. Great Fate, help us!" He rose and faced Glass, grateful to have his aid. "You're right, I will need your help. But remember, Thorin, we're outlaws in Liiria. If Akeela or Trager or anyone else discovers us, we're dead."

"I've been dead before," said Glass with a shrug.

"And what of Jazana Carr? Doesn't she frighten you?"

Glass grimaced. "I admit, that will be more difficult."

"She loves you, Thorin." Lukien grinned at his friend. "Don't ask me why, but she does. If you leave her. . . ."

"I'll handle Jazana," said Glass. "When do we leave?"

"Well, there's no time to waste. We'll have to leave tomorrow or the next day. But Jazana—"

"I told you, I'll handle her," Glass repeated. He was all sobriety suddenly, the same grim man who'd once led the House of Dukes. "You tell Breck and the boy about your decision. I'll tell Jazana."

"When?" asked Lukien.

Baron Glass headed for the door. "Right now, Ryon."

"Thorin, wait," Lukien called after him. When Glass paused to face him, he said, "Don't call me Ryon anymore. From now on, my name is Lukien."

37

Jazana Carr hadn't always been wealthy. She was the only child in a family that wanted sons, a family that struggled until her father had staked his claim to a small diamond mine thirty years ago. Until then, the Carr family had enjoyed very little. Northern Norvor was a rugged place, and the Bleak Territories were infamous for fickle weather and failed farms. Gorin Carr, Jazana's father, had lost his little farm to the whims of a Norvan drought. Finally driven to madness by deprivation, he had murdered the rightful owner of his little diamond mine and used the proceeds to buy protection. It was the first time Jazana had heard the word "mercenary," and she had learned it well. Finally, there had been food on the table and the chance at a future. But there were still no sons.

When Jazana Carr was fourteen, her mother died. Her father, an ugly man by any standard, did not turn to other women to satisfy his lusts. He had a budding daughter at home and that was enough for him. Jazana Carr didn't know the word rape then, but she learned its meaning nonetheless. She endured her father's bed for three gruesome years, never telling anyone and barely acknowledging the gnawing shame within her. But by seventeen she was a grown woman and had gathered the courage to refuse her father's demands. He had never touched her again, never spoke of it nor apologized nor made good for his acts in any way. She was a daughter, he reminded her, a powerless woman. Without a man, she was useless and unable to make her way in a world ruled by his kind.

By the age of twenty-one, Jazana Carr was finally free of him. Gorin Carr was dead from a gangrenous wound he'd gotten while hunting, and Jazana was his only heir. The diamond mine was hers, and Jazana Carr squeezed every last gemstone from it. She used her workers like slaves and built a tidy fortune from their efforts, hoarding the small diamonds they chiseled from the earth until she had enough to expand her empire. She brought another mine and then another, and in time she grew wealthy. And in those years she had a string of lovers, men she knew were attracted to her wealth and comely body, but who never lasted long. They were Norvan men, too proud to bow to a woman. They had tried to wrest control of the gem mines from Jazana, and when she refused they had left her. One by one, they disappeared.

Thorin Glass knew the sad history of Jazana Carr like an old lullaby. She had told him her tale shortly after they'd met and had been repeating it ever since. It was utmost on his mind when he went to speak with her. He knew she'd be hurt by his leaving; he hoped she wouldn't cry. He loved Jazana but she could be so emotional at times. . . .

He found her where he expected, in the stables with her horse, Wolfsbane, a beautiful stallion that was Jazana's pride and joy. Like a lot of males, Wolfsbane was spirited but Jazana's crop kept him in line. Except for Jazana the stable was empty. Thankfully, Rodrik was nowhere to be found. As Glass entered the stable he found Jazana in Wolfsbane's stall, absently brushing his splendid chestnut coat. She had her back turned to him and seemed to be brooding. Her hand moved over the horse in long, deliberate strokes. A strong scent of hay permeated the air but Glass could still smell Jazana's perfume. She looked beautiful, even amidst the hay and musty wood.

"I've been waiting for you," she said suddenly, not turning to face him. "When you sneak up on me I know you have bad news. He's leaving, then?"

Glass walked up to her. "Yes."

Jazana paused. Her shoulders slumped and the brush dropped to the ground. "Damn him."

"It's for Cassandra," Glass explained. He had never told

Jazana everything about the queen, and was careful now. "She sent a letter for Lukien. She wants him to come back."

"After all these years?"

"You knew it could happen someday, Jazana." Glass bent down and picked up the brush. Handing it to her, he said, "We've talked about this. You said Lukien could go any time he wished."

"Thanks for reminding me," hissed Jazana, snatching the brush from his hand. She went back to grooming. "After all I've done for him, this is how he repays me. Did you at least try to talk him out of it?"

Glass steeled himself. "I'm going with him, Jazana."

This time, Jazana Carr was still as stone. She didn't drop the brush. She didn't move a hair.

"I have to," said Glass quickly. "I owe—"

She turned like an adder and tossed the brush at him. "You're going with him?"

Glass held his ground. "I am."

"You're not."

"I *am*." Glass didn't blink. "You can't talk me out of it, Jazana. I've made up my mind. Lukien needs me. I owe him my life."

"You owe *him?*" asked Jazana, flabbergasted. "What about me, Thorin? What about us?"

"There is still us, Jazana." Glass reached out and touched her cheek. "When I'm done with this—"

Jazana swatted his hand away. "When you're done with this you'll be dead! You're an old man, Thorin. And if Akeela finds you he'll skin you alive."

"That's a chance I have to take," said Glass. He tried to smile at her, to make her understand. "I can't let Lukien go alone, not after he risked his life saving me from Woe. I'm a man, Jazana. You can't expect me to ignore my responsibilities."

"Oh, yes, a man," sneered Jazana. "What about your responsibilities to me? What about all we've worked for? I thought you wanted revenge on Akeela. Who else can give you that, eh? Only me!"

"It doesn't matter. We can still do those things, after I help Lukien."

"Doesn't matter?" Jazana turned away and drifted toward

the stable gate. "Have you any idea how many times I've heard those words from men? Nothing matters to any of you. Not even love."

Glass went after her. "I do love you, Jazana."

"No. You love my money and my body and what I can do for you. If you loved me you'd stay. If you loved me you wouldn't make me beg like this!" Frustrated tears began running down Jazana's cheeks. "I forbid you to go," she spat. "You hear? I forbid it!"

Very carefully, Glass looked at her and said, "Jazana, I'm not your servant. I am Baron Glass of Koth. No one rules me."

"I do!"

"You don't," said Glass, growing angry.

"Dog!"

Glass snapped. His hand shot out and slapped her face. Jazana stumbled back, her face contorting, tears flowing in hot streaks. She looked about to spring on him, but checked herself. Instead she straightened like a monarch.

"Go," she said, her voice breaking. "Be gone by the morning."

"Jazana, I—"

"*Go!*" she cried. "But know this, Thorin—you're not welcome here ever again. When you're done with your little quest, there'll be no home for you in Hanging Man. And not in Liiria, either. I'm going to take Liiria someday, and when I do I'm going to find that family of yours. And I'm going to kill them."

Glass couldn't believe her threat. "Don't say that. Don't ever say that."

"Go ahead, Thorin, leave," challenged Jazana. She wiped her tears with her sleeve. "You don't believe I can conquer Liiria? You think your family is safe from me?"

"Stop, Jazana. . . ."

"In a year I'll have King Lorn on his knees. And then it's Akeela's turn." Jazana's face turned the color of bruised fruit. "I'll do it just to spite you, Thorin. I'll do it just to prove what I can do!"

There was no arguing—Glass knew she was beyond reason. And now her threats had slammed the door on him. There was no way he could relent.

"I leave in the morning with Lukien," he said. "Don't try to stop us. If you do, there'll be trouble."

Jazana laughed through her tears. "Don't flatter yourself, old man. I can find another lover. One with both arms!"

"And don't you dare harm my wife or children," Glass warned. He stepped directly into her face, summoning all his thunder. "If anything happens to them, anything at all, I'm going to blame you, Jazana Carr. And nothing in the world will save you from me."

They stayed that way for a long moment, staring at each other, on the verge of blows. Glass could feel the coiled rage in Jazana, how she longed to rake her polished nails across his face. But she did nothing. She said not a word.

And Baron Thorin Glass knew there was nothing left for him to say, either. Shaking with anger, he turned from the woman he professed to love and strode from the stable.

38

After four days of ceaseless travel, Lukien and Gilwyn finally arrived in Koth. The homecoming left the Bronze Knight speechless. It was nearing dusk and the city was darkening. Shadows grew in the avenues. Lukien scanned the skyline of his forlorn home, awed by it. It had changed in the sixteen years since he'd left, but it was unmistakably home.

"Koth," he whispered. From the confines of his cowl he could barely see Gilwyn in the wagon next to him. The disguise had done a good job of keeping away the curious, and Lukien suspected that no one would have recognized him anyway. During the four day ride north they had stopped only once to speak with other travelers, and Lukien had hidden from them behind his hood, pretending to rummage through the wagon for supplies. But the biggest test was yet to come.

"Look there, Lukien, on the hill." Gilwyn pointed toward a tor in the distance, a huge overlook dominated by a single, remarkable structure. "See it?"

Lukien saw it easily. The great library was like a beacon, shining on its hill for all to see. Even in Norvor Lukien had heard stories of the place, but he had never seen it. It had been one of his greatest regrets about leaving the city, that and losing Cassandra. Now he stared at it, unblinking. Akeela's great dreams of the past rushed at him.

"What a shame," he whispered.

"What is?" Gilwyn queried.

Lukien didn't answer. He couldn't explain all that Akeela had dreamed, not even to a bright boy like Gilwyn. "We should get going," he said. "I'm anxious to see Figgis."

He snapped the reins and sent Tempest on his way again, driving the old horse toward the east side of the city. Around them, the old constructs of Koth rose up like bad memories, crowded with people and the familiar accent of city folk. Skirting along the perimeter of Koth was the quickest route to the library, and allowed Lukien a safe view of his former home. In the distance, he could see the ruins of Chancellery Square, now abandoned but for the barracks and headquarters Trager had built. It was garish and impressive, and it frightened Lukien to see all that his nemesis had accomplished. Trager was a general now, leader of the Royal Chargers and all the Liirian military. There were no more chancellors to question his orders. According to Gilwyn, not even Akeela contradicted him. He had gotten what he'd always wanted, and the thought curdled Lukien's homecoming. Had Thorin been with him, Lukien knew that he, too, would be sickened by the sight of the demolished House of Dukes. But Thorin and Breck had left them earlier in the day, heading north toward Borath and the safety of Breck's farm. If all went well, they would meet them there in a day or so with Cassandra.

"I think you should put Teku in your lap," Lukien cautioned. "We don't want to draw attention to ourselves."

"Don't worry," said Gilwyn. "No one knows me around here."

"No? Even with that monkey with you?"

Gilwyn shook his head. "I don't really get out of the library much." He coaxed Teku down into his lap. "The only people I meet are scholars, and they don't stick around or talk to me."

"Now that is a shame," said Lukien. He hadn't talked much to Gilwyn himself the last few days and was starting to regret it. "A boy your age should get out and be with friends. Run and play."

Gilwyn turned and frowned at him. Lukien felt his face flush.

"Sorry," he offered. "I forgot." Then he studied Gilwyn's clubbed hand a moment more, adding, "But you seem to get along very well, even with your problems. And that shoe . . . did Figgis make it for you?"

"Yes," said Gilwyn. "How did you know?"

"Who else would make such a thing? Your mentor is a genius, boy."

Gilwyn nodded. "I know. I miss him. I hope he's all right."

"I just hope he has good news for us," said Lukien. From their place in the street he could see only the tops of the buildings in Chancellery Square, so he didn't know if Trager's army was still on the parade ground. Perhaps they'd already left for Jador. Perhaps they were too late to warn the Jadori. He took solace in the coming darkness though, knowing that even if Trager were around, he wouldn't recognize his old captain. "Tell me something, Gilwyn—is this where you saw the witch of Grimhold?"

"No, that was on the other side of the city," said Gilwyn. "Koth has some bad areas now. I probably shouldn't have gone."

"But she saved you," Lukien mused. "Curious."

Gilwyn didn't answer, for just then another wagon crossed them in the street, coming close enough to overhear. Lukien hurried Tempest past them, toward the waiting library. As the road gradually rose, the crowds thinned and the shops grew farther apart, until finally they were alone on an avenue of trees and wildflowers. A breeze stirred the leaves and the cowl of Lukien's cloak. Up ahead loomed the library, its twin doors of dark wood shut tight. There were dozens of windows to the place, but only a few rooms in the main tower were lit, rooms that Lukien supposed belonged to Figgis. Yet even in dusk the library was not an eerie place. It was beautiful, full of clarity. Lukien wondered for a moment if he'd ever seen such a lovely structure, for even Lionkeep was marred by its status as a fortress. Not so the great library. There were no ramparts or battlements or dentate gates, only sweeping arches and clean limestone and a gracefully turned tower, all constructed to invite learning. It was just as Akeela had promised, just as he'd envisioned before his dementia.

"Where now?" Lukien asked. "Those doors?"

"That's the main way in," Gilwyn replied. Tempest came

to a dutiful stop at the doors, and Gilwyn and his monkey climbed out of the wagon with some effort as the boy favored his bad foot. Lukien watched but offered no help. Something told him Gilwyn preferred to do everything himself.

"I hope your master is expecting us," he said as he got out of the wagon. Around him, the sounds of the city filled the emptiness like the buzzing of insects, but there was no sound from the library. He went to the door and tried to pull it open. "Locked," he said, dismayed.

"I have a key," said Gilwyn, which he produced after rummaging through his pockets.

"Why's it locked?" asked Lukien. "I thought the library was opened to everyone."

Gilwyn fit the key into its hole. "It is, usually. But it's been closed since Akeela found out about Grimhold. I told you, he's had Figgis working like a madman." He turned the tumbler until it clicked. As he pushed open the door he said, "Try to be quiet. We don't want to run into Della."

"Della?"

"The housekeeper," Gilwyn said. "Nice lady, but nosy."

He pushed open the door, and Lukien instantly forgot his questions. The beauty of the main hall rushed at them, revealing a shimmering interior of torchlight and polished wood. A barrel-vaulted ceiling hung overhead, decorated with stout beams and iron chandeliers. Lukien looked down the tunnel of the hallway to the vast chamber beckoning beyond, a field full of bookcases stuffed with countless manuscripts. He followed Gilwyn over the threshold and into the hall, his breath catching at the awesome sight of so many books.

"Amazing . . ." Slowly he scanned the distant shelves. "I didn't think there were this many books in the world!"

Gilwyn laughed and closed the door behind him. "That's just some of them. There's a whole other wing."

"And you know them all?" asked Lukien incredulously. "I mean, you know where everything is?"

"Figgis has a catalog that keeps everything organized," said Gilwyn. "But yes, I remember a lot of it. All the books are specially arranged, you see. Subject, dates, that sort of thing."

Lukien was awestruck. He drifted toward the waiting books, but was suddenly startled by a figure rounding the corner.

"Oh!" cried the woman, putting her hand to her chest in fright. Her eyes darted between Lukien and Gilwyn, then suddenly relaxed. "Gilwyn! I thought I heard someone come in. Welcome home!"

"Thank you, Della," said Gilwyn. He swallowed nervously. Lukien froze, trying not to seem conspicuous. The old woman looked at him, confused.

"I just got back," Gilwyn continued. "The door was locked so I let myself in."

Mistress Della stayed focused on Lukien as she asked, "Were you able to find the books Figgis wanted?"

"Oh, yes," said Gilwyn easily. "No problem. They're out in the wagon."

"And you've brought a guest, I see." The woman smiled, but Lukien couldn't tell if it were welcoming or not. "Shouldn't you make introductions, Gilwyn?"

"Yes, absolutely," fumbled Gilwyn. "Mistress Della, this is Ryon."

"From Marn?" the housekeeper asked.

"Marn?" replied Lukien.

The lady looked at Gilwyn. "You did go to Marn, didn't you?"

"Oh, *Marn*," said Lukien. "Yes, I'm from Marn. Well, around Marn. The outskirts, actually."

Gilwyn hurried to change the subject. "Um, is Figgis around? I'd like to see him, show him the books we brought back."

Mistress Della was still studying Lukien. "I must say, you don't look like a scholar."

"Ah, you must get all sorts here, dear lady," said Lukien with a smile. "And I must admit I look atrocious from the road. Forgive my appearance."

"Oh, yes, the road. Terrible." Gilwyn took Lukien's arm and led him away. "Mistress Della, is Figgis in his study?"

"He's—" Mistress Della stopped herself with a smile. Ahead of them, Lukien saw another figure drift into the hallway.

An old man in wrinkled clothes stood there, staring in

disbelief. Lukien knew at once it was Figgis. He looked older, grayer, and more withered than ever, but the eyes betrayed the old wisdom and the face was decidedly friendly. Lukien grinned, stepping toward him, but was immediately cut off by Gilwyn.

"Figgis, hello," said the boy suddenly. "This is Ryon, the scholar I told you about."

Figgis didn't miss a beat. "Greetings, Ryon," he said with a smile. "I'm glad you could make it."

Lukien gave his old companion a secret smile. "Me too."

"Uh, Mistress Della, do you think you could make us some tea?" Figgis asked. "It's been a long ride from Marn and I'm sure Gilwyn and Ryon are tired."

"Of course," said the housekeeper. "Welcome to our home, Ryon. We'll try to make you as comfortable as we can. Will you be staying long?"

"No, I shouldn't think so," said Lukien. "But thank you, Mistress Della. You're very kind."

"Go and make that tea now, please," said Figgis, shooing her away. He directed Lukien toward another hall. "We can talk in my study, Ryon. Gilwyn, why don't you come with us?"

"I'll have the tea ready straight away," said Mistress Della, then disappeared down an opposite corridor.

Figgis led the way silently toward his study, not looking back or saying a word until he was sure the housekeeper was out of sight. Then he paused, leaned against a wall, and let loose a giant smile.

"It's you," he sighed. "I can't believe it!"

"Nor can I, old friend," said Lukien, thrusting out a hand. "It's good to see you, Figgis."

Figgis took his hand and shook it vigorously. "You look so different, I hardly recognized you! And that eyepatch . . . a disguise?"

"Alas, I wish it were. It's the real thing I'm afraid."

The old man's exuberance dimmed a little. "I'm sorry. It must have been very hard for you. Breck's wife came and gave me a letter from him. It said you were in Norvor."

"That's right," said Lukien. "Not the most gentle place in the world, I'm afraid."

Figgis turned to Gilwyn and gave him a hug. "Norvor!

When I heard where you'd gone I was beside myself!" He released his embrace and gave the boy a worried inspection. "Are you all right? You weren't hurt or anything?"

"I'm fine, Figgis," said Gilwyn. "We found Lukien and came back as quickly as we could. Breck came back with us. He's waiting for us back at his farm with Baron Glass."

"Who?"

"Baron Glass," said Lukien seriously. "Figgis, he was with me in Norvor."

"Baron Glass? But he's dead!"

"No, Figgis, he's not," said Gilwyn. "I met him. He was with Lukien in Norvor, fighting with Jazana Carr."

"Jazana . . ." Figgis shook his head and sighed. "You'd better tell me all about it. But not here. I don't want Della to overhear. Come."

Knowing the way to Figgis' study Gilwyn went first, apparently giving Lukien and Figgis space to get reacquainted. Lukien wasted no time in asking about Cassandra.

"I have to know, Figgis—is Cassandra all right?"

"Near as I can tell, yes. But wait; I'll tell you all about it in the study."

The study, Lukien quickly learned, was a small room made even more cramped by the stacks of books and manuscripts littering the desk and floor. There were two chairs, one for the desk, the other piled with books. Figgis removed these and set them aside in one of the few bare spaces on the floor, then bade Lukien to sit. Gilwyn propped himself comfortably on the edge of the desk. Along the walls, dusty shelves bowed with the weight of fat books. Figgis lowered himself down in his own chair. The leather groaned as he fell into it.

"Tell me about Glass," he said at once. "He's still alive, you say?"

"Alive and well." Lukien quickly explained how he had saved Glass from the Isle of Woe, and how they had been in Jazana Carr's employ ever since. The tale fascinated Figgis.

"Amazing. And Jazana Carr—she treated you well?"

"Well enough," said Lukien. He didn't want to tell too much about the warlady, because somehow it felt like betrayal. "I fought her battles for her and Thorin made her strategies."

"Thorin?"

"Baron Glass. He was close with Jazana Carr. We both were." Lukien paused, noticing Gilwyn's uneasiness. He decided to skip the part about Thorin and Jazana being lovers, and about the warlady's plans for Liiria. "Glass returned with me because he owes me a debt," Lukien added. "He didn't have to but I'm grateful for it. I'm going to need all the help I can get. Now, tell me about Cassandra."

Before Figgis could answer, Mistress Della pushed open the door. In her hands was a tray of steaming tea and cups.

"Here you are," she said cheerfully. "Gilwyn, I brought some of your favorite biscuits." She looked around, frowning at the state of the room. "Look at this place! Why don't you all come into the kitchen and eat properly?"

Figgis groaned and took the tray from her. "Really, this is fine. Thank you, Mistress Della."

The housekeeper huffed. "Whatever you say. Gilwyn, you're welcome to come into the kitchen when you're done here. I'll fix you something nice." She smiled at Lukien. "Your friend, too."

"What about me?" asked Figgis crossly.

"Drink your tea, old man," said the housekeeper, then turned and left the room. The grin on her face told Lukien she enjoyed teasing Figgis.

"Well, Figgis?" he asked when the woman was gone. "What about Cassandra?"

"She's well, or at least I think she is," said Figgis. "It's hard to tell. I haven't heard anything from her since Gilwyn left to find you. I haven't heard from anyone."

"Not even Lady Jancis?" asked Gilwyn. He cleared some clutter from the desk so Figgis could lower the tray.

"No, not Jancis, not anyone," said Figgis. "I think Akeela's growing suspicious. And Trager's been keeping a tight rein on things."

"So they haven't left for Jador yet?" asked Lukien hopefully.

"No, not yet, but soon." Figgis looked grave as he sat back down in his chair. "Trager is planning to set out in two days."

"Two days? You're sure?"

Figgis nodded. "That's what Akeela told me. He sent a

messenger to the library yesterday, telling me to hurry up with my information because he's leaving in two days, with or without my help."

"He knows you're stalling," Gilwyn guessed. He took two biscuits from the tray, giving one to Teku and sampling the other himself.

"He knows my opposition," agreed Figgis. "I haven't been giving him any new details about Jador or Grimhold, mostly because I haven't found any. But Akeela's impatient and Trager's army is all but ready to march." He looked apologetically at Lukien. "I'm sorry, Lukien. I can't stop him."

"Then we haven't much time," said Lukien. "We have to get Cassandra out of Lionkeep as soon as we can. Tonight, if possible."

Figgis grimaced. "It's not going to be easy. There's something I haven't told you yet."

"What?" asked Lukien.

"Gilwyn, this is hard for me to tell you," said Figgis. He reached out and gently touched the boy's hand. "Warden Graig is dead."

Gilwyn's face collapsed. "Dead? No!"

"He slipped and fell on some wine," said Figgis. "Broke his neck."

"I can't believe it," said Gilwyn. "When did this happen?"

"A day or two after you left, at night." Figgis shook his head, sighing. "Seems like a stupid way for a man to die."

Gilwyn gave his mentor a comforting smile. "He was old, Figgis. Old bones break easy."

"What a shame," said Lukien, saddened by the news. In the days before his banishment, he'd been close with Graig. He'd even hoped, perhaps foolishly, to see the Head Warden again someday. "But Gilwyn's right, Figgis. If you take a bad fall and your bones can't take it, well. . . ."

"That's not it," said Figgis absently. "I know Graig was old. It just seems a bit odd, the way he died. I know he had some trouble getting around lately, but he wasn't a clumsy man."

"What are you saying?" asked Lukien. "You think something else happened to him?"

"Not just me," said Figgis. "You know how the wardens hate Trager. Some of them think he had Graig killed."

Gilwyn laughed at the idea. "That's ridiculous."

"Is it?" asked Figgis. "Lukien, you know how jealous Trager always has been. He hates anyone with access to Akeela. With Graig out of the way, he'd have one fewer person to contend with."

The notion was dismaying. Lukien thought about it for a moment, knowing full well the atrocities Trager was capable of committing. But murder?

"I don't know," he said, shaking his head. "Maybe Graig really did slip and fall."

"Maybe," said Figgis. "But the wardens have been on guard since Graig died. They're not letting anyone into Lionkeep without checking them completely first. There's just no way to get a message to Cassandra."

"There has to be a way," Lukien insisted. "I've come too far to be deterred now."

"You can't just walk into Lionkeep and take her, Lukien," said Figgis.

"No, but I wasn't expecting to do that," replied Lukien, losing patience. "I expected you to have some ideas when I got here! Haven't you at least thought about it?"

"Don't bark at me," said Figgis, getting out of his chair. "I've been a little busy trying to come up with a way to keep Akeela from invading Jador! And how was I supposed to know you'd actually show up? You were gone for sixteen years!"

Lukien groaned. "Great."

"Wait," said Gilwyn. "Maybe the two of you haven't considered a way to get Cassandra out of Lionkeep, but I have." Smiling, he gave his simian companion another biscuit.

After another uneventful night in her chambers, Cassandra retired early to her bedroom.

Since her astonishing meeting with Gilwyn two weeks ago, she had once again been forced into the prison of her own home, unable to touch the outside world. Her two brief encounters with the boy had made her hunger for more, yet she knew she could not risk it. So she resigned herself to waiting, not even attempting to contact Figgis at the library to see what—if anything—was happening. Akeela had come to her only seldom over the subsequent days, mostly to torment her with updates on his progress. As the time for his march on Jador drew nearer, he became more and more aloof and moody, more subtly cruel to her. He had not been the same since their argument when he'd torn the curtain between them. His moments of kindness were fewer now. She could hear the growing agitation in his voice, how impatient he was to find the other amulet. In two more days he would leave, he had told her yesterday. And when he returned he would have the fabled other Eye. No more did he speak of it as a loving promise, though. Now he threatened her with it.

This night, however, Akeela had not come to her bedroom, and Cassandra was glad. She had begun to lose faith in her wild scheme to find Lukien, and now hoped only that Akeela would leave for Jador and that his mad quest would kill him. Surprisingly, her ill wishes for him caused her no guilt. He was insane, she reasoned, and would be better off dead.

It was a shame what had happened to him, though. For that, Cassandra had regrets. She dragged herself into her windowless bedroom, took a sip of cold tea from a cup on her bedside table, then blew out the candle. There was no reason to stay awake and she was tired from thinking too much. Her private wing of Lionkeep echoed with its usual, ruthless silence, making the thoughts in her mind seem louder. Tonight she was plagued with images of Akeela and Lukien, and what she had done to them both. She wanted only to sleep.

Sleep, however, did not come easily. And when it did it was fraught with restless dreams. Cassandra tossed in her sheets for the first hour, trying to banish her phantoms, then heard an insistent voice calling her name. Her eyelids fluttered open to see the dark room and a figure standing over her.

"Cassandra, it's me," said the voice. In her stupor it took a moment to for Cassandra to recognize it.

"Jancis?"

"Yes. Can you see me?"

Cassandra sat up in alarm. "Barely. What's wrong?"

"Look!" said Jancis, holding out her hands. It took a moment for Cassandra's eyes to adjust. Jancis was backlit by lamplight from the adjoining room. In her hands was something small and round.

"What?" Cassandra asked, reaching out for the object. The thing squealed at her touch, making Cassandra jump. "Great Fate, what is that?"

"The monkey!" said Jancis. She hovered over the bed, still holding the object out for Cassandra. "Remember? From the boy Gilwyn!"

Cassandra blinked uncertainly. "Monkey?" She shook her head, tossed her naked feet over the bedside, and studied the thing in Jancis' hands. Gradually her sight improved, revealing the furry mass in Jancis' hands. It was indeed a monkey.

"Where'd you find it?" asked Cassandra quickly. "Is Gilwyn here?"

"I don't know," shrugged Jancis. "I was asleep myself when he woke me, just a moment ago! He scared me to death!"

"Teku is a she, Jancis, not a he," said Cassandra. "Gilwyn must be around somewhere. There was no note with her?"

"Not this time," said Jancis. "Unless I'm missing it."

Cassandra studied the monkey, but in the dim light could see nothing. She was excited that Gilwyn was back, because surely only he could have sent Teku looking for her, but without further directions she didn't know what to do. She thought about going into the other room where there was light, then realized in a flash what needed to be done.

"The garden!" She reached out and gently touched the monkey, patting its furry head. "Teku, is Gilwyn in the garden? Will you take me to him?"

The sound of her master's name made the monkey bob her head.

"Put her down, Jancis," directed Cassandra.

Jancis replied, "With pleasure," then spilled the furry creature onto the floor.

"Is Gilwyn near, Teku?" Cassandra asked softly. "Is he in the garden?"

The little monkey chattered and moved toward the door.

"What's it doing?" asked Jancis.

"She wants me to follow!" Cassandra took a step toward Teku to test her theory and was rewarded with another movement toward the door.

"It understands you?" asked Jancis incredulously.

"I think so. Gilwyn told me she was smart, and obviously she knew enough to find you. I'm going to follow her, Jancis, see if she takes me to Gilwyn."

"Cass, you can't go to the garden now. You're not even dressed!"

"I have to, Jan." She started toward the door. "Gilwyn's probably waiting for me. Lukien might be with him."

"Wait!" cried Jancis, stumbling after her. "Take slippers at least!"

Cassandra groaned in frustration, located her slippers beside her bed, and hurried into them. "Don't follow me, Jancis. I don't want to make any more noise than I have to. And if Akeela comes looking for me. . . ."

"I'll tell him you're sleeping," sighed Jancis. "Go. But be careful!"

"I will," said Cassandra, then hurried after Teku. The monkey led her from the bedroom into the main chamber, then out toward the open hallway. She moved quickly but with silence, letting Cassandra skulk after her as she scurried through the corridor. Cassandra mimicked her silence. She was chilly suddenly and regretted not bringing a shawl, but she was too intent on reaching the garden to think much about it. She followed Teku to the end of the hall, near the kitchen where Freen worked. Luckily, the cook had long since gone to bed and neither Megal nor Ruthanna were around. Both Cassandra and Teku kept to the wall as they rounded the kitchen. They were approaching the edge of Cassandra's private wing now, and for a moment Teku looked confused. She studied her surroundings, sniffed the air then looked at Cassandra, her yellow eyes full of concern. Cassandra squatted down beside her.

"Are you lost, Teku?" she whispered.

The monkey merely grunted.

"The garden's the only place he could be," Cassandra mused aloud. "Is that where Gilwyn is?"

Teku headed toward the door again. This time, though, Cassandra caught the monkey, scooping her into her arms.

"It'll be quicker this way," she explained. Teku seemed

to agree, climbing onto her shoulder. Cassandra smiled as she plunged further into the dark corridor. "Just tell me if I'm going the wrong way, all right?"

She knew the way better than the monkey, and soon found herself near the scullery again, where on that first night she had ventured out into the free world. The hall was dark, as always, and a chill crept beneath her nightgown. Her ears picked up some far away movement, but she was free of her servants now and knew they wouldn't discover her. All that was left was to reach the garden.

The last few moments were the worst as she pushed through the unlit scullery hall, where the rusted pots and pans hung like dead men from pegs and the unseen spiderwebs surprised her skin. Searching for the door, she reached out. . . .

"Cassandra?"

Cassandra gasped and fell back in alarm. At the door was Gilwyn, almost invisible in the blackness.

"Gilwyn, you scared me!" she cried.

"Shhh," scolded Gilwyn, coming forward. "I'm sorry, but I couldn't risk being seen." He beamed at his pet, taking the monkey from Cassandra's shoulder. "Good girl, Teku. You found her!" He kissed Teku and hoisted her onto his own shoulder. "I was worried she couldn't find you. I sent her out almost an hour ago."

"She found Jancis," Cassandra corrected. She looked over Gilwyn's shoulder toward the door, noticing with disappointment that he was alone. Gilwyn caught her glance and smiled at her.

"I found him, my lady," he said. "I found Lukien. He's waiting for you not far from Lionkeep, in the apple orchard."

The news was like beautiful music. "Really?" Cassandra asked. "Lukien's back? How is he?"

"He's fine, but there's no time to talk. You'll see him soon enough." Gilwyn reached out and took her hand. "Come on, we have to hurry."

"What, right now?" Cassandra pulled her hand back. "I can't leave dressed like this."

"My lady, please don't argue," implored Gilwyn. "This is the only chance to get you out of here before we're discovered. My wagon's not far from here, waiting for us.

I was able to get inside the keep because I said I was delivering books. They checked my wagon and that's what they saw—books. They won't check me again on the way out, but we have to hurry!"

Cassandra's head was spinning. She was barely dressed, it was the middle of the night, and she hadn't even said good-bye to Jancis. But Gilwyn's earnest face told her he meant business. Lukien was waiting, and couldn't wait forever. If she didn't leave now. . . .

"Please, my lady," said Gilwyn nervously. "We've got clothes waiting for you in the orchard. But we must hurry."

Cassandra glanced back down the dark corridor. The utensils of the scullery stood out stark and ugly. But it in an odd way it was home. Leaving it might kill her. Or worse, Jancis if her treachery was discovered.

"I'm not sure I'm ready," she laughed nervously. She looked at Gilwyn for support, and got one of his encouraging smiles.

"We can make it, my lady, I know we can. But we have to hurry."

It had all come down to this, a getaway in a wagon full of dusty books. Cassandra had waited sixteen years, and in that time had imagined many escapes, all of them more grand than this one. Beneath her nightshirt the Eye of God gave off its reassuring glow, the only warmth for her cold body.

"All right," she agreed. "Let's go."

Gilwyn didn't say a word. Like a phantom he turned in the darkness, opened the door to the breezy outside, and led Cassandra toward freedom.

Alone atop his black charger, General Will Trager trotted toward Lionkeep after a long day with his lieutenants. All was in preparation for his departure to Jador, and the general was in an excellent mood. The lights of Lionkeep drew him forward like a moth. He had good news for Akeela and knew that the king would still be awake, so he had decided not to wait until morning. They were on schedule to march, finally, and could do so as soon as Akeela wanted. If need be, they could depart tomorrow, a full two days earlier than anticipated. Will Trager was proud of himself. His pride glowed in his bearded face. The lateness of the hour had made his trip from Chancellery Square particularly pleasant, without the usual choking traffic. He had even whistled a little while he rode, pleased that he no longer needed to face Warden Graig before meeting Akeela. Akeela had taken old Graig's death hard but it had been worth it; now Akeela listened only to him. Not even Figgis had much access to Akeela these days, an added bonus Trager hadn't expected. Akeela was growing impatient with the old librarian, sure that he was stalling. Like Queen Cassandra, Figgis opposed the invasion of Jador. That made him less useful to Akeela. Trager grinned in the moonlight. It was a very good night, indeed.

Up ahead stood the gates of Lionkeep. A pair of wardens were posted, each with a spear and a black helmet. Since the death of Graig, they had been particularly keen on guarding Lionkeep. Even Trager had to announce himself. He watched them as he rode nearer, slowing his mount a bit. They were suspicious of him and he knew it. There were bold rumors afoot that Graig had been murdered, and though nothing could be proven, the wardens were taking no more chances. Trager was merely yards from the gates when he noticed another pair of wardens arriving, relieving the first pair, who after a quick exchange of formalities disappeared into the darkness. The new sentries fell into position, noticing the approaching general at once. Through the bars of the gates, Trager came under their suspect glare.

"Open up," he commanded. He had no interest in pleasantries and wouldn't have wasted them on wardens, anyway. The sentries studied him with undo care. "Oh, hurry up," he shouted. "I have business with the king!"

"Yes, sir," replied one of the men. It was easy to catch the rancor in his tone. With his partner he opened the gates, bidding Trager inside. But just as the general crossed the threshold, he noticed a wagon coming toward him from within the keep.

"Wait," ordered the first sentry. He held up a hand to stop Trager.

"Wait? What for?"

Both sentries fixed on the wagon. There was a single rider in the conveyance, a boy Trager thought he recognized. Behind him, in the buckboard, was a lumpy pile covered with a tarpaulin. The boy looked pale in the moonlight.

"You boy, hold up," said one of the wardens. He stepped in front of the wagon and raised a hand to halt it. The boy grimaced and reined in his horse, a tired looking old beast with drooping eyes and lopping gait.

"Is there a problem?" he asked the warden.

"Where are you going?" replied the warden pointedly.

"Back to the library," said the boy. He sighed. "Look, I already explained everything to the last sentries. I'm Gilwyn Toms, from the library."

Suddenly Trager remembered the boy. He watched the happenings with interest.

"We know who you are," said the warden. He spied the wagon's contents, frowning. "What's all that stuff?"

"Books, of course! And if you recognize me, will you let me pass, please?"

"Sorry, boy." The warden took a step toward the wagon. "We're checking everything that comes in and out, you know that."

"But I just came in!" Gilwyn Toms protested.

"Doesn't matter," said the warden. He walked over to the side of the wagon, reaching into it to pull off the tarpaulin. "We have our orders."

"Stop being ridiculous," barked Trager. His loud command stilled the warden's hand. "The boy just wants to get home to bed."

The wardens seemed shocked. "General, we have our orders," said one of them.

"Orders," spat Trager. "Let the boy pass. Those are *my* orders, warden."

Hesitantly, the sentries stepped back from the wagon. Gilwyn Toms looked remarkably relieved. And for Trager, the tight grimaces of the wardens was priceless. He laughed, shaking his head in disgust.

"Really, do you think stopping a crippled boy is what Warden Graig would have done? You're pathetic." Trager turned toward Gilwyn Toms. "Go on, boy, get back to the library."

The boy broke into a peculiar smile. "Thank you, sir."

"All right," grunted Trager. "Safe home, now."

Self-satisfaction filled him as he watched the boy snap the reins and head out through the gates with his wagon full of books. The wardens watched the boy go too, shaking their heads and sighing. Trager rode past them with disdain.

"Idiots," he sneered. "All you wardens ever do is waste people's time."

Cassandra lay motionless beneath the tarpaulin, clinging desperately to the amulet against her chest. The soft glow of the Eye's gemstone warmed her cold skin. Through the tarp she had heard the voices of men, then Gilwyn's insistent arguing. The voices had been very close, but now the wagon was moving again. Were they free? Cassandra held her breath. Her body rocked to the movement of the road, pinned on all sides by sharp-edged books. Her awkward position in the wagon had quickly become painful, but it would all be worth it to escape Lionkeep. She said nothing as the wagon moved off again, waiting for a sign from Gilwyn. At last it came.

"We made it, my lady," came the boy's excited whisper. "We're out of the keep! Don't move; we'll be safe soon."

Cassandra didn't move, but she did smile. She wrapped her fingers around the amulet, gleaning its needed warmth, and prepared herself to see Lukien.

39

A thin mist rolled through the apple orchard, brightened by moonlight and the distant glow of Koth. Except for the crackle of a small campfire, there was no sound between the perfect rows of fruit trees, only the scent of apples and the soft, dewy earth. A tawny colored horse stood motionless in the firelight, burdened with packs for a long ride. Lukien squatted by the fire, listening, watching. Down the orchard row he could see mist breezing through the trees. The fog had cut visibility considerably, but he knew he was alone in the orchard, and that worried him. For two hours he had been here, waiting for Gilwyn to return with Cassandra. So far there had been no sign of them, and Lukien was despairing. He put his hands up to the fire, staring pensively into its flames. Smoke from the dry kindling irritated the wound beneath his eyepatch. The horse Figgis had managed to find him chomped lazily at the ground, occasionally finding a fallen, unripe apple. She seemed a good horse, good enough at least to speed him and Cassandra to Breck's farm, where his own mount awaited him. From there they would ride to Marn. It was a decent plan and Lukien was satisfied with it, but none of it mattered unless Cassandra came. As the minutes ticked by, that seemed less and less likely.

And for a moment, Lukien thought that might be for the best. He had nothing to offer Cassandra, really, just his love. He was an outlaw. He wasn't even welcome back in

Norvor. And unlike Cassandra he had aged over the years, badly. She, on the other hand, was as beautiful as when he'd left her, or so said Gilwyn. She deserved a life better than he could offer, but maybe she didn't see that. Maybe she was just too desperate to escape her gilded cage.

Lukien picked up a gnarled stick and poked the flames, sending up a shower of sparks. He had kept the fire small to avoid being seen, but he knew that Cassandra would be cold when she arrived and grateful for the fire.

Lukien corrected himself. *If* she arrived.

Dawn would soon be upon them. Only a few more hours of darkness remained. Lukien had hoped to have some time with Cassandra before fleeing to Breck's, but the coming dawn made that less likely now. Unless she arrived soon, they would have to make the most of the remaining dark, get as much distance between themselves and Lionkeep as possible. . . .

He heard a noise. Alarmed, he hunched down next to the fire, shielding its glow with his cape. Down the tree-lined avenue the mist swirled in the breeze. The noise of horse hooves reached him, coming toward him. His hand went instinctively to his sword. His muscles coiled to spring. If Gilwyn had been discovered there would be dozens of wardens in the orchard, closing around him like a noose.

But only one horse approached, its nose breaking through the mist. Brown and plain and moving with a tired gait, it dragged a familiar wagon behind it. Lukien's sword hand fell loose at his side. Slowly he rose to his feet. The horse was Tempest and the wagon was Gilwyn's. The boy sat in the bench seat, searching the mists. And he wasn't alone.

Beside Gilwyn sat Cassandra.

Dark-haired and lovely, untouched by time. Her body was wrapped in the wagon's tarp, but her face was unmistakable in the moonlight. For a moment Lukien couldn't breathe. He could barely even think, for the sight of Cassandra was so strange to him, as if time had stood still and they were both alone in the orchard again, making love for that first time. As the wagon drew closer Gilwyn noticed him beside the campfire. The boy waved excitedly. Cassandra's head lifted, her eyes meeting Lukien's.

"Great Fate, it's a miracle. . . ."

A great, sad smile stretched across Cassandra's face. Her

hand appeared from beneath the tarp to wave at Lukien, who rushed forward to greet them, sprinting through the mist. Gilwyn reined in Tempest, and when the wagon halted Cassandra jumped to her feet. The tarpaulin she'd been wearing fell from her shoulders and she stood exquisitely exposed, thrusting out her arms for her coming lover.

"Lukien!"

The exuberant call echoed through the orchard. Lukien raced ahead, not stopping until he was at the foot of the wagon. There he paused, looked straight into Cassandra's beautiful face, and put out his hands for her. Without a word she dropped into his embrace. He scooped her from the wagon, laughing, twirling her around in a giddy waltz.

"Lukien!" cried Cassandra again. "It's you!"

"It's me, my love, it's me," sang Lukien. She was weightless in his arms. Tears streaked her glowing face as she looked up at him, her arms stretched around his neck. Not a drop of time had touched her. Lukien stopped spinning long enough to embrace her, holding her without a sound, listening to the remarkable noise of her breath in his ear. She was more than young and beautiful. She was *alive*.

"I can't believe it," he sighed. "I never thought I'd see you again." He pressed her head to his chest and kissed it. "You're free now, Cassandra, free!"

"Free," Cassandra echoed, her voice breaking. She pulled from his embrace and studied his face. Her expression was profoundly sad. "Look at you," she sighed. "Oh, Lukien . . ." Her fingers lightly touched his cheek, tracing the area of his damaged eye. "What happened?"

Lukien took her hand away and kissed it. "I'm well, Cassandra. Don't be afraid. Age has caught up with me, that's all."

"But your eye. . . ."

"It's nothing, Cassandra, nothing."

"No," she insisted. Her smile was pained. "You look so different, so. . . ."

"There's much to tell you," agreed Lukien, nodding. "But time enough for that later." He smiled widely. "Time enough for everything now." Beneath her nightgown he saw the red glow of a jewel and knew at once it was the Eye of God. "So it's true," he said, reaching out to touch the thing. "I guess I never really believed it." There was so much to say, yet so few words to express it. In the end, all he could speak was her name. "Cassandra. . . ."

She returned his smile, almost grinning, the way she always had in the past. "I love you," she said simply. "I knew you'd return for me."

It hurt to hear the words. She had so much faith in him. "Sixteen bloody years. I never should have left you."

From atop the wagon, Gilwyn cleared his throat. "Uhm, pardon me, but don't we have some clothes for the lady?"

Lukien had hardly noticed Cassandra's near nakedness. "Yes, of course," he said quickly. "I have clothes for you, Cassandra, and boots for riding. And a coat."

"First the coat, please," laughed Cassandra, drifting toward the fire. "I'm frozen from riding in that wagon."

Lukien went to the horse and began fumbling with the saddle roll where he'd folded up Cassandra's clothes. He said to Gilwyn, "I was worried about you. You were gone a long time."

Gilwyn climbed down from the wagon with Teku. "It was tougher to find Cassandra than I thought. But Teku found her eventually."

"And you got out of the keep all right?"

Gilwyn and Cassandra glanced at each other. Lukien unrolled the long coat he'd brought and went to Cassandra.

"What happened?" he asked. "Did someone see you?"

"No, but it was close," said Gilwyn. He began to laugh. "You won't believe this, Lukien, but Trager was the one that saved us!"

"Trager?" Lukien draped the coat over Cassandra's shoulders. "What happened?"

"The wardens at the gate stopped us," Cassandra explained. "They were about to look under the covers where I was hiding. General Trager told them to stop hassling us and sent us on our way."

"Can you believe the luck?" crowed Gilwyn. "We left Lionkeep right under his nose!"

Lukien was too nervous to see the humor of it. When the coat was on Cassandra, he directed her back toward the fire. "Here, warm yourself. I'll get the other clothes for you."

But before he could turn, Cassandra snatched his hand, pulling him back. "Wait," she said, smiling. "Let me look at you."

"My lady, I really think you should hurry," said Gilwyn. "It'll be light soon. Once they discover you're gone—"

"I've waited sixteen years for this moment, Gilwyn Toms," interrupted Cassandra gently. "I won't be rushed." She patted the ground next to her. "Sit with me, Lukien. There's so much we need to say to each other."

After all these years, the thought of being alone with Cassandra was too tempting to ignore. Lukien gave Gilwyn a little nod. "There's time yet before we have to set out. Why don't you go keep a lookout, Gilwyn. If anyone comes near, let us know."

Gilwyn gave a sly smile. "Right."

He shuffled off with Teku on his shoulder, soon disappearing into the mist. Once again there was only the sound of the fire and Cassandra's gentle breath. She took Lukien's hand again, pulling him down beside her. Her expression was inscrutable. Lukien longed to know what she was thinking. There was a surprising ease between them, as if no time had passed at all.

"Gilwyn told me about Norvor," she said softly. "And about Baron Glass."

"Good," said Lukien, relieved. "Then you know we're heading to meet with him?"

"At Breck's farm. Yes, I know." Cassandra shifted closer to him. The warmth of the fire mingled with the warmth of her skin. It was the most marvelous sensation Lukien had felt in years.

"I'm not what you expected, I know," said Lukien. "I know I've changed. But life in Norvor is hard, Cassandra. I've had to fight to stay alive."

"Fighting is what you are best at, Lukien. It always has been."

Lukien nodded. "Perhaps. But I'm older now, slower. Great Fate, look at me—I look like your father now!"

"Hush," said Cassandra, putting a finger to his lips. "To me you are beautiful. One eye or two, it doesn't matter."

Her smile told him she wasn't lying. Lukien melted at her touch.

"I still love you, Cassandra," he said. "I never forgot about you, never."

Cassandra chuckled. "I'm not your confessor, Lukien. You don't have to tell me about your other women."

"No, that's not it," said Lukien. "I just want you to know

I was always thinking about you. I always hoped that someday you would send for me, and now you have."

"And you came," said Cassandra. "Thank you."

There was no need for thanks. Lukien knew he would have
crossed an ocean at her call. Being with her again reminded
him of why he loved her. She was beautiful, true, but so much
more. She was that unattainable thing that all men raised on
the streets seek. Her love for him was redemptive.

"It's been so long," she said. "All the years I had to
think about it, I imagined what you'd look like now." She
sat up straight. "Tell me about Norvor. Gilwyn said you
were with a woman there, the warlady Jazana Carr."

Lukien shrugged. "I had no choice, really. Like I said, it
was either fight or die. I chose to fight."

"Is that how you lost your eye?"

Lukien toyed with one of the campfire sticks, picking it
up and studying its burning tip. He didn't like talking about
his missing eye, and wished Cassandra would stop fussing
over it. "A Norvan blade did this to me," he said casually.
"Nothing really to talk about. It hurt for a few weeks, but
now I hardly feel anything."

Again Cassandra seemed sad. "I'm sorry about what happened to you, Lukien. I would have stopped Akeela if I
could have, but he wouldn't listen to me. He won't even
let anyone speak your name."

Lukien plunged the branch into the flames. Even after
all these years, Akeela's rancor toward him still hurt.
"Baron Glass is very grateful to you, Cassandra. You were
able to save him, at least."

"I kept him from being executed, that's all," said Cassandra. "You're really the one that saved him, Lukien. Is that
why he came back with you? Because he owes you?"

"Pretty much," said Lukien. He knew now was not the
time to tell Cassandra anything more. She was still married
to Akeela, after all, and talk of his overthrow would surely
upset her. "He's a good man. He never deserved what
Akeela did to him."

"I know," sighed Cassandra. "But Akeela's not well.
None of us can really blame him for the things he does."

"Hmm, I'm not so sure I'm ready to forgive so easily,
Cassandra. I blame Akeela, and so does Thorin." Then
Lukien softened, asking, "How is Akeela?"

"Oh, how can I answer that? He's demented. He's been so for years now, but he gets worse as he gets older."

The concern in her voice surprised Lukien. "You're sad for him."

"I am. I know you hate him, Lukien, and I suppose you have reason. But he's been kind to me, mostly. And I can still remember what he used to be like, before . . . well, you know."

There was a long pause between them. For a moment, Lukien recalled what Akeela had been like, how good and generous he'd been. He missed his old friend sometimes. The truth was, he had never been able to hate Akeela.

"You have no idea what it's like to see a good man deteriorate so," said Cassandra. "And the worst part is that he still loves me. Can you imagine that? After all these years?"

"Why not?" said Lukien with a grin. "I still love you."

"No," said Cassandra. "You love me like a man should love a woman. But Akeela's love is terrible. It's maddened him. It's turned him into a murderer." She looked at Lukien earnestly. "Gilwyn told you what he's planned, hasn't he?"

"He plans to go to Grimhold for the other Eye," said Lukien. "Yes, he told me."

"Not just Grimhold, Lukien. Jador. And when he gets to Jador he plans on massacring them if they don't help him find the Eye. That's not Akeela the Good, not the man we knew."

"True," agreed Lukien. "But have no illusions, Cassandra—what you're planning is dangerous. If Akeela doesn't find and kill us, then maybe the desert will. Or maybe the Jadori. Are you sure you want to warn them of Akeela?"

"I must," said Cassandra. "I can't let them be massacred."

"Don't expect them to look kindly on us. Even if we reach them, they may remember me. And they'll want their amulet back. Have you considered that?"

Cassandra lowered her eyes. "Yes."

"You'll die without it, you know."

"Perhaps. Perhaps not. If Grimhold exists, then they had enough magic to make this amulet. Maybe they have some other means to help me."

"Not likely," said Lukien.

"No," Cassandra admitted, "but I have no choice. I can't

live like this. To be honest, I'm hoping that Akeela calls off his invasion. Once he knows I'm gone, maybe he won't bother searching for the other Eye."

"I wish that were true, but I can't believe it. Akeela will hound us relentlessly. And he's got a taste for Grimhold now. He's not going to stop. Even if he doesn't go there himself, he'll send Trager to Jador."

"Then you see why I must warn them, Lukien." Cassandra pulled the coat tighter around her shoulders, staring fretfully into the fire. "I've stolen enough life. I won't let the Jadori be massacred because of me. We must go to Jador. And if you won't go with me, then I'll go myself."

"Brave," said Lukien with a smile. "But I can't let you do that."

She looked at him. "What do you mean?"

"You're not going to Jador, Cassandra. I'm going, with Glass. You're going to Marn."

"What . . . ?"

"I'll ride to Jador to tell them what's coming, but you're not going with me." Lukien gripped her hand firmly. "I won't let you die, Cassandra. I won't let you give back the amulet."

"Lukien, I must. No matter what else happens, I can't live like this. Look at you. You said yourself how you've aged. Am I to go on forever, without you, losing everyone I care about?"

"If you remove the Eye you'll die, Cassandra."

"We don't know that. Perhaps my sickness is cured and it's no longer growing. Perhaps—"

"No," snapped Lukien. "The Eye has kept you alive and you must stay alive! I won't let you risk yourself, not even for a thousand Jadori. I'll go to Jador myself and tell them about Akeela. You will stay behind, Cassandra, and you will live!"

His voice carried through the dark orchard. Stunned by the outburst, Cassandra reared back. She did not seem frightened by him, though.

"Why would you do this thing?" she asked. "Why would you risk yourself for the Jadori?"

It was the question Lukien had long dreaded. He knew now that no one had ever told her how the Eye had really been won.

"Cassandra, I owe the Jadori a debt."

Cassandra squeezed his hand. "Tell me."

"It's difficult. It happened so long ago, but it still haunts me sometimes." Glancing away, Lukien distracted himself by studying the flames. In their orange glow he saw the face of Kahana Jitendra. "When we took the Eye of God from Jador, something happened," he began. "Kahan Kadar, their ruler . . . he welcomed us into his palace. He treated us like royal guests. But the Eye was his, you see."

"You stole it from him," said Cassandra. "I know that, Lukien."

"No, we didn't just steal it," said Lukien. "We killed for it. *I* killed. I killed Kadar's wife."

There was no sound from Cassandra. Lukien couldn't bring himself to look at her.

"She was in Kadar's bed the night we went to steal the Eye," he continued. "I thought Kadar was in that bed, but it was Jitendra. She screamed, Kadar burst in on us, and I accidentally stabbed her. And the worst part. . . ." He drew a breath, hardly able to go on. "The worst part was she was pregnant."

Lukien braced himself for Cassandra's reaction. To his surprise she reached out and brushed the hair from his forehead.

"My sweet Lukien," she said softly.

"Sweet to you, perhaps, Cassandra, but not to the Jadori. To them I'm a monster."

"Sixteen years, Lukien. A long time."

"Not long enough to forget the death of a wife," said Lukien. "You weren't there, Cassandra. You didn't hear Kadar. If I live to be a hundred, I'll never forget the sound of his cries. So you see? I have to go back. You don't owe the Jadori anything. I do."

"We will go together, then," said Cassandra. "I won't leave you to them alone."

"I won't be alone. Thorin will be with me."

"Thorin Glass is an old man, Lukien. Whereas I—"

"No, Cassandra," Lukien begged. "Don't argue with me, please. We've talked about this, Thorin and I. You'll be safe in Marn. No one there knows you, and we'll come back for you as soon as we can."

"And if you don't return?" asked Cassandra.

Lukien shrugged. "If I don't return, I'll die knowing that you're safe. Now please, no more talk of this." He smiled at her, trying desperately to change the subject. "It's been so long, I want to enjoy this. And Gilwyn's right, you know. There isn't much time before we have to leave. In fact, you should be getting dressed. I've brought good clothes for riding. Food, too."

"Yes, all right," Cassandra agreed. "Will you fetch the clothes for me? It's nice by the fire."

They both rose, Cassandra standing by the fire, Lukien going to the horse. He expected Cassandra to disrobe and wanted to give her privacy, but she called to him a moment later. Lukien turned. She was blinking, confused. Her arms were spread and her eyes dropped down toward her legs. There, in the space between her thighs, a bloom of crimson stained her nightgown.

"Lukien . . . ?"

Cassandra's breathing grew erratic. The bloody stain spread like ink down her legs. She groaned, softly at first, reaching for her stomach.

"Lukien!"

Lukien hurried toward her, catching her just as her knees buckled. Her skin turned deathly white as an anguished cry leapt from her throat. The blood was spreading; Lukien felt it warm against him.

"What's happening?" she gasped. She clutched her stomach, slipping from Lukien's embrace and buckling to her knees. Back and forth she rocked, screaming. Lukien stood over her, confused and terrified. And then he saw the amulet beneath Cassandra's gown, burning a hot and furious red. Cassandra, shaking, looked down at the thing. "The curse. . . ."

Lukien felt panic rising. He knelt down beside Cassandra, watching in horror as her flesh curdled to a milky white. Her body spasmed as he held her. Cassandra's hands clutched at his cape, clawing at him for help.

"What's wrong, what's wrong?" asked Lukien desperately. "Cassandra. . . ."

She couldn't answer. Her wide eyes looked at him a moment, then shut tight as pain wracked her anew. A strangled cry rose up from her throat, loosed with a fountain of blood. The blood sprayed across Lukien's face.

"The cancer," she gurgled. "I feel it!"

Lukien wrapped her in his arms, bathed in her blood, hoping to somehow stem its tide. She was choking, bleeding from her mouth and thighs and barely able to speak. Beneath her gown the Eye of God shone with wrathful light. Cassandra's fingers crawled toward it, resting on its shining surface. Lukien barely heard her throttled words.

"I'm . . . dying. . . ."

"You can't die, Cassandra, you can't!"

But she was, and Lukien knew it. They had broken the Eye's power. They had, though it seemed impossible. Cassandra pulled at the amulet's chain.

"Return . . . it," she gasped. Weakly she collapsed into Lukien, choking up blood. A giant spasm shook her body. She wailed in his ear, crying for help.

"Tell me what to do," he pleaded. "Tell me and I'll help you!"

But Cassandra was beyond words now. There was no more warmth from her body; her skin lost its hue. Even her shaking subsided. A final, violent spasm rippled into smaller ones, slower, slower. . . .

And stopped.

"Cassandra?"

In the moonlight of the orchard, Lukien's voice was small.

"Cassandra, don't do this to me."

There was no answer.

Lukien knelt with Cassandra in his arms, her head bobbing lifeless on his shoulder. The red light of the amulet went out like a candle.

Across the orchard, Gilwyn was relaxing when he heard the scream. He had found a clearing a respectable distance from Lukien and Cassandra, one with a good view of Koth and anyone that might venture into the orchard after them. With Teku on his shoulder, Gilwyn was sitting against a tree, feeling wonderfully satisfied. But the scream he heard shattered his calm.

He bolted upright at the sound, then knew it had come from the camp. Lukien? He sprinted forward as quickly as his bad foot allowed, gripped by terror. The scream was unholy, an ongoing, anguished wail. Teku's tiny hands clung tightly to his coat as he hurried toward it. The light of the campfire cut through the fog. Next to it was Lukien, on his knees. The knight was rocking Cassandra in his arms. Gilwyn halted. Cassandra wasn't moving.

"Fate above . . ."

The shocking scene weakened his knees. Blood soaked Cassandra's face and gown as though she'd been butchered. The stench of her blood hung heavy in the orchard. Lukien was weeping, hacking up great sobs as he clung to Cassandra's lifeless body. Unable to move, Gilwyn simply stared, horrified at the grisly scene and Lukien's inhuman cries.

"Lukien, what happened?"

Remarkably, Lukien heard his query. The Bronze Knight turned his tear-streaked face toward Gilwyn.

"You told me it was a hoax!" he snarled. "You promised me!"

"Promised you?"

"The curse! You promised me it was a lie, you wretched little beast!"

"It was!" cried Gilwyn. His head reeled as he looked at Cassandra's death-white body, splattered with her own bright blood. "I swear, Lukien, it was a hoax. I looked at her. I saw her with my own eyes!"

"Then look at her now!" roared Lukien. He rose with Cassandra in his arms, holding her out toward Gilwyn. "Look what's happened!"

Gilwyn could barely stutter a response. "I'm sorry! I didn't know!"

Lukien fell to his knees, dropping Cassandra gently to the ground and collapsing over her. He hid his face in his hands, shaking. The sight of the broken knight shocked Gilwyn. Not even when his own mother died had Gilwyn grieved so violently. He stared at Lukien and Cassandra's ghastly corpse, letting Lukien sob out all his misery. It was long moments until the knight finally composed himself. When he did he drew a sleeve across his tear- and blood-stained face, gazing hopelessly down at Cassandra.

"Lukien, we have to go," said Gilwyn shakily. He didn't like making the suggestion, but knew that their danger had just increased a hundred-fold. "Do you hear me? We have to go, before Akeela—"

"I heard you," said Lukien. Then, to Gilwyn's surprise

he reached down and took the amulet from around Cassandra's neck. His free hand went to her face and lightly touched her sunken cheek. It was as if all the life she had stolen for years had gone out of her in one enormous wind. Gone was the beauty that had driven men mad. In its place lay a drained husk.

"Why are you taking the amulet?" Gilwyn asked. He chanced a step closer to Lukien, hoping the knight wouldn't strike him. But the rage had left Lukien. When at last he turned to Gilwyn, there was only sorrow in his expression.

"We're bringing the Eye to Jador," he said. "You and me."

Gilwyn said nothing. He knew he couldn't return to the library. Once Akeela discovered Cassandra's death there would be no safety for either of them. And Akeela *would* discover Cassandra eventually, because they couldn't take her with them.

"I won't leave her to the rats," said Lukien. "We'll bury her here, before it gets light." His voice had lost its friendly timber. Now it was flat, as dead as Cassandra. Once again he went to his knees. "You'll have to help me."

"Lukien, we don't have a spade."

But Lukien was already digging, using his fingers to claw up the loamy ground. Without a word Gilwyn knelt down beside him, using his good hand to join the gravedigging. It needn't be deep, Lukien told him, just deep enough to keep the vermin away until Akeela could find her.

"Akeela will bury her well," said Lukien through tears. "He loved her, too."

40

The next morning, Akeela discovered Cassandra was missing.

He had risen early to meet with his wife and tell her the good news—that General Trager's army was ready to march, and that they would be departing on the morrow. He had expected to break his fast with Cassandra, sipping tea together through the partition while Megal and Ruthanna served them. He had been in an excellent frame of mind. But at the doorway to Cassandra's wing, he found Jancis.

The blind handmaid looked stricken. She told Akeela that she had only just arisen herself, and that she had gone into Cassandra's chambers to check on her. But Cassandra wasn't there, she said. She was gone.

"Gone?" asked Akeela, not quite believing it. "Gone where?"

"Gone, my lord!" said Jancis frantically. She was crying real tears, but Akeela was immediately suspicious. "We've looked for her everywhere. She's left!"

"You looked for her?" hissed Akeela. "*You?* You're blind, woman! Why didn't you report this immediately?"

"I told you, my lord, I've only just woken up myself. I went in to say good morning and she didn't answer. I felt around her bed, thinking she might have fallen out. . . ."

Akeela shoved Jancis aside and raced forward. Megal and the other servants were in Cassandra's quarters when he arrived, calling out her name, blindly searching the opulent rooms. Ruthanna was in tears as she bumped into furniture. Gone was her usual, inhuman poise. Now she was hysterical, her voice hoarse from calling for her mistress. Freen, the cook, was with her, his consoling arm wrapped around her shoulder. It was bedlam in the chambers and Akeela didn't know what to do. He stood in the center of Cassandra's main living area, staring dumbly at the chaos, his jaw slack. A terror like he'd never felt before crept up his spine.

"Cassandra?" he called.

Freen and Megal turned their blind eyes toward him.

"King Akeela?" asked Freen. "Is that you, my lord?"

"Great Fate, Freen, where is she?" asked Akeela.

"I don't know, my lord. We've been looking, but—"

"She's got to be here somewhere!" cried Akeela. Madly be began searching the rooms, dashing into Cassandra's bedchamber and finding the sheets rumpled with sleep. Obviously she had been here before leaving. But how could she have left? It was unthinkable. If anyone saw her she'd. . . .

"Jancis!" bellowed Akeela.

He ran out of the chambers, back out into the main hall of the wing. Jancis was still there, waiting for him. She stood like a statue at the end of the hall, her white eyes blinking and teary. Akeela stalked toward her, his anger cresting. Behind her, wardens were rushing forward, led by Egin the fuller. The wardens halted at once as they noticed Akeela, giving him a wide berth as he closed in on Jancis.

"You were supposed to protect her," Akeela seethed. "You were supposed to watch out for her!"

"My lord, I'm sorry," pleaded Jancis. She dropped to her knees, putting her hands together in a prayerlike plea for mercy. "I don't know what happened, I swear. I went to sleep after she did. When I woke up she was gone!"

"It's true, my lord," said Egin. The fuller inched cautiously toward Akeela. "I went to bed after the queen myself. She turned in early because she said she was tired. That was the last any of us saw of her."

"Saw of her? Saw of her?" Akeela began to laugh hysterically. "How could any of you fools see anything? You're all bloody blind!"

"We'll start searching the grounds for her, my lord," said one of the wardens quickly. "If she's here, we'll find her."

"If you find her she'll die!" thundered Akeela. He put a hand to his head, unsure what to do. Surely there was no choice but to search for her. "Yes, all right," he agreed. "Find her. And find General Trager, too. Tell him to tear Koth apart if he must!"

The wardens bowed and hurried out of the room. Akeela looked down at the kneeling Jancis. He wanted desperately to strike her. Megal and Ruthanna drifted into the hall. Along with Egin, they watched him with wide, sightless eyes.

Are they all against me? Akeela wondered. The little nagging voice in his head whispered treachery in his ear.

"I'm sorry, my lord," sobbed Jancis. "I didn't know. . . ."

Akeela's hand was quaking, poised to slap her face. His breathing came in erratic, angry bursts. This woman had failed him. He had entrusted his most precious thing to her, and she had failed him. Worse, he didn't believe her claims of innocence. She and Cassandra were thicker than thieves. There was no way his wife would have fled without telling Jancis.

Unless she simply wanted to protect her.

So instead of striking Jancis, Akeela reached down and seized her face in his hands, pinching her jaw tightly between his fingers and pulling her to her feet.

"Now you listen to me, you blind bitch. If I find out you're lying to me, I'm going to dig out your eyeballs with a spoon."

Jancis groaned but didn't say a word. Akeela studied her face a moment, then pushed her, sending her sprawling at Egin's feet. Neither the fuller nor the maids said a word. Horror-struck, they merely stared blindly.

"If any of you have betrayed me, I will kill you," Akeela warned.

Then he stormed off, leaving them in dazed confusion. His mind was on fire as he hurried through Lionkeep, calling out for General Trager. His frightened, half-crazed voice rang like thunder through the halls.

For the rest of the morning Akeela held vigil in Lionkeep, waiting for word about Cassandra. The wardens continued to search the grounds, but found nothing. General Trager and his men had fanned out through the city, hoping to find a clue to the queen's whereabouts. Lionkeep fell into a mournful silence, and all the good feelings Akeela had felt just hours before were gone, replaced with the most crushing misery. It was very likely now that Cassandra was dead. Akeela supposed she had risked her life to escape him, that eternity with him was simply unthinkable to her. It was a theory that hurt Akeela, because he knew he had always been good and kind to Cassandra, and had given her everything a woman could want. He had not given her freedom, of course, because that wasn't in his purview to grant. But he had tried to give her love. Why couldn't she have seen that?

Within hours of Cassandra's disappearance, Akeela's depression was total. He was brooding on his balcony, staring out over Koth, thoroughly drunk from the bottles of wine he'd consumed. His servants tiptoed around him, attending his needs without question. At last, Akeela was quiet. No longer was he mad or shouting threats. Instead he waited as patiently as he could for word from Trager, finding solace in the good wines of his cellars. Looking out over the city, he supposed that Cassandra's body was there somewhere, lying in a ditch, victim of the first set of human eyes to sight her. Akeela wondered if her death had been painful. He hoped not.

Hope. There was still that, he supposed. Perhaps Cassandra had gotten away without being seen. She was clever, after all. Akeela rolled his wine goblet between his palms, seizing on the notion, praying for its truth.

"My lord?"

The voice startled Akeela. He turned to see a pair of Knight-Guardians, General Trager's bodyguards, at the end of the balcony. Their faces were characteristically stoic. Akeela's stomach tightened.

"You have news?" he asked in a slurred voice.

"My lord, we've found something," replied one of the men. "In the apple orchard. General Trager sent us to bring you."

"What have you found?"

The man hesitated. "The general asked that we bring you, my lord. He thought it was best you see for yourself."

Fine, thought Akeela. *No more questions.* He did indeed need to face this himself. Pushing his wine glass aside, he got to his feet, a little wobbly at first. His brain sloshed in his skull, but he was able to straighten up.

"Take me there."

The Knight-Guardians had their horses waiting in the courtyard, but it took time for the squires to find a mount for Akeela. They were plainly shocked to see him, for Akeela the Ghost seldom ventured out of the keep. Soon, though, a warden who had been searching the grounds offered Akeela his own steed. Akeela mounted the beast unsteadily, his head spinning. As the Knight-Guardians hurried off, Akeela followed, his black cape snapping behind him. He knew the way to the apple orchard, though he hadn't been there in ages, and as he rode a bad memory came back to him It was something he had almost forgotten, buried deep by his own anger. The apple orchard had been where Trager had first discovered Cassandra's infidelity. It was where she had soiled herself with Lukien.

A blackness descended over Akeela's groggy brain. His teeth began to grind, bottom jaw against top.

Lukien.

It was unthinkable, yet there it was, staring Akeela in the face. Mocking him.

"Great Fate," he whispered. "If it's you. . . ."

Long minutes of riding brought them at last to the outskirts of the orchard. The morning mist had long ago burned away, revealing the rows and rows of perfect fruit trees. The Knight-Guardians proceeded into the orchard, bidding Akeela to follow. Akeela steeled himself. Up ahead he saw a group of Royal Chargers, some mounted, others milling near their horses. The Knight-Guardians slowed as they approached. In the center of the throng was Trager. The general's bearded face contorted as he noticed Akeela. Surprisingly, he looked sad. It occurred to Akeela that he had never seen that expression on Trager before.

"My lord," Trager called, waving. The Knight-Guardians brought their horses to a halt. Akeela slowed his mount, trotting up to the group cautiously. He noticed suddenly that the men were arranged in a half-moon, standing around a mound of freshly dug earth.

Akeela's heart began racing, hammering loudly in his

ears. He brought his horse to a stop, letting two of Trager's men help him down. Suddenly he could barely move. The mound—what looked like a grave—drew him dreadfully closer.

"What is it?" he asked softly.

"I'm not sure," replied Trager. "We didn't want to disturb it in case. . . ." He shrugged. "You know."

"Dig it up," said Akeela.

Trager merely gestured, ordering two men forward. They had already fetched spades and set to work. Akeela watched, stone-faced, trying hard not to break down. For a moment he thought he might faint. Each man had taken only three shovelfuls of dirt when they paused.

"What is it?" Trager asked.

"Feels like something just below the surface," replied one of the diggers. He probed at the ground with his spade, unearthing a hand. A gasp went through the men. The digger blanched and glanced at Akeela.

Unable to speak, Akeela nodded for the men to continue. They did so carefully, uncovering the body beneath the dirt with their spades and, soon, with their hands. When they brushed the soil from Cassandra's face, Akeela nearly collapsed.

"Oh, help me," he groaned. "Oh, no. . . ."

Trager was there in an instant, his arm around Akeela to keep him from falling. Akeela's nausea spiked, sending vomit spewing from his mouth. As he bent over, hacking up his meal of wine, Trager patted his back.

"Let it out," he counseled.

The men continued pulling Cassandra's body from its shallow grave. Akeela struggled to catch his breath. Sweat fell from Akeela's forehead, stinging his eyes. Next to him, Trager was staring at Cassandra's body. With effort Akeela straightened. Except for where it was spattered with blood, Cassandra's corpse was bone white. The knights around her parted as Akeela shuffled closer, kneeling beside her. Trager stood over Akeela's shoulder, studying the body.

"Akeela, it's gone," he whispered.

Akeela nodded. He had already noticed. The Eye of God had been taken. Then, something else caught Akeela's gaze. There was an object tied to Cassandra's right hand. Akeela poked at it, brushing away the dirt and found it was a slip of paper. Someone had tied it to her wrist like a bracelet.

"What's that?" asked Trager.

Slowly, carefully, Akeela pried loose the folded paper. Trager ordered his men to step back, to give the king some room. But the general himself stared over Akeela's shoulder, intently watching as he unfolded the note. And it *was* a note, Akeela was sure. He didn't even need to read it, for he was dreadfully sure of its contents. In shaky penmanship the letter read:

To my mad brother,
You weren't the only one who loved her. Forgive me.

It was signed simply, *Lukien.*

"Lukien," sighed Akeela.

"Lukien!" hissed Trager.

Akeela rose to his feet. The nausea that had plagued him fled in an instant, replaced by a ground-shaking rage. With a trembling fist he crumpled the letter and tossed it into the empty grave.

"He takes everything from me," he snarled. "The only thing I loved, the only thing left to me!"

"We'll find him, my lord," Trager vowed. "And when we do, we'll cut his heart out."

"No," said Akeela. "You won't find him. He's already gone."

"Yes, but where?"

Akeela closed his eyes. An enormous headache threatened to crack his skull. "I don't know, but I know someone who can tell us." When he opened his eyes again, Cassandra was still at his feet. Still dead. "Get her out of here," he told Trager. "See that she's cleaned and readied for a proper burial. Then, bring me the librarian."

He turned and went back to his horse. On the orders of General Trager, the Knight-Guardians followed him home. Finally, when he reached Lionkeep and was alone in his study, Akeela wept.

41

Akeela sat alone in the vast dining chamber of Lionkeep, pensively sipping a glass of wine and surveying the feast laid out on the table. His cook had done an excellent job with the meal and had prepared many grand dishes. The aromas in the chamber were enough to tempt anyone to eat, Akeela was sure. Akeela, however, did not eat. Satisfied with his liquor, he simply admired the delicacies laid out on the table. The scents of roast duck and spitted venison filled his nostrils. Fresh breads and biscuits sent up wisps of steam. Across the table, a single place setting had been arranged with a metal goblet of wine. Moonlight came through the stained glass window, alerting Akeela to the time. Nearly two full days had passed since he'd discovered Cassandra's body, and he hadn't eaten a thing. Neither had Figgis. Now it was time to reward the old man for cooperating.

Surprisingly, Figgis had lasted longer under persuasion than Akeela had thought possible. Old bones break easily, Trager had assured him, but for the first full day the librarian had stuck to his story, swearing to every god and devil that he knew nothing of Cassandra's whereabouts. Lukien, he insisted, had not contacted him. Akeela supposed Figgis thought him incapable of torture. And for that first day, there had only been the threat of it, for Akeela had always liked Figgis. The thought of resorting to violence was almost abhorrent to him. But time was of the essence and he needed information, and he knew that Figgis was the lone link in the chain to lead him to Lukien. No one else would have dared contact Cassandra on his behalf, or so Akeela had thought. It was why he had originally left Breck out of his theory. Breck had a family now, too much to risk. And how strangely incriminating that the boy Gilwyn Toms had run off. Figgis had sworn ignorance about this, too.

Akeela set down his goblet. *It's a shame that no one can be trusted*, he thought. *A shame that people make me do such things.*

In the end, Figgis had cracked like an eggshell. Lukien and Gilwyn Toms were on their way to Jador. Surprisingly, Breck was with them, or had simply fled his home in Borath. Knight-Guardians sent to Breck's farm had reported that the place had been abandoned.

There was no doubt in Akeela's mind that Lukien had the amulet now, and that he and his cohorts intended to warn the Jadori about the coming invasion. Most curiously of all, though, was the presence of Baron Glass. Akeela's mind turned on this fact, troubled by it.

All my enemies gather against me.

He was determined not to let them win. The amulet meant nothing to him now. What life was there without Cassandra, anyway? It was his, and he would reclaim it, but he doubted he would use it. He wasn't such a great king, and he knew it. There was no reason for his reign to last forever.

A knock at the chamber door broke into his thoughts. As he called for his guest to enter, General Trager opened the door. He looked wretchedly tired, his face drawn from the fatigue of his unpleasant duty. He looked toward Akeela at the table.

"We've brought him," he said.

"Bring him in," replied Akeela.

Trager stepped aside, revealing two of his soldiers. Hanging between them, supported by their outstretched arms, was Figgis. The old man's face was bloated and contused. Blood caked his swollen lips and both eyes sported black bruises. The effort of walking to the dining chamber had winded him so that his breath came in grating rasps. Seeing him made Akeela flinch. Figgis lifted his face, saw Akeela seated at the elaborate table, and let out a mournful groan.

"Don't, Figgis, please," said Akeela. "It's done, I promise you. No one is going to hurt you any more." Akeela gestured to the soldiers. "Sit him down."

The men did as ordered, half dragging Figgis through the chamber and propping him into the high-backed chair so that he sat across from Akeela. Figgis could barely hold up his head, but he struggled valiantly to do so, squaring his shoulders as he stared at Akeela over the feast of platters.

"Should I stay?" Trager asked.

"No," said Akeela. "Wait outside and take your men with you. I'll call if I need you." He offered Figgis a reconciling grin. "Leave me alone with my friend for a while. We have some things to discuss."

Trager and his men left the dining chamber, closing the doors behind them. When they were gone Akeela smiled across the table at Figgis. The old man looked ghastly in the light from the candelabras. His face seemed to droop; pain glowed in his blackened eyes. Exhausted, he leaned back against his chair, his head lolling on his shoulders. Red welts marked his neck where Trager had worked the garrote. Finally, Figgis spoke.

"Why . . . ?"

The voice dribbled from his swollen lips. An expression of pain and sadness contorted his face.

"I had to know the truth," said Akeela. "You were lying to me; I could tell."

"I'm an old man, my lord. We're. . . ." He paused. "We were . . . friends."

"Yes," said Akeela, nodding. "But you betrayed me, Figgis. You sold me out to Lukien. And you killed Cassandra."

"We didn't know," Figgis groaned. Weakly he leaned forward, his elbows banging clumsily into the table. "We thought the curse was a hoax."

"So you've told me," said Akeela. "But dead is dead, and now I'll never see Cassandra again. That's murder, isn't it? People should pay for murder, shouldn't they?"

Figgis said nothing, but his eyes widened in alarm.

"Don't worry. I'm not going to kill you." Then Akeela laughed. "Who else could I get to run that confounded library of mine?" He sighed, spreading his hands in friend-ship. "Well, it's over. Tomorrow I leave in search of Lukien and Glass, and that troublesome boy of yours. But you and I will speak no more about this, agreed? When I return, it will be just like always between us. No grudges."

Figgis began to shake. Akeela realized he was sobbing.

"No, don't weep, my friend," said Akeela gently. "Look, I've set out this great feast for us. A peace offering."

"I'm not hungry," rasped Figgis.

"Oh, yes you are. You must be. You haven't eaten in days, and neither have I. Go on, eat. Let's both forgive ourselves for what we've done, eh?"

The table was full of temptations. Akeela could see the hunger on Figgis' face, even through his contusions.

"Please," urged Akeela. "There's nothing more you can do. Now that I know where Lukien has gone, I'm going to find him. You won't be able to save him, you know that. You might as well ease your own suffering."

Predictably, Figgis' resolve broke in moments. With one shaky hand he reached for the nearest platter, filled with joints of game birds. His fingers trembled as he held the bird to his lips, eating with effort and pain. Akeela watched him devour the food, pleased to seeing him enjoying it.

"Good," he said softly. "I want peace between us, Figgis. And I want you to at least try and understand why I did what I did."

Figgis didn't answer. He picked up his goblet and drained its contents, pouring half of it down his soiled shirt.

"You do understand, don't you, Figgis?"

The old man nodded, but Akeela knew it was just to shut him up. He let the librarian continue gorging himself. Figgis reached out for another piece of fowl, took a few bites, then dropped it into his plate. He began to cough as though a bone had lodged itself in his throat.

"My lord," Figgis gasped, staring at him with bulging eyes. His face began to redden as his windpipe involuntarily constricted. Banging on the table, he cried, "Akeela!"

Akeela watched impassively, surprised by the speed of the poison. Figgis put a hand to his throat, gasping. There was still remarkable strength in him, even after the beating; his thrashing impressed Akeela. But it wouldn't matter. The poison had already done its work. Figgis knew it, too.

"Akeela . . ." His gasping reminded Akeela of a chicken, squealing with its neck on the block. His eyes flared in utter disbelief. "You can't! My library. . . ."

It took effort to understand him. Akeela watched Figgis change color as the poison choked his words. "It isn't your library, Figgis," he said. "It's mine. Just like Cassandra was mine. Why doesn't anyone understand that?"

Past the point of answering, his remaining life ebbing fast away, Figgis gave Akeela a merciless sneer. Then he collapsed face first into his plate.

The room fell deathly quiet. Akeela stood up and went to his old friend, feeling his bruised neck and getting no pulse. A wave of sorrow overcame him.

"Why does everyone betray me?"

The dead man gave no answer. Akeela pulled back Figgis' head, sitting him up properly and carefully wiping the food from his face. The old man deserved some dignity, he supposed.

"Will, get in here," he bellowed.

Instantly Trager opened the doors. When he saw Figgis slumped dead in his chair, he smiled. "It's done. Good."

"Yes," said Akeela, "and don't look so glad about it. He was a good man."

Trager smirked. "No, my lord. A good man wouldn't betray you."

"Many good men have betrayed me. Now be ready to set out in the morning. We leave at dawn."

"For Jador, my lord?"

"Of course," said Akeela. "That's where we'll find Lukien."

"And the amulet, my lord."

"Yes, the amulet, too."

"Will we try to recover both of them?"

Akeela shrugged. "If the freaks of Grimhold stand against us, we will make them pay. If they have the amulet, we will take it."

"We'll have to fight, have no doubt," warned Trager. "Lukien will try to help them. For that, they will protect him."

"Then they will die," said Akeela.

Trager couldn't conceal his grin. "We'll make Lukien pay for what he's done to you."

"Indeed we will," agreed Akeela. Regretfully he regarded the dead Figgis. "Friends, Will—they're the worst enemies of all."

"Yes, my lord," said Trager, then turned and left the chamber, leaving Akeela alone with the feast of poisoned food.

PART THREE

THE

MISTRESS OF GRIMHOLD

42

Jador was far away.

In the heat of the desert the sands moaned, shifting and obscuring the white city in the distance. Beneath his black gaka, Kadar chafed under the sun. He could barely detect his city now, for he had traveled far in the hours since morning. Only the tips of Jador's spiraling towers could be seen above the dunes, like tiny needles shining on the horizon. Ahead of him, a rugged collection of tall reddish rocks erupted out of the desert sands. Kadar spied the rocks. The sun was dazzling, blinding him with its hot light. Little beads of perspiration fell from his brown brow, stinging his eyes, the only part of his face not covered by black cloth. He was still as stone as he watched the rocks, as was his kreel, Istikah. The great lizard felt the caution in her master's mind. Understanding perfectly, she mimicked Kadar's quiet. The thick scales along her hide shifted colors, turning from their usual green to approximate the golden sand. Like Kadar, Istikah sensed the danger ahead. Her tongue slid from her long, reptilian snout, tasting the air. In the bond that had grown between Kadar and his mount—the bond that always formed between rider and kreel—Kadar could sense Istikah's alarm. The rass was very near. They had discovered its hidden lair. But Istikah gave Kadar no sense of fear. In the tongue of Jador, the lizard's name meant "courageous," and she had always lived up to her name. She and Kadar had confronted rass before, and they had always been victorious against the great snakes. Though the rass were the natural enemies of the kreel, giant hooded cobras with an insatiable appetite for kreel eggs, Istikah did not fear them. Rather, she seemed to hate them with an almost human zeal. It was why she was so effective against them. And it was why Kadar had bonded with her so well, better than with any kreel before her. Both were driven, perhaps irrationally, and both had no fear of death.

It hadn't always been so for Kadar. In the days before the coming, he had loved life and dreaded its eventual end. With the amulet's help, he had buried many wives. But none had he loved so much as Jitendra. With her death, the lure of immortality lost its strange appeal.

Kadar's eyes darted carefully over the rocks. There were mountainous regions like this one throughout the desert, where both kreel and rass made their homes. The rocks protected the creatures from the relentless sun and collected water when the scarce rains came. Yesterday Kadar had visited a kreel nesting ground in a range of red rocks much the same as this one. And he had found to his horror that the clutches of eggs had been devoured; the kreels protecting them driven off. The sands of the desert did a poor job of maintaining tracks, but a few long trails protected from the wind told a very ominous tale, and a single scale left behind had confirmed Kadar's fears. They were after a rass of enormous length, thirty feet across at least and as wide around as a stout man. It was an old rass, certainly, no doubt new to the region. Left alone, it would dominate the other snakes and eat its fill of the precious kreel eggs, for it had fangs the size of scimitars and could easily best the biggest kreel.

Sitting atop Istikah, Kadar knew he should be frightened, but he was not. He had never hunted a rass so large, but back home in his palace he had a collection of jaws from the beasts. There were eleven of the gruesome trophies now, polished to an ivory sheen and propped open to reveal their curving fangs. One more would make an even dozen. Or he would die. There were no draws when hunting rass. There was no quarter. The rass were swift and lethal, and immensely aggressive in guarding their lairs. To enter one was to invite their wrath, but Kadar had come prepared. Beneath his layered gaka was an armored suit formed from the scales of dead kreel, a remarkably tough but light plating that even the jaws of rass had difficulty piercing. Kadar had worn the armor to hunt many times. Tethered to Istikah's harness was a spear with a long, thin blade, sharp enough to penetrate the rass' lightly armored skin. He had a shield with him also, covered in kreel scales. Most importantly, though, he had his whip, the weapon of choice for kreel riders. Once, before the coming, the whips had simply been used to train the kreel. But losing Jitendra to the northerners had shown Kadar the need for the Jadori to defend themselves, and the whip had evolved into a potent weapon. Just like the rass, the whip was lightning fast. And at fifteen feet in length it could keep even an enormous opponent at bay. Kadar and his men had become experts with the weapon, easily capable of taking down a man or beast from the back of a kreel at full gallop. They had perfected the whip's rolling, snapping techniques, and none of them ever left the palace without it. Not since the coming.

Just like his city and its people, Kadar himself had changed since the coming of the northerners. He was older now, physically. With the power of the amulet and its great spirit removed, he had aged. His dark hair was streaked with gray and he no longer had all his youthful vitality. Most of all, though, he missed Jitendra. She had been his most precious thing, his greatest reason for living. He often wondered if her death was why he tested himself against the rass, why he never heeded the calls of his advisors to send younger men after the beasts. He was kahan, he told himself, and so killing the rass was his responsibility. But even he knew he didn't have to ride off after them alone. He chose to be alone. Maybe to die alone. He had responsibilities to Jador and to Grimhold, but if he died out here in his beloved desert, he supposed he really wouldn't mind.

Istikah's tongue continued probing the air. She had not moved a muscle since her scales had turned gold. The link between them told Kadar Istikah smelled rass scat. And something else. There was the usual scent of the enemy snakes, which equated in Kadar's human mind to something like leather. But Istikah picked another scent out of the air, one that it took both kreel and rider a moment to comprehend. Old skin.

The shedding time.

Kadar gripped Istikah's reins tighter, sensing her excitement. Like all snakes, the rass periodically shed their skins. It was at this time, during the shedding, that they were most vulnerable. If they could surprise the creature in its lair while it was shedding. . . .

Kadar didn't like the idea of rushing into the rocks, but they needed to hurry to take the advantage. Istikah sensed his decision in a wordless instant, moving slowly toward the rocks. Such was the bond between them, so strong now that Kadar hardly needed tack at all. Istikah wore a saddle, which Kadar was strapped onto at the thighs to keep from sliding off her pitched back. A few light squeezes of his thighs, some gentle tugs of the reins, were all that was needed to control the kreel. They had become one. When they were together, they were more than a pair. Istikah picked her way over the sands, her powerful, biped limbs making no sound. She had sharp claws on her front limbs, which were much shorter than her legs but excellent for close combat. As she moved toward the rocks, she lowered her reptilian head, her large eyes narrowing, her tongue still pricking at the air. Kadar untied the shield from her harness and slid his left arm into its straps. With his right arm he took up the spear. Crouching low on his mount, he kept the spear out before him. If he'd suspected the rass would be out in the open, he would have chosen his whip, but if the beast was shedding he might be able to deal a quick killing blow without first subduing it.

Istikah's wide feet stalked through the sand, and the ground began to harden as they entered the rocks. An archway of stone bid them entrance, and soon they were in a mountainous pass, very narrow and tall. Two walls of steep rock climbed above them, creating an avenue that split off into various, winding directions. Istikah paused, taking measure of their surroundings. Kadar watched carefully, assuring himself that the rass had not seen them. If, as he suspected, the rass was shedding, it would be too preoccupied to sense them, and they had entered downwind of the rocks, giving Istikah and her sharp senses the advantage.

Kadar didn't need to tell his mount what he wanted; Istikah probed the air for a moment, then chose her direction. The scent of the skin was strongest to the right. Kadar hefted his spear, still crouching behind his shield as Istikah approached the scent. Blood pumped like thunder in his temples. He was on a razor's edge, lusting for the coming battle. All the rage he had felt at Jitendra's death had been channeled toward these monster serpents, and Kadar knew his anger would sustain him. Twenty feet, thirty feet, a hundred feet or more; it didn't matter how big this creature was. He could slay it because he was Kadar. He was cursed to live without his beloved, and no rass, however fierce, could interfere with that destiny.

At the edge of another narrow canyon, Istikah again paused. There were rocks in the way and she dropped down behind them, letting her long neck move her probing eyes and tongue along the scene. This was it, she told her master silently. Her primitive brain relayed the fact as clearly as speech. The shedding rass was beyond these rocks, hidden somewhere in the narrow gorge. It was easy for the snake to make its way into the crevice, and Kadar knew that rass often shed their skins in such places, away from prying eyes. Again he sensed the serpent's vulnerability, sure that he could easily spear the beast before it noticed his attack. With luck it might not even be able to turn. The gorge was only about eight feet wide, and the rocks on both sides formed two sheer walls. There was light at the other end, space enough for the creature to flee, but if he speared it fast and true, there would be no escape.

Kadar pulled the wrappings from his face. He drew a slow, silent breath. He could feel the strength of his armor against his chest and legs and arms, but he hated the confinement of helmets. They were the garb of northern cowards. Good men of Jador wore no such defenses. They faced their opponents bravely, with full, unmasked faces.

At his command, Istikah stepped up over the rocks, staying as low as her big body would allow as she entered the lair. Sunlight slanted down from the stone walls, but much of the gorge was obscured by shadows and jutting rocks. Kadar studied the tunnel of stone, looking for a trace of the serpent. Anxious thoughts raced between him and Istikah through their arcane, silent link. Kadar could feel the reptile's sharpness, her sureness of foot and lust for revenge. She was a fierce creature at times like this, as frightening as any rass. Her hooked claws twitched at her sides, eager to open the snake's belly. Her keen tongue tasted the air, homing on the scent of shedding skin. Uninterrupted by Kadar, she slinked forward, her long, spiked tail straight out behind her.

As usual, Istikah spied the rass first. Her mind sent the message to Kadar. Together their eyes moved toward a hint of color in the distance. There, obscured by rocks and shadows, was the stout tail of the serpent. Half its long body was exposed but shadowed, while the other half was completely invisible. There was no movement from the creature, but that didn't surprise Kadar. The shedding was a long and tedious process, and often came in fits and starts. It was common for the snakes to rest between bouts of struggling free. Kadar couldn't help but smile. Only halfway through its shedding and trapped in this narrow gorge, the rass would be easy prey.

Gently now, he told Istikah. He raised his spear. *Closer. . . .*

The kreel obeyed, and the multicolored skin of the serpent became clearer. This one was black and speckled green, swirled with golden cobra markings. Drawing closer revealed its breathtaking size. For just a moment, Kadar felt the tingle of fear. He had never seen such an enormous rass. There was a brief flash of regret as he remembered his friend Ralawi, pleading with him not to hunt the creature alone.

But I am kahan, Kadar told himself. *I am better than this beast.*

They were well into the gorge now. Each step brought them closer to their prey. Kadar grew suddenly uneasy as he spied the monster, still unmoving. Istikah sensed his apprehension and reinforced it with her own confusion. Both agreeing, they took another cautious step, then another, and realized with shared dread that they weren't seeing the rass at all—they had stalked its dead and shed skin. Kadar felt the spear slacken in his grip. He was about to order Istikah out of the gorge when he felt a cold shadow climbing over his shoulder. Slowly turning, he looked into a pair of lidless, primeval eyes.

The great hood of the rass blocked out the sun. Two long fangs split its red mouth, and its horrible forked tongue vibrated as it let out a dreadful hiss. Its newly exposed skin glistened in the sunlight, moist and sparkling like a rainbow. A gleam of triumph sparkled in its strange eyes. Kadar froze under its glare. He was trapped now and he knew it. He gave the rass credit for its cleverness. With no time to turn, he raised his shield.

The rass struck like a thunderbolt, driving its hooded head against him. Istikah crouched as the blow smashed into Kadar's shield. The quick maneuver kept them from sprawling, and Kadar quickly countered, jabbing his spear at the rass just as it backed away. The serpent hovered from side to side, watching, safely distant from Kadar's weapon. Kadar knew he couldn't flee. To turn and run meant certain death. At this range the whip would be best, but there was no way to use it in the confines of the gorge. There was only one way out.

So Kadar raised his spear and charged, screaming a war whoop. Istikah lowered her head and ran for its belly, her sharp claws tearing at the air. Surprised, the rass reared for a second, then brought its tail around to stop them. Istikah leapt. Almost bounding over the tail, the last bit of it caught her, sending her tumbling into the sand. The concussion of the ground rattled Kadar. Still strapped to the saddle, he looked up to see the snake's jaws snapping toward him. His shield was up in an instant, battering back the reptilian head. Istikah hurried to her feet, but the rass quickly coiled its big body around, blocking their escape. Istikah charged its exposed underside, a doglike howl tearing from her throat. Her slashing claws caught the rass, ripping a wound in its belly. Enraged, the rass attacked again, striking for Kadar. Again his shield met the attack, again he drove it back. His spear jabbed at the moving target, missing as the rass easily dodged his attacks. Istikah moved like a dancer in the narrow gorge, her scales angrily speeding through colors. Kadar knew they had one chance. He needed to rope the beast to control it, to slow its great speed and give them the advantage. Quickly he tossed the shield aside, snatching the long whip from Istikah's harness. *One more charge,* he ordered his mount. *Get us free!*

The kreel obeyed, driving forward with a snarl. This time

the wounded rass protected itself, curling away. Kadar
knew it would strike in a moment. Barreling past it, he
turned in the saddle and uncoiled his whip, snapping it with
blinding speed. The weapon quickly ensnared the shocked
rass, hooking it beneath its wide hood. Istikah continued
forward, dragging the monster with them. Its head hovered
over Kadar, its jaws opened wide to grasp him. He rammed
the spear into its mouth, pushing it past its upper palate
and through its head. The serpent's crown exploded with
blood as the spear exited. Kadar released the spear but
held tight to the whip. At his command Istikah kept running, dragging the writhing beast behind her, out of the
dangerous gorge. Finally in the open, the kreel turned.
Seeing the badly wounded rass, she raced in for the killing blow.

There was nothing the rass could do. It was half dead
anyway. Istikah's claws slid like knives through its soft
scales, tearing open its belly.

When the rass was dead, Kadar ordered Istikah back.
The kreel's snout and claws were covered with blood. He
unstrapped himself from her saddle, dropping down into
the hot desert sand to take full measure of the beast, certainly the largest one he'd ever slain. Remarkably, he was
unscathed. He decided once again that immortality was
worthless. The kind of skill he possessed now only came
with age.

He pulled back his gaka and drew a dagger from his
belt, then went to the dead rass and began cutting free its
enormous jaws.

An hour later, Kadar was on his way home. The spires and
rectangular towers of Jador rose clearly above the desert
sands, but he did not hurry. It was satisfying to be alone
with Istikah, satisfying to glance down at the rass jaw hanging from his saddle, still wet with blood and bits of flesh.
It was mid-afternoon, and the sun was unbearable. The
cloth of his dark gaka burned with its heat. The scales of
Istikah's tough hide had turned a dusty shade of green,
reflecting the worst of the sunlight. The kreel's mind was
quiet as they rode. She, too, was satisfied. When they returned to the palace they would rest, Kadar decided. He
would take a bath in rosewater to soothe his aching mus-

cles, and Istikah would be well fed and rubbed. They had earned it. Kadar smiled and patted his mount's long neck. He loved the feel of her scales, like armor. Together they crested a dune and saw Jador sprawled out before them, rising like a great oasis out of the desert. In the last decade the city had grown. The outskirts reached a mile into the sands now, and more of the Ganjeese had come to live and trade among them. It was still a pretty city, though, white and sparkling. The Jadori had much to be proud of, Kadar knew. They were strong in a way they had never been before, more capable than ever of protecting Grimhold. Kadar considered this as he spied his city, then noticed a single rider coming toward them. Curious, he ordered Istikah to halt, then watched as the rider came into view, clearly having sighted them at the top of the dune. The rider changed course toward them. Wearing a black gaka with red piping, Kadar recognized the man as one of his own. He supposed it was his friend, Ralawi, come in search of him. He waved at the approaching rider, who returned the gesture.

He will be glad to see me alive, thought Kadar. He ordered Istikah toward him. It was indeed Ralawi, because as they got closer Kadar recognized his friend's kreel, a great, ill-tempered male with dark green streaks along its back. When they were but a few paces apart, Ralawi undid his cowl to show his face. Like all Jadori, he had beautiful dark skin and piercing eyes. He smiled at Kadar, and at the jaws hanging from his saddle.

"You are alive, I see," he said in a mocking voice. "I had not thought you would be."

"Ah, alive and victorious," replied Kadar. He rode up to greet his friend, patting the jaws at his side. "See the size of it, Ralawi? I swear to Vala, it was a monster."

"Twenty-footer, by the look of it," said Ralawi.

"Thirty, and you know it," jibed Kadar.

Ralawi's smile was warm. "You look uninjured. I'm glad."

"You were worried?"

"Of course. If you were smart, you'd have been worried too."

Kadar looked up into the sun. It had taken a long time for Ralawi to come looking for him.

"I know what you're thinking," said Ralawi, "but I didn't come out to rescue you."

"No?"

"Your order was to obey you, Kadar, and that is what I did. But I have news. Ela-daz is here."

Kadar was surprised by the statement, though gladdened. In the tongue of Jador, Ela-daz meant "little one." He said, "Ela-daz? When?"

"She's only just arrived. I told her you would be back soon and she said she would wait for you, that there was no hurry to speak with you. But I thought you would like to know."

"Indeed, Ralawi, thank you," replied Kadar. It had been months since Ela-daz had been to Jador, and he was anxious to see her. "Is she alone?"

"The big one is with her."

"Always," said Kadar. "Anyone else?"

"She has brought two young ones as well."

Kadar smiled. It was good when Ela-daz brought more into her fold. Kadar liked to see Grimhold growing. It added purpose to his life.

"Come," he told Ralawi. "I don't want to keep her waiting."

Forgetting his bath, Kadar directed Istikah toward the city, eager to see his old companion. Though she had been out riding for hours, Istikah was far from exhausted, and carried her master with swift ease. Ralawi and his own kreel kept pace, striding quickly across the desert sand. As they rode, Kadar told of his encounter with the rass, and how he and Istikah had slain it. Ralawi listened, shaking his head, and Kadar could feel his old friend's disapproval.

"You wish to die," said Ralawi as they neared the city. "That must be it."

Kadar didn't answer. He rode into the outskirts of the city where his palace stood, guarding the mountains in the distance. The gates of his home, which had been erected after the coming, opened as he approached, controlled by a pair of sentries. As he passed the gates and entered one of his many gardens, he asked the sentries about Ela-daz. She was in the aurocco, they replied, waiting for him.

Waiting for him. Kadar chuckled, reminded of her endless patience. He dismounted, asking Ralawi to look after Istikah, and made his way to the aurocco, unraveling his headpiece as he went. It would not do to greet his friend

with a covered face. She was not of his kind, but she understood their customs well enough, and expected certain
things. More importantly, Kadar respected her. They had
been friends for many decades.

The aurocco was located on the side of the palace facing
the mountains. It was a vast, open air chamber with dozens
of arches and pillars, a place of prayer devoted to Vala.
Whenever she came to the palace, Ela-daz always visited
the aurocco. As Kadar entered the antechamber, he heard
his footsteps echo through the stone structure, bouncing
back and forth between the ancient arches and columns.
There was dazzling artwork on the ceiling and floors, geo-
metric mosaics made of multicolored tiles arranged in ro-
settes and star patterns. The architecture of the place
invited contemplation before entering the even more imposing aurocco. Because the aurocco was so large, it took
a moment for Kadar to locate Ela-daz among the pillars.
But soon he heard her, her gentle voice wafting through
the chamber. Silently he followed the voice, hiding behind
the pillars as he approached. Then he saw her, pointing out the
mosaics to the youngsters she had brought with her. They
were a boy and a girl, twins from the looks of them, both
with canes to bolster their badly twisted legs. The boy's
back was rounded with an ugly hump, while the girl had
no such deformity. To Kadar's eye, they looked no older
than eight years old.

Ela-daz, on the other hand, looked typically timeless. Because she wore the amulet, she was without age. Standing
apart from her was Trog, her bodyguard. He was first to
sight Kadar among the pillars, but did nothing to alert his
mistress. Kadar gave the giant a smile of thanks, pleased
that he could watch Ela-daz for a while. The sleeves of her
colorful coat swirled as she pointed out the many marvelous artworks in the aurocco, her elfin face split with a wide
grin. Ela-daz always took great pride in showing off the
aurocco. And she always told her young charges the same
thing—this was only the first of many wondrous sights.

Ela-daz, or Minikin as she was called across the desert,
lifted her face to smile at Kadar. He stepped out from the
shadows to greet her.

"Discovered," he laughed, speaking in her language.
"How long did you know?"

"I heard you approaching a few moments ago," replied the little woman. She put her small arms around the children and ushered them forward. "Kahan Kadar, this is Gendel and Keir, from Kana."

"Brother and sister?" asked Kadar.

Ela-daz nodded. "Their parents are dead. They had no one to care for them. They were in the streets when I found them."

"Starving from the look of them," said Kadar. The boy was horribly emaciated, and the girl's clothes, though clean, hung from her like cloth on a pole. He gave the children the warmest smile he could muster. "Ah, but you will be well now, certainly. Ela-daz will take good care of you."

The girl frowned in puzzlement. "Ela-daz?"

"A term of endearment, child," replied the little woman. "It is what they call me here."

"What does it mean?" asked the boy.

"Just the same as my regular name," said the woman. "It means 'little one.' Now. . . ." She directed the children toward Trog. "Wait with Trog while I speak to Kahan Kadar, all right? I shan't be long."

The children obeyed, going to Trog and standing beneath his tall, protective shadow. Ela-daz turned and went toward Kadar, looping an arm through his and leading him away from the children.

"It's good to see you, Shalafein," she said. "I've missed you."

Kadar was happy. He enjoyed being called *shalafein,* a word that in his dialect meant "great protector."

"It's been too many months, my friend," he agreed. "I had begun to think you had forgotten us."

She laughed at the absurdity of the idea. "It was time to come and visit."

"Yes, the little ones," said Kadar. "Will you be leaving with them soon?"

Ela-daz shook her head slightly. "No. I'll send them on without me. I'll be staying here a little while. I have . . . things to discuss with you."

Kadar stopped walking. "Bad things?"

The little woman's face became grave. "Shalafein, there is trouble coming from the continent. We must prepare for it."

43

Condors wheeled in the desert sky, sailing the winds above the hot sands. A breeze blew across the shifting, golden earth, forever changing the horizon. It was high noon, and the sun was a relentless ball of fire burning the backs of the drowas and cooking the men in the tall, cloth-covered wagons. Behind them, Ganjor and its pools of clean water were a desperate memory. Ahead, the Desert of Tears taunted them with its shimmering heat. The caravan had traveled for two days now, leaving Ganjor and its safety for the scorching unknown of the desert. Headed by a desert leader named Grak, the caravan had six of the unusual desert wagons and twelve drowas, all heavily laden with waterskins and goods for Jador. Grak's eight children hung from the sides of the wagons, talking and laughing as the caravan slowly crawled across the desert. And in the last wagon, crammed between sacks of grain and water skins, a trio of northerners shielded themselves from the blistering sun, having spent their last few pennies on passage to Jador.

Upon Cassandra's death, Gilwyn, Lukien, and Baron Glass had fled Liiria as quickly as possible. They had met Breck at his little farm in Borath, telling him what had happened and warning him that Akeela would soon be after him, too. Knowing there was nothing to do but flee the farm he'd spent years building, Breck and his family abandoned their home, heading north into Jerikor to es-

cape. Before doing so he gave his friends what little money
he could spare, enough to get them to Marn. Baron Glass
and Lukien had enough gold for the rest of the trip, and
assured Gilwyn that they would make it safely to Ganjor.
It had been an arduous trip. They had only two horses
between them, because Tempest was too old to make the
trip. So they hitched Gilwyn's library cart to a pair of geld-
ings given to them by Breck and headed south, first to
Farduke and then on to Dreel, carefully avoiding the Principality of Nith. All the while as they traveled they looked
over their shoulders for Akeela. They took turns driving
the wagon, and even one-armed Baron Glass did his best.
He was a stoic man and Gilwyn had come to like him in
their brief time together. Since the death of Cassandra, he
was the only one who spoke to Gilwyn. Lukien generally
said nothing to anyone. Cassandra's death haunted him. He
spoke only when necessary and ate very little, and he did
not seem at all perturbed by their predicament. Rather, he
seemed bent on reaching Jador, no matter the cost. With
his golden armor still locked safely in the chest Breck had
given him and the Eye of God wrapped in a burlap sack,
Lukien was like a dark messenger, bent on delivering his
bad news to the Kahan of Jador and returning the amulet
that had caused so much misery. Of the few things he had
told Gilwyn on their trip south, one still rung in Gilwyn's
mind.

"This amulet has destroyed me," he had said one night
in Marn. "I will see it back to Kadar, and if he kills me,
then so be it."

The gloom of those words haunted Gilwyn now as he
spied Lukien, sitting apart in the wagon, his head bobbing
in half-sleep. Gilwyn sat near the opening, alternatively
watching Lukien and the blue sky above. Between them
sat Baron Glass, also silent and half asleep. There was little
to do on the long trek through the desert, and talking
wasted precious strength. They had paid Grak the very last
gold they had for passage to Jador, and Grak had happily
agreed. He did not strike Gilwyn as a greedy man, but his
eyes had lit up at the sight of the Liirian coins. For that he
promised safe passage to Jador, food and water along the
way, and no guarantees when they reached the white city.
Jador, Grak explained, wasn't open to foreigners any more.

Only Ganjeese were allowed in the city, and only then in manageable numbers. The Ganjeese of Jador kept to their own ghettos, too, little pockets of the city that had sprung up in the past decade. But northerners, whether from Liiria or Marn or Reec, were strictly forbidden in Jador. Grak had been honest enough to warn them that they might be killed on sight. Lukien had merely shrugged at the suggestion. And Baron Glass, who had done almost all of the bargaining and planning on their trip, agreed to the passage with his usual stoicism.

Gilwyn turned away from Lukien to stare at the ever-changing sands. Even with the shade of the wagon, the heat was choking. Like Glass and Lukien, he wore a dark gaka to stave off the worst of the sun, but beneath the cloth he itched and perspired. Teku was asleep in his lap. Being from Ganjor herself, the little monkey had taken well to the heat, spending much of her time sleeping and eating dates. Gilwyn stroked her lightly as he watched the desert, rocking gently with the motion of the caravan. In the wagon up ahead he could hear two of Grak's sons arguing, but he didn't understand the words. Of the family, only Grak spoke the tongue of the north, another reason Glass had chosen him for the journey. At first, the children had been curious about Gilwyn and the others, especially Glass. They had stared at the stump of his arm, making the baron bristle. And they had been enamored with Teku as well, but only for a short while. Monkeys like her were common in Ganjor. Eventually they had all settled down, leaving the trio to the dreary confines of the wagon where Glass always slept and Lukien never said a word.

It had been weeks since they had fled Liiria, but to Gilwyn it seemed like years. He had never expected his life to take such turns. At the library he had been happy. He'd had a good life there with Figgis. Now he was an outlaw. And Figgis? Dead, probably. Baron Glass had explained it to him. Mercy, he had said, should not be expected from Akeela. Lukien had silently concurred. To both of them, Akeela was a monster beyond redemption. Yet even as he fled his home, Gilwyn couldn't quite believe that. He remembered what Cassandra had said about King Akeela, how he was mad but still sweet in his own, demented way.

The caravan continued through the day and into the night,

finally stopping when the sun dipped below the sands. As the wagon came to a halt, Lukien finally stirred. They were all eager to stretch and so vacated the wagon, dropping down into the hot sands and watching as Grak and his family made camp. The desert became remarkably cool at night, so Grak's three sons began making a fire while his wife and daughters prepared food. It was the best part of the day and Gilwyn's stomach immediately began to rumble. He had trouble walking in the soft sands, even with his strange boot, but he approached the boys and helped them with the fire. While they worked, Lukien leaned against the wagon, absently watching the stars appear. When the food was ready he sat apart from the others, leaving Gilwyn and Glass alone to eat with Grak's family. Gilwyn watched Lukien take his plate aside, sitting against one of the tall wagon wheels and picking at his food. He looked old and miserable, and Gilwyn felt sorry for him. Baron Glass noticed his expression and jabbed him lightly with his elbow.

"Don't worry about him," he said softly. "He'll come around."

Gilwyn gave Teku a date then sent her off to play with Grak's daughters. "He blames me for Cassandra dying," he said.

Glass shook his head. "I shouldn't think so."

"No, he does," replied Gilwyn. "And I don't blame him. I told him that the curse was a hoax. But I was so sure. . . ." He shrugged and stared down at his food. "I don't know what happened."

"It's not for you to know, Gilwyn," said Glass. "It is the Fate that decides such things."

The notion made Gilwyn scoff. "I don't believe that."

"No? Well you should, because it's true. We're all given a purpose in life. Even Cassandra's death has a purpose. If Lukien believed in the Fate, he would not be so miserable now. He would take solace in the knowledge that there's a reason for everything."

"If you say so," replied Gilwyn. He wanted to ask the baron what possible purpose there could be for losing an arm, but he thought better of it. "I don't know what to believe. All I know is that Cassandra is dead, and Figgis is probably dead, too, and Breck and his family had to leave their home and here I am on my way to getting beheaded."

Glass laughed loudly, and suddenly Gilwyn was laughing with him. Grak looked at them across the camp fire and smiled. Lukien heard them, too. The knight cocked his ear in their direction without turning around.

"I don't think Lukien cares what happens to us in Jador," whispered Gilwyn. "I think he wants to die."

"If you think that, then you do not yet know Lukien," said Glass.

The answer perplexed Gilwyn, but he decided not to pursue it. Instead he ate his meal in silence, satisfied with the good food and the gentle music of the desert. When he was done he set down his plate and went to Lukien. Hovering over him, he noticed at once that the knight had hardly touched his supper.

"You should eat, Lukien," said Gilwyn. "It does no good to starve yourself."

Lukien set his plate down on the sand. "Gilwyn," he said, "I heard what you told Thorin, about me blaming you. I don't."

Gilwyn flushed. "No?"

"No. I did, but not anymore." Lukien patted the soft sand beside him. "Sit with me a while. I haven't talked much, I know, but I'm ready for some company now."

Grateful for the invitation, Gilwyn sat down at once. Near the campfire he saw Baron Glass look at him and smile before turning away. Lukien stared up at the sky. There were thousands of stars and a bloody red moon.

"Lukien?" asked Gilwyn.

"Yes?"

"What will you do when we reach Jador?"

Without hesitation, Lukien replied, "I will give Kadar back his blasted amulet. Then if he wants to kill me, I'll let him."

"You won't fight?"

"I won't fight Kadar."

"But you brought your armor," Gilwyn observed. "Why?"

"Because I owe Kadar a debt," said Lukien. "And I'm going to repay it, any way he wants."

There was no more to say, so Gilwyn said no more.

For two more days the caravan traversed the desert, suffering in its heat and obeying its fickle whims, until at last

Jador appeared on the horizon. It was much as Lukien had remembered, and much different, too. The first thing he recalled was its beautiful white towers, rectangular works of limestone that reflected the sun like a beacon across the sands. The towers had hardly changed at all, but there were more of them now. In the last sixteen years, Jador had sprawled. It seemed taller to Lukien now, and far less compact. Sixteen years ago, the sight of Jador had impressed him. Now, sadly, it frightened him. He leaned out over the side of the wagon, marveling at the city and watching Gilwyn. The boy's fair skin was sunburned, despite the gaka, and redness surrounded his eyes. The trip had exhausted them all, but the sight of Jador heartened them. Thorin leaned over with them, struggling to support himself with his one arm. They had pulled back the canvas cover to get a better view, and the sun was hot on their backs. Grak's family chatted happily among themselves, pointing at their destination and smiling. They had all fared well, even the youngest children. Their heartiness surprised Lukien, who himself was spent from the long voyage and eager to see fresh water again. Remembering Jador's fresh, sparkling fountains, he let out a languid sigh. It would be good to take a bath, just one at least before Kadar killed him. He wondered if the desert ruler ever granted final wishes.

Thorin whistled as Jador grew on the horizon. "Amazing. I never thought it was so big."

"It's grown," Lukien admitted. "It wasn't that big when I was here."

"Are you ready?" asked Thorin gravely.

Lukien shrugged. "It's a bit late to turn around now."

None of them really knew what to expect in Jador. According to Grak, Kahan Kadar was still in charge, and didn't take well to foreigners. Lukien wasn't sure if the kahan would remember him by sight; he had aged badly over the years. But once he turned over the amulet, he was sure Kadar would remember him. After that, who knew? They might all be killed simply for setting foot in Jador. Even Gilwyn. Lukien glanced at the boy, who wore a peculiar expression. Lukien couldn't tell if the boy was afraid or simply awed by the city.

"I'll do the talking when we get there," Lukien explained. "I'll try to get Kadar to listen to me, and hopefully spare the two of you. You're innocent, after all."

"If we get that far," said Thorin. "The Jadori might kill us on sight."

"I don't think so," said Lukien. "They're a peaceful people, or at least they were. And once they see the amulet, they'll let us see Kadar."

"Peaceful? That's not what Grak says," said Gilwyn. "They've changed, Lukien, remember."

"He'll speak to us," said Lukien. "Even if it's just to spit in my face."

It took another hour for the caravan to reach the outskirts of the city. The tall towers and elaborately turned spires of central Jador dropped off into collections of squat brick homesteads and marketplaces. Around the old city towered a giant stone wall, while the outskirts themselves were unprotected, with barely a shadow of the old city's beauty. The Ganjeese lived in the outskirts, Grak had explained, because foreigners weren't welcome inside the city proper. Lukien and his companions kept their faces hidden as the caravan entered the narrow avenues of the outskirts, choked with traders and running children and stray dogs. Grak had promised to take them directly to Kadar's palace, but had warned them that they might be searched at the city gates. They made no sound as they neared the gates, trying to look inconspicuous inside the wagon. Better to be taken directly to the palace, Lukien had decided, but if guards stopped them at the gates he wouldn't fight them. Beside him, Gilwyn held Teku in his lap, silently stroking her. The avenue widened as they approached the iron gates, revealing four guardians, all in black gakas trimmed with crimson cloth. Two of the guardians were mounted on kreels. The sight of the enormous lizards startled Lukien. They looked nothing like the docile beasts he remembered. These were far more muscular and fierce, with heavy armor plating and stout bridles fixed in their fanged snouts. The mounted men held spears. Long, coiled whips dangled at their sides. Their reptilian mounts blinked slowly in the heat, hardly stirring.

"Are those kreel?" whispered Gilwyn. "They don't look anything like the ones in Ganjor."

"No," agreed Lukien, "they don't. I don't know if we'll be able to get past the guards."

"Let's wait and see," suggested Thorin.

Lukien went to the back of the wagon where he kept his iron chest. Opening it, he found the burlap sack with the Eye of God atop his bronze armor. He took the sack then quickly closed the chest and went back to his companions. Gilwyn looked at him curiously.

"What's that for?" he asked.

"An invitation to the ball," said Lukien, then sat back to wait.

The caravan wound its way to the gate, led by Grak atop his drowa. There, he stopped the caravan and began talking to the guards. The two who were on foot listened and nodded. Lukien and his companions strained to hear the exchange. It was in Jadori, so he didn't understand a word, but there seemed to be trouble. He spied Grak through the confines of his cowl. The desert man was cajoling the guardians, obviously trying to explain that his caravan carried nothing dangerous. The mounted guardians moved their kreels closer to the caravan, peering into the wagons from the backs of their reptiles.

"We should get out there," Lukien told the others quickly. "I don't want to put Grak or his family at risk."

"No," said Thorin. "Wait."

The mounted guards drew closer, inspecting each wagon in turn. Lukien listened as they questioned the people in each one.

"They're going to discover us," he said. "Let's not make this any harder than we have to."

Holding the burlap sack, he climbed out of the wagon and into the street. One of the mounted guards noticed him and turned his kreel.

"Lukien, get back in here!" hissed Thorin.

Up ahead, Grak's eyes went wide. The guardians at the gate pointed at Lukien, asking questions that made Grak stutter.

"It's all right, Grak," Lukien called to him. "This is far enough." Then, with the Jadori guards watching, he unwrapped the cowl from his face. The Jadori looked at him in astonishment, but made no threatening moves. When he was sure it was reasonably safe, Lukien called to the others.

"Thorin, Gilwyn, come down," he said. "There's no sense going on."

Sputtering in anger, Thorin was the first out of the wagon. He helped Gilwyn down the best he could, then turned to face the Jadori. With Teku perched on his shoulder, Gilwyn removed his facecloth and smiled nervously at the guards. Thorin did the same, still muttering at Lukien.

The mounted guards moved cautiously closer. Lukien stood firm as the kreels sniffed the air with their tongues and narrowed their dark eyes on him. He expected the men to raise their spears, but instead they merely watched, shocked and fascinated. Grak's family had fallen silent, too afraid to make a sound. Grak himself was still talking to the foot guards, hurriedly explaining the presence of the foreigners. He shot Lukien an angry glare.

"Tell them the truth, Grak," Lukien advised. "Tell them who we are and that we're here to see Kadar."

Grak shook his head in exasperation. "You are very stupid, Liirian."

"Tell them."

Grak obeyed, and the Jadori guards listened, perplexed by the tale. The one nearest Lukien ordered his kreel a bit closer, studying him intently.

"They want to know why you wish to see Kadar," said Grak. "What should I tell them?"

"Don't tell them anything," said Lukien. "Let me show them."

In all the days he had traveled with Grak, Lukien had never revealed the real reason they were going to Jador. Now he slowly reached into the sack and pulled out the Eye of God. Beside him, he heard Thorin whisper a warning. The guards frowned, raising their spears a bit. But when they saw the amulet emerge, they nearly dropped their weapons. Grak and his family gasped at the sight.

"Inai ka Vala," Lukien proclaimed. Then he leaned over to Gilwyn and asked, "That's right, isn't it?"

Gilwyn nodded, swallowing nervously.

"Inai ka Vala," Lukien said again. "For Kadar."

The sight of the Eye amazed Grak. He stepped forward, ignoring the guards and staring at the amulet in Lukien's hand. The ruby at it center caught the bright sun, sending its light spiraling across his face.

"Where did you get that?" asked Grak angrily.

"It doesn't matter," replied Lukien. "Tell them it belongs to Kadar."

"We know who it belongs to! That is Inai ka Vala, the life amulet!"

Lukien nodded. "I've brought it back for Kahan Kadar." He looked at the guards, trying to make them understand. "Kadar," he repeated. "Inai ka Vala for Kadar."

"They know that," said Grak. "But how?"

"Tell them to take us to the palace," ordered Thorin. His big voice made the guards take notice. "Kadar," he pronounced. "Take us to him."

The guard closest to them raised his spear and put out his hand.

"He wants the amulet," Grak explained.

"Make him promise to take us to Kadar," said Lukien.

"Liirian, you do not understand," said Grak. "You are being arrested. They will take you to Kadar if Kadar wishes to see you, but you have no choice. Give him the amulet."

Lukien hesitated, but Thorin encouraged him to surrender. "Grak's right, Lukien. We've come all this way to deliver the amulet."

"And to deliver our message," Lukien reminded him. "Grak, tell them it's very important that we see Kadar. Tell them we have vital news for him. Life and death news."

Grak sighed but did as Lukien asked. The guards listened, then once again pointed their weapons at the foreigners. The one in the lead insistently kept his hand outstretched, insisting that Lukien hand over the Eye.

"Well?" asked Lukien. "Do they agree?"

"It's as I said," replied Grak. "They will tell Kadar you are here. It is up to the kahan whether or not he will speak with you."

"I think that's the best we can hope for, Lukien," suggested Gilwyn. "Give him the amulet before they kill us."

Seeing no choice, Lukien acquiesced. He handed the Eye of God over to the guard. The man took it carefully, as if holding something holy. Then he took the sack from Lukien as well, putting the amulet safely away. He spoke to Grak as he gestured at Lukien and his companions.

"He says you three are to follow him," Grak explained.

More incomprehensible words from the guard. Grak nodded.

"He says that you will go alone. My family and I are to stay behind, outside the wall."

"I'm sorry, Grak," said Lukien. "I didn't want you to get in trouble."

Grak gave a broken smile. "We are not in trouble. But I think you may be." He put out his hand for Lukien. "Luck to you, my friends."

"And to you," said Lukien. "Thank you for taking us this far. Will you look after our things for us? Hopefully we'll be back."

Grak agreed, telling Lukien that they would wait in the outskirts for them to return. The guard stepped between them, pushing Lukien toward the gate. His unmounted companion did the same with Glass, but was more careful with Gilwyn once he saw the boy's uneven gait. Lukien led the way through the tall iron gates, followed closely by Thorin and Gilwyn. Two of the Jadori guards escorted them, one on foot, the other mounted atop his snorting kreel. As they stepped into the city, the eyes of curious Jadori fell on them. Whispers moved through the crowd. Lukien avoided their stares. He glanced ahead and saw the magnificent palace of Kahan Kadar against the sky. It was just as he remembered, beautiful and bright. Behind it stood the silent mountains. The guards steered them toward the palace with rough commands, pointing with their spears. The crowds of people in the street parted to let them pass.

"Is that Kadar's castle?" asked Gilwyn.

Lukien nodded. "That's it."

"At least they're taking us to see him," said Thorin. The baron spied the palace, sizing it up. "Impressive."

The guard at their backs urged him to continue. Lukien did nothing to anger them. He obeyed without question, heading quietly toward the palace. When at last they reached its sprawling grounds, crossing through another great gate and into a green and verdant garden, the guards finally stopped to confer with some companions, two more Jadori men in similar black and red garb. These new men listened to the story of the trio's capture, plainly shocked when the Eye of God was handed to them. One of the guards turned to Lukien.

"You have come to see Kadar?" he asked.

The words were spoken perfectly, startling Lukien.

"You speak our tongue?" he asked.

The man nodded. Like the guards who had brought them here, he and his own companion bore spears and long, serrated swords at their belts.

"I know your words," he said through his black face cloth. "You have brought Inai ka Vala. Where did you find it?"

"We'll tell that to Kadar," said Lukien.

"Who are you?" pressed the man.

"Let's just say Kadar knows me. Please, let us speak to him."

The man conferred with his comrade, speaking in Jadori. Finally, he asked, "Do you have weapons?"

"No," said Lukien. "We're unarmed. We left our belongings with the caravan that brought us here. To be honest, we have valuables with them still, things that are important to us. If you could—"

"Your things will be found," the guard interrupted. "Come with me."

He turned and walked through the garden. None of his fellow guards followed. The man on the kreel pointed his spear, directing Lukien and the others after him. Lukien exchanged a surprised glance with Thorin, then proceeded after the guard, following him toward the palace. Around them the garden bloomed with pink flowers and gurgled with the sounds of crystalline fountains. The white walls of the courtyard blanketed the grounds with shadows. Gilwyn looked around, marveling at the many plants and statues. A gaggle of children tumbled on the lawn, stopping their playing to stare at them.

"What a beautiful place," Gilwyn whispered.

At last they reached the main structure of the palace, finally passing through an unguarded door and into a splendid corridor. Just as they had been sixteen years ago, the walls of the palace were a smooth, cool white. Lukien glanced around, pleased to see that not everything had changed. The place still had its old, welcoming charm.

After a few moments, the guard stopped at a chamber

with a wooden door. He pushed the door open to reveal a small room flooded with sunlight from rectangular, glassless windows. There were some chairs in the room and a small table. Except for these things, the chamber was empty.

"You will wait here," said the man.

Lukien peered inside. The room seemed unthreatening, even comfortable. "You'll get Kadar for us?"

"I do not *get* the kahan," replied the man. "You will wait."

Lukien smiled. "Right." He entered the chamber, followed by Gilwyn and Thorin. Gilwyn quickly took a seat, glad to relax his bad foot. Teku climbed down from his shoulder to rest on the table. The windows were low and easily wide enough for a man to pass through, but the courtyard beyond seemed unguarded. The guard left the room, still carrying the Eye of God in its burlap sack and closing the door behind him.

Now there was nothing to do but wait, so Lukien joined Gilwyn near the small table. Thorin paced uneasily about the room, then settled to looking out the windows. His face was tight and serious. Long minutes ticked by without any of them speaking, until Gilwyn mentioned he was thirsty. Lukien agreed, hoping that someone would soon appear and let them out. Surprisingly, the door seemed unguarded. It would have been an easy thing to step into the garden and drink from a fountain. But none of them suggested the idea. Thorin continued staring toward the mountains in the distance, sighing as the minutes mounted.

Then at last they heard footfalls. The door opened. Lukien expected to see the guard again, but instead a lone figure stood on the threshold. The man's face, though older, was immediately familiar. Lukien rose at once.

Kahan Kadar had changed over the years. He was lean and stern looking now, with streaks of gray in his dark hair and beard. His olive skin sagged a little from long days in the sun but his eyes were bright and clear as he stared at Lukien. He barely bothered to glance at the others, keeping a steely gaze on the man who had slain his wife. Even before crossing the threshold, the room filled with his presence. Not knowing whether to speak or bow, Lukien simply stood there enduring his fiery stare.

"It is you," said the kahan finally. "By Vala, I never would have believed."

"Kahan Kadar," said Lukien. He bowed slightly. "I'm honored you've come."

In his hand Kadar held the Eye of God by its golden chain. He lifted it to show the foreigners. "You've brought me this," he said. "Why?"

"My lord Kadar," said Thorin, smiling diplomatically, "we've come on an urgent mission. The amulet—"

"Silence, one-arm," snapped Kadar. "I'm speaking to the man who killed my wife." Keeping his eyes on Lukien, he said, "Explain yourself. Why are you here, and why have you returned my amulet?"

It was a simple question, yet the answer was so complicated. "My friend speaks the truth," said Lukien. "We've come on a mission."

Kadar smirked. "A peace mission, perhaps? Like last time?" At last he glanced at the others. "And who are these you've brought with you? More thieves?"

"Let us explain, please, your lordship," said Thorin. "My name is Baron Thorin Glass, from Liiria." He pointed at Gilwyn and said, "This boy is named Gilwyn Toms. And you already know Lukien."

Kadar stepped forward, taking immediate notice of Gilwyn's strange boot and twisted left hand. Remarkably, he smiled at the boy. "Gilwyn Toms."

Gilwyn returned the smile. "Yes, my lord."

"You are welcome here," said Kadar. The statement startled them. Kadar turned quickly back to Lukien. "You are the one called the Bronze Knight. The one who killed my Jitendra."

"Yes, my lord," said Lukien. "And I'm truly sorry for it."

"And this?" Kadar asked, dangling the amulet in Lukien's face. "Was this not worth it to you?"

"No." Lukien's tone was flat. "It was not."

"Something happened to bring you here. Tell me."

"You speak very well now, my lord," Lukien observed. "Have you studied since we met last?"

"I've had time, Bronze Knight, and the need to learn about your people. Now, tell me what brought you here."

"We're trying to tell you," said Glass. "If you'd just listen, we have important news."

"No," said Kadar, shaking his head. "I want to know why you decided to bring the Eye back to me."

"All right," said Lukien, barely checking his anger. "Your blasted amulet is cursed. It's cost me everything, and everyone I care about. Is that what you want to hear?"

At last Kadar seemed satisfied. There was no joy on his face, but rather a look of complete understanding. And, for a moment, a glimpse of sadness. He gestured to the three chairs. "Sit."

Lukien hesitated, unnerved by Kadar's expression. But he did as asked, and his companions did the same. Teku slid onto Gilwyn's shoulder. Kadar watched the amulet for a time, turning slowly on its chain. He hardly seemed surprised by what Lukien had told him, or even pleased to have the life-giving Eye back.

"You've come to give me news," said Kadar. "Fine. But first, your story." He looked directly at Lukien. "Speak."

"If it satisfies you, I'll tell you," said Lukien, then proceeded to explain his sorry history. He started from the beginning, when he had first stolen the amulet, explaining how it had been needed to save Cassandra's life. It was not his idea, he told Kadar, but rather Akeela's, his king. Kadar nodded at the name, but did not interrupt. Lukien told him how the amulet had saved Cassandra, arresting her cancer for sixteen years. But Akeela had gone mad in that time, and he himself had been banished from Liiria. As he spoke, Kadar listened intently, his face barely showing any emotion. And when at last Lukien got to the part of Cassandra's death, Kadar only nodded and stroked his bearded chin.

"So you see, Kahan Kadar? I've lost everything. And so have these others." Lukien ended his story with a shrug. "Before she died Cassandra asked me to return the Eye to you. She had planned to come herself, but the curse killed her."

Kadar turned away to stare out the window. He was quiet for a long moment. The amulet hung loosely from the chain in his fist. At last he asked, "Did you not wonder why I never hunted you?"

"I did," said Lukien. "We escaped you easily, and I always wondered why. At first I thought you would come after us, but you never did."

"I never had to," said Kadar. He lifted the amulet. "This did it for me. It destroyed you."

Lukien understood. "It's cursed," he sighed. "Truly."

"It is protected," Kadar corrected. "I am the Eye's rightful owner, and you took it from me. The spirit of the Eye did what it had to."

"Spirit?" asked Lukien. "What do you mean?"

Kadar ignored the question. To Lukien's surprise, he did not put the amulet back around his neck, but rather let it dangle uselessly in his hand. "My wife died the night you left," he said. "Have you always known this?"

"No, not really," said Lukien. "But I always suspected it. Kadar, I'm sorry. I never meant for her to die, nor the child she was carrying. I'm not asking you to forgive me, but I want you to know it was an accident."

Kadar was unmoved. "Accident or no, she is dead."

"And I regret that more than I can say. That's the reason I've come back, partially. To give you back what is rightfully yours."

"And to warn you, Kadar," added Thorin. He rose from his chair and stood face to face with the kahan. "You can silence me after I've said my peace, but you need to know that you're in danger. We haven't come all this way just to give you back your bauble, but to tell you of an invasion."

"Indeed?" Kadar smiled thinly. "I am listening."

Thorin looked at Lukien, plainly surprised by the kahan's lack of interest. Lukien got to his feet and said, "My lord Kadar, you should listen to us. We speak the truth. You and your people are in great danger. My king—"

"Former king," corrected Thorin.

"Yes, our former king, Akeela, has formed an army to take back the Eye. He knows we've come here, and he wants it. He's marching for Jador even as we speak."

"For the Eye?" asked Kadar suspiciously. "Or for you, Bronze Knight?"

"Kadar, it doesn't matter what you think of me. You're right—Akeela is coming to kill me. But his army will slaughter you just the same. He wants that amulet just as much as he wants me."

"And something else," added Gilwyn. He got unsteadily to his feet. "My lord, King Akeela is looking for Grimhold."

Finally they'd said something to get Kadar's attention. "What does he know of Grimhold?"

"He knows that's where the Eyes of God come from," Gilwyn replied. "And he knows that it's somewhere in the mountains beyond here." Gilwyn studied Kadar. "Is that true, my lord? Is there really a Grimhold?"

Once again, Kadar gave the boy an enigmatic smile. "A great story, perhaps."

"My lord, we know about the amulets," insisted Gilwyn. "And we've seen the Witch of Grimhold. We know she exists."

Kadar's eyebrows shot up. "You continue to surprise me, boy. You say you've seen the Witch?"

"I have, my lord," said Gilwyn. "She entranced me so that I'd forget, but I remember her. I know she wears the other amulet, just like that one."

"Where did you see her?" asked Kadar. "In Jador?"

"No, in Liiria," said Gilwyn. "But I know it was her."

Kadar stepped lightly toward the window and stared out into the bright day. "If this witch is in Liiria, then why would your King Akeela come here for her?"

"He's not looking for the witch, my lord," said Lukien. He was growing frustrated now and went over to stand behind Kadar, trying to make him listen. "Akeela doesn't even know the witch exists. We told you, he's after your amulet. And there's someone else with him; a general named Trager. He'll be after Grimhold and whatever else he can get."

The desert leader did not turn from the window. He said simply, "No doubt you have seen how we've changed. We can protect ourselves."

"With respect, Kahan Kadar, I disagree," said Thorin. The baron went to Kadar's side, pressing him between himself and Lukien. "You don't know Akeela or what he's capable of. We've seen your men and their lizards. They're impressive. But they're no match for Liiria's army. You're in great danger."

"Do not be concerned," said Kadar. "We Jadori can look after ourselves."

Frustrated, Lukien glanced at Thorin, who seemed equally confused by Kadar's attitude. He didn't mind the kahan being evasive about Grimhold; he had expected that. But to turn a blind eye to the coming invasion seemed ridiculous.

"Kahan Kadar, we've come in good faith," he said. "I know you think I'm not to be trusted, and I don't blame you for that. I came here expecting to be punished however you decide. But—"

"There will be no punishment for you," said Kadar.

The reply made Lukien pause. "No punishment?"

"Have you not already been destroyed?" asked Kadar. "Have you not said so yourself? What more could I possibly do to you? You came here prepared to die. I know what that is like. That is enough."

Enough. The word surprised Lukien. Despite the suffering of his last sixteen years, he still expected cruelty from Kadar. Instead he was getting mercy.

"Then let me help you," he said suddenly. "You're going to need my help against Akeela."

"Lukien, easy," said Thorin.

Lukien ignored him. "Kadar, listen to me. Akeela *is* coming. You have to believe that. And if you're not going to kill me, than at least let me try to repay you for my wrongs. Let me help defend Jador."

For the first time, Kadar smiled at him. "You can never repay me for taking my Jitendra. But now you know what that hole in my heart is like. It is impossible to fill." He moved to the door. "I will think on what you've said. You will wait here in the palace. Rooms will be prepared for you."

"My lord, wait," pleaded Lukien. "There's no time for you to consider things. You have to act at once. You have to start preparing yourself for Akeela's invasion."

Kadar put up his hand as if uninterested. "No more talk. Rest. Food and drink will be brought to you. We will speak again."

Before he could leave the room Lukien was once again on his heels. "Wait, one more thing," he said. "How did you learn to speak our tongue? You didn't speak it sixteen years ago, I'm sure."

"I had a good teacher, Bronze Knight," replied Kadar. "And I had your people to worry about. It was time for me to learn."

With his strange reply hanging in the air, Kahan Kadar left the room, leaving the door open and his visitors blinking in confusion.

44

Akeela leaned back in his chair beneath the shade of a tree, studying the game board and his opponent's passive face. He had already lost his best pieces to the man, but was determined this time to best him. Around him, the noise of his army continued, a constant distraction. He reached over the table for his wine, drinking it down as he considered his predicament, then pouring himself another big goblet. Lieutenant Leal looked relaxed and confident. Akeela felt anxious and cross. It had been a very hard road south and it had taken them far longer to reach Farduke then he'd hoped or expected. He was tired and irritable, and playing crusade was his only comfort, beside the drink. As soon as they had reached the border of Nith, Akeela had called Leal to play with him. Their relationship had been awkward at first, because he was not used to being around his king and hardly knew how to react. But an odd friendship had quickly grown up between the two, at Akeela's insistence. Today they had been playing crusade for three hours straight, wasting the bulk of the afternoon while Trager and the other officers made camp. The day was warm and pleasant beneath the tree; the army had chosen a good spot to rest, just over the valley of Nith in a wide plain dotted with elm trees. The plain was more than large enough to accommodate Akeela's two thousand men, plus all their horses, wagons, weapons, and supplies. And because the men were used to traveling now, the tents had gone up quickly. Cooking fires had been started for the evening meals and now lit the land for acres, like stars in the sky. General Trager's voice came to Akeela over the breeze. The general was shouting orders in the distance, organizing his troops and making sure their horses were tended. It should have been mayhem with so many men, but Trager had a real gift for organization and things were going remarkably smoothly. According to their maps, there was a stream about half a mile east of their position, a tributary of the Agora River. Trager was having the various companies take turns watering their horses, making sure they all returned by sundown.

"My lord, it's your move," said Leal.

Akeela's eyes tilted up from the board. "I know," he said. "I'm thinking."

"Sorry, my lord."

"You're trying to distract me, Leal. It won't work."

He was a good man, the lieutenant, and according to Trager an excellent soldier. But when it came to playing crusade, he was a giant and had beaten Akeela in almost every game. And of the few games he had won, Akeela suspected Leal had deliberately not played his best. At last he reached for a game piece, moving his general across the board. Leal considered the move for only a moment, then brought out a catapult. The speed of the lieutenant's decision irritated Akeela.

"Are you sure that's the move you want to make?" he asked. "You didn't even think about it!"

"I did think about it, my lord," replied the soldier. "I knew if you moved your general, I'd move my catapult."

"Fine."

Akeela sank back into his own dark thoughts. Though he was losing badly, he was grateful for the distraction of the game. Since losing Cassandra, his mind had been a wasteland of misery and drink. He missed Koth and the comforts of Lionkeep, and he missed knowing his beloved wife was only a few steps away, safely locked in her private wing. Now all those things were gone, and all that remained were bad memories. And though it had been many years since he had left Koth, he derived no pleasure from their current travels or the beautiful countryside. He wanted only to reach Ganjor, and then Jador. And then, to find and kill Lukien.

"My lord?" asked Leal suddenly.

"Yes?"

"Do you think Prince Daralor will let us cross?"

"I'm sure he will," replied Akeela, surprised by the forwardness of the question. "One way or another."

Leal glanced away from the board, looking southward toward Nith. So far, their heralds had not returned. But Akeela wasn't worried. He expected an answer from Daralor soon, quite probably by nightfall.

"The people of Nith are proud, my lord," Leal reminded him.

"Now you sound like Trager," said Akeela. "Don't let his pessimism rub off on you, Leal. Once Daralor sees the size of our army, he'll let us pass, just as all the others have."

The words seemed to comfort Leal. Since leaving Koth, their army had met no resistance. Instead, the kings and princes of the lands they traveled had welcomed them, no doubt frightened by their size and reputation. Akeela supposed Trager was to thank for that, for the general had built the Liirian military into the terror of the world. In Marn and Farduke, they had even been greeted as heroes. They had been showered with gifts and good food and their supplies had been replenished, all thanks to the hard work of Will Trager. Akeela was grateful to his surly general. Now that Graig was gone, Trager was his only friend in the world.

"The general thinks we should go around," said Leal. "He says it would only cost us a day or so."

"We will not go around," said Akeela. His eyes narrowed on the game pieces, wondering if he should take Leal's catapult. "We don't have the time to spare."

"The general thinks we do, my lord. He's worried about crossing Nith."

"The general doesn't make those decisions," said Akeela. "Now be quiet and let me think."

In his annoyance he quickly moved his cavalryman, taking Leal's catapult. Leal smiled, then moved his war tower to take the cavalryman. Akeela's head began to pound.

With an angry grunt he picked up his goblet and took a long drink, the only thing that ever deadened his pain. When the goblet was drained he slammed it down on the little table, sending the game pieces jumping.

"I'm sick of this," he hissed. "I'm sick of being out here in the middle of nowhere, and I'm sick of all this bloody noise!"

The men around him making camp shot him nervous glances. Embarrassed, Akeela took a deep breath. Very carefully, Leal started to replace the pieces Akeela had toppled.

"We could start a new game, my lord," he suggested.

"What, and surrender? Forget it, boy. We continue."

"As you wish, my lord. It's your move."

As always, the arrangement of the pieces favored Leal. Akeela wasn't sure there was any point in continuing, but he was determined not to let talk of Nith throw his game. For some reason he couldn't fathom, the little principality had made his vaunted army nervous. Even Trager had been hounding him to go around Nith rather than through it, a detour that would have wasted precious days. As he considered the board and his dismal options, Akeela remembered Trager's warning.

"Bloody brigands," he muttered.

"My lord?"

Akeela looked up at Leal, suddenly realizing he was talking to himself. "Nothing. I was just . . . thinking."

He tried returning his attention to the game, but was disturbed by a peculiar call out in the distance. Both he and Leal turned to see riders approaching from the south. They were his heralds, returning from Nith. Behind them rode a small band bearing the blue-and-gold standard of Nith. Akeela grinned. General Trager saw the riders approaching, then glanced across the field at him.

"I knew they'd come." Akeela waved the general over to him. "You see, Leal? I know how rulers like Daralor think."

Lieutenant Leal got to his feet as his general approached. Trager gave him a sour smile.

"Having a good time, Lieutenant?" asked Trager sarcastically.

"At ease, General," said Akeela. "He's only doing as I've asked."

Trager gestured to the coming horsemen. "Looks like you got your wish, Akeela. That's Daralor himself."

"Is it?" asked Akeela. He got to his feet and stared out over the field. Besides his heralds, there were seven men approaching from the valley. The one in the lead wore a bright green cape and a golden crown on his head.

"There, you see, Will?" he said happily. "I told you they'd come to talk, and here's the prince himself."

"Don't congratulate yourself yet, Akeela," warned Trager. "Daralor might just be coming out to spit in our faces."

Prince Daralor rode quickly once he saw Akeela's pavilion, which was larger than the rest and topped with the blue flag of Liiria. The Liirian heralds now rode at his sides, their silver armor brilliant in the sun. Daralor himself wore no armor, but instead dressed in a fine red tunic and brown breeches. His emerald cape billowed behind him. He looked stunning on his white horse, the very picture of royalty. From across the plain he smiled warmly. Akeela's fears instantly vanished. Like all the other kings and princes, he knew Daralor would yield.

The heralds rode up to Akeela and dismounted. They bowed first to Trager, then greeted Akeela.

"Prince Daralor, my lord, as you asked."

Daralor brought his horse to a stop ten paces away. His armored knights fell in behind him. When he dismounted, his men did the same. But they did not approach Akeela as the prince did. Daralor went alone to greet Akeela. When he was almost in Akeela's shadow, he fell to one knee and hung his head.

"Your Grace, welcome to Nith. I am Prince Daralor."

He had a voice like music and a handsome, hairless face. It was hard to imagine him a military hero, yet legend held he had freed Nith from Marn. Seeing him reminded Akeela of all his own past glories, and how so many of them had fallen to ashes.

"Thank you, Prince Daralor," said Akeela. "Arise, please."

Daralor rose then quickly gestured to one of his men, who stepped forward bearing a small wooden box. The prince took the box and, smiling, presented it to Akeela.

"For you, Your Grace. A gift from the people of Nith."

Akeela beamed. "A gift?" He turned to Trager. "Well, what do you think of that, Will?"

Trager scowled but said nothing. Akeela happily opened the box, finding inside it a brilliant gold ring with a giant, sparkling diamond.

"A small token of our esteem, Your Grace," said Daralor. "When your heralds told me you had come, I knew I had to greet you myself."

"You honor me, Prince Daralor," said Akeela. "Thank you." He took the ring from the box and admired it. The flawless facets of the diamond twinkled in the sunlight.

"Your Grace is pleased?" asked Daralor.

"Very," said Akeela. "It's beautiful. And it's very welcome, Prince. Some of my men were worried you would turn us away. I'm gladdened to know you welcome us."

"Your Grace comes with a great army," said the prince. "Word of it reached us some days ago. We have prepared for your coming."

Something in the statement made Trager bristle. "Prepared, Prince? What exactly does that mean?"

Akeela said quickly, "This is my general, Will Trager. I'm afraid he doesn't trust you, Prince Daralor."

"Your Grace has our best wishes and kindest thoughts," said Daralor, "but there is truth in your general's counsel."

Akeela's face fell. "Oh?"

"The Principality of Nith is very small, Your Grace, very easily gone around." The Prince smiled. "Would it not be simple for your army to skirt our valley?"

Trager gestured angrily at Daralor. "You see, Akeela? I told you this would be his way."

"Shut up, Will," snapped Akeela. He returned Daralor's unnerving grin. "Prince Daralor, I'm not sure you understand the importance of my journey. I'm hunting the man who killed my wife. Time is of the essence. I cannot waste any time taking my army around Nith."

Daralor refused to be shaken. "Your Grace is wise, and I feel for your loss. We in Nith know of your queen's death and are saddened. But we have a history of our own to protect. There have been no foreign soldiers on Nithin soil since the war with Marn. I'm afraid we cannot allow it."

"We come in peace, Prince Daralor, I assure you," said

Trager. "We want nothing from Nith but a quick route to Ganjor."

"I understand," said the prince. "But how long could it possibly take you to go around our valley? A day? Two, perhaps? You have already traveled many weeks from Koth. What could two more days mean?"

"We have indeed traveled many weeks, Prince," said Akeela, "and we're very tired of the journey. And any time wasted is time for my quarry to escape me, time for him to enjoy freedom he doesn't deserve. I thank you for your gift, but I must ask you to reconsider. After all, other countries have allowed us to pass."

"They have allowed it because they fear you, Your Grace."

"And what about you?" asked Trager pointedly. "Don't you fear us?"

Prince Daralor frowned. "We are Nithins. We fought and defeated Marn. We fear nothing."

There was challenge in Daralor's tone. Behind him, his armored knights stood erect. The arrogance of their expressions made Akeela's insides clench. He took a small step forward, held the diamond ring out daintily in two fingers, then let it drop to Daralor's feet.

"I don't like your argument, Prince," he said. "And I don't like anyone standing in my way. You have seen my army. You know that we can best you easily. Will you yield?"

"No, Your Grace, we will not," replied the prince. "What you ask is impossible, and I can't allow it."

"Tomorrow morning we break camp," said Akeela. He pointed southward. "We're going that way, right through your valley. It's the quickest route to Ganjor, and we won't be dissuaded."

"Then we will defend what is ours, Your Grace," said Daralor. "We will not let our sovereignty be trampled."

"You'll be crushed," warned Trager. "Prince Daralor, reconsider."

"Go around," said Daralor.

"We won't," said Akeela.

The two rulers locked eyes. It infuriated Akeela to know Daralor thought them equal. At last the prince stooped and picked up the ring he had presented Akeela, dusting the dirt from its diamond.

"I will wear this on the battlefield," he told Akeela. "And if you still want it, you will have to take it from me."

Then he turned to go, quickly mounting his horse. His knights did the same. Before riding off Daralor gave Akeela a final, disdainful glare. As the Nithins rode away, Trager shook a frustrated fist.

"Now that was brilliant," he spat. "Fate above, Akeela, what were you thinking? Now we'll have to go around, and hope they don't ambush us."

Akeela looked at Trager as if he'd heard the highest treason. "No, General, we won't be going around. We're not going to waste another blasted minute. Lukien is in Jador, waiting for us. He's living free, while Cassandra rots in her grave. So we're going straight through this damnable country. At dawn, with swords drawn. And if anyone tries to stop us, they will die."

He sat back down at the table and once again considered the game pieces. Trager and Leal hovered over the board, staring at him.

"I suggest you prepare your men for battle, Will," said Akeela. "And Leal, sit down and finish this damn game."

At dawn they broke camp. Doing so had become a common ritual for the traveling army, and they did it with their usual efficiency. Within an hour they were on their way to Nith. The green valley gently sloped down into a blanket of morning mist, obscuring the distance and the tall, ancient elm trees. Despite the noise of the wagons and horses, it was an eerily quiet morning. Akeela, riding at the head of his army, listened to the drone of insects. At his side rode Trager, nervously scanning the fog and trees. He was sure an ambush was coming, and had warned his men to expect it. Throughout the night he had pleaded with Akeela to reconsider his decision. Akeela sat high in his saddle as he rode, daring an assassin to kill him. Unlike Trager he feared no ambush, secure in the knowledge that Daralor would never stoop to such tactics. There had been too much pride in the young ruler's eyes.

"Stop looking around, Will," said Akeela. "The men will see you're frightened."

"I'm not frightened," growled Trager. "Just wary."

"Don't be. Daralor will meet us out in the open, proudly

and stupidly." He glanced over to his left, where Lieutenant Leal was riding behind Colonel Tark, Trager's second-in-command. "Leal, are you afraid? Or do you trust me?"

Leal hesitated before answering. "I'm sure you know what you're doing, my lord."

Trager laughed. "Ha! You hear that? He's watched you play crusade."

"No faith," sighed Akeela. "But you'll see. Just keep your eyes forward."

But the seasoned companies Trager had chosen were too convinced of an ambush to relax. As the men and horses weaved through the fog, they kept a wary watch on the trees. The stray sounds of the surrounding forests made the ears of the horses twitch. Akeela took it all in stride. He knew that Prince Daralor wouldn't run and hide, but he wouldn't ambush them, either. There would be a battle, very soon. Oddly, Akeela didn't mind. Trager had honed his men to a razor's sharpness; there was simply no way the Nithins could best them. That they were foolish enough to try simply wasn't Akeela's fault, and so he felt no remorse.

A few minutes later, the ground flattened into a wide field. The trees on either side thinned, and the morning mist parted in a breeze, revealing a line of mounted silhouettes in the distance.

"There," pronounced Akeela. He stopped his horse and let the various companies slowly fall in behind him. Trager peered through the fog at the stand of knights. It was hard to make out their numbers, but they could see at least a hundred men in the front rank, all mounted and armed with lances.

"You were right," said the general, sounding relieved. A small smile crept onto his face. "They've come to face us."

"They will try again to talk before fighting," Akeela predicted. "Bring up some bowmen."

Trager passed the order down to Colonel Tark, who called for archers. Two men quickly dismounted and came to stand beside Akeela. They had bows in their hands and quivers on their backs. Without being asked they nocked arrows in their bowstrings.

"Don't fire unless I order it," Akeela ordered.

The men nodded and kept their arrows pointed downward. Trager pulled his horse a little closer to Akeela's, waiting for the inevitable heralds to arrive. Next to them, Lieutenant Leal shifted uneasily in his saddle. Colonel Tark was still as stone. Soon a figure broke from the fog, riding out of the ranks. Another followed him, bearing the standard of Nith. The herald rode purposefully forward, the feathered comb of his helmet bouncing in the breeze. He wore Nithin armor and a gold breastplate that reminded Akeela of Lukien's. The standard bearer rode a full pace behind him. Akeela's army closed ranks as the herald approached, the noise of their movements echoing through the morning like the rolling surf. In the distance and obscured by fog, Prince Daralor sat defiantly atop his white stallion, easily recognizable in his splendid cape and silver armor. When the herald was only five yards away, he removed his helmet and placed it in the crux of his arm. Carefully he surveyed the army, coming to a slow stop before Akeela. The archers raised their bows and drew back their strings, taking aim. Remarkably, the herald barely glanced at them.

"On behalf of Prince Daralor of Nith, sovereign lord and protector of this valley, I come to you, King Akeela," declared the man. His ruddy face was resolute as he delivered his proclamation. "The prince humbly asks that you turn and head back, or face the peril of his rage."

Akeela glanced toward Daralor's troops. The morning sun was burning off the haze now, bringing them into better focus. It was quickly clear to Akeela that their numbers, though formidable, were no match for his own.

"Your prince has seen our army," said Akeela, "just as we now see his own. You are no match for us. You should yield."

"Prince Daralor requests you reconsider, Your Grace. This is sovereign land, fought and bled for. He is prepared to battle for it."

"So it seems," said Akeela. "And you, herald? Are you prepared to die as well?"

Without hesitation the herald said, "I am."

"That is well, because you're standing in my way. By delaying me, you are protecting my greatest enemy."

With a mere nod Akeela gave the order. The archers loosed, sending their shafts whistling forward. One caught the herald in the throat, slicing through his windpipe and coming out the other side. The other found the standard bearer, puncturing his helmet and cracking his skull. Both men teetered in stunned silence. The herald gasped for air, then dropped from his horse. The standard bearer dropped soon after, his flag falling like a tree. Across the field a gasp rose from the Nithin ranks, followed by a chorus of cries. Now there was no turning back, and Akeela knew it. He turned to Trager.

"Attack."

Trager drew his blade and went to work, calling to his waiting men. It would be the Royal Chargers who would do the bulk of the work and send Akeela's terrible message. Swords sprang from scabbards and horses churned the earth, and all around the world erupted in noise. Colonel Tark galloped forward, the first to follow Trager into the melee. With them went their seasoned company, bent on cutting a path to Ganjor.

Safe in the fog atop his white stallion, Prince Daralor of Nith watched in shock and horror as his heralds were murdered. His first emotion was disbelief, but watching the flag of his homeland totter snapped reality into focus. A great, angry cry went up from his men. Across the field, he saw King Akeela give the order to attack. General Trager raised his sword and rallied his armored cavalry. In a moment they were charging.

Daralor's men looked to him for orders. His mind roiled in rage. He took his own sword from its scabbard and raised it high above his head, crying, "Charge!"

His lancers roared, rushing forward with their weapons. At their lead rode Daralor, his stallion tearing up the earth. Ahead came a wall of silver steel and horse muscle, the cream of Liiria, swords high, bodies bent behind ornate shields. Daralor knew his chances were hopeless, and he cursed himself for his many miscalculations. It was said in Nith that Akeela was mad, and now he knew the truth of it. But there was one slim hope to save the day . . . if he could slay Akeela.

Daralor's knights met the Liirians. Around him the air exploded as lances and shields. His charging lancers slammed into the rushing Liirians, sending some sprawling.

But most met the clash easily, parrying the lances with expert speed and countering with slashing swords. Daralor looked wildly about the melee, finding a target. An onrushing Liirian raised his sword, hacking down toward Daralor's head. Easily parried, the blow glanced off the prince's blade. Daralor countered, slicing his sword in a low arc and connecting with the man's midsection. Wounded, the man doubled to favor his damaged armor, bringing up his sword too late. Daralor's blade found his neck, cleaving through his gorget. The severed head spun through the air as the body tumbled from the horse. All around Daralor the battle raged. He was in the thick of it now, with his men badly outnumbered. Waves of Liirian cavalry flooded the field. In the distance, King Akeela sat upon his horse, watching the misery from the fog. Daralor gritted his teeth and urged his horse forward. If he could reach Akeela, he could end it. He slashed his way through the ranks of knights, taking the best of the Liirian blades. In the eight years since winning Nith's freedom, his renown with a sword hadn't diminished, and seeing his skill rallied his men. They grouped around him, fighting back the hordes of Chargers as they inched across the field toward Akeela. The king himself was not unprotected. There were men around him still, and General Trager no doubt nearby. But to take him down was the surest way to end things, so Daralor plunged ahead.

Now there were half a dozen men with him, slicing a bloody path through their foes. Daralor's horse snorted and reared, battling the press of men and beasts. Screams and the sounds of combat filled the air. Liirian archers opened fire. Next to Daralor, the head of a companion shattered as an arrow found its mark. Daralor continued on, waving his sword like a flag.

"Follow me!" he ordered his band. "To Akeela!"

More men rushed at them, fresh troops from Akeela's side. Daralor could see General Trager now, himself engaged in battle. The general's sword was everywhere at once; Daralor had never seen such ferocious speed. Akeela's face grew troubled as inch by inch Daralor drew closer. A Charger raced toward him, swinging a flail. Daralor ducked the weapon and plunged his sword into the man's breast. Another came and then another, and Daralor dispatched them easily. A mad frenzy was on him now. But he knew his men were losing the fight. One by one they fell to Liiria's numerous blades.

"Onward!" he roared, mustering his men. A handful heeded the call, joining his assault. Beneath him his horse bucked as it plowed through Liirian swords. They were mere yards from Akeela now. Daralor could see the king's surprised grimace. Finally, hope showed its elusive face. Daralor battled forward, four men at his side. General Trager glimpsed his approach and fought harder to put down his opponents. Blood and steel blinded Daralor. A young knight, who had long been at Akeela's side, finally sprang forward. The prince let out a wrathful cry. Sword to sword, they battled before Akeela. Daralor realized dreadfully that the men he'd been leading were already gone, cut down by the overwhelming number of Liirians. The young knight protecting Akeela was skilled and fresh, and Daralor struggled to parry his blows. Akeela himself sat alone on his horse, not even drawing his sword. There were still endless ranks of men behind him, waiting for his orders. His confidence enraged Daralor.

"I'll kill you!" he bellowed.

A second later, he threaded his blade through the knight's defense and punctured his heart. The man fell from his horse, revealing Akeela's angry face behind him. Finally, the king drew his blade. He looked about to charge when another wave of Chargers raced forward, this time led by Trager. The general let out terrible cry and an explosive flurry of blows, driving Daralor back into a waiting circle of Liirian blades.

"No!" bellowed Akeela. "Don't kill him!"

Trager pressed his attack, raining blow after blow down on Daralor's weakening sword. The others encircling him kept back, letting them duel. There was no escape for Daralor now. He had become the general's sport.

"Damn you!" he hissed, sweat flying from his brow.

"Surrender!" cried Trager. His face reddened with effort as he loosed his attack. The archers at Akeela's side held their bows at the ready. Remarkably, they didn't fire, waiting for orders like dutiful dogs. Daralor desperately dodged Trager's attacks. Exhausted, his sword dipped a moment too soon, letting Trager's blade slip down his gauntlet. A fiery pain shot through his hand. Daralor dropped his sword in horror as two fingers flew through the air. The flat of Trager's sword slammed into his chest, sending him sprawling to the ground. The force of the fall rattled his skull. When he finally looked up, his horse was gone and Trager was floating over him. The general's fellow horsemen closed around him like a noose.

"Now," said Trager, pointing his blade down at Daralor's throat. "Will you surrender?"

Exhausted, his hand bleeding and screaming with pain, Daralor could barely find his voice. "Piss on you," he croaked.

Trager trembled in rage. Daralor was sure he would die. But the general's sword didn't move. Instead, Akeela's voice drifted over his shoulder.

"Leave him," ordered the king. The circle of knights parted as he trotted into their circle. As the battle raged on just yards away, Akeela looked down at Daralor, shaking his head. There was no glee in his eyes, only sadness. "You are a fool, Prince Daralor."

Daralor got unsteadily to his feet, teetering with blurred vision as he stood to face Akeela. "Kill me, butcher," he said. "Give me the dignity of death, at least."

"I don't want to kill you, Daralor," said Akeela. "I've never wanted to kill you, or your men. But you've given me no choice. Do you not see that? Did I not tell you how important my mission is?"

"Madness," gasped Daralor. "This is nothing but madness."

King Akeela shook his head and got down from his horse. He looked around the battlefield, and when his eyes came to the young knight who'd been protecting him, he let out a deep sigh. "Such a good man," he whispered. Then he searched the ground near Daralor's feet, where blood still spilled from his wounded hand. There in the dirt were Daralor's fingers, still encased in the metal of his gauntlet. Akeela stooped down and, to Daralor's horror, popped the fingers from their metal casings. The first one he dropped to the ground without interest. But he smiled at the second one, happily plucking a diamond ring from it. The mockery of the gesture sickened Daralor.

"All this for a diamond?" he asked. "Great Fate, was it worth it?"

Akeela looked hurt by the question. "The diamond is yours, Daralor," he said. "As is Nith."

He held out the ring. Daralor looked at him, stunned. Sticking his ruined right hand beneath his armpit, the prince reached out and let Akeela drop the ring into his left hand.

"I don't want your diamonds, Daralor, and I don't want your country," said Akeela. "All I want is to find the man that killed my wife." He turned to Trager. "Take him, General, but don't harm him."

Daralor shook off his surprise. "No! Kill me, you bastard! I demand it!"

"Daralor, look out onto the field," said Akeela.

Daralor looked. Past the horses and men he could see the last of his own knights fleeing the field. Bodies lay everywhere. Hot blood bubbled on the earth.

"There's been enough death for you," said Akeela. "And a good man shouldn't want to die so easily."

The words shocked Daralor. "How can you do this?" he asked. "How can you let me live after all you've done?"

"I did what I had to do, Daralor, nothing more. You tried to stop me, I made my point. Now we are finished."

"So?" spat the prince. "What will you do with me?"

Akeela climbed onto his horse. "After we tend our wounded and rest, we ride again for Ganjor. You'll come with us. Once we reach the border, you'll be freed." Again he turned to Trager. "Take care of his hand. And make sure nothing happens to him."

General Trager nodded. Then he and his men dismounted, beginning the dirty work of separating the injured from the dead. Daralor was speechless. He let the Liirians strip the dagger from his belt. An old captain began inspecting his hand. Trager walked casually into the battlefield, calling to his men to break off their chase.

And through it all Akeela sat upon his horse, untouched by the battle, silent and imperious.

45

Two days after arriving in Jador, Gilwyn and his companions were still waiting for Kadar. After their first meeting with the kahan, they were given a room to share in his palace, a ground floor chamber that was comfortable, clean, and unguarded by Kadar's black-robed sentries. But Kadar himself was nowhere to be seen. He had simply told his guests that he would call for them when he was ready. In the meantime, they were to wait and to rest. Food and clean linens were brought to them, and fresh water scented with roses to clean themselves was constantly replenished in their washbasin. The weather outside their room's single window never changed; the sky was perfectly blue, and the heat remained unbearable. Gilwyn had spent the first day in and around the chamber with Lukien and Baron Glass, sure that the kahan would want to speak with them soon. But Kadar had never come, and as the day slipped into night Lukien began to wonder what was taking Kadar so long.

"He'll understand when he sees Akeela's army," Lukien had predicted sourly. Baron Glass had only sighed and nodded. Of the two, the old baron was far more patient, but Gilwyn knew his silence belied his own anxiety. Since leaving Norvor, Baron Glass almost never spoke of his troubles with Jazana Carr. Still, Gilwyn could tell he was troubled and worried about his family in Koth, a family he hadn't seen in many years.

By the second day, Gilwyn had decided to explore the palace. It was, he soon discovered, a remarkable structure, much more beautiful than Lionkeep and without its cold stone and decay. Kadar's palace was a golden marvel, full of ornate mosaics and sunburned colors and smooth stonework that rose and fell in graceful arches and rounded, glazed domes. Most remarkable, though, were its inhabitants. The beautiful, dark-skinned people of Jador did nothing to hamper Gilwyn's exploration of the palace. They gave him ample room whenever he passed by, occasionally offering a deferential though suspicious smile. He was an outsider, after all, and outsiders had killed their kahana.

It was mid-afternoon when Gilwyn found himself outside on the palace grounds. As usual, Teku rode on his shoulder. Kadar's home was surrounded by gardens, and Gilwyn liked to listen to the many gurgling fountains, so refreshing in the desert heat. Because the sun was high and hot, most people had gone indoors, but Gilwyn was tired of the palace and went instead to the outer gardens, a ring of fruit trees and desert flowers bordering the encroaching sands. From here he enjoyed an unobstructed view of the mountains, dark and foreboding in the distance. Gilwyn strode along a winding path of perfectly square bricks, the air thick with the scent of flowers he'd never seen before. Except for the sounds of tumbling water, the garden was remarkably quiet. He sat down on a huge stone and listened, content with his surroundings. As he stared out across the sands, he wondered about the mountains and what might lie beyond them. And he wondered about home, too, and how far he had come. Liiria was very far away, and he was in a different world now. He didn't feel afraid, but he did feel out of place. Even if Kadar kept his word and decided not to punish them, what would happen to them now? None of them could return to Koth. And the library? A dead dream. The thought saddened Gilwyn. Without Figgis, the library would be cold and empty. All the work his old mentor had poured into it had been for nothing. Gilwyn looked down at his feet and studied the strange boot Figgis had made for him.

No, he corrected himself. *Not for nothing.*

The library had given him life. Without it, he would have been a simple cripple, forced to beg on the streets.

Gilwyn was about to rise when a strange noise reached him from the other side of the garden. Teku's little ears picked up the sound, turning toward it. Like a small cry, the sound peaked and was soon gone. But soon Gilwyn heard it again, this time much louder. He sprang to his feet, trying to locate its source. It was like a howl, inhuman and frightening. Alarmed, Gilwyn put out his arm for Teku, who quickly scrambled up to his shoulder. The sound was certainly an animal, for no human could make such a noise. The cry rang through the garden, growing louder but no closer. To Gilwyn, it sounded like a wail of pain. Not sure of the danger, he moved quickly toward the sound, heading straight through the garden. The cry went on and on. Suddenly Gilwyn recognized the sound; he had heard it several times since arriving in Ganjor.

A kreel. . . .

One of the great lizards of the desert people. And this one was in pain, hissing and howling as though caught in a trap. Gilwyn cut across the rocky garden, at last coming to its end. There he saw the kreel with three stout ropes around its neck, being dragged to the ground by a trio of men. A fourth man stood apart from the others, a great, shining blade in his hands. The kreel thrashed against the ropes in fright. It was smaller than the other kreels Gilwyn had seen, and slightly off color. But it fought like one of its larger siblings, straining against its bindings yet refusing to lash out with its razor-sharp claws.

"*Stop!*" Gilwyn shouted.

The startled men turned, almost losing their grip on the ropes. But when the kreel tried to bolt they jerked the ropes harder, dragging the creature forward until it collapsed. The man with the blade took a step toward Gilwyn while his comrades subdued the kreel, hurriedly working more ropes around its legs.

"Don't!" Gilwyn demanded. "You're hurting it!"

The man with the blade held up his hands, barking at Gilwyn to stay back. He looked confused by the interruption, uncertain how to deal with it.

"What are you doing to that poor thing?" Gilwyn shouted. He pointed to the curved blade in the man's hands. "Are you going to kill it?"

The man seemed to understand. He lifted the sword and nodded.

"But why?" Gilwyn protested. "Why kill it?"

"Because it is a runt," came a surprising reply.

Gilwyn whirled to face the new voice. What he saw shocked him even more than the screeching kreel. A woman was standing before him. *The* woman. Small as a midget with white hair and a swirling, colorful coat.

"You!"

The woman gave an enigmatic smile. Next to her stood the same giant Gilwyn had seen with her in Koth, the mute monster with bulging shoulders and tree-trunk- sized arms. The man with the blade lowered his weapon at once. To Gilwyn's surprise, he bowed to the woman.

"Ela-daz."

Confused, a bit afraid, Gilwyn gasped, "You're the Witch of Grimhold!"

The woman laughed and wrinkled her nose. "Welcome to Jador, Gilwyn Toms."

"You know me! Just like in the alley!"

"I know you. But I am no witch."

"Who are you, then?" Gilwyn asked. "*What* are you?"

"You have questions. I have answers. Gather your friends, Gilwyn. It's time we talked."

The woman turned and started off, trailed by her enormous guardian.

"Wait," Gilwyn called after her. "What about the kreel. Are they going to kill it?"

"Yes," said the woman. "I'm sorry, but that is the way of things here. The kreel is a runt of its breed. It is too small to hunt for itself."

As she spoke, the kreel continued to howl and struggle against its bindings. The men hovered over it, unsure what to do. The one with the blade questioned the little woman in Jadori. She replied in his own tongue.

"Do not feel too badly for the kreel," she told Gilwyn gently. "There is nothing to be done."

"But it's fine!" Gilwyn cried. He rushed to its side, standing between it and its executioner. "There's nothing wrong with it. It's strong. It was fighting these men and everything!"

"Gilwyn, please, come with me," said the woman. "There's much to discuss, much more important things."

"No," said Gilwyn. "Not if they're going to kill it. Not because it's small. It's not right!"

The woman looked at him oddly. "We are guests here, you and I, Gilwyn. It is not our place to question how they do things."

"But . . . !"

"Hush," said the woman. She turned back to the men, exchanging a string of sentences. The men nodded reluctantly. "All right, Gilwyn," she continued. "They will wait because I have asked them to. Now will you come with me?"

"Will they kill the kreel when we're gone?" asked Gilwyn.

"Go and gather your friends," said the woman simply. "The time has come to talk."

Lukien and Baron Glass walked alone through the aurocco, admiring its dazzling mosaic ceiling. Like Gilwyn, they had also tired of their small chamber in the palace and so had decided to explore its impressive grounds. After an hour in the gardens, they had discovered the aurocco. The place so mesmerized them that they lost track of time. As he stared up at the ceiling, ornamented with countless fragments of tiling, Lukien could hear the soft breeze echo through the many arches. The long shadows of the columns gave the place a mazelike feel. Yet despite its complexity, the aurocco was anything but disorienting. It was peaceful and cool and invited contemplation, and Lukien felt at home. Next to him Thorin whistled, impressed by the amazing mosaic overhead. The sun-washed colors of a billion tiny tiles reflected in his dark eyes.

"It's like a church," he mused. "You think?"

Lukien nodded. "A place to worship Vala, maybe."

Vala, the one god of Jador, seemed to possess every tiny tile. Lukien knew almost nothing of the deity, but he knew the deadly power of the amulet, and he was sure that something magical dwelled within Jador. God or no god, this was a place of miracles. His gaze drifted from the ceiling, surveying the dozens of sandstone columns and arches.

"They've changed so much."

Thorin glanced at him. "What do you mean?"

"Look at this place. This is the kind of place they used to build, before I came and changed them."

The old baron snickered. "Don't exaggerate."

"It's true," said Lukien. "Now they build walls and train their lizards to fight. We changed them, me and Trager and Figgis." Lukien's gaze fell upon a fountain in the center of the aurocco, dry but nonetheless beautiful. A figure of a maiden stood in its bowl. Dressed in flowing robes, she held a single stone flower in her hand. Lukien at once thought of Cassandra.

Had it all been worth it?

He listened to the breeze, but heard no reply.

"I want to go now," he said softly. As he turned to leave he saw a figure approaching from the garden, one of Kahan Kadar's ubiquitous guards. The man called to them, waving them forward.

"What's this about?" wondered Thorin.

The guard went to them, gesturing toward the palace. He spoke, but the only word Lukien understood was "Kadar."

"Kadar wants to see us?" Lukien probed.

"Kadar," said the man, nodding. He went on in Jadori, pointing toward the palace.

"Well, it's about time," sighed Lukien. He turned to Thorin. "Ready?"

Thorin made a sour face. "Ready to hear what Kadar wants to do with us, you mean? Personally I can wait."

"He said he wouldn't punish us," Lukien reminded his friend. Then he told the guard, "We'll come with you."

The guard led them out of the aurocco into the bright sun of the garden. Lukien and Thorin shielded their eyes as the stabbing light bounced off the white walls of the palace. Kahan Kadar's home was attached to the aurocco, making it a short walk. Once inside the palace, the guard led them through its golden halls. The usual mass of people passed them, but this time there were no suspicious looks. Lukien tried to subdue his excitement as he followed the man toward Kadar. He was sure the desert leader would keep his promise not to punish them, but Lukien was after more than that from him. He owed Kadar for the things he'd done, and hoped the kahan would let him repay his debts. With Akeela's army drawing closer, Kadar needed every able swordsman.

When at last they reached the end of the hall, the guard stepped aside to reveal a shimmering, beaded curtain. He gestured for Lukien to step through it. Lukien glanced at Thorin warily. He could hear voices beyond the curtain, muffled by the beads. The guard grunted.

"All right," said Lukien. He took a breath to steady his nerves then parted the beads. A round chamber of yellow tiles and emerald tapestries greeted him, centered by a long, squat table. There were no chairs, just silky, multicolored pillows strewn on the floor along with elaborate rugs. Lukien paused halfway through the curtain, stunned by the people gathered in the chamber. At the head of the table sat Kadar, cross-legged on the floor. He was talking but stopped just as Lukien entered. At his left side was Gilwyn and Teku. The boy gave a relieved breath when he noticed Lukien in the threshold. Across from Gilwyn, at Kadar's right, sat a woman Lukien had never seen before, a tiny thing with shocking white hair and elfin ears and a coat that seemed alive with color. Behind her stood a barrel-chested giant, at least seven feet tall. The little woman gave Lukien an inscrutable smile.

"Ah, here he is," she said. She leaned to one side to see past him. "And not alone?"

Lukien stepped inside so that Thorin could enter. He, too, was stunned by the gathering. He looked carefully from face to face, finally coming to rest on Gilwyn.

"Gilwyn, is everything . . . all right?"

Gilwyn shrugged. "I think so. We've been waiting for you. Lukien, this is the woman I told you about. The—"

"The Witch of Grimhold," Lukien whispered.

The woman clapped her tiny hands and chuckled. "Does everybody call me that? No, Sir Lukien, I am no witch. But I am the Mistress of Grimhold."

"Enter, both of you," commanded Kadar. He waved them in, his expression stern. Lukien hesitated, unsure of what he was seeing. The little woman hardly looked human, and her monstrous companion was frightening to behold. Except for the rasping of his heavy breath, he made no sound. Lukien and Thorin both stepped toward the table, wondering if they should sit or stand in the kahan's presence.

"You sent for us, my lord?" asked Lukien.

"I did," said Kadar.

"And the boy, too?" asked Thorin.

Kadar motioned to some pillows next to Gilwyn. "Sit. It is time to talk."

Lukien sat down beside Gilwyn, never taking his sight from the enigmatic woman. Baron Glass slowly and awkwardly dropped down next, carefully balancing himself against the table with his single arm. Together the three Liirians waited in silence for someone to speak. Incense burned on the table, wisps of smoke coloring the air a fragrant purple. Lukien looked past the smoke, studying the woman directly across from him. Amused by his curiosity, she tossed him a playful wink. Only then did Lukien notice the glowing amulet around her neck.

"Yes," said Kadar. "She wears the other Eye of God."

"Who are you?" Lukien asked the woman. "Are you really the Witch of Grimhold?"

"I am called that by some," replied the woman. "My name is Minikin."

Thorin was incredulous. "Are you from Grimhold?"

"I have said so already."

"She's the woman I saw in Koth," said Gilwyn. "I remember her."

"Yes, and you shouldn't," said the woman. "Shame on you, Gilwyn Toms."

Lukien remembered what Gilwyn had told him, how Figgis had reawakened his memory of the witch. "So it was magic that made you forget her, Gilwyn? Really?"

"I've explained it to her," said Gilwyn. "I told her about Figgis, and how he helped me remember her. This *is* the woman I saw in Koth, Lukien. This is the Witch of Grimhold."

The little woman rolled her eyes. "My name is *Minikin.*"

"Yes, so you claim," said Thorin, half laughing. "Minikin from Grimhold. I don't believe it."

"She wears the amulet, Thorin," said Lukien. "It must be her."

"That's meaningless," Thorin said, staring hard at the woman. "Kadar gave you that amulet, am I right?"

"You are wrong," said Kadar. From beneath the table he produced the other Eye of God, slapping it down on the wooden surface. "Let us hear no more of your doubts. This is Ela-daz, the Mistress of Grimhold. And my honored friend."

Lukien still couldn't believe it. Even after all he'd been through, Grimhold still seemed like a fairy tale. "Kadar," he said carefully, "we mean no disrespect, but you have to understand how hard this is for us to believe. Where we come from, Grimhold is a myth."

"I assure you, Sir Lukien, I'm no myth," said the woman. "Nor are these amulets. And I know you've already seen their powers. It would be wise for you to believe what we're telling you. There is a Grimhold, and I am its ruler."

"And I am its protector," said Kadar. "And that is why the amulet was given to me."

Gilwyn nodded as if he understood. "So Figgis was right. Grimhold really is beyond Jador, in the mountains."

"Not far from here, yes," said Kadar. "You cannot see it because the mountains hide it. But it is there, to the west."

"Who lives in Grimhold?" Lukien pressed. "Are they really monsters?"

Kadar frowned at the question. The little woman called Minikin lost her cheery smile.

"We are not monsters, Sir Lukien. And Grimhold is not some kind of asylum for freaks. It is my lifelong creation. It is a sanctuary."

"A sanctuary?" asked Gilwyn. "For who?"

"Why, for people like you, Gilwyn Toms. For people who might not be able to fend for themselves in the so-called normal world. I take them to Grimhold. I teach them how to live and defend themselves. I give them power."

"You mean magic?" asked Thorin.

"Magic is a word the ignorant use," said Minikin. "But yes, Baron Glass, you may say so. Like the magic of these amulets, I teach my Inhumans how to use the power of the spirit world."

"Inhumans? What are they?" asked Lukien.

"That is what we call ourselves," replied Minikin. "The world looks at us and thinks we are inhuman, so that is our name."

"But that's an insult," Gilwyn protested.

"Words, Gilwyn," replied Minikin. "That is all they are. Cruel names are meaningless. That is why we accept the slurs others pin on us, to remind ourselves that we are far more than just someone's misguided opinion. I call myself Minikin because I was called that when I was young. My friend behind me is named Trog, because cruel men called him a troglodyte." She turned to her mute companion, beaming warmly. "But you see? Trog does not mind. He has learned to ignore the insult, and now it cannot hurt him."

"I still don't like it," said Gilwyn. "Inhumans. It's a terrible name."

Minikin's smile widened. "That's a great shame, Gilwyn. Because you see, you're already one of us."

The statement hushed the gathering. Minikin's twinkling eyes watched Gilwyn, who simply stared back in disbelief.

"What do you mean?"

"Gilwyn, haven't you wondered why you were able to look at Queen Cassandra without breaking the spell of the amulet?"

Gilwyn nodded. "Yes. . . ."

"You were marked as an Inhuman," said Minikin. "So you did not look upon Cassandra with *human* eyes." She smiled sadly at Lukien. "I am sorry, Sir Lukien, but Gilwyn didn't know. He was able to look upon your beloved without harming her. Not so with you, I'm afraid."

"What?" sputtered Lukien. He looked at Gilwyn in shock. "He's one of you?"

"Am I?" asked Gilwyn. "What do you mean, you marked me?"

"When you were born I heard about your deformities," began Minikin. "I went to your mother and told her I could take you to a place where the problems of your body would not limit you, a place where you would be safe and cared for. But your mother was certain you would be safe in the castle. She assured me that your new king, Akeela, would not let any harm come to you." The little woman glowed with pleasure. "Obviously your king kept his promise. But I couldn't know for certain that he would, so I marked you with a kiss. That way, part of you would always know that Grimhold exists, and that you could come to us if you were ever in need."

Gilwyn was ashen. "I . . . I don't believe it."

"Every word of it is so," said Kadar. He reached out and gently touched Gilwyn's clubbed hand. "You were marked as someone special, boy. You have always been one of the Inhumans. And hear me—there is nothing for you to fear."

"Inhuman," whispered Lukien. A great feeling of regret rose in his chest. "I looked at Cassandra. I killed her because I'm not one of you."

Thorin put his hand to Lukien's shoulder. "You couldn't possibly have known."

"No," agreed Minikin, "you couldn't. The amulets protect themselves from falling into the wrong hands. I have no control over the Akari inside them."

"Akari?" repeated Gilwyn. "That's the second time you mentioned them to me. What are the Akari?"

"It is a lot to explain," said Minikin. "The amulets are home to powerful spirits. It is they who grant what you call magic."

"And you've worn the other amulet all along," said Lukien with a sigh. "Great Fate, what fools we were." He looked apologetically at Kadar. "Forgive us, my lord. Figgis, the man who sent us here, was mistaken. He was a great scholar, but he thought the other amulet was worn by your wife."

"Your scholar was not so mistaken," said Minikin. "I am not Kadar's wife, it is true. But he is my zirhah. Do you know that word?"

Both Lukien and Gilwyn nodded. "Zirhah," Lukien repeated. "That's the word Figgis used. It's Jadori for wife."

"It is Jadori for wife *and* for servant," corrected Minikin. "Figgis told you what he read in the old texts, yes?"

"Yes," said Gilwyn. "He said that the master of the place beyond the desert wears the amulet, and that his zirhah wears the amulet's twin."

"And the place beyond the desert is Grimhold, not Jador," said Lukien. "Figgis had that part right at the end."

"But the Master of Grimhold isn't Kahan Kadar," added Gilwyn. Like Lukien, he too was beginning to understand. He looked at Minikin and said, "*You're* the Master of Grimhold."

"And Kadar is my zirhah," said Minikin. "My servant. That is why we call him Shalafein, the great protector. He protects me and the other Inhumans from the outside world. Because of that he was given the amulet long ago."

"But why?" asked Thorin, still confused. "Why do you protect them, Lord Kadar?"

Kadar's face tightened. "It is not important for you to know. All that matters is my oath to them. And why you have been called here."

"Tell us," said Lukien. "What do you want of us?"

Kahan Kadar leaned back and considered Lukien as if he were the only person in the room. "I have been thinking of you, Bronze Knight. Ever since I knew of your coming."

Lukien and his friends glanced at each other.

"Yes," Kadar continued, "I knew. Ela-daz told me. I waited for you, and I wondered what I should do. But my rage is dead, you see. As I told you, I cannot punish you more than you have been punished already."

"Then you'll let us help you?" asked Lukien hopefully.

"We have an army of our own to fight your King Akeela," said Kadar. "We will defend Jador and Grimhold against him. He has only horses, and he does not know the desert."

"He's strong, my lord, make no mistake," warned Thorin. "And he has all the riches of Liiria, too. He'll buy whatever transport he needs to bring his army across the desert, horses and all."

"It does not matter," said Kadar. "We will fight him. To our deaths if we must."

"Then let us help you," Lukien pleaded. "We know Akeela and Trager. We know their tactics. If we fight with you, you'll have a better chance."

"Much better," stressed Thorin. "And still it won't be easy."

"But we have some time left," said Lukien, suddenly excited. "Akeela's got a whole army with him. He can't travel quickly. That will give us time to form our defenses. If—"

"Stop," ordered Kadar. "There's no need to speak of Jador's defense, Bronze Knight. I will see to it. You will go to Grimhold."

"Grimhold? Why?"

"They have need of you," said Kadar. "You will help defend them."

"Excuse me, my lord, but that's foolish. You're going to make your stand here in the desert, right? So then that's where I should be."

"You will go to Grimhold with Ela-daz," said Kadar evenly.

"But why, damn it?" Lukien jumped to his feet, surprising them all. "Kadar, I'm a fighter. And I'm damn good at it. Please don't make me go and nursemaid a bunch of cripples!"

As soon as he said the word, Lukien regretted it. From the corner of his eye he saw Gilwyn's hurt grimace. Minikin's face was icy.

"Sit down," ordered Kadar. His voice was calm but steely. Lukien obeyed, kneeling again next to the table. Kadar continued, "You came here because you wished to right a wrong, yes?"

Lukien nodded. "Yes."

"Did you not slay my wife? Do you not think you owe me something?"

"Yes, Kadar, but—"

"Then you will go to Grimhold with Ela-daz. You will help to defend it from the army of your king. One more man with a sword will not make a difference here. But Grimhold is a mountain keep. And they have no soldiers there. They will need your skills."

Lukien sighed and shook his head. None of it made any sense to him. "Kadar, I'm a soldier, and I know General Trager's tactics."

Kadar waved the comments off. "It is decided. You will go to Grimhold. Baron Glass will stay in Jador."

"Me?" blurted Thorin. "Why?"

"Do you not also know the tactics of this general?" asked Kadar.

"Well, yes. . . ."

"Good," said Kadar. "Then you will stay, Baron Glass. You will help us. The Bronze Knight will go to Grimhold. The boy, too." Kadar turned to Lukien. "You will leave in the morning."

"No, I still don't understand," argued Lukien. "Explain it to me."

"Sir Lukien, Kahan Kadar has explained it," said Minikin gently. "Do you not agree that you owe him a debt?"

"My debt is to Jador, not to Grimhold," snapped Lukien.

"Your debt is to me," said Kadar sharply, "and I will claim payment any way I wish!"

His shouts rattled the room, so that even Minikin's mute bodyguard glanced at him. Kadar looked away, smoothing out his vestments as he composed himself.

"Go," he commanded. "All of you but the Bronze Knight."

Minikin quickly rose. Smiling, she held out her hand to Gilwyn. "Come, Gilwyn, let's walk together."

Gilwyn hesitated, but Lukien shooed him off. "It's all right," he said, "go on. You too, Thorin."

Thorin looked wary. "Are you sure? I could stay."

"I wish to speak to the knight alone, one-arm," said Kadar. "Leave us."

Thorin relented, following Gilwyn out of the chamber with the midget woman and the giant. When the beads of the curtain stopped moving, Lukien stood up.

"All right, the truth now," he said. "There's something you're not telling me. Why are you sending me to Grimhold?"

"To defend it," said Kadar.

"But why?"

"Because my daughter is there!"

The words came in a torrent. Kadar's face reddened. He looked away, annoyed with himself.

"Your daughter?" asked Lukien. "What daughter?"

"The child my wife was carrying," said Kadar bitterly. "The one she birthed the night you killed her."

"Great Fate," whispered Lukien. "I thought the child would die."

"She did not die," said Kadar. "She was born that night. Jitendra drew her last breath expelling her from her womb. But she was born too soon. She was . . ." Kadar searched for the right word. "Let us say she was born like the folk of Grimhold."

"You mean deformed?" asked Lukien. He felt the same stab of pain as the night he'd killed Jitendra. "Kadar, I'm. . . ."

"Sorry?"

Lukien nodded. "Yes. I know it's worthless, but what can I do but apologize?"

Kadar replied, "You can go to Grimhold and protect my daughter. You owe me a debt, Bronze Knight. You will be her shalafein, her great protector. If I die fighting King Akeela, then at least she will have you to defend her."

"I don't understand," said Lukien. "If you love her so much, why did you send her away? You could have cared for her here."

"No. The heat and light of Jador is too much for her. That is why she stays in the mountain of Grimhold. You will understand when you meet her." Kadar's expression filled with hope. "Will you do this for me? Will you protect my daughter?"

The request was almost a plea. Lukien agreed eagerly. Finally, there was something he could do right.

"Yes," he said, "I'll defend her. I'll do my best for her, Kadar. I promise."

At Minikin's request, Gilwyn followed her out of the chamber with her bodyguard Trog as they headed back toward the palace gardens. She had asked Baron Glass to leave them alone for a while, so that she could explain some things to Gilwyn privately. Ever protective of his young charge, the baron had hesitated to leave Gilwyn's side, but Gilwyn had reassured him. For some reason he couldn't explain, he felt perfectly safe with the white-haired lady, and even her monstrous bodyguard did not frighten him. Now Gilwyn and Minikin strode slowly along the garden's flowered lane, Trog's enormous shadow blocking out the scorching sun behind them. Minikin had been very quiet as they walked, but her smile never wavered. When she was sure they were far from eavesdroppers, she paused.

"I hope you're not angry with me, Gilwyn," she said. "I know the things I've told you were a shock, but I did what I thought was right. Marking you as one of my Inhumans was the best way to protect you."

"But I didn't need protection," said Gilwyn. He was still confused by all he'd heard. "I grew up in Lionkeep. Nothing would have happened to me there."

Minikin nodded. "You're right, but I couldn't know that.

And you have lived a sheltered life. You were fortunate to grow up with people who could protect you. Many like you are not so lucky."

Gilwyn flexed his clubbed hand. He had always known that Akeela's goodness had protected him. "I know," he admitted. "And I don't blame you for marking me. But I'm still not sure what that means. Am I cursed like the amulets?"

"Not at all," said Minikin. She directed him toward one of the garden's stone benches, then sat down beside him. "There's no reason for you to be concerned. Being marked as an Inhuman is not a curse. It simply means you have an Akari looking after you."

The strange word still frightened Gilwyn. "Is that some kind of ghost?"

"In a way. All the Inhumans have Akari. They are like spirit guides. I like to call them angels."

"Angels?" The name surprised Gilwyn. In Liiria, some people believed they were creatures of the heavens that looked after people. "So they are good spirts, then?"

"Most certainly. They help us to overcome our maladies. And they protect us, keep us safe from harm. If you had ever been in danger—if you had ever needed a home— your Akari would have spoken to you. She would have told you that Grimhold exists, and that you have a place there."

"She?" blurted Gilwyn. "You mean my Akari's a girl?"

"Not exactly," chuckled Minikin. "But she was a woman once, a very long time ago."

"You mean she's dead now?" Gilwyn shook his reeling head. "Gods, I don't believe this. . . ."

"It's true, Gilwyn. When we die we don't simply blink out of existence. We continue. Our spirits are eternal. Even in Liiria, with all its varied beliefs, most people hope for that, don't they?"

"Well, yes, but no one knows for certain."

"I know for certain," said Minikin. "I know that we go on when we die, all of us. And sometimes, spirits do not pass into the next world, but rather stay here to assist others. The Akari are like that."

The claim confused Gilwyn, but then he remembered his strange recollection of Grimhold months ago, when he'd first seen Minikin. "Yes," he whispered. "I remember now.

When I first saw you in Koth, I thought of Grimhold. I couldn't get it out of my mind. Was that my Akari speaking to me?"

"Indeed," said Minikin. "And as you come to know her better, you will learn how she can help you."

"You mean with magic?" Gilwyn asked.

"Something like that," said Minikin. "You see, Gilwyn, the spirits that help us are from a very special people, an ancient race that left the world a long time ago. These people were what you might call magicians and witches. They knew the secrets of summoning."

"Summoning?"

"Calling those from other realms," explained Minikin. "They were called the Akari, and they lived beyond the mountains where Grimhold lies now."

"What happened to them?" asked Gilwyn.

The little woman's smile retuned, albeit faintly. "That's not something you need to know just yet. The important thing for you to know now is that your Akari is with you always, and that she is not going to harm you."

Fascinated, Gilwyn asked the obvious question. "Does she have a name, Minikin?"

"Yes. Her name is Ruana. And when she died she was about twenty years old." Minikin's grin grew sly. "She was very pretty. Still is, in fact."

"What? You mean you can see her?"

"It's what I do, Gilwyn. I can see and communicate with all the Akari spirits. That's why I'm the Mistress of Grimhold."

Suddenly curious, Gilwyn glanced over his shoulder, but he saw no one there but Trog. The sight of the big man intrigued him. "Minikin, does Trog have an Akari, too?" he asked.

"All the Inhumans have an Akari spirit if they need one, Gilwyn. It's what makes us what we are. Trog's Akari is named Ozmalius. He helps Trog to hear, even though he's deaf."

Gilwyn looked at Trog, feeling sorry for him. "Was he always deaf?"

"Since birth, yes," said Minikin.

"And mute?"

This time Minikin measured her reply. She got up from

the bench and went to her companion, taking his giant hand and stroking it. "Trog isn't a true mute," she said. "Because he could not hear while growing up, he never learned to speak in anything but grunts." She gave Trog's hand a loving squeeze. "I don't know who, but someone couldn't take his noises anymore. They cut out his tongue."

Trog didn't even blink at the story, but Gilwyn was horrified. Minikin turned to him with a sad grimace.

"You see?" she asked. "The rest of the world isn't like Liiria. Akeela might be mad, but he made a good place for you in Koth, a far better place than many on the continent have. That is why I marked you, Gilwyn—to spare you the cruelty of the normal human world."

Seeing Trog and Minikin's love for him left Gilwyn sad and confused. His mother had always told him he was as good as anyone else, and Figgis had reaffirmed that belief. But he had always known that a cruel life befell many with deformities. It was only by the grace of the Fate that he had avoided such a life. Or was it the intervention of Minikin's unseen spirits?

"I don't know what to say," said Gilwyn at last. "Everything you've told me; it's all so strange. I'm not sure I believe it."

"You will believe when we get to Grimhold, Gilwyn," said Minikin. "Once you see the wonders the Inhumans can do, you won't doubt any longer."

"When will I learn to speak with my Akari?" asked Gilwyn eagerly. "I'd like to get to know this Ruana better."

"In time," replied Minikin. "But you'll have to be patient, perhaps more patient than you've ever been before. There is much I need to do when I get back to Grimhold. But when this crisis is over, I will teach you."

Gilwyn didn't hide his disappointment. "But I'd like to learn now. I mean, if she's always with me, can't she at least show herself?"

"It isn't that simple," said Minikin. "Communicating with the Akari isn't like having a talk with a friend. You don't just sit down to tea with them. You need to be prepared, and only I can do that for you. And I will when I have time, but not soon." Then she brightened and said, "Ah, but you're forgetting something, aren't you?"

"Huh?"

"The kreel?"

Gilwyn hurried to his feet. "I forgot!" he said, looking around madly. "Which way?"

Minikin held up her hands. "Do not worry, Gilwyn, they won't kill it."

"What? How do you know that?"

"Because I told them not to," said Minikin. She started off again down the garden path. Gilwyn hurried after her. As they left the garden, she said, "You reminded me of something, Gilwyn. Of all people, we Inhumans shouldn't condemn an imperfect creature."

"So they'll save it?" asked Gilwyn anxiously.

"If I say so, yes," replied Minikin. Then she paused again and looked at him. "But hear me well, Gilwyn—killing is an easy thing. Living is much more difficult. If you want to save this kreel, then you will have to look after it. Are you prepared for that?"

"Me? But I don't know the first thing about kreels!"

Minikin pointed to Teku, still perched happily on Gilwyn's shoulder. "You do fine with monkeys. I think you'll do fine with kreels, too."

"But—"

"Do not argue, Gilwyn. Kadar's men will not look after a runt kreel. If you want to save the creature, you'll have to take it to Grimhold with you. So, will you do that?"

Gilwyn needed to think, but it was all happening so quickly. Then an exciting notion occurred to him. "Will I be able to ride it?" he asked. "I've never been able to ride a horse before, not with this." He held up his twisted hand.

Minikin reached out and wrapped her small fingers around his hand. "A boy with a clubbed hand can do many things, Gilwyn. You will learn that. In Grimhold, we will teach you."

46

Early the next morning Lukien and Gilwyn said a quick good-bye to Baron Glass, then set off for Grimhold before the sun grew too hot. With them was Minikin and the ubiquitous Trog, along with a handful of Kahan Kadar's black-robed guardians. They traveled on drowas through the rocks and hard sand, while Kadar's men rode their enormous lizards. Gilwyn's lizard, who he had already named Emerald because of her glistening skin, traveled behind them, tethered by her snout to the back of Gilwyn's drowa, a brown and hairy beast that he shared with Lukien. Minikin and Trog shared the drowa ahead of them, making an odd looking couple as Minikin leaned back against Trog's enormous chest, almost disappearing there.

The road to Grimhold wasn't really a road at all, just a straight line through the desert toward the red mountains in the distance. The mountains seemed to grow no closer as the sun rose in the sky. Lukien adjusted his dark headdress, trying to block the worst of the sun's rays. His one eye felt blinded by the light, but he found controlling the drowa an easy thing, something he was sure Gilwyn could do alone, even with his bad hand. The boy sat in front of him, his monkey Teku in a small metal cage dangling on the side of the drowa. With his simian friend and new lizard, he reminded Lukien of a Kothan animal act. But Gilwyn seemed not to notice the absurdity. For some reason, he was enthralled with the idea of reaching Grimhold, and

Lukien wondered if Minikin had enchanted him again. Despite her claims to the contrary, Lukien still thought the midget a witch. According to Gilwyn, she had told the boy she could see and control spirits, the souls of the dead, and Lukien had no reason to doubt her claims. After seeing the awful power of the amulets, he doubted very little now.

Yet Lukien did not fear Minikin. There was too much sincerity in the woman to think her dangerous. She had always kept Gilwyn's best interests at heart, even when she'd marked him as a baby. And she was a strange and compelling creature. With her white hair and peaked ears, she was unlike anyone Lukien had ever seen before. And if she had a gift for speaking to the dead, it did not mean she was evil. She was simply different. Lukien thought about this as he bounced across the desert. It intrigued him that the little woman could see spirits. If true, there were those he would like to speak with himself.

He reached down and unhooked a waterskin from the drowa's harness. Teku chattered for some, so he unplugged its stopper and poured some through the bars of her cage. The monkey's tiny tongue caught the falling water, happily lapping it up. When she had drunk her fill, Lukien took a swig himself, then thrust out the skin for Gilwyn. Gilwyn turned awkwardly and took the skin in his good hand, taking the time to shoot Emerald the kreel a concerned glance.

"You all right back there?" he shouted to the lizard. The kreel looked straight at him as it loped along the sands. "Minikin told me that they bond with their owners," he said. "Once she gets to know me, I'll be able to ride and control her." An expression of pride flooded Gilwyn's face. "I always wanted to ride. When I was younger, I used to dream of being a Royal Charger, like my father. But I could never do it, not with a hand and foot like mine."

"Then a kreel suits you well," said Lukien, happy for the boy. "Just take it easy, all right? They look vicious."

"I'll be fine." Gilwyn settled in again confidently on the drowa's back. "I just wish we'd get to Grimhold. The heat's killing me."

Minikin had said it was a full day's ride to Grimhold, and neither of them had been anxious to face the desert again. Back in Jador, Thorin had been relieved to be spared the misery of the ride. He had wished Lukien good fortune on his mission, though. And his own mission was far more dire. Soon Akeela's army would come across the desert, maybe in as soon as a week. Though Thorin had told Lukien not to worry about him, his own fears were evident. But he had also seemed eager to help Kadar, and that pleased Lukien. Thorin was a good man and a great tactician. If anyone could help Kadar, it was Baron Glass.

After traveling for several hours, the Jadori men called for a rest. They were in a wide canyon with shallow sloping walls of red rock and hard earth that made walking easier. As they dismounted, the Jadori broke out food and water, instructing the others to do the same. Lukien helped Gilwyn down from their mount, then got out their own food as the boy quickly freed Teku from her cage. The monkey hurried to her perch on Gilwyn's shoulder. Lukien tossed them both some dates from their packs, which Teku quickly devoured. As the monkey ate, Gilwyn went to Emerald and petted her scaly snout, cooing to the creature like a kitten as he undid her harness. Lukien was about to stop Gilwyn, but was quickly fascinated by the boy's easy manner with the lizard. When he unlooped the harness, Emerald did not run. She simply stared at him with her cool eyes, as if communicating some primal thanks.

"The boy has a way with the kreel," said an unexpected voice. Lukien turned to see Minikin smiling at him. She had a wedge of bread in her hand. Some distance behind her, the giant Trog was rummaging through their packs and gobbling up the food.

"Yes," said Lukien. "It seems so."

Minikin drifted closer. "Why don't you bring some food and sit with me a moment?" She pointed toward an outcropping in the rocks. "We can sit there, in the shade."

Lukien hesitated, but the woman's expression encouraged trust. He found himself some bread and dried meat and followed her toward the rocks, where a great ledge overhung the canyon wall like a swollen lip. There she sat down, smoothing her long coat along her backside. The amulet around her neck looked enormous against her small figure. It glowed in the strong light, but her colorful coat was surprisingly muted. She waved Lukien closer, urging him to sit down next to her. Together they ate their food, enjoying the shade as they watched Gilwyn in the distance.

"So," said Lukien, "Gilwyn says you talk to spirits."

Minikin laughed. "You are very direct, Sir Lukien. Is that what concerns you about me?"

"I'm not sure what you mean."

"You have been watching me all morning. I've felt your eyes on my back. You don't trust me. Or perhaps you fear me; I can't tell which, and I prefer not to crawl around your mind to look for the answers."

"What? You're a mind-reader, too?"

Minikin smiled. "Only when I have to be."

Lukien didn't know whether or not to believe her. "You're different, that's for sure," he said. He chewed on his bread, wondering how not to offend the little woman. "To be honest, I've never met anyone like you, or your man Trog. And you have to admit, you are a rather odd pair."

"I admit only that we are strange to you," replied Minikin. "You don't know the ways of the people here, or their beliefs. You're a Liirian, and Liirians have many disparate beliefs. Perhaps you believe in the Fate?"

"I don't believe in anything, really," said Lukien.

"Ah, yet you believe in the power of the amulets. You must."

"Yes," Lukien admitted. "Because I've seen their work. But I don't believe that there's a great god named Vala." He regarded her. "Is that what you believe?"

Minikin was evasive. "The peoples of Jador and Ganjor say there is a god that is supreme over all others. Many people in the world believe this. Even some in Liiria believe in a one great god. In Jador and Ganjor, they call him Vala."

"You're not answering me. I want to know if *you* believe in Vala."

"I believe in this," said Minikin, lifting her amulet on its chain. "I believe in the Akari, because they speak to me. And it was the Jadori who first called the amulets the Eyes of God, not I."

"So they named the amulets after something that they understood?"

"Precisely," said Minikin. "Kadar and his people worship Vala, and I have no reason to question them. The Akari believed in Vala, too, at least some of them. But they have never told me what it's really like on the other side, or if Vala truly exists."

The cryptic answer didn't satisfy Lukien. "Tell me about the Akari. Gilwyn told me that you can see them, even though they're dead."

"That's right."

"So you do see spirits?"

Minikin grinned. "You are asking two questions."

"What do you mean?"

"You don't just want to know if I can see spirits, Sir Lukien. You want to know if I can see spirits around *you.*"

Lukien flushed in embarrassment. "Yes, all right. I mean, if you can see the dead. . . ."

"Let me put you at ease, then. I can see only the spirits that aid my people, the spirits of the Akari. They have chosen to speak through me and make themselves visible. But I can't see other spirits."

The revelation deflated Lukien.

"You wanted to know if I could see Queen Cassandra," said Minikin gently. "I'm sorry, I cannot. But that doesn't mean she isn't with you, Sir Lukien."

Lukien tried to smile. "No, of course. It was a stupid idea anyway." Eager to change the subject, he said, "So what about these people, the Akari? You told Gilwyn they knew magic. Is that so?"

"I told Gilwyn that they knew the secrets of summoning," corrected Minikin, "and that they could commune with the spirits of their ancestors. In a sense, they could do what you would call magical things. Some of them were very powerful."

"So what happened to them?"

Minikin became pensive. "That's a long story, and not very pleasant."

"I'd like to know," said Lukien. He smiled at her, trying to coax her to speak.

"Very well," she sighed. "The Akari died off a long time ago, decades ago, really. They lived beyond the mountains, where Grimhold lies now. Grimhold was their stronghold. It was where they performed their summonings, and it was how they protected themselves from the outside world. But they could not protect themselves from everyone. Kadar's people—the Jadori—feared the Akari. They feared their might and powers." The little woman's face grew grave. "Eventually, Kadar's people slaughtered the Akari. They killed them all."

"The Jadori? But they're so peaceful."

"As I said, it was a long time ago, long before Kadar was even born. Back then the Jadori were different. They were far more aggressive and fearful." Suddenly Minikin's face brightened. "Oh, but Kadar changed them. He made them beautiful people."

"How'd he do that?"

Minikin's eyes seemed to fill with good memories. "I met Kadar years ago, when he was a young man and I was . . . well, far younger than I am now. I came here looking to flee the normal world, because of what I was."

"You mean . . . small?" Lukien ventured.

Minikin smiled. "It wasn't always easy for me, Sir Lukien. The world beyond Jador is cruel."

"How well I know that," said Lukien with a sigh. "So when you came to Jador you met Kadar?"

"That's right. He'd only been ruler of Jador a few years, but he knew the history of his people, the horrible thing they'd done to the Akari. Kadar is a good man, Sir Lukien. You need to believe that."

"I do," said Lukien. In the distance Gilwyn was still working with Emerald. He remembered the kindness Kadar had shown the boy.

Minikin continued, "Kadar welcomed me, just as he welcomed you when you came with your companions all that time ago. He was determined to change his people, to make them less warlike and fearful of outsiders. He and I quickly became friends. And I loved living in his palace. I was free for the first time in my life, surrounded by people that didn't judge or ridicule me."

"And it didn't bother you what the Jadori did to the Akari?"

"No," said Minikin. "I knew Kadar's heart was good, and when he finally told me about the Akari I realized why he had become such a good man. But I made him take me to their land in the mountains. That's where I found Grimhold . . . and the spirits."

Fascinated, Lukien said, "You mean the spirits of the Akari spoke to you?"

"Like a bell! They screamed at me from across the years. I was the first person to encounter them in many decades, and they could never have trusted Kadar or one of his people." Minikin gave a humble shrug. "So they chose me."

"To tell their story?"

"Yes, I think so. And to live on through me, and the people I brought to them. Not all of the Akari were willing to cross into the next life. Most of them, of course, but the strongest ones wanted to live on."

"So you bring people for them to attach themselves to," said Lukien, suddenly understanding.

"That's right. As I told Gilwyn, they are like what you of the north might call angels. The Akari spirits get to live on through my Inhumans, and the Inhumans are helped by them to overcome their problems. If they're blind then they can see. And if they're deaf like Trog, they can hear."

"Amazing." Lukien took a deep breath and glanced at Trog. The big giant was oblivious to their conversation, still eating the provisions they had brought, though more slowly now. "What about Gilwyn's Akari?" he asked suddenly. "What good will that spirit do him?"

"I don't know yet," Minikin confessed. "When I marked the boy it was simply to make sure he'd know of Grimhold. If he'd ever needed us, his Akari would have spoken to him, guiding him to us." She gave a wide smile. "But Gilwyn doesn't seem to need help."

Lukien glanced down at the amulet around her neck. "You still haven't told me about the Eyes," he said. "Did you find them in Grimhold?"

"I did," said Minikin, "along with other things, like this coat."

"Yes," said Lukien, "what about your coat? It changes colors."

"It helps me to blind the minds of those who see me," Minikin explained. "Like the amulets, it too is possessed by spirits of the Akari. They control what people see. They work on the minds of men. That's one of the things the Akari summoners did best."

The explanation frightened Lukien. "So there are spirits in the amulets? They're the ones that make the magic?"

Minikin nodded. "Some of the Akari were more power-

ful at the summoning than others. The amulets were made
years ago to contain the essences of two great summoners,
a brother and sister. It is they that hold the power, and
keep people from aging."

"But you gave one to Kadar," Lukien said. "Why?"

"To forge the bond between us," said Minikin. "That
was why the amulets were forged, to be a great gift, something worthy of the task set upon the wearer. Kadar feared
death, like any man. When I told him of the amulets he
was more than pleased to wear one and I the other. He
agreed to protect Grimhold and I agreed to bring people
there for the Akari. And after all, our bargain worked out
well for many, many years."

"Yet now he won't wear the amulet," said Lukien with
a frown. "I brought it back for him, but he refuses it."

"Kadar has changed, Sir Lukien. He no longer wants to
live forever, not without his wife."

Lukien shook his head regretfully. "I understand that. I
wish there was something I could do, but she's dead."

"You are doing your part," said Minikin. "You've agreed
to protect his daughter."

"Yes," nodded Lukien. "Tell me, what's she like?"

The enigmatic smile returned to Minikin's face. "You
will see when you meet her."

"Why won't you tell me?" said Lukien. "Why the great
secret?"

Minikin got to her feet and brushed the crumbs from her
lap. She said, "Grimhold has many secrets, Sir Lukien.
When we get there, you'll see what I mean."

Then she walked off, leaving Lukien alone on the rocks.
He watched her go to Trog and wipe a stain from his shirt,
like a mother caring for a child. And though she had told
him a great deal about herself, she was as inscrutable as
ever to Lukien, a great puzzle yet to be solved.

By dusk they had reached the base of the red mountains.
An hour later, they saw Grimhold.

Lukien reined in the drowa, and his and Gilwyn's eyes
drifted up toward the strange fortress. They were in a flat
clearing of hard earth, with the sheer walls of the mountains rising up on all sides. The giant face of Grimhold
stared down at them with a menacing leer. At ground level,

a huge gate of black iron bars formed the giant's mouth, a black maw guarded by a single armored sentry, a huge man whose bulk rivaled Trog's. Above the gate, staggered on both sides, rose high-columned turrets sculpted into the blood-red rock, with glassless windows that gazed down on them like a hundred unblinking eyes. The ancient ramparts at the tops of the turrets had been worn smooth by countless sandstorms so that the fortress seemed invisible, hidden by the shadows and twists of the mountains. Lukien had never seen a more impressive sight. For all its dismal beauty, Lionkeep paled in comparison to the marvel of Grimhold, and Jazana Carr's Hanging Man seemed a trifle. Grimhold was unimaginably tall, taller than Koth's highest spire, and the effort to mold so much rock boggled Lukien. He knew when he saw it that Minikin had not lied to him— the Akari had been powerful indeed.

"Great Fate . . ."

Lukien dismounted then helped Gilwyn down from the drowa, all the while keeping his gaze on Grimhold. A great wind bellowed through the canyon, yet all else was silent. In the distance the huge sentry shifted his massive sword from hand to hand. Minikin waved to him as she dismounted. The sentry nodded and folded his naked arms across his chest.

"This is amazing," said Gilwyn. His awestruck expression made Minikin smile. "It's even bigger than the library."

"There are many of us, Gilwyn," said Minikin. "Grimhold must be big to shelter us all."

The Jadori guards did not dismount from their kreels, but rather kept their distance. Lukien gave them a puzzled look.

"They will not come any further," Minikin explained. "They'll rest for the night here, then return to Jador in the morning."

"Why? Are they afraid?" Lukien asked.

"Grimhold is a sacred place," Minikin explained. "And they are still mindful of the spirits within it, and what their people did to them." The little woman walked toward Gilwyn and took his hand. She said, "This is your home now, Gilwyn, for as long as you wish it to be. You will always have a place here."

"Like the library," said Gilwyn sadly, and Lukien could

tell he was thinking again of Figgis. The boy shrugged. "I don't know what to say. It's overwhelming."

"Grimhold has that effect on people," said Minikin. "Don't worry, you'll get used to it."

"Who's that?" asked Lukien, pointing toward the lone guardian.

"That is Greygor," replied Minikin. "Guardian of the gate."

"He's big, like Trog."

"Almost as big; not quite." Minikin winked at her body-guard. "Come now, Trog. We're going."

"What about Emerald?" asked Gilwyn. "Can we take her inside with us?"

"Not yet. We have to make a place for her." Minikin turned to the Jadori men and said a few words. The men nodded. Minikin turned back to Gilwyn, saying, "They will look after the kreel for the night. In the morning, we will find a place for her in Grimhold."

"What place?" asked Lukien. He studied the fortress. "Have you got some sort of stable in there?"

"You are full of questions, Sir Lukien. But your answers are at hand. Come. . . ."

With Trog at her side, Minikin made her way toward the gate. Lukien glanced at Gilwyn. The boy's expression was elated. Together they followed the little woman until they stood just before the gigantic gate. Torchlight gleamed beyond the thick iron bars. Figures moved within the fortress' dim recesses. But blinded as he was by the hot sun, it was hard for Lukien to make out much beyond the bars. The only detail he could see was a flickering flame, glowing, it seemed, in someone's palm. As they neared, the man called Greygor swept his huge sword aside and gave a fluid bow, so quietly he barely ruffled the air. He was covered in spiky black armor and wore a helmet that hid his face behind a tusked facade. A long queue of black hair trailed down his back. The soundlessness of his greeting startled Lukien.

"Rise, Greygor," commanded Minikin. The guardian of the gate did so, fixing his gaze on his mistress. Minikin smiled at him. "You're a welcome sight, my friend. Raise the gate and sound the horn."

Greygor did as commanded, turning toward the gate and

using his sword to rattle the bars. It was odd hearing the soundless man make noise. Within moments came the din of chains being pulled, then the enormous creaking of the great gate lifting skyward. Inside the fortress, a horn released a bellowing note. Lukien stepped back and watched the huge portal slowly rise. Minikin stood her ground, unmoved by the clamor. The giant Greygor stood aside to let them pass, as implacable as his mistress.

"The guardian," whispered Lukien. "Why doesn't he talk?"

Minikin replied simply, "He chooses not to."

The answer puzzled Lukien. "How's that?"

"Greygor is from Ganjor, Lukien," Minikin explained, "and the Ganjeese are desert people, very quiet. Before coming here he guarded a harem for a Ganjeese prince." She kept her voice low, and if Greygor heard her he didn't seem to care. "Greygor loved a woman in that harem. When he was discovered, he was banished. But not before his bones were broken. In his arms and legs, even in his hands."

Lukien studied the man in amazement. "His bones? How can that be? He moves like no one I've ever seen."

"The Akari, Lukien. I told you—they help us overcome our maladies. Just as they kept your Cassandra alive, they hold together Greygor's bones. They give him the grace you seem to marvel at. You will never find a more skilled warrior than Greygor, Lukien. That, too, the Akari have gifted him. He is as silent as a breeze now, and quicker than a cobra."

"But he never speaks?"

"Greygor does his work here and speaks to no one unless he must," said Minikin. She looked momentarily sad. "Perhaps he fears caring too much for us, I don't know."

Slowly the massive gate reached its apex. The hellish screeching stopped, but now there were other sounds, the muffled noise of voices and the scraping of feet. Lukien squinted in the bright light, trying to peer into the dimness of Grimhold. Amidst the oily torchlight he saw movement and figures. Again he caught the glimpse of flame, jumping in an open palm but barely lighting the cowled face of its bearer. The deepness of Grimhold seemed to go on forever,

far, far into the belly of the mountain. A strange fear seized
Lukien as he realized there were eyes in the darkness,
watching.

"Fate above," he whispered. "Who are they?"

"They are my children," pronounced Minikin proudly.
"My Inhumans."

Stepping over the threshold of Grimhold, the mistress of
the place held out her hands and beckoned Lukien and
Gilwyn forward. Lukien put his hand on Gilwyn as they
walked forward together. Leaving the desert's blinding
light, the great interior of Grimhold slowly revealed itself.
Unfolding like a book, a huge, tiered palace with balconies
and staircases appeared in the dark rocks, with layers of
wooden beams supporting the expansive ceiling. The entire
place glowed with a soft orange opalescence, lit by torches
staggered along the walls. There were no windows, nor the
smallest drop of sunlight. And unlike other castles, there
were no statues or greenery or portraits or tapestries. Instead, the walls of Grimhold were smooth stone, dark and
featureless but for the landings and balconies and beams.

Most astonishing of all, though, were the people lining
the floor and staring down from the high balconies. They
were an awesome lot, a cross-section of nature's strange
diversity. There were stunted midgets like Minikin and
freakish giants like Trog, milk-skinned albinos and dwarves
with heads too large for their diminutive bodies. Clubfooted children like Gilwyn gave the strangers a welcoming
smile, seeming to know instantly that one of their own had
arrived. Even men like Baron Glass were in the crowd,
who had lost limbs to battle or some defect of birth. And
amid them all was the darkly cowled figure with the flame,
its face obscured behind folds of fabric, the little flicker of
light still dancing in its open palm. Perhaps he was a leper;
Lukien couldn't guess. The sight of so much odd humanity
made his head swim, for though they were strange and
difficult to comprehend, they were not the beasts the stories
had claimed. No matter their maladies, they smiled at Minikin and the strangers she had brought, and Lukien could
feel the warmth from them, stronger even than the desert
sun.

Grimhold is a place of monsters.

The old words from the fairy tale pushed their way into Lukien's mind. Instantly he pushed them out again.

"Not so," he whispered.

At his side, Gilwyn was too awestruck to speak. The boy's gaze darted over the odd procession, taking in its strangeness. There were dozens of Inhumans; at least two hundred had turned out to greet them. To Lukien's surprise, Gilwyn seemed to be trembling. He put his hand on his shoulder, steadying him.

"Do not be afraid," Minikin told them both. "You're welcome guests here, and my children won't hurt you."

She turned and raised her hands and face to the Inhumans, beaming a smile into the highest balconies. Those who could clap did so. And those who could speak raised their voices in a call of praise, though the cowled figure remained silent.

"Thank you, friends," said Minikin, clasping her hands before her as if in prayer. "You honor me. And you honor our guests, too. But we have work now. There's danger ahead."

The Inhumans nodded and became grave. Minikin's smile faded a little.

"There are dark times coming for us. But this man is here to help us." She gestured to Lukien. "He and his friends know the ways of our enemies. Together we can turn the tide."

"Yes!" the crowd agreed, and there was a raucous chorus of chants and banging. Lukien looked at the faces of those on the floor and then up toward the balconies where more Inhumans cheered. In many ways they did seem like children, naively sure that Minikin would save them. Lukien wanted to speak suddenly, to tell them all that Akeela's army was far worse than anything they'd imagined. In a week they might all be dead. But he could not say it. More than anything, he wanted to help them.

"There is work ahead of us, my children," cried Minikin, "and we will all need to do our best. Grimhold is our homeland. We must do our best to defend it!"

More banging ensued, more cries of agreement. A man with one arm stamped his feet on the tiled floor, while a hunchback beside him dully clapped his palsied hands.

Together the misfits of Grimhold let loose such an outcry
that Lukien had to hold his ears against the echoing clamor.
As he did, a single figure stepped out from the dimness, a
slim and beautiful girl with a white dress and amber skin,
the kind of skin that made the Jadori so beautiful. A waterfall of raven hair ran down her back, straight and shiny
black. She smiled as she neared Minikin, her teeth dazzling.
But as she neared Lukien saw the horrible flaw in her, for
her eyes were bone white and blank. She moved slowly but
surely, drifting over the tiles with her dress billowing out
behind her, and when she reached Minikin she took the
midget's hand and kissed it.

"Minikin, welcome home," she said in a musical voice.
She was much taller than Minikin, so stooped a little to
hug her. "I've missed you."

"And I you, child," replied Minikin.

"How is Father?"

The question struck Lukien like a hammer, and he knew
in an instant that this was Kadar's daughter.

"Your father's well," said Minikin. "He's sent us ahead
to prepare." Then she held out her hand, gesturing for
Lukien to come closer. "And he's sent someone to look
after you."

The girl turned her featureless eyes toward Lukien. Though
she was surely blind, she looked directly at him. "Hello."

"This is Lukien, the Bronze Knight of Liiria," said Minikin. "The one who killed your mother, White-Eye."

There was a pause in the girl's motion, but only for a
moment. She let Minikin put her hand into Lukien's, then
remarkably she smiled at him.

"Welcome, Sir Lukien," said the girl.

Lukien could hardly speak. "Thank you," he managed.
"I'm honored to meet you." He studied her face and perfectly blank eyes. There was no way she could see him, yet
his manners made the girl giggle.

"I am not as blind as you think I am, sir."

Startled, Lukien cleared his throat. "I'm sorry. It's just
that . . . did Minikin call you White-Eye?"

"That's my name now," said the girl. "Appropriate, don't
you think?"

"Um, yes, I suppose," said Lukien. "You are Kadar's
daughter?"

"I am."

"Then it is you I am here for." With all the Inhumans still looking on, Lukien dropped to one knee before then girl and, still holding her hand, looked up into her pretty face. "I have wronged you and your father. I've slain your mother. To atone I pledge myself to your protection, White-Eye. While I live, I will defend you."

There was silence in the vast chamber. Staring into White-Eye's face, Lukien saw the most sublime forgiveness.

"Rise then, and be my protector, Sir Lukien."

As Lukien got to his feet, Gilwyn shuffled into their circle.

"Can I introduce myself?" he asked. There was a tinge of nervousness in his voice. When Lukien saw his face, he knew why. In his eyes was plain lovesickness, the same surrendering love Lukien had seen in Akeela's eyes when he'd first spotted Cassandra. Not surprisingly, White-Eye turned her dazzling smile on Gilwyn, enough to make the boy's breathing quicken.

"Yes, right," said Lukien. "White-Eye, this is Gilwyn Toms. He came with me from Liiria."

Gilwyn put out his good hand for her. "I was an apprentice librarian there," he added quickly. So enamored was he by the girl that he forgot Teku on his shoulder. When the monkey cried a protest, Gilwyn said, "Oh, and this is Teku. She's a friend of mine."

It took a moment for White-Eye to notice the monkey. Like everything she did, there was a tiny delay in her reaction. "Oooh," she cooed, then reached out to scratch Teku's head. "She's very pretty. She's Ganjeese, yes?"

"That's right," said Gilwyn. "But I got her a long time ago in Liiria."

They were talking as if they were the only two in the world. Lukien gave Minikin a furtive glance, which she returned knowingly. Again she raised her hands to the gathered Inhumans.

"Your welcome is appreciated, my children," she said. "But now I must rest. And then we must all work. So go now, and we'll all speak again soon."

Like loyal soldiers the Inhumans began to disburse, though White-Eye remained. Minikin waited for them to go before turning back toward Lukien.

"You are tired, I know, Sir Lukien, but there's someone I think you should meet before you rest."

"Oh?" asked Lukien. "Who is that?"

Minikin turned to White-Eye. "Child, why don't you take Gilwyn Toms and show him some of Grimhold? I'm sure he'd like that."

"Yes," said Gilwyn quickly. He looked adoringly at White-Eye. "Very much."

White-Eye nodded. "Where will you go, Minikin?"

"To see Insight." Minikin grinned at the two young people. "I hope I can trust you both together."

White-Eye laughed and Gilwyn flushed, and Minikin turned away from them, bidding Lukien to follow. "Come along, Sir Lukien," she said. Trog trailed close behind her.

"Where are we going?" asked Lukien. "Who's Insight?"

"You'll see," Minikin replied. She headed quickly toward one of the halls sprouting out from the great chamber. Like all the others, this one was dark but for the light of distantly-spaced torches. When Lukien caught up to Minikin, he decided to ply her with more questions.

"So White-Eye is blind?" he asked.

"Obviously."

"And she sees with the help of an Akari?"

Minikin kept walking. "That's right."

"But why can't she stay with her father in Jador? Kadar told me I'd understand when I met her, but I don't."

"Because of her eyes," Minikin explained. "They are too sensitive to light for the bright sun of Jador. It is very painful to her. So she stays here within the mountain."

The answer only added to Lukien's guilt. "Oh." He glanced around as they moved through the halls, passing more of the strange Inhumans on their way. Trog kept back a pace or two, characteristically quiet. The interior of Grimhold continued to amaze Lukien. The deeper they went into the mountain, the less like a mountain it became. The walls grew smoother and more even, so that except for the lack of windows, it seemed like any other castle. Each hall snaked into another, each bend revealed a new stone stairway expertly cut into the rock. Lukien could only wonder at the skill of the Akari engineers. Grimhold was certainly formidable, and would make a good stronghold against

Akeela and his army. But who would defend it? The Inhumans? The disabled folk of Grimhold were hardly soldiers.

They walked together for long minutes, until the hallway narrowed into a quiet wing full of doorways. It was, Lukien supposed, where the sleeping quarters were located. The lack of noise told him most of the rooms were empty. But near the end of the hall he saw a door half open and candlelight spilling over the threshold. Minikin slowed as she went to the door, Trog's enormous shadow on her back. Carefully she peered inside.

"Here she is," she said softly. "Come."

Gently she pushed open the door and went inside. Lukien stepped cautiously after her, leaving Trog at the door. Inside he saw two figures, both females, one much older than the other. The younger figure sat in a plain wooden chair with an equally spartan table at her side. The older woman hovered over her, slowly spooning food into the girl's barely moving mouth. As Lukien and Minikin entered, the older woman gave them a mild smile. She was normal by the look of her, without any obvious maladies. Sadly, the same couldn't be said of the girl, who stared blankly at the wall, unblinking and barely breathing.

"Minikin," said the older woman. "You're back."

Minikin went to the woman and stood on her toes to kiss her cheek. "Just arrived," she said. "And I've brought someone. Lukien, this is Alena, Insight's mother."

The older woman nodded at Lukien. "We were expecting you," she said. "Welcome."

"Expecting me?" Lukien asked. "What do you mean?"

"Insight told us," replied Alena. She lowered the spoon into the bowl, which Lukien could now see was full of porridge, then began wiping the girl's mouth. Lukien looked questioningly at Minikin.

"The girl Insight came to us three years ago, Sir Lukien," said Minikin. "She has a disease of the brain that makes reaching her impossible. She can't speak and she can't care for herself. But she can hear. Believe me, she's listening to everything we say."

"And her name is Insight?" asked Lukien. He knelt down in front of the girl, looking into her hazel eyes. "Because she can see the future?"

"With the help of her Akari, yes," said Minikin.

"Insight wasn't her real name," added Alena. "That's only what she's called here."

"Her birth name was Jenna," said Minikin. "I found her in Koth, not far from Lionkeep. Alena's husband had abandoned them. They were on the streets. I took them here to help them."

"So not everyone in Grimhold is . . . well, you know. . . ."

"Alena is one of the only plain people here, Lukien. I couldn't take Insight away from her, of course, and she wanted to come."

"We had nowhere else to go," said Alena. "Minikin saved us."

The child called Insight stared back at Lukien, but there was nothing in her eyes save the smallest glint of life. It was pitiful to see her, and Lukien wanted to look away. But he knew that Minikin had brought him here for a reason, so he tried to smile at the girl.

"Insight, if you can hear me, my name is Lukien."

"She knows who you are," said Alena. "I told you, she said you would be coming."

Lukien looked up at Minikin. "Is that right?"

"I'm sure it is," replied the little woman. "You see, Insight's Akari allows her to communicate with the outside world. But it can also see the future, or a semblance of it."

"Really? How's that possible?"

"All Akari spirits have this 'sight,' but not to the degree of Lacaron, Insight's spirit. In life he was a powerful summoner."

"Lacaron." Lukien studied the girl. "Will Lacaron speak to us, then?"

"Through Insight," said Minikin. "That is why I brought you here—to find out what might be coming."

Lukien nodded and took a deep breath. He had never been in any sort of seance before, but he wasn't skeptical any longer. After seeing the things Minikin could do, he was already a believer. Minikin went to Insight's side and put a hand to her head, lovingly brushing the strands of hair from her eyes.

"It's me, Insight. Minikin." The little woman's voice was softer than a lullaby. "I'm back now. We're all together now."

The girl's blankness didn't change.

"Insight, can you tell me what Lacaron sees? There's trouble coming to Grimhold. An army of northerners. Do you see them?"

There was silence in the room. Then a single remarkable sound.

"Yes."

The voice made Lukien quiver. He could hear the child in it, but only as though from a great distance. Something else laced the voice, something masculine and strong.

"Good," crooned Minikin. "Keep looking, child. Keep looking at the army. What's Lacaron showing you?"

"Hello, Mother," said the voice.

Alena broke into a sad smile. "Hello, my darling."

"Hello, Minikin."

"Hello, child," said Minikin. She continued stroking Insight's head. "You are strong today?"

"I am . . . strong enough."

"Is Lacaron showing you the army?"

"I can see the army."

Lukien held his breath and stared at Insight.

"Tell us what you see," said Minikin gently. "What is Lacaron showing you?"

"The army and the river," said the strange voice. As it spoke the girl's face barely stirred. "Big. Silver. Many."

Minikin glanced at Lukien, who nodded.

"That could be them, I suppose," he whispered. "They'd be following the Kryss south."

"Where are they now, Insight? Can you tell?"

"They have fought," replied the girl. "In the little country. They have killed." She paused. "The one who seeks is very angry."

Akeela, thought Lukien.

"Go on," urged Minikin.

The girl was silent for a moment. When her voice returned, it was deeper, slower. "They will come across the desert soon. Very near now. Very many."

Minikin paused for a moment and the amulet around her neck pulsed. "Lacaron, look to the future," she said. "Tell us what you see."

"I see death."

The voice sounded ancient. It chilled Lukien's soul.

"Go on," said Minikin.

"I see Grimhold."

"Yes?"

"I see ruins."

Minikin opened her eyes and stared at Insight. "You see Grimhold ruined?"

Insight paused. Then, "Yes."

"When?" asked Lukien. "When are they coming?"

"Lukien, stop," ordered Minikin. "Lacaron, are they coming soon?"

"Soon," said the voice. "Very strong. Very many."

Lukien backed away shaking his head. "Great Fate. . . ."

There seemed nothing else to say. Even Minikin appeared shaken.

"Lacaron, can you tell us anything else?" she asked. "Anything useful?"

Again there was a pause before the spirit spoke. Lukien supposed it was thinking.

"The one who leads them struggles," said the voice. "His mind is lost, like the child's. Too much rage. Broken."

"He's talking about Akeela," said Lukien.

"Anything else, Lacaron?" asked Minikin. "Anything useful?"

"The desert," said the voice from the girl. "Blood. A battle. And a one-armed man with the kahan."

"Baron Glass."

Minikin put a finger to her lips to quiet Lukien. The voice continued.

"One will die."

Lukien's heart sank. "Oh, no. Don't say that."

Suddenly the girl's head fell forward, as if sleep had instantly come. Alena came forward quickly and held her daughter. Minikin let out a sighing breath.

"That's it," she said. "Lacaron's gone." She stroked Insight's head, saying good-bye. "Let her rest now, Alena. Take your ease. I'll see you later."

Minikin headed to the door. Stunned, Lukien hurried after her. "That's it?" he asked. "That's all she can tell us?"

"That's it." Out in the hallway Minikin found Trog. She smiled at him. "You must be hungry. Come; let's eat now."

"Wait, Minikin," Lukien insisted. He ran in front of the

woman, blocking her way. "Didn't you hear what was said in there? Grimhold's going to be ruined!"

Minikin shrugged her tiny shoulders. "Perhaps. Perhaps not."

"But Insight saw it! And what about Kadar and Baron Glass? She said one of them would die!"

"Lukien, it doesn't have to be that way," said Minikin. "What Lacaron saw was just one possible future. There are still things we can do to change it."

The answer vexed Lukien. "Possible future? But a likely future, right?"

"Yes," admitted Minikin. "It may be our fate to die here, I don't know. But you're here now. You can help us change things. We can defend Grimhold and defeat your mad king."

"Minikin, we can't," said Lukien. "Grimhold is formidable, yes, but there's only a handful of people here able enough to defend it."

The familiar grin returned to Minikin's face. "Don't underestimate the Inhumans, Lukien. We can do some amazing things."

Lukien pointed down the hall. "We can't lead those cripples back there into battle, Minikin. Not against Akeela and Trager. They'd be slaughtered."

"If some must die to defend the rest, then so be it," said Minikin.

"No! That can't happen. I won't let it. Not because of me!"

The little woman put her small hand into Lukien's. "Akeela's wrath has come to Grimhold because of what you did to him. You can't change that. But you can change the future, Lukien. It's still in your hands. You can help defend White-Eye and all the others here. And if we die, then we die in a just cause."

With her faint smile dimming, she let her hand fall from Lukien's then turned and walked away with Trog. Lukien stood silent in the middle of the hall, watching her go. In his mind Insight's disembodied words rattled over and over again, forming a picture of Grimhold in ruins. And it was all because of him, and his love for Cassandra. He looked around the dim hall, and he could not recall a time when he'd ever felt so empty.

47

Akeela sat alone in a small chamber overlooking Ganjor, silently sipping a strong local liquor and cursing the stifling heat. The large window of his room was open wide but there was no breeze from the city, only the stink of overpopulation. Down below the streets were choked with livestock and the dark-skinned people of Ganjor. Their ceaseless chatter rose up into Akeela's chamber, a confusing language of rolling vowels and grunts. It was afternoon, a peak time for the marketplace, and the noise of the city was enormous. Past the outskirts of Ganjor, Akeela could see his army spread out on the distant sand, waiting for his return. They had arrived two days earlier and were all grateful for the rest. Akeela and Trager and a procession of Knight-Guardians had ventured into the city to make arrangements for the trek across the Desert of Tears and to find Akeela proper accommodations. In Ganjor, it seemed proper accommodations were anything with a roof, even for a king. So Akeela had stayed in his moderately sized room at the top of a shabby boarding house, getting drunk on the local wines while Trager searched for a guide to take them across the desert and the house's strange little proprietor did what he could to make his guest comfortable. Surprisingly, there had been no word from the ruler of Ganjor, a weak and minor king named Baralosus. Akeela suspected that word would come soon, along with an invitation to the royal residence, but he really didn't care. He hoped to be out of Ganjor very soon. Trager had been making arrangements since they arrived, and the resourceful general had overturned a remarkable gem. There was a caravan leader named Grak who had just arrived in the city from Jador. More amazingly, Grak had recently escorted another group of northerners across the forbidding desert.

Akeela wiped sweat from his brow and took another drink of the strong wine. The lightness in his brain told him he was already drunk, but he was used to the sensation these days and so didn't curb his thirst. Since Cassandra's death, he had spent most of his time in that netherworld between drunkenness and sobriety, holding onto just enough of his wits to do the work at hand. He looked around the room, studying the foreign decor. A well-worn carpet with a strange, crimson pattern dominated the center of the chamber. Colorful silk pillows dotted the floor. There was a small desk and a few ornate wooden chairs, and oil lamps along the walls that gave off a pleasant if peculiar scent. On the table next to Akeela sat a silver platter of exotic canapes, leaves stuffed with dates and ground meat and unusual fruits drizzled with oil. These Akeela ignored. His appetite had never really returned, and he continued to lose weight. Once again he turned toward the window and stared down into the marketplace. Somewhere in the distance a dog was barking. Children played among carts in the streets, all seemingly alike with their dark hair and skin. They were a handsome people, though, Akeela decided. And they had been gracious to him. He wondered if the Jadori were similar. If so, it would be a shame to harm them.

At last a knock came at the door. Akeela swiveled in his chair. "Come," he called in a slurring voice.

The door opened, first revealing Will Trager. The general wore a triumphant smile. He stepped into the chamber, then moved aside for two of his Knight-Guardians, who bore another man by the arms between them, a frightened looking Ganjeese fellow of middle age. The soldiers led him roughly into the center of the room, and when he saw Akeela across the chamber he started. Trager pushed the door closed with his foot.

"This is him, my lord," he said. "Grak."

Akeela smiled dispassionately. "Grak. You speak our tongue, Grak?"

"Uh, yes, my lord," replied the man nervously.

Akeela waved a hand at the Knight-Guardians, who immediately released the man. "Don't be afraid," he told Grak. "We don't want to harm you. We just want some information, and perhaps your help with something."

"My help, my lord?"

"What have you told him?" Akeela asked Trager.

"Only that you wanted to see him."

"And he arrived in the city yesterday?" Akeela looked back at Grak. "Is that so?"

"Yes, it is so, my lord," said Grak. Rubbing his arms, he studied the soldiers who had manhandled him. "I have eight children, my lord. And a wife that depends on me."

"I told you, we won't harm you. You have my promise," said Akeela. He decided to offer the man a drink. "Would you like some wine?"

Grak shook his head. "No, my lord."

Akeela put his own glass aside. "All right, to business then. My man Trager here tells me you're a caravan leader, that you lead people across the Desert of Tears."

"Yes, my lord," replied Grak. He licked his lips. "It is my business. I trade with the Jadori."

"And you've just returned from Jador, is that right?"

Grak nodded.

"You took northerners across this time, did you not? Northerners like us?"

Grak glanced at Trager and the soldiers before nodding. "I did, my lord."

"Describe them."

"There were three of them. They were light-skinned, like you, my lord," said Grak. "And one of them had light hair and an eyepatch."

"Eyepatch?" The answer surprised Akeela. "But he was a tall man, yes? And there was a boy with him?"

"That's right," said Grak. "And a man with one arm."

Trager's face soured. "Baron Glass."

"Yes, I think that was his name," said Grak. He looked apologetically at Akeela. "My lord, I meant no harm. If

these men are outlaws, I did not know it. Or that they had
the amulet."

"Amulet?" Akeela finally got out of his chair. "You saw
the amulet?"

"Yes," answered Grak, seeming confused. "Is that what
you seek?"

"You don't ask the king questions," snapped Trager.

"No," said Akeela, "that's all right." He smiled at Grak,
for he was immensely pleased by the news. "Yes, that's
what we're after, the amulet and the men who stole it from
us. They're in Jador now?"

"They were taken to Kadar, the Kahan of Jador," replied
Grak. "After a while Kadar's men came back and got their
belongings. I do not know what happened to them after
that, my lord, I swear."

"Oh, you've told us quite enough, my friend." Akeela
sank back in his chair with a huge grin. "Thank you very
much. But now you can do us a service."

Grak grew puzzled. "A service, my lord?"

"You've seen my army outside the city?"

Grak nodded. "They are easily seen, my lord. I saw them
yesterday, when I returned."

"I need to get them across the desert. All of them. And
with all their horses and equipment. I need a man like you
to help me do it."

"Me, my lord?" said Grak, plainly stunned.

"You know the desert, and you've made the trip before."
Akeela smiled. "And since you helped my enemies across,
I think you owe me some assistance."

"But to move such an army would take much, my lord."

"If you mean gold, I have enough," said Akeela.

"Gold and effort, my lord." Grak frowned, considering
the enormous task. "It is a great distance, and horses cannot travel quickly. The ground is soft until you reach
Jador."

"But horses can travel the desert," said Trager.

"Yes," said Grak, "but not easily. They will need water,
lots of it. And feed. They are not like drowa."

"If there's enough water in the city then there's enough
to bring with us," said Akeela. "We'll use drowa to carry
it."

Grak smiled politely. "My lord does not understand. To hire that many drowa would be very expensive."

"I know," spat Akeela. "Every move my army has made has cost me a fortune. I didn't expect this to be any different. There is gold waiting with my army, enough to pay for this excursion and your troubles, Grak. If you agree I will send for it so that you may start making arrangements."

"And if I don't agree?" asked Grak.

Trager stepped forward with a sneer. "If you don't agree—"

"If you don't agree I will hire someone else," Akeela interrupted. Then he sighed and said, "But it would be a great loss to you, Grak. I would pay handsomely for your services."

The desert leader thought for a moment, weighing his options. Akeela could tell he was still afraid, but he didn't want Trager's threats intimidating him. Grak was right; it would be a difficult and expensive undertaking. It was best to have someone loyal for the job.

"I will help you," decided Grak finally. "But it will take some time."

"I want to leave the day after tomorrow," said Akeela.

Grak's eyebrows shot up. "That is very soon."

"Time is of the essence. I don't want my enemies escaping me."

"Yes, but—"

"The day after tomorrow," declared Akeela. He picked up his wine glass again and rolled it between his palms. "General Trager will tell you what we need and answer any of your questions. And I'll send word to my army right away to bring your payment, and the gold you'll need for supplies, drowa, whatever." He took a deep swallow of his wine, satisfied with the deal he'd made. Trager began showing Grak the door. But before he left, a different notion seized Akeela. "Wait," he called to Grak. "I'd like to speak to you a moment more."

"Yes, my lord?" asked Grak.

Akeela thought for a moment, then said, "Will, I'd like to speak with Grak alone. Take your men outside and wait for him."

"Alone?" Trager's eyes narrowed. "Why?"

"Because I wish it," snapped Akeela. "Now go."

Not hiding his hurt feelings, Trager turned with a grunt and left the room with his Knight-Guardians, shutting the door behind him. Akeela listened for a moment, then, satisfied Trager had moved off, gestured toward a nearby chair.

"Sit down, Grak," he said.

The Jadori said nervously, "I can stand, my lord."

"Don't be an idiot. Just sit," ordered Akeela. Awkwardly Grak pulled the chair forward and sat down before Akeela. Besides his own, there was one other glass on Akeela's table. He picked it up and poured some wine into it, then reached over to hand it to Grak, who took it haltingly.

"I am confused, King Akeela," confessed Grak. He didn't sip at his wine or even look into the glass. "Why am I here?"

"Because I want to ask you about the man with the amulet," said Akeela. His head was suddenly pounding. The drink had hit him hard. "He had an eyepatch you say?"

"Yes," nodded Grak.

"And was he called Lukien?"

"He was, my lord."

Just hearing the name made Akeela grimace. "So he's lost an eye," he said absently. For some reason it struck him as sad. "But otherwise he was well?" he asked.

Grak shrugged. "I believe so, my lord. Truly, I cannot say." The Jadori smiled awkwardly. "Why are you concerned for this man, my lord? Is he not your enemy?"

Akeela started to answer, but couldn't form the words. Instead he merely nodded. He knew it was the drink making him weak, but for a moment he could see Lukien's handsome face, and he regretted its maiming.

"I will take you to find this man," said Grak. "And when you do, you can have your revenge on him."

Akeela nodded. "Yes." He took another gulp from his glass, draining it. Reaching for the wine bottle, he poured himself another tall drink. It would be a long night; tonight he would be haunted. He said to Grak, "It's fortuitous you came. Now I know my hunt hasn't been for naught."

Grak replied, "If you are prepared for the expense, my lord, then I will see you and all your men safely across the desert."

Akeela laughed grimly. "The expense means nothing to me. I've spent every penny I have on this vendetta. After we cross the desert, my pockets will be empty."

"My lord? I don't understand."

"This is it, there's nothing left," said Akeela. "I've spent every coin in Liiria's coffers on this escapade. Once we've paid you to take us across the desert, I'll be penniless. And so will Liiria."

Grak's expression was grave. He looked toward the door, then whispered, "My lord, do your men know this?"

"No," said Akeela. "And you're not to tell them or breathe a word of it. If you do, I will kill you."

The threat made the Jadori sit back and stare. He nodded slowly. "My lord," he said cautiously, "if this is so, what will you do when you return home?"

Akeela beckoned Grak closer with a finger. Grak leaned toward him and Akeela whispered, "I don't intend to return home." Then he sat back with a maniacal smile on his face, watching Grak's stunned expression. "There's nothing left for me in Liiria. Nothing left for me anywhere. Once I've killed Lukien, my work will be done."

48

For three days Lukien and Gilwyn waited in Grimhold, and for three days Lukien fretted over the fortresses' defense. They had been given a modest room on the ground floor of the keep, not far from the room Insight shared with her mother. Like all of Grimhold's chambers, this one had no windows; only a pair of oil lamps lit the entire room. But it was comfortable enough for the weary duo, and that first night they had slept sound and peacefully, awakening to a breakfast brought to them by a young blind boy who could somehow see remarkably well. His name was Farl, and he explained to them that he would be their attendant while they were in Grimhold, and that they were to call for him should they need anything. After breaking their fast, Lukien and Gilwyn went their separate ways. Gilwyn was anxious to have Emerald, his kreel, brought into the keep and to see White-Eye again. And Lukien still had to tackle the enormous task of defending Grimhold.

It was a harder task than it should have been. Grimhold was an extraordinary stronghold, and the people who'd designed it had done a fine job. Its walls were thicker than any normal castle, and its many high peaks provided a perfect firing platform for archers. It was also well hidden in the mountains, but with an excellent view of the canyon leading to it, so that a company of skilled bowmen could have an excellent killing field. But there was one fatal flaw in any such plan—Grimhold had no bowmen. There were plenty of weapons stored deep in its cellars, but nobody able enough to use them, and Lukien knew there was no way he could turn the Inhumans into a fighting force. They were eager and they had magic, but they were also limbless and blind, hunchbacked and crippled, and no amount of Akari help could make them capable of facing Trager. They simply weren't soldiers. And this more than anything deflated Lukien, for he knew that even a great fortress like Grimhold could not stand without men to secure it.

On his second day, Lukien came across Minikin in the great hall of Grimhold. He had been looking for her, but the little mistress had been difficult to find. She was talking with one of Grimhold's many mutes when he found her, a fellow that could only communicate in the most rudimentary sounds. Yet somehow Minikin understood every word. She stood there nodding as she listened, and when they were done she turned to Lukien and winked at him from across the hall, as if she knew he was there all along. She asked Lukien how things were going, and if he needed anything.

"Yes," he had replied. "I need about a thousand soldiers."

Minikin had merely smiled at the remark, assuring him that the Inhumans were able to defend themselves, and that he was not to fret too much over their lack of training or experience in combat. He was merely to familiarize himself with Grimhold, she said, and think of ways that Akeela and his army might try to attack them.

"That's easy," Lukien had shot back sarcastically. "He'll come through the front gate with a battering ram and keep going until everyone is dead."

At that Minikin had turned away, telling him "Have faith."

Regrettably, Gilwyn had been no more helpful than Minikin. The boy had disappeared into his own little world, as though he had forgotten that an army was coming. His lovesickness for White-Eye was more than plain, and he would lie awake in bed at night staring into the flame of the oil lamp. Lukien knew the symptoms and tried to sympathize, but he was strangely angry over the amount of time Gilwyn spent with White-Eye. It wasn't jealousy; Lukien simply needed a friend. And Gilwyn was an intelligent boy. He was sure he could have contributed something to their defense plans rather than wasting time pining for a pretty girl. If they lived, he would have all the time in the world to court Kadar's daughter. But if they didn't, none of it would matter at all. Their growing affection for each other would be snuffed out like a candle.

Depressed and confused, Lukien took to wandering Grimhold's mazelike halls, but by his third day in the fortress he had had enough. He was tired of the Inhumans and their many maladies, and he was sick at heart from the burden he had been given. He missed Cassandra terribly, and none of the Inhumans, no matter how friendly, could ease his loneliness. Oddly, it was this loneliness that drove Lukien into wanting to be alone. He wanted sunlight and solitude. Without a word to Minikin or Gilwyn, he headed for the main gate of Grimhold. There he found Greygor, the huge, broken-boned guardian of the keep, reclining on a large wooden chair just inside the iron portal. He looked up at Lukien but was characteristically soundless.

"I want to go out," said Lukien. "Please open the gate."

It was plain that Greygor was used to being disturbed, because he rose without question and banged on the gates with the pommel of his sword. Up on a dark landing, a pair of the guardian's cohorts began pulling on the thick chains, lifting the great gate. They were twins, from the looks of them, and seemed to have no maladies at all, but Lukien had already learned that looks were deceiving in Grimhold, and wouldn't have been surprised if the twins were blind cripples with leprosy. As the gate went up Greygor stood aside to let Lukien pass. Even his ornate black armor made no sound.

"That's it?" Lukien asked. "You'll let me go just like that?"

Behind his iron helmet Greygor blinked but did not answer. There was a frown on his face that told Lukien he didn't like being questioned.

"Fine, I'm sick of talking to you people anyway," said Lukien, then hurried out of the fortress into the fresh, clean air of the mountains. At once the hot desert sun struck his face, but Lukien didn't mind at all. It was good to feel the warmth, even if it burned. Behind him, Grimhold's iron gate began descending, shutting away the secretive Inhumans. Lukien took a few steps forward without looking back then paused. He had nowhere to go, really. He had just wanted to leave. Curiously he looked around, surveying the clearing and the high cliffs hiding the fortress. The ledges would make a good defense, he knew, if only he had fighters to man them.

"Enough," he told himself. "No more thinking."

He had wracked his brain for days with war plans, and now wanted only peace. So he chose a particularly inviting cliff far in the distance, deciding it would be a good place to relax and clear his troubled mind. It took him long moments to reach the base of the cliff but he didn't mind; it was good to be away from Grimhold's stifling air. The thought of being all alone spurred him on faster, but when he reached the base he discovered a figure there, kneeling with its back to him. Lukien slowed. He could make out nothing of detail, for whoever it was wore a black cloak that covered body and head completely. A fire was burning in the sand before the figure, consuming a pile of dried twigs. The figure slowly suspended its hands over the fire, as if giving a silent incantation. Lukien didn't want to disturb the person, but he was too curious to turn back.

"Hello?" he called.

At once the figure jumped, leaping to its feet and turning on him. Its gnarled hands shot up and hurriedly closed the hood around its face, obviously frightened. Pity was the first thing Lukien felt, because he was sure suddenly that the person was a leper, and no doubt ashamed of his appearance. Quickly Lukien put up his hands.

"Don't be afraid," he said. "I'm Lukien, from the keep. You've heard of me, yes?"

For a moment the figure didn't move, but then the cloaked head nodded.

"I came out to get some fresh air," said Lukien with a smile. "I guess you wanted the same, eh?" He glanced down toward the fire at the figure's feet, remembering the strange glowing flame he had seen in the figure's palm days earlier. "A bit warm for a fire, wouldn't you say?" he asked.

Still the figure said nothing. Surprisingly, it put its hand out over the fire, a good four feet above the flames. The flames extinguished instantly, and without a word the figure lowered its head and dashed past Lukien, hurrying back toward Grimhold. Astonished, Lukien looked at the dead fire then back at the fleeing figure.

"Wait," he called. "Don't run off!"

Surprisingly, the figure stopped and turned toward him. Still clutching the hood around its face, a female voice said, "I came out here to be alone, Sir Lukien. Please let me be."

"You're a woman," said Lukien. "I mean, forgive me, I'm just surprised." Gradually he tried coaxing her trust. "I didn't mean to disturb you. I came out here to be alone myself, but I can go and leave you to whatever you were doing." Again he glanced at the extinguished flames, looking at the ashes and wisps of smoke. "What exactly were you doing?"

The woman came no closer, yet neither did she retreat. "Minikin has asked us all to be welcoming to you. I do not wish to go against her, but I am a private person, Sir Lukien. If you would let me be, I would be grateful."

She had a pretty voice, clear and youthful.

"It's a big mountain," said Lukien. "We can share it. And just now I think I'd like some company."

"I thought you wanted to be alone," the woman observed.

Lukien shrugged. "A change of heart." He held out his hand for her. "Come back, please. I swear I won't judge you, if that's what you're afraid of. I've seen a lot of things in my time, far worse than you're hiding behind that hood."

"You're very bold," said the woman. Lukien couldn't tell if she was offended or not, even as she walked toward him. "Maybe I can do with some company as well," she sighed. As she approached she let her hands fall back to her sides, letting the crevice of her hood hang open a bit. Lukien tried not to stare.

"Good," he said, "then sit with me and show me what you were doing with this fire. How did you blow it out like that?"

"That is my secret curse, Sir Lukien. All the Inhumans have them. Haven't you noticed?"

"You brood, my lady," said Lukien. He sat down cross-legged near the smouldering twigs. "Sit with me, and tell me your name."

Again the woman hesitated, but soon sat down across

from him, to Lukien's great pleasure. He was careful not to lift his gaze toward her, an avoidance she noticed at once.

"I don't want to be shunned, sir," she said flatly. "That is why I came to Grimhold. Look at me if we're going to talk."

"I'm sorry," said Lukien, lifting his head. "I didn't want to stare or make you uncomfortable."

"I'm constantly uncomfortable. That's my lot in life."

"Why?" asked Lukien. He could barely see her green eyes in the depths of her hood, but he had noticed her hands, which were deeply and horribly scarred. "Are you a leper, my lady?"

"If I were shouldn't you be afraid of me?"

Lukien shook his head. "No. Death no longer frightens me."

The woman seemed intrigued by this, and within her hood her green eyes softened. Slowly she nodded. "I understand what that's like," she said. "I'm not a leper, Sir Lukien. I have burns. My face, my hands . . . my whole body, really. They make me look like a leper."

Without knowing why, Lukien said, "Show me."

And amazingly, the woman did so. Her ruined hands went to her hood, slowly drawing back the fabric and revealing locks of long blond hair. Her right side was beautiful, wholly unmaimed, and her green eyes sparkled hopefully as she watched Lukien, gradually revealing herself. But unlike her right side, her left was carved with deep, red scars running down toward her neck and disappearing beneath her cloak. Lukien steeled himself, refusing to flinch. It was a tragedy to behold, the two faces of the woman, so unalike, but he was steadfast. Instead of grimacing, he smiled.

"That's better," he said.

The woman laughed. "Better? You're either very kind or blind in both eyes."

"I mean it," said Lukien. "You shouldn't go around hiding your face the way you do. And why here? Minikin told me the Inhumans do not judge each other."

"I hide my face as much from myself as from anyone," said the woman. "I can't bear to look at it and never could."

"Was it fire?"

She nodded. Her pretty green eyes looked away. "When I was very young the house I lived in caught fire. My father and mother were both killed, but I was able to get away. My clothes were on fire when I ran into the street. Before anyone could douse the flames. . . ." She shrugged and put a hand to her damaged face. ". . . this happened to me."

"That's a terrible story," said Lukien. "I'm sorry for you."

The woman gave him an appreciative smile. "I was around twelve when it happened. At first I thought I would be all right, that my skin would grow back and I'd be normal. That's what everyone told me. But of course I got older and I never got better, and I still have to live with the pain of it."

"How did you come to Grimhold?"

"How does anyone come here? Minikin found me, about two years ago. I was an outcast, Sir Lukien. I had no family, and of course I had no husband. Do you have any idea how men react to a woman like me?"

"Yes, I'm afraid I do," said Lukien. Suddenly he was the one feeling embarrassed and wished for a cloak of his own. The woman read his feelings at once.

"There's no shame in being a man, Sir Lukien, and you are kinder than most. No man wants to wed a monster."

"Come now," said Lukien, "I thought that word wasn't allowed here. And you're no monster. I don't want you calling yourself that, not in my presence at least." He made sure he spoke directly to her without averting his eyes, and was surprised to find her easy to look at. "You still haven't told me your name."

"Meriel is my name," she said.

"Meriel, nothing more? I thought the Inhumans had special names."

"I never wanted an Inhuman name," said Meriel. "I never really wanted to be an Inhuman, and Minikin didn't make me take on a name. Before coming here people called me horrible things, Sir Lukien. I don't care to hear those slurs again. I'm just not strong enough to endure them."

"Then I will gladly call you Meriel," said Lukien. "But you are an Inhuman—I saw what you did with the fire."

"Yes," said Meriel, staring down into the still smouldering twigs. "Fire is my curse."

"You mean your gift, don't you?"

"I mean what I say—fire is my curse. It's part of my body; it's inside my skin. I live with its pain still after all these years. I have an Akari to help cope with the pain, but. . . ." She paused and looked up. "You know of the Akari, yes?"

"Yes," said Lukien. "Minikin told me about them. You have an Akari spirit that helps you."

"That's right. And if not for him my life would be constant agony. I'm grateful for Sarlvarian's help, but I would gladly give up my abilities to have my real skin back. That's why it is a curse, sir."

"You can control fire?" guessed Lukien. "Because it's part of your skin?"

"Fire made me what I am, that's what Sarlvarian says. He's my Akari, and he helps me control the pain as well as any flame."

"That sounds like an amazing gift to me," said Lukien. "Hardly a curse. To be able to make fire with a thought—"

"I cannot make fire," said Meriel. "I can only control it. But if there's any spark at all, any little ember, I can make an inferno from it. It was one thing that the Akari summoners could always do. The most powerful Akari, Amaraz, is a master of fire. Amaraz taught Sarlvarian to master fire so that Sarlvarian could help me."

"Will you show me?" said Lukien. "I'd like to see."

Meriel smiled at him. "Sir Lukien, I do these things with fire to entertain myself. By controlling fire, I can control the pain of my condition. That is the only reason for my. . . ."

"Gift?" injected Lukien with grin.

"If you say so."

"When I came to Grimhold I saw a figure with a flame in its hand, standing with the other Inhumans. That was you, wasn't it?"

Meriel nodded.

"It was very strange and beautiful. That's what you are, Meriel. You're compelling."

The woman chuckled for the first time. "What a charmer you are, sir. As I said, you must truly be blind."

"Oh, I see quite clearly. I've already seen many wondrous people here in Grimhold, and I count you among them. I don't think you're cursed, Meriel. If there is a cursed person in Grimhold, it is I."

"Yes, I see that in you," said Meriel. "You walk like one of the damned. Minikin has told all of us your story. I am sorry for you, Sir Lukien. You've lost a great deal."

Lukien looked at her, surprised to hear such words from a woman who'd lost so much herself. Unlike the other Inhumans, Meriel had still not come to accept her maladies. Yet even she pitied him.

"I should go now," said Lukien, standing suddenly. "I've got a lot of work to do."

Meriel quickly grabbed his hand. "Wait," she said. Gently she pulled him down beside her again. "Let me show you something."

Lukien knelt beside her, confused. "Meriel, you don't have to show me what you can do. I should not have pushed you."

"No, I want to," said the woman. "I want to do something for you."

From out of the ashes of her fire she produced a single twig, its tip glowing faintly crimson. She blew on the twig to increase its light, then focused, producing a funnel of flame from the twig, a fire that did not burn down the length of the stick but rather expanded in the air around it. Enchanted, Lukien leaned in closer, marveling as the woman used her other hand to coax the flame upwards. As Meriel twirled her fingers the flame danced to her rhythms, following her fingertips, even changing color.

"Remarkable," laughed Lukien. "Meriel, that's amazing."

"Wait," said the woman. "I'm not done."

The flame at the tip of the twig widened, changing color to a deep red, pulsing with magical life. Meriel concentrated, making the flame twirl in on itself, shaping it into folds. Lukien watched, transfixed, as the woman worked the dancing fires into a remarkable, living sculpture.

"A rose," said Lukien, recognizing the shape instantly. The fire-rose leapt on the tip of the twig, alive and delicate. Meriel smiled proudly, handing her gift to Lukien.

"For you," she said. "For being kind to me."

Gently Lukien took the rose, careful not to douse its

strange life. A huge grin split his face as he twirled it, watching tiny sparks leap out from its center.

"It won't last," said Meriel. "I can't hold such complex shapes very long."

Looking at the rose, Lukien felt a satisfaction he'd seldom known. "That's all right. Nothing so beautiful lasts forever."

"Look," said Meriel sadly. Already the rose was fading. They watched it together until the shape collapsed and the twig was just a twig again. The death of the rose made the woman's face wilt.

"No, don't be sorry," said Lukien. He laid down the twig and looked at Meriel, and in that moment decided she was beautiful. Leaning forward, he kissed her cheek. Not the pretty, soft cheek but the hard, scarred one.

"Thank you," he said to her. "That was very beautiful. I don't think a monster could have made such a thing."

Meriel's hand lingered on her face where he had kissed her. She seemed dumbfounded, unable to speak. Lukien didn't want her to say a word. He merely rose to his feet, said good-bye to the strange woman, and went back to Grimhold, determined to find a way to save the Inhumans.

In less than an hour Lukien found himself once again in the keep's lowest levels, where the armory was kept, still stocked full of weapons and Akari armor. To Lukien, who had spent his life as a warrior, the place was like a quiet refuge, something of a temple. It was dusty and dim and deathly quiet, but he loved to wander around the suits of armor, all of which were lovingly arranged against the wall and periodically cleaned by Inhuman attendants. As Lukien lit the oil lamps along the wall, the armory sprang to life. The metal suits tossed dancing shadows along the stone walls; ornate helmets with wings and horns glistened. At the far side of the chamber a rack of spears stood erect, their tips still sharp after years of disuse. Akari swords were piled high in forgotten corners. Lukien went to the swords and chose one from the pile, blowing the dust from its blade. It was large and slightly curved and remarkably light. He swept it through the air to test its balance, finding it perfect. A little smile curled his lips. The Akari had been a remarkable race. It was a shame that they were gone, a

shame that the Jadori had wiped them out. According to
Minikin, they had abandoned their own warlike ways for
art and culture, and to develop their magical abilities of
summoning. But none of that had helped them against the
Jadori. And years later, when the Inhumans had discovered
the Akari's armory, nearly ruined and rusted, they had
brought the weapons back to life with the forethought that
someday they might be needed. Now that day had come,
but there was no one skilled enough to wield them well.
Lukien lowered the sword back into the pile. Perhaps that
was simply the way of things, he mused. Perhaps the history
of the world was the story of the strong slaughtering the
weak, and now it was the Jadori's time to be slaughtered.
The thought depressed Lukien, but seemed horribly true.
And what else was he but a pawn in that great game?
Had he not done the will of Akeela's father, battling the
Reecians? And was he not Jazana Carr's pawn as well,
slaughtering Norvans because he could and because the pay
was good?

Lukien leaned against the cold wall and let his shoulders
slump. He had sworn to protect White-Eye, somehow. He
owed that to Kadar. And now there was Meriel to protect
as well, and all the other Inhumans who'd been kind to
him. It was a great burden, and Lukien knew it could
break him.

Suddenly he noticed another door at the far end of the
chamber, a door he hadn't noticed in his previous visits to
the armory. From beneath the door crept a glowing light.
Lukien took a small step forward. It didn't surprise him he
hadn't noticed it before, but now that he did he was intrigued. He approached to it carefully, imagining the trea-
sures he would find inside but knowing there was probably
nothing more than dozens of rusty swords. When he
reached the door, he paused to listen. There was no sound.
A rusty bolt on the door had been slid aside, an open
padlock dangling beside it. He tried the doorknob and
found that it, too was unlocked, so he pushed the door
slowly open. It creaked and groaned with heaviness, revealing a warmly lit chamber that was impeccably clean and
startlingly bright. All the walls were bare, smooth stone.
The chamber was empty, except for one remarkable artifact
that glowed at its center, rising up like a dragon from the

floor. Lukien's hand fell away from the door. His jaw dropped in awe.

It was a suit of armor, perfect and unblemished, and it shone with an inner light that made it look as though it were made of black sunshine. It stood erect on a small dais, as though filled with an invisible body. Even the helmet hung in the proper place, a great, horned thing with a death's head mask and rings of black chain mail. The breastplate shone like a mirror, and the shoulders were bolstered with sharp spikes. Greaves and sabatons made up the legs, while vambraces and gauntlets created the arms, giving the illusion of a living thing. It was as if the armor itself was alive, pulsing with preternatural light. Lukien stared at the armor, stunned by its brilliance and dark beauty. He had always prided himself on his own bronze armor, thinking it the most beautiful ever made. But his was like dust compared to this marvelous suit. His breathing slowed as he took a tentative step into the chamber. The armor on its dais rose up high before him. It was hard to fathom something so perfect, yet here it was, completely unmarred by battle, flawless in every detail. Lukien longed to touch it but did not. There was something forbidden about the armor, something that spoke to his brain on a primal level, warning him. So he merely stared, spellbound. He did not know how long he stood there, for he was entranced by the armor and quickly forgot the mission that had brought him to the cellars. But then he heard a voice calling his name. The sound broke his stupor, and he turned back toward the armory in time to see Minikin picking her way toward him. This time, her ubiquitous smile was gone.

"What you are doing?" she asked. "You shouldn't be in there, Lukien."

"What is this?" Lukien asked, pointing to the armor. "I've never seen anything like it."

"No, I'm sure you haven't," said Minikin. "Come away from there now."

Lukien wouldn't budge. He stayed in the shadow of the magnificent armor, forcing Minikin to come to him. "It's beautiful," he whispered. "And look—it's completely unmarked. It's perfect."

"Hmm, not as perfect as you think," sighed Minikin. "That is the Devil's Armor, Lukien."

Lukien turned. "Devil's Armor?"

"That is what it's called," Minikin replied. "An apt name."

"I don't understand."

"Step away and I will explain."

Lukien shook his head. "No, I want to look at it. I've never seen armor like it before. What is this metal?"

He was about to reach for it when Minikin quickly seized his hand.

"Don't," she commanded. She held fast, pulling him away from the armor. "The Devil's Armor isn't to be touched."

"Sorry," said Lukien in confusion. "I didn't mean any harm. I came down here to see what kind of weapons there were. There was light under the door so I came in." He turned back toward the armor. "That's when I found this . . . thing."

"How did you get in here?" asked Minikin. "That door was locked."

"It wasn't. It was open when I arrived."

Minikin's face darkened. She looked angry, and a bit afraid. "Open? That's the truth? You didn't pry it open yourself?"

"Why would I do that?" asked Lukien. "I'm telling you, it was unlocked."

Minikin grimaced and said, "I believe you. I should have warned you about it before you stumbled down here yourself. The fault is mine I suppose."

"How did you know I was down here, anyway?"

"I was told," said Minikin simply.

Lukien was about to ask by who, but then decided he didn't want to know. She had already told him there were spirits in Grimhold. So instead he asked, "What is this armor, Minikin? Why is it called Devil's Armor?"

"*The* Devil's Armor," Minikin corrected mildly. "And it's called that because the man who made it was a devil. He was an Akari named Kahldris, and he was a great summoner. But he was also a butcher. He lived many years ago, many years before the Akari were destroyed. That," Minikin pointed toward the armor, "was his greatest creation. And his most infamous."

"Why infamous?" asked Lukien. "What did he do?"

"Kahldris was a general," said Minikin. "A great military leader of the Akari, back when they cared about such things. Back then there were many people in this part of the world, I think. I don't know for sure, because the spirits don't tell me everything. But they did explain the armor to me. It was Kahldris' greatest weapon. It was supposed to live on after he died. And it has, because just like the Eyes of God, that armor is possessed . . . by Kahldris."

Lukien studied the armor, still confused. "So why is it so dangerous? This Kahldris was a butcher, you say? But he's dead now."

"No," said Minikin. "He lives on within the armor. He possesses it, Lukien. You must understand what that means. Any man who wears the armor will be driven by Kahldris, owned by him. The armor may be invincible, but—"

"Invincible?" Lukien looked at her hard. "Say that again?"

"It's true," said Minikin darkly. "The armor is invincible to blade or arrow. No one wearing it can be destroyed, at least that's what the spirits say. But before you get any ideas understand what I'm telling you. No man can control it. To wear it would make you a killing machine. Like Kahldris, you would be a butcher."

"Oh, that's just great," said Lukien sourly. "So why did he create it? If it can't be used what good is it?"

"I'm not quite sure," confessed Minikin. "Maybe Kahldris created it so that he could live on forever. But none of the Akari would wear the armor. Not even when the Jadori came and slaughtered them."

"That seems very stupid to me," said Lukien. "This armor could have saved them."

Minikin shook her head. "No. The Akari preferred to die rather than have their minds eaten by Kahldris and his poison."

"But if no one even tried it how could they have known? Maybe they could have controlled it. Maybe—"

"Stop now, Lukien, and listen to me. The Devil's Armor is an evil thing. The only reason it's still here is because I've never discovered a way to destroy it."

"But this armor could be our salvation! If I could wear it in battle against Trager—"

"No!" snapped Minikin. She fixed her coal-dark eyes on him. "That armor is never to be worn. Not by you or any-one else. There's no way you could control Kahldris, Lu-kien. And there's no way I would let you try. Kahldris still has sway in the world. That door didn't just unlock itself."

Lukien almost laughed. "You mean Kahldris opened it? Just to get me in here?"

"How many things do I have to show you, Lukien? When will you believe that there are forces in Grimhold you don't yet understand?"

"I'm sorry," said Lukien. "You're right. I don't under-stand. But is it better that the Inhumans should die, then? You won't even take a chance on saving them?"

"The Inhumans will not die, Lukien. You underesti-mate us."

"You keep saying that!" cried Lukien. "But I've looked all around Grimhold, and I haven't seen a single thing to convince me we can defeat Akeela."

Minikin smiled. "You've looked all around Grimhold?"

"Yes. And I'm telling you that all your magic tricks aren't going to help us. It doesn't help that some mute girl can see the future or that a burned woman can make a rose out of fire. I need people who can fight, people who can pick up a mace and smash a man's head in!"

"And there's no one here who can do that?"

"Why are you asking stupid questions?" Lukien sput-tered. The frustration of everything overcame him. "Look around, Minikin. Some of your people don't even have arms!"

Minikin said calmly, "Lukien, I think it's time I showed you something." She took his hand and led him out of the chamber, careful to close and lock the door on the Devil's Armor. As they left the armory she was characteristically quiet, which only infuriated Lukien further. Halfway up the cellar staircase, he yanked free his hand.

"Where now?" he asked with a sigh. "Minikin, I need to talk to you."

"We will talk," said Minikin, "after you've seen what I want to show you."

So the little woman kept walking, up the stairs and into the feeble light of the hall, then down the hall and up another flight of stairs, passing Inhumans along the way

and giving them her gentle smile. Lukien followed with a
frown on his face, wanting to stop and ask her questions
but knowing he'd only get more of her meaningless replies.
When at last they reached one of the keep's numerous
turrets, revealed inside by a great bulge in the wall, Minikin
opened a large door to uncover yet another stairway, this
one coiling upward in a tight circle.

"We're going up," she said. "Prepare yourself; it's a
long climb."

And she was right. After a few minutes of climbing, Lukien was puffing and his thighs burned. Minikin's little legs
carried her effortlessly up the stairs, as though she'd made
the climb a thousand times. The walls of the turret were
smooth and lit with more of the familiar oil lamps, but
there were very few and so the way was dark and treacherous. Occasionally the stairs gave way to landings, where
shuttered windows were cut into the mountain and plat-
forms jutted out onto battlements, complete with arrow slits
for Akari archers, now long dead. But Minikin did not
pause at any of these. Instead she continued spinning upward until Lukien thought he would faint from exhaustion.
It was hard for his eye to adjust to the light. Minikin noted
his discomfort and told him the top was not much further.

"And what's at the top?" he asked.

She replied, "You'll see."

"Why so bloody high?"

"Patience, Bronze Knight. You'll like what I show you."

Her claim didn't fill Lukien with confidence, so when, at
last, they reached the top of the turret, he looked around
skeptically. They entered a round room, nearly bare but
for a few chairs and tables and some odd looking equipment near a large shuttered window. Lukien recognized
one of the items at once. It was like a long tube on a tripod
made of gleaming metal. A spyglass. Akeela used to have
one in his study. There were charts on the wall with amateurish scribblings and other instruments of measurement
strewn along a nearby table.

"What is this place?" Lukien asked.

Minikin went to the spyglass and began unclasping the
shutters, but she did not open them. "An observatory.
We're in the highest part of Grimhold now. You can see
everything from here. This is where I teach the Inhumans

about the stars and their magic." Then she shrugged. "Well, those who can make the climb, anyway."

"So why bring me up here?" asked Lukien. He went to the spyglass and ran his fingertips over it. The metal was smooth and cool. It was larger than the one Figgis had made for Akeela, and of an unusual design. Lukien supposed it was Akari.

"Have you ever used one of these before?" asked Minikin.

Lukien nodded. "Yes. Akeela had one. He used to like to watch the stars. Figgis, his librarian, told him a lot about the heavens. Sometimes we used to stay on his balcony for hours, just stargazing and talking."

Minikin smiled at the lament. "Sounds nice."

"It was," said Lukien. "But that's not the Akeela you'll be facing, Minikin."

"Which brings me to my point," declared the little woman. "Look through the spyglass for me."

Lukien frowned. The spyglass was pointed toward the shutters. "But the window is closed."

"I'll open it," Minikin assured him. "Just do as I say, all right?"

With a shrug Lukien stooped and looked into the lens. As expected, he could see only blackness. "Very interesting," he said dryly.

"Wait now," urged Minikin. "And don't look up. Just keep your eye on the lens."

"I will."

When Minikin at last opened the shutters, sunlight flooded the room and the lens of the spyglass. It stabbed Lukien's eye, and it took a moment for him to adjust. When he did, he saw the colors of the desert spring to life. But unlike Akeela's spyglass, this one was shockingly clear, revealing its contents in crisp detail. Yet at first Lukien didn't know what he was seeing. The browns and reds of the desert flooded his vision, but also strange white shapes that looked like. . . .

"Homes. . . ?"

A second later, he knew it was a village. He bolted up from the spyglass and stared out the window. In the distance he saw it—a rolling white village of homesteads and avenues, spreading out in a sunken valley between the mountains. The sight shocked him. Blinking in disbelief, he leaned out over the open window.

"By the Fate, what's that?"

"That," said Minikin, "is Grimhold."

"That's a village! With people and everything!" Lukien could see them in the avenues, lugging water and holding children, safe from the world beyond the mountains. "Minikin, I . . . I don't understand."

"That is Grimhold, Sir Lukien," said Minikin with a chuckle. "The real Grimhold."

"But I thought this fortress was Grimhold!" Lukien rushed back to the spyglass for a better look, laughing with delight as he scanned the village. There were Inhumans, all right, but also able-bodied men and women in the streets and working in the fields circling the homesteads. There was even a small pond fed by a mountain stream, with women drawing water from it. It was a beautiful village, a picturesque dream, and Lukien couldn't contain his glee. "I don't believe it!" he crowed. "It's huge! How many people are there?"

Oh, at least a few thousand now."

"What?" Lukien lifted his gaze and stared at Minikin. "All Inhumans?"

"And not all of them deformed," replied Minikin. "Lukien, this fortress isn't Grimhold. It's only part of it."

"But how?" sputtered Lukien. "How so many people?"

"Think about it, Lukien. If you do, you can figure it out for yourself. As I once told you, Grimhold has existed for many, many years. There was no way this fortress could hold so many people after a while, not once they started having children."

Lukien was aghast. "Children? You mean the Inhumans have been breeding?"

Minikin laughed. "Why should that shock you? We're people, Lukien, just like you."

"But that would take decades," said Lukien. He went to the window and leaned over the sill. What Minikin had told him was mind-boggling. Surely most of these people had been brought here, otherwise. . . .

He turned very slowly toward Minikin, regarding her carefully. "Minikin, how old are you? I mean, if there was no one here when you arrived, how could you have possibly brought this many people to Grimhold?"

"I did not bring them all, Sir Lukien. I told you—most of those people were born here. It's been generations now."

"Generations? But that's impossible. That would make you ancient!"

"Well, not ancient precisely," joked Minikin. "But I do look young for my age." She reached for the amulet around her neck. "This has kept me alive for many years. Probably more years than you can comprehend. Haven't you wondered why the myth of Grimhold has persisted so long? The story is nothing new; it was around long before you were born."

"I know but. . . ." Lukien shrugged. "How's it possible?"

"The amulets, Lukien. They're very strong. They've kept me alive since the beginning. And the beginning was long ago, indeed." Minikin looped her arm through his and guided his gaze back out the window. "Look out there. There are thousands of us Inhumans now, and the number grows every year. This is why I told you not to worry; we are not as weak as we first appear."

"Those people down there, the ones that are, well, normal—are they Inhumans too?"

Minikin nodded. "Everyone who dwells in Grimhold is an Inhuman, but not all of them have Akari spirits as guides or helpers. Those who are able-bodied do not need them. But they're the offspring of the people that I've brought here. Some of them were born disabled, like their parents. But many are what you call normal, Lukien."

"Do they know of the outside world?"

"Of course. They aren't prisoners. I don't keep secrets from them. Everyone knows why they're here and how they came to be, and they know that Grimhold is a secret place, the only place where the Inhumans are truly safe. They work the fields and build homes and haul water, and they are fit enough to defend Grimhold." She nudged him with her elbow. "Enough to make an army out of, eh?"

"Yes," said Lukien softly. "Yes, perhaps you're right."

It was a tantalizing notion. With so many people, even Akeela's men would be hard pressed to defeat them. And they had weapons. Besides those he'd found in the armory, he supposed there were more in the village below. But there wasn't much time. And there was still Insight's dismal prophecy.

"Minikin," said Lukien, "what about what Insight saw? She saw this place in ruins. I admit there are many people to defend Grimhold now, but they're not soldiers. Even if they can carry weapons, they might be slaughtered."

"I know," said Minikin, "and so do they. But this is their home. They are willing to die for it."

Lukien had to look away. "But I don't want them to die, Minikin, not any of them. It's not fair. I brought Akeela here. Why should all these people have to pay for my mistake?" He shook his head regretfully. "I wish I could stop it. I wish. . . ." He shrugged, unable to finish. There were simply no answers.

"Lacaron sees the future as if through broken glass, Lukien," said Minikin. "The things he tells Insight do not always come to pass. People have power to change things."

"I don't know," sighed Lukien. It wounded him to think of the good people down below, and the plague he had brought them. "I don't know if I can lead them."

Minikin grinned like an elf. "I have more faith in you than you have in yourself. Remember—you are the Bronze Knight of Koth."

"That was a long time ago," said Lukien.

"No," Minikin insisted. She punched his chest with her fingertip. "What is needed is still inside you. Now you must summon it. We still have time before Akeela and his army reaches us, and he may not reach us at all. He has to get past Kadar first."

"He will," said Lukien darkly. "Insight saw it."

Minikin grumbled in frustration. "You're not listening. The future is still ours to make. Kadar is strong, and so are his warriors. They will make Akeela pay for crossing the desert. And if your king does reach Grimhold, we will be ready for him. You will make sure of it." The Mistress of Grimhold fixed him in a furious glare. "Do you understand?"

Lukien looked over the miraculous village, remembering his promise to Kadar. If he was to defend White-Eye, then he needed to defend her home as well. "I'll do my best," he said finally. "And may the Great Fate help me."

49

Akeela swayed to the gentle loping of his horse, baking beneath the hot sun. The Desert of Tears roiled around him in every direction, an endless sea of sand and dunes and red mountains standing dauntingly in the distance. It was late afternoon and the sun was starting to descend. The procession of men and horses and drowa plowed their way relentlessly west, strangely quiet in the all- consuming sands. Ganjor was now but a distant memory. Akeela thought about his modest chambers at the top of the boarding house with genuine longing. He and his army had only been in the desert two days, but he craved the comforts of Ganjor and its wines as if he'd been away for weeks. Grak had done a remarkable job of getting the things they needed. They had left Ganjor on time, two days after hiring the caravan leader. Once he'd seen the amount of gold he'd had to work with, Grak had no difficulty purchasing the scores of drowa and countless water barrels for their trips. Now the train of drowa strung out behind Akeela in a long, winding line, their backs burdened with food and tents and skins of water. Progress had been slow. Although horses could travel the desert, they could only do so slowly and needed frequent rest. The heat was an incessant enemy. Grak had purchased gakas for the men and white covers for the horses, so that they looked like ghostly beasts lumbering across the sands. Beneath his own black gaka Akeela itched and sweated, cursing the misfortunes that had brought him to this desolate place. Truly, the Desert of Tears had been forsaken by the gods, for never had Akeela seen so much nothingness. Not even Norvor, with its rocks and stretches of burned earth could rival the desert for bleakness. Here there was nothing to see for hours on end, only mountains that never seemed to get closer. Akeela pulled back his gaka, unable to take its stifling heat a moment longer. Cursing, he wiped a slick of sweat from his forehead. Next to him, General Trager rode in stoic silence, his own face hidden beneath black cloth. Beside the general rode his aide, Colonel Tark. The colonel was as silent as his commander. Miraculously, the entire army was silent. Except for the occasional grunts from the drowa, there was no sound. Even when they rested, the desert gave them little to talk about. There was water and food and almost no other comforts, and Akeela knew his men longed to return to Liiria. They had served him well and he was proud of them, and he wished he could repay their loyalty. But he knew that he could not.

Grak had promised that they would be in Jador in less than a week. Along with his brother Doreshen, they had so far done a good job of leading the caravan. Grak had left the rest of his family behind in Ganjor, promising to return soon. The decision had pleased Akeela, for he did not know what kind of fight they would face in Jador, and he didn't want Grak's wife or children at risk. It would take a week, Grak had claimed, because the horses required much rest and enormous amounts of water, water which was heavy even for the drowa to carry. It was a great undertaking, but Akeela had taken such bold moves before. It was like building the library, he told himself. Some said it couldn't be done, but he knew better. And just as he could build a library on a mountaintop, he could move an army across the desert.

Watching the afternoon sun, he retrieved the waterskin from the side of his mount and took a long drink of the sweet liquid. Grak had warned him not to drink wine while in the desert, claiming it would sicken him. It had been tempting for Akeela to ignore the advice, but in the end he heeded it. It had been the first time in weeks he'd been completely sober, and he found the sensation odd. Not refreshing or pleasant, just odd. Most remarkably, though, the desert had quieted his fevered mind. Here where there was nothing to disturb him, he did not feel the heavy concerns of kingship. Though the sun always blazed, there was something about daytime here that reminded him of night. Akeela reveled in the solitude.

When nightfall came they made camp. The two thousand soldiers began the work of unloading tents from the backs of the drowa and the cooking fires were lit. Akeela's own pavilion was erected, larger than the rest, at the head of the camp near the tent that Trager shared with his top aides. Grak and his brother also had a tent nearby, because Akeela liked keeping them close. He knew that he had erred in confiding so much in Grak, but he also liked the desert man's company, and they often ate together, enjoying the plain food. On this night, Akeela was particularly tired from the day's ride, so after his meal he went off to the outskirts of the camp to get away from the noise and smoke. There he found Grak, stargazing alone. Like all the nights in the desert, this one was astonishingly clear. Akeela had never known there were so many stars in the heavens. He came up behind Grak quietly, but he knew Grak could hear him.

"A beautiful night," he remarked, staring up at the sky.

Grak nodded but did not look at him. "It is." There was weight in Grak's voice, as if he were deep in thought. Akeela regarded him curiously.

"You're troubled?" he asked. "Are we not on the right path?"

"No, my lord," said Grak. "We make good progress. Do not worry."

"But you are troubled, I can tell." Akeela decided to push him. "Why?"

"There are things that concern me," said Grak. He still did not look away from the stars.

"About this trip?"

Grak nodded.

"What, precisely?"

"I am wondering," said Grak. "What will you do with so many men when you reach Jador? You say you are after the man called Lukien, but it does not take an army to hunt a single man."

His boldness surprised Akeela. Normally he wouldn't

have accepted such forwardness from an underling. "That is my business," he said simply. "You're getting paid to take us to Jador, not to concern yourself with their welfare."

"But I do worry, my lord," said Grak. "They trade with me, make me money. And they are good people. I would not want to see them harmed." Finally he looked at Akeela. "Or have a part in it."

"Then you should have said so before you took this commission," said Akeela a bit angrily. "I didn't hide my army from you. You could have refused me."

"I was afraid," Grak confessed. Then he surprised Akeela by smiling. "But perhaps I should not have been."

"What do you mean?"

"I have been watching you, my lord. You are not what I expected. In Ganjor you are called *Jahasavar*. Do you know what that means?"

Akeela shook his head. "Tell me."

"It means mad. You are the mad king, and not just in Ganjor. All know of you and think you are brainsick. But I have seen your concern for my family and the good way you treat your men. And now you come out here to look at stars." Grak grinned. "I think you are not what they say you are, my lord."

"Oh?" asked Akeela. "What do you think I am, then?"

"I think you are the man they used to call you. I think you are Akeela the Good."

The term rattled Akeela. He looked away. "That was a long time ago, when I was naive and stupid. And before I had so many enemies."

"The desert is a magical place, my lord. It affects all men differently. For you, it has been cleansing. Do you not feel it?"

"I do," Akeela admitted grudgingly. "So what's your point?"

Grak shrugged. "Perhaps nothing. Or perhaps that you should listen to the good man still inside you."

"I *am* a good man," hissed Akeela. "I have always been and always will be!"

"A good man would spare the Jadori, my lord."

"You're speaking very bravely," warned Akeela.

"To slay them just to reach the man who wronged you—"

"What do you know of him?" cried Akeela. "Nothing!" His voice carried easily to the camp as he ranted, "You have no idea of the wrongs Lukien has done me. He must pay, and he will!"

"All right, my lord," said Grak easily. His voice was soothing. "All right." He smiled. "Let us look at the sky, then, and forget our troubles, eh?"

Akeela took a deep breath, struggling to contain himself. Anger crested in him so easily, yet Grak had a way of easing his mind. "Yes," he sighed. "Yes, all right."

Like a little child he turned his gaze back toward the heavens. For almost an hour he stood there with Grak, neither of them speaking, until it was time for sleep.

Akeela shared his pavilion with nobody. He slept alone because he enjoyed the quiet and was not afraid of the desert, though he did have two Knight-Guardians posted at his tent entrance. Tonight, Akeela's sleep was restless. Nightmares consumed him, visions of slaughtered Jadori. He dreamed that he was at the front of a large army, driving hordes of Jadori women before him, naked and weeping for the men he had slain. The ugly image jolted him awake and he lay in his silk sheets, panting. There was not a sound in the world, and the silence was like an anvil, pressing the breath from his lungs. He looked around the darkness, spotted a single candle glowing against the murkiness and fixed on it, trying to remember where he was and convince himself that everything was all right.

"Fate help me," he groaned. "What has become of me?"

No one answered. Within a few moments Akeela had composed himself. His eyelids began to droop and his head floated down to his pillow. He was asleep for only a moment when he heard an inhuman cry. Again he bolted up. Outside his tent he heard a terrible noise and the sounds of men shouting. There was a commotion suddenly as sleeping soldiers awakened throughout the camp. The scream came again, a strangled, guttural cry. Akeela flung his sheets aside and jumped up. Moonlight splayed through the fabric of his pavilion. Against it he saw an enormous shadow creeping skyward. He stared at the wall of his tent, dumb-founded.

"What the . . . ?"

Still in his bed clothes, Akeela sprang for the exit. His Knight-Guardians had left their post, then he saw why. A nearby tent was torn and flattened—Grak's tent. Over it hovered the most enormous creature Akeela had ever seen, a monstrous serpent with a long, stout body and oily, scale-covered hide. Two crimson eyes glowed in its spotted head, shadowed by an enormous hood. The mouth was open, hissing and spitting, revealing a pair of saberlike fangs. Akeela skidded to a halt, frozen by the sight. Coiled in the creature's tail was Grak, raised high above the sands and screaming. The Knight-Guardians had their swords drawn, holding them out impotently before them. All around the camp men were waking to Grak's cries and the monster's awful noise.

"By the Fate, what's *that?*"

Akeela spun to see Trager sprinting toward him, half-naked, sword drawn. The general grabbed Akeela's collar and dragged him backward.

"Stay back!" he ordered.

"It's got Grak!" Akeela shouted.

Trager shoved him back. "Get away!"

The Knight-Guardians were quickly joined by others, who formed a broken circle around the serpent. It hovered over them, threatening them with snapping jaws as it squeezed Grak to a ruddy purple. Grak's brother Doreshen crawled out from beneath their flattened tent, his face bloody, his hands clawing the sand.

"Grak!"

The serpent spun at the sound, whipping its neck forward and bursting through the line of men, sending them scattering. Trager roared forward and slashed his sword before the beast.

"Down, you motherless whore!" he cried.

"Will, get back here!" ordered Akeela.

Seeing their king unprotected, the Knight-Guardians swarmed over Akeela, forming a shield and pulling him toward safety. He watched as Trager lunged for the snake, driving his sword again and again at its underbelly. But the monster already had its prize. With Grak still entwined in its tail, it darted away from Trager and slipped swiftly into the desert gloom, Grak's gurgling screams echoing behind.

Akeela broke free from his guards. "After it! We have to follow!"

Trager fell to his knees and shook his head. "No," he said breathlessly. "It's too late."

"It's got Grak!"

"I know!"

More soldiers came, a pair of whom helped Doreshen to his feet. His eyes were terror-filled as he watched the darkness that had swallowed his brother. Akeela went to him at once.

"What was that thing, Doreshen?"

"A rass," gasped Doreshen. He broke from the soldiers and cried, "Grak!"

"He's gone," said Trager. "Bitches and whores, I lost him." He got to his feet, his sword dangling weakly in his fist.

Doreshen slumped into the sand, weeping. Akeela stood over him, unsure what to say. All the men were staring, their faces ashen. The echoes of Grak's screams still seemed to fill the night.

"A rass," whispered Akeela.

He had never heard the term before, but he knew now that the desert had deceived him. Grak was wrong. The desert wasn't peaceful or full of magic. Like everything else, it was evil and not to be trusted.

50

For Baron Thorin Glass, there was no greater disgrace than having to share a mount. In his youth, before his maiming, he had been a peerless horseman, but there were few horses in Jador and none of them could compare to the quick and powerful kreel. Worse, he had only one arm these days, and so could not ride the way he used to, galloping with perfect balance over any terrain. That was a luxury lost to him. Though he could still ride he could not do so with the skill and ferocity of his youth, and it pained him.

Tonight he had ridden out into the desert with two of Kadar's men, sharing the back of a kreel with one of Kadar's closest friends, a warrior named Ralawi. Ralawi spoke little of his tongue but the other scout was well-versed in the northern language, a lucky break for the baron, who had picked up no Jadori in his days with Kadar. The moon was rising when they'd left the palace, and now the sands shimmered in its silver light. Far in the distance, Jador sat uneasily on the horizon, a city bracing for battle. Thorin had been with Kadar when the first scout had returned, bringing the bad news.

Akeela's army had been sighted.

Baron Glass chose to investigate. Only he could properly surmise their enemy's strength. And since he could do no actual fighting, he was anxious to do his part. No sooner had the scout given his news then he had ridden from the palace himself. An hour later, he was crouching with Ralawi and a scout named Benik. A great dune hid them and their two kreels from the army on the western horizon. Thorin Glass lifted his eyes over the dune and let out a dreadful groan. He had never expected Akeela to bring so many men.

"Great Fate," he whispered, shaking his head.

Ralawi only nodded. The first scout had reported a large force, but had not stayed long enough to really see their numbers. But now the moonlight revealed the truth to them. Akeela's army was vast indeed. Thorin counted the mass and put their numbers at perhaps two thousand. Among the horses and men were scores of drowa, which had no doubt been used to carry the bulk of supplies. The cost of the operation boggled Thorin's mind, and he knew that Akeela had spent a fortune, maybe more than he really had. A great blackness seized the baron's heart. It was *his* money Akeela had used to prop up his reign, his and the money of other noblemen. Now he was essentially penniless, while Akeela continued to squander gold. More than anything, Thorin wanted to battle in the morning. There were years of crimes needing to be avenged.

"So many," he whispered. "I did not expect it."

"No," agreed Ralawi.

Benik was defiant. "By the morning we will be ready," he declared confidently.

"So will they," retorted Thorin. "They'll be expecting us."

He could tell by the way their camp was arranged that Akeela's army didn't plan on staying long. Relatively few of the tents were erected; men milled about in alert pockets with pikes and lances, or grooming their horses or sharpening their swords. These were battle preparations; Akeela and Trager knew they'd been seen. Even now they knew Jadori scouts were in the dunes, watching them. The cockiness of their stride was meant to intimidate and frighten.

Ralawi asked a question in Jadori, which Benik translated. "He wants to know where they will attack," said Benik, "In the city?"

"Yes," replied Thorin, "unless we take the fight to them."

Ralawi understood well enough. A grimace gripped his

face. "Bad," he said. They all knew Kadar wanted to fight on the sands, rather than risk the people in the city. More, that's where they would have the advantage. The desert terrain was well-suited to their swift kreels. They had hoped it would be enough to offset the size of Akeela's force, but now that he saw the Liirian army, Thorin lost that hope. He knew now they would need a miracle. He had spent his time in Jador training Kadar's warriors, telling them what to expect, the tactics Trager might employ. And he had been impressed with the Jadori and what they and their kreels could do. They were fierce and skilled fighters, and if the odds were even could easily have bested the Liirians. But the odds were heavily skewed. Akeela had come with every Royal Charger and a dozen other companies. Kadar's kreel riders numbered barely three hundred.

"We will win," said Ralawi, his face hard. He had learned the term from Thorin and repeated it constantly, like a mantra. He looked at the baron for support. "Win?"

Thorin bit his lip. "I don't know." With his one arm he rolled himself onto his back, feeling the warm sand beneath him and looking up into the stars. His mind was reeling. Back in the palace, Kadar was hurriedly preparing for battle, hoping to ride out and meet the invaders at dawn. He was a brave man who truly loved his people, and Thorin hated the idea of him dying. He wished Lukien were with him, and wondered how the Bronze Knight was faring in Grimhold. As he stared up into heaven, he decided that the best they could do was take out as many of the Liirians as possible, giving the Inhumans a fighting chance.

"We go back now," he said.

Ralawi and Benik looked at each other. Benik asked, "What do we tell Kadar?"

With effort Baron Glass got to his feet and brushed the sand from his breeches. "We tell him it's time for battle," he said, then turned and walked toward the waiting kreel.

Kahan Kadar's army was ready before the sun rose.

With the advice of Baron Glass, they had arranged themselves at the crest of a long dune, so that the rising sun struck their kreel-hide armor and glinted off their spear tips. Kadar had mustered his three hundred riders, with another hundred or so warriors guarding the gates of the city. If the Liirians broke through here, Glass supposed the warriors would have little chance. After that, it would be up to the people of Jador to defend themselves. Glass hoped Akeela would be merciful.

He sat astride a kreel with Benik, who had been ordered by Kadar not to leave Thorin's side. Neither of them were to join the fight. Neither man appreciated the order, but both understood. Thorin would be little use in battle, Kadar had told him frankly, and would be more valuable in warning Grimhold of the outcome. Kadar himself was grim-faced as he sat upon Istikah, his own magnificent kreel. Both were armored in heavy green and brown scales, a light and flexible suit that made the pair seem like a single reptilian beast. The kahan wore no helmet. His gray hair shone in the sun, proud and disdainful. At his side was a whip. In his left hand he held an erect spear decorated with white feathers. Like his kreel, he was silent. Istikah's tongue darted out to test the air. Her sparkling eyes watched their distant enemies with almost human hatred. She had sharp claws that she flicked from time to time, eager for combat. She was beautiful, though, and Thorin admired her. If only there had been more time; he knew they could have built an army strong enough to best his old countrymen.

Three hundred yards away, Akeela's army stood at the ready. Ranks of heavy horsemen waited at the forefront, bearing lances and swords, their silver armor reflecting sunlight in all directions. They were arranged in a line, as Thorin had predicted, with lancers in front. One by one the lines would be called into battle. There would be no distance fighting with archers this time. It would be a clash on the sands, hand to hand and hoof to claw. Behind the lines sat Trager atop his black charger. The general looked splendid, his helmet held in the crux of his arm as he surveyed his Jadori foes. A standard-bearer sat next to him, boldly displaying the Liirian flag. The air was breezeless and the flag hung still. Thorin wondered if Trager recognized him up on the dune.

Then out of the camp rode Akeela, his white stallion prancing through the sand as he joined Trager. He wore no armor, just a kingly tunic and royal cape. On his head sat his golden crown. He looked older to Thorin, even from

the great distance, with a serious expression that enhanced
his twisted reputation. Kadar bristled when he noticed
Akeela, letting out a low growl.

"The snake of Liiria," he pronounced loudly. Down the
line his men affirmed the accusation, rumbling their hatred.
The kahan turned to Thorin. "He will offer terms?" he
asked.

"I don't know," confessed Thorin. He was uncomfortable
sitting behind Benik on the kreel, so he slid off the creature's back. Kadar scowled. "I can't see a damn thing up
there," Thorin shot back in frustration. At his side he wore
a sword, in case a lucky opportunity arose. He felt like a
coward letting others do his fighting, and thought of pleading with Kadar to let him join the fray. But it had already
been decided. He let out a disgruntled sigh as he watched
the distant Liirians. "Akeela wants Lukien," he said finally.
"He may offer something in return."

"Your king is a fool if he thinks I would give up a comrade so easily. He thinks I am like him, a whore?" asked
Kadar angrily.

"As I said, I don't know," replied Thorin.

"Get back on your kreel."

"I can direct the battle better if I can see, don't you
think?"

"I direct the battle," said Kadar. "And you will be safer
on the kreel. Mount."

Baron Glass ignored the order.

"I see Glass," said Akeela with a frown, "but where's
Lukien?"

Trager snorted, "Hiding, no doubt."

The answer irked Akeela. "I've come all this way for
Lukien, and he doesn't even bother to face me?" He
craned his neck to see past the cavalry. On the dune far
ahead were a line of mounted warriors, ready on their
kreels. In the center of the line was a man Akeela supposed
was Kadar. He was an impressive looking leader, tall and
spartan, with dark skin and a hard expression. Next to him
stood a man with one arm. Akeela had immediately recognized his old adversary, Baron Glass.

"Not only does he flee, but he helps my enemies," he
seethed. "Well, we will make short work of him."

"Agreed," said Trager. His aide Colonel Tark rode through the ranks, barking orders at the men. The lancers would go first, followed by a wave of swords. It was a good plan, Akeela supposed, but not being a military man he couldn't say for sure. Trager, on the other hand, was supremely confident. When he had seen how they outnumbered the Jadori, he had grinned like a schoolboy. Still, Akeela was unsure. Before his death Grak had warned him of Jadori skill, and the ferocity of their kreels. "They could tear a man's throat out in an instant," Grak had told him, and his brother Doreshen had echoed the sentiment. Doreshen had led them the rest of the way to Jador after Grak's death, and now was safe in the rear with the drowa, but his warning still rang in Akeela's head like a bell.

"Why do they wait?" Akeela asked. "For our terms?"

"Probably," surmised Trager. "And to hold the high ground." He considered the Jadori position. "A good tactic. It will make this tougher."

"But we will defeat them, yes?"

"Of course. But then we'll have to secure the city."

There was an unhealthy gleam in the general's eyes. Akeela warned, "I want no massacres, Will."

Trager replied, "My lord, if they oppose us, we'll have no choice. Don't get soft on us now."

Akeela said, "For the sake of our men, then. Have a herald come forth. I wish to deliver my terms."

Trager was incredulous. "Terms? What terms?"

"I see no point in a slaughter if they'll hand over Lukien and Glass." He thought for a moment, wondering if he should demand Gilwyn Toms in the bargain. "The boy is not really a concern. Just the traitors. And the amulets."

"Akeela, we've come all this way to punish your enemies. Not just Lukien, but his allies as well." Trager pointed to the dunes where Kadar waited. "Would you have that barbarian go free?"

The words gave Akeela pause. He had been so full of anger on the trip, but he was tired now and just wanted to rest, and he admitted to himself that he was afraid of the coming fight. Visions of his long ago battle in Norvor flashed through his mind.

"All I want—all I've ever wanted—is Lukien," he said. "If they turn him and Glass over to me, I will spare their city." He smiled, pleased with himself. "That is my bargain. Once Kadar hears it, he will agree. No king would risk his own city."

"You did," muttered Trager.

Akeela shot him an angry glare. "What was that?"

Trager took a steadying breath. "It's a mistake. If you let the Jadori go they'll attack us as we retreat. We must destroy them." He leaned over and whispered, "They're your enemies, Akeela."

Akeela licked his lips. "Yes . . ."

But something else was in his mind, a memory of Grak and their last conversation, and of being called Akeela the Good so very long ago. He began rubbing his temples.

"No," he said, shaking his head. "No. Have my terms delivered."

"Akeela . . ."

"Do it!"

General Trager looked at his aides, young lieutenants that followed him everywhere. Their faces were distressed. He said finally, "Very well. I'll deliver your terms myself."

"You?" blurted Akeela. "Don't be ridiculous."

Trager turned his eyes toward the distant Kadar. "I want to get a closer look at this scrapper."

Trager's arrogance didn't surprise Akeela, and he didn't want to argue. "Very well," he relented. "But be quick about it."

Baron Glass waited patiently beside Kadar and his warriors, refusing to give up the high ground by attacking first and wondering if there was enough humanity inside Akeela to offer them decent terms. After long minutes of waiting, a small group of horsemen broke from the Liirian ranks and approached across the sand. To Thorin's great astonishment, Trager was among them.

"I don't believe it," he said with a grin. "The devil's minion himself."

Kadar was confused. "That is the general?"

"Trager," nodded Thorin. "Coming to deliver the king's message."

"Why would a general come himself to give terms?" asked Kadar.

"I'm not sure." Glass narrowed his eyes suspiciously. "To see us for himself, I suppose. Arrogant pisser."

Kadar straightened in his saddle. "Then we will face him. Mount your kreel, Baron. I want to see this soiled dog myself."

With Benik's help Thorin mounted the kreel, holding fast to the extra set of reins looped to the beast's saddle. Kadar called two more of his riders forward, and together they rode down the dune to face Trager. They were many yards from each other but the two leaders kept their eyes locked as they closed the gap. More than anything Thorin wanted to be alone on his kreel; it pained him to face Trager as a cripple. He had never cared for the brash soldier, not even when he was young. But Trager wasn't young anymore. As they drew near him, Thorin could see the age on his face, the bit of gray in his beard, and leatheriness of his skin. Sixteen years ago, he'd been oddly handsome. Now he simply looked cruel. The general brought his horse to a stop and raised a hand to halt his company. Kadar rode until they were only a few yards apart, then reined in Istikah. Benik and the others fell in close behind. Trager's eyes immediately went to Thorin.

"Well, old man, I never expected to see you again," he said.

Baron Glass grinned. "I'm a hard man to kill, Trager."

"Yes, I see that," replied Trager. "But you're still a coward, Glass. Still hiding behind others."

The insult tempted Thorin to dismount. His hand twitched, aching for his sword. "You've brought that poison adder Akeela into Jador," he said. "He'll be sorry for that."

"We shall see who's sorry," laughed Trager.

"Enough," growled Kadar. "What is your message, murderer?"

Trager's smile was infuriating. Casually he gazed over Kadar's shoulder. "Where is that coward, Lukien? I'd hoped to see him and finally cut his heart out."

"Deliver your message, dog," spat Thorin. "Does Akeela offer terms?"

"Is Lukien hiding?" asked Trager. He seemed delighted by the notion. "Somewhere in the city, maybe?"

"Your message!" thundered Kadar. "What is it?"

"Only this, barbarian—Akeela of Liiria says that you are a fool and he curses you. He says that by day's end you will be a portion for vultures, and your city laid to waste." Trager's mocking grin spread across his face. "That's what you get for hiding Lukien."

Kadar cursed in Jadori and raised his spear.

"No!" shouted Thorin. "Don't, Kadar."

Trager laughed. "No, the baron's right, Kahan Kadar. He knows I can best you too easily." Before Kadar could answer he whirled his horse around and headed back toward his army. He called over his shoulder, "But don't worry, Dirt-King—we will battle soon enough!"

Seething, Kadar prepared to toss his spear. Thorin pleaded with him to stop. "No, that's what he wants! Your men would be leaderless without you."

Kadar slowly lowered his spear. Trager was already out of range, his escorts trailing behind him. "You are right," he hissed. "He is the devil's own!"

Quickly he turned Istikah and headed back up the dune. Benik and the others followed. When Kadar took his place back among his warriors, he raised his spear and his voice in angry challenge. Thorin didn't understand the words but the meaning was clear. The Jadori fighters let loose a loud war whoop. Their reptilian mounts joined the song with a bloodcurdling cry.

"Do we attack?" shouted Thorin over the noise.

"We do!" cried Kadar, then ordered his first hundred riders into position.

Down in the valley of sand, Trager watched as the kreel riders took position on the dune, forming a defensive line while Kadar and Glass and the others fell back. There the riders waited, their monstrous kreels letting out a terrible war cry. For a moment Trager was impressed. It would be difficult for his lancers to make it up the dune, but he knew there was no other choice. Kadar wasn't stupid enough to give up the high ground. As the Jadori warriors waited, taunting them, Akeela rode up to Trager's side.

"They want a fight, my lord," sighed Trager. "There was nothing I could do about it."

Akeela's lips disappeared in a tight grimace. "They spit

on my offer," he rumbled. "Well, they will pay for that. Attack, General. Destroy them all."

The words were like music to Trager. "Yes, my lord," he replied. He turned to Colonel Tark, who was waiting dutifully at his side. "The order's given, Colonel. First line attack."

"First line attack," repeated Tark, then called the order to his lieutenants. At once the horsemen in the front line raised their lances. "Up the hill and over!" cried Tark. "Attack!"

A second later the lancers exploded forward, sand flying out behind them like a desert storm. They moved with perfection, charging across the desert, their weapons poised, their armored heads bowed. Trager watched, impressed by their movements even in the difficult terrain. They were slower, certainly, but more surefooted than he'd thought. As the horsemen reached the bottom of the dune, the second line—swordsmen—readied to join them. Their lance-wielding brothers struggled up the high dunes toward their adversaries. At the top of the dunes, the kreel riders held out their spears, the muscular haunches of their reptilian mounts ready to attack. When the horsemen crested the ridge, the kreels sprang.

They were like screaming lightning, and Trager hardly saw them. With spitting snouts and slashing claws the beasts barreled into the horsemen, ducking the lances and slamming into their armored flanks. The shocked horses whinnied and reared; the stunned horsemen nearly fell from their mounts. Suddenly, the kreels were everywhere, and their riders with them, stabbing with their spears and working their whips, pressing their advantage. Some of the Liirians broke through, impaling kreels or riders on their lances, but most were muddled, dazed by the quickness of their enemies and struggling for footing. With appalling ease the claws of the reptiles tore into the Liirian armor, slashing leather straps and finding the soft flesh beneath. The horses bellowed as the beasts opened their guts with razor claws. The lancers dropped their clumsy weapons, turning to regroup as the monsters fell on them. Jadori whips snapped through the air, snatching men from saddles and dragging them to the sand. The lancers drew their swords to counter, slicing through the blinding shield of scales.

Back in the Liirian ranks, Trager watched in horror as his men were slaughtered. The lances had been a debacle. He had never expected the quickness of the kreels; he had never seen creatures so fleet. A worried murmur swept through his men. Colonel Tark looked at him for guidance. Next to him, Akeela's face was tight with fury.

"Not a good start, General," he grumbled.

Quiet, you ass! thought Trager. He didn't need a coward's backtalk now. He needed action, so he gave the order for the next lines to charge. The lieutenants made the call, and two hundred more horsemen galloped forward. They drew their swords and raised them high, shaking the air with their thunder. Up on the dunes, the kreels and cavalry were locked in combat, clashing claws and swords and screaming in bloodlust. The kreels were everywhere, outnumbered but impossibly fast, bounding between horses and dodging blades, their long jaws snapping off limbs. A huge cloud of dust rose from the dunes. Trager rode forward for a better view, leaving Akeela safely in the rear. He knew that somewhere, Kahan Kadar was waiting for him, eager to meet him in combat.

For almost an hour, Thorin and Kadar watched the battle unfold, safe from their position on a nearby dune. Their first wave of warriors had done remarkably well, but their numbers had dwindled and needed bolstering from fresh fighters. Kadar had ordered more of his men into the melee, and Trager had met them with his own seemingly inexhaustible supply of troops. Thorin knew Kadar was worried. He had always known his kreels were better than any horses, but the overwhelming numbers of Liirians had virtually negated that advantage. Worry shone on the kahan's face, and a kind of quiet resolve. It was just a matter of time. Thorin scanned the battle, hoping for a miracle. He had wracked his brain since the fight began, trying to think of some new tactic to give them an advantage. If they had mobilized the people of the city they might have been able to beat back Akeela's army, but Kadar wouldn't hear of it. It was his charge to protect his people, and he would die before letting untrained farmers take up the fight.

Soon enough for that, thought Thorin blackly. Once his old countrymen defeated the kreels. . . .

The battle raged on. Kadar ordered more and more of his men into the fray, until there were barely fifty men left with the kahan. Thorin pleaded with Kadar, begging him to let him fight. It didn't matter that he had one arm, he insisted. He was good with a sword, promising to take down at least ten Liirians before falling himself. The boast made Kadar smile.

"You will ride to Grimhold," he told Thorin.

"But I can fight!"

Kadar shook his head. "Grimhold is more important than anything," he said. Thorin knew the kahan was thinking of his daughter.

A few minutes later what Thorin dreaded most came to pass. Out on the dust-filled dunes, the Jadori warriors began to falter. Exhaustion overtook them and their stout-hearted mounts. Across the distance Trager prepared his final assault, organizing the rest of his cavalry to charge, still over a thousand strong. It was the end and Kadar knew it.

"Go now, Baron Glass," he said. "Get to Grimhold, tell them what you saw here. Tell them what is coming."

Thorin's throat tightened. "Kadar, let me—"

"Go to Grimhold," repeated Kadar. He hefted his spear and took a deep breath. He said to Benik, "Ride quickly. Be sure to get him there."

Benik nodded but didn't say a word. Like Thorin, he hated the thought of abandoning the kahan. Kadar's hard face softened enough to give Thorin an encouraging smile.

"Be well, Baron Glass. And see that the Bronze Knight protects my daughter."

"I will," said Thorin. He took a final look at the dune where the battle raged. Off to the east, Trager and his cavalry were about to charge. Never had the baron felt more cowardly.

He told Benik he was ready, almost choking on the words, and the two fled the battlefield for the safety of Grimhold.

Kahan Kadar of Jador watched the foreigner from Liiria ride off, carrying his greatest hopes with him. He hadn't expected to like the big baron or to trust him with the life of his daughter, but he supposed he was living in a remarkable time. And it occurred to him that he had lived a long life, burying many wives and friends and seeing miraculous things. He was glad he had given the amulet back to Eladaz. He was ready to die. But not before settling a score. He did not expect to reach the mad Akeela; that was asking too much. But if could slay the general in battle, he would happily leave this world.

"Men of Jador," he called in their tongue. "This is our last stand!"

His remaining warriors raised their spears willingly. Kadar called the attack and charged into battle, haunted by the image of his beautiful, blind daughter.

Will Trager rode at the head of his cavalry, leading the final assault up the dunes. Through the visor of his helmet he saw Kadar racing into the melee and knew what he sought. Fifty more kreel riders were with him, the last of them, Trager supposed. The odds were heavily in his favor now, and he didn't expect to lose many more men. He could tell the Jadori were tiring. Even their lizards were slowing. As his black stallion tore up the sand, he drew his sword and pointed it at Kadar.

"I'm going after the kahan!" he roared to Colonel Tark. "Take the men into battle!"

Veering from the rest of the line, Trager steered straight for Kadar. The kahan saw him from the top of the dune, saw his intent, and ordered his kreel down after him. As the Liirian cavalry rushed by, Kadar ignored them, focusing on Trager. His spear was up and his head was lowered. Trager prepared himself, quickly studying Kadar's attack and drawing back his blade. He would now go for the kahan himself.

As the Jadori sprinted forward, Trager expertly evaded the spear and brought his sword low. He had jousted with the best a hundred times and easily ducked the blow, slamming his sword into the kreel's neck. He heard the lizard cry as it raced past, felt the blade cleave the armor and the skin beneath. As he turned to see the damage, the kreel skidded headlong into the sand, spraying blood. Trager let out a triumphant shout as Kadar spilled from the kreel's back. The kahan tumbled, losing his spear. Trager spun his horse around. It had all been over so quickly; he had expected more from the vaunted Kadar.

"I told you we would meet, Dirt-King," he taunted. Behind him on the dunes, the sounds of battle raged on, but Trager ignored it as he pranced toward Kadar. "Tell me now, who is your better?"

Kadar sneered and clawed the sand for his spear. Trager let him take the time to find it. When he did the kahan sprang to his feet. The kreel was crying beside him, desperately struggling to raise itself even as blood sluiced from its wound.

"A remarkable beast," said Trager. "Loyal. But not enough to save you, savage."

"Fight me!" roared Kadar. He bared his teeth as he poked the air with his spear. "Come and face me!"

Mounted, Trager knew he had the advantage. And if he were Kadar, he would try to even the odds by striking for the horse. Without a shield to protect him, Trager realized he was still in danger. Then, far in the distance, he noticed Akeela watching him. The Liirian king was on his horse, surrounded by guards. Trager knew he could easily call for help, but knew also that Akeela was judging him, just as he always had. Was Akeela thinking of Lukien, he wondered? Did he still think the Bronze Knight his better?

"I don't need help to defeat you!" Trager shouted, then kicked his heels into his horse, sending it springing forward. Kadar braced himself for the clash. An angry Trager brought up his sword, poised to trample the kahan. Kadar stood firm until the last moment, then moved like a cat and smashed the butt of his spear into Trager's chest, catching him cold and driving him from his saddle. Trager's world winked out of existence. He felt the blow, felt himself falling, then the awful impact of the ground rushing to meet him. The air flew from his lungs but he held firm to his sword, opening his eyes just in time to see the screaming Kadar racing forward. He rolled, barely avoiding the spear tip, then brought up his weapon and knocked it aside. Bounding to his feet, he felt a stabbing pain in his ribs and knew he'd cracked some. Kadar was before him, swinging his spear. Trager ducked and the weapon swooshed overhead. He tried to counter but Kadar was too quick, falling back before the blade caught him. Trager panted and gripped his side. Kadar staggered on his feet, still dazed from his own fall. The sounds of battle erupted in their ears. The pain in Trager's ribs was searing.

Akeela's watching! he told himself. *Win!*

With desperate strength he flung himself at Kadar, his sword whistling. The dazed kahan brought up his spear to block the blows, one by one parrying them all. But Trager was beyond stopping now. He pressed his attack, hacking down again and again until at last the spear splintered and the blade smashed Kadar's breastplate. The blow buckled the armor. The kahan stumbled back, wounded. His eyes scanned the ground desperately for a weapon, but found only useless sand. Trager knew he had him. One more strike and Kadar was finished. He twisted his grip on the pommel and with both hands sliced at Kadar's chest, cracking the damaged armor and biting into flesh. Kadar fell back as the blade came away, blood dripping down his armor. He tumbled into the sand and stared up at the sky, sweating and panting. Slowly Trager stalked after him. He stood over the wounded kahan and put the point of his sword to his naked throat.

"Now you die," spat Trager, his own face covered in dirty sweat. "Any last words?"

Kahan Kadar of Jador did not flinch as the blade pricked his flesh. He looked up at Trager with utter contempt. "You will not win," he declared. "The folk of Grimhold are stronger than you!"

Trager added pressure to the blade. "We shall see," he said bitterly. "After we take your city, we ride for Grimhold."

Then he lowered his weight on the pommel, sending the blade effortlessly through Kadar's throat and into the sand beneath. There was a spasm and a gurgling cry as Kadar slowly died. Trager watched him every moment, his eyes locked on his foe's twisted face. Blood soaked the earth under Kadar's head, running quickly into the sand. When he was finally dead, Trager drew back his blade and stood, letting the soiled weapon dangle from his fist. He wobbled a moment, his side screaming with pain. A quick look toward the dune told him the battle continued, but that the day was his. Gazing eastward, he saw Akeela waiting on his horse, still watching with detachment.

"So?" Trager gasped. "Did you see? Did you finally see?"

Clutching his side, he staggered toward Akeela, forgetting the horse and the raging battle.

"I'm better than Lukien, better than all of them," he groaned.

He knew Akeela couldn't hear him, but it didn't matter. He had seen, and that was enough.

51

When the battle was over and Trager had bandaged his damaged ribs, the army began taking care of their wounded and preparing for their march to the city. It was nearly afternoon, and Akeela was eager to reach Jador. He had no intention of spending another night out in the desert, and still expected a fight at the city gates. While his men made ready, Akeela finally trotted out from the safety of his guards and onto the battlefield. It was eerily quiet. All the men, including Trager, were shaken by their losses. From the top of the dune Akeela could see Jador in the distance, waiting for him. The desert sands were littered with bodies, most of them dead, others that would soon expire. The odd calls of the near-dead kreels floated up through the air, faint and ghostly. A stink began to rise, driven by the heat. Trager had estimated their dead at nearly eight hundred. An appalling loss, and Akeela grieved for them. He had lost men in Nith and now in the desert, and was sure to lose more when they reached the city. He hoped enough would remain to eventually capture Lukien. That was all he wanted now.

After resting a few hours, Akeela ordered the men back on their horses, and together they and their caravan of drowa set off for Jador. Akeela took the lead this time, with Trager and Colonel Tark close behind, both of whom barely spoke, so rattled were they by the losses they'd endured. Akeela didn't need Doreshen anymore and so relegated the Ganjor man to the back of the column. He wouldn't like what was about to happen in Jador. Neither would Grak have. But Akeela was still angered by the way Kahan Kadar had refused his generous terms, and so felt no remorse for what he was about to do.

It is Kadar's will that they should die, he told himself as he rode.

An hour later the army reached the outskirts of Jador. They found the avenues choked with people, some armed, most not. These were Ganjeese, mostly. The Jadori, Akeela knew, were behind the city's wall. But of the armed he found a hundred of Kadar's black-robed warriors, standing in a defiant line before the city, blocking its major avenue. They had spears and curved swords in their hands. Their faces were resolute. Clearly they knew their kahan had perished, yet they seemed determined to fight on.

So be it.

Akeela brought his diminished army to a halt at the outskirts of Jador. The Jadori defenders were a mere twenty yards away. Beyond them, he could see people hanging out of the windows of the dingy towers. And beyond the towers, the city wall of Jador stood, also burdened with onlookers. They would yield or they would die, and with only a few hundred warriors left to defend them, either option was all right with Akeela. He had hoped to spare the lives of the citizens, but he was beyond caring now, really, and so accepted what the Great Fate handed him.

He didn't ask Trager if his men were prepared to fight. He didn't ask the defenders to surrender. He simply called out to them across the remaining stretch of desert.

"Your kahan is dead," he shouted. "And soon so shall you be."

There was no reply from the staunch defenders. Akeela doubted they understood him. Sighing, he turned to Trager and said, "Kill anyone who tries to stop you. Spare the citizens, if you can."

Without hesitation, Trager's Chargers went to work.

52

Minikin stalked through the halls of Grimhold, a thousand troubled voices screaming in her mind. She moved quickly, not talking to anyone, not even Trog. The cries in her mind threatened to split her skull, yet she could not understand their pleas. The Akari were speaking all at once, a jumble of alarmed and weeping voices. It was late afternoon, and Minikin had been taking her midday meal at the usual time, sitting with Trog in her chamber and enjoying the view from one of the keep's only windows. Then the screams had started; it was like getting hit in the head with a stone. Minikin's tea cup had dropped from her hand and shattered. She fell back in her chair, trying to make sense of it all and realizing something terrible had happened.

When at last she reached Insight's room her head was spinning. She tried the door but it was locked.

"Damn it!"

She banged on the door, hoping Alena would hear her. "Alena, are you in there? It's Minikin."

There was no answer. The spirit voices in her head went on and on, refusing to talk directly to her in their grief and anguish. They were a fickle lot, the dead Akari, and when they were sad or angry they tortured Minikin.

"Trog," she gasped, "open the door."

Trog didn't bother trying the knob himself. Instead he slammed his shoulder into the door, splintering the jamb.

The door burst open with an explosive bang. The noise would have frightened anyone else, but the only occupant of the chamber didn't stir. Insight sat in her lonely chair by the light of a candle, staring at the wall in her silent stupor. Her mother, Alena, was nowhere to be found. Minikin supposed she was somewhere doing chores.

"Wait here," Minikin told Trog, then went into the room and quickly knelt down before Insight. The girl didn't acknowledge her, even when Minikin took her hand. "Insight, child, listen to me," Minikin pleaded. "I need you to help me. I need you to tell me what's happened in Jador."

As always, it took a few moments for the girl's consciousness to stir. She did not blink or turn her head, but slowly her mouth began to move with the unseen aid of her Akari spirit.

"Minikin. . . ."

"Yes, child, it's me. Can you summon Lacaron? Is he with you?"

"Lacaron is here," said the voice. Minikin couldn't tell if it was the girl or the spirit talking.

"Lacaron? Can you hear me?"

This time the voice was solidly male. "Lacaron can hear."

Minikin knew the Akari spirit had seen the trouble, whatever it was. She braced herself as she asked, "Which one is it, Lacaron? Kadar or the Liirian?"

"They have battled," said the voice. "They are defeated."

"Who?" Minikin demanded. "Who's defeated?"

For the first time that Minikin could remember, Insight's face actually flinched. Her voice shook as she said, "Kadar."

Minikin fell back on her heels. Though she had known it in her heart, it was unbearable to have her last flame of hope extinguished. "No. . . ." She closed her eyes. "Please don't say so."

"The kahan is dead," said Lacaron through Insight. "The man with one arm comes to tell you."

Minikin knelt, unable to speak. There seemed nothing else to ask the spirit. She did not want Lacaron to continue, but the spirit did so.

"Many men, many dead. On the field and in the city."

Insight's young face fell as she gave the terrible news. "Kadar is gone."

For long minutes Minikin remained on the floor beside Insight, unable to lift herself from the spot. She didn't know what she would do without her old friend. And she couldn't imagine telling White-Eye the news. Outside the chamber, Trog peeked his head over the threshold. She could feel his concerned eyes watching her.

"I . . ." Her words choked off. "I need some time, Trog," she managed. "I need to be alone."

Reluctantly, Trog turned and left his mistress in the dim chamber. When he was gone and she was sure he would not hear her, Minikin wept.

The sun was off their backs as Gilwyn and White-Eye rode in the protective shadows of Grimhold. Emerald, Gilwyn's kreel, moved across the sands at a gentle trot. It was a good day, clear and pleasant despite their many worries, and they had been riding for almost an hour without rest. In his short time with Emerald, Gilwyn had easily bonded with the beast, and now could command her almost completely with his mind, a strange and wonderful sensation that the boy had quickly found addicting. When he rode, he was not a cripple or an object of ridicule—he was like the grand horsemen of Liiria's past, and as good as any other boy. More, Emerald had become a true companion, like Teku or even Figgis, a creature he could really call a friend. Since coming to Grimhold, he had not busied himself with the keep's defense as Lukien did, but instead had indulged himself with things he never thought possible. Like riding. Or being with a girl.

White-Eye had been remarkably kind to him, and Gilwyn adored her. He supposed she felt much the same, or at least a bit so, for she spent great amounts of time with him and had been the first to show him the "real" Grimhold. With Minikin's permission, they had come out to explore the village from a safe distance, in the daytime when the risk to White-Eye was greatest. At first Minikin had refused, saying it would be dangerous for the girl, but White-Eye had desperately wanted to ride with Gilwyn, and so they had fashioned a blinder for her, a thick strip of dark cloth that covered her eyes, shielding them from the relentless sun. It was odd looking but functional, and Gilwyn didn't mind. How could he, when she didn't even see his own oddities? He didn't know if the spirit that guided her had described his clubbed foot and hand to her; he had never asked her. White-Eye simply didn't seem to care, and that was good enough for Gilwyn.

The cooling shadows of Grimhold shielded them as they rode. Gilwyn did his best always to keep the sun off them. He could tell by the way White-Eye sometimes winced that even this was painful for her, but then she would smile as if nothing in the world was wrong. She knew that her father was back in Jador, worrying about her and waiting for Akeela's army to come. Yet even that couldn't spoil the joy of the ride, and as Emerald trotted quickly through the valley Gilwyn could feel her breath on his neck as she laughed. It was good that they were enjoying themselves, he supposed. Tomorrow or the next day might bring tragedy, but for now they were safe and happy, happier than Gilwyn had ever been in his life. He had seen very little of Lukien lately, and though he felt some guilt over that, he convinced himself that he was not really needed. Lukien was the military man, after all, and was already doing an excellent job making the Inhumans into an army.

Today is mine, he told himself happily.

And maybe, if he was lucky, so was White-Eye.

Emerald quickened a bit beneath them, sensing Gilwyn's happiness. The boy had one hand on the reins and both legs strapped to the saddle so that he couldn't fall—there were no stirrups on a kreel's saddle and no reason for a clubbed foot to hinder him. White-Eye kept her arms wrapped tightly about his waist. Silently he told Emerald to slow down, worried about the girl. In her strange reptilian language, Emerald seemed to tell him not to fret.

Deciding to take a break, Gilwyn brought the kreel to a stop at the top of a swale. They were in the shade of one of the fortress' tall turrets, with Grimhold's town clearly visible in the distance. As Emerald came to a halt, White-Eye took her arms from Gilwyn's waist.

"Why are you stopping?" she asked.

Gilwyn carefully slid down from the kreel's back. "I thought you might be tired."

"No," said White-Eye.

"Well, I am," said Gilwyn. He took White-Eye's hand and helped her down. "There's a great view here and. . . ." He stopped himself, shocked by what he'd said, but White-Eye only laughed.

"Don't worry," she told him. "You can't offend me. Faralok shows me all I need to see."

Faralok was White-Eye's Akari guide. She had rarely spoken his name, and it intrigued Gilwyn. He led her away from Emerald toward the edge of the tor. It was dim and cooler in the shadow of the keep, yet she still squinted beneath her black blinder.

"How are your eyes?" he asked. "We can go back now if you like."

"No, I don't want to go back. It's good to be outside." White-Eye took a deep, soulful breath. "I'm glad Minikin let us go. It's been ages since I rode a kreel. My father took me once, a long time ago."

Gilwyn guided her down and together they sat on the sands overlooking the town. He stared at her, entranced by her dark beauty. Lukien had once confided in him during the long ride south that he had loved Queen Cassandra the moment he'd set eyes on her. It had been that way for Gilwyn, too; instant love. He wondered if White-Eye knew he was staring, and if Faralok made her aware of such things. He had so many questions for the girl. In the few days he had spent in. Grimhold, he had already learned a great deal. But the Inhumans were full of mysteries.

"It's very pretty here," he said. "I wish we'd. brought some food. We could have picnicked."

"Tomorrow, maybe," replied White-Eye. Then she smiled. "If Minikin lets me out again."

"Hmm, I doubt it," said Gilwyn. Convincing the mistress to let them go had been difficult enough. "You're very close to Minikin, aren't you? She acts like your mother."

White-Eye thought for a moment. "Yes, she is, in a way. She's protected me since I came here. She's taught me everything I know, especially how to use Faralok."

"Is it hard?" asked Gilwyn. "Controlling the Akari, I mean? Is it like controlling the kreel?"

"I don't know what it's like to bond with a kreel, Gilwyn. But no, it isn't hard to control Faralok. And control isn't a good word, really. He speaks to me. With his help, it's like I can really see."

The answer intrigued Gilwyn. "So you're always talking with him? Even now?" he asked. "And he just tells you what's around you, just like that?"

"At first it was like that," said White-Eye. She leaned back on her palms so that her dark hair fell back. "But now it's easy. It's not even like talking." She shrugged. "I just know what's around me."

Gilwyn slumped down to one elbow, leaning and studying the girl. "I wish I knew what it was like to talk to my Akari," he sighed. "Minikin told me she would teach me, but she's been too busy. All that I know is that her name is Ruana. But I don't know what she's for or anything."

"If Minikin granted you a spirit, there must be a reason, Gilwyn. You should trust her. When the time is right, she'll teach you about Ruana."

Gilwyn's mind reeled with the possibilities. "I don't think she'll be able to help me walk any better," he mused. "But maybe she'll help me to see in the dark like you, or do magic like Minikin. I saw her summon the Akari once in Koth. They were like pillars of fire! I'd like to do that someday."

White-Eye chuckled at the idea. "The Akari are to help us, Gilwyn, not to entertain us."

"I know," said Gilwyn. "But it would be nice to have some power for once, to not feel so helpless." He grimaced as he looked at his clubbed hand, so useless and deformed. His sudden silence caught White-Eye's attention.

"What are you thinking about?" she asked.

"Oh, nothing," Gilwyn lied.

"I don't believe you," said White-Eye, grinning. "You're wondering if I know what you look like."

Her deduction made Gilwyn flush. "Well, yes," he admitted. "I have wondered that a little." He glanced away. "*Do* you know what I look like?"

White-Eye nodded. "As much as I can, yes."

"And you don't mind?"

"Gilwyn, I live with people with far worse deformities than yours. How could you ask me such a question? Do you mind that my eyes are so ugly?"

"They're not!" said Gilwyn. "I think they're beautiful."

White-Eye laughed, but he could tell she loved the compliment. "You're a very polite liar," she said.

"I'm not lying, White-Eye," said Gilwyn. He slid a little closer to her. "I think you're the most beautiful girl I've ever seen."

White-Eye didn't move. She merely stared ahead. Her lips pursed. Gilwyn could tell she was nervous. A fluttering sensation went through his stomach. Should he kiss her? Would she stop him? He leaned closer, his lips barely brushing her cheek. . . .

. . . then was startled by a sudden cry.

"White-Eye?"

Gilwyn jerked back and looked around. White-Eye sprang to her feet. Up the tor walked Minikin, accompanied by Trog. Gilwyn felt a stab of terror when he saw her, sure that she'd somehow read his intentions. But when he saw her distressed expression he knew something far worse had happened.

"Minikin?" White-Eye called to her. "What is it?"

Minikin climbed the tor without speaking, facing the girl. She swallowed hard. Gilwyn had never seen her this way, and it frightened him. She was obviously bracing herself. White-Eye began to tremble.

"Minikin?" she asked. "Has something happened?"

The tiny woman's voice shook as she answered, "Baron Glass, the Liirian. He's on his way to Grimhold."

White-Eye was deathly still. She whispered, "My father?"

Minikin took the girl's hand. "I'm sorry, child. He's gone."

Gilwyn couldn't move. His grief for White-Eye overwhelmed him. White-Eyed bitterly stripped the blinder from her face and tossed it to the ground. It was strange to see her peculiar eyes crying, but the tears came fast.

It was nearly nightfall when Thorin Glass finally reached Grimhold. He was exhausted from the ride, a nearly non-stop sprint across the desert, and when at last they reached the mountains Glass thought he would faint from hunger and thirst. Benik, his guide, drove their kreel into a wide canyon with high, red peaks rising around them. Shadows grew in the crevices between hills. Benik said nothing as he concentrated, spying the scraggy hills for the right direction and always deciding quickly. Thorin held tight to the reins as they rode. His one good arm ached from the effort.

"Is it near?" he asked hoarsely.

Benik slowed their mount and nodded. "Very near."

A moment later, they turned a corner in the canyon and saw torchlight in the distance. Thorin fought to focus his eyes. They were in the shadow of a gigantic mountain. A wide iron gate opened into it, revealing an interior of orange light. There were figures in the light. They shouted when they noticed the newcomers.

"Thorin, over here!" cried a voice. A waving man stepped out from the gate.

"Lukien!"

"Grimhold," pronounced Benik. He let out a weary sigh, then pointed at the shadowed figures. "They await you."

Thorin dropped eagerly off the kreel's back and hurried toward the keep. It was an awesome sight, tall and forbidding, but the welcome shouts from Lukien settled his fears. There was a giant outside the gate who Thorin thought was Trog at first, but soon realized was some sort of guardian. The midget woman Minikin was at the gate as well, her diminutive figure cloaked in shadows. Lukien hurried out from the gate toward Thorin, meeting him halfway. A smile of huge relief graced his face.

"Thorin, thank the Fate you're all right!" cried Lukien. As they met he embraced the baron. The hug squeezed the strength from Thorin's body.

"Easy, Lukien," he laughed, "I'm ready to drop from that bloody ride!"

Lukien stood back and inspected him. "You look like death," he said. His smile waned, becoming sad and crooked. "The battle. Very bad?"

Glass nodded. It was hard to think of how he'd abandoned Kadar. He looked toward the dimly lit gate, realizing that Gilwyn hadn't come to greet him. "Where's the boy?" he asked.

Lukien replied, "Comforting Kadar's daughter."

Thorin looked at him. "How'd you know about that?"

"There's a lot to explain to you, Thorin. Minikin was right—some of her people can do amazing things."

"I don't understand," said Thorin, puzzled.

Lukien put an arm around the baron and led him toward the keep. "I'll explain it to you," he said. "But first you need to rest."

"Gods, yes," groaned Thorin. "Food and drink, if you please." He gestured toward Benik behind him. "For him as well. We're both starved and exhausted."

"We've already prepared something for you. Come."

"Already? But how'd you know—"

"No, no more questions yet," said Lukien. "We'll have a hundred from you soon enough."

He led Thorin into the gate where Minikin was waiting. The little woman's expression was bleak. Around her stood the strangest people Thorin had ever seen. He stared at them, shocked by their deformities. Minikin stepped forward and took his hand.

"Welcome to Grimhold, Baron Glass," she said. "And thank you for all you've done for us."

Thorin shook his head. "Do not thank me, madam. I left your good kahan to die. Now, if you have food for a coward, I would appreciate it."

"The food is this way," she said, gesturing down a hall, "but it's for a hero, not a coward."

"If you say so, my lady," replied Thorin. He let the tiny woman guide him into the miraculous keep, deep into its stone halls. Lukien followed close behind but did not say a word. Somberness infused the air. The Inhumans, as they were called, stood and talked in little huddles, their voices muted. Thorin knew they were worried, and with good reason. He dreaded the news he had to deliver, even though it seemed they already knew it. Soon they reached a large chamber off the hallway. The doors were open, revealing an interior well lit by candles and a wooden table filled with food and drink. The sight of it buoyed Thorin. He sat down without invitation, tore a chunk from a loaf of bread and poured a tall mug of ale as he chewed. Lukien took a chair across from him while Minikin closed the door, obviously shutting out unwanted ears.

"Well?" Thorin asked between bites. "Tell me what you know."

Lukien did the talking. He told Thorin about Insight, an amazing girl who could see the future, and how she had told them of Kadar's death. Thorin listened as he ate, skeptically enthralled. But he was distressed to learn that Insight hadn't told them everything; they still didn't know what had happened to the rest of Kadar's men.

"Dead," said Thorin as he lowered his mug. "I'm sure of it."

The news struck Minikin hard. "All of them?" She seemed unable to believe it. "How could your king be so ruthless?"

"He's not our king," said Lukien darkly. "He's not the Akeela we served, not anymore."

"Speak for yourself, Lukien," said Thorin. "I could have told you the moment I met Akeela what a demented little snake he was."

"You're wrong, Thorin," argued Lukien. "You never really knew him."

Thorin was incredulous. "How could you defend him? I just told you—he massacred those warriors! Probably the folk in the city, too!"

"He wouldn't," said Lukien. "Not the Akeela I knew."

"Oh, Great Fate. . . ." Minikin held up her hands. "It doesn't matter. His army is coming now and we must prepare ourselves."

Thorin looked at Minikin. "No offense, my lady, but I've seen what you have to work with here. They're all cripples and blind men."

Lukien gave a short laugh. "Believe me, Thorin, all isn't what it seems," he said, then proceeded to tell the baron about the real Grimhold, the town beyond the fortress, and how it was filled with legions of ablebodied men. "I've been training them and they're quick learners, Thorin," he said. "And there are plenty of weapons here, enough swords and shields for all of them."

Thorin was skeptical. "Akeela still has over a thousand men at least, Lukien."

"And we'll have at least that many ourselves, and this fortress to defend us," Lukien countered. "I know they don't look like much, but these people will surprise you, Thorin."

Thorin smiled. "They already have," he admitted. "All right, then. I'll help you with this army. But it won't be easy, and there's not much time."

"Rest first, Baron Glass," said Minikin. "There'll be time enough for war talk in the morning." She rose from the table and went to the door. "I'll leave you two now." But before she left she turned one last time and said to Thorin, "You've honored us, Baron. You may not think so, but you have."

As she closed the door behind her, Thorin pushed his plate aside with a heavy sigh. Suddenly he'd lost his appetite. "Ah, she has me wrong, Lukien. What kind of coward would leave a ruler's side like I did?" The stump of his arm began to itch, the way it always did when he was troubled. "Half a man, that's what I am. And not even a quarter of a soldier."

"Thorin, don't," said Lukien. He reached across the table and took the mug, pouring his friend another round. "Just rest now. There's no point in thinking about it."

"You weren't there, Lukien. You didn't see." Glass took the offered mug, but didn't drink. Instead he stared into it, and his own reflection sickened him. "He was magnificent, a real leader. He made his men proud. And I just left him there to die." He glanced up at Lukien. "How did he die? Did this girl tell you?"

Lukien shrugged. "He was killed in battle I suppose."

"Yes, but by who? Was it Trager?"

"I don't know," said Lukien. "Why do you ask?"

"Because that serpent came to deliver terms before the battle," spat Glass, "and he baited Kadar to fight him." He ground his teeth at the thought. "I just know he was the one that killed him. I just know it."

"It's what Kadar wanted," Lukien said softly. "It's what he had to do."

"I should have been out there fighting with the rest of them." A sudden rage boiled up in Glass. "Damn it all, look at me! I'm no better then these cripples we're protecting!" He suddenly wanted to fling the mug against the wall. "If I could have ridden after Trager. . . ."

"He would have killed you," said Lukien.

Thorin looked up angrily. Lukien was grinning. His companion's expression defused the baron's anger. "Probably," laughed Glass. "But it would have been a better death than to stay here and let him slaughter us."

"He won't slaughter us, Thorin. We can beat him."

"You're so sure?" Thorin asked. "Are these people so exceptional?"

"They're willing to fight, Thorin, and die if necessary."

"Ah, well, it's good that they're willing to die," said Thorin, "because Akeela is more than willing to kill them."

Lukien sat back, unamused. "It's their home," he said. "They want to defend it."

"And I admire that, truly," said Thorin. "But many will die, Lukien, you know that."

Nodding, Lukien replied, "I know. But maybe we can win. Doesn't that count for something?"

"It counts for everything. I taught you a long time ago that there's no honor in defeat. But even if we win, how many of these people will die?" Thorin leaned back, contemplating the horror of it. "Akeela's not a good man, not anymore. There's not a shred of decency in him. And he won't stop till he has you, Lukien. I just hope these people are prepared for that."

The Bronze Knight didn't answer. He fiddled with the pitcher of ale, obviously distracted.

"Lukien?" probed Thorin. "Are you listening to me?"

"Uh-huh."

Thorin leaned forward. "What are you thinking about?"

Lukien's lips twisted as he debated divulging his thoughts. Finally, he said, "Thorin, there's an armory down below this keep. It's full of old weapons that the Akari made years ago. I saw something down there that I just can't get out of my mind."

"What's that?"

"A suit of armor," Lukien replied. "But not just any suit. It's magical, like the amulets. It's possessed by one of these Akari spirits, a man who used to be a summoner."

"Summoner?" The word confused Thorin. "What's that mean?"

"I'm not really sure," confessed Lukien. "A summoner is someone like Minikin, I think. Someone who can summon spirits to help him. Anyway, this armor was remarkable. It was like nothing I've ever seen before, all black and shining like it was alive. And perfect, too, like it's never even been nicked by a blade. You can't even see where the hammer forged it; there's not a single mark."

"Interesting," said Thorin. "But I don't see your point."

Lukien glanced over his shoulder, then whispered, "It's called the Devil's Armor, Thorin. Minikin says the Akari gave it that name because the spirit that possesses it is evil. But listen—she says whoever wears the armor is invincible."

"Invincible?" laughed Thorin. "How's that possible?"

"I don't know; how's any of what the Inhumans do possible? The point is that Minikin really believes it, and after what I've already seen here I don't have any reason to doubt it. And if you saw this armor you'd know what I'm talking about."

Thorin immediately began getting ideas. "If what you say is true, this armor could be our savior."

"That's what I thought, too," said Lukien sourly. "But Minikin won't let me touch it. She says it's too evil, too powerful to be controlled. She claims that anyone that tries would come under the spell of the armor's spirit, or something like that." He sighed, shaking his head. "If only I could wear that armor. Then we could really even things up."

"Yes," agreed Thorin. His mind raced with the possibilities. Such armor could make him whole again. "You say Minikin has forbidden you to wear this armor?"

Lukien nodded. "Sadly, yes."

"Just you?"

"I know what you're thinking, Thorin. Forget it. Minikin won't let anyone use the armor, not us or one of her Inhumans. She told me the only reason it's still around is because she can't figure out how to destroy it. Imagine! Armor that can't be destroyed!"

Thorin did imagine it. The stump of his arm itched with anticipation. "Perhaps I can convince Minikin," he suggested. "If she sees that there's no other hope. . . ."

"It won't work," said Lukien. "I tried that on her already." He slumped back miserably. "What a waste." To Thorin's surprise he got up from the table.

"Where are you going?" asked the baron.

Lukien went to the door. "To think," he replied, then quietly left the room.

That night, Lukien did not sleep. He did not go to the room he shared with Gilwyn, for he did not want to face the boy, and he did not see Baron Glass again. Nor did he see Minikin, or anyone else. Instead he wandered the grounds of Grimhold for hours, alone with his thoughts, considering the mess he had made of his life and the bleak consequences he had fostered on the Inhumans. He went up to the observatory Minikin had shown him and stared at the village in the distance. It seemed safe and lovely to him, a haven for the Inhumans and their offspring. There, under the canopy of stars, he made his decision.

Lukien quickly made his arrangements.

Eventually he went to the stable where the horses and drowa and Gilwyn's kreel, Emerald, were kept. Minikin had showed him the stable on his fourth day in Grimhold, after she had revealed the full truth of the place. The stable, like the fortress, was built into the mountain itself, but faced the village side of Grimhold to keep it hidden. There were not many horses in the place, for most were kept in the village proper. Therefore, there was only one person needed to tend the animals, a hunchback with the horrible name of Monster. Lukien had been shocked when Minikin had told him Monster's name, but she had gently reminded him that such was the way in Grimhold—a place where slurs were worn proudly to show their ineffectiveness. And of course, Monster was nothing like his name. He was gentle and soft-spoken and always carried a cat with him, which he cooed to like a child and fed the best scraps from the kitchen. He was also immensely strong, stronger than any man his height could be by nature. As with all the Inhumans, Monster's abilities came from the supernatural, and he was so endowed with it that he could lift a boulder and move with the grace of a dancer, despite his horrible hump.

Because it was very late, Monster had gone to sleep long before Lukien arrived at the stable. Not surprisingly, the stable was unlocked. The few animals in the wooden stalls looked at him curiously as he entered, unaccustomed to being disturbed so late at night. Lukien had a lantern with him that shone in their eyes and on the saddles and tack along the stone walls. It was a remarkable place, really, capable of housing many more animals than the Inhumans had. Lukien carefully looked into each stall, knowing the animal he wanted. She was a mare named Gallant, a particular favorite of Minikin's and a stout-hearted beast. The little woman had showed her off proudly to Lukien, for she had been a gift from Kadar. Lukien found her stall and paused. The chestnut mare looked up at him, her face expressionless.

"Yes, you remember me, don't you, girl?" whispered Lukien. "Good. Don't be afraid. I won't hurt you."

He scanned the walls and saw a suitable saddle, the one Minikin herself used on the rare occasions that she rode the mare. More precisely, she was taken riding, she had told him, because her legs were too short to reach the stirrups. Lukien smiled as he recalled the story. Minikin was a remarkable woman. She didn't deserve to die.

As he stood in the darkness of the stable, Lukien realized that the plan had really been with him all along but it had taken Thorin's unwitting counsel to convince him of its rightness. The old baron was right—it wasn't about the amulets or vengeance on Grimhold. It was about him. The cold fact was that he had driven Akeela insane, because he had betrayed him and stolen his wife. And he'd been running from that fact for sixteen years. Tonight he would stop running.

For a brief time, he considered the Devil's Armor. It still seemed a shame to him that such a weapon should go to waste. But of course Minikin would never have given her permission. He would have to steal the armor, and he didn't want to steal again. Stealing—whether amulets or women— had ruined his life.

He glanced out through the stable doors, knowing dawn would soon arrive. But there was enough moonlight left to escape, and that was good. Outside he left waterskins and other essentials, and would secure them to the horse once her tack was ready. With no time to waste Lukien set to work. He got the saddle and all the other tack from the wall, working quietly but quickly to put them on Gallant. The mare was of an excellent temper and let him work without protest. She seemed to sense the urgency in him.

"Good girl," he said gently. "It's for the best, you'll see."

But of course the mare wouldn't return, and that saddened Lukien. Minikin would miss him, he was sure. And oddly, he would miss her, too, and Gilwyn and Thorin and all the Inhumans.

When he had saddled Gallant and secured his supplies to her tack, Lukien mounted the mare and rode her out of the stable. He glanced around to make sure no one was watching, then rode off into the waning moonlight for Jador.

53

Just past dawn, Gilwyn finally returned to his chamber after a long night with White-Eye. He was weary beyond words and eager for his soft bed. It had taken White-Eye hours to fall asleep. The news about her father had devastated her, and Gilwyn had been afraid to leave the girl alone. Suddenly life seemed to be spinning out of control. From one moment to the next he had gone from bliss to heartache, but at least he had been able to comfort White-Eye a little. He supposed that was something. As he walked the quiet hall to his chamber, he realized he might have very little time left with her. Foolishly he had assumed that Baron Glass and Kahan Kadar would be able to hold back the Liirians. He had been wrong, and he was ashamed now that he had not listened better to Lukien or helped the knight form his army. He'd been too lovestruck to see the truth, but that was all going to change now. Lukien and all of Grimhold needed him.

When he reached his chamber the door was slightly ajar. He paid it no attention as he slipped inside. The sun was already up, but if he could just get a couple of hours sleep, he'd be useful enough to help Lukien. He entered the room quietly, not wishing to disturb the knight. To his surprise Lukien was not in his bed, and the sheets looked undisturbed. Had he been working all night? The thought only worsened Gilwyn's shame. Exhausted, he went to his own bed across the room, sitting down to pull off his shoes. But as he worked the buckles on his unusual boot a fleck of white caught his eye. He turned to see a piece of folded paper on his pillow. He stopped unbuckling his boot and picked it up, at first thinking it was from White-Eye but then realizing that was impossible—he'd just left her. Lukien, perhaps? Or Minikin? When he read the note the contents shocked him to the core.

"Fate above," he whispered. "What the . . . ?"

The note was brief and succinct. It read simply,

Gilwyn,
I have gone off to Jador to face Akeela. He does not want the amulets. He just wants me. For the good of Grimhold do not follow.

It was signed *Your friend, Lukien.*

Then, almost as an afterthought, another line was written under the signature. Gilwyn's heart nearly broke when he read it.

One more thing—thank you for letting me see Cassandra again.

Gilwyn sat in stunned silence, unsure what to do. Lukien was a dead man now, surely. There was no way King Akeela would let him live.

"Gods, Lukien, what have you done?"

And what could be done, Gilwyn wondered? He didn't even know when Lukien had left the note, or how much of a lead he'd have already.

"It doesn't matter. I've got to do something. . . ."

Hastily Gilwyn rebuckled his boot and hobbled from the room as quickly as he could, carrying the little note in his hand. He needed to find Thorin at once. If they were to have any chance of catching Lukien, they would need to leave quickly. But he didn't even know where Thorin's chamber was, for he'd spent the night with White-Eye. Helplessly he looked around the hall of closed doors. Thorin might be in any one of them, or none of them. Gilwyn felt a twinge of panic. Every second lost was more assurance of Lukien's death, and he couldn't bear that. He had to do something. Finally, in angry frustration hé shouted, "Thorin, where are you?"

His call resonated in the stone hall. He heard grumbles from behind a number of doors, but no answer. So he again he cried, "Thorin!"

Down the hall a door flung open. The hunchbacked Monster stuck his angry face into the hall and hissed, "What are you doing, boy? Trying to wake up the whole keep?"

"Monster, I'm looking for Baron Glass. Have you seen him?" asked Gilwyn desperately.

"Baron Glass? Who's that?"

"He arrived last night from Jador," Gilwyn explained. "I need to find him at once."

The hunchback shook his big head. "Don't know him. Go back to bed."

"I can't, I have to find him," said Gilwyn.

"Well hold it down then!" snapped Monster, slamming his door in Gilwyn's face.

Frustrated, Gilwyn stood in the dark hall, madly trying to think. Then he remembered Farl, the houseboy assigned to him and Lukien. He hadn't seen much of the boy since that first day, but he knew his room was up on the next floor. Somewhere. So he hurried for the stairs at the end of the hall. The staircase wound up into another dark hall, this one also full of closed doors—except for one. In the center of the hall was an open door with candlelight flickering over its threshold. Gilwyn went to it at once and made a miraculous discovery.

"Farl!"

The boy was on the edge of his bed, pulling on his shoes. His blind eyes looked up at Gilwyn in alarm.

"Master Gilwyn!" he asked. "I was just getting up to fetch you and Master Lukien some breakfast."

"Forget breakfast, Farl. I need your help. Lukien's gone."

Farl got to his feet at once. "Gone? What do you mean?"

Gilwyn showed him the note. "He left this for me this morning," he said. "He's gone off to Jador. He must have left some time last night."

Farl didn't bother looking at the note. "Does Mistress Minikin know?"

"No, I don't think so," said Gilwyn. "Farl, I have to go

after him. But I need to find my friend, Baron Glass. Do you know where his room is?"

"Baron Glass? Oh, you mean the one that came last night! Yes, I know where his room is," said Farl. "It's just down the hall. But he's not there. I saw him with Mistress Minikin not long ago. She came to get him."

"Get him?" asked Gilwyn. "For what?"

"I don't know, Master Gilwyn. It's not my place to ask such things."

Exasperated, Gilwyn pressed, "Where did they go, Farl? Do you know?"

The boy shrugged. "Sorry, I don't. But you can try Minikin's chamber. Do you know where it is?"

"I'll find it," said Gilwyn, then hurried out of the chamber and back down the stairway. He knew Minikin's own chamber was somewhere on the ground floor of the keep, on the same level as his own chamber. Its exact location was a mystery, but he supposed someone would be walking the halls and could tell him. But as soon as he'd left the familiar area of the living quarters, Gilwyn regretted not waiting for Farl. Grimhold was a maze of hallways, and finding Minikin's chamber would be a nightmare. So instead of trying he headed for the main hall of the keep, the great entry hall where the gate was located and where he and Lukien had first entered the keep. There were always guards on duty there, men who would certainly know the whereabouts of Minikin's chamber. It took long minutes for Gilwyn to reach the hall, but when he did he found it nearly deserted. The keep was deathly quiet, but up ahead he heard voices from one of the great hall's chambers. Rounding a corner, he came to a room with an open door and the soft light of candles. The room was large and well-appointed, with a long wooden table and numerous chairs. He peaked his head carefully inside the chamber and saw Minikin at the head of the table. To Gilwyn's great astonishment, Thorin was with her. The two of them looked up from their cups of tea with troubled faces.

"Gilwyn, what are you doing here?" asked Thorin.

"Looking for you," replied Gilwyn. He entered the chamber, waggling the note in the air. "I got this note from Lukien. He's left, Thorin."

"We know, Gilwyn," replied Minikin. "That's what the baron and I have been discussing. Sit down, please."

"You know?" asked Gilwyn. "How?"

Minikin's smile was wan. "The Akari tell me things. Now sit, please."

Confused, Gilwyn took a chair next to Thorin. The baron sipped pensively at his tea, then put down the cup and looked at the boy. "Minikin came to my room an hour ago," he told Gilwyn. "She told me the news about Lukien. We knew you were with White-Eye and thought it best not to bother you. We didn't know he'd left you a note. May I see it?"

Gilwyn handed the note to Thorin. Minikin asked him how White-Eye was faring.

"She's all right, I think," said Gilwyn. "As good as can be expected, anyway."

Minikin smiled. "I'm glad she has you to comfort her. White-Eye is fond of you, Gilwyn."

Gilwyn felt his face go hot. "Thanks."

Baron Glass passed the note to Minikin. "Nothing really. It just says he's on his way to Jador."

Minikin frowned as she read the note. "Your friend is a stubborn man."

"Minikin, we have to go after him," said Gilwyn.

"We will," she replied.

The answer relieved Gilwyn. "Good. If Thorin and I leave now, we might be able to catch him before he reaches the city. I don't know what time he left, but—"

"Gilwyn, stop," said Minikin. "You're not going. Neither is Baron Glass."

"What? Why not?"

"Would I be sitting here drinking tea if I were going after him?" asked Thorin sourly. "Minikin has another plan."

"What plan?" asked Gilwyn angrily. "There isn't time for this! We have to go after him right now!"

"Easy, boy," commanded Minikin. "I want Lukien back as much as you do. But sending you or the baron after him isn't the answer. I've got someone better in mind. Someone with particular talents for the job."

"Who?" asked Gilwyn indignantly.

An unexpected voice replied, "Me."

Gilwyn turned to see a figure standing in the doorway, reedy-thin and shrouded in black cloth. He was taller than Gilwyn but his voice was young. Two pale gray eyes sparkled beneath his dark gaka, the only visible part of his face. Even his hands were clothed, covered in dark gloves. As he stepped into the room, he gingerly removed the gloves, laying them on the table and revealing a pair of bone-white hands. He then unwrapped his face and stooped to greet Minikin with a kiss. When he stood, his shocking features came fully into view. Gilwyn stared at him, astonished. He was barely a man, not much older than Gilwyn himself, with bright white hair and skin the color of milk. There was no color in him at all, not even in his silvery eyes. He drew back his bloodless lips in a thin smile, obviously entertained by the reaction of his audience. Minikin rose and took his hand.

"Gilwyn, Baron Glass . . . this is Ghost."

The young man inclined his head slightly. "Good to meet you," he said.

Thorin politely stood. "Uh, good to meet you, too . . . Ghost, is it?"

"That's right. Not a name I would have chosen for myself, but it's probably appropriate."

Thorin gave an uncomfortable smile. "Yes, I would say so."

Gilwyn stared at Ghost, perplexed by his snowy skin and icy gray eyes. "What are you?" he asked.

Before the man could reply Thorin said, "He's an albino. And you're staring, boy."

"Sorry," offered Gilwyn. "It's just that, well, I've never seen a person so white before. You really do look like a ghost."

The young man stuck his face into Gilwyn's. "Boo!" he shouted, then laughed. Gilwyn reared back, horrified by him and his odd humor.

"I sent for Ghost, Gilwyn," said Minikin. She took her seat again, guiding the strange fellow into the chair next to her. She continued, "He lives here in Grimhold, but he was out in the village visiting his children."

The thought of the man having children made Gilwyn squirm. A picture of weird, milk white babies flashed through his mind. "I've never seen an albino before," he said. For some reason, he already disliked the man. "Is that why you wear those robes, because of your skin?"

"That's right," replied Ghost. "If I went out without them I'd roast like a chicken." He chortled at his own joke, revealing teeth as white as the rest of him. "So," he said, "do I frighten you? I've frightened a lot of people, even my so-called parents."

"I'm not afraid of you," said Gilwyn. "I'm just. . . surprised."

"Ghost came to us when he was very young, Gilwyn," said Minikin. "I found him in Norvor. He wasn't as lucky as you, though. His mother didn't want him, and neither did anyone else in his village."

It seemed to Gilwyn that Minikin's words were meant to soften him. For her sake he replied, "I didn't mean to stare, Ghost. I'm sorry. I'm just upset. My friend Lukien has gone off for Jador."

Ghost nodded. "I know your troubles. That's why I'm here."

"Yes," said Thorin. "Explain that to me. Minikin, this is the man you mean to send after Lukien?"

Ghost said, "My appearance shouldn't trouble you, Baron Glass."

Glass smiled. "You know my name, eh? Lukien was right—you Inhumans are full of surprises."

"I think we should go after Lukien ourselves," Gilwyn piped in. "He's our friend and we owe him. And at least we know what he looks like."

"Gilwyn, be quiet," ordered Thorin. He looked plaintively at Minikin. "The boy does have a point, madam. I'm not sure what your reasoning is for sending Ghost here after Lukien. You told me he was perfect for the job, but, well, he's a bit odd looking. He'll only attract attention." He said to Ghost, "No offense, young man, but if you can't even go out in the sun. . . ."

"Ghost can handle the sun as long as he wears his coverings," said Minikin. "And he's well suited to the task."

Baron Glass frowned. "Tell me."

"I'll do better than that," said Ghost. "I'll show you."

He sat in his chair, smiling like a maniac at the two Liirians and not saying a word. Gilwyn and Glass watched him curiously, watched him sitting with his arrogant grin, then watched as he silently faded from view. The air around him wavered a moment, swallowing him up.

"What the seven hells . . . ?" Thorin got to his feet.

Minikin remained seated as if nothing had happened.

"Where is he?" asked Gilwyn.

"I'm still here," came Ghost's disembodied voice.

"Where?" asked Gilwyn.

"What are you, blind?" The voice laughed delightedly "Here!"

Minikin laughed too. "Seen enough?" she asked.

"I don't see anything!" said Thorin.

"Maybe not, but I assure you Ghost's here," replied the mistress. Gilwyn looked around the room, sure there was some trick to it. But when he felt a tap on his shoulder he shrieked.

"Get off me!" he cried, springing from his chair. The room filled with invisible laughter.

"All right Ghost, that's enough," said Minikin. "Let them see you."

As quickly as he'd disappeared, the albino became visible in a moment of shimmering air. He stood behind Gilwyn with his weird white grin on full display.

"That was amazing," said Glass breathlessly. "But how?"

"It is a lot to explain to you, Baron Glass," said Minikin, "but the Akari spirits allow us certain abilities. You have heard how the blind here can see and the deaf can hear, yes? It is the same with Ghost's spirit. With his help, Ghost can work on the minds of men. He was here all the time, of course, yet the spirit told you he was gone. And your mind believed it."

"Incredible," said the baron. He laughed, shaking his head in disbelief. "Truly amazing."

"If I'd kept talking your mind would have realized I was here," said Ghost. "You would have seen me eventually. But if I stay quiet, I can remain unseen much longer."

"Now you see why I've chosen Ghost to search for Lukien." Minikin leaned back in her chair, beaming proudly at her albino friend. "If Lukien has reached the city, he's already been captured. And if he's been captured, only Ghost will be able to find and get him out."

"That won't be easy," warned Thorin. "He doesn't even know what Lukien looks like."

"That's right," said Gilwyn. "We should go with him, at least."

Minikin shook her head. "No. I won't risk it. If either of you are seen you'll be captured on the spot. You'll be taken to Akeela and probably killed. At least Ghost would have a chance to escape."

"But he's our friend," Gilwyn protested. "We can't just sit here and do nothing!" He looked at Thorin pleadingly. "I'm right, Thorin, you know I am. Lukien needs us."

Thorin sighed heavily. "Gilwyn, I've already been through this with Minikin. I want to save Lukien too, but if there's any chance at all I think this fellow can do a better job than either of us." He told Ghost, "You have my blessing, son."

"Well he doesn't have mine!" Gilwyn flared. "What happens when he gets to Jador? How will he even reach Lukien?"

"I'll decide that when I get there," said Ghost. He'd lost his earlier humor and now was hard as nails.

"You call that a plan?" Gilwyn groaned.

"Do you have a better one?" snapped Ghost. He pushed Gilwyn's shoulder. "Well?"

"No," said Gilwyn. The admission angered him. "But I still think he needs us."

"Gilwyn, try to understand," said Minikin gently. "If you go to Jador and are captured, you'll be killed. What good would you be to Lukien then, hmm? Ghost at least can get past any guards. If Lukien is still alive, he'll have the best chance of helping him."

It was logical. Gilwyn knew Minikin was right. Yet it did little to ease his guilt. "I know," he said glumly.

"It's for the best, boy," added Thorin. "All right?"

Gilwyn nodded but said nothing.

"Good," said Minikin. She turned to the albino and said, "There isn't much time, Ghost. You'll have to leave at once."

"I'm ready, Minikin," said the young man with confidence.

"Just get to Jador and find out what you can," the mistress ordered. "Akeela has probably taken over Kadar's palace. If he has, that's where you'll find Lukien. There's a dungeon under the palace. Check there if you can."

"I will," said Ghost. He walked toward the door.

"And Ghost. . . ."

The albino paused. "Yes?"

"Just find Lukien. If you can help him, good. But if you can't, don't try to be a hero."

Ghost grimaced. "Are you in my head again, Minikin?"

Minikin's voice was iron. "Just remember your task. Don't try to go after Akeela. We're not murderers, remember."

The young man cocked a surprised eyebrow. "How could you think such a thing?" he asked mockingly.

"I'm not jesting, Ghost," said Minikin. "Now go. Be as quick as you can."

The albino bowed with a flourish then left the room, his dark robes trailing out behind him like a bridal train. When he was gone Minikin got to her feet and stretched her little body.

"I'm tired," she pronounced. She looked unimaginably exhausted. "I should go and check on White-Eye." Before leaving she paused in the doorway. "Baron Glass, we'll need to talk later. With Lukien gone, it will be up to you to the lead the Inhumans."

"I know, madam," replied Thorin. "I've been thinking about that."

"Good. If you have any ideas, let me know later."

She left the room, leaving Baron Glass and Gilwyn alone. The baron sat back in his chair, fiddling with his tea cup but not drinking. Gilwyn could tell he was worried about Lukien.

"Do you think he'll find him?" Gilwyn asked.

The baron shrugged. "I don't know. But it's best this way. If that miraculous boy can't find Lukien, who can?"

Gilwyn was about to reply, but bit back his answer.

Gilwyn stayed with Thorin for a few more minutes, talking about Lukien and how he had sacrificed himself. The baron was downhearted, not only because Lukien had left them, but because it reminded him how he had been unwilling to do the same himself. He told Gilwyn about how he'd left Kahan Kadar to fight alone, and how Trager had probably killed him. He hated himself for that, and the admission bothered Gilwyn. He knew Thorin was a good man. He knew his reputation and how he had once been a fine leader, and he knew Thorin wasn't a coward. Yet that was how Thorin saw himself now, and it troubled Gilwyn. So he stayed and talked to the older man longer than he wanted to, hoping to cheer him and rouse him from his self-pity.

"The Inhumans need you now," he told Thorin. "Now you can prove yourself."

The notion seemed to ease the baron's mind. "Yes," he agreed. "Yes, perhaps so. Lukien seemed sure he was making an army of these people. Do you think so, Gilwyn?"

Gilwyn had to admit that he hadn't spent much time with Lukien, or helped him form his army. "I don't know, Thorin," he said. "But you'd be a better judge of that anyway."

"Indeed I would," Thorin pronounced. He stood and nodded, the old arrogance coming back to his face. "Yes!"

Finally, he left Gilwyn in the council chamber. Gilwyn cursed his bad luck. He had lost a precious hour. Dashing out of the chamber, he glanced around the hall to make sure Minikin wasn't around, then proceeded back to his chambers where he found his gaka, still dirty from the ride to Grimhold. This he rolled into a bundle and stuffed under his arm. He looked around the room to see if there was anything else he wanted to take with him. There wasn't, but when he saw the chest near Lukien's abandoned bed a twinge of emotion caught his throat. It was the chest in which Lukien kept his bronze armor, and he hadn't even bothered to wear it.

"He doesn't plan to fight," whispered Gilwyn to himself. "He just plans to let them take him."

Taking a final glance around the room, Gilwyn left and rushed down the hall, heading toward the rear of Grimhold and the stables where Emerald was kept.

54

Lukien rode the mare as far as he could, stopping for rest only occasionally. But by the time Jador was finally in sight, Gallant collapsed beneath him. He had exhausted her, killing her, and abandoned her to the burning sands. But he knew he had to go on without her. It had taken them all day to come this far, and Gallant had served him valiantly. She seemed to have sensed the importance of his mission and so put every effort into helping him. Lukien was grateful. He stroked her unmoving head, little beads of sweat dripping from his forehead onto her chestnut coat.

"Minikin would be proud of you," he told the mare. His voice was hoarse from thirst and the desert's relentless dust. Overhead the sun beat down on him and the mare's prostrate body. Lukien hoped she would die quickly. Up in the bright sky, the black dots of wheeling buzzards appeared.

He went on.

Jador twinkled on the horizon, clearly in view yet still tauntingly far. He trudged through the sands, his throat screaming for water. An hour ago he had drunk the last of it, thinking he would make it easily. But the desert mercilessly sucked the moisture from him, and within an hour of walking he was ready to collapse. His blistered feet burned in their heavy boots; his thick hair suffocated his scalp. He had only the clothes on his back to weigh him down, yet he moved as if through mud. Finally, he reached the outskirts of Jador. Exhausted, he fell to his knees and looked upon the city, and what he saw appalled him.

Against the backdrop of bright buildings stood dozens of crudely erected crosses. From the crosses hung figures, men in black uniforms. They hung motionless from their ghastly perches, the hot sun bleaching their bloated faces. They had been arranged like a fence, each of them turned toward far-off Grimhold. The sight withered Lukien. He remained on his knees, staring at the grisly trophies, finally comprehending the depth of Akeela's madness.

"Great Fate. . . ."

He had heard the stories for sixteen years. But they had been like rumors to him, almost fantasies. He had never really quite believed them. Now, seeing the crucified warriors, his gentle memories of Akeela vanished. For a moment he thought of turning back, of going off to die in the desert and sparing himself the same heinous fate. But slowly he rose to his feet, resolving to go on. If Akeela was mad, he had made him so. It was right that he should die today.

He trudged along, his swollen feet dragging through the sands, and within a few long minutes came to the first section of road where the crosses were erected. The city was quiet. A few stray voices reached him, but no children, no happiness of any kind. He supposed the Jadori were huddled in their homes. Or worse. Through the streets he heard the clip-clop of hooves. Looking into the city he saw small groups of Royal Chargers on patrol. Exhausted, he leaned against one of the crosses, looking up at a dead figure hanging from its wrists. Dried blood ran down from its wounds. The head was tilted, staring down at Lukien. A buzzard picked at the lifeless eyeballs. Catching his breath, Lukien staggered into the city. He headed straight for the nearest patrol, calling out to them, his hoarse voice ringing through the avenue.

"Over here, butchers!"

The trio of horsemen turned, shocked at the sight of him. They galloped forward, drawing their swords. Lukien, unarmed, stood his ground. If they cut him down he wouldn't be able to face Akeela, so he shouted, "I'm Lukien of Liiria!"

The Chargers quickly drew back their steeds, sur-

rounding him. A young cavalryman lifted the visor of his
helmet and stared, plainly confounded.

"Lukien? The Bronze Knight?"

The others raised their visors to inspect him. "I don't
believe it," said one. The other squinted uncertainly.

"It is I, dogs," said Lukien in disdain. Despite his exhaustion he squared his shoulders.

"It can't be!" said the young one.

"Look at me!" growled Lukien. "Who else would I be,
idiot? I've come to see Akeela. Take me to him."

The horsemen looked at each other in confusion, neither
striking Lukien nor taking his word. Frustrated, Lukien
shouldered past them and continued on.

"Fools. Where is your bloody king?"

"Halt!" ordered the youngest soldier. He sped up behind
Lukien, slapping his back with the flat of his sword and
sending Lukien sprawling into the street. His jaw hit the
paving stones hard, splitting his lip. When he looked up the
three Chargers were over him again.

"You might just be stupid enough to be Lukien, traitor,"
said the young one. "Get up."

Lukien rose unsteadily to his feet. The young solider ordered one of his companions to ride ahead to the palace and
inform Akeela of their prize. The Charger galloped off
while the remaining two took up positions alongside
Lukien.

"That way," ordered the young one. With his sword he
pointed down the avenue. Up ahead stood the sparkling
palace of Kahan Kadar.

Satisfied, Lukien lurched forward.

Akeela had been in the palace's throne room when he'd
heard of Lukien's capture. The news had hit him like a
hammer. He had been studying Jador through the chamber's many splendid windows, watching his men secure the
city. But when the soldier had burst in with his story,
Akeela had nearly fainted, hurrying to the throne to sit
down. A few moments later, Trager had exploded into the
chamber. The general was thrilled by the news. A weird
giddiness twinkled in his eyes. They would wait for Lukien
together, he pronounced. Akeela hadn't argued with him,
for he could barely speak. His mind reeling, he had stayed

on the throne until his legs stopped wobbling. Then he crossed to a giant window and looked out over the city, awaiting Lukien. The vast throne room was silent except for the anxious tapping of Trager's foot. There was no one else in the chamber, and Akeela didn't bother talking to his general. He knew Trager would never leave him alone with Lukien, and he supposed that was for the best. It might be that Lukien had some trick up his sleeve and was coming to slay him. Or it could be as the soldier had claimed, that Lukien had come simply to speak to him. Akeela pondered the possibilities as he gazed out the window. Lukien might be planning to plead for mercy, if not for himself then for the wretches of Grimhold. If so, Akeela decided he would listen. He hadn't liked massacring Kadar's men, just as he hadn't enjoyed killing the Nithins. But they were all his enemies, he knew, and had stupidly opposed him.

"Why?" he asked himself.

"What's that?" asked Trager from across the room.

Akeela shook his head. "Nothing. I was talking to myself."

Trager laughed. "You've been doing that a lot lately."

"Quiet, you fool."

Trager's tittering abruptly stopped. Akeela continued staring out the window. It was very large, like everything in the throne room, and gilded with gold. Kadar had spared no expense in building his palace. It was beyond comfortable, and Akeela had relished his short time in it. He had even tested the dead kahan's bed, a huge and fluffy thing with lots of silk pillows and a soft, downy mattress. Akeela smiled when he thought of it. It hadn't taken much to occupy the city, not once they'd killed its last defenders. And crucifying them had been a master stroke. As Trager had predicted, the grisly act had kept the rest of the populace in line. After that, taking the palace had been effortless. Disheartened by the loss of their kahan, his servants had put up little fight. Trager and his army had spent the rest of the time resting and preparing plans to march on Grimhold. They had even been torturing townsfolk to find its exact location. So far, no one had given it up. They knew only that it was westward, in the mountains. But they would find it, Akeela knew. And when they did. . . .

Long minutes ticked by. Trager began pacing the throne room impatiently. Akeela remained arrow-straight at the window. There was a dagger in his belt for his own protection, one that he had never drawn in his entire ride south. Now he rested his hand on its pommel, waiting. Like the crucified on their crosses, he didn't move, not even when he heard footsteps approaching the throne room.

"It's them," Trager said excitedly.

Akeela nodded, not taking his eyes from the outdoors. "Bring him in here."

Trager went to the doors. Akeela could see his reflection in the glass. As the great doors to the throne room parted, in stumbled a man Akeela hardly recognized. Behind him came two guards, who pushed him roughly into the chamber. Trager stepped back, inspecting him. Even in the glass Akeela could see the general's triumphant grin. The man that was Lukien was barely in the room before Trager's fist slammed into his stomach. The blow jolted Akeela, but he didn't move or say a word as Lukien sank with a cry to his knees.

"Is it him?" Akeela asked.

Trager replied, "Yes!"

Akeela didn't know what to feel. He was both elated and frightened, and still unable to turn away from the window. He said to Trager, "Dismiss your men and close the doors."

Trager did as ordered, leaving the three of them alone in the throne room. In the glass Akeela saw Lukien struggle to his feet. He stared across the room at Akeela's back. Trager stood beside him with his arms folded, grinning.

"I can't believe you've come here, Captain," said Trager acidly. "You've saved us all a great deal of trouble."

"Akeela, look at me," croaked Lukien. His voice was hoarse. He chanced a step forward. "Akeela—"

Trager struck him again, buckling him. "You don't address the king, dog!"

"Don't, Will," Akeela ordered. "No more."

Finally he found the courage to turn around. Lukien was before him, tottering to his feet. But he was not the beautiful man Akeela remembered. His hair was rough and filthy, full of sand, and his face was streaked with age and dirt. A patch covered his left eye; the other one was bloodshot. Yet still it was Lukien. Still, after sixteen years, he was unmistakable. When he saw Akeela his lips twisted into what could have been a smile, but his one eye showed his remarkable sadness. For Akeela, the sight of him was heartbreaking.

"You shouldn't have come," said Akeela softly. "You still might have escaped me."

Lukien's expression didn't change. "No more running," he said wearily. "I've come to give myself up to you, Akeela. Do what you will."

"Where are the amulets?" Akeela asked.

"I don't have them." Lukien shrugged. "They weren't ours to begin with, Akeela."

Trager came forward and seized his arm. "Where are they?"

"I don't have them," snapped Lukien, shaking off Trager's grip.

"Who does, Lukien?" pressed Akeela. "Are they in Grimhold?"

Lukien's gaze narrowed on him. "Did you kill Figgis, Akeela?"

The question rattled Akeela. It was like they were young again, with Lukien in control. "I'll ask the questions," he said.

"Did you?" Lukien's expression was grave, as if he already knew the truth. "He was a good man, Akeela. He was your friend."

"I have no friends!" raged Akeela. Spit flew from his mouth as he stepped toward Lukien. "Were you my friend, Lukien? Was Cassandra?"

"Yes," replied Lukien. "We loved you."

The answer enraged Akeela. His hand shot out and slapped Lukien's face. "How dare you!" he seethed. "How dare you speak of love to me! Would a man who loved me take my wife? Would a wife who loved me betray my bed? Answer me, you gutter rat!"

Lukien's face was forlorn. "Yes," he said simply. "We would."

"Why did you come?" asked Akeela. His voice was shaking. So were his hands. "Why give yourself up to me?"

"For the sake of the Inhumans," said Lukien. "The people of Grimhold."

Akeela blanched. "Inhumans? This is what they call themselves?"

"Yes, but they're not what you think. They're special people," Lukien argued. "They have deformities, some of them, but they're not weak. And they're not worthless. They deserve better than to have you slaughter them."

"Ha!" laughed Trager. "You won't save them, Captain, or earn our pity."

Akeela raised a hand to silence him. He asked Lukien, "Did you think you'd find mercy in me? After what you've done to me?"

"I've come to give myself up," replied Lukien. "It's me that you want, I know that. Now you can do whatever you want with me."

"To save Grimhold?" asked Akeela bitterly. "Nothing more?"

"And because I've wronged you," said Lukien. He looked straight into Akeela's eyes. "I've wronged you, Akeela. And I've made a monster of you."

Akeela stood there, staring and shaking. A monster. Was that what he was now? Did the whole world think so?

"I am not a monster," he declared. "I'm a great king. I brought wisdom to the world."

Lukien shook his head. "No. That was your great dream, but that was a long time ago. You're merciless, Akeela. Look outside that window. Look at the men you've crucified."

"Enemies, Lukien. Men who opposed me. Enemies like you."

"Then I was right," said Lukien. "All this is because of me. Well, it can end now." He stretched out his hands to show how helpless he was. "I'm here, Akeela. I'm yours. Kill me and end this horror."

"Oh, you will die," Trager assured him. "But not before you tell us where Grimhold is." He smiled like a wolf. "And I'm going to enjoy persuading you."

Lukien ignored him. Instead he kept his gaze on Akeela. "You can torture me but I won't tell you. The Inhumans are good people and I won't betray them."

"No," spat Akeela. "You'd never betray a bunch of freaks. Just your own king!"

"Look at me, Akeela. I'm finished. You've beaten me. Spare the Inhumans. They've done nothing to you."

Akeela studied Lukien's ruined face, the deep lines in his red skin. The sight was overwhelming. "Yes," he said softly. "I have beaten you, haven't I?" He reached out and gingerly touched Lukien's eyepatch, carefully probing the flesh. Lukien winced but did not pull away. "How did this happen?"

"In Norvor," replied Lukien. "A long time ago."

"It changes you. You look . . . older."

"We've all changed, Akeela," said Lukien. "Especially you. You used to be a good man, remember? You used to be loved."

Akeela gave a bitter grin. "They loved a fool, then. I'm not that stupid any more."

"But you can still be good. You can still do one good thing," urged Lukien. "You have me now. You don't need to ride for Grimhold."

"If you think that will save you from me, think again," said Trager.

Lukien turned on Trager. "Torture me, then!" he cried. "Torture me, kill me, do whatever you want! But I won't tell you where Grimhold is, Trager. And Akeela, I know there's good left in you. You can kill me, you have that right. But if you kill the Inhumans you'll just be a murderer."

Unable to stand it, Akeela looked away. The accusations were stinging. And just seeing Lukien again made him weak. He turned back to his window. "You will die, Lukien," he said. He didn't want to make the decree, but he had come too far now. Too much had happened to simply forget. "On the morrow, at dawn. I will kill you myself."

He saw Lukien's shocked expression in the glass.

"I must do this, Lukien. You must die for what you've done, and I must be your executioner."

To Akeela's surprise, Lukien simply nodded. "If that's your wish, I accept it. But what of Grimhold?"

Akeela turned to regard him. "Aren't you listening? You're going to die, Lukien."

"I heard you. Now please, answer me. Will you seek out Grimhold?"

Akeela was dumbstruck. "Why are you thinking about

them? Your life is over! Doesn't that mean anything to you?"

"They're worth saving," argued Lukien. He went to Akeela, almost pleading. "I've been with them, and I know they're good people. They've done you no harm. And. . . ." He hesitated a moment. "And Cassandra thought they were worth saving, too."

"What?" Akeela's face contorted.

"It's true," Lukien went on. "When she learned of your plans to ride for Jador, she sent for me. She wanted to come here with me, to give back the amulets and warn them about you."

"That's not true!"

"It is!" insisted Lukien. "She saw the madness in you. She told me it was like a disease, and now that I'm here looking at you I can see it too."

The revelation staggered Akeela. He fell back against the window. "Cassandra loved me," he whispered. "I know she did."

"She did, Akeela," said Lukien. "But she knew how sick you are. And she would never have wanted you to kill the Inhumans. If her memory means anything to you—"

"Her memory is all I have because you took her from me," Akeela groaned. "And you killed her." He looked at his old friend in disbelief. "You killed her, Lukien. How could you have done that? You say you loved her yet you killed her."

Lukien looked down at the floor, unable to meet Akeela's accusative gaze. "That's why I deserve death," he said softly.

"And die you shall," said Trager. He took hold of Lukien's arm again. "Let me take him below, Akeela. Let him sweat out his last hours in a cell."

Still shaking, Akeela said, "Yes. Yes, take him below."

Trager spun Lukien toward the door. "Come along, Captain. We've got a nice room prepared for you."

"Akeela, tell me you'll spare them!" Lukien shouted.

"Move!" ordered Trager, nearly pushing him over.

"Akeela, tell me!"

"Take him to the cellars," said Akeela. Then, "I will think on what you've told me, Lukien."

"What?" erupted Trager. He stopped shoving Lukien

and glowered. "Akeela, don't listen to his lies! You've come all this way. Don't turn back now."

"Should we kill good people, Will?" asked Akeela.

"They have your amulets!" said Trager. He pointed at Lukien. "And they've harbored this scoundrel! Good people? Freaks, Akeela. Enemies!"

Akeela thought for a moment, his mind shredded by the two arguments. Desperate to be alone, he waved at Trager to go. "Take him," he ordered. "And leave me alone."

Trager grunted unhappily, then opened the doors of the throne room. Two soldiers were waiting there. Immediately he barked at them to take hold of Lukien. Akeela watched as they dragged the knight from the chamber. When they had all gone he slumped down into the ornate throne. The meeting had rattled him. He heard Lukien's voice over and over in his head, speaking of Cassandra. Suddenly he was desperate for a drink.

No, he corrected himself. *Not just one drink.*

Tonight he wanted to get horribly drunk. Without the help of alcohol, he knew he'd never be able to face the dawn.

55

After a full day's ride, Gilwyn finally reached Jador at dusk. The city gleamed across the sands, beckoning him forward like a beacon in the ebbing sunlight. He was exhausted, but he still had enough water in his pouches for a celebratory drink. He undid one of the waterskins from Emerald's harness and took a long, satisfying drink. He was proud of the journey they'd made, and conveyed this pride to the kreel with his mind. The reptilian response was like a silent purring in his brain. They had snuck out of Grimhold without incident, and no one had followed. Gilwyn didn't know if Minikin had discovered he was gone, though he supposed she had by now. It didn't matter. He had reached Jador. Simply by pointing the kreel's nose east and telling her to find "home," she had sprinted across the desert almost nonstop. And though Gilwyn could feel her exhaustion, he could also tell that she was eager to go on, to finish the journey they had started together.

But they couldn't go on. Just in sight of their destination, Gilwyn got down from her back.

"That's it," he told the creature, patting her long neck. You can't go any further with me."

The reptile's eyes blinked at him in confusion. He smiled sadly at her.

"You have to wait for me here," he explained. "I can't risk losing you, Emerald. The Liirians might kill you on sight. And if I do make it out again, I'll need you to take me back to Grimhold."

Emerald replied with a silent, almost human apprehension. Gilwyn knew she objected to the word if.

"All right, *when* I make it out," he told her. "Either way, I'll need you here." He looked back the way they'd come. There were some hills in the distance with dry, scraggly shrubs. "There." He directed the kreel's attention toward the hills. "If you wait there for me you won't be seen. And it's getting dark. You'll be safe."

If Emerald were human she would have shaken her head. She looked toward the city.

"No," said Gilwyn, "it's not that far. I can make it even with my bad foot." Gently he stroked the creature's neck. "I'll take water with me. I'll be fine."

His reassurance hardly assuaged the kreel, but Emerald lowered her head submissively.

"Good," said Gilwyn. "Now go. I'll be back as soon as I can." He tied the waterskin to his belt, then turned toward Jador. The dark was coming quickly—he would have to hurry. He took a few steps then turn back to see Emerald dutifully watching after him. "Go!" he shouted. "I mean it!"

Emerald turned and walked toward the hills. Gilwyn smiled. She was a fine kreel, and he had begun to understand the often talked about bond between a soldier and his horse. Like Teku, Emerald had already become a friend. He was already missing both of them, but he turned back toward the city and walked slowly toward it, his bad foot sinking awkwardly into the sand with each step. Jador quickly took shape in the darkening sky. Gilwyn immediately noticed the palace near the edge of the city; if that's where Lukien was, he would find him quickly. But then he noticed other structures as well, things he'd never seen before. He squinted across the last stretch of desert, trying to make out the shapes. They were crosses. Curious, he continued toward them. A minute later came the grisly revelation. There were men on the crosses. Dead men. Gilwyn stopped in his tracks, his feet frozen, his heart pounding in his chest. He stared at the crucified figures, shocked yet unable to look away. They were ghastly, motionless and bloated, their heads lolling forward in death. Buzzards and other birds picked at their faces, feasting on the soft flesh. A wave of nausea overcame Gilwyn. He sunk down to his knees, thinking he might vomit. Quickly he undid the waterskin from his belt and took a drink, trying to steady himself. Suddenly his idea to save Lukien seemed doomed. He stared at the city, wondering if he should go on, or if one of the gruesome figures hanging from the crosses was Lukien himself. But no, he didn't think so. From the looks of their black garb they were Jadori warriors, probably the last of the city's defenders.

"King Akeela," he whispered softly. "How could you?"

It didn't seem possible that the man who'd built Liiria's great library could do something so horrid. Not Akeela, not a man who so loved books and learning. It was incomprehensible to Gilwyn, and he refused to believe it. He recalled his brief encounter with General Trager, and all the terrible things Lukien had said about him.

"It's Trager," he said to himself. "It has to be."

His resolve strengthened, he got to his feet. He had come for Lukien and he wouldn't retreat, no matter how many frightful warnings Trager hung in the streets. So he trudged forward, blocking the crosses from his mind and heading straight toward Kadar's usurped palace. He was almost at the outskirts of the city when a voice made him jump.

"Toms!"

Gilwyn let out a surprised cry, spinning to see who was behind him. Ten feet before him was a black-robed figure on a large kreel. Gilwyn panicked, not knowing who it was until the man unwrapped his headpiece, revealing his bone-white face.

"Ghost!"

Ghost rode angrily toward him. "What are you doing here?" he demanded.

"How'd you find me?" asked Gilwyn.

"I've been camped outside the city, waiting till dark," said Ghost. "Now answer my question."

"I've come to help Lukien," declared Gilwyn firmly.

Ghost got down from his kreel and towered over the boy. "And just what do you think I'm here for, the view? Does Minikin know you're here? No, of course she doesn't. You came out here on your own, didn't you?" He looked around. "How did you get here?"

"Well, I didn't walk," snapped Gilwyn. "Obviously I took a kreel, like you did. She's in those hills a little way back."

"Good. Then you can just go on back there and ride home to Grimhold." Ghost took his arm and shoved him toward the hills. "Move."

Gilwyn angrily shook off his grip. "I'm not going anywhere. I've come to help Lukien and I'm not leaving without him."

"You can't help Lukien, you stubborn fool! Didn't you hear what Minikin said?"

"Shhh!" urged Gilwyn. Quickly he glanced toward the city, afraid someone would hear. "Keep your voice down."

"I will, just as soon as you stop arguing with me," said Ghost. Now that the sun was down he kept his face exposed to the air. Remarkably, his expression softened. "I know you want to help your friend, but there's nothing you can do. You don't have my abilities and you're. . . ." He paused. "Well, you know."

"You mean I'm deformed, is that it?" asked Gilwyn. "Well don't go looking in any mirrors, friend."

"I didn't mean—"

"I know what you meant," said Gilwyn angrily. "You think just because I have a clubbed hand and foot that I can't do anything. Well, I got all the way out here on my own, didn't I? By the Fate, I've come all the way from Liiria! I can take care of myself. And I can help Lukien."

Ghost sighed and looked toward the city. "Someone's going to see us," he muttered.

"That's right," said Gilwyn. "And if they see you arguing with me then your plan is finished."

"So what are you saying, that you want to get caught?" asked Ghost. He frowned. "Just what do you expect to do here? Walk right in and demand they release your friend?"

"Something like that," said Gilwyn. He hadn't really thought about it much, but seeing the grisly crosses had given him an idea. "I'm going to see King Akeela. I'm going to plead for Lukien's life."

Ghost laughed, covering his mouth to keep the sound from carrying through the empty streets. "Oh, yes," he chortled. "That's a great plan. Brilliant! What makes you think that madman Akeela will even listen to you?"

"Because I know him," argued Gilwyn. "I know what he was like before all this madness happened to him. If I can just get him to listen—"

Ghost abruptly turned his back. "Go home," he said as he mounted his kreel. "Go back to Grimhold where it's safe."

"I won't!" Gilwyn shouted.

"Quiet!"

"I don't care who hears me, Ghost," Gilwyn warned. "If I'm captured they'll just take me to Akeela."

"Or kill you," said Ghost.

Gilwyn shrugged. "Maybe. But if they find you with me then you'll die too."

"Great Fate almighty," groaned the albino. "What do you want from me?"

"I want you to come with me," said Gilwyn. "Make yourself so people can't see you, then follow me. I'll get you into the palace. Then maybe we'll both be able to free Lukien."

To Gilwyn's surprise Ghost considered the plan. His gray eyes narrowed in thought. "I'll admit, I don't really have a way of getting inside the palace," he said. "But I won't be able to help you. Once you're inside, you're on your own. If I have to save both of you—"

"Don't worry about me," said Gilwyn. "Just stay with me. Let me try to talk to Akeela if I can. At least I'll be able to find out where they're keeping Lukien."

"Sure," said Ghost with a laugh, "as they take you down into the dungeon, that's where I'll find Lukien!"

Gilwyn had to admit that was a risk, but it was one worth taking. "If I can just get to see Akeela," he said hopefully. "Maybe I can convince him to let Lukien go."

"You're a fool to think so," said Ghost. Then he smiled and added, "But you're brave, I'll give you that. Start walking, Gilwyn Toms. I'll be with you."

"Will I be able to see you?" Gilwyn asked.

"Probably. It depends on how much you concentrate. But don't worry—I won't leave you, not unless I must." Ghost got down from his kreel again, then patted the creature's rump as he directed it toward the hills. He turned back to Gilwyn with a mischievous grin and gestured toward the waiting palace. "After you."

Taking a deep breath to steady himself, Gilwyn proceeded into the city. He moved cautiously, trying to quell his fear as he looked down the narrow avenues. The streets of Jador were deserted, the homes and shops closed up tight. With evening came the moonlight and a few candles in the windows, though most were shuttered and lifeless. There was very little sound, only the stray voices of Liirian soldiers, carrying endlessly through the echoing streets. Once proud and beautiful, Jador was now a silent, somber place, and even the palace seemed to be mourning. Gilwyn could see it clearly on the edge of the city, surrounded by its lovely gardens and mosaic statues. The first soldiers came into view, milling around gardens without care. Gilwyn braced himself.

"Ghost," he whispered, "are you with me?"

The answer was as faint as a breeze, heard mostly by the mind rather than the ears. "Behind you. Not far."

Gilwyn turned to search for the Inhuman, but saw no one. He paused, concentrating, then detected flashes of the albino against the nearest building. Ghost was smiling.

"Go on," he urged quietly. "I'm with you."

"All right," said Gilwyn. His nervousness spiked as he entered the grounds of the palace, passing a wall of high, well-manicured hedges, the outer ring of the garden. Ahead of them, a foursome of Liirian soldiers, all Royal Chargers from the look of them, were carousing in the garden, stretching out on the ornate stone benches and laughing. So lost were they in their good humor that they did not see Gilwyn until he was almost upon them. Once again that nagging yen to turn and run came over Gilwyn, but before he could decide one of the men glanced over at him, looked away as if nothing was interesting, then looked back with his mouth agape. The soldier sprang to his feet. Terrified, Gilwyn nonetheless stood his ground.

"You there," the soldier called. He seemed more shocked than angry. "What are you doing here, boy?"

The foursome all got to their feet and headed toward him. Gilwyn held his breath, then heard Ghost's reassuring voice in his head.

I'm right here, said the voice. *I've got my knife and I won't let anything happen to you.*

Gilwyn found the comment only a little reassuring.

Though the soldiers didn't draw their weapons, they quickly encircled him.

"Who are you, boy?" they demanded. One of them stared hard at Gilwyn, then gasped when he noticed Gilwyn's hand and boot. "You're the boy from the library!" Quickly he grabbed hold of Gilwyn's arm, shaking him. "You're Gilwyn Toms, aren't you?"

"Yes," said Gilwyn shakily. "I've come to talk—"

The soldiers drew their blades. "Where are the others?" they demanded. They quickly scanned the garden and beyond.

"I'm alone," Gilwyn insisted, sure now that they couldn't see Ghost. Nor in his fear could he. "I've come to talk to King Akeela."

"What?" The man holding him pulled him into the garden. "What are you talking about? You bring a message?"

Thinking fast, Gilwyn said, "Yes, a message. I have word from Grimhold."

"What word?" asked one of them. He put the tip of his blade to Gilwyn's chest. "Speak it."

"I can't." Gilwyn put up his hands pleadingly. "I can only tell my message to the king."

"You've come for the Bronze Knight, haven't you?" the men pressed.

"No! Lukien came on his own, to give himself up. I bring a message from the Mistress of Grimhold herself, I swear!"

Ask them if Lukien still lives, came Ghost's voice suddenly. *Find out where he is.*

The voice was like an annoying fly buzzing in Gilwyn's head. "Please," he told the guards, "I'm not armed. I'm just a messenger. If you could take me to see the king."

Lukien!

Shut up! Gilwyn cried silently. He smiled nervously at the guards. "You can look for yourselves," he said, "but you'll see that I'm not lying to you. There's nobody with me."

"We'll do that," sneered the man with the sword. He snapped his fingers at two of his comrades, ordering them to check the area. "I'll take care of the boy."

"You'd better take me to Akeela," Gilwyn warned. "I have important news for him. If he finds out you've delayed it he won't be happy."

The man thought for a moment, then nodded. "I don't see the harm in telling him you're here. But if you're lying. . . ." He pushed on the sword until its point bit through Gilwyn's shirt and cut the skin. "I'll peel you like a grape." Then he sheathed his sword and walked off, ordering the remaining soldier to bring Gilwyn along. Relieved, Gilwyn stumbled after them as quickly as he could. His foot ached but he kept on, keeping pace with the soldiers as they left the garden and entered the palace. There, more soldiers were on patrol, though most of them were hardly at attention. When they saw Gilwyn they forgot their tasks and peppered their companions with questions. The men leading Gilwyn said they were taking him to the king and asked where Akeela was.

"In his chamber," one of them replied. He pointed down the hall toward a polished marble staircase.

His chamber? wondered Gilwyn. Certainly they meant Kadar's, which he already knew was in a tower of the palace. The soldiers led him toward the stairs. Halfway up the marble walkway, a grim figure blocked their way. The soldiers stopped abruptly.

"My lord," said the lead man in a panic. He and his companion bowed. Gilwyn looked up into the confused face of a man he'd never seen, yet whose identity he knew instantly. The man stared back at him.

"Charger?" asked the man. "Who is that boy?"

The soldier replied, "My lord, I'm sorry to disturb you. We found this boy in the garden. He claims to have a message for you from Grimhold."

Gilwyn was nearly speechless. King Akeela was an awesome sight, the very epitome of madness with his twisted features and rumpled garb. He clung to the wall of the staircase, his nails digging between the bricks to keep from falling. His eyes glowed an itchy red.

"King Akeela," said Gilwyn. He brushed past the soldiers and took a cautious step upward. "My lord, do you know who I am?"

The king's eyes tried to focus. "I don't know you."

His voice was badly slurred. Gilwyn tried to smile, knowing this was his only chance. "My lord, my name is Gilwyn Toms. My mother was Beith Toms. She worked for you in Lionkeep for years." He held out his clubbed hand for

Akeela to see. "You sent me to work in the library, remember?"

Akeela drifted down the stairs until he faced Gilwyn. There he studied him, his heavily alcoholed breath striking Gilwyn's face. "I remember," he said softly. "Yes, the library boy. The cripple."

"No, not a cripple, my lord." He lifted his foot. "See? Figgis made this boot for me so I could walk."

Akeela's expression collapsed. "Figgis."

"My lord, you should go back to your chamber," suggested one of the soldiers. "You're . . . indisposed."

"I am not," Akeela shot back angrily. But his face softened as he said to Gilwyn, "You're a traitor, young Toms. You sided with my enemies." The fact plainly saddened him. "Why?"

"My lord, I must speak to you," said Gilwyn. "Could we talk, please? I have important things to tell you."

"Please, my lord," interrupted the lead Charger. "You really should get back to your chamber." He took hold of Gilwyn's arm again, waiting for the king to reply. "My lord? Your chambers?"

"Yes. Yes, all right," Akeela agreed. He pointed a bony finger at Gilwyn. "But I tell you, young Toms, if you've come to plead for your friend Lukien you're too late." He turned and started back up the stairway.

"Too late?" asked Gilwyn. "Gods above, you killed him?"

"Not yet," said Akeela, "but I will. He dies at dawn. Now come and tell me your news."

Gilwyn breathed a sigh of relief. In his mind, Ghost did the same. He was glad the albino was still with him, and still apparently invisible. As the soldiers pushed him up the stairs, he concentrated, trying to catch a glimmer of Ghost. He couldn't, but supposed the man was somewhere behind him. At the top of the stairs Akeela continued down another fabulous hall, swaying as he walked. The way was lined with gilded mirrors and golden sconces, each of them aglow with a separate candle. Gilwyn prepared himself, his mind racing with ideas. He still wasn't sure what he would say to the king—he obviously had no message from Minikin. But if he could just talk to him, just for a little while, he might be able to breach the king's insanity.

The hallway quickly gave way to a giant, doorless chamber with a high-domed ceiling and silvery-white walls. Exquisite furniture with turned, brightly polished wood decorated the tiled room, while a beautiful starburst mosaic spread its orange fingers to all corners of the room. The requisite collection of colorful Jadori pillows were scattered about, inviting relaxation.

Moonlight poured through the many windows, bouncing off the chamber's many mirrors. It was a place fit for a king, but Akeela had apparently abused it, for there were dirty glasses everywhere and half-drunken pitchers of wine. Akeela's own cape lay unceremoniously on the floor near the entrance. Boot marks on its black fabric made it look like a doormat. Akeela meandered to a tall chair near one of the room's windows and plopped into it wearily. Next to it was a pedestal with a pitcher of ruby-red wine and a filthy, tipped over glass. Akeela took the glass and poured himself a liberal helping of the wine. As he sipped he waved the soldiers out of the room.

"Leave me with the boy," he said.

One of the soldiers smiled politely and said, "Perhaps that's unwise, my lord. We can stay and protect you."

"Protect me from what?" asked Akeela. He jerked a contemptuous thumb toward Gilwyn. "Him? He's a cripple."

"Yes, my lord, but—"

"Oh, shut up and wait outside," said Akeela wearily. "Toms, sit down with me."

As the soldiers departed, Gilwyn moved warily into the chamber. Akeela's red eyes studied him, not even hinting at his intent. Gilwyn wondered about a man who would grant him such easy access. Clearly, he truly was mad. One look around the room could tell a blind man that. There was a long couch opposite Akeela's chair. He gestured to it with his glass, slopping wine over the edge.

"Sit down, boy," he commanded.

Gilwyn did so, falling into the soft green cushions. Frantically he groped for an argument, some way to reach the king. Earlier, when he'd spoken to Ghost, the first inklings of a plan had come to him. Now it was time to test his theory. Terrified, he wondered if Ghost was still with him, but in his nervousness couldn't concentrate enough to see him.

"So you bear a message you say," said King Akeela. "Speak it."

Gilwyn hesitated, fumbling for words. "My lord honors me with this audience," he said. "I'm truly humbled."

The king yawned. He looked unspeakably tired.

No, thought Gilwyn then. *He looks pathetic. It's like talking to a little boy.*

"My lord," he continued, "my word from Grimhold is just this—they aren't your enemies. They're just people like me, the kind of people you once wanted to help." He put out his bad hand again. "You're right, my lord—I can't hurt you. Neither can the folk of Grimhold. And they don't want to. They just want to live in peace and be left alone."

There, he'd said it. He watched Akeela for a reaction. Surprisingly, the king let out a jaded laugh.

"You make the same argument Lukien did, young Toms," he said. "I'm not impressed. And if that's all you have to tell me, you can join your traitorous friend in the cellars."

A ripple of panic went through Gilwyn. "No, my lord, listen to me—"

"You haven't come to tell me anything new," Akeela interrupted. "You've just come to plead for Lukien." He put down his glass with an angry groan. "Fate above, that's always the way it is for him! Always he has the power of men's hearts. . . ." He closed his eyes. "Don't tell me how good a man he is, Gilwyn Toms. Don't tell me how his heart is true and how sorry he is. He killed my wife."

"I know," said Gilwyn. "I haven't come to argue his innocence. He's wronged you, my lord. But surely there's forgiveness in you." Gilwyn smiled at him. "I know there is. Why else would you even be speaking to me?"

"Because it amuses me," said the king.

"No," said Gilwyn. "You want to talk to me. I risked coming here because of all the faith Lukien still had in you. And because I know from Figgis what a special man you used to be. And look, here you are, talking to me instead of throwing me into a dungeon." Gilwyn leaned forward for emphasis. "You're still Akeela the Good."

Akeela laughed bitterly. "Akeela the Drunk, you mean. Akeela the Butcher. That's what they're calling me, you know. Even my own men. They don't think I hear them whispering, but I do."

"Then they're wrong about you, my lord," pressed Gilwyn. "They don't know the man you were."

"And you do?" asked Akeela. "Hmmph. A young boy's faith. How charming and useless."

"I do know what you were like, my lord," said Gilwyn. He knew he had to press on, to not be deterred by the king's madness. "I know that you loved reading and books, and that you loved Cassandra more than anything in the world."

Akeela's face grew sad. "Yes," he nodded. "I did."

"And I know that you loved Lukien, too."

Again Gilwyn watched for a reaction. This time it was slower to come, but soon Akeela's sad expression twisted into something like agony. He couldn't speak. He seemed on the verge of tears. Gilwyn seized the chance. He rose from the coach and approached the king, dropping to one knee in front of him.

"My lord," he said gently, "I really do have a message for you."

With bloodshot eyes Akeela looked up hopefully. "Do you? Tell me."

"This," said Gilwyn. Once again he put out his hand for Akeela, this time laying it in his lap. The king looked at it curiously, but did not understand.

"Your hand? What of it?"

"My hand and my foot have been clubbed since I was born," said Gilwyn. "In another land, I might have been discarded. Once my mother died there would have been no one to care for me. I would have been a beggar."

Slowly Akeela began to understand. He said with a drunken smile, "But you're not a beggar."

"No," said Gilwyn, "because I had a place to go. A place that you built, my lord. My mother told me about the time you first saw me. Do you remember that, my lord?"

"Yes," said Akeela softly. His mind tripped back through the years. "I remember. . . ."

"You told my mother—"

"I told her that there would always be a place for you

in Lionkeep." Akeela didn't look at Gilwyn as he spoke. His eyes were glassy, staring into space. "I told her that I was making a new Liiria."

"That's right," said Gilwyn. "And you succeeded, my lord. You made a place for me when you built the library. You brought knowledge to Liiria." His voice shook a little as he spoke, but there was one more thing he needed to say. "You saved my life, King Akeela. And I've never been able to thank you until now." He sort of shrugged. "I guess that's my message."

A single tear welled up in Akeela's right eye. It dropped down his cheek, rolling onto his soiled shirt. "I tried so hard," he whispered. "To know that I helped you . . . that is a great gift, boy."

It was astonishing to see the change in him. The angry, time-twisted face softened as if lit by the sun. Gilwyn knew he was reaching Akeela. Somehow, his simple words of kindness were thawing Akeela's frozen heart.

"My lord," Gilwyn continued, "I know that you're a good man."

"I'm insane, Toms," choked Akeela. He glanced down at himself in disgust. "Look what the world has made of me. I'm a drunkard. And I've lost everything. Everything. . . ."

He began to weep, great hacking, drunken sobs. With an angry sweep of his arm he knocked the wine pitcher from the pedestal, then put his filthy hands over his face.

"I don't care what anyone else says about you, my lord," said Gilwyn. "To me you will always be Akeela the Good. You'll always be the man who saved me."

Akeela put up a hand. "Don't," he begged. "I can't bear it. . . ."

Gilwyn leaned back on his heels. "My lord," he said gently, "Lukien loves you."

"Stop!"

"He does, whether you want his love or not. That's why he gave himself up. Not just to save Grimhold, but to see you again. I just know it." Gilwyn waited for his words to sink in, then he asked the impossible. "Please, my lord, can't you forgive him?"

In the windowless cells beneath the palace, time lost all meaning. The unbearable heat stretched out the hours. A thick veneer of dust covered the stone floor and walls, undisturbed for years, and the iron gates of the cells shed flecks of rust when they opened, screeching with the strain. There was very little light, only the glow of a single torch. Lukien had counted five such cells. His was in the middle. The torch lay against the opposite wall, illuminating the passive face of Trager as he leaned back on an old wooden chair, balancing it on two legs. He didn't seem to mind the heat or dust; he was far too pleased to notice such things. Lukien sat on the floor of his cell with his back against the wall. Despite the heat the wall was cool, providing him his only bit of comfort. His hands were tied behind his back, an unnecessary precaution given the iron bars, but one that Trager indulged anyway. The general had a dagger in his hands that he twirled from time to time, occasionally whistling as he whiled away the time with his prisoner. He had promised Lukien that he would remain with him all night. It was, Trager had explained, his reward for all his years of patience. Lukien did what he could to block Trager from his mind. The darkness of the cell crowded around him. Given other circumstances, he might have been frightened. But he was not. He had made his choice and was satisfied. And if Akeela kept his promise, he would die at dawn.

"You know," said Trager suddenly, launching into one of his long-winded speeches, "I've been thinking, Captain. It didn't have to be this way." He happily rolled his dagger between his fingers as he spoke. "Imagine what your life could have been had you not poked Cassandra. You would have remained Akeela's favorite forever, and I wouldn't be here now, having so much fun."

Lukien ignored the comment.

"Not that I blame you for bedding the queen, Captain. Oh, she was a beautiful wench. Raven hair, dark eyes. And that bosom!" Trager smacked his lips loudly. "That must have been tasty, eh?" Casually he flipped his dagger into the air, catching it by the handle on its way down. "What a waste for you, though. All those years on the run, selling yourself to that bitch in Norvor for a few pennies, disgracing yourself. Who knows what you might have made of yourself in Liiria? You might have been a baron now, or a duke."

"How was that going to happen?" Lukien jabbed. "Akeela outlawed the noble houses, remember?"

"Hmm, yes, that was a pity," replied Trager with a wild grin. "A shame about Baron Glass and his fortune. I'll mention that to him when I see him." He mocked Lukien with his grin. "When do you think that will be, Captain, soon?"

Once again Lukien fell silent. It didn't matter what was done to him; he would never divulge Grimhold's location.

"We'll find it, you know," said Trager. "You don't have to tell us anything. I'll enjoy the hunt. And when I do turn over that rock, I'll squash all of those insects you call friends, including that old bastard Glass."

Lukien sighed. "Gods, don't you ever shut up?"

Trager got out of his chair and stuck his face between the bars. "I have much to say to you, Captain. And just one night to say it."

"Then say it," spat Lukien, "and spare me your insipid voice!"

"All right," chirped Trager. "I'm your better."

Lukien finally looked up at him. Trager grinned.

"Yes, that's right," he crowed. "I'm your better and I always have been. And today we have the proof, because you're rotting in a cell and I'm out here, free as a lark. I'm more loyal than you, more respected. I've turned the Royal Chargers into the best cavalry in the world. You couldn't have done that. And do you know why?"

"I'm sure you'll tell me," groaned Lukien.

"Because you were too busy playing your part! Always the Bronze Knight, the king's golden child. You couldn't let a single good looking woman go by, not even the king's wife!" Trager smugly laced his arms over his chest and stood back from the bars. "That's it, Captain. That was your downfall. You just loved to look at yourself in the mirror."

Lukien didn't want to think about the accusation, yet it struck him as horribly true. He had no retort for it.

"You know I'm right, don't you?" asked Trager. "That's why I'm a general, and you were just a stinking captain."

The sudden sound of approaching footfalls finally silenced the general. Two of his soldiers came down the hall, saluting as they faced him.

"What is it?" asked Trager tersely.

"The king has asked us to bring the prisoner to him," replied one of the men.

Trager's face lit up. "Ah! You hear, Lukien? Akeela just can't wait until morning to kill you!"

"No, sir," said the soldier. "I don't think that's it. The boy Gilwyn Toms has come. He's with the king now."

"What?" Trager erupted. "That little troll from the library?"

Lukien sprang to his feet. "Where is he?" he demanded. "Is he all right?"

The soldier glanced at him, about to answer. Trager roared, "Look at me, you idiot. What's that boy doing here?"

"Sorry, sir," said the man. "The boy says he has a message from Grimhold. He's with Akeela now."

"What message?" pressed Lukien.

When the soldier didn't reply, Trager barked, "Well? What message?"

"I don't know, sir," said the soldier. "The king met with him alone. His lordship sent us down here to bring the prisoner."

Trager's face purpled. Whirling on Lukien, he hissed, "What is this? Some kind of trick?"

"No trick, Trager. I don't know what the boy's doing here."

"You must know," Trager insisted. "Don't lie to me. I can make your last hours very unpleasant."

"I'm telling you I don't know," swore Lukien. "Now open this god-cursed gate and take me to Akeela."

Seeing he had no choice, Trager reluctantly agreed. Muttering obscenities, he plucked the key from the wall and opened the cell's lock. One of the soldiers opened the rusty gate, which squealed as it swung outward. The other took hold of Lukien's arm and pushed him out of the cell.

"Both of you, keep hold of him," ordered Trager. "Follow me."

He led the way out of the cellars with a string of curses. Lukien followed as best he could. The soldiers kept tight hold of him, dragging him along as he struggled to keep his footing. It was awkward walking so quickly with his hands tied behind his back, but Trager wouldn't let up. He took the musty stairs two at a time, and when he reached the top he bellowed down for them to hurry. The soldiers half carried Lukien up the steps, pushing him out into a well lit hall. Moonlight poured through the windows, stabbing Lukien's eye.

"Hurry up, you damn fool," ordered Trager. He continued quickly on his way. "Where is the king?" he asked his men.

"In his chambers, sir," one replied.

"His chambers? He's meeting with the boy in his own rooms?" Trager laughed and shook his head. "The man gets more demented every day. Come on, then."

The news struck Lukien equally as odd. Why was Gilwyn in Akeela's chambers? He didn't know whether it was a hopeful sign or not, but he supposed it meant the boy was safe, at least for now. He quickened his pace, following Trager through the palace and up a flight of marble stairs. This, he knew, led to Kadar's opulent living area. At the top of the staircase Trager paused, waiting for Lukien. He reached down and looped his arm around Lukien's, dragging him up the final step.

"Stay here," he told his men. "I'll take the prisoner in myself."

Neither soldier argued, releasing Lukien to Trager, who roughly shoved him toward the chamber up ahead. The doors to the area were open wide, revealing the splendid interior. Lukien could tell Trager was apprehensive by the way he wet his lips, his pink tongue darting out nervously. Just before they reached the chamber, Trager called out for Akeela.

"My lord, I've brought him," he said loudly. "What's going on . . . ?"

His voice trailed off when he looked inside the vast room. There was Akeela, on his knees in the middle of the tiled floor, weeping. Over him stood Gilwyn. The boy looked at Lukien helplessly.

"Great Mother of Fate," whispered Trager. Cursing, he shoved Lukien into the chamber then hurriedly shut the doors behind them. He turned on Akeela like a cobra. "Akeela, what's wrong with you? What are you doing down there? Get up!"

Akeela lifted his head, but didn't look at his irate general. Instead he gazed at Lukien. His tear-stained cheeks were puffed and red. Lukien gasped at the sight, going to him at once.

"Akeela, what's wrong?" He glanced at Gilwyn. "What happened to him?"

"I was talking to him, Lukien," said Gilwyn. "And he just broke down."

Trager surged forward. "What did you say to him, you little brat?" He took hold of Gilwyn's shirt, shaking him. "Tell me!"

"Let go of him!" cried Lukien.

"Or what?" Trager pushed Gilwyn backward and turned on Lukien. "What will you do, Captain?"

"Lukien. . . ." Akeela staggered to his feet. Lukien could tell instantly that he was drunk, for he could barely hold himself erect.

"Akeela, talk to me," Lukien urged. "Please. . . ."

Akeela sobbed, then laughed, then sobbed again, his shoulders shaking as he alternated through emotions. His hand went to his belt and slowly pulled forth his dagger. Trager snickered in triumph.

"Yes, Akeela, do it!" he urged. "Kill him!"

Slowly Akeela wobbled forward, his manic face twisting as he neared Lukien. Lukien stood his ground, unable to believe it would end this way. But Akeela was unreadable. The only thing for certain on his face was madness. An inscrutable smile broke on his face as he raised his dagger.

"Lukien . . ."

"King Akeela, no!" cried Gilwyn.

"Do it!" laughed Trager.

Lukien didn't move. He didn't even flinch. Akeela's nose practically touched his chest. The hot breath and stink of liquor was unbearable. Akeela whispered, "Turn around."

"What?" asked Lukien puzzled.

Akeela tried to spin him around. "Turn," he said. "I'm going to free you."

"What?" exploded Trager. "You can't!"

Lukien couldn't believe his ears. Nor could Gilwyn, who beamed at him. Lukien turned so that Akeela could cut his bonds. "Akeela, my friend." His voice choked on the words.

"No!" roared Trager. "I won't allow it!"

He reached out for Lukien and dragged him forward, sending him sprawling. Lukien's skull collided with the floor. For a moment he was dazed, but when he opened his eye he saw Trager standing before Akeela with his own dagger drawn.

"After what I did for you?" he seethed. "You'd let this bastard free!"

Gilwyn ran between them, shouting. Trager grabbed his neck and tossed him aside. He hit the wall hard and sank to his knees. Lukien struggled to his feet.

"Get away from him!" he cried.

Akeela just stood there helplessly, as though he couldn't believe what was happening. "Will?"

Gilwyn shouted, "Ghost, do something!"

Lukien staggered forward, rushing for Trager. The general easily sidestepped him, knocking him aside. Again Lukien skidded across the floor, and again Gilwyn cried out for unknown help. But it was too late. As Akeela stood with his own dagger dangling in his hand, Trager slashed at him, opening a red gash in his neck. Akeela dropped his blade and hovered there, blood filling the slit in his throat. Lukien lay on the floor, frozen in horror. Akeela stood, dazed and drunk, his hands going to his wound. Then he floated like a leaf down to his knees, all the while staring at Trager.

"Die, you ungrateful bastard!" cried Trager.

"Oh, Gods, no. . . ." Lukien got to his feet, intending to charge ahead, but an unseen hand held him back.

"Don't!" whispered a voice.

"What the . . . ?"

Blood raced down Akeela's rumpled shirt. He fell forward, his face smashing into the floor. Trager stood over him, his face a twisted mass. He stared down at his wounded king and let the dagger fall from his hand.

"Damn you! You made me do this!" he cried.

Gilwyn hurried toward Lukien, helping him to his feet. "Ghost," he whispered, "where are you?"

"I'm here," said the unseen voice. Lukien knew instinctively it was one of the Inhumans. Amazingly he felt the ropes being cut from his hands. "Go now," he ordered. "I'll take care of Trager."

"No!" said Gilwyn.

"*Go!*" roared the voice.

Trager was on his knees beside the gasping Akeela. When he heard the strange voice he turned in its direction. His hand frantically searched for the blade he'd dropped.

"Hurry," urged the voice. "It's your only chance!"

"Who is that?" demanded Trager. He got to his feet with his dagger in hand, scanning the chamber. Lukien looked around too, trying to see his unknown benefactor. Now that he was free he could get to Akeela. If he could reach him, pull him away from Trager. . . .

"Ghost, or whoever you are, get Trager!" he cried as he made his way to Akeela. Trager made to stop him but was instantly bowled over by some unseen force. The blow stunned Trager, who looked around in terror for an opponent he couldn't see. The invisible warrior blocked the way between Lukien and Akeela. Lukien could hear his unseen blade slashing through the air. Amazingly, Trager ducked and parried each one, falling back against the wall, twirling to avoid his invisible enemy.

"Akeela, it's me," said Lukien desperately as he reached his fallen king. Blood trickled down Akeela's neck. He was still alive, though barely. Lukien quickly studied the wound. It wasn't as deep as it could have been, but it was bad. Akeela looked up at Lukien and tried to smile.

"I die, Lukien. . . ."

"No," Lukien argued. "I won't let you. Not here. Not like this. Gilwyn, help me with him. We have to get him out of here."

"Lukien, he's finished," cried Gilwyn. Behind him Ghost and Trager continued battling. breaking everything in the room around them.

"Get out of here!" shouted the Inhuman. "Before he sees me!"

Lukien ignored the voice, struggling to get his arms beneath Akeela. The thought of killing Trager flashed across his mind, but he only had one chance to save Akeela, and he wasn't going to waste it. With a grunt he pulled the wounded king off the floor and lifted him in his arms, easier than it should have been because Akeela had wasted away.

"Come on, Gilwyn," he cried. The boy hobbled after him, stealing a last glance at Trager and the still invisible Ghost. The thought of leaving Trager alive was unbearable, but to Lukien the thought of Akeela dying was worse. He knew his king didn't have much time, but if somehow they could reach Grimhold maybe Minikin could save him.

"Kill that son of a bitch, Ghost!" he cried as Gilwyn pulled open the chamber doors.

"No!" shrieked Trager. Again he tried to lunge for them, and once again Ghost was there to stop him. For a moment Lukien caught a glimpse of him, a frenzied flash of white skin, and knew that whatever magic kept him invisible was fading. But he couldn't stop to help the albino—a pair of Liirian soldiers were outside in the hall.

Lukien's harried mind groped for an answer as the soldiers blankly stared, shocked by the sight of their bloodied king in his arms. Gilwyn hurried to produce an explanation.

"The king has fallen," said Gilwyn earnestly. "He's badly hurt!"

A sudden shout from within the chamber galvanized the soldiers. Trager's voice echoed over the combat in the room.

"Stop them!"

A large crash finished his words. Lukien heard Trager's anguished cry. Confused, the soldiers in the hall reached for their swords. Burdened by Akeela, Lukien knew he was finished, but a second later the white-skinned terror exploded from the chamber with a furious scream. The Inhuman called Ghost raced past Lukien and Gilwyn, slamming his sword into the first soldier before his own weapon was drawn. The other soldier fell back in horror at the sight of Ghost, recovering in just enough time to bring up his blade.

"Move!" ordered Ghost as he pressed his attack. "Get out of here, both of you!"

Lukien glanced back to the chamber. Inside was Trager, alive or dead. Over his arm Akeela gurgled with rasping breaths. The awful sound made Lukien's mind up for him. There were only seconds, and really only one choice. They had to get out. Now. Lukien looked around wildly, desperate to save Akeela but with no way out.

"Did you bring horses?" he asked Gilwyn quickly.

Gilwyn nodded. "Better. A kreel. She's fast."

"She'd better be," said Lukien. "Because we have to run like the wind."

"But how do we get out?"

Before Lukien could answer the man battling Ghost gave a terrible cry. Lukien turned to see him sliding down the wall, his heart punctured, just as Ghost pulled free his blood-soaked blade.

"Ghost!" cried Gilwyn. "Are you all right?"

The albino man nodded, barely able to breathe. "I'm all right," he gasped. "We have to move."

Lukien shot a glance into the chamber. "What about Trager?"

"I don't know," said the Inhuman. "Maybe dead, maybe unconscious. I hit him pretty hard."

"Then we'd better hurry," said Gilwyn desperately.

"No!" cried Lukien. "We can't let Trager live!"

"And we can't let Akeela die, either," Gilwyn argued. "We have to get out now!"

"How?" cried Lukien. "There's no way through. The others will see us."

Ghost grinned through his exhaustion. "Just follow me," he said, then herded them toward the stairs.

Trager awoke to the faces of worried men. His head throbbed from the blow he had taken, a blow he hadn't seen coming. As his eyes fluttered open through a stream of blood, he realized that he hadn't even seen his assailant. It had been one of the gods-cursed freaks from Grimhold. He tried to sit up, then felt a shooting pain in his side.

"Argh!"

"Don't try to move," urged one of the men. Trager realized suddenly it was Tark. The old colonel looked concerned. "You took a bad hit in the head. And your ribs again."

Trager felt nauseous, as though he might faint. He struggled to speak. "Where are they?" he gasped.

Tark looked away, studying Trager's wound. "You're bleeding," he said. "You've been stabbed."

"Tark, where are they?" Trager demanded.

The colonel said haltingly, "I don't know. They got away."

Trager's head fell back, barely able to stay up. He stared at the ceiling, swearing. There were others in the room, mumbling to themselves as they saw his terrible condition.

"General, I don't know how to tell you this," said Tark. "King Akeela's gone. There's blood outside and all though the palace. I think they took him."

"They killed him, Tark," said Trager. "They slit his throat. I don't know why they took his body, but they did." He closed his eyes, feigning disgust. "Probably for some cursed ceremony. Human sacrifice, something."

Tark looked ashen. "Fate above. . . ."

"It was Lukien, Tark," he said. "I tried to stop him, but. . . ."

"Shhh, don't talk," urged the colonel. "You need rest. And when you're better we'll hunt down that king-slayer scum and make him pay."

"Yes," said Trager. "We'll find him, make him suffer. . . ."

As Colonel Tark wrapped a bandage around his wound Trager sat motionless on the floor. Guilt gnawed at him, devouring his thoughts. But Akeela had deserved it. After all he'd done for the king, how could he have turned yet again to Lukien?

"Tark, tell the men what's happened," said Trager. "Tell them I'm in charge now."

"I will, sir." Tark applied pressure to the wound in Trager's side, stemming the blood.

"Tell them Lukien killed Akeela," Trager went on. "Tell them we're going to Grimhold to get the king's body back and to punish that treacherous filth."

"I will. Now hold still."

There was nothing else to say, so Trager closed his eyes and let Tark work. In his mind he saw Lukien defeated, and the amulets of immortality around his own neck. He saw himself returning triumphantly to Koth, to a country without a king and desperate for a leader. If he was clever—if he could lead his men against Grimhold and win—he could have the thing he'd always prized.

The respect of the world.

56

Lukien and the others rode as far and as fast as they could, leaving behind the city and the gruesome shadows of the crucified. They had taken the fleet-footed kreels to the confines of a row of high, sandy dunes, hoping to escape the Liirians with their speed and the aide of Ghost's remarkable magic. The strange albino had worked his miracles on the minds of the Liirians, getting them out of the palace without being seen. Remarkably, Akeela had lived through the ordeal, silently laying in Lukien's arms as if he knew they were escaping and wouldn't make a sound to betray them. Hoping that they could make it to Grimhold, Lukien had let Ghost ride up ahead with Akeela crudely strapped to the albino's kreel. Since he couldn't ride a kreel himself he had to share Gilwyn's, and he wanted to give Akeela the best chance of reaching Minikin and her powerful magics. The amulet would save him, he told himself as they hurried over the dunes. If only Minikin would let Akeela have it. It was a gamble but it was also Akeela's only chance, and Lukien had risked everything to take it, even letting Trager live. Ghost didn't know for sure if he had killed the general, offering only vague assurances that he had done his best. But Lukien knew it would be worth it if only he could keep Akeela alive. It was the only thing he wanted in the world now.

Then, when Lukien felt confident they were far enough from Jador to make it safely home, he watched Ghost's kreel in front of him come to a skidding halt. The albino, exhausted from his magical efforts to save them, looked down at the bloodied figure slumped in front of him in the saddle. Stricken, he turned and called to Lukien.

"Mother of Fate, no," groaned Lukien. Gilwyn hurried Emerald up to Ghost's kreel. It was dark and they could barely see Akeela, but the moonlight on Ghost's white face exposed the Inhuman's grim expression.

"He's asking for you, Lukien," said Ghost. Then he shook his head slightly with a sad expression. "I could barely hear him."

Lukien dismounted from Emerald's back as quickly as he could, then went to Akeela and very gently lifted his head. The bandage he had fashioned around Akeela's throat was filthy with dirt and saturated with blood. Akeela's eyes lolled back in his head, but on his lips was Lukien's name, over and over. Seeing him now, Lukien knew that he'd failed. Akeela had lost too much blood and was too near death to make it to Grimhold.

"Gilwyn," he said softly, "help me get him down. I want to be with him."

"Lukien, we have to keep going. If there's any chance—"

"There is no chance, Gilwyn. You were right."

Lukien began undoing the straps keeping Akeela on the kreel while Ghost dismounted. With the albino's help Gilwyn was able to free Akeela's legs and ease him into Lukien's arms. Cradling him like a withered child, Lukien stood in the moonlight, unsure what to do. Gilwyn and Ghost were watching silently. Realizing that he wanted to be alone with Akeela, Lukien turned and walked off toward the dunes. His companions didn't follow. Akeela continued whispering his name as he was carried away, occasionally fluttering his eyes, struggling against death.

"It's all right, Akeela," said Lukien. "I'm here with you now and I'm not going to leave you."

He took Akeela far from Gilwyn and Ghost and their waiting kreels, setting him down in the sand and propping his head up with his hand. There he knelt beside the dying man. Akeela's breath was heavy, coming now in short, choking gasps. He managed to open his eyes just enough to recognize the face hovering over him.

"Lukien . . ."

"It's me, Akeela," Lukien reassured him, stroking his face as though he were a child, though Akeela looked impossibly old.

"You came back," rasped Akeela.

"You knew I would. I had to. You're my brother, Akeela."

For the briefest moment the dementia left Akeela's face. "Brothers fight sometimes."

Lukien smiled, remembering the many times he had said that same thing. "That's right. But that doesn't mean they don't love each other."

"Thank you for being my brother, Lukien." Akeela tried to reach up and touch Lukien, but he was too weak. His hand trembled with effort. Lukien took his hand and held it, and knew that it held the very last of Akeela's strength.

"If I had the amulet I could save you," he groaned. "I'm sorry." He fought back tears. "I've killed you, just as I killed Cassandra."

Akeela coughed, his body wracked with pain. "It was me," he gasped. "I killed us all."

Then he closed his eyes and his grip slackened in Lukien's hand. The bubbling of blood around his bandage went on, but his breathing slowed and his face softened.

And then he was dead.

Lukien held his hand and did not let go.

"Akeela?"

When he heard no reply, the tears came at last.

57

In a small, quiet room in a seldom used wing of Grimhold, Minikin knelt with her palms on her knees and her eyes shut. Before her stood an altar of white stone, the only object of any size in the chamber. On the altar stood two glowing candles. Between the candles rested the amulet of the dead Kadar. The Eye of God lent its ghostly red light to the illumination of the candle, bathing the little room in its warm glow. Minikin felt its heat on her face, saw its radiance against her closed eyelids. Physically, she was alone in the room. Mentally, her mind sang with voices. She could sense them swimming through the air around her, their formless feet and hands like wisps of smoke. Her breathing steadied as she completed her trance, raising her mind to the consciousness of her Akari hosts. Their invisible fingers caressed her, taking her into their dead realm. The presence of Amaraz rose from the amulet to greet her. In her mind she could see his wizened face, ancient but gentle, shimmering as it came into focus. She kept her eyes closed and concentrated on him. To a novice at the summoning, the little chamber would have seemed empty. Not so with Minikin; to her it was filled with beings. Amaraz' presence subjugated the other Akari. Their ethereal bodies drifted to the back of the room and up to the ceiling, anywhere to make room for the amulet's spirit. Amaraz' shimmering face smiled at Minikin.

Long since you've summoned me, he said. His voice was

soothing, gentle. Typically, his first concern was for his sister. *How fares Lariniza, Minikin?*

Lariniza inhabited Minikin's own amulet. As the great spirit spoke, Minikin felt his sister pulse within the jewel around her neck.

She is well, Amaraz, replied Minikin. *She greets you.*

Minikin loved Lariniza. She was her protector, her life-giver. She and her powers had kept disease and age from touching Minikin's mortal body, just as her brother had long done for Kadar. Together they were not only the rulers of the Akari, but their protectors as well. It was why the amulets had been formed, and their spirits forever encased within them. Now Lariniza spoke to Minikin, gentle, reassuring words. The spirit of the Eye told her not to be afraid. She urged her human friend to ask her questions.

I worry, Amaraz, said Minikin to the incandescent face. *About Grimhold. Ghost is still gone, and I have lost young Gilwyn, too. Tell me please,* she begged, *can you see them?*

Amaraz' face smiled, his teeth like glowing fog. *You are a treasure, my Minikin,* he said. *Do not fear. The albino is well, and the young Liirian. I have been watching them.*

Minikin let out a sigh of relief. From the rafters in the ceiling she heard the chorus of spirits do the same. Of all the Akari, only Amaraz could see so clearly. Not even Lacaron, Insight's spirit, was as powerful as he at seeing the world beyond Grimhold. For Lacaron, the world appeared as a fractured mirror. Not so with Amaraz. His vision was as clear as sunshine.

That pleases me, said Minikin. *Thank you, Amaraz.*

There is more, said the Akari. *Your champion is with them.*

Lukien? Minikin was overjoyed. *He's still alive?*

They return to Grimhold even now, said Amaraz. *They are uninjured.*

Are they near? asked Minikin excitedly.

Very near, replied Amaraz. Moment by moment his face grew more clear as the bond between them grew. It was as if Minikin had left her body behind in an alternate Grimhold, and now she was one of the Akari, floating with them in their own preternatural realm. Amaraz stretched out a hand for Minikin, a hand that had almost taken form and flesh. She even felt the warmth of his touch. *There is more news, my Minikin,* said the spirit. *The mad Akeela is dead.*

Dead? Minikin couldn't believe it. *How?*

Slain by his general. The Bronze Knight tried to save him. But be warned— the one called Trager still lives.

Minikin didn't know what it meant. Without Akeela, there might be the chance that the Liirians would retreat. It was unlikely, she knew, after what she'd heard about Trager, but there was always the chance. Perhaps this was the hope that she'd told Lukien about, the unforeseen event that changes the future. She had never imagined that Trager would slay his-king.

Will they still come? she asked hopefully. *Can you see, Amaraz?*

Amaraz never couched his answers in riddles. He said simply, *They will come.*

Minikin's mood fell. *But without their king. . . .*

They will come, Minikin, repeated Amaraz gently. *I do not need to see the future to tell you this. The Trager is wounded, but resolute. When he recovers, he will ride for Grimhold.*

Of course he will, thought Minikin bitterly. There seemed no way out of this trap. *Then we will be ready for them,* she declared. *Baron Glass has been preparing our defense, and Lukien will soon return to aid us.*

Amaraz' warm hand tightened on her own. *You will do your best, I know,* he said. *But I must warn you, my Minikin, I will not allow this hallowed ground to be soiled. The invaders must not breach the gate.*

Of course, Amaraz, said Minikin. *We'll do our best to defend it.*

You do not understand. Amaraz' breath seemed to sigh. *I cannot allow Grimhold to fall into foreign hands.* He looked up and around the chamber, which had magically expanded now to accommodate hundreds of Akari. The faces of the other spirits were grave. *We have spoken, Minikin, and we have agreed. Grimhold must not fall.*

Amaraz, I don't understand, said Minikin. *Explain yourself, please.*

Amaraz kept his gentle grip on Minikin, lifting his other hand toward the ceiling. *You may fight outside these walls,* he said, *but inside we are the masters.* A flame grew in his palm, like the fire of a torch. *We are only spirits now, Minikin. We have no bodies to be destroyed.*

So? asked Minikin. She guessed at Amaraz' meaning and hoped she was wrong. *What are you saying?*

Watch!

The fire in Amaraz' palm grew until it consumed his hand, then exploded out in all directions. Minikin felt its heat but no pain, watching in horror as the searing light engulfed the room. The rafters in the ceiling burned, the bricks ignited and tumbled. And all around her the hall of Grimhold filled with fire, like a rushing torrent of red water, until all was in flames and burning. The Akari spirits watched the holocaust from the safety of the air, their faces drawn but resolute. Minikin stood in the center of the room, unscathed, her clothes magically retarding the flames. Slowly she turned to Amaraz and nodded.

Enough, she said. *I understand.*

Amaraz closed his fist, instantly extinguishing the inferno. His expression was grim as he looked at Minikin. *If you cannot defeat the northerners beyond these walls, then I will do so within them.*

Minikin tried to compose herself. *If you do that, all my Inhumans inside the fortress will die.*

Then you must make a choice, my Minikin, said Amaraz. *Do you have faith in the Lukien and the army he has made? If not, then take your children out of here. Bring them to the village. They will be safe there from my power.*

They'd be vulnerable in the village, said Minikin. *Without these walls to protect them. . . .*

Then let them remain, said Amaraz, *and have the Bronze Knight protect them.*

But if he cannot—

Minikin, I have protected your people for years, more years than even I can remember. But I must protect my own people, too. My powers are greatest inside Grimhold. I will not be able to destroy the Liirians outside these walls.

Minikin nodded. His logic was horrible but flawless.

This is our sacred place, the only home left for the Akari. I cannot let it fall into the hands of foreigners, not again. We will not allow it. Take your children away from here.

The walls of Grimhold can withstand my fire. The Inhumans will be able to return once it is over.

They will be dead by then, Amaraz, said Minikin. *The Lüirians will not send all of their men into the fortress. There will be enough to slay my children in the village.* She let her hand slip out of Amaraz'. *But I understand. You have been good to us, Amaraz. And we have only been guests, after all.*

The Akari looked profoundly sad. *More than guests.*

Minikin smiled crookedly. *More than guests, though not quite family it seems. Do not fear, Amaraz. We will defeat the Lüirians somehow.*

Before the Akari could reply Minikin opened her eyes, severing the trance. The room around her was again quiet and small. Above her head the rafters were empty. The two candles glowed on the altar. Between them, the amulet of Amaraz burned like spitting fire. Minikin glanced down at her own amulet and saw that its jewel was pulsing sadly. She heard Lariniza's voice in her head, almost apologizing, but Minikin did not want to hear it. Instead she rose from her knees and left the tiny chamber in search of Baron Glass.

It was almost dawn when Lukien and his entourage finally reached the mountains of Grimhold. They had ridden through the night on their two kreels, Gilwyn on the smaller Emerald while Lukien shared a beast with Ghost. The albino was silent as they rode. Exhausted from all they had been through, he spared Lukien conversation, letting the Bronze Knight mourn Akeela instead. They had buried Akeela in the dunes, digging a shallow grave for him with the help of the kreels and their sharp claws. It was a horrible grave, just enough to keep the vultures off his corpse.

How should I remember him? Lukien wondered as they rode. The moon had fallen and the sky was melancholy, matching his mood. He was glad that he had enjoyed a last moment with Akeela, that in the end they had been brothers again. It was good to see his face untainted by madness, however briefly. That's how he would remember Akeela, he decided. The way he was before the madness.

But the thought of Akeela's reclamation did little to leaven Lukien's mood. There was still the awful matter of

Trager. Had Ghost killed him? The albino seemed to think so, but he couldn't be sure. Lukien flayed himself for fleeing the palace without finishing off his nemesis. It would have been so easy, but Akeela was bleeding and time was so short, and. . . .

Enough, he scolded himself. If Trager still lived, he would deal with him. He would have to.

With dawn breaking over the barren horizon, they came at last to the canyon where Grimhold was hidden. Emerald sniffed her way forward with her tongue, leading the way. Even in the darkness the kreels could see perfectly, their strange eyes widening to catch every glimmer of light. Lukien nudged Ghost as they entered the canyon.

"We're here," he said softly.

The albino's white head scanned the rising walls of rock. "Thank the Fate." He let the reins slacken in his hands. "The kreel will take us the rest of the way."

Up ahead, Lukien could barely see the mountain fortress in the distance, camouflaged by darkness and its own rocky facade. He was about to call out to Gilwyn when another voice startled him from above.

"They're here!"

Ghost bolted upright, and together the trio scanned the cliffs above, but could see nothing but darkness and the sharp contours of rock. Gilwyn jerked Emerald to a halt and whirled her about.

"Who was that?" asked the boy.

Ghost shrugged.

"Ho, there, Lukien!" said the voice again. It seemed to come from everywhere and nowhere in particular. "Here!" the voice directed. "Above you!"

Lukien focused on the cliffs, at last catching a glimpse of movement. Directly above them a man was perched, waving down at them.

"Lukien, it's me, Darren," said the voice. He leaned out carefully so they could see him better. Lukien recognized him at once. Darren, one of the Inhumans from the village, had a bow in his hand and a beaming smile on his face. As he came into view others joined him, dozens of men with bows and spears who'd taken up position in the rocks.

"Darren, what are you doing up there?" Lukien called to him.

"Baron Glass' orders, Lukien," said Darren. "We're on guard for an attack."

Lukien counted up the defenders, all of whom waved down at him. There were women in the cliffs, too, like the dwarf Jasine, who had insisted that she could throw a spear and had proven herself among the best. Lukien saw her on the cliff to his right, her small profile set against the darkness. She raised her spear overhead in greeting.

"Is there an attack on the way?" asked Gilwyn.

"No, I don't think so," said Lukien. "I'm sure they're just drilling. I told them I wanted them to get used to being in the cliffs. That'll be our first defense." Again he looked up at Darren and shouted, "Where's the baron, Darren? I need to speak to him."

"Baron Glass is at the gate," cried the man. "We've all been waiting for you."

Lukien waved at him in thanks, then told Ghost to head onward. The albino did so, ordering his kreel toward Grimhold. Gilwyn followed at their side. He smiled at Lukien.

"Not a bad army you've got there," he joked.

Lukien couldn't help but feel proud. "They're keen, that's for sure," he replied. He was eager to find Thorin and tell him what had happened in Jador, but he suspected that Minikin had already told him. Then he laughed and said, "They do look good up there, don't they?"

"They do," agreed Ghost. "You see, Liirian? You're not the only one who can fight."

In a few moments they reached Grimhold. The huge iron gate was open with the giant Greygor standing guard. Near the gate milled a dozen men and women, all of them conscripts in Lukien's Inhuman army. They had swords and bows and spears in their hands, all the old Akari weapons from the dusty armory. With them was Baron Glass, talking loudly as he explained the importance of surprise and stealth. The Inhumans listened to him, enraptured, standing around him in a semicircle as he imparted his hard-won wisdom. So entranced were they that none of them saw Lukien approach.

"Stop here," Lukien ordered. He climbed down from the kreel as Ghost brought it to a halt, then walked out of the darkness with his hands raised and a bright smile on his face. "Don't you need me anymore?"

Glass and the Inhumans turned to look at him, then broke into a chorus of shouts and warm greetings. Gilwyn and Ghost came up behind him, receiving the same hero's welcome. Thorin hurried toward them and slapped his hand on Lukien's neck.

"You crazy bastard, it's good to see you!"

As the Inhumans crowded around, Lukien laughed. "What is this?" he asked, gesturing toward the cliffs. "You're starting to look like a real army!"

The men and women smiled and told Lukien how glad they were he was back. All were careful to include Gilwyn and Ghost in their comments.

"Gilwyn!" cried a distant voice.

Lukien and Gilwyn both turned to see White-Eye standing in the gate, her expression bittersweet. She had obviously been worried about the boy and looked on the verge of happy tears.

"White-Eye!" Leaving the others behind, Gilwyn hurried toward her. With all the Inhumans watching, they embraced. When they kissed, the gathered broke into applause.

"I see the boys brought you back safely," quipped Thorin. "What were you thinking, you damn fool?"

Lukien's smile was forlorn. "Thorin," he said softly. "Akeela's dead."

The baron nodded. "I know. Minikin saw."

The comment surprised Lukien. "She saw already? Gods, keeping a secret from that woman is impossible. Did she tell you it was Trager that killed him?"

"She did." Thorin pulled Lukien closer, his arm hugging him like a father might. "I'm sorry, Lukien. I know what Akeela meant to you."

"I thought I could change him, Thorin. I just had to see him one more time, you know? And he did change. I saw it."

Thorin looked at him askew. "What do you mean?"

"He released us, Thorin. That's why Trager killed him. I tried to get him here to Grimhold, to get the amulet around him and save him. But I didn't make it."

"You tried. That's what matters."

"I was so close," said Lukien. "All I needed was a little

more time." Then he smiled, adding, "Oh, but you should have seen him, Thorin. That last moment, it was like the old Akeela again."

Though he'd never had any use for Akeela, Thorin was pleased for Lukien. He put a hand on the knight's shoulder. "I'm glad for that. But there's more news, Lukien. Trager is still alive."

Both Ghost and Lukien froze at the news.

"What?" gasped Ghost. "Are you sure?"

"Minikin saw it, just as she saw Akeela's death. He's still alive, and he'll be coming for Grimhold."

The news shattered Lukien, who balled his hands into fists. "It's my fault he's still alive."

"No, Lukien, it isn't," said Ghost. "He was mine to kill and I failed."

"I should have gone back and finished him!"

Ghost shook his head. "You couldn't have, there was no time. You had to save Akeela."

The reasoning did little to comfort Lukien. "But I didn't, did I? I let Akeela die and Trager live!"

"Minikin says he'll be on his way," said Thorin, "just as soon as he's recovered. We may have a week, maybe a bit more." He looked at Ghost with a wicked grin. "You should be proud of yourself, my boy. You came closer than most to killing that piss-bucket."

Ghost nodded dully. "I just wish I'd finished the job."

Thorin smiled. "There's still time for that. Get inside now. Get some rest."

Ghost excused himself from the gathering and staggered toward the open gate. Lukien watched him go.

"The boy's too hard on himself," he said when Ghost was out of earshot. "It's not his fault Trager's still alive. It's mine. And now I've left us open to attack. Great Fate, what a fool I am."

"You were trying to save Akeela, Lukien," said Thorin. "That makes you a hero, not a fool. And there's nothing to be done about it now. I say let Trager come and attack. We'll be ready for him."

Lukien looked around, wondering why all the Inhumans were out so early. "So what is this?" he asked. "Drilling at this hour?"

"There's not much time, Lukien," said Glass. "I've been instructing them on how to ambush the Chargers when they come through the canyon."

"Did you see them up there, Lukien?" asked Garvis. He was a blacksmith from the village, a big man with arms like pythons who could wield two swords at once, though not deftly.

"I saw them," said Lukien. For the benefit of them all he added, "They looked damn good to me."

The defenders of Grimhold broke into proud smiles. Baron Glass puffed a little at the compliment.

"They're yours once more, Lukien. But it was an honor to command again, I'll say that." He pointed down the canyon. "And these walls will be a great defense. I've been drilling them with bows and spears. If we can set up a crossfire here, we'll have Trager's men pinned. We can take out a third of them before they even reach the fortress."

"I'm sure," said Lukien, trying to sound impressed. The idea had already occurred to him, but he liked seeing the change in Thorin. "Minikin says we have a week?"

"Give or take a few days," replied Thorin. "She's waiting for you inside the gate. She has something to talk to you about."

"Oh? Trouble?"

Thorin shrugged. "She wouldn't say. She just wanted me to send you inside when you got here."

"All right, then, carry on, Thorin," said Lukien. He left the baron and his soldiers behind and headed for the gate. There he found Gilwyn with White-Eye, sitting together in a quiet corner. Gilwyn had his arm around the girl, comforting her. He couldn't help but smile at the boy's good fortune. But when he saw Minikin inside Grimhold, his smile melted away. The little woman was leaning against a wall, waiting for him, her face sullen. Trog was with her, as silent as ever. Minikin barely smiled when she saw him. At first Lukien thought she was angry with him for going off to Jador, but he quickly realized from her drawn expression that something far worse preoccupied her.

"Minikin?" he asked when he reached her. "What's wrong?"

Her face lightened only a little. "Welcome back, Lukien. I'm glad you're safe."

"Baron Glass told me you wanted to see me," said Lukien.

Minikin nodded. "Walk with me a little, Lukien."

Lukien did as she asked, following her away from the gate and unwanted ears. The sudden secretiveness made him apprehensive, but he asked no questions as she led him further into the hall. Because it was so early the hall was mostly deserted. She came to a stop under one of the many sconces. The oily light revealed the exhaustion on her face.

"You look like you've been up all night," said Lukien. "Doesn't anyone in Grimhold sleep anymore?"

"Not when there's so much to do," replied the midget wearily. "Baron Glass has told you what I've seen?"

"Yes," said Lukien. "He's told me."

"Lukien, I'm sorry for you. Your loss is truly great."

Lukien didn't know what to say. "I thought I lost Akeela sixteen years ago, Minikin. I'm not sure why I feel the way I do."

"Losing a friend is never easy," said Minikin.

"No, I suppose not," said Lukien. "I just didn't realize that Akeela was still my friend until it was too late. Now, tell me what's bothering you."

She surprised Lukien by laughing. "Ah, what isn't bothering me?" she said. "The battle, Lukien. I am afraid."

"No, it's more than that, I can tell," said Lukien. "Come on, the truth now."

Minikin fiddled with the amulet around her neck, avoiding his eyes. "We must defeat your countrymen, Lukien," she said gravely. "It's even more important now."

"I know that," said Lukien. "With Akeela gone I thought there might be some hope, but Thorin told me Trager's still alive. I'm furious with myself for letting him live. Now he'll be coming."

"He'll be coming just as soon as he is able," said Minikin, "And I'm sure he seeks the amulets just as much as he seeks revenge."

"Then we'll beat him, Minikin." Lukien felt his rage boiling over. "I promise."

"You want to kill him for what he did to Akeela, I know," said Minikin. "But that won't be enough. This isn't

about a vendetta anymore, Lukien, not yours and not
Akeela's. This is a war for survival."

"Minikin, you don't have to explain it to me. I know
what's at stake."

"No," said Minikin, "you don't." She continued to toy
distractedly with her amulet. Lukien could tell something
was troubling her, something more than just his coming
countrymen. He waited for her to find just the right words.
Finally she said, "The Liirians must not breach the gate.
They must not take the fortress or even set foot in it. If
they do. . . ." She glanced away, unable to finish.

"Tell me," Lukien urged.

Minikin caressed her amulet mournfully. "If they do, the
Akari will destroy them, and everyone else inside Grim-
hold." She looked up at Lukien, her eyes full of fear. "The
Akari will burn the halls with fire if the Liirians set foot in
Grimhold. They won't let their home be taken, Lukien. Do
you understand that?"

Uncertain exactly what it meant, Lukien decided to be
encouraging. "It means we have to defeat the Liirians out
in the canyon. And we will, Minikin, I promise."

"You don't understand," groaned Minikin. "What will
happen if the Liirians defeat you? What if they take the
keep? What of my Inhumans? They'll be killed, Lukien,
burned to death." The little woman leaned miserably
against the wall, shaking her head. "That musn't happen. I
couldn't bear it."

Lukien still didn't comprehend the Akari or their ways,
but he knew they had the power to carry out their threat.
He said, "Then take the Inhumans to the village, Minikin.
They'll be safer there."

"No they won't," said Minikin. "After the fortress falls
the village will be next, you know that. Even if the Akari
kill the Liirians inside the keep, there will be many left
outside." She looked at Lukien helplessly. "They'll find the
village, Lukien. They'll kill my children."

For the first time since he'd known her, Minikin looked
truly afraid. Lukien bit his lip, trying to think of a way out
of their dismal predicament. He knew Minikin was right—
if the Liirians defeated them, they would storm the keep
on foot, but others would remain behind, enough to discover the village and pillage it. And if the Inhumans re-

nained in Grimhold, they would die in the Akari fire. It
seemed horribly cruel to Lukien, but he had no reason to
question the Akari. Grimhold had been their home for
ages, and they had already lost it to foreigners once. As
unthinkable as it was to kill the Inhumans, Lukien could
almost understand their decision. That left only one option
for them.

"Then we'll have to defeat Trager," he said. "There's no
other way."

Minikin nodded. "And I will keep the Inhumans inside
the keep. They'll be safest there, I think."

"Agreed. The fortress is their best chance for survival."

It was their only chance for survival, and both Lukien
and Minikin knew it. The Mistress of Grimhold put out her
tiny hand and took Lukien by the fingers. She did not speak
for a long moment. Rather she simply looked at him, sharing the moment. There was very little time left, and neither
of them wanted to waste it.

"Minikin," said Lukien gently, "don't forget what you
told me. The future is always in question. We have the
power to change it."

The little woman finally smiled her bright, enigmatic
smile. "I know," she said. "I just hope I don't soon regret
those words."

"You won't," promised Lukien. "One way or the other,
I'll make sure the Inhumans are saved."

Minikin frowned. "That's a promise you can't keep."

"But I will," Lukien insisted. He squeezed her hand.
"Now if you'll excuse me, I've got a lot of work to do."

"No," urged Minikin. "Rest first. You've been traveling
all night."

"It doesn't matter. Like you said, there's no time to
waste."

He bent and gave her cheek an unexpected kiss, then
walked off to join Baron Glass and their blossoming army.

58

General Will Trager sat alone in a dark corner of the cell, watching the handiwork of his subordinate, Sergeant Marrs. The room was dim save for the light of a single torch and the glowing embers of a brazier filled with coals. The cellars were deserted; Trager wanted no witnesses. He knew that men like Colonel Tark were loyal but squeamish sometimes, and torture had never really been part of the Royal Chargers, a unit founded on more lofty stuff. But these were dire days and called for extreme measures. And that was why Sergeant Marrs was here, doing what the gods had gifted him to do. Marrs was a man with no remorse and a heart as hard as iron. He had never flinched in battle nor mourned the death of a friend. To Trager's knowledge, the sergeant had no friends. He was a loner but a good soldier, and today his particular dispassion was being put to good use.

Sergeant Marrs stood in the center of the cell. In his hand was a metal rod, its tip glowing red. There were three other such rods in the brazier, warming up for the dirty business at hand. Two long chains dangled down from the ceiling, with two stout manacles to hold their naked prisoner. His name was Benrian. And like all the servants in the palace, Benrian had claimed no knowledge of Grimhold. But Benrian was as close to Kadar as any servant had been. He had been the dead kahan's body servant. And though Benrian still claimed otherwise, another of his fellow servants had not been so resilient under the whip. A woman named Dreana had broken quite easily after only a few lashes, exclaiming in her pain that Benrian had been to Grimhold before. It had taken days for Marrs to get to Dreana, systematically working his way through the palace servants and seeming to enjoy every moment. Trager himself had not bothered with the preliminaries. Like Tark, he didn't really have the stomach for torture, and he had needed to rest his wounds. He was still very weak, and had to hold himself up with effort. The wounds the Inhuman had given him had laid him up for days, and it would be days more before he could ride against Grimhold. But they were near now to learning the keep's location, and Trager wanted to hear the words himself.

Surprisingly for a body servant, Benrian was extremely resistant. It was well past dawn now, and Marrs had been working on him for an hour. He had started with the whip, turning Benrian's dark skin into a coagulated mass of scars. When the whip failed, he had turned to the pokers. The stink of brimstone filled the dank chamber as the coals in the brazier burned. The single torch made unusual shadows on the opposite wall. Benrian looked like some sort of twisted dancer, dangling in his chains as Marrs worked his naked body. Trager pitied the man. He had come to respect the Jadori in his brief time among them and didn't like torturing them, particularly the women. It was not what he was raised to do, and he knew his father wouldn't approve, though his father had beaten his mother as if it were meaningless, swearing it was his right as a husband. Trager had daydreamed about his mother while the woman Dreana was in the chains. Their cries had been so similar.

Sergeant Marrs replaced the poker he was holding with a fresher, hotter one from the brazier. He twisted it before Benrian's eyes, which widened horribly at the sight of it. Marrs' thick voice carried through the chamber as he spoke to his victim.

"I'm getting tired of you," he whispered. Slowly he directed the glowing end of the rod toward Benrian's left eye. Benrian let out a muffled cry through his thick gag, pleading for mercy. He shook his head wildly. Marrs smiled and pulled back a little. "No? You want to keep both your eyes? Then tell me what I want to know!"

Benrian began to sob, and Trager could see the struggle within him. Unable to take it anymore he rose from his chair and went to the dangling man, shoving Marrs aside.

"Benrian, look at me," he ordered.

The Jadori kept his eyes closed, sobbing. Trager roughly grabbed hold of his hair and jerked his head forward.

"Open your eyes!" he growled.

When Benrian looked his eyes were red and full of tears. Badly garbled words spewed from his gagged mouth, begging Trager to end his torture.

"You know what I want to know, and you know I'll find it sooner or later," said Trager. His head and ribs screamed with searing pain, but he hardly felt it in his rage. Like many in the palace, Benrian understood his tongue, though not well. "There's no reason for you to endure this. You know where Grimhold is. Now tell me."

Benrian stifled his sobs and shook his head.

"Tell me!"

Still Benrian said nothing.

Trager whirled on Marrs and snatched the poker from him. "Give me that," he snapped, then turned back toward Benrian. Holding the Jadori's head firmly in one hand and the poker in the other, he began carefully pointing the burning rod toward Benrian's eye. The man screamed and slammed shut his lids. Trager singed the lashes. "Closing your eyes won't help," he warned. "This beauty will burn right through your head and come out the other side. You want that? You want to go bumbling around the desert like a blind chicken?"

Benrian choked on his own breath as he pleaded.

"Then tell me what I want to know," said Trager. "Stop protecting those cursed freaks!"

"Just do it, General," urged Marrs. "He'll break once you do, I'm sure."

But Trager didn't want to do it. So much of his humanity had already been stripped away. "Don't bloody make me, you black-skinned bastard," he hissed. His hand was shaking, and so was Benrian. "Speak! You saw what I did to those warriors of yours!"

Finally Benrian screamed, breaking into a chorus of sobs and wildly nodding his head. Trager lowered the poker and stepped back. A wave of relief washed over him. He reached out and yanked down the gag from Benrian's mouth.

"I take you," sobbed the man. He tossed his head and stared at the mildewed ceiling, weeping. "I know Grimhold."

Satisfied, Trager plunged the poker back into the brazier, sending up a shower of sparks. "Release him," he told Marrs. "Get some clothes on him and let him rest. If he's hungry give him food."

Marrs gave a gruff, "Yes, sir," as Trager left the cell. Eager to be gone from the stinking cellars Trager went at once to the slimy stone stairway and made his way back up to the livable regions of the palace. He was breathing hard and wanted desperately to return to his bed and rest. Worse, the tortures had taken a toll on him, and the way his men viewed him They were following him now because Akeela was gone—probably dead—and they wanted to avenge themselves on Lukien, but Trager knew he could easily misstep. He had to be cautious, he knew, and not break the fragile hold he had over his men.

Up in the palace, he went in search of Colonel Tark. Before he could rest he had to tell the colonel the news. After making inquiries among his soldiers, he found Tark out in the garden, sitting around a stone table with his lieutenants. The men rose to attention as Trager limped into their midst.

"At ease," said Trager. "Sit."

The officers took their seats again as Trager stood before them. Colonel Tark looked tired and disheartened.

"Cheer up, Tark," said Trager. "We've found our way to Grimhold."

All the men but Tark cheered. Trager noticed his aide's ill-humor but ignored it. Instead he told them all to make ready, they would be leaving for Grimhold within days. The news heartened the lieutenants, who promised to have their troops ready to move on his orders.

"As soon as I've recovered," he told them. It embarrassed him to admit it, but he was hardly ready to face the Inhumans yet. "What about you, Tark?" asked Trager. "Are you ready?"

"I've been ready for days, sir," replied the gray-haired colonel. "The question is how are you? You don't look well."

"I'll be ready to ride, don't worry about that. I just need a few more days. That should give you enough time to get that sour look off your face." Trager said to his lieutenants, "You men have work to do now. Get to it."

There were salutes as the officers dispersed. Colonel Tark leaned back in his chair and stared out toward the mountains. "So, you've found the way to Grimhold?" he asked.

"I have." Trager took one of the vacated chairs, grateful to be sitting again. The wound at his forehead threatened to crack his skull. He rubbed it as he asked Tark, "Do you have a problem with that?"

"Not all the men know how you've been coming by your information, sir. I'm not sure they'd approve."

"I see," said Trager. "And you don't approve, is that right?"

Tark was characteristically frank. It was one of the things Trager had always liked about his aide. "I didn't mind killing warriors. They were soldiers, like us. They were well prepared to die. But these people in the palace are servants. They're civilians, General. And we're Royal Chargers, after all."

"Colonel, I do what I must."

Tark shrugged. "Some of them think you go too far. Some of them say you dishonor yourself, and the Chargers. They say the Bronze Knight would never torture people."

The statement stunned Trager. "They say that? How dare they speak that brigand's name? This is war! And I'll do whatever it takes to win."

Tark grinned. "Is this a war, General? Or just a vendetta?"

"Both," declared Trager. "And it's not just my vendetta, Tark, so stop looking at me that way. Lukien murdered the king. He dragged Akeela's body off for some sick ceremony. He's become one of those damned Grimhold freaks. He must be punished for that."

The old colonel nodded but didn't seem convinced. "You're right about that, certainly."

"But?" pressed Trager. "Go on, Tark, speak freely."

Colonel Tark looked at Trager, his expression gloomy. "You're a fine soldier, General, and a good leader. The men will follow you anywhere, as long as you don't cross any lines."

"What lines?"

"The same lines King Akeela crossed, sir. We follow you because you're stable, because we know we can count on you. Have you not always had our loyalty?"

Trager nodded, seeing what his aide was getting at. "I have," he said. "And I've been grateful for it. But Lukien maddens me, you see?"

Tark smiled. "Just don't go over the edge," he said. "If you remain the man who rebuilt the Chargers, we'll follow you anywhere." He leaned forward. "Anywhere, General. Even to the throne of Liiria."

Excitement pulsed through Trager suddenly. He did his best to control it. "You're a good man, Tark," he said. "You give good advice. Now let's get our army together, eh? We've got a war to win."

Four days later, Trager rode out of Jador at the head of his twelve hundred strong army. Beside him at his right rode Colonel Tark. To his left was Sergeant Marrs, leading a pack mule carrying the still dazed and battered Benrian. The former servant of Kahan Kadar wore a white gaka to stave off the sun and to hide the embarrassing bruises on his face and arms. He did not speak, and probably would not until they neared the distant mountains. He had only told Trager to point his army westward. There, hidden in the high rocks, they would find Grimhold. Trager felt wonderfully good this morning. His ribs still twinged but that was nothing; he was finally, at last, going to face Lukien. Buoyed by his conversation with Colonel Tark, he kept himself erect in his saddle so that all the men could see him. He did not wear his silver armor, nor did any of his men. The wretched heat of the desert would have roasted them, so they carried their armor and heavy weapons with a train of pack animals. The sun was already hot, bearing down on his army as it made its way across the desert sands. Most were glad to be leaving Jador behind. Subjugating the city had been unpleasant business. And because they were soldiers and eager to avenge their king, they voiced no complaints about the heat or the long ride ahead. It was only two days, after all. They would endure it. On kreels it would have been quicker, Trager knew, but he was in no great hurry any longer. There was nowhere for Lukien to hide.

Grimhold will be his final hiding place, he told himself as he rode. The city fell away behind him.

They rode through the day, breaking often. At midday Trager went to Benrian, offering him a drink. The Jadori was shocked by the small kindness, but took the drink gratefully. Trager watched him as he drank, sizing up his loyalty.

"Do well and we won't harm you further," he told the man. "Just take me to Grimhold. Then I will release you with a horse and enough water to return to Jador."

Benrian handed him back the waterskin and nervously licked his lips. "I will do as you ask," he promised. The terror in his eyes was plain. Satisfied, Trager left him and ordered his men back onto their horses.

They rode through the afternoon, until finally the mountains seemed to grow closer. Benrian told Trager that they were more than halfway to Grimhold. Trager told Tark that they would go on a few hours more, hoping to get close enough to Grimhold to be able to reach it early the next morning. After more riding and resting, the sun finally began to dip. Exhausted and still smarting from his wounds, Trager ordered the companies to stop for the night. Sergeant Marrs drove a tent stake into the ground and tied Benrian to it, a precaution Trager thought unnecessary given the rugged terrain and the possibility of attack by one of the desert's giant serpents. But he let the sergeant do as he thought best, then rode through his men, directing them as they made camp.

The night was blessedly quiet. Because they had no tents with them, they laid their bedrolls onto the warm sand and slept looking up at the stars. The aroma of cooking fires reached Trager as he rested, reminding him how hungry he was. Once his wound had healed his appetite had returned with a vengeance, so he ate heartily before going to sleep. Guards milled nearby as he blanketed himself in his bedroll. When he closed his eyes, sleep came quickly, and with dreams. He dreamed about the amulets and the power they would give him, and about a glorious return to Koth with an army behind him and no one to oppose him. And he thought of his father, too, and how proud the old man might have been. And how shocked. Even as he slept, Trager smiled.

Tomorrow, he would finally meet his destiny.

59

Alone with Gilwyn in the council chamber of Grimhold, Lukien sipped thoughtfully on a glass of wine and tried to keep his mind focused. Outside the keep, Baron Glass and his army of Inhumans had begun taking their positions, waiting for the Liirians. Inside the keep, those Inhumans who couldn't fight had remained, readying themselves to fight or die just as their comrades out in the rocks would. Among these was White-Eye, who had promised Minikin she would stay by her side, no matter what. As Lukien and Gilwyn awaited word from the mistress, the boy fed Teku from a handful of nuts. The monkey seemed to sense the tension in the room and so ate quietly. It was well past dawn now. Ghost and the other scouts had reported that Trager had made camp last night just a few miles east of them. They would be coming; there was no doubt of it now. Lukien was eager to get outside and take up position with his comrades. He was proud of the men and women he'd trained, impressed with their willingness to defend their home. And the chance remained that they might actually win against the well-armed Liirians, though that chance was slim.

Too slim a chance for Lukien to risk, though he hadn't confessed that to anyone.

He waited. He took some nuts from Gilwyn and gave them to Teku. He sipped at his drink again and found it had no taste, a sure indicator of his own agitation. Time was precious and he didn't like Minikin wasting it. But before he grew too impatient, the door to the council chamber finally opened. Minikin stepped inside, looking drawn and serious. With her was Trog. The big mute had chosen a suit of armor from the cellars, a great spiked affair that made him look even more massive than usual. He had a sword at his belt and a mace in his hand, which dangled loosely from a giant, gauntleted fist. Lukien himself wore his own bronze armor. He had spent the night polishing it until it gleamed.

"Well?" he asked Minikin.

The tiny woman didn't bother taking a seat. "They are coming."

"How close?" asked Gilwyn.

"Very close. A mile away, maybe a bit more. They have paused to suit themselves in armor. Amaraz says they will be here within an hour."

Lukien got out of his chair. "That's it, then. There's no more time to wait."

Minikin merely nodded.

Gilwyn put out his arm and let Teku climb onto his shoulder. "I'll be up in the turret with White-Eye," he said. "Will you be coming, Minikin?"

"As soon as I'm able," said the mistress. Like White-Eye and Gilwyn, she had agreed to remain inside the fortress, and would watch the battle from one of the keep's towers. They would be the first to know when the Liirians broke through. Trog would wait with Greygor by the gate. The two giants would be the keep's last guardians.

Lukien asked Minikin, "Did Amaraz tell you anything else? Is he still prepared to go through with it?"

"Amaraz does not change his mind, Lukien," replied Minikin. "If the Liirians defeat you and enter Grimhold, he will burn them. And all of us with them."

"Minikin, remember my promise," said Lukien. "I'm not going to let the Liirians defeat us. Trust me."

Minikin smiled and beckoned him down toward her with an index finger. When Lukien stooped, she kissed his cheek and said, "You're a very good man, Bronze Knight. But even I don't expect miracles today." She turned and went toward the door. "I must go see to the others. They'll want me to speak to them before the battle. Gilwyn, get up to the tower with White-Eye. Wait for me there. I'll be up presently."

Lukien waited for Minikin to leave before speaking to Gilwyn. The boy gave him an encouraging smile, but there was sadness in his eyes. It occurred to Lukien how much Gilwyn had come to mean to him. Just as he couldn't let the Inhumans die, he couldn't let Gilwyn be harmed, either.

"Did I thank you yet for coming to save me?" he asked.

Gilwyn nodded. "You did." His expression grew serious. "Did you mean what you told Minikin? Do you really think you can defeat them?"

"I intend to defeat Trager once and for all," replied Lukien, not wishing to elaborate. He went to Gilwyn and put a hand on his shoulder. "You've been a good friend. You would have made a good Royal Charger."

"Hmm, I don't know," joked Gilwyn. "The Chargers aren't what they once were."

"Because they've been corrupted by an evil man," said Lukien. "Don't forget that. Don't forget what the Chargers used to stand for, and what they could be again."

"I won't," said Gilwyn. He stepped back to inspect Lukien. "I've never seen you in your armor before. You look. . . ." He shrugged as he groped for the right word. "Well, you look the way I expected you too, that's all. Good luck, Lukien."

Lukien pulled the boy to him and kissed his forehead. "And to you. Protect that girl of yours."

Outside, Lukien quickly located Thorin near the gate. The baron was directing his people into position, telling his archers to take the higher ground and the spearmen to position themselves just below the bows. It was a good plan that Lukien and Thorin had devised together, and they had made sure that each man and woman was also provided a sword so that they could join the fighting quickly once the initial assault was over. Thorin turned toward Lukien when he saw him, waving him over. The baron wore a mismatched collection of armor he had scrounged from the armory and had tied a strip of blue cloth around his upper arm, the color of his noble house back in Liiria.

"Ho, Lukien," he called in greeting. "What word?"

"An hour, maybe less. They're suiting up for battle." Lukien raised his voice so that all the Inhumans could hear. "Are you listening, my friends? The Liirians are on their way. Take your positions and wait for my orders. And don't let them see you!"

"Where will you be, Lukien?" asked Darren. The farmer was halfway up the rocks with his bow on his back. "We'll need to see you."

Lukien pointed to the head of the canyon. "I'll be there, on the southern slope," he told his people loudly. "Baron Glass will be back here with you, there on the north slope. Those of you who won't be able to see me will hear my orders, don't worry."

Darren nodded and continued climbing the path they'd cut in the stones. His companions did the same, one by one taking up their hidden positions in the high rocks. Lukien braced himself for Thorin's reaction. It came quickly.

"The southern slope?" railed Thorin. "You and I are taking the north slope, Lukien, back here near the fortress."

"Change of plans, Thorin," said Lukien. "I've had an idea."

"You've had an idea?" Thorin sputtered. "What are you talking about? It's all been arranged!"

"I know, but I want Trager to see me first, before he sees anything else," said Lukien. He didn't want to explain himself to Thorin, for he knew he'd only end up arguing. "Those are my orders, all right?"

Thorin frowned. "What are you up to?"

Lukien chuckled, trying to defuse the baron's anger. "Don't be so suspicious, Thorin. It's still the same plan. I just want to get a good look at the army, that's all, to see what we're up against."

"That makes no sense at all, and you know it. Come on, Lukien, talk to me. What's your plan?"

"My plan is for you to take the north slope and for me to take the south," said Lukien. "Now get up there into position." He began walking toward the front of the canyon but paused. "And Thorin, one thing—if anything happens to me, you'll be in charge. Do whatever it takes, but make sure those Chargers don't take the fortress."

The old baron didn't argue. "All right, Lukien. But whatever fool idea you've gotten into your head, just be careful, all right?"

"I will," said Lukien, then headed for the southern slope. He looked up at the high rock walls as he walked, satisfied that his army was invisible against the bright sky. He was sure Trager wasn't expecting an ambush. As far as the Liirians knew, there were no soldiers in Grimhold, only cripples.

"Time for a surprise, Trager," sneered Lukien as he began hiking up the rocks. He and his people had chiseled out channels and footholds to make the climb easier, but it was still a difficult task, especially in armor. Lukien chose the most gentle slope. It took long minutes, but when he reached the top he surveyed the canyon floor far below. His position was perfect. Closer to Grimhold he could make out some of the Inhumans among the rocks, their bows poised and ready. He himself was on a granite shelf that jutted out over the canyon like a jaw, the perfect platform for his performance. He turned toward the east and squinted. The first hints of Trager's army showed itself—a cloud of dust rising up from between the mountains. Lukien watched closely, trying to gauge their numbers and distance. They were very close, but their numbers remained hidden by the rocks. He took a deep breath to prepare himself. For a moment he thought of praying to Vala, the Jadori god who'd caused him so much trouble.

"Vala, if you're listening, watch over us," he whispered. Then he turned toward the defenders in the rocks. "They're coming!" he shouted. "Make ready!"

Trager led his men into the winding canyons, his mind alert to every sight and sound. The rocky way was narrower than he would have liked, though Benrian had promised him there was a clearing near the entrance to Grimhold from which his men could organize and fight. Colonel Tark kept close to the general, protecting him as he looked ahead and wound his way over the rough ground. Sergeant Marrs rode near to Benrian's mule, cursing at the Jadori and promising to skin him alive if he didn't find the proper route soon. Benrian looked around nervously, his bruised eyes scanning the many paths. The way was like a maze, and Trager wasn't surprised by the man's difficulties.

"I have not come here many times," Benrian explained nervously. "But I know it is here."

"You'd better be right," warned Marrs, "or I swear I'll sharpen my dagger on you."

"Marrs, shut up," snapped Trager. "You're frightening him. Benrian, think now. Which way?"

Benrian looked around desperately. "This is the path, I think," he replied. "We keep going."

Behind them the army began to mutter. Trager ordered his lieutenants to steady them. He himself was a little on edge, for he hadn't expected to get trapped in this maze of rock walls. But Benrian wasn't lying, he was certain.

"We go on," he told his men, then led the way deeper into the gorge. His horse stepped lightly over the rough terrain, careful not to loose its footing. Trager didn't rush the stallion, and warned his men to go slowly, also. As the column picked its way forward, Benrian noticed another bend in the path.

"There," he exclaimed. "That is the way." He turned toward Trager hopefully. "You go that way. I go now?"

"When we find Grimhold you'll go home," said Trager. "Come on."

His mood lightened, Trager directed his horse through the bend in the path and saw for himself what Benrian had predicted. The path instantly widened into a large clearing, showcasing a giant mountain looming up ahead of him. Trager's eyes lifted toward its summit, stunned by its immensity and formidable beauty. He could see turrets cut into the mountain and a huge iron gate. On both sides of the clearing the mountain walls rose up in sheer cliffs, as though a raging river had blasted through the place a thousand years ago.

"Grimhold," he whispered. Colonel Tark and the others trotted into the immense clearing after him. One by one the jaws of the soldiers dropped as they noticed the forbidding fortress.

"You see?" said Benrian. "Grimhold! I go now, General, yes?"

Trager nodded. He didn't need the man anymore. "Take

your mule and go," he said, too distracted by their discovery to even turn around. Slowly he trotted deeper into the canyon, mesmerized by the sight. Colonel Tark and his lieutenants ordered as many horsemen as would fit into the clearing, until they filled it with the noise of horse hooves. Yet the gorge and its fortress were curiously quiet.

"Tark, what do you think?" asked Trager as he scanned the silent cliffs. "Where is everyone?"

"Holed up in the keep would be my guess, General," said Tark. His lieutenants nodded in agreement. Trager wasn't so sure. He looked toward the great gate and noticed it was unguarded, though he supposed that really wasn't a surprise. It was stout enough to withstand a good bombardment, and they had no battering ram. He thought for a moment while his troops continued filing into the gorge, considering his options. If Lukien and the freaks were in the fortress, they were well protected. He ordered men to continue taking up positions in the clearing, eager to get them out of the confines of the narrow paths. When most were safely inside, he turned to Tark.

"We should explore the area, see if there's any other ways in or out of the keep," he said. "Then we can—"

"Welcome, murderer!" exclaimed an echoing voice. "Up here!"

Startled, Trager scanned the cliffs for the voice. What he saw took his breath away. There on a lip of the southern slope stood Lukien, his bronze armor shining so that he looked like a golden god. He was on the edge of the cliff, gazing down disdainfully. His taunting echoed through the canyon.

"Surprised to see me?" he shouted. "You shouldn't be, you disloyal snake. Did you really think I'd let you get away with killing our king?"

Another murmur instantly rippled though the Liirian ranks. Colonel Tark and the lieutenants looked at Trager in horror.

"What's that?" said Tark. "General, what's he saying?"

"You didn't tell them, did you, Trager?" mocked Lukien from his high perch. "I'm hardly surprised. You've always been a traitor."

"And you're a liar, you wretched bucket of scum!" Trager shook his fist at Lukien. "It was you that killed the king, and all these men know it! Where's his body? What did you do with it?"

Lukien laughed. "These men know you well enough, Trager. They know the truth, I'd wager."

The knight's voice shook the soldiers on their steeds. They began shifting in their saddles, unsure what to believe. Trager knew he had to act fast or he'd lose them.

"Liar!" he spat up at Lukien. "You'll pay for your murdering, Kingslayer! You and those monsters you're protecting!"

"You're the monster, Trager," shouted Lukien. He looked beautiful in the sunlight, the very epitome of his own undying memory. "What kind of man kills his own king? What kind of monster?"

Enraged, Trager glanced desperately at his men. "He lies! He wants to turn you against me!" He glared up at Lukien, blinded by his bronze armor. "How dare you taunt me, you traitor! All these men know how you abandoned Liiria! They all know I'm better than you!"

Again Lukien filled the cliffs with his mocking voice. "If these men follow you, Trager, then they'd better be prepared to die!"

"Ha!" chortled Trager. "That's a big boast, one-eye! We've got the weapons, remember?"

Lukien surprised him with a wink and a smile. The Bronze Knight turned toward the fortress and shouted through the cliffs, "Defenders of Grimhold, show yourselves!"

Instantly the rocky walls came alive with figures, men and women in mismatched armor bearing spears and bows, all pointed downward at Trager's army. There were hundreds of them or more, too many to count. The horses whinnied in panic as stones tumbled down from the cliffs. Trager swiveled in confused panic, watching as more and more of the armored heads appeared in the cliffs.

"Gods, now what?" asked Colonel Tark. He looked toward Trager for answers the general didn't have.

"Not a bad army for a bunch of freaks, eh Trager?" crowed Lukien. His hand rested confidently on the pommel of his sword. "Don't try to flee. If you do I'll give the order to fire."

It wasn't a bluff and Trager knew it. Immediately he put

up his hand, ordering his horsemen not to move. "A good gambit, Lukien," he called, "but not good enough. There'll still be enough of us left to take your precious Grimhold."

Lukien shrugged. "Maybe," he shouted back. "Want to find out? They may not look like much but they've got good aim. I'm sure we'll take out a bunch of you."

Trager ground his jaws together, desperate for a plan. Having Lukien best him was unbearable. And just his presence on the cliff was affecting his men. He could see the adoration in their eyes, mixed with their very real fear of death. The army in the hills kept them sharply in their sights, ready to rain down their arrows and spears. Trager knew he was trapped. The last bit of control in him collapsed.

"Damn it!" he cried, shaking his fist. "I'm your better!"

Lukien's gaze narrowed hatefully on him. "Prove it."

The challenge was intolerable. All his life had come down to this single moment, and suddenly Trager didn't care about anything else, not the amulets or Grimhold or the possibility of ruling Liiria. He didn't even care about the lives of his men. He just wanted to beat Lukien in front of them.

"Name your bargain, traitor!"

"You and me, to the death," said Lukien. "Why risk all these men, when all you really want is me?"

The hunger to avenge himself for a lifetime of wrongs made Trager pull the sword from his scabbard. "Get down here and face me!"

Lukien shook his head. "No way, murderer. If you want me, you fight me up here, where everyone can see us."

Before he knew what he was doing Trager jumped from his horse. He scanned the cliffs for a way to scale them.

"General, no!" cried Tark. "What's the matter with you? He's baiting you, can't you see that?"

Trager looked at his aide, desperate for him to understand. "I know, Tark, but I must. And you watch, all right?" He called out to all his men, "All of you, watch me! Watch me defeat this vermin once and for all! Then you'll see who the best really is!"

Under the threat of Grimhold's arrows, the hundreds of Liirian horsemen watched helplessly as their leader turned away and started hiking his way up the cliff. As Trager climbed he heard Tark calling after him, cursing.

"You're as mad as Akeela!" cried Tark.

Trager ignored the colonel's charge. None of them understood. None of them could ever understand.

"You didn't grow up in that bastard's shadow, Tark," he grunted as he slogged up the rocks. Tark couldn't hear him, but it didn't matter. His destiny was waiting at the top of the cliff.

High in the northern turret of Grimhold, Gilwyn waited with White-Eye and Minikin, watching the extraordinary events unfolding outside. They had waited until they'd heard Lukien's order before opening the shutters, and had experienced a wonderful but brief surge of pride. Seeing her Inhumans so well prepared for battle had made Minikin almost weep. Gilwyn had felt the very same. But then Lukien had started talking, and everything went astray. Minikin almost hung over the window in disbelief as she watched Trager begin shimmying up the cliff. At the top was Lukien, swishing his blade and stretching his muscles in preparation.

"Vala's Grace, what's he doing?" exclaimed the little woman. White-Eye joined her at the window, as dumbstruck by the knight's actions as her mentor. With the help of her Akari she could see everything that was going on. She turned toward Gilwyn for an explanation.

"Gilwyn? What's he doing?"

Gilwyn pushed past her for a better look. The Liirian soldiers were hardly moving. In the cliffs were the countless Inhumans, aiming their weapons down on them. He could see Baron Glass on the northern slope, standing in dumb surprise with his mouth open. Apparently he didn't know what Lukien had planned either.

"He's going to fight Trager himself," said Gilwyn.

"Why?" shrieked Minikin. "He doesn't have to do that! He'll be killed!"

The lump in Gilwyn's throat grew as he realized Lukien was sacrificing himself. "If he can take out Trager. . . ."

"But he can't!" said Minikin. "The man's only got one eye!"

Gilwyn reached for White-Eye and took her hand. "He's doing it for us," he said. "The Liirians won't attack if they lose Trager."

White-Eye nodded but was unable to speak. There was still every chance in the world that they would soon burn in Amaraz' fire.

Lukien waited at the top of the cliff, exercising his sword arm and listening to Trager curse as he hiked his way up the rocks. In the distance he could see Minikin in Grimhold's turret, her face tight with shock. Baron Glass was on the northern slope, calling orders to their comrades and periodically shooting Lukien an admonishing glare. Lukien knew the old baron had figured out his plan. Clearly, he didn't approve. But Lukien was past caring. He had been prepared to die since fleeing for Jador, and he knew the consequences of his actions. In fact, he was content and pleased with himself.

How well I know you, Trager, he thought as he sliced his sword through the air. How easy it had been to coax him up.

In a few minutes Trager had bested the cliff and appeared on the ledge to face Lukien, stepping out from behind a huge outcropping of brown rock. He had sheathed his sword and let it rest at his side as he watched his opponent. His eyes took measure of the ledge and smiled.

"You've chosen quite a stage for our showdown, Lukien."

Lukien let his sword fall to his side. Trager was a pitiful sight, his once gleaming silver armor now scratched and filthy from the hike. He noticed the way his old nemesis favored his side a bit as he breathed.

"Your wound," he said. "Still hurts?"

Trager's grin was maniacal. "Not enough to save you."

"I knew you'd come," said Lukien. "I knew you just couldn't resist trying one more time to beat me."

"Why shouldn't I try?" sneered Trager. "I've had to live with your memory every day of my life. Now I'll finally get a chance to prove to everyone what a bag of wind you are."

Lukien gestured toward the waiting Liirians below. "You're losing them, you know. They don't believe I killed Akeela. They know what you are, Trager."

"They follow me, Lukien, in a way that no one ever followed *you*." Trager took a step forward, his face reddening. "I made them the greatest soldiers on the continent. But do I get any praise for that? Does anyone talk about me the way they speak of you? You're a gods-cursed traitor and they still revere you. They don't know what you're really like!"

Lukien shook his head, almost pitying the man. "They see the truth in you, that's all."

"The truth? You made me, you bastard! I was the one who held Akeela together when you ran out on him!" Trager spit at Lukien's feet. "You sicken me. You call me a coward, but I was there to pick up the pieces after what you did to Akeela. And he never once thanked me for it. Never once!"

"You both went mad," said Lukien. "But that doesn't mean you should be allowed to go on." He hefted his sword. "You need to be put down, Trager. Like a rabid dog."

Trager's eyes gleamed as he unsheathed his blade. "I've waited a long time for this," he said. "I'm going to love watching you die."

There was hardly time for Lukien to raise his blade. Trager charged, swinging his sword in a blinding arc and nearly catching his torso. Lukien's blade slashed down to parry, then twisted to repel the attack. At once Trager came at him again, slashing at Lukien's blind side, a tactic the Bronze Knight had expected. He was stunned by Trager's swiftness, amazed that a man could move so fast. Again and again Trager pressed, pushing Lukien toward the edge of the cliff. The ground beneath him began to crumble. Lukien heard the stunned gasps below, felt the rocks giving way. Snarling, he gritted his teeth and counterattacked, desperately holding his ground, putting all his strength into an inch-by-inch advance. The sudden burst surprised Trager; Lukien watched his eyes widen. He pressed his one advantage, going for Trager's wounded ribs and catching his torso with the flat of his blade. The armor dented as the blade found its mark. Trager hollered in angry pain, falling back and saving Lukien from the edge. Lukien kept on, swinging his blade for Trager's legs. The wounded general's weapon parried every blow, dancing from point to point with expert speed. Countering, he brought up his armored forearm and smashed it unexpectedly into Lukien's face. Lukien felt his nose explode in pain, saw the blood erupt in a blinding spray. He staggered back, instinctively bringing up his blade to block the blow he knew was coming. The sword clattered as Trager's blade slide down its length, barely missing his armored fingers. Blinded and in pain, Lukien fought to clear his face of blood. The awful pain drove him on, and again he pressed his attack, catching the surprised Trager once more in the torso. This time the general doubled over as the blade pierced his armor. But again he brought up his sword too soon for Lukien. Despite his pain his blade was everywhere, countering every blow Lukien mustered. Finally Lukien broke off, exhausted and blind. This time Trager didn't counter. Both men took a much needed rest, panting as they paced around each other like maddened tigers. Lukien wiped the blood from his eye and saw that Trager was staggering, favoring his wounded side. Blood ran down the general's silver armor.

"You won't beat me," Trager seethed. "I won't let you!"

Lukien thought his lungs would burst. Fighting to catch his breath he spat, "All talk, Trager. Always all talk!"

The insult baited Trager into striking. He plunged madly ahead, his sword out before him like the horns of a bull. Lukien danced aside and brought down his blade, catching Trager in the back of the thigh. But Trager didn't howl. Instead he brought his blade about and smashed it into Lukien's back. The stroke paralyzed Lukien. The last bit of air shot from his lungs in a jolt of pain. He stumbled, falling to his knees, his back on fire with agony. Hardly able to move, he looked down and saw he was again at the cliff's edge. Again the rocks beneath him threatened to give. Far below, the wide eyes of Trager's men watched in horror. Lukien struggled for strength. Trager was behind him somewhere, stalking slowly forward. There was only one chance left, and he had to time it perfectly.

He didn't turn or listen for the approach. He barely even moved, Instead he watched the faces of the Liirians, sure that they would betray the death blow. A second later he saw their eyes widen just as Trager's shadow fell on the rocks. With his last bit of strength he lifted his sword and moved aside, pushing it into Trager's descending belly.

Trager's blade fell from his fingers and tumbled into the canyon. Lukien lay gasping on his knees, his old adversary impaled like an insect on his sword. A ball of blood gushed from Trager's mouth. Lukien held him there for all the world to see.

"You're beaten," he whispered hatefully. "I'm still the best!"

Exhausted and dazed, his back screaming with pain, Lukien pulled his blade from Trager's belly and got to his feet, kicking the general onto his back. He stared down into the man's contorted face. Trager looked up at him, coughing blood from his punctured innards. A strange smile swam on his face.

"I'm right, you know," he gasped. "You were always Akeela's favorite."

The words struck Lukien as hard as any sword. He knelt down beside the dying Trager, looking at a man who might have been so much greater, if only he hadn't been forced to contend with a legend. He realized that he had won, and that never again would Trager haunt him. It was time to give the man his due.

"I know," he said softly.

Trager's expression became suddenly calm. "Finish me," he croaked. "Don't let me die like this."

"A man like you deserves the worst of deaths," said Lukien. "I should let the vultures eat you."

"But you won't," gasped Trager. His odd smile twisted. "You owe me. You know you do."

Lukien's vengeance fled as he stared down into Trager's brainsick face. Without malice he picked up his sword, raised it high above his head, then lowered it like a guillotine and chopped off Trager's head. His strength quickly ebbing, he picked up the head and stood on the edge of the cliff.

"Here's your general!" he cried, then tossed the grisly trophy down into the clearing. "Leave this place!" he ordered. "Or die like your demented leader!"

The world around Lukien grew blurry. It was all he could do to hold himself up. Far below, the ranks of Liirians began talking among themselves. Lukien wavered on his feet, about to faint from the pain. Down his back he felt hot blood sluicing from his wound.

Then a figure rode out from the ranks of horsemen, who took off his helmet to reveal his weathered face. He stared up at Lukien in dumb amazement. Lukien stared down at him, sure he didn't recognize the old soldier, doing everything he could to keep himself from falling.

"Bronze Knight," cried the man. "I am Colonel Tark. Will you join us?"

The question shocked Lukien. He staggered forward to stand at the very edge of the cliff. "I have killed your general, and I will kill you too if you don't leave us in peace."

"You are one of us, Captain Lukien. You're a Lirian. And I do not believe you killed our king." Colonel Tark swept his hand over his dwindled army, who began nodding agreement. "None of these men truly believe it. You don't belong with these people, Captain. You belong with us."

The wound in Lukien's back was agonizing. Even breathing was an effort. "I . . . I cannot," he gasped. "That time for me is over. Go now. And never return."

Colonel Tark's expression was grave. "We need you, Captain. We need a leader. What will happen to us now?"

Lukien tried to answer but couldn't. Pain overcame him, coursing through his back and brain. The world around him spun rapidly around, and the last thing he heard was Colonel's Tark's cry of alarm. Then he collapsed to the ground, and all went dark.

60

Amaraz' fire never came.

Colonel Tark and his Liirians left the canyon without Lukien, letting the leadership of the band fall on Tark's shoulders. Once they'd seen Trager fall, they knew there was nothing they could do to save themselves. The Inhumans were too numerous, and they had lost heart and honor following their demented general. In the final hours Tark had seen that, but it had been too late. The old colonel regretted his life in service to Trager, and told his men that they were murderers, not at all like the Royal Chargers Lukien had commanded, and that they should be prepared to die for what they'd done. With the last shreds of honor left to them, many of the Chargers obeyed Tark's call to surrender. Most, however, were like Sergeant Marrs, who refused to turn himself over to the folk of Grimhold, and rode out of the canyon alone.

But with Minikin and her people, Colonel Tark found a mercy he didn't expect. He and his men were sent back to Jador weaponless, guided by envoys from Grimhold with assurances that the Jadori were not to harm them. This was the word of White-Eye, the new ruler of Jador. At Gilwyn's pleading she had let the Liirians live, though they had killed her father and slain hundreds of her countrymen. It was the greatest act of kindness Gilwyn had ever seen, and it made him adore White-Eye even more. He knew that she had done it for his sake alone.

In Grimhold, the Inhumans quietly rejoiced in their victory, though Lukien had been badly wounded and lay near death. For two days he remained in bed, motionless, being comforted and watched over by Gilwyn, White-Eye, and Baron Glass. His death was imminent now. The knight had lost a great deal of blood, and the wound in his back had begun to fester. And try as Minikin might to reach his mind, it was clouded and dark inside his brain, with only the slightest stirrings of life. Despite their victory, a pall fell over Grimhold.

By the end of the third day, Gilwyn had lost all hope. He had White-Eye now and a new home, but his closest friend was dying, and he could not bear the loss. He sat alone in his chamber, the one he had shared with Lukien, staring into the light of a candle, brooding over memories. He missed Figgis more than ever. If the old librarian were here, he would have known what to say to comfort him, but he was dead now like everyone else. Just like Gilwyn's mother. Just like Lukien was soon to be. A plate of food that Farl the houseboy had brought him lay cold and untouched on the nearby table. The halls outside his chamber were silent. All the Inhumans had stopped celebrating their victory now, because they knew the man that had won it for them was dying.

"Gilwyn?"

Gilwyn looked up at once and saw White-Eye in the doorway of his chamber. She moved like a ghost and always surprised him. It was a pleasant surprise, though, so he smiled at her.

"I'm sorry, I didn't mean to disturb you." White-Eye shrugged. "Your door was open a little so I came in. Baron Glass said you had come here." Her blank eyes had a peculiar way of questioning him, and did so now. "Why aren't you with Lukien?"

"What good would it do?" Gilwyn looked down at his plate and pushed it further away. "He's dying. Minikin said so."

White-Eye came into the room and knelt down beside him. She took his hand and gazed at him. "Then you should be with him, no?"

"I can't," said Gilwyn. "I can't face it. Looking at him like that. . . ." He stopped himself before grief could choke him off.

"I would have given anything to have been with my father when he died, Gilwyn," said White-Eye. "You have this chance. You should take it."

"Why?" Gilwyn flared. He wrenched his hand away from her, not wanting to be comforted. He wanted to be angry. "Why does everyone have to die? Why won't Minikin save him? She has the bloody amulet. She could save him in a moment."

"And let him live like your Queen Cassandra? A prisoner from his own people? You know he wouldn't want that, Gilwyn. And only the spirit of the amulet can decide who may wear it with honor."

Gilwyn didn't want to hear her logic, or any more of Grimhold's magical riddles. Lukien was dying, and that was all that mattered to him.

Minikin knelt alone in her little prayer chamber, communing with Amaraz. She thanked him for sparing Grimhold and confessed her anger with him, explaining how worried she'd been for her children, the Inhumans.

Amaraz listened patiently.

He was pleased that their alliance would continue, but he could also sense her melancholy. Up on the altar, the amulet that held his essence pulsed in quiet sympathy. Minikin told Amaraz how worried she was about Lukien, and how guilty she felt over his impending death. Lukien was not to blame for the things that had happened to him, she explained.

Amaraz continued listening, patiently.

The Mistress of Grimhold chose her words carefully. She had a great favor to ask the spirit. She explained to him how Lukien had saved them, how he had battled Trager to keep the Liirians from Grimhold and to spare his "army" from even one death. He was a good man despite his faults, she told Amaraz, and though Amaraz already knew the story he continued to listen.

Finally the spirit of the amulet asked his mortal friend what it was she wanted from him.

With all the deference she could muster, Minikin made her request.

For what seemed like an eternity, Lukien drifted in darkness. It was not like a dream or nightmare, not like conscious thought at all. It was wholly different, black and terrifying, a maze from which he could not escape or glean a sliver of light, or even find a voice to scream. He was in emptiness, barely aware of himself. Occasionally other voices reached him, breaking through the darkness to offer words of love and encouragement. But Lukien could not answer them. The voices were familiar but intangible. Lukien could not remember who they were or even why they had come to him. He was in blackness and in pain, and that was all he knew.

And then there was a light and the first stirrings of memory. The familiar voice came again, stronger this time, blowing the cobwebs from his mind and flooding him with sunshine. The voice coaxed him forward. He groped for it madly. Slowly the world he knew was his again, replacing the void with the familiar heaviness of sleep.

Lukien, he told himself. *I am . . . alive?*

It took great effort to open his eye. A blurry world swirled around him. Remembering his wound he expected to feel pain, but he did not. There was only peace in his mind and a warmness through his body. He blinked, once and then again, his eyelids fluttering to focus his vision. A smiling, elfish face greeted him.

"You're awake," said the voice that had pulled him from the void.

It took a moment for Lukien to remember her name. As the grogginess lifted he whispered, "Minikin."

Minikin put her tiny hand on his forehead. Like a mother she gently brushed the hair aside. "You're alive, Lukien. You made it."

It surprised Lukien how quickly his strength was returning. Second by second he felt more invigorated. "Alive?" he asked. Then he laughed hoarsely. "I'm alive!"

Minikin's smile lit the room. There was an unusual ruby glow on her face, though her amulet was buried beneath her coat. "How do you feel?" she asked.

Lukien mentally checked his body. All his parts seemed to be with him. He remembered battling Trager on the cliff, then the world going dark. "I'm fine, I think," he said. "But I shouldn't be. My back. . . ."

"Shhh, don't fret," said Minikin. "You are well again. That's what matters."

Lukien glanced around the room. "Where's Gilwyn and Thorin?"

"They are well, do not worry," replied the mistress. "We are all well, Lukien. The Liirians are gone. Gilwyn and Baron Glass are in no danger."

Relieved, Lukien sighed. "Thank the Fate. But where are they, Minikin? I want to see them."

Minikin smiled. "I sent them away, just for a little while. I needed to be with you alone." She put out her hand. "Can you sit up?"

"I think so."

With his renewed strength it was surprisingly easy for Lukien to move. He lifted his head from the pillow, expecting it to jolt him with pain, but again there was nothing but a warmth coursing through his body. He sat up without needing Minikin's help and leaned against the headboard. The strange ruby glow on Minikin's face shifted as he moved. Confused, Lukien looked down and noticed the glow emanating from his own chest.

"Fate above. . . ."

Around his neck was the Eye of God, thrumming with supernatural light.

"What is this?" he exclaimed. "Minikin, what have you done?"

"It was the only way," said Minikin quickly. "Your wound was very bad. You would have died without it."

"Died? I wanted to die!" cried Lukien.

He reached for the amulet and frantically tried to rip loose the chain. The pulsing Eye burned when he touched it. He cried out just as Minikin caught his hand and pulled it toward her.

"Don't, Lukien," she pleaded. "Let me explain."

"Explain what? This thing killed Cassandra. It ruined me, Minikin. It ruined all of us!"

"You are wrong," said Minikin. She kept her remarkable grip on his hand. Lukien leaned back and let out a miserable sob.

"Get it off me," he gasped. "I don't want it. I don't want to live this way! I'm a Liirian!"

"Lukien, listen to me—the spirit of the amulet has granted you this gift. You are not cursed. As long as you wear it you are its sanctified owner. You can go wherever you wish, be looked upon by anyone."

"But it's evil, Minikin. . . ."

"It is *not* evil," Minikin insisted. "It didn't kill Cassandra, it saved her! And the Eye isn't to blame for your life. It was Akeela's madness that caused all that." Minikin sat down at the edge of the bed, her hand loosening on Lukien's, her touch mild. She said, "You can take off the amulet any time you wish. That's your choice. But—"

"Fine," snapped Lukien. "Then take it off me now."

"*But*," continued Minikin firmly, "if you do the infection in your body will return, just like Cassandra's cancer. It will kill you, and Grimhold will lose its defender."

Lukien frowned. "What do you mean?"

"Grimhold needs you, Lukien. I can't defend it by myself, and without Kadar we will be in danger." Minikin's eyes were steely as she spoke. "We've been discovered. The normal world will not leave us alone now. And you made a promise to Kadar. Do you remember?"

Lukien remembered perfectly. "I protected White-Eye from Akeela," he said. "I've fulfilled my promise."

"Perhaps," said Minikin with a shrug. "Perhaps not. If you die then we will lose you. We will have to face the perils of the future without you. All of us, including White-Eye. And what about the Jadori? They need you too. White-Eye will lead them now, but she'll need a defender. And so will Gilwyn."

"Gilwyn?"

Minikin nodded. "He's one of us, an Inhuman. He won't leave here. This is his home now. And if I'm not mistaken, you don't have a home to go back to."

It was all too much for Lukien. He looked away and felt the great warmth of the amulet envelop him. He knew there was a spirit in the Eye, and that spirit was with him, bonding with him. "I'm not one of you, Minikin," he said. "I'm not an Inhuman."

"As long as you wear that amulet, you are one of us," Minikin replied. "You can be our protector. Amaraz has willed it."

Looking up, Lukien saw Minikin's enigmatic smile. She was just as she had been the first day they had met—supremely confident. It was good that she was still alive, and her Inhumans with her. Lukien realized his plan had worked, that his gambit on the cliff had saved them. He could die in peace but for the unknown, threatening future. He lifted himself higher, sitting upright, and flexed his fingers. They were strong, stronger than they'd felt in years. He still wore his eyepatch but the itching and constant throbbing was gone.

"So," he asked, "Gilwyn will stay in Grimhold?"

"Yes," said Minikin, obviously pleased with the idea. "He and White-Eye are close now. He won't leave her." She grinned. "Will you, Lukien?"

Lukien thought for a moment, considering his promise to Kadar. He had broken too many promises in his life, and he wasn't yet sure if he'd fulfilled this one or not. He slipped his legs over the side of the bed, testing their strength. They held him easily, so he rose. He took a deep breath. The air was fresh and good in his lungs. Minikin remained on the edge of the bed.

"Lukien," she said softly, "you don't have to answer me today, or even tomorrow or the next day. But you will think about what I've said, won't you?"

Lukien glanced around the room for his clothes, finding them draped over a chair in the corner. Minikin watched him as he put on his shirt and pulled on his boots. He stood up and asked, "Where's Gilwyn? I'd like to see him."

Minikin didn't press him further.

Gilwyn rode alone through the valley between the village and the fortress, glad to be away from the stifling air of Grimhold. He knew what Minikin had planned and how upset Lukien would be, but he also hoped desperately that her plan would work, and that the amulet would be able to save Lukien. Emerald loped along the ground, sensing his fear and confusion. He did not command the kreel directly but instead let her take him wherever she wanted. It was simply good to be with her, to taste the warmth and air and be reminded of better days. To the west he could clearly see the village, now back to normal, its lanes filled again with people, its many fields being tilled by farmhands. Just to the east rose the fortress, still bustling with busy Inhumans. There was a lot to be thankful for, Gilwyn supposed. At least White-Eye was safe, as well as all the other

Inhumans. And Thorin was still with him. At least if Lukien died he'd still have the old baron.

"No," he rebuked himself. "No, he won't die."

There had to be enough life in Lukien to save, he wished fervently. If he had the will to live. He looked up impatiently at the sun, deciding that he'd been gone long enough. Unable to wait any longer, he steered Emerald back toward Grimhold. Halfway there, he caught a glimpse of a horseman riding toward him.

"Lukien!"

The Bronze Knight looked fit and exhilarated as he galloped along the sands. Around his neck bounced the golden amulet.

"It worked," whispered Gilwyn. "It worked!"

Overjoyed, he sped Emerald onward. The kreel dashed ahead, kicking up a storm of sand. Lukien reined in his horse as Gilwyn approached, greeting him with a raised arm. Gilwyn came up next to him and slapped his good hand into Lukien's.

"You're back!" he exclaimed. "And look at you!"

Lukien took a deep breath and exhaled loudly. "I'm a new man, Gilwyn."

"You were almost a dead man! What were you thinking, going after Trager like that? He could have killed you."

Lukien shrugged. "It was a chance worth taking." He glanced back toward Grimhold with satisfaction. "And it worked, after all."

"Yes, it did," said Gilwyn. With his chin he gestured toward the amulet. "To be honest, Lukien, I didn't expect to see you wearing that."

"Nor did I," said the knight. His face became pensive. "Minikin has given me much to think about, Gilwyn. If I remove the amulet, there's every chance I'll die."

"I know," admitted Gilwyn. "But you're one of us now, Lukien. You won't have to live as a shut-in like Cassandra. You were given the amulet freely."

Lukien regarded the boy and very quietly said, "It will make a prisoner of me nonetheless. I am already its slave. Have you heard? I'm to be Grimhold's defender."

"Only if you choose to be, Lukien," said Gilwyn. He raised a hopeful eyebrow. "Do you choose to be?"

The knight looked up at the sky and smiled. "It's a good day," he said. "Perfect for riding."

"Lukien, White-Eye and the Jadori need you. Grimhold needs you. We all have to know. Will you stay with us?"

Lukien ignored the query. He continued scanning the sky and the desert horizon.

"You're not going to answer me, are you?" said Gilwyn.

Very gently Lukien snapped the reins of his horse and sent the beast trotting toward the distant village. "Ride with me," he said.

Gilwyn spun Emerald about and followed the knight, riding close beside him. He waited long minutes, not saying a word, sure that Lukien would speak again. At last the Bronze Knight was ready. He did not look at Gilwyn as he spoke but rather kept his one eye on the horizon.

"A week ago I wanted to die," he said. "But today, I'm glad to be alive."

Satisfied, Gilwyn rode quietly at Lukien's side.

Tad Williams

THE **WAR** OF THE **FLOWERS**

TAD WILLIAMS

Memory, Sorrow & Thorn

"THE FANTASY EQUIVALENT OF *WAR AND PEACE*...
readers who delight in losing themselves in long complex
tales of epic fantasy will be in their element here."
–*Locus*

THE DRAGONBONE CHAIR
0-88677-384-9

STONE OF FAREWELL
0-88677-480-2

TO GREEN ANGEL TOWER (Part One)
0-88677-598-1

TO GREEN ANGEL TOWER (Part Two)
0-88677-606-6

To Order Call: 1-800-788-6262

TAD WILLIAMS

TAILCHASER'S SONG

"Williams' fantasy, in the tradion of WATERSHIP DOWN, captures the nuances and delights of feline behavior in a story that should appeal to both fantasy and cat lovers. Readers will lose their hearts to Tailchaser and his companions."
—*Library Journal*

"TAILCHASER'S SONG is more than just an absorbing adventure, more than just a fanciful tale of cat lore. It is a story of self-discovery...Fritti faces challenges—responsibility, loyalty, and loss—that are universal. His is the story of growing up, of accepting change, of coming of age."
—*Seventeen*

"A wonderfully exciting quest fantasy. Fantasy fans are sure to be enthralled by this remarkable book." —*Booklist*

0-88677-953-7

To Order Call: 1-800-788-6262

DAW 43